MW00574724

A STORY SPUN IN SCARLET

TALES OF
WONDER AND WOE
BOOK 1

R. DUGAN

COPYRIGHT

Book Cover by: The Odd Seed
Map by: Lizard Ink Maps
ISBN: 978-1-958927-10-6
First Edition 2024

DEDICATION

For all the writers who ever stared down a blank page, hoping the ending would come.

And for every reader who knows the power of a story that can change the world.

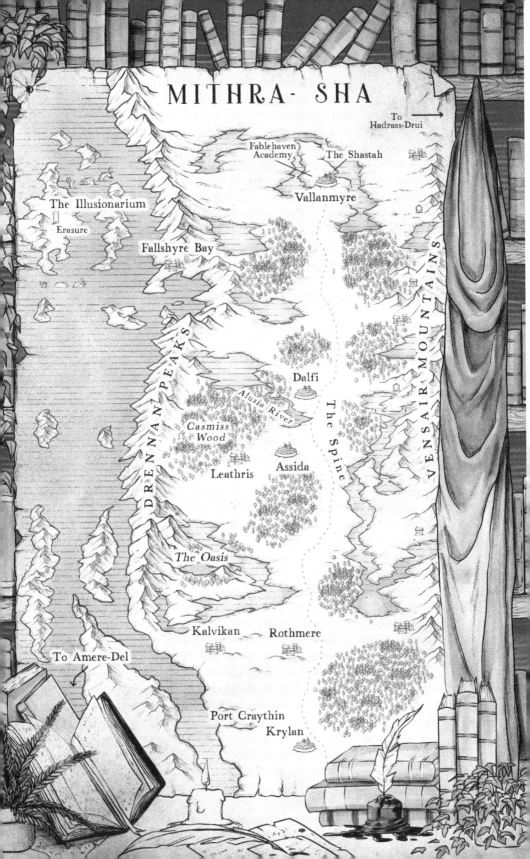

MITHRA- SHA

To
Hadrass-Drui

Fablehaven
Academy
The Shastah

Vallanmyre

The Illusionarium

Erasure

Fallshyre Bay

Dalfi

Alusia River

Casmiss
Wood

Leathris

Assida

The Spine

The Oasis

To Amere-Del

Kalvikan

Rothmere

Port Craythin
Krylan

DRENNAN PEAKS

VENSAIR MOUNTAINS

CHAPTER 1
A PERFECT, POWERFUL MOMENT

et me tell you a story.

The public square was dismally hot, baked in the sort of midday misery that made laborers cringe and gardeners look twice for wilted leaves and drooping stalks. The kind that only those burdened by absolute necessity would endure…which was what had me sitting on the hand-hewn wooden bench in the dusty center of Rothmere, another forgettable town in a forgettable corner of a Luck-forgotten country.

Necessity was the thing scratching in my gut that demanded my perch beneath the blazing sunlight, wearing a drab gray cloak that in times past might have been red or green, blue or gold—any number of colors to delineate rank and status. Necessity made me kin to the people scurrying around the dusty circle of shops hooping the center of Rothmere, the occasional ramshackle home clapped between them; frantic eyes flitted to me and away, settling longer on my gathered audience than on the woman speaking to them.

That was the pool I plucked my listeners from: the desperate, harried mothers caught between errands, their sweating, cranky children lured in for a moment's respite so these women could finish their tasks in peace. I'd realized long ago that children made for the best audience, many of them too young to understand how I was broken. How all people like me were, and how that broke the world around us in turn. And often their parents were grateful enough to shell out a few coppers or even a silver, if Luck smiled on me, for the simple act of keeping their little ones occupied so they could finish their chores.

Opportunistic, perhaps. But these days, all of Mithra-Sha thrived on opportunity—one perfect, powerful moment offering us the chance to do better. To *be* better. To try and spin our luck favorably and write our stories in such a way that today, at least, they ended happily.

Or at least ended without empty bellies and sunken spirits. Sunken eyes. Haggard faces of all ages begging for more than this country could give them.

Those sunken eyes in too-young countenances watched me with rapture as I bent my elbows on my knees and inclined toward them.

"*Let me tell you a story,*" I breathed, and an expectant hush fell over the cluster of dirty, delighted faces. With their gazes trained on me, I tapped into the power that simmered in my core…not quite extinguished, but mere embers compared to the roaring inferno it had once been.

Still. Embers might be more than enough, particularly on this hottest of days, to warm us all in the right ways.

Once upon a time, in a land so ancient time forgot it, there lived a man they called the Prince of Mirrors.

To hear his name, you might think him a vain lad, consumed with the beauty of his own reflection. And lovely he was indeed, fair of hair, bronze of skin, tawny of eye. But nothing about him was so lovely as his heart…a pure and fair prince, a future ruler beloved, the Prince of Mirrors was. To be his friend was to see your own face reflected back to you—all the truths of who you were, shown kindly and without contempt. He was confidant and advisor, defender and provider. There were few who did not crave to be in his presence, to obtain his council, to be called by name from his mouth.

But where goodness plants its garden, the weeds of envy often thrive. So it was that the Prince of Mirrors came by his name…not for how he reflected the faces of his friends, but for how he was nearly felled by his foes.

A few small gasps floated up from my young audience, and my heart soared with the sound.

Yes, this was good; a mysterious and adventurous tale, full of enough danger and daring to scintillate young minds, and whimsical enough to tempt older ears to remember what it was to feel that love was a power which could conquer all.

There was a cruel man in this nameless kingdom…a man who wished for all the notoriety and fame the Prince of Mirrors held. He did not see that these things were obtained through kindness and patience; instead he sought them through cruelty and possession. And when he failed to achieve such high regard for himself, he sought to steal it from the Prince of Mirrors.

There was an attack!

I flashed my arms wide, and the children yelped and leaped in their skin; a few passing errand-runners chuckled, slowing their stride to bend a listening ear my way as I went on, the blazing air shimmering before me while the tale played off my lips.

The envious man set upon the Prince of Mirrors in a hall of no windows…a place where his own cruel act would not be reflected back on his sinister face. Yet as the Prince bled and died from a wound to the heart, he clawed his way from that darkened hall intended as his tomb, and found the arms of his lover instead.

She was beauty incarnate, this woman…not of the features alone, but of the spirit. A woman of untold power who served the Prince's family as her ancestors had, a mighty enchantress who could bend the fabric of nature itself to her will.

The enchantress was no healer. But she was clever, and full of love. And love, as we are all aware, is a force strong enough to alter the shape of the world. It can restitch the seams of all we know to be true and possible. And for the Prince who had shown her the truth of her own face, who knew her heart as no other did, the enchantress did the impossible.

She took her dying lover, the very essence of him, and sealed it within the gilded mirror in her chambers.

A collective breath caught among the children as they all mustered up, scooting closer on their haunches, captivated by the tale that tumbled from my tongue with almost painful haste.

I could see it unfolding, a mirage on the humid air clogging the public square, the strands of the story spinning together—the Prince of Mirrors with his palm pressed to one side of the pane of glass, the Enchantress with her fingers flattened to the other. Near enough that they reflected one another, hand against hand…but eternally apart.

Together forever, but never again to touch. That was the gift and the curse of the Enchantress's action…for though nearly every act in creation has a counteraction, to stay death one must pay a price that rends the world in equal measure. The loss must be felt the same, though the world may not demand a life for a life.

So it was that the Prince of Mirrors became true to his name. His dominion turned from lavish halls to a realm of windowpanes and gilded frames, endless corridors of glass only he could travel through. Now the people came to consult him in their own reflections, seeking his advice and presence, desperate to cool the ache of his loss with a glimpse of his face by mirror and window.

Day after day, he met the people he had once counseled and courted, laughed with and loved, their voices and faces distorted by shimmering glass. And night after night, the Enchantress slumbered with her brow pressed to the mirror in her chambers, whispering herself off to sleep with words of love lost to the man who waited beyond the pane.

And he whispered back.

Words of love, at first. And then, as the chasm between them widened, as his fingertips forgot the sensation of her hair wound between them, as his stomach ached like a shard of glass rammed through it for the pain of missing her nearness, he began to scheme.

He would not allow this to be the end. He would be the Prince of Mirrors no more, but a King of Glass. And glass he would shatter, if it meant returning to the living, somehow. To the kingdom that needed him to rule it. And to the woman who still craved his love.

Oh, this was a *very* good tale. It had all the right trappings…danger and boldness, desire and denial, pain and pleasure. The things that captured hearts and minds and did not let go. And at the core, love…the love of another, the love of a kingdom, the love for the craft I worked over them all.

The scenes sizzled to life in my mind's eye, so vivid it was as if I lived them myself; and in my chest, that forgotten, fantastical thing stirred, purring and arching, a vibrant cord of power, of *otherness* coming awake.

Joy arced through me when I wove that cord around my fingers, when I cradled my rousing power. It tasted of wild waters and icy climes, of all the beautiful places in the world yet to be discovered.

The stories yet to be told.

The tale sparkled a lurid green, like the heart of a forest, like rotted envy, like new life. It rose up out of me, demanding to be told, felt, *experienced*.

It had potential. It had the potential to be *finished*.

And so the Prince of Mirrors broke the halls of his domain, shattered the glass corridors through which he had walked for so long. And upon the breaking, he found that what lay beyond was not another endless span of glass reflecting his own tired face back at him.

Instead, there was a world beyond…a reflective realm of shards and shattered dreams, which had collected all the prayers and promises breathed in a tacky fog against washroom mirrors, begging for strength and wisdom. All the hopes of boys and girls pressing kisses to their done-up reflections, desperate to find true love. All the tears sobbed against windowpanes with faces turned away from friend and foe alike to hide the breaking.

The Prince of Mirrors, the King of Shattered Glass with a crown of splinters and shards, would take these things. And he would use them to build a bridge back home.

The children weren't the only ones enraptured by the tale now; mothers and fathers, shopkeepers and errand-runners halted in their tasks and duties to look twice. They leaned in shop doorways and perched on the stoops of dwellings, all inclined my way, eyes dancing with the pure joy of *forgetting* as my tale wove around them.

Like water in this horrid, endless drought, the words carried them away to places of wonder. Of pure living.

Deluded hope swelled in my chest. Perhaps this time, the right words would come to me. Perhaps I would manage what no Storycrafter in Mithra-Sha had done in years.

Perhaps this was a story I would *finish*.

Fingertips singing at the notion, the tale spooling out of me faster and faster in its own gilded sheen, I leaped to my feet; the children leaned away with a burst of delighted giggles, dodging the whip of my soiled gray cloak as I pirouetted before them, arms flung out, portraying the vastness of the world within the mirror.

The Prince of Mirrors set off into this realm of glass, this kingdom gifted him by his Enchantress; and within he found far more than he had ever dreamed. Mountains built of silver fractals, striking between breath-fog clouds! Rivers of tears streaked on glass, flowing away to seas reflecting a sky of whispered dreams! On and on he traveled, until he found a corner of his realm that reeked of far darker things.

Shadowed halls. Mirrors covered. Cloth cast over dastardly deeds done in the dark…in places where one hides the mirror for fear that something or someone, somehow, may be watching from beyond.

Well. The Prince of Mirrors was watching. And in the farthest, darkened edge of his new domain, he found…

My tongue stumbled over the last word. My feet caught beneath me, stilling me in place.

The emerald surge of power unspooling in my chest went limp all at once, a sail cut off from its wind, a tether severed by the cruel blade of two-faced Luck. The dazzling tale of the Prince of Mirrors and the Enchantress withered on my lips, my excitement for it perishing, the inspiration going sour, and despair bladed straight through my core when the words simply *abandoned* me.

My mind went utterly, brutally blank. A void.

Silence smothered the public square. The children exchanged glances, weighty, wondering…but resignation wrote itself on their parents' faces; it etched itself, too, into the fallen countenances of the older children hefting themselves to their feet with grumbles, slouching off to escape the heat.

"No!" I lunged after them, hand extended. "Wait! The Prince of Mirrors found...he found..."

The air shimmered at the tips of my fingers, a flare of life sputtering...dying.

The emptiness crashed over me, and I slumped to my haunches on the handcrafted bench that had been my perch.

"What did he find?" one of the youngest boys had the courage to ask—his eyes round and wide, waiting to reflect the rest of the tale.

He was so small. So full of trust still. Too naïve to realize how things went in this world...how they had been going for years.

I tried to write a smile across my face, but there was not enough ink in the world to script joy into my tone when I murmured, "I wish I knew."

Slowly, parents wandered forward to collect their little ones. Some hung pitying smiles on wan faces as they shelled over a few coppers at my feet; they knew that, opportunity aside, I was no charlatan bribing their children with false tales. I was doing the best I could.

Every Storycrafter in Mithra-Sha was doing the best they could...but all it ever amounted to anymore was enough coppers for a warm meal or two, a roof over our heads if Luck smiled on us.

Luck did not smile on me today. Just four coppers sat in the dust before me when they all departed, hastening to escape the heat and the misery that swam humid and thick in the dismal public square.

I hadn't hoped for much more. There were no happy endings, after all.

There were no endings at all anymore.

CHAPTER 2
WHEN WORDS FAIL

It was some relief, at least, to warm myself with a bowl of homecooked food at Rothmere's only public house following the disastrous attempt at Storycrafting that afternoon. I'd grown tired of foraging for berries and edible tubers on the long road here.

Long roads seemed to be all that were left to me anymore; and while I fought to foster a spirit of gratitude that I could travel and forage at all, when so many others in Mithra-Sha had far less opportunity, my selfish tongue ushered in bites of oxtail stew with a burning haste that would have made a liar out of my humblest parts.

Tucked away in the dimmest corner of the public house, I was content to nurse my bowl and my latest failure in solitude. It was rare that anyone looked on a Storycrafter with anything but pity on the fairest days anymore. On the foulest, it was contempt that overshadowed the hunger pangs and perpetual fretting in their gazes. And though none of this was my fault, I couldn't begrudge them their own grudges in turn.

It used to be that the presence of a Storycrafter was a cause for celebration. Feasts and fetes had been flung up in our honor. Particularly in small towns like this, barely a nib's scratch on the wide-reaching map of Mithra-Sha, little else counted for a good Luck charm but to be graced with the presence of a traveling Storycrafter. Now it was all sour disappointment curdling the air, if not false politeness as potent as the herbs flavoring this batch of stew—a pungent, rosemary tang covering up for the lack beneath, the touch of age and weariness to the batch.

Want and lack were everywhere I turned. They twisted the skin tight over rib bones and spines; they shoved strong heads and proud shoulders into slopes and stoops. They whispered in the void of coinless pockets and the unspoken things neighbors kept to themselves, reticent to impress their own needs on their equally-needy friends.

And it was impossible not to blame Storycrafters for it all, whether or not we were responsible for the loss of our stories' endings.

No one looked twice my way while I ate, which I had come to expect. Once they realized I was no different from the rest of my kind, my tales as threadbare and short-lived as anyone's, I faded like my colorless cloak into the weathered grain of the woodwork around me. Just another rare traveler in Rothmere, and not even one worth looking at twice.

Just another Storycrafter without a finished story to tell.

Even after all these years, dwelling on those thoughts too long picked at the stitches over a wound ripped wide open in me the night I'd gone to my parents' home and learned precisely what they thought of their daughter without a story to finish; when they had told me, bluntly and without a hint of warmth, "We have no daughter named Audra Jashowin."

I evaded the memories of their curt dismissal and how they'd cast me out just as smoothly as I would a handsy traveler looking to write a lascivious scene into their own tale. Instead, I scoured the public house with my gaze, eyes snagging on the notice board hung behind the counter where patrons like myself had retrieved their food and drink.

That board was the clearest sign that Rothmere was a town adjacent to the long, winding road that was the Spine; though this settlement was small and unassuming, and the broadest throughway in the country not visible from within the town proper, papers and parchments and announcements were nailed to the wood in such excess that they spoke of travelers' hopes long gone on before me.

Announcements of performing troupes, hoping to beckon others traveling behind them to come and witness their shows. I wondered how many of them were still performing together and how many had fallen apart, scattering to more lucrative work while their notices frayed and yellowed on their settings.

A pang of an old, buried longing rose up within me…hopes sundered, memories that were good for a bit of warmth, at least, before my eyes traveled on.

Services offered on parchment—farriers, woodworkers, tailors, smithies, repairmen of all sorts for all kinds of travel. Invitations for luck-altering trysts and tokens. And there, on darker parchment than most and written in gold-leaf lettering…

Amplifiers.

I shuddered at the evocative decoration of moons and stars on the blackened parchment, an almost ethereal beckoning from those who promised they could assist Storycrafters with enhancing their power. Perhaps help them bring to life a finished story, after all.

Every Storycrafter knew about amplifiers…we had been warned about them from the time we told our first tales. Whether by potion or herb or Luck itself, they coaxed out among the most powerful stories of all. But the cost…

Nightmarish manifestations birthed of the stories they told, ravaging Mithra-Sha. Storycrafters themselves so addicted to their craft, they went mad, drowning themselves in substance, forsaking their loved ones and life itself, Luck-bent on bringing their next tale to bear. They became greedy, desperate, *feral* for the satisfaction of another wondrous tale to sweep away not only their audience, but themselves.

And particularly in years recent, when stories found no end, no satisfaction, no culmination to lay the Storycrafter's heart to rest…it was too great a danger even to consider. Only the most desperate would seek to amplify a Misspoken tale.

I was not so desperate.

Not yet.

Tearing my gaze away from the bulletins beckoning one to consider even the smallest amplification in hopes of telling a tale to its end, I untucked my writing journal from my cloak's inner pocket and flipped it open on the table. Around my bowl of stew, I studied the small, gnarled map by which I'd plotted my course down through Mithra-Sha.

I'd almost come to the end of my southward travels. Mithra-Sha was a country of impressive size, its sprawl dotted with forests and jungles, deserts and wetlands, mountains and mines. I'd taken a bit of everything I'd seen and garnished it throughout my stories, sights and wonders beheld while traveling down the Spine—the road forged of unbreaking glass that joined Mithra-Sha from end to end.

But there was only one place of note left along the Spine: Krylan, the Tailbone at the end of the Spine, a haven for immigrants from the neighboring country and a military outpost of sorts before our land met with the borders of Amere-Del; it was the farthest you could go from Vallanmyre, capital of Mithra-

Sha, the Head atop the Spine...and it was still another fortnight's walk at least from Rothmere.

In Krylan, I hoped to find enough migrant Ameresh ears that weren't numb quite yet to the disappointing, unresolved stories that came from our country. I could ply my Storycrafting talents, pitiful though they were, hopefully long enough to develop some other sort of talent...something that would earn me more than a few coppers.

Perhaps then I could finally settle in, finally stop fleeing from shadows, peel my feet off the ground that had compelled them into frequent flight. And if not...

Shaking a quill down from the inseam of my sleeve, I traced an idle path on the map with the bare nib; north again from Krylan, off the bend of the Spine, into Mithra-Sha's wildlands. Those simmering bogs, those secretive dells, those treacherous mountains...the sorts of places I preferred to tell stories about, rather than actually visit.

Krylan was, quite possibly, my best hope. I was tired of an empty stomach gnawed with hunger pains. I was tired of sleeping beneath the stars, my cloak as my only cover. I was tired of telling disappointing stories with near-empty pockets to show for them.

I wanted somewhere to come home to. And ever since the moment my parents had slammed the door in my face, the bluster of its shutting like a rogue wind pushing me out onto the Spine for the first time, beginning my endless southward trek...I hoped I was drawing near to it. I couldn't shake the sensation that in Krylan, I might learn what *home* truly meant.

The notion goaded me with enough hope to risk flipping through the pages of my journal, past cramped squares of written prayers to the Maker of all stories, all left unanswered—and many left as unfinished as the tales they begged for. My thumb skimmed the feathered edges with a cautious sort of unconcern, as if I could deceive my own talents. Like one might approach a skittish animal, feigning a lack of interest until they could scruff it by the collar, I paged idly through the contents, never settling on one.

Then I slapped the book open, feverishly taking in the page, mind racing as if I could outrun the inevitable death of inspiration that came when reviewing my own work.

A story I knew so well: a tale of a cloth-spinner who learned she could weave fate into the threads on her loom; her ungracious father had shut her away in the cellar when he discovered her talents and forced her to spin endlessly, until her hands bled and her back broke with sobs. She suffered in the dark while he profited off her labor, rising swiftly in notoriety until the King himself took note of the man's product.

He'd armored his entire fighting force in fate-touched threads, and invited the girl's father into a lavish estate as a show of gratitude; and the father had snapped up the offer like the vicious opportunist he was, leaving his daughter in the cellar to await his regular visits while he cast himself into the King's good graces.

That was where the father's schemes had come undone. An injured traveler had stumbled into the abandoned spinner's home and found the young woman imprisoned below. And as he'd tended her mangled hands and heard the story from her lips, his rage had grown and grown on her behalf, until...

Until nothing.

Until the page went blank. Until this story, like every other one I told, forfeited its potential and became nothing but an empty tale without conclusion.

Setting my teeth so hard my temples throbbed, I pressed the point of the quill to the end of the last sentence I'd written...dropped in mid-word. The blankness beyond haunted me like the vacant stares of skulls I'd spotted littering the edges of the Spine, a testimony to robbers and worse who prowled the most inhabited road in Mithra-Sha. The mere notion of them had herded me nearer to pockets of strangers than I had any right to go, hoping no sinister eyes would see me for what I was.

A woman traveling alone. Someone who had *been* alone since the punctuated slam of a door in her face, marking her forgotten. Disowned. Dispensable. Someone who would not be missed if she were to go abruptly and eternally missing on the road to Krylan.

Long ago, I could've handled even the foulest pack of thieves myself with a few Wellspoken words...before fickle Luck had flipped its razor-edged coin against me. Now this hanging-off story taunted me, like those empty-eyed skulls had taunted me, a reminder of just how little I had to my name with the endings of all our stories ripped away.

"Would you just *do something?*" I snarled under my breath at my useless, empty mind. "It doesn't even have to be a *proper* ending! Just *some kind* of one!"

But nothing came. Not even a few simple sentences that would preemptively tie up the story and send the spinner and the stranger off.

I was a woman who'd built her life around the power of words. And now words failed me.

Cursing rotten Luck and its two-sided token, I cast down my quill and shoved my empty stew bowl away with my arms folded on the table, burying my face in them.

The chatter of the public house engulfed me as I resigned myself to wallowing for a moment in the misery of the day's predictable outcome. The clamor told a tale of its own right—dwindling numbers as the last few patrons and suppliers trudged off to their homes or lodgings. My last two coppers hung weightlessly in my pocket, a featherlight reminder that I would be sleeping out on the Spine tonight…not enough coin even for dwelling indoors.

Those who remained around me spoke of the weather, the unbearable heat and humidity that had put more strapping young men to bed with exhaustion and dizziness than could be tallied. Some had even died with their hand to the plow, trampled or simply dead of exertion before the rest of their laboring families were near enough to notice their absence.

Streams running dry. Crops plagued with disease, herds diseased with a plague. Lack of food. Lack of trade. Lack of *hope*.

It was the same tale I'd been hearing since I set out from Vallanmyre. Every year, it worsened; and every year, there were more scathing looks than sympathetic ones when I fumbled yet another worthless tale. That there was any kindness at all in Rothmere made me never want to leave it; if I could just sink into the warm, textured tabletop still imprinted with the heat from my first fresh meal in Luck only *knew* how long…

The creaking open of the public house's door heralded this time not a reduction in the noise, but an increase in it; curiosity pulled my head up from the sulking sanctuary of my folded arms.

And then a familiar fear did the rest.

I jolted upright, sinking back into the shadowy recesses of my chosen corner, gaze hunting across the nine armor-clad bodies crowding at the counter.

Mithran soldiers. A whole pack of them.

While they joked among themselves and made their requests for bowls of stew, my heart thundered in time with their boisterous banter. My eyes darted to the notice board above their heads, raking over not only announcements and beckoning bulletins now; there was an entire section dedicated to arrest notices. Bounty lines.

Some of those faces, I knew. Some I'd seen in passing on the Spine and only realized it after, in other establishments like these, when I'd beheld their hair-raising countenances crafted by an expert hand on notices warning of murderers, bandits, and worse. What I did know was that not a single one looked like me; only one was a woman at all, and we were nothing alike—I'd seen her notice plastered in enough public houses by now to assure myself of that.

There was not even a name to her picture, unlike most of the others; and that picture had been rendered in the vaguest terms, almost as if she had been drawn from guesswork and shoddy memories. Even then, there was enough to tell she would have been arresting in person…something imperious in the column of her neck, the tilt of her chin, the hardness of her jaw and those void, undetailed eyes. Black hair falling in a straight sheen to her back. Lips rendered rose-red.

By contrast, I truly faded in with the wood. A gray cloak cast over an unassuming frame, neither lacking enough to garner taunts nor endowed enough to garner appreciation. Brown hair and brown eyes of unremarkable hue. I was the essence of nondescript, which was how I liked it best…it made traveling the Spine so much easier when I drew eyes for absolutely no cause whatsoever. And it made my stories shine brighter, even when they were doomed to fail.

But though no soldiers looked my way, and no one sought out my face…still. That didn't stop the panic scratching at my insides like the incessant scrawl of a quill, writing unease into the parchment of my bones.

Get out. Two words, repeated over and over again. *Get out.*

Run.

The same words that had set my feet to the Spine years ago. That had me ducking in and out of places whenever I caught a glimpse of a Mithran soldier in the distance. That made me feel like I was running from something, though no one chased. No one ever pursued.

That didn't stop me gathering my journal, casting up my hood, and slipping swiftly and silently out the back door.

CHAPTER 3
SOMETHING TO BELIEVE IN

I did not breathe easily again until I'd left Rothmere behind. The town shrank behind me, its clapped-together edifices and modest public square a splash of graying wood amidst the drought-browned grasses when I crested one of the steep hills that encircled Rothmere proper; from that height, far more than the town was visible, and the iron band of unease finally pinched free from around my ribs.

Letting out the breath that had been trapped in my lungs while I'd wound through the backways of Rothmere, looking over my shoulder for Mithran soldiers at every corner, I laced the front of my cloak with flying fingers. It gave the energy fizzing in my fingertips somewhere to go, and it defended against the blustery wind combing the stunted grass at the hilltop while I let my gaze measure the distance to my next destination.

The Spine was a road that could only have been woven from a story; it was a shimmering beacon, a path forged entirely of unbreakable glass. No matter how many wheels or feet passed over it, not a single crack ever disgraced its surface. It glittered like liquid gold in the setting sunlight, a gilded ribbon twisting away through the hillcountry of southern Mithra-Sha.

My heart swelled and weighed heavy at the sight of it. Nowhere to go but back that way, still bound for Krylan. My feet ached at the prospect; the Spine might be unshattering, but my soles certainly were not. And a ball of despair bobbed in my throat at being run out of yet another town—if only by my own anxious thoughts.

I wasn't certain I would ever stop running, at this pace. I wasn't certain I

Sighing, I folded down on the hilltop, wrapping my arms around my knees and balancing my chin on them as my gaze wandered back the way I'd come…north, toward more populated cities, toward Vallanmyre and the life I'd left behind.

The world seemed kinder out here, in some ways; this hill certainly offered an uncongested view of Mithra-Sha's beauty. Even with drought dipping the grass in tawny gold, even with crops withering under the relentless sun in a patchwork span of sickly gray-greens and browns on either side of my perch, there was plenty to admire here. There was always the Spine, never more than a few miles from the places I scuttled into to ply my useless Storycraft; and there was the sky, painted in pastel yellows and pinks as sunset encroached, dotted with tufted clouds and airships that drifted lazily among them, buoyed up by harnessed balloons.

Traveling by those, I would have made the journey to Krylan in weeks, at most—but airships were reserved for use by the ruling Sha and his family, by the military, or by those who ferried goods to the most desperate corners of Mithra-Sha.

Lately, it seemed every corner was desperate.

It hadn't always been this way. Only a handful of years ago, Storycrafters had ensured the Mithran people wanted for very little. A Wellspoken tale from a powerful Storycrafter could conjure storms on a cloudless horizon; it could coax crops to grow and flowers to bloom. Airships and cities had been spun to life by stories; rivers had carved their paths into barren lands by the curl of a Storycrafter's clever tongue. The Spine itself had flourished from the words spoken by a Master Storycrafter long ago, his epic tale woven so beautifully it had brought the farthest reaches of the country together.

Such power had ridden the current of words spoken over this country that we'd been ranked by the tales we could tell, our might delineated by the color of our cloaks. And I still tasted the bitter despair that had choked me the day I'd drawn my cloak from its fastenings in my closet to find it a dull ash-gray—how I'd poured its hem through my fingers, searching frantically for a flicker of color, any color…and found none.

That despair had redoubled when all my fellow Storycrafters had come about sporting the same cinder shades, each of us brought low in the likeness of one another: taletellers without any power left in their stories.

And now those stories brought only a shimmer of illusion, a gasp of a mirage to tempt wanderers in this barren desert of dreams. A story without its end could conjure little, if anything; and those who tried to circumvent their circumstances with amplifiers had Misspoken more and more tales in recent years, those nightmarish manifestations adding terror on top of the anguish Mithra-Sha already suffered.

Word along the Spine had it that the soldiers and Storycrafters in service to the Sha had their arms full, gathering up the manifestations of those broken tales that could not be easily destroyed, and ushering them out of the country to the Isle of Misspoken Stories where they could harm no one. It was a lucrative task, one that offered a small sense of comfort to the beleaguered country.

But the whispers of them remained. The threat of what they could do. What *we* could do.

So we Storycrafters had become useless at best. At worst, at our most desperate, we added to the suffering around us.

Perhaps that was why my spine bristled whenever a Mithran soldier breathed the same air as me. Their widespread presence was a reminder that if I did grow desperate enough to taste an amplifier's power, I would be pounced on. Jailed. Enfettered like the young woman in my unfinished story, a cellar my prison, my weaving left for worthless tales no one would ever hear.

It felt too close, sometimes. Inevitable.

And no one would miss me when I was gone.

Dampness scuffed my sleeve, and I hastily thumbed away a second tear before it could escape my eye. Drawing my knees nearer to my chest, I hugged them close and stared down the slope of the hill to the Spine, dimming into a freckled silver sheen as the sun was lost behind the hill. Soon, it would gleam like moonlight instead...an icy river through the shadows, a current that would carry me onward.

But for now, I lingered, and watched the sunset paint the countryside in splashes of color. And I let myself remember a time when Storycrafters had been to thank for those things...when tales had endings at all, good or bad.

When we were something to believe in.

CHAPTER 4
AT THE GATES OF KRYLAN

*W*allowing in self-pity was a difficult mindset to maintain when one had places to go and tales to tell.

With my satchel of meager belongings retrieved from beneath a bush abreast of the Spine, I put Rothmere and my failures there at my back; and for weeks more, I walked.

It was not an uneventful journey—travel on the Spine never was. A few caravans ushered me in for the trade of attempted tales, and even though they abandoned me when those floundered, the disappointment was worthwhile for the swift bouts of safety their presence afforded.

Without them, I hurried alone, tracking the thickening undergrowth as the drought-dusted, emaciated foliage of the dells gave way to thicker evergreens fed by seawater instead; a tinge of salt soaked the air that spoke of the narrowing land and the inlet sea encroaching on its edges.

There were memorable faces to stamp my days, characters of bustling salespeople and coy Luck-tellers, curt caravan matriarchs and jovial troupe frontmen weaving themselves into the tales I told when I moved on from them. They all glittered just as brightly as the road we walked together, leaving sizzling imprints on my mind like sunspots long after we parted ways.

And we parted ways more frequently as the scenery changed—as the Tailbone City drew nigh.

The soldiering presence thickened along the Spine the nearer I journeyed to Krylan, and almost of their own volition, my habits shifted; I found myself sleeping often during the day in pockets of shade off the side of the glass road, dodging the suffocating heat as well as the keen eyes of Mithran soldiers.

During the night, I walked—more vulnerable by far, but I appreciated the silence, the broad spans of nothingness between pockets of caravans and fellow travelers I passed. And there was something arresting about the path forged of utter moonlight beneath me, the lonely tread of my steps on its shimmering face soft as music.

But then there came the night when not even late hours of travel spared me the crowds; they flocked the Spine in frenzied clusters from the moment I crawled out of my foliage shelter at sundown, and as I walked, they only thickened. Excitement swarmed the air in a captivating hum that nudged my own enthusiasm up from its sleepy repose; despite the alarming number of Mithran soldiers weaving through the herd of people, my feet stuck to the Spine rather than steering off of it.

And perhaps that was for the better, because no one looked twice at me...not even in my drab Storycrafter gray. Some selfsame, giddy rush urged us all along with the feverish haste of a quill scratching out the perfect tale, delighting in every stroke made word; even the soldiers laughed and talked in spirited tones that lightened my heart.

For a moment, I belonged to something, even if I didn't quite understand what it was. That intimacy towed me along, setting me weaving through the crowd more quickly than most could move in caravans and companies of three or more—so I was swifter to round a bend in the dense evergreen swath and find the end to this particular tale that all our haste wrote us in together.

We had reached the gates of Krylan.

The first sight of the city knocked the breath out of my chest; the gate alone was cathedral-like, a soaring set of mint-green doors in rich currant frames edged by dust-gold, spire-topped towers—the color of healthy grainfields in the height of harvest. The Spine led straight to those doors, manned by an uncountable swarm of soldiers, the glass ending perfectly at the city's threshold like the final flawless whisper of the Master Storycrafter whose tale had laid the road itself.

Now I saw, too, why the road was so crowded; everyone who passed through those gates had to submit to a search from the soldiers.

For the first time since the buzz of frenetic energy had scooped me up out of my resting place and swept me off in this sea of people, my heels scraped to a stop against the glass. A few caravanners knocked into me, but their bodies hardly jostled me forward.

Sweat dewed the small of my back. My voice stuck in my throat.

I was not welcome here.

I didn't know how I knew it, but I was as certain of that as I'd once been of my story endings. Whether for the drab cloak marking me a consummate failure, or that Luck-lost feeling of being watched and judged from afar, the city gates of Krylan felt no different now from the door of my parents' home.

Something else waiting to be slammed in my expectant face.

A heavy weight barged into me from behind, an impatient salesperson bellowing at me to *stop holding up the line*. Borne on the tide of eager bodies who had no reason to fear, I stumbled forward through the Spine's glittering glow, the trees around us paved in silver sheen from the light beneath our feet, our faces sculpted in the refracted glow of mint, amber, and crimson from the gatehouse. And through its seams as we drew closer…

I lost my breath again at the sight of Krylan proper—a city built of stories.

Flushed in shadows, much of it was nondescript, waiting to be revealed in the light of glorious morning; but the moonlight and lanternlight within revealed enough of its peaked towers and arched streets to be awe-inspiring. Thin bridges laced its many turrets together, with domed caps scattered between; everything seemed to be built of sharp, spired angles—from cathedral naves where people invoked Luck with coin and prayers to many-tiered corridors of housing set above shops. Revelrous sounds floated from the inner streets, music and laughter and friendly shouts weaving perfectly in with the fevered chatter of the folk around me, fighting to lift my spirits.

There was no turning back, no fleeing now; I'd prayed myself hoarse all the way here, and all I'd found was more disappointment, more failure, more loneliness.

Krylan was a coin-toss I hadn't tried. Ready or not, welcomed or not, here I came.

With a fortifying breath, I stepped up to the broad stone turnstile that funneled visitors through; praying to the Maker that my pounding heart wasn't audible to the line of more than fifteen soldiers holding the turnstile and the gates beyond it, I hitched my satchel tight against my shoulder and tugged on a smile. "Evening, sirs."

"Evening, ma'am." One of the soldiers flashed a grin in return, barely visible through his thick, salt-and-ink beard; he held a ledger in the crook of his arm, quill poised to write, and though he must have been about this business since long before sundown, his beaming expression remained unworn. "Name and origin?"

"Audra Jashowin. From Vallanmyre." Though both those things were true, somehow the weighted stares of his fellow soldiers made my neck prickle as if I'd been caught in a lie. One of them in particular watched me with a heated intensity I would've assumed should be kept for gamesmen entering the city with crossbows and blades; his thick, ruddy brows mashed low over a storm-gray gaze that didn't falter as he beheld me.

"Mmhmm." The soldier scratched his ledger. "And what brings you to Krylan, Miss Jashowin?"

"Work, I hope." Peeling my lips back in what I prayed was a disarming adjustment to my own smile, I gave my bag a rattle. "If not, I'll be out of your streets soon."

"Mmm," the soldier hummed again, eyes flicking to me and hastily away again as he jotted down far more than what I'd just spoken.

My stomach plummeted; he'd taken in my cloak, likely noted it for what it was...not a simple traveling cape, but a Storycrafter's ashen attire. And he would do with that as he willed—whether he saw it as an advantage or a detriment to the city.

Of all the rotten luck...why hadn't I balled the thing into my satchel before I'd reached the gate?

I was too used to it from the Spine; too used to being innocuous, unassuming, or simply passed by. Here in Krylan, it would be different; here, I would have to stash it away before my reputation ruined itself.

But it was too late now for this band of soldiers; I could do nothing but hold my ground while the officer made his notes and finally, *finally* looked at me again. I wasn't certain if I imagined that the light in his gaze had dimmed a bit, caution creeping into the cracks of his stare. "You may find work is a bit lacking in Krylan at present, Miss Jashowin."

His tone, at least, remained kind—almost too kind. It held the same sickly edge of pity as the glances of the townspeople in Rothmere when they'd thumbed out a few coppers for my trouble.

He didn't expect me to stay long. He expected nothing at all from me...disappointed before I'd even set foot into the city.

Anguish spread like an inkblot through my middle; I fought to scrub it away with a fresh tilt to my smile. "I'm sure there will be *some* kind of work! I'm not above shoveling slag off the streets or running errands all day long."

That, at least, earned me a chuckle. "That attitude may carry you places yet." He sidestepped, sweeping an arm to beckon me through the turnstile. "Welcome to Krylan."

My heart lunged into my throat and tears surged in my eyes. Feeling half like a figment within one of my own tales, I floated past him into the shadow of the open gates; every sense beckoned me toward the promise gripped in those shadow-soaked streets, beckoned with hope—a vocation that did not end in failure, a chance to *belong* somewhere—

Rough fingers snagged hold of my satchel strap, yanking me off-balance and then thrusting me into the shadow of the open gate.

I stumbled into the deep vee of darkness between the green iron and the tawny tower beside it, righting myself with a hand to the stone. Whirling, heart leaving its floating grace to plunge straight to my toes, I faced the redheaded soldier who'd watched me so keenly.

Now the bulk of him filled up the gap between door and tower, barring my escape.

CHAPTER 5
THE TWO-SIDED COIN

very fear of Mithran soldiers I'd ever held, even without a cause or story to pin it to, swirled in a suffocating lump in my throat as the officer stalked into the vee after me, his muscular contours bristling with restrained violence.

I darted forward, aiming to duck around him; but before I had taken more than a step, his hand was around my satchel strap again, between my shoulderblades. He wrenched the braided cord harshly against the side of my neck as he backed me deeper into the vee—until my shoulders crammed stone and iron so hard they pinched with agony, and a yelp burst from my lips.

"I know what you are, *Storycrafter*." His snarl stank of ash and tobacco, spinning my already-whirling head into fractals of knee-quaking fright. "You're nothing but a charlatan selling useless *lies*, and I'm not about to watch you take advantage of the poor in this town with your make-believe."

Somewhere, defiance and indignation found a foothold in the swirl of terror that his crowding, overbearing presence evoked. I slid my thumb under the strap where it chafed the side of my neck, tugging it away just enough that relief gave me the strength to speak. "I've done absolutely *nothing* wrong. *Nothing* to warrant this kind of treatment—"

"*Yet*." With a twirl of his fingers, he tightened the strap, pinning my thumb to my collarbone and spiking pain into my hand. "But you *will*. You're a talentless little trickster, and you'll do what every one of your kind does…steal from honest folk with stories that have no power. And when you do, do you know what happens next?" He bent into my breathing space, his snarl harsh against my tingling face. "You'll soon notice you are the *only* Storycrafter in

Krylan. Do you need me to tell *you* a story about what happened to all the others?"

The air tumbled from me in a rush, and blind terror stiffened my limbs so viciously I no longer felt the satchel strap cutting into my neck or digging into the base of my thumb.

I had *always* been right about these Mithran soldiers.

The man's lips peeled back in triumph at whatever emotion scrawled across my face. "I'll be watching you, Storycrafter. The first moment I catch a *whiff* you've started plying your tricks, there won't be enough flips of Luck's two-sided *coin* to save you from what I'll do with your lying, cheating hide."

Staring into the hateful gleam of his eyes, there was no question he meant it. Every word. Whatever havoc Storycrafters had wreaked in Krylan before me—if they truly had, and this was not merely prejudice for what we could or couldn't do with our unending tales—he was prepared to retribute it into *my* flesh.

As he might have done to those like me, who were no longer in this city.

"Galan!" The shout winnowed around the door, bringing the soldier's shoulders stiffly together. "Man your post, will you? Where in flipping Luck did you run off to?"

"On my way!" He gave one last wrench of the strap, jerking me flush against him, then flinging me back so hard I landed on my seat, teeth slamming together, pain grinding into my temples. Water flooded my eyes, but I didn't dare rise to meet his all-knowing sneer; nor did I move when he sauntered off, back to his post.

Tears blurred the seam of the street I could see beyond the gap, and I grasped blindly for the tower's harsh edge. But when I tried to rise, the shaking in my legs put me back down in an instant, folding up like a cut streamer.

I gripped the sculpted tower and turned my face against it, squeezing my eyes shut and caring nothing this time for the tears that escaped down my face; my own mouth tasted of tobacco and ash.

Huddled between the door and the tower, I shivered and sobbed.

Not wanted in Vallanmyre. Not wanted in Dalfi, the last city where I'd hoped against hope there was someone who wouldn't turn me away. Not wanted in Krylan, either, and I'd only just set foot over its threshold.

Nowhere in Mithra-Sha seemed to have a space for Audra Jashowin anymore. If all the stories in our country had no end, mine had ended too abruptly.

Sometimes it felt as if I had died. As if I was a displaced spirit gliding among the people, belonging with no one, wanted by no one.

An old wound broke open and bled at that notion, a harsh, hurting word hissing in the back of my head: *expendable.*

Face still buried against the back of my hand, I peeled one eye open to watch the folk from the Spine funnel past the door, into the city; no one looked twice my way. No one knew or cared for a forgotten Storycrafter wrapped in shadows, knees still quaking from a vicious and unearned threatening. An assault meant to send me fleeing.

Expendable. Unwanted.

No one would miss me here. No one anywhere missed me. No one would notice if I came or went.

Except that soldier. *Galan.*

He would notice. He was awaiting my failure. Awaiting the opportunity to make me the brunt of his hate, as I'd fretted every soldier I'd crossed paths with might do.

It had finally come to pass. That thing I had so long feared—I was on the other side of it. I had tasted it.

I had *survived* it.

Something flickered in the depths of me—some brash notion that breathed strength into my shaking limbs.

Now he would track me. Stalk me. Watch me.

Because I *existed.* Because I was a living, breathing Storycrafter who still tried. Even if I had been discarded by some, forgotten by those who raised me, abandoned by someone I once thought of as a sister…I could forge new bonds. And if I could make enemies simply by stepping into a city, then I could make friends, as well.

Friends and enemies. Good and ill. The two sides of fickle Luck's impartial coin.

Fingers tightening around the jagged edge of the tower, I hauled myself up to my quivering legs, planting my feet, yanking my satchel off and switching it to the unchafed side of my neck. When I fingered that mark carved into my skin, my resolve stuck to my heart like ink bonded to a page—words set and dried in parchment.

Inerasable. Undeniable.

Audra Jashowin would not be run out of one more city. She would not run at all…not anymore. There was nowhere else to go.

I had reached the end of my southward journey—there would be no better place to plant my heels and make a stand. Against all of the fear that had driven me from inhabited places; against the feeling that I could not belong anywhere.

Though I had not expected the likes of this Officer Galan…if I was going to fortify my courage against any soldier, I craved it to be him. The sort of man who made all my misplaced fears seem true.

So. If he wanted to make me his enemy, I'd make his city my playground.

CHAPTER 6
FAREWELL TO THE GRAY

The way my heart thrilled at the challenge laid ahead in Krylan made me feel, in some ways, like a stranger to myself. I had never really been the sort to stir up trouble, and these last handful of years in particular, all I'd wanted was as quiet a life as my useless Storycrafting talents could render me.

But my scrape with Galan awakened something ugly and *angry* seething in my chest, and it would not be quieted. It wanted to prove wrong, not only him, but every pitying look and sad headshake that had haunted me down the Spine. Every unspoken notion that I was as withered and used-up as my craft.

I hardly slept that first night in the city; finding refuge in the clotted shadows beneath one of Krylan's lower bridges, I wiled away the hours in thought. Plotting my course and strategizing keenly had kept me alive on the Spine; I had faith it would do the same now.

So instead of sleeping, I planned; step by step, piece by piece. What I would do next, where I would go. How I would act and carry myself to a certain point, beyond which I couldn't see…but I would weave it together as I went.

It was no different from plotting out a story—something I had done often while I traveled in the meager hopes that some foresight would help bolster an ending.

But this was not an ending; it was a new beginning, and I was determined to make it the best one I could.

So when dawn broke against my face, rousing me from just a few fitful hours of sleep, I dutifully rose, servant to my own schemes—if a reluctant, grumbling one—and stowed away the cloak I'd used as a pillow last night and for so many before it.

I grazed my fingertips lightly over the ashen folds with one last dismal wish to Luck's fickle flip of the coin that a shimmer of color might appear in the creases.

Nothing. Just as drab gray as ever.

A corner of my spirit wilted, lying tucked away in the satchel with my cloak as I tugged it shut, hoisted it over my shoulder, and scrambled from the recess beneath the bridge to explore Krylan as the sunlight revealed it.

By night, the city had beckoned and shivered in shadow-dipped secrecy. By day, it was a flower abloom in a riot of colors. Tawny spires and emerald domes dominated the Mithran portion of the city, and towers and bronze minarets the Ameresh immigrant quarter. Cathedrals loomed on every other street corner, built of white magnesite on one half and ebony quartz on the other—the sharp contrast of Luck's two sides. Statues outside depicted Luck itself as a tall, narrow figure wearing a two-faced mask, a coin on its fist with thumb tucked beneath, ready to flip that sharp-edged token and change the path of the future.

I strode beneath its unseeing mask—one half weeping, the other side grinning—without glancing back.

Today, and every day after, I was determined to make my own luck.

So I spent my last coppers—the two from Rothmere, and a third I'd earned by the mercy of a caravan matriarch after I'd scrubbed out the inside of every iron pot in all four of her family's carts—on new attire: a simple tan tunic, a corset more for show than support, and a thick wool skirt that would serve as a blanket until I could afford to sleep somewhere other than beneath a bridge.

I tugged my hair into braids and washed my face in a rain barrel at the corner of one of the markets shared by Mithran and Ameresh vendors shouting good-natured abuse at one another.

And then I set off to do what Galan would want to see: I went to beg for a position at every public house and tavern I could find.

It was not a swift venture; it was not a simple one, either. Work was indeed scarce, particularly in a city brimming with both Mithran hopefuls having nowhere else to search, and Ameresh immigrants looking to begin a new life safe from the troubles that afflicted their own country.

But after three days and a rotation into nearly every establishment making meals of any kind, I found *The Tiller's Tankard*—a tavern that served the laborers in and surrounding Krylan. Errick Dubain, the tavernkeeper, had himself been a farmer of some repute before an injury with a scythe had cost him his lower left arm.

"Fieldworkers and farmhands deserve a hot meal and a full tankard as much as any bladesmith or trader or those Luck-loved actors my fellow tavernkeepers prefer to serve," he grumbled while I sat fidgeting at the table across from him, taking in the dingy sweeps of his establishment. Long and high-roofed, it was reminiscent of a stable in ways that made me suspect it had been converted from such. It certainly had all the trimmings of it, from the shape down to the mounting block at the far end, converted to a stage where bards performed, paid only half-mind by the patrons.

But that wasn't why I fidgeted.

There was an absolute abundance of Mithran soldiers here, overflowing at the tables within the small, private stalls that might have once housed horses. Their chatter hummed in my ears as I fought to pin my focus on Errick and remain in the conversation.

They were not here because of me. But still, my skin crawled.

"I don't mind serving whoever," I lied through my tight smile, holding Errick's sun-stamped, wrinkled gaze. "I just need the coppers."

"Aye." He folded his arms loosely over his barreled chest, one elbow-length leather glove dragging forward to reveal the cuff on his stumped arm. "You should do nicely, then. I only demand three things: a hardworking ethic, a bright disposition, and that you not run out in the dead of night."

I blinked. "Oddly specific."

"That was what the girl you're replacing did," he grunted, shifting his seat. "I had high hopes for Madellah, I really did…seemed she'd been down on her luck for some time. Used to be a Storycrafter, was my understanding. Then one night, she missed her rotation, and that was the end of that. Never saw her again."

Horror sheared down my spine, my gaze flipping back to the tables of Mithran soldiers as my perception of this establishment tilted abruptly.

The stage—not only for bards and actors, but a temptation irresistible for Storycrafters hoping to sell an unfinished story. And soldiers like Galan, perhaps even Galan's own company, frequented this place. Watching for charlatans. For liars.

For people like *me*.

This hadn't been *precisely* part of the plan; I'd intended a public façade for whenever Galan chanced a glance my way, not to place myself directly beneath his beady gaze.

But then again, he couldn't accuse me of shifty behavior if I worked proudly beneath his very nose and the noses of his fellow soldiers; and the obviousness of my daily trade might just serve as a deterrent for him looking any closer at the other dealings I intended to kick up in the dust of fleeing footfalls into the other side of the city whenever he wasn't looking.

So I crafted on my most charming smile, reached a hand across the table, and met Errick's stern gaze. "Those three things, I can do. Consider my talents yours…and don't worry, I'm a quick learner."

He snorted. "We'll see about that."

But he clasped my hand. And just like that, I had an honest trade.

CHAPTER 7
STORIES SPOKEN IN SECRET

If only an honest trade were enough.

I was grateful, of course—so grateful to collect enough coppers to pay for one of three beds in a small room at a boarding house. Particularly when the autumn rains began to roll in off the coast, smashing the city rooftops with needle-sharp raindrops. I didn't mind learning from the rest of the barmistresses and barmasters who'd served at *The Tiller's Tankard* longer than me; I didn't even mind the patrons, soldiers aside.

But it *wasn't* enough.

Not enough to keep me fed and in clothes; not enough to pay for a different establishment I didn't have to share with too many bodies packed together, snores echoing from either side of the thin wooden walls that I slept—or tried to sleep—between. It didn't keep the hungry gazes of the other boarders from hanging on my coinpurse, or quiet my craving for my own space where I didn't have to sleep with one eye open, fearing the creaking of the door that would signal someone had decided to flip Luck's coin in their favor by stealing mine.

And it wasn't enough to quiet the itch for Storycraft that rubbed under my skin.

I'd worried that might be the case, though I'd never had to pursue the possibility while I'd traveled the Spine. My whole life, I'd been telling stories; and even though they'd been relatively fruitless these past few years, the disappointment didn't dim the craving to spin tales and weave narratives. I ached for even the rawest beginnings of a story to carry my tired mind away from the

Tankard where eyes were always on me, and the boarding house where it was the same, if for different reasons.

So at night, I crept out of the boarding house in different attire than I'd entered, wearing a different cloak—core black, bought for paltry coppers from a man who couldn't stitch a straight seam to save his life—and hiding my hair beneath a scarf. It never seemed that Galan or his friends pursued me...or, if they did, I was better at evading them than I thought.

Those three days searching for work had taught me a handful of ways into the Ameresh district. Now I took them, different ones every night, never settling on a pattern; and they always brought me to the nightlife markets.

Glass lanterns paved the midnight marketplaces in splashes of raucous mosaic; all sorts of instruments peppered the air with a dizzying array of notes, somehow separate and blended all at once. Fragrant cooking spices and rich honeyed drink notes floated on the back of the music, beckoning, enticing. Hawkers brayed and even some children laughed, playing at their parents' feet as if they'd never tire. In the late hour, the vibrant, jeweled tones of the immigrants' attire—all classic Ameresh dress—half-blinded me with their vivid beauty.

They danced. They bought and sold. They argued and discussed, they sang and laughed. And in the shadowed avenues between their minaret towers and broad stone homes, a Storycrafter told half-finished tales.

It was everything I'd dared to hope for; the Ameresh immigrants had not yet grown as jaded as my Mithran countrymen...perhaps because, prior to arriving in Krylan, they had never known the full array of what Storycrafting *could* be.

Sha Lothar, ruling from Vallanmyre, did not permit Storycrafters to immigrate to Amere-Del; we were to keep to our own borders, safe from what I took to be quite a bit of conflict and danger seething within the Ameresh borders. So our neighbors had tasted little of the wonder-working power of a story before, and they had far less to be disappointed in.

I won more grateful smiles and coppers in their district than in any one town or city along the Spine—particularly from parents who offered grateful grins when they carried away their children, small bodies lulled to sleep before my stories ever faltered.

In time, I learned to tell my tales more slowly, more rhythmically...to turn broken ones without endings into lullabies that floated off into silence. It was a bandage over a broken bone, but it helped to have purpose again. Even if it didn't mend the stories, perhaps it could mend *me*.

I served meals and drinks to rowdy patrons. I told tales to sooth children in the shadows. In time, I moved on from the boarding house to a room nearly just as small, situated in one of the windowed complexes framing Krylan's bustling streets; but it was mine, and *only* mine.

It was a life, or the beginnings of one…something I could finally call my own. And though I lived it walking the razored edge of Luck's coin, waiting with bated breath for the balance to flip against my favor, I *lived*…I lived the most out of every day.

Days passed.

Weeks passed.

A month passed. Then two.

And then it happened.

CHAPTER 8
A CITY CALLED HOME

I t was a day that dawned like any other.

The splash of the waterclock on my bedside shelf jolted me from a deep, restful slumber; the gears, cranked to the precise hour of my intended waking, cut free at last—tipping a gentle deluge from the gathered handbucket that had slowly filled overnight into the bowl below.

It was the same sound that greeted me every morning. A rhythm. A routine.

I came to with a smile to greet the day, dipping my fingers into the bowl and splashing water on my face to wake myself fully before I clambered off the foot of the bed into the long, narrow space that made up my room. It was only scarcely broader than my armspan across, but I'd made the most of it; repurposed wood from scrap heaps across the city strung up as shelves, displaying my meager collection of secondhand books and neatly folded clothes; a washbowl and a pitcher on the same narrow wooden nightstand that housed my satchel and the single mauve-and-ivory orchid I'd indulged in to brighten up the space.

Dressing was an art I'd mastered over time, pulling elbows to avoid knocking into the walls. With hair finger-combed and tied back, corset laced and feet shoved into my well-worn boots, I made my way to my second-favorite indulgence: a small bakery tucked away on the corner of the same street I now had the pleasure of calling my home.

Most of my meals came from *The Tiller's Tankard*; since I spent my afternoons and evenings there, it was only fair Errick provided stew and bread in between serving tables. But the first meal was the most important of the day, and now that foraging was no longer my primary source of food, I didn't mind shelling out the coppers for a hearty breakfast. Particularly when a friendly face accompanied it.

The whisper of layered chimes cascaded after my arrival in the warm, wood-walled space like a gusty sigh…different from the ringing bells most vendors employed, a mark of how the space differed as well. The bright silks adorning the walls and rugging the floors, the particular blend of savory and sweet spices held for different pastries, loaves, and even potted pies, all delineated the Ameresh flare of this place. And that was before one laid eyes on its proprietor at the kneading counter, working over a batch of dough and calling out at my arrival, "I'll be with you as soon as I can make this cheese loaf *behave!*"

"Is that *any* way to refer to a customer?" I joked, winding between the already-stocked shelves loaded with fresh-made breads to reach the counter.

The shop's patroness snorted. "Ah, Addie. Just you."

"Ah, Lio. Just me," I grinned, folding my arms on the counter and leaning my weight into them. "Who's the misbehaving cheese loaf?"

"This *blasted* thing." She pummeled the dough with one fist, then straightened, hands perched on her broad hips, long sleeves cuffed to cover her wrists and speckled in flecks of flour. "That is the last time I use Farmer Tillion's raw cheddar, I'll tell you that much."

I couldn't stifle a laugh at the smirk she shot me; Lionyra Vara was an Ameresh immigrant around my age who'd left her own district behind, trading the certainty of profit among her kin for the chance of being the most renowned Ameresh baker and pastry-maker in the Mithran district of Krylan. And from what I had tasted—and broadly lauded—of her wares, she had a better than decent chance of securing the title.

It wasn't only that her goods were delicious, either; Lio exuded the sort of honest benevolence that made one eager to befriend her, even at the expense of looking the fool. She dressed like royalty despite her humble station, a gold hoop in her left nostril, her well-pared nails always lacquered the same shade as her traditional jewel-toned Ameresh attire; her dark hair, bound beneath a matching silk handkerchief, was a sleek black that married well with her rich brown skin, and her smiles came often and easily, beckoning in customers far more gracefully than even the well-rendered sign above the door, sporting the bakery name: *The Secret Ingredient.*

I'd tried to craft a character like her into one of my tales soon after we'd met, but I'd never quite managed it. Something about Lionyra Vara defied imitation, as if there really was some secret thing about her that no tale could capture; as if she was someone who must be experienced purely in the flesh, not by the spoken word.

"Anyway," Lio winked, dusting her hands clean and peeling off her apron, trading the role of the baker for the saleswoman with a neat pivot, "what will you have today, Addie-cat?"

Her deep, hoarse voice and rich Ameresh accent played mischievously with the nickname she'd given me the first day I'd ducked into her shop to escape a violent deluge of autumn seaside rain. Soaked and shivering on her stoop, I'd bought a pastry just to be polite; she'd looked me over with those thick, dark brows arched, and declared, "You look like a half-drowned alleycat."

When I'd introduced myself as Audra, she'd announced herself a woman of nicknames—"Lionyra, but you'll call me Lio"—and then she'd decided I was Addie. And from that, with a roguish grin at the sound of the name rolling off her own tongue, she'd added, "A half-drowned *Addie-cat*."

I'd been coming to her every morning since, even when I could make a loaf or pastry last me two breakfasts; because Lio's shop was warm, but Lio herself was warmer. She was the closest thing to a friend I'd had since my disastrous detour to Dalfi on my southward travels, when another person I'd thought of as a friend—as a sister, even—had politely dodged conversation with me. Then dodged *me* with increasing agitation. And then broken her sweet disposition to threaten my arrest if I didn't get off her doorstep and sober up in solitude.

Another door slammed in my face, the echo of it still ringing in my ears.

Lio did not slam the door; she stood behind the coin till, watching me expectantly, and I clawed myself out of that painful pocket of the past to answer the question I'd left hanging far too long to be polite. "Rosemary and garlic loaf today, if you've got one, Lio?"

"*If I've got one,*" she scoffed. "I'd *better* have one, or what was I up three hours before sunrise doing?"

"I assumed you were spending all that time on your schemes to overthrow Krylan and establish a guild of bakers. Fair, but not afraid to douse you in flour and toss you into the brick ovens if you misbehaved."

"You are always so full of nonsense, Addie-cat." She flicked her fingers at me like dusting water off the bright magenta sheen that coated her nails; then she hurried around the counter to one of the display stands, where she rifled among the contents with the practiced care of the same one who baked and stocked the contents each day. "Plans for citywide dominion don't take three hours. One, at the most."

"Ah, of course, I'm forgetting," I laughed. "This is Lionyra Vara I'm speaking to."

"And never forget it again!" She pitched the wrapped loaf to me underhand, and I caught it, the impact in my hands puffing a fragrant waft of rich spices into my nostrils. My mouth flooded with water, and I almost moaned.

"You are truly a gift, Lio," I said fervently as she circled back around to the till. "I don't know how you manage all of this."

"Years and years of being in the kitchens when I ought to have been anywhere else." She flashed a hand to me, brightly-tipped nails curling. "Now. Payment?"

"Obviously." I fished out a copper and flipped it to her like Luck's own coin ready to turn favorably on the day; and with the savory aroma still floating from the loaf in my hand, that was not difficult to believe.

Lio slipped the coin into the till, then leaned her elbows on the counter. *"And?"*

I rolled my eyes; this other half of the payment was something she'd first demanded after a night of tension and poor treatment from soldiers at the *Tankard* had driven me to her doorstep for my usual loaf in an absolutely foul mood. It was the first time she'd called me her friend—and the first time, but not the last, that she'd invited me into her spacious back room for sweet Ameresh dessert tea, where I'd poured out as much of my life's story as I dared.

And ever since then, she'd demanded dual payment for every loaf of bread.

"All right, all right, you greedy goose, let me think." I propped my elbows backward on the counter, resting the loaf over my midsection and worrying into the crust with my fingernails. "One good thing that's happened in the last day…"

"Anything at all," she prodded.

"I said, let me think!" I swung around to swat her with the edge of the loaf, which wasn't enough even to shift her from her incline, chin balanced on her palms, awaiting my report. Blowing out a breath between rounded lips, I hunted around for the details of the previous day. "Well, Errick's been in an exceptionally good mood, though none of the other bartenders know why. But he let me go home early yesterday…barely after sunset."

Lio straightened, grinning. "That's fantastic news, Addie!"

And she knew it was; Lio and I had first crossed paths in the Ameresh district where she'd manned a cart while I told tales. Though my memories of her presence had been sketched in charcoal shadows, she'd recalled me clearly;

she'd told me I glowed when I wove my stories. She knew I returned almost every night…and how much more I could do on a night when Errick didn't k us working to miserable hours.

"It was a good night," I agreed, halving the loaf with a single rip now tha my payment was complete. "Tonight will be even better. We're still on for tea.

"Yes, and finally you will let me teach you how to play *Poor Man's Dice*." S stabbed a finger several times into the counter between us. "I know there is a good gameswoman in there somewhere, and I will draw her out by any means necessary."

Snorting, I stuffed a piece of bread into my mouth. "The greatest baker i Krylan, a tutor in Ameresh games, a well-dressed citizen…how *do* you manage all?"

Lio spread her palms in a wide shrug. "What if I told you I am also the runaway Delina of Amere-Del who has been hunted for many moons, seeking better luck in a life of peasantry and humble servitude?"

"Right," I deadpanned. "And I'm the Master Storycrafter in disguise."

We both burst into laughter, and as the chimes tumbled above the door again—ushering in the morning rush, which I was always determined to beat— backed away, lifting my half-loaf high. "Perfection itself, as always, Lio!"

"Until tonight, Addie-cat!"

I walked with the wind in my steps from *The Secret Ingredient*, winding through Krylan's familiar avenues with joy blooming in my chest.

It had taken only the turn of a single day for my parents to shut me away. For everyone I'd known and loved to shun me like a stranger. Every morning when Lio still treated me like a friend was a gift I didn't intend to squander; no could I ever explain to her how *that* was the best thing that happened to me, da after day.

I took my time making my way toward the *Tankard*, just as I did every day—enjoying half of the bread loaf while I lingered at open plazas where actin troupes performed short skits for the crowd. I clapped and cheered with all my might, the essence of the performing soul in need echoing my own desperate refrain from all my years wandering down the Spine, seeking somewhere to belong. I tossed a few coins into their collections box and hoped they would fi that belonging here, just as I had.

I wound through the markets next, purchasing items for a few coppers more—always carefully budgeted, exact to the razor-edge of the coin I had to spare, but enough to bring smiles to whichever vendors seemed the most despondent. And if I couldn't use their wares myself, I brought them with the other half of the bread loaf to the beggar's quarter, just a stone's throw from the *Tankard*, and handed them off.

Items for trade, and a bit of sustenance. It wasn't much to give, but there were too many poor and destitute to count, and two months in the Tailbone of Mithra-Sha had not shaken the sense that much of the suffering in our country was every Storycrafter's fault. Helping with what little I could spare seemed the least I could do…and I was glad to do it.

With empty hands and lighter pockets, and a heart brighter by far, I reached the *Tankard* moments before the midday swell, when farmers and tillers and poorer laborers flooded into the converted stable for a hot meal and a stein of cider swiftly served before the latter half of their workday began.

I danced inside with a pirouette, waving a greeting to Errick as I passed him just off to the side of the rolled-aside doors; he didn't even glance away from the boy he was engaged in some deep conversation with, but that was all right. A half-dozen greetings floated from my fellow barmistresses and barmasters as I retrieved my plain gray apron and slipped it over my head.

For just a moment, the ashen fabric caught in the corner of my vision, and a pang of melancholy shredded through me—so potent it ripped the breath from my lungs and birthed a stitch beneath my ribs. Memories of another gray costume flickered in my mind…a notion of days I didn't quite *miss*, but—

"Look lively, Audra!" Nolin, one of the barmasters, tossed me a thin wooden serving tray. "Here they come!"

Shaking off the fit of nostalgia, I scrawled my broadest smile across my face and hastened to the nearest table in one of the stalls as our afternoon patrons poured in.

There was no time to reflect on forgotten gray cloaks or the past, after that; my life's own story was made up of unforgettable characters—the farmworkers with their dirt-clotted nailbeds and sun-worn stares, the tillers with broad shoulders and strained scowls, the laborers of various trades marked by old scars and burns healed over, the small nicks of fishing hooks in fabric and flesh, the callouses of tailoring scuffed with fabric dyes.

I moved relentlessly, circling to and from the counter, arms laden with trays, hands laden with tankards, over and over while the slant of sunlight through the open doors shifted and changed, lowered and lowered.

This life was nothing like I'd known before…but I truly loved it. The bustle, the busyness, the quirks and characteristics of our patrons that would always, without fail, find their way out in the stories I told in the Ameresh district long after dark. And though I wouldn't be telling tales in those streets tonight, I could tell Lio about them, and that was nearly as satisfying.

A friend. A paying trade. My stories my own secret in the dark.

Contentment surged in my throat as I paused between the rushes to sip warm water from a tankard left out for me by Nolin—and then I yelped when broad fingers gripped my upper arm, and the stern leather of a cuff rapped against my opposite wrist.

"Come with me, Audra." Errick tugged me down to the far end of the counter where it was quieter, the span of untreated wood extending nearly to the full aft of the old stable; when he spun me to face him, everything else fell away behind him, blurred out of focus.

There was only Errick, paler than I'd ever seen him, his eyes bloodshot and his mouth trembling as if he might weep.

I had never seen the sturdy old farmhand *weep* for anything.

Alarm rocked through me, and I shifted nearer to him. *"Errick?"*

"I have some trouble, Audra," he croaked. "I need your help."

CHAPTER 9
A CURSE FOR COIN

I bit off a protest the moment before it could emblazon itself on my tongue. No one had needed *my* help in as long as I could remember. Forcing myself to breathe steadily, I asked instead, "What's the matter?"

"I had an acting troupe booked for the colder season," Errick rambled, sliding his hand back through his graying chestnut hair. "Had them on the list for *months*. Well, they just sent a runner this morning to cancel on me. Couldn't even do it to my face themselves, they sent an *errand boy* to do it…"

No wonder he'd paid me no attention at my arrival. "Errick, please tell me you hadn't already paid them."

"No, but that might have been my mistake…seems they had a better offer. They're performing elsewhere until the spring."

I dropped my elbow against the serving counter, rubbing my brow. "Well, that's rotten of them, but it could be worse. At least you aren't out the coin."

"Not this time. But, Audra…" He swept a glance at the other tenders, then lowered his voice, "the *Tankard* struggles in wintertime. Fewer crops to sell at market means the sort of folk we cater to have less coin to spend on frivolous meals out-of-house. This performance was meant to usher in a newer crowd…younger, fresher faces. The sort who find other work to fill up their days during the cold times. I was betting my hand on the new coin they'd bring, to help keep the place afloat even after the troupe moved on. So I wouldn't have to trim down on my hires."

The way his gaze bored into mine, desperation and apology mingling in the depths…

My stomach plummeted.

He was talking about trimming back *me*.

Suddenly, selfishly, every copper I'd spent at Lio's shop in the past two months, every coin I'd shelled out to actors and vendors, every scrap I'd ever given away felt like foolish expense. Not kindness, but overconfidence. As if with one flip of Luck's coin, I'd never want for those things again. As if I hadn't been giving away the surety of my own wellbeing.

As if Luck's mask couldn't swivel, the grinning jester traded for the weeping miser aimed my way.

This life I'd built, this future I'd been working for, wavered and shimmered at the edges like one of my dazzling half-tales, dying even as I struggled to breathe life into it. "What can we do?"

Errick hesitated a moment, drumming his fingers on his bearded chin. "You wouldn't happen to have any mentionable talents, would you?"

Winter might have come early for how the air around me froze. My breath shuddered in my lungs; I darted a swift look around the *Tankard*, but mercifully there were no Mithran soldiers at the tables. Their shifts rotated in the early evening; the last afternoon group had already packed away to their posts, and the first round of nightly patrons had yet to change from their soldiering attire and make their way to our tables.

Still, I struggled to catch my wind. "I don't..."

"Audra, I'm begging you. What've you got? Musical talents? An acting knack? Anything? *Anything* to show off."

"Nothing that would matter."

He stared at me, long and solemn, a thin trace of disappointment winding through his gaze like the lazy curl of the last letter in an epic tale. "I haven't said a thing, because I figured it was your own choice to make. But we heard talk of another Storycrafter arriving in Krylan from some of the soldiers here, just a few days before you came asking for work. I saw how you clammed up when I mentioned Madellah being a Storycrafter, and what became of her."

The unspoken words hung between us, siphoning off what little breath I'd retained: *I know you're one, too.*

My tongue knotted around a well-written lie. So much of what I did these days felt false and failed. I didn't want to fail him, too.

"Fine. I'm a Storycrafter," I spat the words at last. "That doesn't make me an actor or a musician! I can't give your friends what you invited them for."

Errick scrubbed the back of his neck. "It just so happens, what I promised them was a performance to remember. I didn't happen to mention what sort of performance it would be."

I railed silently as that excuse slipped my grasp. "Errick, I truly don't think—"

"I'll repay you," he cut across me so harshly, the words shriveled on my tongue. "Everything I was set to pay the troupe."

Sense wailed at me to keep the two halves of my new life from overlapping; but the tentative question still wiggled out between my half-numb lips. "How…how *much* coin are we—?"

"Fifteen silvers."

I *choked*.

Fifteen silvers would settle my pay for the whole winter, and then some. It would let me *save* a bit. It would put to death any fear of an empty stomach if the cold season turned harsh, if the farmhands and tillers stopped frequenting their usual stools.

It would mean security. It would mean I could hold together this new life of mine, and continue to give to others, even if the worst should come; even if Errick revoked my assignment here.

I didn't even know how Errick Dubain of all people had *come* by that much coin—and a bitter piece of my heart resented him using it to pay performers rather than to pay all of us to stay on for the winter.

But I understood that decision, too; it was business sense. Fifteen silver spent to keep haunches on his seats and patrons returning would pay for itself and then some by spring.

And all those silvers could be mine, along with my pay as well. All I had to do was tell a story.

"They won't want to come back after they hear me." It was my last feeble attempt to convince him. To convince *myself* not to do this. "I don't bring people near…I push them away."

I didn't explain it was more than just my stories that did it. That *I* was a luckless talisman, mostly good for having doors shut in my face.

"We could stretch out the tale," Errick offered. "Don't tell it all…just tell a bit tonight. We'll promise them the next portion tomorrow. And more the day after." Excitement lightened his gaze. "There, what do you think of that? *The Undying Tale*, we'll call it…a new portion every night you work."

That was *far* more than a single story…and it strayed dangerously close to something Galan might consider looking at twice. Something like *charlatanry* and tricking people out of their coin…deceiving among the most hardworking and least profitable in Krylan with a story that would never end.

Bringing them back night after night to spend their coin and listen to me weave the next portion of the tale. To turn the next page…just the next one. No frantic thumbing through in search of an ending that always hung just out of reach. I wouldn't flirt with an ending; I'd flee from it, stretching out the story as long as possible, until I'd wrung every drop of it dry.

There was too much danger in that half-spun plan. Too much of a coin-toss to bet my luck on.

I hated that I *loved* it. I hated that his scheme made *sense*. I'd been chasing stories with hopeless, elusive endings for so long, I'd never considered telling one that deliberately *avoided* such an ending.

What if I could strangle enough power out of an unending story to do something *better* for Errick's establishment…to truly make this place memorable?

I drummed my fingers on the counter next to my elbow, pretending to decide, even though my racing thoughts had long since made the decision for me. "One condition."

"Name it."

"I want you to make it clear from the outset this was *your* idea. Not mine. And we keep the payment between us…no one else is allowed to shell over a single coin for it."

Errick's brows knitted in the center of his wrinkled forehead. "You expect people to believe you're telling this tale for free?"

"Call it a part of my earnings. Just as long as it's clear you *asked* me for it."

He studied me a long moment more; then his forehead settled, his mouth curving into a smile. "You're an odd one, Audra, there's no denying it. But I give you my word, I'll do it just as you say."

"Ah!" I said when he turned away. "*Coin*. So I'm honor-bound, in case I receive a better offer."

"Clever girl," Errick chuckled, beckoning me with a jerk of his head.

A moment later, it was done: a satchel of silvers retrieved from a locked chest behind the counter, which only Errick held the key to. Giddy disbelief rocked through me when the purse bounced against my hand, and I hastily tucked it under my corset, letting out the laces just a bit.. The dimpled coins kissed my ribs through the thin fabric of my tunic.

I was all the gladder I'd moved on from the boarding house; there was no chance I would've been left alone with this much coin on my person.

I'd walk home cautiously anyway.

CHAPTER 10
THE UNDYING TALE

t was nearly impossible to focus on my tasks the rest of the evening; my ears strained for Errick's prompting and my mind was in a clamor, dodging orders from customers in favor of concocting the beginnings of a tale.

I refused to consider how I would even *attempt* to weave some satisfactory conclusion for it; instead, I trained my focus on how expansive it could be.

Daydreaming, it turned out—something I rarely indulged in at the *Tankard*—made for poor side-wages from unimpressed customers, but it certainly made the time pass more quickly. It felt as if I'd only served a handful of tables when Errick's shout from the mounting block dragged my galloping thoughts to heel. "I've promised you all a performance, and now it's time to deliver!"

The boom of rowdy cheers jolted me to a halt; bracing the edge of the serving platter against my stomach and folding both hands on its far edge, I twisted in place to find *The Tiller's Tankard* was poured in to the brim of the inkpot with fresh-faced farmers and day-laborers; most of them were younger than our usual clientele and fit enough to sway between professions when crops ran scarce.

Errick's salvation—and mine, if I hoped to keep this honest wage—all watched with expectant eyes as his gaze, too, roved the crowd. Some still mingled amongst themselves and chatted, but others hung on his every word, waiting for the next.

I was one of them.

"You'll not find another performance like this in all of Krylan," he said—which was true, thanks to Galan— "nor in all of Mithra-Sha, perhaps! I had to plead and beg this extraordinary and humble young woman to grace our establishment with her talents…so be sure to stay a while and not make me look a fool for it."

Laughter burst like dust kicked up in a rain-thirsty drought, and heat stained my cheeks. Though it was all for show, and I'd practically begged *Errick* to employ me…still, the compliment warmed me from the inside out.

It was lovely to hear I was wanted, even if it was part of the act.

"Brace yourselves for something exceptional." With a wink, Errick tipped his head and signaled me up to the mounting block. "*The Tiller's Tankard*, and we alone, proudly present *The Undying Tale*…and Audra Jashowin, its Storycrafter!"

A hush gripped the *Tankard*, and the heat in my cheeks dripped into my belly in a pool of sizzling dread.

I wished I'd asked him not to give them my name.

But there was no turning back now; the eyes of my fellow tenders were on me, a riot of intrigue and skepticism darkening their faces; and when the patrons around me realized where others were looking, they took notice, too.

Suddenly, the edge of the serving tray pressed into my gut was no different from the wicked edge of Luck's coin, already tossed…already twirling in the air, waiting to land for or against me.

Swallowing my panic, I threaded between expectant patrons to join Errick at the mounting block. He offered his broad hand to me, gratitude and reassurance bright in his eyes; and with the silvers pressed against my ribs, their weight woven into the encouragement of his single swift nod, I stepped up beside him to face the crowd.

Still no soldiers…not yet. Maybe Luck was smiling at me tonight, after all.

Errick stepped down heavily off the block, clapping his one hand on his thigh as he went, leading the room into a broken smattering of polite applause; most watched me with a touch of interest but little faith. They were practical, hardworking people in need of some sensible distraction for the night.

The acting troupe would have done far better. But all they had was me.

Luck, let me be enough.

I gathered my breath and smoothed down my skirts as I settled into the seat Errick had arranged on the back of the mounting block. "Let me tell you a story."

And as an expectant hush blanketed half the *Tankard*, I began my unpracticed tale.

This story begins where many do: in a land that seemed nearly perfect, except for those who wanted what they could not have. Those who loved what was not theirs to love. Those who coveted what begat danger even to gaze upon. And those whose honest trade was turned against them.

A few new heads swiveled my way, and my heart bounded up a step along my ribs.

Good. They were listening.

This was the Land of Arinsethe, and its beauty was held in subjugation to an ambitious king and the conjurer who ruled at his side. She was a woman of such profound beauty and estimable power, it was said that even to gaze upon her would enchant the strongest of men.

Hair of charcoal and eyes of jade, skin pale as a winter dawn and red lips the shade of new blood…they called her the Frost Queen. All who turned an eye to her bent the knee to him…and thus Arinsethe remained a kingdom of fealty and control.

It would seem as if few suffered in such circumstances…but the common folk knew far better. The beauty of Arinsethe was built on the backs of their labor. The roads were made pristine by bitter taxes; the cities of alabaster and white stone flourished by the calloused hands of those who would never be permitted to see the outcome of their wretched work.

Day after day, they toiled to lay feasts on the tables of the wealthy, with hardly enough kept behind for the starving mouths of their own families. While the greedy flourished, the humble starved.

Appreciative scoffs floated on the mead-honeyed, tallow-rich air, mingling with the fragrance of food and drink and sweating bodies, and another stitch loosened beneath the taut muscles of my chest.

I'd chosen this angle with care; it was a mirror held up to the faces of those I'd met in my travels down the Spine and in the corners of Krylan, day by day and night by night. Common folk, humble farmhands and laborers and traders who scraped for their next meal, who watched the droughted land with harrowed gazes and felt the hunger pangs of famine's threat stamped into their aching bellies and the lean bodies of their families, their friends, their neighbors.

This story was my apology, my penance. If I could not give them the truth of a world made right, a world where their struggle was eased, then I would write the broad sweeps of their suffering into a story. I would give them absolution in fiction, and hope for the actuality of it…something to hold onto until, someday, their pain was made right.

So they chose for themselves champions. Champions to remove the Frost Queen from her throne, for it was said that she was both shield and blade poised at the King's hand. Uprising would be futile so long as his conjurer drew breath…and after so many years of anguish, the people sought change.

The sort of change that only bloodshed and rebellion can bring.

Sparks like bitten ice danced along the aft of my tongue, glints of dazzling silver and moody blue-green as the story took shape before me…the brilliant thread of its path, the details beginning to anneal in my mind's eye. Shoving my chair back, I paced along the narrow mounting block, articulating with my hands—a habit I'd never been able to overcome, even when teachers had long ago warned me it distracted from the tale itself.

I couldn't help it. A good story deserved *enthusiasm*, not only from its audience but from its orator.

One by one, the strongest among the Arinsethes rose up to make their challenge known against the Frost Queen.

Farmers, with sickles and scythes!

A bawdy cheer from the dirt-scuffed farmhands among the crowd—

Blacksmiths, their muscles firm as their steel!

Whoops and hoots from another pocket of patrons, their brawny arms flexing proudly—

Shapers and creators, as crafty as they were keen!

Fists and feet pounded on the bartop, tables, and floors, and across the room I caught Errick grinning at me while he aided in filling tankards and plating food, his single hand as nimble as any pair of another tender's.

Riotous laughter at the doors stilled my breath a moment and slashed my heartbeat to a halt, my pace slowing on the mounting block.

Soldiers. A flock of them, entering the *Tankard* all at once, a few with arms around one another—some still in their black-leather uniforms though their hair was newly washed and cheeks freshly shaven. No doubt they hoped for a cheaper meal for their rank…perhaps even a free one. Perhaps even one they would badger and threaten out of Errick.

None were more than fleetingly familiar…none were *Galan*. But several sets of eyes found me on the mounting block, and the brand of their gazes scorched me with wary recognition and dislike.

They knew precisely who I was. *What* I was. And they had not been present for Errick's spiel at the start, the half-truths that claimed me innocent of deception and thievery.

Sweat budded beneath my collar. The story's thread wavered within me, this time not because I was anywhere near to its ending, but because *my* ending felt as if it had just set its feet inside the *Tankard*.

And all perished.

A hush gripped so much more of the room than I'd anticipated; several heads spun my way, a few of the soldiers' among them. Hovering at the edge of the mounting block, I stared down the men in their military garb, my heartbeat thundering in the base of my throat.

One by one, they rose up. And one by one, the Frost Queen brought them low. For with a word, this conjurer Queen could bring to life tines of ice that impaled the best-armored bodies. She froze the hardiest farmhands with a cold that not even their most abysmal days of toil could touch. She created mazes of glistening, slick snow that turned the craftsmen around until they wandered to their deaths, frostbitten and forgotten in the endless coils of their eternal cage.

So the King remained content. The Frost Queen's ill repute grew. And their hard labor continued, unmitigated, unrepaid, as the taxes worsened, as the demands grew and grew…

A few grumbles ruffled the air. The soldiers retrieved their tankards and laid claim to tables in a pair of adjacent stalls, laughing still, bantering among themselves so loudly it drowned out a good deal of the conversation around them, nevermind my tale.

But still, some of them watched me. Subtly, from the corners of their eyes, making note of every word.

My gaze lunged back to Errick. His grin slipped several notches, and he bared his palm, shoving it out toward me in a *go on* gesture one might use for a reluctant horse.

Swallowing, I grasped wildly for the thread, finding just enough purchase to weave it back between my fingers and tug another tight, tense coil of the story loose from within me.

And then the hunter came.

Nomad, they called him. Vagabond, to some. It was a secret shrouded in deepest shadows why honest labor never agreed with him. Though his blood was Arinsethe red, his soul carried a stain none could wash clean. His fingers were too handy with a blade, his steps too silent to be natural, and everywhere he journeyed, death followed.

Touched by darkness, they claimed. Luck's coin had flipped and fallen on its bad side a cursed half-dozen times the night of his birth. He was born with a solemn mouth downturned, and wore the mask of Luck's sinister misery. He had been driven out long ago by the unease of kith and kin...and yet in Arinsethe's darkest hour, he returned, flighty as the last shadow that clings to the world at sun's break.

He arrived in a whisper of hidden blades on a body robed in black, and he told them simply: "I will put an end to the Frost Queen, for a price."

Some swore it was desperation that drove them to accept. Others were meek enough to admit morbid fascination guided their assent. But from each of them, the hunter demanded a single piece of payment: a plain silver coin, the dross rendered utterly from it.

With these, he disappeared into the craggy mountain halls surrounding the King's castle. In their depths, he forged a blade of pure silver without taint or tarnish. And with this blade, he set off to the hunt.

Though I'd planned this portion of the tale, the words felt wrong, off-kilter, clumsy on my tongue; weak and wavering like the stumbling steps of a drunkard forgetting how to trust the floor beneath her feet. My collar itched with the thick tack of sweat gathering underneath it, staining the tan fabric a sickly yellow; and now that their own kind had been unseated from the hero's role, the patrons looked askance about the *Tankard*, their interest as frayed as the thread of Storycraft drooping in my grip. And with the lack of their curiosity, the smug scrutiny from the soldiers sharpened, like a bandit's blade pressed to my kidney.

My floundering enthusiasm was not enough to breathe life into *The Undying Tale*.

I was not enough.

Heat seared my eyes as more and more people looked away from me, back to their tablemates, back to their food and drink. Disinterested. Discarding me.

I was expendable to them. Forgettable.

The hunter...the hunter came upon the King's halls in the dead of night, and...

Barely an eye flicked my way. This was not like the towns and cities I'd risked my talents in along the Spine. The story was not failing me...I was failing the story. Withering and rotting beneath the scrutiny of the Mithran soldiers, beneath the weight of an audience who did not want me. Who had no *use* for me.

The tavern blurred before my eyes, stains of moving bodies shifting as another wave of farmhands and laborers pulled away from the serving counter, where they'd placed orders for food and drink—

And for the first time, I saw him.

Perched on a stool at the counter, arm propped on the sleek wood, fingers drumming a tune between thumb and smallest finger, over and over, the middle joining the dance every fifth pass or so.

With a single blink, my vision cleared. I saw him *truly*...not a smear made by tearstained eyes, not a man among many. But a face that leaped out from the crowd, bright and brilliant like a mirage of my own storytelling.

Like I'd spoken him to life.

CHAPTER II
A GARDEN COMES ALIVE

I caught my breath.

All at once the soldiers mattered less. My heart lunged like a thread of the story itself had gripped my hand and given it a reassuring squeeze...and I knew why.

This farmhand looked *precisely* how I saw the hunter in my mind.

Tawny hair a mess between chestnut and gold, hanging in unruly waves at shoulder-length; skin the sort of bronze that shook hands between sunkissed and heritable. Muscled arms and mirthful eyes and just a hint, a *glimpse* of something dangerous in the way he smiled when a barmistress brought him food and drink.

It was so rare, so *unspeakably* rare that I saw someone who begged to be made a character—someone like Lio. A face, a habit, a way of being that pleaded without speaking for a place in a story. And it was rarer still to find someone who already matched a character in a tale I told, like one of my own creations made manifest.

This was a kiss of the inspired from the Storymaker Himself, an answer to prayers penned in the press of my journal pages—never spoken, only thought. And when the farmhand looked at me, his expectant eyes the deep brown of tilled dirt to match the stains on his broad hands and the smudge just above his left eye, the thread of the story held limp in my hands leaped to life, a fresh radiance of silver and teal singing in my chest.

This time, the words didn't stumble out of me. They *burst* free.

Up and up into the Frost Queen's tower, the hunter climbed. Though guards came to meet him, alerted by the errant breath of his passing, the whisper of some dark presence flitting among their master's halls, none drew breath for longer than a moment in his presence.

By storm and shroud, he ascended to the very pinnacle of the south-facing turret…for in Arinsethe, it was said that all power rose from the south, from beneath, from below. And there he found the Frost Queen's chamber, guarded by nothing but tines of ice piercing outward. For what need did the most powerful conjurer in Arinsethe's antiquity have of mortal guards? Particularly guards who fell so readily to this hunter's blade.

But the hunter had seen much in his travels since they banished him from Arinsethe. He did not fear ice and snow. He did not fear conjuring or blade. He did not fear death or women forged of it.

So, through the door he entered…and he laid eyes on his greatest prey of all.

The farmhand watched me, fascination lining the tilt of his head; and though I was dimly aware others were listening again, the soldiers among them, the hook of their gazes did not pierce me. If they frowned, if they smiled, I did not know.

I was telling this to him. *For* him. This character come alive, whose face had found a home in the tale.

The Frost Queen perched at her vanity, gazing into a mirror that held no reflection. Whether glass or ice, the hunter could not say. He only knew that she could not see him approaching at her back, silent as a shadow, steps making no sound at all…and that the blade he carried was all a man needed to end a conjurer.

Blade of silver, cold as frost.
Pure as snow, no hint of dross.
Tip of dagger, sharp as ice.
Bleeds the heart when dug in twice.

With this in mind, the hunter came to a blade's length of her, and raised the weapon to drive twice into her heart from behind.

And here was the moment where the story would pivot. Where *The Undying Tale* would veer sharply into a quest, rather than a hunt.

"Who are you?" The Frost Queen's voice halted him in place. It was not the sheer rasp of ice against rock, but the soft sift of gently falling snow.

For a moment, the hunter was as frozen as the ice-coated angles of that chamber, certain that death had turned on him at last, naming him prey rather than predator. But when she did not conjure a spear of ice to pierce him through the heart, he told her: "They call me Faxon."

Only a name. But a name none had spoken since he was driven out...not even the hunter himself.

"Have you come to end me, Faxon?"

He did not answer. Luck whispered in his ear that his own had run dry...that death awaited within those words.

But even fickle Luck does not always anticipate where the turn of the coin may land. For the next words the Frost Queen spoke were nothing like he had ever dreamed.

"Please, tell me you've come to end me."

And she turned to him, and all at once, the world changed.

For the Frost Queen wept before him, snowdrops sliding down her frigid cheeks.

The farmhand leaned his chin on his fist, biting and tearing from a hot roll, his gaze never leaving mine. I could see him here, but also I could see Faxon in him, the hunter driven out, standing with blade lowered in the Frost Queen's chamber.

Silver and teal, white and amber. My skin ached at the riot of colors and words shuddering beneath it, pleading to be set free.

"I'm begging you," the Frost Queen wept. "Arinsethe is my home. I was born in these mountains and carried into service for my talents. The King makes me a weapon lashing the backs of my own people. I do not want this anymore. I would rather be dead than be his blade."

It was a death Faxon could have easily given. It would have sated his thirst for battle, the need to kill…that darkness that had seen him driven out of Arinsethe as a boy.

The stain that he had spent many long years learning to master. The blight that his time in exile had seen him paint over in brighter shades. The very shadow he had returned to prove did not define him…that he was master over it, not the other way around.

And so Faxon lowered his blade. He knelt at the Frost Queen's feet and caught her tears with his gloved fingers around her chin, erasing their cold path against her jaw.

"We don't have to be what they make us," he said. "We can be whatever we make ourselves. We can rewrite this story. We can tell it however we want."

"You truly believe that?" she asked.

And he spoke as only one who has fought darkness and emerged to light truly can: "I've done it before. I can show you how."

Dimly, awareness nudged the back of my mind…this tale had taken a path even I did not anticipate. But it was far too late to halt its course now; its very essence was a living thing churning in my heart. The mirages danced in my mind's eye as I paced the mounting block, flying hands sculpting the lay of the scene as I saw it…the hunter on his knees before the conjurer, embraced in walls of slippery, sleek ice. A cage of its own sort, a prison with no guards for a woman who could not escape her own misdeeds.

Her iron bars were fear, her warden the whispers in her mind of all the ways in which she had failed, the reasons for which she would be cast out or killed if she left the castle. And over her shoulder, the looming presence of the King who used her without remorse, his cruel voice warning her that she was unlovable, unredeemable. That she had no purpose if not with him.

Warmth kissed my cheeks as the story solidified before my eyes, from a mirage to a scene made true and pure.

"Show me," the Frost Queen pleaded. "Help me mend this. Please."

He took her hands and lifted her to her feet, and he said, "I will show you, as it was shown to me."

And in that moment, the darkness in him and the shadow in her looked into each other's eyes…and in the meeting of their gazes, they found the likeness they had sought all along.

So it was that ice and shadow left the south-facing tower that night, gone in a blink. For some time after, all of Arinsethe would tell the tale of the missing conjurer, of how she was murdered with no trace…not even a stain of blood left behind. They would breathe fearful tales of the hunter and hope he never set foot in their land again.

Only two knew the truth.

The hunter laid down his life's only dream, his final hope and wish of returning home. He sacrificed his chance of redemption to give the Frost Queen hers. And in so doing, he gave redemption into every hand in Arinsethe. For in her absence, the people rose up again.

Farmers, with sickles and scythes. Blacksmiths, their muscles firm as their steel. Shapers and creators, as crafty as they were keen. All together, they laid siege to the castle and overthrew the cruel King; they made for themselves a land in the shape of their dreams, a fair and just one.

And far away, in another land where miracles laugh in the face of Luck's two sides, Faxon and the Frost Queen built a life together. They learned how to shed light on the deepest darkness, how to thaw the thickest ice. For themselves, they sowed a garden of redemption…and every year, the dim and frigid cold gave way to sunlight so bright and blooms so beautiful, no trace of cold or shadow could hope to remain.

The story's very fabric pulsed and leaped like a second heartbeat in my chest.

And then it *erupted.*

Flowers burst from every tabletop in a riot of vivid hues, from blistering blood-scarlet to rich midnight-blue; glaring, noble purples marrying lurid shades of pink and yellow and orange. Hanging moss surged out of the knots in the serving counter, spilling down to kiss the wooden seams of the floor…those weatherworn panels between which grass erupted, a meadow carpet dotted with white, whimsical peeks of wildflowers. Ivy tendrils and climbing roses spun down along the *Tankard's* walls, wrapped the posts of the doorless stalls, embraced the columns that propped up the roof, and unleashed a heady fragrance that softened the scent of mead and meals.

And I...I froze.

We *all* froze.

Every eye in the tavern fixed on me. Every breath snagged all at once. And as the shimmering mirage cleared from before my vision, bringing the farmhand's awestruck face into sharp relief, his mouth rounded in a silent, awestruck whistle, I realized what I'd done.

I'd ended *The Undying Tale*. A story meant to go on night after night, ushering in patrons to the *Tankard,* earning profits for Errick...

No. That didn't matter.

I'd *ended a story*.

And somehow I knew, with a certainty rooted in me as deeply as Storycrafting itself, that this farmhand was the reason why.

CHAPTER 12
WHAT THE STORIES KNOW

The whispers started the moment I lunged off the mounting block, landing in a heap of springy moss that cushioned the strike of my heels. Storming to the counter through a swath of ankle-nipping grass also muffled the urgency that bristled in every fiber of my being, but there was no slowing. Not when the tide of murmuring at my back bore me forward.

I slammed to a halt at the counter, brutally aware of the eyes hanging on me from every side. Some of the patrons had gone back to conversing among themselves, or pretending as if they were; but far too many were still watching me when I met this farmhand face-to-face.

He blinked at me. I glared at him. "Who *are* you?"

"Mmm!" Wiping his hand hastily on his trousered thigh, he offered it to me. "Jaik Grissom. That was some story...sorry I missed the beginning of it." His broad grin became fixed, somewhat; a small frown pinched between his brows. "You know, it's wild...I almost feel like I've heard one like that before."

"Would you be quiet for one *second?*" I hissed, and he blinked again, hand falling limp in his lap. "How did you...how did you *do that?*"

He just stared me down, head tilted a bit to one side.

"*Well?*" I snapped.

"What? You told me to be quiet!"

"Oh, by the Maker's *tales*—!" I pushed myself up onto the stool next to him. "I need to know who you *really* are."

His eyes narrowed slightly, beholding me the way one might a drunkard hawking lavish tales on the curb outside a tavern just like this one. "Last I *checked*, I was just a farmhand from outside the city walls." He flashed his inner wrist to me—marked by a black smudge of a brand that I assumed noted him a denizen of Krylan who could pass through the guard's turnstile without enduring the daily lines. "Heard about a performance at Dubain's tavern tonight, and I've got to say...you delivered."

"You don't *say*," I muttered.

His lips twitched, fighting a smile the moment far from allowed for. "I just did."

"No, you half-wit!" I slammed my hand down on the counter, a blow once again cushioned by greenery—greenery of my own making. "Don't you realize what I just did?"

"Told a story, stormed over here, started insulting me—"

"*I finished a story!*" My snarl fanned another inquisitive wave of silence out around us, and chills whorled down my spine. I buried my face in my hands, dodging the exact sort of attention I *didn't* crave. "Faxon and the conjurer *running away together*, of all the *luckless*, rotten *things*..."

"Was that not what was supposed to happen?"

"No!" I lifted my head to pin him with a glare. "No, they were meant to duel, and after she *beat him*, he would go on a quest beyond the borders of Arinsethe to find a trove of powerful objects and allies to wield them. That way, they could defeat the conjurer *together*, and then Faxon's people would finally see him for the hero he was born to be. But you..."

The words died on the tip of my tongue.

I'd just done it again. Without even *meaning* to.

The Undying Tale hadn't *had* an ending. I'd known about the trove, known about the allies, but I'd never tried to scheme up a conclusion. That was the ending I'd been fleeing from.

He'd just unspooled it from me. From *nothing*.

My hands fell into the tangles of hanging moss, gripping until the tiniest threads of greenery nibbled my skin. "What *are* you?"

The words emerged on a puff of wonderous breath, hardly more than a whisper; and now the biting mirth faded from his crooked grin. The frown reappeared, driving a deep vee between his brows—so deep he might have worn it more often than he squinted beneath the daylight. He certainly lacked the sun-stamped creases of his contemporaries gathered along the counter and at the tables, watching us from the corners of their eyes.

"Not sure what you're looking for," he said, "but I'm just a farmhand."

Lie. The word cracked through me, swift as a bolt of lightning and equally senseless of where it struck.

I had no right—*no right*—to call this man a liar. I didn't know him. I knew nothing about him at all.

Nothing but that he'd walked into my life tonight, wearing the face of a man from my story; and that in his presence, I'd ended not one tale, but two.

I had a word for what he was, but it made no *sense*.

Darkness slithered on the corners of my vision, abrupting my bewildered thoughts: Mithran soldiers shoving back their chairs, throwing coppers on the bouquet of a tabletop, and hastening out through the *Tankard* doors.

My pulse drummed in my veins. *No, no, no…Maker have* mercy…

I lunged down from my own stool, pulse thudding in my wrists and temples, ushering in a headache. "I need you to come with me."

The farmhand—Jaik—snorted with laughter, fishing a few coppers from his own pocket and drizzling them onto the counter. "Yeah, listen, you seem like a nice enough lady, and all…except, oh, wait, you *don't*. You really think I'm going to go galivanting off into Krylan with you when you just ignored my handshake, called me names, and snarled in my face like a tiger that got its tail pulled?"

"You're not *listening to me*." Desperation seethed under my tone no matter how fiercely I fought to steady it. "Whatever you are, you're not *just a farmhand*…and now everyone here knows it!"

He swigged the rest of his mead and stood; on his feet, he was nothing short of impressive. My height was as average as the rest of me, but even so, he loomed so tall I had to tilt my head back to meet his enigmatic stare. "So, what am I, *tiger*?"

The way he breathed that word—wrapped with challenge and taunting and a hint of casual intimacy—raised the hair all along my body.

"You're an amplifier," I whispered. "A *human* amplifier."

Something I had never even heard of before—not in whispers down the Spine or tales told by fellow Storycrafters. Not in all my years of schooling. But here he stood before me, a man who'd sketched a story's ending in my head, who'd pulled me from the despair of unsatisfying tales for the first time in years.

A living, breathing talisman.

Again, that cocky slant to his head. "And that means *what* to me, precisely?"

"It means every Storycrafter who hears a breath of what happened in this tavern tonight will be on the hunt for you. Which is why you need to come with *me*."

His brows arched. "Right. Go with you. And *you* are…what? The only Storycrafter who's *not* on the hunt?"

My jaw unhinged at the faint accusation that flavored his words. And before I could fasten it back into place and script some sort of retort, he shook his head and scoffed.

"I'm out of here."

"No—*stop!*" I grabbed for his sleeve, but he tucked his elbow out of reach, winding out through the tavern doors.

Stripping off my ashen apron, I bolted after him, ignoring the cries from Errick and my fellow tenders…ignoring the eyes and shouts that followed me out into the brisk autumn night.

"Stop!" I bellowed again, catching up to the long-limbed farmhand several paces down the street. "Jaik—stop!"

He spun on me, his expression shifting from that gentle mockery to a thunderous warning that seemed unfit for a farmhand. It set me back on my heels, suddenly mindful I knew nothing about him at all…nothing but that my stories came alive in his presence.

"Listen, tiger, I'm not going anywhere with you," he snapped. "I've got a life here that has nothing to do with you. That means a farm to help tend and a cat to care for. I have everything I ever wanted here in Krylan. You're just the entertainment I heard about between the cornstalks…nothing special."

Shrugging off the potent pain those words jabbed into my gut, I stepped nearer to him, spreading my arms to emphasize the vastness of what we'd unwittingly stumbled upon tonight. "You don't happen to think the first *finished story* in *years* is more important? It's a *cat*, Jaik, it can fend for itself!"

He jabbed a finger at me. "All right, first, you don't know a thing about Sheeba. Second, why do your problems suddenly have to be *my* problems? *I don't even know you!*"

"But my stories know *you!*" The steam of my breath enshrouded our heads as I pushed in nearer again, gripping fistfuls of his stained vest and hauling him close. I had never been a person of physical prowess—had never possessed enough strength or resilience to *be* that person—but tonight, to keep Jaik Grissom and his strange power within my grasp, I was willing to cross uncourted lines. "I don't have the first notion of what that was, how that was even possible! But I do know this: I ended the first tale that's been finished in *years* because of you. So I am not letting you go, Jaik Grissom. Not without a fight."

His gaze raked up and down the length of me, mouth quirking to one side. "You really don't want to do that. I could dump you like a sack of potatoes."

"Now who's being rude?"

"It's not rude. It's self-defense."

But he didn't make good on his threat; instead, his broad hands, roughened with callouses on and between every finger, wrapped around my wrists. And with a bolt of pressure to the pulse at the heels of my palms, he broke my hold and shoved me staggering back into one of the lantern posts shedding a rich ocher glow over the empty street.

My foot caught against a slag pail laid out for the street cleaners, and I nearly fell to my seat; I caught myself against the post just in time, the cold iron biting into my palm, dragging a hiss from between my teeth.

Jaik froze, and a flicker of something like regret slashed across his gaze. But in a single blink, it cleared.

"As far as I'm concerned, Storycrafters are rotten luck." He enunciated each word with the same cold precision as a Mithran soldier sharpening a blade on a whetstone. "I've seen that in this city. Seen it everywhere. I don't get involved. Now go and see if someone *else* in that tavern is making your stories dance, because I won't be back."

He meant it. He absolutely meant it.

And that was why I acted how I did.

The pail was in my hand. My feet were flying down the street before he'd fully turned away.

And I slammed the slag bucket against Jaik Grissom's unruly golden-chestnut hair, dropping him in a senseless heap on the Krylan cobblestones.

CHAPTER 13
FAREWELLS FORGED IN SHADOW

*W*ell. That was not how I'd foreseen the evening unfolding.

Nor was this how I'd seen it ending: me, huddled on the foot of my bed, arms curled around my ankles, hair damp from dunking my head into the washbasin just to assure myself this was not a dream; and Jaik Grissom, sprawled out, taking up the rest of the sunken mattress, absolutely unconscious and far too large for my sleeping space.

At least I'd possessed the half-muddled presence of mind—after towing his deadweight through the streets and feigning his drunken stupor to any suspicious-eyed folk we passed—to bind his hands. In front of him, not behind; I didn't want him *utterly* incapacitated, just enough to not make good on his threat to dump me like a sack of potatoes.

Because I'd surely given him a reason to. Something far beyond idle threats leveled against his person, his position, or his cat.

I'd taken him prisoner. Taken a man *hostage*.

I didn't even know the woman I'd caught staring back at me with wide-eyed disbelief from the rippling surface of the washbasin. This woman who knocked innocent farmhands unconscious; this woman who had fifteen silvers to her name.

Who'd told the end of a tale tonight. *Twice.*

Burying my face in my knees, I inhaled the scent of florals still pressed into the creases of my skirt. Flowers I'd spoken to life…a gift of beauty and wonder for Errick that hardly touched the weeks and weeks of storytelling I'd squandered with an inadvertent ending.

How was I going to face him when I went back?

Could I ever go back?

The thought dug daggered talons below my ribs, shredding my insides to tatters.

A story completed had never seemed like it could be bad luck; but the way Errick had stared at me, the mingling of shock and awe and even suspicion amidst the whirling conjecture in his gaze, bloomed to life behind my squeezed-shut eyes now that I had a quiet moment to think. To reflect on precisely what had transpired in the *Tankard*.

There had been more than admiration in that look. Covetousness…the same way every Storycrafter who heard of the man on my bed would want *him*.

I'd wished for so long that my Storycraft could carry a sense of purpose again. But I'd never imagined it would feel like this—like the eyes of the whole world rooting me in place, holding me captive to their need for a tale full of power.

As if I was any better.

I peeled my heavy head up just enough to peer over my knees at Jaik. He truly was a sprawl of a man, taking up so much of the bed his feet nearly landed over mine, his head slumped sideways on my pillow and his bound hands resting in his lap. Aside from his height, there was nothing remarkable about him…and nothing at all that should suggest he held any sort of power that would bring stories to their absolution.

I didn't understand how the answer to Mithra-Sha's greatest problem could live beneath the bronzed skin of a nondescript farmer living outside the walls of Krylan. It made no sense. *He* made no sense.

And being near him, *I* made less sense to myself than I had since I'd first struck out on the Spine.

A whisper of footfalls on wood brushed my ears, jolting me up straight on the bed. The echo had barely issued when knuckles rapped lightly on the door.

Soldiers wouldn't knock. *Galan* certainly wouldn't knock.

"Addie-cat? Are you there?"

All the breath whooped out of me at once, and I slammed a hand over my mouth.

Tea. In the chaos of the night, I'd utterly *forgotten* about Lio.

"Maker's *tales*," I hissed, scrambling backward off the bed and standing frozen in the center of the small, narrow room. What was I going to tell her— why I'd neglected our planned meeting, when my eagerness for a friend had always made me early rather than late? And if she saw Jaik here and assumed the wrong thing—that I had abandoned her for a strange man, of all things—

"Addie!" Lio's voice sharpened, and the knob rattled in its fastenings. "I can see your shadow. I know you're in there. Let me in, or else—"

"All right, all right! Hold your donkeys." Hastening to the door, I unlatched it, opened it a hair—then wedged my foot into the seam and blocked her view of the room.

A diamond-patterned, beaded shawl strung around her back and draped in the crooks of her folded arms, Lio regarded me with dark eyes in chaos between irritation and a simmering concern that punched right into the core of me. "You look like a half-drowned alleycat again, and it isn't even raining. What is *happening* with you?"

The words stuck in my throat—a wild, hysterical retort, a gush of truth that slammed against the backs of my teeth. "I'll show you, but I need your word first that you will understand something: this is *not* what it looks like."

Slowly, her dark brows sketched upward. "All right?"

"And you have to swear to me you won't report me to the city soldiers."

Now her brows plunged, scrunching into a frown so swiftly, my stomach twisted. "Addie-cat, you're frightening me. What is the *matter*?"

"I may have possibly…" The words deserted me. I peeled the door wide. "Just look."

Lio slipped sinuously into the room, then halted beside me, staring at the bed. Staring at the stranger *in* the bed, still thoroughly unconscious from my well-aimed blow.

"Audra," she said, slowly, carefully, as if her words danced on the edge of a knife, "what is this?"

I shut the door and leaned back against it, arms folding around my middle. "I would think you'd recognize a man when you see one."

"A man, yes. An unconscious farmhand, in your *bed*?"

I winced at the bite in her tone. "It's not how it looks."

She pivoted to face me, shawl straining against her taut arms. "Then how is it?"

In a rush of breath, the tale poured out of me…the story of everything that had unfolded at the *Tankard*. And as I told it, we shifted: I sank down with my back to the door, and Lio settled on the foot of the bed near Jaik, her gaze slowly revolving from my face to his. The tension in her shoulders eased, but a fresh streak of wariness tightened her spine and set her fingers tapping in the creases of her elbows, stirring the raindrop crystals that dangled from the hem of her shawl.

"This…" she breathed when I finally fell silent, hoarse from talking, "this is *remarkable*, Addie-cat."

"I know." I thumped my head back against the door, once, twice, the resonance of wood against bone ringing through my skull and settling me slightly. "I've never seen anything like it. Like *him*. And when he tried to walk away from me, I didn't know what to do, except…"

I gestured vaguely to the bed. Lio grimaced, sliding her thumb over her lips. "Yes, that is the *other* matter. You know that taking hostages is a punishable offense in Krylan. That to force anyone against their will is—"

"An imprisoning crime. I know. I went to the same immigrant orientation as you." For three mornings after my arrival to the city, in the public room of the boarding house, my neighbors and I had undergone a detailed lecture on the rules and requirements leveled on Krylan's citizens. To live in the Tailbone City, all did their best to contribute. And those who infringed on the safety of others were dealt with swiftly and without mercy.

Something I hadn't considered when I'd swung the pail at Jaik Grissom's head.

"I suppose my *hope* is if I can talk to him without all that charming hostility," I crossed my legs and balanced my wrists on my ankles as I bent forward, "he'll see this for what it was: a rescue, not a ransom."

Lio's head slanted slightly. "*Is* that what it is?"

Bitter offense scoured the back of my throat, sitting me up sharply against the door. "*Lionyra.*"

"*Audra.*" She leveled the same biting tone back at me. "You have a man chained on your bed…a man you assume gave you the power to finish a tale, something you have coveted for *years*. Look into my eyes and tell me you took him for pure and selfless reasons."

A readied retort jammed in my throat when I held her glittering black gaze.

There was something about Lio that made half-truths and complicated things seem like precisely what they were: a guise for what slunk below the surface, ashamed to show its face. She had a knack for trawling up secrets and refusing to let go until they lay naked and exposed in the light, no matter how painful it was.

She was a bit like Naomi in that way.

It was a pang of melancholy at the thought of another friend I'd lost—and the fear that my mistakes tonight might lose me the one before me—that brought the quiet answer to my lips: "I don't want to hurt him. And it was wonderful to finish a story, I can't lie. But not like *that,* Lio, not for the way they were all looking at me. At *us.*" When I blinked, I saw Errick's face again; the faces of those Mithran soldiers. A shudder wracked through me. "I *do* want answers to what in the Maker's many *stories* happened tonight. And I'm never going to get them if I let him go. Because if it isn't just me he can do this to, then every Storycrafter in Mithra-Sha will be after him."

"And that matters to you, why? If he is not merely a talisman?"

Her question was searching, not accusatory. So it did not account for the fire that flushed up under my skin, the way a throb manifested itself in my temples with three stuttering heartbeats.

"Because *no one* deserves to be used for their power!" I snarled, shoving up to my feet. "No one deserves to be treated like a charm hung around some wealthy person's neck and flashed at fetes and parties. He is a living, breathing *person,* and I'm not going to huddle in the shrouded corners of this city and watch *Galan* and his luckless guards lay hands on him and throw him to whichever Storycrafters pay the highest price!"

Lio blinked, slow and steady—which was as good as a dropped jaw from her.

And I couldn't blame her. As suddenly as the heady rush of rage had filled me up, it emptied me, knocking me breathless back against the door, apologies crowding my tongue.

I'd never given much thought to notions of how people were used, their talents manipulated. Certainly, I knew it had to be happening…the Sha, after all, while a fair and devoted ruler, was desperate to combat the afflictions that came with unfinished tales and suffering lands. That necessitated some level of strain on the backs of our country's most capable citizens.

But the notion of a man chained and collared in habit if not in true deed, the purpose of his life siphoned off to feed the heart of Mithra-Sha…

I despised it. I despised it even if I *had* put shackles on the man himself.

For a long moment, Lio and I stared at one another, helper and hypocrite; then Lio said, quietly, "And what do you want to do?"

Relief brought on a different rush altogether, and I drank it in with deep gulps of air while I settled back onto the floor and schemed.

"I think I need to get us out of Krylan," I decided at last. "Just far enough away that we outpace the gossip about what happened tonight. I know if we can have a civil discussion, he'll come around…he'll understand that this is important. And then we can piece together *why*."

"And if the combined wit of a farmhand and a Storycrafter yields no truths?"

Notions sparkled in the recesses of my mind, the fine fragments of tales told long ago set alight again. "We have options…possibilities."

None of which mattered if Galan had his way with the pair of us. He was a man for whom reasons mattered far less than results…he'd proven that in the way he'd threatened me the day of my arrival. And if those Mithran soldiers had reported back to him already…

Clammy fear soaked my palms in sweat, and I wiped them hastily on my skirts. "What matters now is that we leave Krylan, before either of us falls into the wrong hands."

Lio swiveled to gaze at Jaik, and I fidgeted, teasing a frayed thread in the high hem of my skirt. I was keenly aware that our luck hung in the balance of how Lionyra Vara flipped the coin tonight. If I couldn't trust her, this woman I'd called friend for scarcely more than a month, then my future was forfeit. And likely Jaik's was, too.

"You're right, Addie-cat," she murmured at last. "No one deserves to be bound against their will to a life they do not want."

Her focus spun back to me, sharp as the steeples of Luck's cathedrals, bright as the beads whispering on the tasseled fringe of her shawl.

"Here is what we will do," she said. "I will make a diversion, down in the Ameresh district. There are enough there who owe me favors that we can raise quite the clamor. In the chaos, you and this farmhand can flee."

Shock parched my throat. "Lio, if they catch you—"

"Then it will be more difficult for me than you can possibly imagine." Her lips tugged in a wicked smile. "But there are risks worth taking, and people worth taking them for."

My vision swam and dampness filled the back of my nose. "I don't deserve you."

"*Do not* say that, Addie-cat." Swinging her legs swiftly off the bed, Lio took the two steps across the room to me, gripping my elbows and shaking me lightly. "You *do* deserve friends who will risk everything for you. You deserve people who put you first. And I know you have lacked that for many years, but from this day on, never forget that someone cared for you. That a friend loved you enough to help with your mad schemes."

I surged forward to wrap my arms around her, and she clung to me just as tightly; and though every bone in my body ached with the finality of it, the sensation of an endless farewell, I infused every scrap of hope I could dredge up into saying, "I'm going to see you again. And I'll tell you *everything* I learn about this. About us."

"I look forward to it," Lio whispered against my ear.

When we drew apart, purpose laid claim to the angles of her face, wiping away all of the earnestness and softness of a moment ago.

"Now, listen carefully," she said. "There is a butcher on the same street as *The Secret Ingredient*. He has a handcart, and he owes me a favor. If you retrieve the cart, you can dump the farmhand into it. Cover him with burlap and be on your way to the gate."

Forcing a stiff nod, I stepped out of her path. "If you could arrange one other thing…"

"Name it."

"He…has a cat," I muttered, sharply aware of how ridiculous and worthless the words sounded. "If you know of someone who—"

"Oh, Addie," Lio laughed quietly, but there was no mockery in the sound. "I *am* going to miss that tender heart of yours."

There were no words for all of the things about her that I would miss. So I only said, "Be safe, Lio."

"And you, Addie-cat." She squeezed my hand in passing. "Get yourself as near to the gate as you can in the next two hours. When you see my signal, you will know. Run, and do not look back."

With a last, grim smile, she ducked out through the door, shutting it in her wake. I locked it with a twist of my hand, then leaned against it; for a moment, burying my brow into the wood, I simply breathed.

This was happening. With Lio on the move, there was no turning away from it. I'd set my own departure from Krylan into motion…willfully chosen to abandon everything I'd built here in the last two months.

A fresh wave of heat bloomed in my eyes, and I let it come—gave space for a breath of time to the tears tracking down my cheeks. A silent farewell to the city I'd come to love, the *Tankard* and the memories made there, to the taste of fresh bread and a friend to drink tea and learn card and dice games with, and a home to call my own.

I couldn't see what lay beyond this night. That was not a story I was ready to tell myself. All I could do was survive this moment. And the next.

The next moment brought me to the nightstand, where I crouched, digging my satchel from the recesses. Freeing the bag of silver coins from beneath my corset, I weighed it in my hand a moment; then into the bag it went, tucked beneath the ashen ball of my cloak—

And there I froze, shock bolting like lightning through my fingertips.

For a heartbeat, I could not breathe.

Then I slammed back on my heels, centering myself while I clawed the cloak out; I spread the hem between my shaking hands, twisting it this way and that in the moonlight falling through the windowpane.

No. I hadn't misjudged. Hadn't imagined it.

The hem of my cloak was a pale, pastel pink.

CHAPTER 14
A THREAD OF TRUST

For a moment, an array of soft, satiny pink colored my world.

A blush of color, one of the weakest in the Storycrafter's palette. But it was color, returning to my cloak.

A sob of disbelief and wonder surged in the back of my throat, and I gripped the cloak taut in my fists, pressing my face into the stale folds. Then I flung it around my shoulders, jerked my satchel shut, and tugged the strap across my body.

It was time. I had to do this.

I straightened from my knees before the nightstand—

Then crashed against its edge as a weight slammed into me from behind, flinging me into the wood so sharply the sculpting bit beneath my ribs. Pain ruptured through my insides, and I toppled sideways, slamming against the wall; dizzied, wheezing, I struggled to bring to focus the figure stumbling toward the door, clumsy with his bound hands.

Rage and fear clapped through me, and I lunged after Jaik. "*Come back here!*"

My scrambled legs tangled with his, and we went down in a heap, his chin striking the floor with a dull *crack* that stirred my guilt at once; but that was easier to ignore when he kept crawling anyway, trying to reach the door.

"Will you *stop*?" I pounced on him again, this time sitting cross-legged on his shoulders; and that, finally, was enough to hinder him.

"You know I could just buck you off," he growled.

"Yes." I blew an errant strand of hair from my face. "But I'm hoping you're enough of a gentleman not to."

"You're one to talk." Forehead pressed into my scuffed wooden floor, he croaked, "What in Luck's fickle, flipping *coin* did you hit me with?"

"A slag bucket."

"A *slag*—" He broke off with a deep-chested groan. "Don't they use those to rinse manure out of the streets?"

"Yes! Now stop squirming!" His hips still rocked a bit, as if he was seeking the best position to flip me from. "I'm trying to think—"

"Oh, right, yeah, of course. Wouldn't want to inconvenience the careful thought processes of the woman who *knocked me out with a slag bucket and took me hostage*!"

"Just listen to me, will you? You're not my hostage."

"Then what are *these*?" Face still mashed to the floor, he reared his bound arms up above his head; the guilt burrowed deeper between my ribs at the sight of his tied wrists.

"Those are…" For the first time in his presence, a practiced story withered on my tongue. Clutching my aching side with one hand, I centered my weight between his shoulders, hoping to keep him down. "I'm not *proud* of this, all right? It's a necessity. I've spent the last few years doing everything I could to survive…now I'm trying to keep us *both* alive."

"Well, excellent job. Really. I feel the most alive I ever have."

"Do you ever shut your ramble-hole?"

"Not when I'm trying to talk a madwoman down from tying me to her bed and doing Luck-knows-*what* to me."

Though the words were scathing, another reckless cut of that caustic wit, they gave me pause.

What must this *truly* seem like to him? If he didn't believe me, didn't think he was the reason I'd been able to end the first completed story in Mithra-Sha in years, then I was simply a merciless stranger who could not be trusted. A woman who'd brushed off his genial greetings, hurled accusations and demands, then dragged him unconscious to my home. Like he'd said—a snarling tiger.

Self-loathing dove deep into my guts, burrowing into the cracks shame had split between my ribs. Dragging in a breath, I laid my hand between his tense shoulderblades. "I'm going to let you up. So we can *talk*."

"Nice try."

His weight surged aside all at once, and I was barely quick enough to unfold my legs and slam a knee down next to his shoulder before he could toss me off. I rocked with his weight instead, and when he rolled over beneath me, I drove my other leg down—trapping him, straddling his hips, his face upturned toward mine.

But he had me, too: his bound arms looped over my head, yanking me down until our brows nearly brushed. The curtain of my hair shrouded the light dripping in through the window, shadows dunking his eyes in murk and myst...

"You let me up," his voice was husky, low, "or I'm not letting go."

"I could put one of my knees right into your groin."

"Could. But then, where's your balance?"

Gritting my teeth, I slammed my chin straight down into his sternum; he swore and seized up, and I whipped my head out from under his arms, pinning them down against the length of his abdomen and spreading my weight over them so he couldn't wriggle them free. I folded my arms over his clavicles for good measure, dug my fingernails into his biceps, and seethed, "I've spent the last too-many years fending for myself on the Spine. Alone. Without my storie to help keep me safe. *Balance* is the least of my concerns. Now, can we *talk*?"

His eyes angled down a bit to catch mine from his vantage point, and something flickered in that gaze—something curious, almost confused.

Whatever he might've said to that, it was buried by a brutal pound of fist wood.

Both of us jolted, and I sat up sharply; Jaik twisted beneath me, laying his bound wrists to the floor, craning to peer over his shoulder up at the door.

It shook violently under the next strike of a hand. "Audra Jashowin and J Grissom, you are both under arrest according to the statutes of Krylan!"

"*What?*" Jaik's voice cracked with disbelief, and he slammed his bound hands into the floor. "I didn't *do* anything!"

"What did I tell you?" I lunged to my feet, stumbling a bit when the clap my heels on the floor lanced fresh pain along my side; I'd no doubt wear a bar of bruises along my midsection by dawn, but that was the least of my worries.

First, I had to survive to see the sunrise.

Panic bubbled in my stomach, bearing the same sweet, cloying mustiness fresh nausea. My gaze lunged around the room as the knocking repeated, intensified, rattled the walls themselves.

Only two ways out: through the door, into their hands; or out the window with its stained-glass pane and a sheer, bone-breaking drop to the ground belo

"Hey!" Jaik bellowed above the pounding on the door. "Hey, I'm innocer She's got me tied—"

"Be *quiet!*" I leaped for him, grabbing to cover his mouth, but he slammec his elbow into my bruised middle and sent me down to the floor in a heap of gasping agony.

"I mean it! I'm not a part of whatever this is, I just want to go *home*!"

The crack in Jaik's tone yanked my head up, a deadly blow dealt against my wounded courage.

I was dragging him away from that. His life. His position. His *cat*.

A pause ensued beyond the door for a moment; then a voice dripped beneath the seam of it, oily with false sincerity. "Don't worry, Grissom, it's going to be all right. Your arrest is a formality while we confirm the events at the tavern tonight. We'll have you home by sunrise."

Dread knocked me back on my seat.

Galan. I hadn't heard his voice since he'd pinned me against that tower wall and cast his hideous shadow over the life I intended to build here…but I still knew it. My mind had replayed it often enough in my nightmares.

Jaik shifted his weight, gaze darting down to me. "And her?"

"She knows what's coming for her. She chose this for herself."

Frustration branded my eyes with tears this time, holding Jaik's stare. I *hadn't* chosen this—it had been done to me. Luck's laughing mask pivoted my way, the coin turned against me. My life in Krylan was over, just when I'd been expecting it to improve.

"So, why arrest *me* at all?" Jaik called back, his tone careful in a way that set my hair on end.

The pause was too long this time—as if something was being conferred beyond the door, between Galan and whatever men followed him.

"We'll be through with you once we know precisely what transpired in that tavern," he said at last.

"Mmm, yeah. That's comforting," Jaik muttered under his breath.

Before I could shift and find my feet, he hauled me up to them, bound hands pinching beneath my arm. He shoved me to one side of the door and pressed his back to the other, grim-faced, head knocked back against the wood.

"Jaik, what are you—?"

"He's about to take an axe to the door."

The last word had barely escaped his lips when metal crunched wood, and the upper tip of a perfectly honed axehead pierced through.

I barely bit back a shriek, tucking myself deeper into the corner as the axe reared and struck again. "Do you still think I'm putting this out of proportion, *Jaik*?"

"Yeah, yeah!" he snarled, chafing his bonds against his thigh. "Who *is* that pedantic pissant?"

I winced as the axehead burrowed in, nearly half of it visible this time. "Galan, one of the city guards."

"*Galan.* Redhead, beard, really nasty smile?"

"You know him?"

"Nope. Never seen him before in my life." Grimacing, Jaik leaned away from the door as wood chips sprayed. "So, what's the plan, tiger?"

What, indeed?

My gaze darted around the small room again, catching on no newer salvation, no fresher course of action revealed by the flying woodchips and the punch of arms and legs as Mithran soldiers broke down the door. All of my usual schemes for eluding handsy threats on the Spine were lost in this narrow matchbox of a space.

The room I'd been so proud to rent had become my coffin.

No. Not yet. We weren't out of options. Low on them, certainly, but I'd been low on them for what seemed like my whole life; that was why I was here. And I'd survived on the Spine with fewer prospects than a failing door, a single window, and a farmhand without a weapon between us.

A farmhand who breathed life into my stories.

The notion struck me all at once, in harmony with the snap of a larger chunk of wood cracking loose.

No time to think. No choice but to fling myself at the mercy of a power I hadn't relied on to save me in too many years.

"Can you get us out of the city?" I cried to Jaik.

His gaze danced over me, sparking with fury and regret. "Like no one else probably can."

"Then you lead. I need to concentrate."

Galan's freckled fingers shoved through the hole he'd made in my door, hunted for and twisted over the latch, at the same moment I reached out my hand to Jaik.

No longer the snarling tiger. Just the Storycrafter begging for a thread of trust. And when his bound hands gripped mine, the new tale exploded out of me.

Let me tell you a story.

CHAPTER 15
AT THE EDGE OF THE WORLD

I yanked Jaik away from the wall, toward the bed, snatching up my satchel as we went; no time to grab for anything else. Not my black, misstitched cloak or my books or my other clothes. We were leaving with all that we had in our hands...and if the Maker wrote the rest of our story tonight, that would be enough.

"Their whole lives, it felt like they'd been running—a pair of pirates, short of luck and long of dreams, crossing over from the land of lost souls to the land of the living, ferrying gold into chests in a land none could reach but by their cursed ship."

"Audra?" Jaik's voice pitched upward with shock and fear as we stepped up onto the bed and hurtled for the window, my hand wrapped relentlessly around the twine that trapped his wrists.

I didn't answer; I poured my vision into the story rolling off my lips, even as the door flung open behind us and the soldiers poured in—

"They crossed over time and again by the Bridge of Souls—black as night, firm as adamant!"

We launched through the window, Jaik's howl of shock abrupted by the slam of his boots and mine on the deep sable arch of black stone that erupted from below the window, sloping down steeply to the ground.

"*What*—?" Jaik's shout broke off into a wild burst of mirthless laughter as I hauled him in a dead sprint down the bridge, into the street.

By the time our feet struck cobblestone, he had taken charge. He tugged *my* hand this time, and we ran, my bruised middle thudding with fresh pain at every step. But I couldn't afford to pay any heed to that.

I had a story to tell.

"Wherever they fled, these two pirate captains, trouble pursued—"

"*Really?*" Jaik peered back at the swearing Mithran soldiers on our heels.

"Would you be quiet? I'm trying to tell you a story!" I stumbled a bit over my skirts; Jaik hitched me back up by the hand, and we kept running, Galan and his men scrambling down from the window to take up the chase.

It was nearly impossible to shut out their curses and cries, to focus on the darkened road ahead—and on Jaik, and how to get us out of this. I just had to trust this story, difficult as that had become.

"Trouble pursued—for they had stolen first what could never be reclaimed."

Yes, that was perfect—the more depth a story possessed, the greater the power it invoked. And the sooner it could manifest its might.

"Before piracy, there was a prison. Before there were open seas, there was a cage. Captain Lyndra had once been Princess Lyndra, fated to marry the cruel son of her father's ambitious archrival in their neighboring land. And though Captain Kidd had stolen her as a ransom long ago to hold against the rulers of both kingdoms, to secure a lifetime's sum of gold, the feisty princess had won his respect over time. And then, his heart."

A gasp wrenched out of me as Jaik yanked me sideways down an alleyway, dodging a guardpost at the corner of a nearby cathedral. Catching myself with my free hand to the narrow brick wall, I panted out the words:

"So they raked in the ransom together and set out to conquer the seas."

Jaik cackled, still tugging me down the alleyway. "All right, now *that's* a twist!"

And it was poignant enough to set the alley walls dancing around us, shimmering like a mirage. Power leaked through my veins, my Storycraft rising, *investing* itself in the tale. Saltwater spray and the hot metal tang of a coin's surface rippled on my tongue; I could *see* the pair of captains, standing on the prow together. Her with dark hair and an untamed smile, him with sandy locks tied in a short tail, his spirited eyes forever fixed on the horizon.

Captains to one ship, sharing the burden of the title and duties rather than squabbling over them. Likeminded. United. A sameness and understanding between them that made my chest hurt to fathom.

We burst out on the alley's far side and slammed to a halt.

Mithran soldiers awaited. *Many* of them.

"Whatever the opposite of a good-luck talisman is," Jaik hissed out of the side of his mouth, "that's what you are."

"Maybe that's what *you* are," I spat back, sidling a step into his shadow.

Not to hide. There was no hiding from the dozen men and women with their fidgeting fingers near their rifles. But I needed a moment to think. To *speak*.

"The captains were pursued to the edge of the world by Lyndra's father and by the man who'd once laid claim to her marriage hand. But wherever they ran, Luck was on their side, tossing the coin in their favor…eager to see how their tale would end."

"Gag her," one of the soldiers jerked his chin at me. "And if either of them tries to run, shoot below the knee."

"How is that fair?" Jaik bared his tied hands, palms out. "I need my legs to work!"

"Then don't *run.*" The soldier's lips peeled back in a snarl as one of his companions sidled forward, freeing a length of cloth from his pocket.

Panic spiked through me, all the blood pooling out of my head, leaving me dizzy and wavering.

I'd heard of Storycrafters being gagged—those who Misspoke tales, those who broke the statutes of Storycraft. But that had never been me...I'd never been miraculous or dangerous.

But tonight was different. They wanted to stop my stories until they could find a way to use them for their own gain. Use *Jaik* for their own gain. They wanted to silence me.

Never. *Never.*

"Wherever the Captains journeyed, the world felt it. The earth itself quaked with fear."

A shudder rocked through the city streets below us, and the soldier halted, casting an uneasy glance back at his commander. I threaded my fingers into Jaik's bonds, gently tugging his hands back down before him.

"These Captains took what they wished. They rode the waves of fortune to victory after victory."

The words tingled with a wild, wide-sweeping cerulean spool of power, half-numbing my tongue with their sizzling might. I couldn't remember the last time I'd felt such an evocative draw to a story, if I ever had.

"Whenever they tempted trouble near, just to see the whites of its eyes, the sea was their ally, carrying them away to calmer waters."

Another groan snaked beneath our feet; the cobblestones cracked and fissured, and with an uproarious *heave*, the aqueducts below Krylan's surface *sundered.*

Water punched up through the cracks in the stones, a furious skyward jettison with enough force to blow us and the soldiers away from one another. Several of them screamed as they plummeted into the stone trench, and I gripped the back of Jaik's shirt, heaving him clear before he could topple after them in wide-eyed disbelief.

"Come *on*!" I bellowed, and then we were running again.

Tearing alongside the trench my story had fashioned, we bolted through the streets; and as we ran, I kept telling. Kept crafting.

The feats of the pirate captains; the way they broke into vaults and burst through chained doors. How they outwitted their opposition, again and again.

My words toppled walls and sprouted trees from nothing, barring the Mithran soldiers into alleys, blocking their pursuit of us. They twisted streets in our wake and raised them up to sheer drops there was no descending from. Powerful word after powerful word chained together in my mind and spewed from my mouth so rapidly I nearly stumbled over them; and as we drew nearer to the city wall, Jaik was doing far more of the leading and running. The hum of potent storytelling in my head turned from a scintillating pleasure to a dull ache throbbing in my temples, marrying with the bruises along my middle and the stitch below my ribs.

I hadn't poured this much of myself into a tale in longer than I could remember…and never for this long. The exertion of thought and the tug of the power-laden words sanded down the edges of my mind until I could scarcely hold the thread of the tale.

Not for lack of inspiration. That was still there, an electrifying jolt that redoubled whenever Jaik touched my elbows or snagged my wrists, guiding me out of more populated streets and down chinks in the city's mapping, evading a fresh rush of Mithran soldiers. But it soured into the sort of inspiration that tasted of rot and madness…the kind that had Storycrafters locked in their chambers, soaked in spirits and strong herbs, trying to speak something to life that could never meet their expectations.

I was almost grateful when Jaik shouldered me into another sidestreet and squeezed in after me—grateful to stop, to measure my breathing and work on the cramp beneath my ribs. But even that relief was short-lived when I looked into his face.

Grim. Beyond concerned. "We need to get higher."

I blinked at him, hoping the sliver of darkness granted to my straining eyes would somehow arrange his words in a way that made sense. "I'm sorry, I don't—"

"We're two streets away from the gatehouse. What's on those streets, tiger?"

"Cathedrals. Apartments." And then my mind caught up at last, unleashing a deluge of dread down my knotted spine. "The *soldiers'* apartments."

The structure of Krylan was perfect that way—enemies coming in or going out would have no choice but to contend with two broad streets full of sharp-edged edifices and the well-honed militants who inhabited them.

And tonight, horrific as it was, *we* were the enemy.

"Mmhmm." Jaik twisted to peer around the corner, then jerked his head back. "If your friend Galan suspects where we're going, then they're most likely watching the streets, waiting to ambush us here. Best way out is up."

"I don't know how much of this story I have left in me." I'd wrung out seven scenarios already for Lyndra and Kidd to escape from—for *us* to escape from—and every drop of my stamina had dribbled away with them. The stone wall of the tailor's shop at my back was the only thing keeping me upright.

"Please. As if I need your story to get us over." He flung out his arms toward me. "Cut me loose."

The curt request cleared my head quicker than a dash of spirits and my face dunked in a washbasin. Suspicion crowded out my exhaustion, and I straightened slightly.

If he was going to run, now would be the time: straight toward the soldiers, or away from them. Either way, he would leave me to take the brunt of their fury, weakened as I was.

"Don't look at me like that!" His terse command dragged me from my uneasy stupor. "Do you want to get out of this place alive? Then cut me loose!"

I cursed Luck's fickle schemes in my head, yanked out my small, defensive blade from my satchel, and rent the twine. Jaik stripped off the fibers, rolled his wrists at the joints, then stepped back against the opposite alley wall, gaze lifted to the stars.

"I'll give you a boost. Then I'm right behind you."

Though my body screamed at the thought of more exertion, there was no use waiting. If he was going to betray me and leave me to the soldiers, best to get it over with and get on with hating him for the rest of my likely brief and miserable existence.

I lurched up from the wall and darted toward him, gripping his shoulders and stepping up into his cupped palms. He flung me upward with a lithe grace like we'd done this a hundred times, and I caught handholds in the different-sized, misshapen stones; then I clambered up in lunges and pulls, flinging myself up to the top of the roof and sprawling out for a moment, gasping, burying my face in my arms.

For a moment, all was quiet save for the rush of my breath in the cavity of my body, the wind running gentle fingers down my back.

The weight of those fingers turned more insistent. Prodding. "*Audra.* You with me?"

Moaning, I towed the upper half of my body up on my elbows and squinted at Jaik, crouched on one knee beside me, rubbing his wrists. "I despise you."

"Oh, good. I was wondering when we'd find some common ground." He jerked his chin at the soaring gatehouse towers, a far fiercer and more fortified threat than they'd seemed when I'd come to Krylan for the promise of a better life. "Ready?"

Once again, we took off running; and though every step jolted pain into my chest and head, I kept on Jaik's heels. He conquered the rooftops like this was woven into his very nature, taking leaps from corners with fearless strength, turning back to steady me when my clumsied feet clipped the edges of jagged architecture and threatened to pitch me into the street below.

"Do you do this *often?*" I grunted.

"Honestly? Not a day in my life." He dragged a hand back through his hair. "Blame the adrenaline."

I was willing to blame—or bless—whatever it was, so long as it got us out of here.

We crossed the two streets in near-silent ease, entering the shadows of the gatehouse steeples, reaching the edge of the furthest rooftop and preparing for our descent with a glance into the vacant alley on the far side—

A rifle hammer clicked at our backs.

"Don't move. Either of you."

Galan's triumphant voice punched rage straight through me, sleeker than the lead in the weapon he carried…another miracle made of Storycraft. Turning the creation of my own kind against me.

"When he says *don't move,*" Jaik hissed under his breath, still crouched on one knee just like I was, though his gaze shot from the street below to land sidelong on me, "are we not supposed to look at him?"

"Don't *speak*." Galan's footsteps brushed the rooftop, stalking toward us. "Thought you were clever, did you, Storycrafter? Thought you could stay one step ahead? I've been hunting your kind because of nights *just* like this." Fabric whispered as he shifted his aim. "Somehow, you always leave a mess in your wake. Mutilated streets. Broken things. *Dead* things. So now you get to pay it all back…and the debt you racked up tonight?"

The small, round muzzle-mouth of that rifle buried itself in my hair, and vomit flooded my throat.

"Pulling this trigger would be justice," he breathed. "And no one would ever look *twice*."

Before I could suck in a breath to steady myself, or brace for the blackness of death, or plead for my life—Jaik slammed his boot into Galan's knee with an audible *crunch*. While the soldier was still howling, Jaik spun up from his crouch, catching the muzzle and jerking the rifle up and away from my head. His boot impacted a second time—Galan's chest—sending him slamming back with a gasp of lost air, his rifle separating and staying in Jaik's hand. And by the time I scrambled to my feet and spun—

Fireworks.

A dazzling, dizzy array of color exploded from the Amaresh district, along with the resounding *crack* of crushing stone and snapping wood. Like bones breaking, like a body caving in, several of the minarets folded in on themselves. They fell like the dead.

Explosion after explosion after explosion. Stunning streamers of red and gold and silver painted the cloudless sky, a storm of falling stars, a crackling beacon—a farewell salute.

"Lio." Her name escaped me as a breath, a prayer to the Storymaker that she and her Ameresh friends would somehow escape with their lives from what we'd unleashed tonight.

And a wish that I would see her again.

Then, below us, a fresh commotion. The guards broke from the gatehouse in a dead sprint toward the source of the latest havoc, leaving only one harried man to hold the murmuring, jostling crowd who strained to see beyond him toward Krylan in chaos.

Galan, wheezing, dragged himself up on his elbow; jolted into motion, I gripped the rifle and yanked it from Jaik's hands, hurling it into the street below. And then I spoke the words that bubbled up in my chest, holding the soldier's hateful gaze.

"For all their rage, all their fury, the rival kingdoms could not catch Lyndra and Kidd…nor could they claim their stolen wealth for themselves. When it seemed they were cornered at last on the edge of the world, the armies of two kingdoms at their backs, the captains and their crew crossed the bridge for the last time…the Bridge of Souls, black as night, firm as adamant."

The structure crystalized audibly behind me, but I did not look back when I stepped onto it, as we descended toward the street. Fear refused to let me turn my back on Galan. I would never do it again.

"So they sailed the beyond together…two captains bound by respect, bound at the heart, and the crew who trusted them. Their lives and freedom were a treasure that could never be taken away."

Our feet touched the cobblestones, and I forced the last words over my trembling tongue.

"Behind them, the Bridge of Souls sealed…never to allow another of the living to pass."

The glossy ebony bridge pulverized to dust, carried on the breath of the tale's end.

Another ending. Three in a single night.

I dropped my shoulder against the edge of the gatehouse tower, giddy and dizzy and nauseous. Jaik snagged my hood, dragging me back upright by it and tugging it up and over to shield my face. "Walk like you belong here."

Without giving me a moment to summon a witty retort, he snagged my hand and dragged me to his side, threading between the towers and moving out toward the turnstile. He kept his face set, but flashed his wrist—showing off the marker on his skin that allowed him entrance to and from the city.

The harried soldier didn't even look twice. And then we were free.

CHAPTER 16
TWISTS OF COLOR, TWISTS OF LUCK

The rush of the waves bashing themselves to bits on the rocky shore of Port Craythin, the nearest inlet of the sea, should have soothed me. It was not unlike the lullaby of falling water that had always drifted in through the high windows of Fablehaven Academy; or my home in Vallanmyre, where my mind had roared like the rush of those same cascading falls on the day everything had changed, with the glimpse of a gray cloak and a tale yawning unfinished in my head.

But tonight, no lullaby would do the trick.

I slumped on a mound of stone, sheltered by the dense, fragrant seaside alpines. They hugged the clifftop whose paths—hewn by hand and tool—spiraled down toward the bay below. That was the direction Jaik had gone...that I'd *let* him go in silent gratitude for seeing us out of Krylan. For sparing me the rifleshot that had itched to bury itself in the back of my head.

My restless fingers dug at the same patch of scalp again, unpared nails worrying through the first layer of skin, rusting blood into my nailbeds.

This entire day and night had the odd, displaced sensation of a dream I might blink awake from at any moment. But no matter how hard I stuck my lashes together or how swiftly I peeled them apart, it was all still the same: the surf, the shadows, the imprint of Galan's rifle pressed to my head.

He would have killed me. He wouldn't have thought twice about it, regardless of the miracle of a finished tale in the *Tankard* tonight.

No wonder I had an intrinsic urge to avoid Mithran soldiers—a sense I should have *listened* to. Now I was more than reviled for being a Storycrafter; I was personally wanted for havoc wreaked by my own hands, my own words.

Worse, I'd dragged an innocent man into the wilds with me, and who knew where we would go from here?

The snap of shifting undergrowth arrested my miserable thoughts, and I sharpened my posture, slamming my hands down on the rock on either side of my body. I was braced to run at the first whisper of a triggering rifle—and only slightly relaxed when Jaik pushed his way through the undergrowth to join me. He'd shed the simple vest worn over his tunic and used it to towel off his damp hair, shy of the back of his scalp where I'd struck him with the slag bucket.

A fresh surge of guilt shoved through me, predictable as the tide. "I'm sorry about your head."

He peered up at me through his lashes, a faint challenge painting the contours of his face. "What—that it's only good for hanging a hat on? That it's had a vacancy sign and no tenants my whole life?"

Dumbfounded, tongue-tangled, I stared at him for a moment; when he didn't crack a smile, I answered sheepishly, "For *hitting* it."

"Oh." He dropped the fist that was wrapped in his vest, the wetted leather hanging limp at his side. "Right. Well…forgiven. I know what desperation does to people…I've scraped with just about every poor and hungry person who's wandered into our fields looking for a mouthful. Just don't make a habit of it, deal?"

"Deal." I shifted aside on the rock, offering him space.

He didn't take it.

Resignation bubbled through me. I knew precisely how the rest of the night would go—and how it would end.

With me alone. With all of my questions unanswered.

Leaning forward over my bent legs, boots planted on the slope of the stone, I trapped my hands between my knees. "What now?"

"You mean, am I heading back to the farm and trying to pretend this was all some fever-dream brought on by sour mead and bad pheasant stew?" Jaik heaved a shoulder-rocking sigh, stringing his vest between his fists. "It's what I *want* to do. But the farm where I'm hired on is still Krylan land. How long do you think it's going to be before your friend Galan comes sniffing around, trying to get his hands on me?"

"Not long." And then we would be right in the throes of everything I feared: Jaik, captured and used for whatever spine-tingling power lived in the depths of him.

"Not long," Jaik agreed. "Especially if you're gone and I'm all they have left."

He strode to the rock, and I shifted aside to offer even more space; this time, he took the invitation, pushing himself up the granite dome and settling half an arm's length from me. Knees cocked, he peered up through the shaggy collar of treetops around us, to the graying dawn above.

"The way I see it, I can't go home," he sighed. "Not until we get some answers, find out what's really going on around here. Something strong enough to stop a berserk soldier from rampaging all over us before we can even get a word in."

"What, you're not going to try to reason with him?" I joked weakly.

"Reasoning implies we have the same mental capacity, and given how tonight went, I'm not up to a coin-toss on those odds. Besides," an edge of steel crept into his tone, "I don't like the thought of me, or you, or just about anyone going up against him without some sort of collateral. I don't like that soldier, something about him…"

"Maybe the fact that he threatened us both and put a rifle against my head?"

"Might be that." Jaik picked at the torn skin around his thumbnail. "So let's try to stay a step ahead of him."

I swallowed a flicker of fear that scratched nib-sharp in the base of my throat; I hoped Lio and her friends from the Ameresh district had evaded Galan's attention. I didn't know if he ranked high enough among the soldiers to manage interrogations, but if it came down to it, Lio against Galan…

I couldn't bear for that to happen. It was almost enough to make me want to march back into Krylan and trade myself for her.

But Lio had believed in me enough to get us out, so that we could find the answers to every anomaly that had been struck to life tonight. I owed it to her not to make that risk and sacrifice be in vain.

And beneath that, some selfish, terrified piece of my heart was not ready to face the man who'd nearly pulled the trigger and ended my life.

"About Galan," I murmured, and Jaik shifted slightly toward me. "How did you know to fight him like that?"

He snorted harshly. "I didn't. I thought every second I was about to take a rifleshot to the face. Don't know how I didn't, either…I've gotten into my share of scrapes, but I'm not really that much of a fighter." He grimaced. "But I couldn't just sit there and let him paint the street with the insides of your skull. I wasn't going to live with that on my conscience, either."

A bead of warmth dabbed into my heart, fanning out like an inkblot spreading across fresh parchment. "Thank you."

"Just be grateful you're alive to thank me. I could've gotten us both shot with that maneuver."

"And instead, you saved our skins." I leaned forward, resting my cheek on my kneecap, tossing a smile his way. "Not bad for a farmhand."

"Not bad for a Storycrafter, either." Settling his weight back on his hands, Jaik mirrored my posture with his cheek to his shoulder, his eyes fixed on me. "Can I ask you something?"

"Clearly."

Another snort. "So, you told that story…about the pirates. And that made all those things happen…the bridges, the aqueduct, changing the shape of the streets…"

I shivered at the memory of the hate in Galan's eyes when he'd warned me what I'd wrought on Krylan must be repaid.

"What I don't get is, why the story? Why not just say '*Jaik and Audra disappeared and reappeared outside the wall,*' and be done with it?"

"That's not how Storycrafting works." Shifting upright again, I skimmed my hands down my skirts from knees to ankles, comforted by the rub of coarse wool against my sweat-damp palms. "Our power brings pieces of the story into manifestation, but it's just that…a story. I can't make Lyndra or Kidd come to life, I can only pull pieces of what I imagine out of the tale."

"Whatever pieces you want?" He shifted his weight, rocking his head to rest on his opposite shoulder. "So if I was to say I had a craving for huckleberry pie—"

A laugh wrung out of me. "*Maybe.* The more skilled a Storycrafter is, the more defined the work of their craft. A low-ranking Storycrafter might be able to tell a story with a pie in it, and possibly be Wellspoken enough to weave *some* sort of pie into reality. But the greater their skills, the more exact things can be. That's how we have airships and rifles and the Spine, you know…they were spoken to life by Storycrafters."

"Right, I think I heard that somewhere."

"You *think* you heard how the greatest road, the best weapons, and the mightiest transportation vessels in Mithra-Sha were made?"

He shrugged, his gaze raking over me with newfound curiosity. "So, you'd have to be pretty powerful to do those things, right? Things like making bridges appear out of nowhere? Altering streets?"

"*Please,*" I scoffed. "That's low-level work. A second-year Academy student could do any of that."

"And you did—what, two years?"

"Ha. I completed the full ten, thank you."

He cocked a brow. "I take it that's supposed to impress me. How high a rank *are* you?" It was my turn to shrug, glancing down at my cloak. Jaik followed my eyes, then straightened up, shifting to rest his wrists on his bent knees. "That's what you were looking at when I...you know, back in your room, when—"

"You hit me from behind and threw me into the nightstand?"

He scratched beneath the disheveled wave of his hair. "Look, at that point I still thought you were a madwoman somewhere between making me your slave or cooking and eating me."

"That's disgusting."

"Well, I thought the same of you." He inched nearer, reaching over to fidget with the blush-pink hem grazing the rock around me. "So, what about this cloak?"

"Storycrafter cloaks denote rank." I tugged it out of his grip. "They twist color depending on the skill level of the wearer they're assigned to at graduation. And when the endings of all the stories withered up, every cloak turned gray."

Silent, we gazed together at the decidedly not-gray strip at the edging of my cloak.

"Flipping Luck," Jaik's tone was guttural with shock. "This is really happening."

A caustic retort seared my tongue, but I swallowed it back and settled for a nod. I'd had the power singing in my veins and the ecstasy of a finished story to make things come alive for me tonight; he was just a spectator to whom my tales had grafted themselves. He deserved time and grace to fathom the incomprehensible on his own terms.

After another long pause, the wonder in his gaze steadied into something thoughtful. Something *scheming*. "You're going to have to hide that thing while we travel. Dead giveaway."

"We?" I echoed. "*Travel?*"

"You know about Storycraft stuff, clearly." He gestured to the length of me. "So you've got to have some idea how to make this right. Find out what's going on with us and fix it."

I mulled that over for a moment, leaning into the same notions that had sparked when I'd spoken with Lio earlier that night. "I might," I offered at last, carefully. "There are two places where we could possibly find answers. One would be…significantly more dangerous than the other."

Jaik groaned, pressing both hands to the small of his back and audibly popping out a kink. "Let me guess, that's the one *you* want to go to."

"Oh, *Maker*, no," I swore, the hair on my arms prickling at the mere thought. "I'd rather face Galan's rifle again."

Jaik unbent from his rigor, peering at me with narrowed eyes. "That bad?"

"The worst. And it's likely gotten *worse* than the worst since the stories lost their endings." Grimacing, I rubbed my arms. "Fablehaven Academy is our best option. The truth we can find there may not be as precise, but the Record Hall houses all the written knowledge of Storycrafting. If there have ever been human amplifiers or stories effected this way, someone will have recorded it."

"You would think if they had, someone else would've found those answers by now. Since Mithra-Sha's just been suffering for years without Storycrafters to help things happen."

Doubt winnowed under my skin, but I scrubbed every trace of it away. "I know Fablehaven. It's our best chance."

Jaik shrugged. "Suit yourself, tiger. Vallanmyre it is."

"So, you don't know how the *Spine* was laid, but you know where the Storycrafter's Academy is?"

He froze in the motion of boosting himself up from the rock, that sharp dip of a frown cutting between his brows again. "Just…deduction, I guess."

Not that it was an unsensible explanation—Vallanmyre was the Head of the Spine, the capitol, home to Sha Lothar in his gilded palace with all of his trusted Storycrafters around him. It was mostly a foregone conclusion that Fablehaven would be nearby.

Still, unease ruffled my back as Jaik slid off the rock and turned to me, jutting out a hand. "Let's try and get a little farther north. We're still too close to Krylan for my liking."

"And mine." I let him help me off the rock, swinging my satchel back over my head and snugging it against my hip. I turned north, heart heavy in my chest, but Jaik didn't follow; instead he peered back the way we'd come, the predawn breeze tugging his hair.

My heart twinged. "Jaik."

"Just…" His voice cracked, and he cleared his throat harshly. "Thinking about Sheeba."

My gut twisted.

Krylan had been my home for only two short months…but how long had Jaik called it that? What friends and family might he be leaving behind for this mess I'd dragged him into? Would he even have a life to return to when this was over?

Apologies stuck in my throat; none would begin to brush against the surface of the pain my presence here had caused him—had caused the entire city. So all I said was, "I…have a friend. With connections. I made her promise Sheeba would be looked after."

His gaze leaped to me, disbelief lighting his eyes, and I braced for the sarcastic retort that brewed beneath the sharpness of that look.

But all he said was, "Thank you."

Then, setting his shoulders and straightening his spine, he brushed past me, leading the way north; and with my thumb woven into the strap of my satchel, with one last glance at the brush-shrouded, faraway smudge of Krylan on the horizon, I left behind the dream I'd fought to build and set off into the nightmare of the unknown with only a farmhand at my side.

CHAPTER 17
DEEP RED, BLOOD-RED

Blood.

Blood stained my hands. Blood spooled between every finger. Blood soaked the bodice and belly of the finest dress I'd ever worn.

Screaming voices. Rifles cocked.

Blood. Blood. *Blood.*

Let me tell you a story...

Shaking hands wrapped around a dagger—a weapon forged from a tale. A nightmare. A daydream.

Let me tell you a story...

Sorrow and shame. Wrath and ruin.

Let me tell you a story...

So much blood, so much death, so much *screaming* around me—

"*Audra!*"

I flailed upright, clawing with my bloodstained hands, raking away the cold kiss of iron shackles before they could close around my wrists. My fingers met frayed trouser knees and the brace of a strong forearm bent against them, distorting my perception.

"Whoa, whoa, whoa," Jaik's voice pierced the chaos in my head. "Take it easy, tiger."

A few swift blinks, and the world oriented itself around me.

No blood. No dresses. No rifles cocked, aimed at my head, burrowing under my hair. Just a forest swathed in alpine timber, its rugged hues full of granite-gray and umber-brown. It could have been any patch of forest I'd slept in

But this wasn't the Spine. It was the wilds, near sunset, after a full day of walking. And I wasn't alone.

Jaik crouched on one knee beside me, forearm still resting on his bent leg, his other hand extended toward me like he was calming a frightened horse.

"Easy," he repeated. "Just a bad dream."

I could see now that was true; but my racing heart didn't care to believe it. Nor did my fingers, tingling with the damp memory of blood in their creases.

Shivering, I flexed my fists, and Jaik breathed out long and low through his parted lips. "Well, that's one way to wake up in the morning."

Humiliation heated my neck; we'd spent most of the day walking, until finally I'd had to plead for rest—had to hope we were far enough from Krylan that Galan and his men wouldn't reach us if we took a moment to catch our breath.

Luck's coin had flipped our way; we were still alone. But it seemed I hadn't evaded the press of that soldier's rifle in my dreams. And I'd ruined whatever sleep either of us had a chance for.

"I'm sorry, that doesn't usually happen to me." My gaze snagged on his forearm when he rubbed his callused palm idly against it, and humiliation simmered over into boiling-hot shame. "Jaik, I'm so sorry."

"What, for those?" He cocked a brow at the pale, raised welts my nails had dealt him when I'd clawed my way back to wakefulness. "Think it'll need amputated?"

"*Jaik.*"

"No, honestly, I've had worse scratches from Sheeba when I bundled her in from a rainstorm." He stretched both arms above his head, then swung them behind himself, lean fingers wrapping his opposite wrist and tugging until his shoulderblades met and his back popped. "If you're looking for something to feel guilty over, you can have the rude awakening. And maybe don't do that again…they say farmhands have the healthiest hearts out of anyone, but I'm not really in the mood to test that old myth for myself, you know?"

It was a peace offering delivered with all of his casual charm, so I accepted it, rubbing my nose on my wrist. "Deal. I really am sorry, I don't…I'm not usually one for nightmares."

"It's not that I blame you. Everything that happened the last day? It'd have most soldiers weeping into a tankard at Errick's." He twisted off his knee to sit bow-legged on the ground, peering around at the patch of forest where we'd chosen to rest. It in no way differed from any of the rest we'd walked through all day—the inlet waters of the sea somewhere to our left, the Spine faraway to our right. "So, now what?"

"Well, I think we've come far enough from Galan's reach that we can plan." I dove into my satchel with fingers eager to be productive, to be helpful—not to be the reason we were both unwillingly awake, dappled in sweat, and him sporting clawmarks on his arms. Bunching my knees to my chest, I opened my journal against them to the map that had guided me all the way to Krylan.

For a moment, my fingers hovered just shy of the page, capturing the absurdity of the moment in a thought that I could never truly put to words. How I'd feared failure in Krylan, and being forced to strike off into the wilds around the Spine to test Luck. And here I was, doing that very thing…yet with more mystery and more hope in my pockets than I could have ever imagined on my long southward trek.

Jaik shifted nearer, his shoulder nearly brushing mine, and the damp scent of the pine needles we'd slept on wafted from his clothing. "Nice map."

"Thank you." I traced my finger over the lower portion of the mottled parchment. "Here is Krylan. So we, roughly, should be in this region." I circled the bare wilds near the Tailbone City with the pad of my thumb, hesitating when my gaze fell on the border of Amere-Del.

Fresh concern for Lio bobbed in a hard knot against my throat. It was difficult to swallow around it, to catch my breath enough to go on.

"Here's Fablehaven," I murmured, tracing my fingertip to the Academy tower rendered in sharp relief at the top of the map, "just on the boundaries of Vallanmyre."

"About as far as you can go," Jaik mused. "You're *sure* that is the better option?"

"In every way."

He shrugged. "Suit yourself. So, what are you thinking? We just…walk? Walk until we get there?"

"Well, I thought we could scoot on our backs for part of the way, maybe crab-walk, or I could carry you—"

"I meant, are we riding *horses*."

"I know what you meant." Embarrassment dampened my spine with sweat. "It's just that I…I'm not…well-versed. In the saddle."

His incredulous gaze pierced me sidelong. "You're afraid of horses."

"I don't know why!" It was some relief that my embarrassment cooled quickly into annoyance. "Just looking at them gives me a headache. I prefer walking."

He snorted. "Scared to fall off?"

"Something like that."

"Well, don't be. If we pack two of us on a horse, I can point us in the right direction and get us there without kissing dirt."

"You're assuming a mount could handle the sort of terrain we'll be crossing." I dragged my thumb along my lower lip while I eyed the map. "We can't travel the Spine, it's too conspicuous. We'll have to stay in the wilds, and that will take us near far fewer towns and cities. Most of the terrain will be boggy, sometimes perilous…even mountainous."

"And you think that's better to face *on foot* than on horseback?"

"*I* made it this far, didn't I?"

There was the subtlest shift in how he regarded me, at that…with more curiosity than contempt. "How long did it take you to get to Krylan?"

"A few years." I traced the way back with my gaze along the map that had kept me company all that time. Rothmere. Dalfi. Every town and city I'd entered, always full of dashed hopes and angry or pitying stares.

If only they could see me now. *Hear* me now, with Jaik as my amplifier.

"Well, listen, we don't have much choice yet," Jaik said at length. "Unless you want to tell a story about a horse that's faster than the wind, we're on foot until we can find a town or trading post. So, let's walk."

"Let's." I snapped the journal shut and handed it to him while I snatched up my satchel and stood; by the time I'd gained my feet, he had the journal open again, flipping through the latter pages. "*Excuse me!* Rude!"

I grabbed for it, but he caught the journal away, peering at one of the tales he'd thumbed to in the back. "You wrote this?"

"I wrote *all* of those," I spat. "What I could of them, anyway. You might remember there was the small matter of incomplete tales?"

"Right," he mumbled, still scouring the page. After a moment, he shook his head sharply, clapped the journal shut, and tossed it to me. "You ought to try finishing them now. See where it gets you."

It wasn't a bad thought—not that I'd ever tell him so. I stowed the journal and map and tugged up the hood of my cloak against a stinging wind barreling down from the north—another impending complication to our plans. I wasn't particularly eager to be out in these climes during winter, but once again, fickle Luck left me no choice.

So we walked.

For most of the day, we did so in silence, and that allowed my mind to wander. Back to Krylan, back to what had transpired there. Back down avenues bucking and writhing with misshapenness and guilt. Back to Lio's parting embrace and the emptiness of her absence. Back to a place I'd called home for so short a time, I'd barely left my mark on it in any way that would matter. After last night, I would only be the Storycrafter who'd somehow managed the ending to a tale…and then left portions of the city in shambles.

What would Errick and the others think?

I didn't want it to matter, but it did. My foolish heart cared that I would be at best forgotten, at worst thought of as a villain in the tales Krylan told from now on. Even when Jaik's name was cleared in all of this and he found some way to return there, I never could.

The quiet life was over for me, at least in the city I'd spent years walking toward, dreaming of. And my only consolation was that I did not leave it alone; instead, I'd dragged a stranger down with me. A man who strolled at my side, whistling beneath his breath—then spoke suddenly, when midday bled toward dark: "All right. Ground rules. We need to lay them."

I arched a brow, thoroughly driven from my miserable thoughts. "*Ground rules?*"

He shrugged. "Every good partnership has them. Back on the farm, you didn't hire on seasonal hands until they agreed to the rules. Keeps everything running like a well-oiled plow."

"So now you want to plow with me?"

"Ah, she banters." He fixed his gaze ahead on the soft palette of browns, grays, and greens that dappled the terrain. "Look, I just think—proprietarily speaking—if we're going to travel, just the two of us, we should have our boundaries."

It was an odd formality, for a farmhand…but perhaps it felt that way because I was unused to being among gentlemen at all. And I could do far worse than travel with a man whose first thought was ensuring we knew precisely where our lines lay.

"All right," I hedged. "We've already established one: no horses."

Groaning, he pivoted on heel, walking backward and facing me. "You can't just *lead* by cutting me off at the knees, Audra!"

"Listen to you…*cutting me off at the knees*. What kind of soldier-speak is that, *farmhand?*" I shouldered past him, digging an elbow into his ribs, and he huffed with laughter. "I mean it. No horses."

"All right, all right!" He flashed both hands, lengthening his stride to catch up with me. "Unless it's *necessary* for our survival. Deal?"

"If *I* deem it is."

"Fair enough." He folded his arms behind his head, stretching. "No cities."

"Agreed." And fervently. I had little desire to repeat any of what had befallen us in Krylan. "Towns?"

Relaxing from his rigor, Jaik tipped his head side to side. "Let's let our stomachs and the weather decide that. We may need to dip in and out, if trapping and hunting gets scarce or frostbite's a threat."

"*Hunting?*" The foreign notion halted me in my tracks.

"Yeah, Audra, *hunting*." Jaik rammed a hand between my shoulderblades, prompting me along. "The farmhand hunts. Next rule…no telling stories."

When shock caught my feet this time, there was no forcing me onward. Jaik's hand barreled right over the side of my arm, and he turned back to face me.

I stared at him, searching his countenance for a hint of mirth; I found none.

"Jaik," I said, "this power, this…*thing* I can do. It could change everything for this country. I can't just keep that to myself."

The steely edge of his expression buffed down to something pained, something nearly compassionate. "I know, and I'm not trying to be cruel. But, *logically*…look what just happened in Krylan, right? Anywhere you finish a story, it's going to send up a beacon. That means Galan—that means *anyone* who's after the pair of us—will know *exactly* where we are and what we're doing. They can maybe even figure out where we're *going* and try to beat us there. So you can't have it both ways."

An inferno of fury and grief washed across my field of vision and stormed my throat.

None of this felt right…not having the power to finish stories again, and not keeping them to myself, either. How could having everything I'd craved be bad luck as much as good?

"Audra." Jaik took a step back toward me. "I need you to agree to this. None of the rest of it really matters if they track your stories."

"Fine," I muttered. "No stories. But I'm at least going to finish the ones in the journal."

"You think you can stop yourself from opening a florist's shop every time?"

"Do you think anyone would notice the *difference* out here?"

"Fair enough," he chuckled. "Fine, I'm amenable to that. What else?"

"We'll have to stop somewhere I can get another, less conspicuous cloak," I flashed my rose-pink hem at him. "Because not wearing this should also be a ground rule. And I didn't have a chance to grab my other cloak on our way out of Krylan."

"Agreed." Jaik eyed the hem as we struck off walking again; this time, he kept perfect stride with me. "I don't think I asked last night…what *are* the colors of those things, exactly?"

"It gradates." I dropped the edge of the cloak to grip a young sapling for balance and stepped up and over the top of a fallen pine in our path. "Different hues through the shades of a rainbow."

"So the pale pink…not impressive?"

I shot a glower over my shoulder as Jaik mounted the pine behind me, then released the sapling—letting it slap him straight in the face.

"I tend to think that finishing a story at *all* is impressive these days," I jabbed over his cursing and flailing while he fought to keep his balance. Only when he descended clumsily next to me and dusted himself off did I deign to admit, "It's not particularly powerful, no. Pastels are low-ranking…what you'd expect from first and second-year Academy students. As they progress, the shades become bolder. Those tend to strengthen and darken through the remaining eight years. Most graduate on shades like apple-red, ginger-orange, golden, and such."

"No black or white?"

This time, I couldn't bite back a smirk. "Tales told in black and white are rarely intriguing."

"I'll give you that." Scrubbing his knuckles over a welt on his cheekbone— one I felt far less guilty for than the scratches raised on his tanned forearm—he added, "So, what's the most powerful shade?"

A streak of color bolted through my mind—a tale, a vision, a dream soaked in blood.

"Red." The word escaped on a quiet breath. "Deep red, scarlet…the farthest you can extend yourself on the gradient."

"Like the color of blood?"

Swallowing proved difficult. "Precisely."

Jaik nodded, untouched by the horror of a nightmare that made my nostrils practically burn with a coppery sanguine stench. "So, how many graduates make *that* color?"

"None." I inhaled deeply through my nostrils, choking down the scents of pine sap and cool, damp wind to stifle the tightness in my chest. "Not from Fablehaven, anyway. Only one Storycrafter wears a scarlet mantle...the Master Storycrafter."

"That one, I've heard of. So, when they get the title, they get the cloak?"

A deep scoff finally cleared the congested feeling from my throat. "No, Jaik. Those with the potential to be Master Storycrafters undergo a series of tests to prove their talent...their ability to tell stories and wield them well. The one who triumphs, *their* cloak changes shade to scarlet."

His eyes rounded, fascination sheening their depths. "Impressive."

"So I'm told."

"Ever seen it?"

Did I need to, in order to conjure a thought of that legendary shade? A color that so many Storycrafters coveted, that Fablehaven students yearned to wear?

Deep red, blood-red, pouring between their fingers—

"I tend to avoid the Shastah." The name of Sha Lothar's palace felt clumsy in my mouth, like a piece of a tale that preferred itself untold. "I'm not fond of politics."

"That makes two of us." Jaik snorted. "So, first town we come to, you'll ditch the tell, tiger?"

I aimed a kick at his shins; that, unlike the branch, he dodged. "I'll find a new cloak, yes."

But I wouldn't toss this one away. It was a piece of a life I'd left far, far behind in Vallanmyre...a life where I'd held my parents' affection, where I'd had friends to rely on. Where the world had made sense, built of something other than broken tales and strange farmhands.

It had served me well on the Spine; it had been a faithful fragment of the past until now.

So I would hold on to it...a piece of the woman I'd been before. Since I was the only one who noticed her absence, or missed her at all.

CHAPTER 18
A LAND OF SPICE AND SECRETS

dle chatter sprinkled the days as we walked, the terrain around us grading slightly from the harsher hills of the alpine coast to the gentler, rolling knolls that encompassed towns like Rothmere. And now that I was in the wilds, it took me by surprise—sometimes enough to silence me midword—that it was not so frightening as I had once expected.

There was even a beauty to it I hadn't foreseen, my heart trained for towns and cities and my feet for the Spine. Though far more rugged, the land beneath my boots belonged to Mithra-Sha itself. In these regions that harbored a more scattered populace, the lack seemed less; the world fed its own and brimmed with game and underbrush, which we ate from often as we walked. It was a relief not to have to watch always over both shoulders and sleep with one eye open, wary of other travelers stumbling upon my sleeping space.

Soldiers, I still listened for with half an ear even while sleeping; but as little as I knew Jaik Grissom, at least I could trust him not to rob me and flee. And most nights, that was all I needed to sleep.

When I could.

Brutal dreams of bloodied hands and vicious tales followed nearer on my heels than any pursuing Mithran soldiers. Often I dozed in lulls and starts, wary of waking Jaik with another fit of flailing—or, far more humiliating, the prospect of weeping or screaming in my sleep.

Galan and his men, it seemed, had dealt my slumbering mind a worse blow than any to my body in the escape from Krylan. But I was determined to manage that as I had everything else since departing Vallanmyre for the Spine: on my

So we walked, and I slept when I could; and it was almost with a pang of melancholy that I turned our course to another town at last by the marker on my map, and by our mutual agreement; it was far enough from Krylan that we shouldn't raise the alarm of any soldiers who happened to be about, and it was time for my cloak to be bundled safely away in the depths of my satchel.

Still, I missed the security that only the anonymity of wilderness wandering could afford. My limbs trembled with more than just the bite of the late-autumn breeze through my thin shirt and skirts when we caught a glimpse of the posts framing the path into town. Fire burned cheerfully above the stone pillars etched with its name: *Kalvikan*.

It was a modest place, a trade outpost for hunters and gatherers and wanderers who tried their luck off the Spine. Most of what framed the path beyond the torches was sculpted of wood and stone, sturdy but weather-beaten. It all held the faintest aftertaste of a noble touch when we slipped in among the humble dirt roads—winks of color here and there, fresh scaffolding affixed to broken arches and storm-pocked homes. Food was cooking on fires along the path that could not have grown in these rugged woodland climes, and spices hung rich on the air that stirred memories like puffs of dust on the drought-stricken roads.

"The Sha's people were here."

Jaik slowed beside me, his gaze swerving from home to shop across the dirt road as it widened. *He* wasn't shivering, though he wore no cloak either—and hadn't since we'd left Krylan in such a rush. "What makes you say that?"

"It smells like home."

Jaik cut me a look of raised brows as we wove between the people dotting the street; to my relief, none glanced our way twice. "Your home smells like manure and dirt roads? What sort of house did you live in?"

I rolled my eyes, privately glad for his prodding; it blunted the sharp edge of nostalgia jabbing at my chest. "Have you ever heard Vallanmyre called the Spice City?" Jaik shrugged, which was of little surprise; if the intricacies of Storycrafting had not made their way to the gossip circles of Krylan's outer farmlands, no doubt the idle chatter about Sha Lothar's wife had not either. "Shadre Calten was affianced to the Sha by her father, Drui Moraven...of our eastern neighbors, Hadrass-Drui. The Land of Spice and Secrets."

"Right. They have the most talented assassins in any country."

My heels snared on the pitted path, and I gaped at him. "Why do you *know* that?"

He flicked a glance over his shoulder and didn't stop walking. "What? You think the *Tankard* was the only tavern I ever went to? Soldiers talk. Get them drinking, and they could tell stories to rival...well, anyone's."

Yours. The notion prodded at my back, spurring me to reach his side again. "Well, that's what I smell. Hadrassi spices, like they sell back in Vallanmyre."

"So, you think Shadre Calten is here?"

I shook my head; Sha Lothar's adoration and concern for the wife he'd romanced for nearly a decade before she ever loved him back was the sort of tale many a Storycrafter revered. We had strengthened our talents on retelling it around cups of steamed cocoa at Fablehaven's great, roaring central hearth.

If she had been present still, we would not have entered Kalvikan without being manhandled.

But she *had* been here. The bursts of muted blue cloaks and clothing, fletched in unassertive yet attractive silver—far too fine for this town, but kissed with Hadrass-Drui's glints of secret shadow tones. The scent of imported food, likely flown by airship straight from the legendary kitchens within the Shastah, prepared to last for at least a season. And the feeling of *hope* that permeated the air when we reached the town square...it was stronger stuff than any of the scaffolding that repaired their storm-damaged edifices.

"Sha Lothar sent aid here," I murmured as we tucked ourselves beneath a hide awning, watching the people bustle to and from their homes and shops, going about their daily tasks. Relief strangled me when I didn't lay eyes on a single Mithran soldier, nor one of the Sha's private guard. If we had come to Kalvikan even days earlier, we might have been leaving in chains.

"He's doing his best," Jaik acknowledged, lounging back against the storefront where we waited. "He sent provisions down to Krylan, too, after we had a hard season last winter. Seeds and grain from the storehouses in Vallanmyre, some cattle to replace a herd that froze to death out in a blizzard. Things like that. Spares what he can when everyone is in about the same straits."

I could hardly fathom the burden on Sha Lothar's shoulders, on his wife's, even on his children's, who were around my age and as embroiled in all of this as their parents—trying to provide for a country that had plummeted so suddenly from little lack to voracious need. Working night and day to fill in the gaps ripped wide in the very fabric of Mithra-Sha by the loss of Storycraft, to plug up the leaking wounds driven beneath the skin as town after village after city floundered and struggled to stay afloat.

Fighting to spread hope as well as provisions when both frayed thin was no small task. And, if the gossip floating up and down the Spine for the last few years was true, he was doing all of it without the same aid and advisement his predecessors had enjoyed.

"He's a good man," I sighed. "They're a good family."

"Know them?"

I wound my thumb into my satchel strap, biting back a shiver as the chilly wind funneled between the buildings and nipped at my uncloaked skin. "Not personally. But I saw the aid he was sending while I traveled the Spine. And I heard he went for weeks hardly sleeping when the stories first dried up, piecing together a plan to make up for what was lost."

It had been a bandage around a shattered bone...something our present circumstances proved all too well.

Jaik clapped his hands on his thighs, startling me from my thoughts. "Well, no sense wandering around, mooning over the man. Sounds like he's happily married. So...how about that cloak?"

I rolled my eyes. "Why don't *you* see to the cloaks, and I'll see to finding us something warm to eat?"

"You know, there are grander gestures to make a man fall in love with you, tiger...but I think I'm happy with that one."

"And it takes plenty of effort to repel a woman *forever*, yet you make it seem so effortless."

He punched a hand over his heart and doubled up, miming a pained wheeze. "*Oof!* You've got good aim, for someone who has to resort to using slag buckets to do her dirty work."

Heat painted itself across the bridge of my nose and tingled in my cheeks. "Aren't you ready to let that *go*?"

He fingered the back of his head. "Welt's still there, so...no, I'll have to say, not yet. Try again next week."

Rolling my eyes, I flipped him a silver coin from my satchel and stepped out into the street, leaving him and his ridiculousness behind.

To my relief, a few moments prowling the square revealed a public house—a small establishment, but likely with enough visitors that my presence wouldn't be memorable. I slipped into a seam between lumberers, carried on the tide of pine sap and freshly cut wood that floated from their thick wool shirts, across the narrow, long parlor to the serving counter. The smell of their clothing clung to me; it reminded me of home in a way that ached.

It reminded me of family—a notion I was swift to distract myself from.

While I waited at the counter, I swept the room; it wasn't deep, only a dozen steps across from the door to the counter itself, but long to my right and left. The tables were mostly full of folks chattering, telling their own stories of Shadre Calten and her son, Shadran Arias, and the aid they'd brought. All their tales wove around me, thawing the chill straight out of my bones—easing the guilt that had so long hampered my heart. While it was true that Storycrafters had failed Mithra-Sha for years now, that had not entirely crippled the Sha's ability to help.

And now, thanks to Jaik Grissom, I was not entirely crippled, either.

Curiosity tapped its quill against my heart when my thoughts turned his way; this was the first time I'd been without him since Krylan. My first chance to try my hand at something I'd wondered ever since.

My turn at the counter arrested my curiosity for a moment, but as soon as I'd ordered food and drink and slid a coin to the beaming attendant, I chose a stool and dug out my journal and quill. Carefully, I thumbed through to the tale of the spinner trapped in her father's basement. Something about it itched at my mind, here in particular…as if it belonged in this public house, amidst the chatter, amidst the warmth and fresh hope.

So I put quill to paper, and I *wrote*.

The stranger's rage, building and building at the injustice dealt to the cloth-spinner. Her plea that he just set her free and forget he had ever met her. And how he couldn't…how he could never abide a person, and one so kind and generous and beautiful at that, being held captive, forced away from the world she longed to discover.

The words were wobbly and weak and uninspired, at first; they could hardly stand on their own, the lettering itself crooked beneath my shaky, out-of-practice hand. But I was making my way toward an ending, the contours of a conclusion I could just scarcely grasp in my mind…what came after the cottage, after he stayed, after they fell in love, and then her father arrived for an unexpected visit—

Until the words blinked out. Vanished. Smothered.

I sat back, quill tapping the counter's edge, my tongue tangling around a bitten-back curse.

So, I'd suspected right; Jaik's amplification had a range. And whatever shop he'd just dipped into or street he'd gone down, he'd stepped outside of it.

It was good to know. But it would certainly complicate things if we landed in danger again.

Flipping the journal shut and stowing it, and the quill, back into my cloak, I let my gaze swim around the public house again. So much eagerness hung on these faces that also wore the stamp of too much time shrouded in worry…and it was a joy they did not need Storycrafters to bring.

It was practical. It was powerful. And some part of me shrank and withered at the relief I ought to have celebrated.

Perhaps Jaik and I had found each other far too late for it to matter. After all, the noblest family in all of Mithra-Sha was making do without the tales only I could complete.

Storycrafting could be replaced. *I* could be replaced.

As if a single dark cloud had entered the public house and opened its deluge above me, I slumped, my happiness sputtering. My gaze wandered to the notice board behind the counter, seeking some form of distraction, and a fresh prickle of warmth slid into my chest at the sheer familiarity of it.

Just like Rothmere. Just like every public house I'd escaped into for warm meals and cold beverages when it was coppers, not silvers, rattling in my coinpurse. Some things never changed…and it was the familiar parts of the world I clung to now. Places that had once made space for me.

And then my eyes snagged on something that stopped my wandering attention. That stopped my luckless *heart*.

My name.

My name, on the notice board, splashed in bold, black letters, a sinister grin of scripted ink—

Audra Jashowin.

CHAPTER 19
FAMILIAR NAMES AND STRANGE FACES

There among the bulletins for Storycrafters who Misspoke, among the thieves and murderers, among the temptations for amplifiers and the pleas for attention, for salvation…my eyes were riveted on my name.

My name.

But not my face.

Feverish heat and suffocating confusion tangled into a hard knot in the base of my throat as I beheld that same familiar, vague sketch of the dark-haired woman whose countenance had been plastered on notice boards all along the Spine. And etched above her striking, unmistakable features…

My Luck-loved name.

It made no sense. It made *no sense*—

But I fled from it.

I slid down from the stool and backed away, bumping into table after table. My hand fumbled behind me, curling over the chilly doorknob; the icy shock of the cold metal biting into my palm jolted clarity back into me, bringing a sharper vision of the public house into relief.

Few faces were turned my way. Those that paid me mind would see no resemblance to that *Wanted* notice; and yet the urge to flee choked me, strangled me as ferociously as it had when I'd seen those Mithran soldiers in Rothmere.

The need to *run*. The compulsion that had driven me ever since I'd put Vallanmyre at my heels.

I backed over the threshold, my gaze fixated on that stranger's bulletin wearing my name—one of us hunted, or both of us, enmeshed by some cruel flip of Luck's coin—

"Going somewhere?"

Burly fingers fastened over my shoulders from behind, warm breath grazing my ear, and *something* tore out of me.

Something brutal. *Violent.*

I rammed my heel backward onto the dead center of the booted foot brushing against mine; gripping my fist in my opposite hand, I hurled my elbow into a chink between my assailant's ribs, bucked upward from my back, and whipped my head skyward. Skull smashed cartilage, and hot blood sprayed my hair like a rifleshot—

A brawny arm banded over my cocked elbow and crooked arm, hauling me into a grip like iron shackles. Spice-harsh, heated breath punched into the side of my head. "*Would you stop?*"

I couldn't. I writhed, twisted, tying myself in knots as I fought to get away, my mind branded with the image of my name sprayed across the notice board to be hunted, captured, caged like an animal.

"*Audra, stop!*"

The crack in his voice finally, finally pierced me through. It froze me mid-struggle.

Jaik.

All the fight went out of me on a wild, strangled gasp of a breath—a fight I hadn't even known I possessed. And he must have felt it; that restraining arm loosened, and Jaik spun me to face him.

Jaik, in his own brand-new cloak, another draped over the crook of his elbow. Jaik, seizing my upper arms, his hands gliding up to cradle my shoulders in a grip surprisingly gentle.

Jaik, his nose cocked halfway through, blood streaming down his upper lip.

I clapped a hand over my own mouth—as if that would do anything for the blood running into his. "*Jaik!* Oh, Maker's *tales,* I'm so sorry, your *nose...*"

"Forget about my nose." His fingers flexed over my shoulders. "You look like you saw a dead body. What's wrong?" When I struggled for words, mouth opening and shutting limply, his bronze complexion sallowed. "*Did* you see a dead body?"

"It's happening, Jaik," I choked, and his eyes widened. "My name is on the notice board. They're looking for me."

His fingers bore down on my skin, and this time they did not loosen. "Me, too?"

Fury punched through my gut, and I wrenched from his grasp. "Is that all you care about? Whether *you're* being hunted by the *Mithran army*?"

The army. The soldiers. All of them after *me*.

It didn't matter if the image was askew, the face wrong, everything about this tilting and twisting itself like a horrific tale; they knew my name. That was enough to flip my life upside-down like a coin turning on its edge, no guarantee at all it would land on the lucky side.

Heat crowded into my space—filled my chest and my head and eyes, blurred the world. And it pressed against me... *Jaik* pressed against me, taking my shoulders again, guiding me in a swift backstep to an alleyway beside the public house.

"I know you're panicking right now," he said levelly, "but here's what I'm thinking: if they're not looking for us both, then I can still dip in and out of towns for the things we need. Now, listen, I need you to help me with something if we're going to make it out of here without getting caught."

Anything. I would do *anything* not to feel shackles on my wrists when I walked from this town.

"Look over my shoulder," he said. "Tell me the first five things you notice out there."

I lifted my chin enough to peer past him, back into the town square. "People." I blinked to bring their blurry shapes into focus.

"Soldiers?"

"No."

"Good, all right, that's two. What else?"

"A few of them are looking this way."

"Do they look curious? Do they think we're doing something naughty?"

The heat cringed back into the core of me. "*Jaik.*"

"That'd be a no. Their loss. Give me two more?"

I shook my head wildly. "How is this helping?"

"Trust me. It's a farmhand thing."

Blowing out a frustrated breath, I concentrated on the sliver of the town square I could see again. "The scaffolding is brand-new."

"And?"

"There's a man out there who looks much more handsome and far less obnoxious than you."

"Good. That's good."

It wasn't good. None of this *mattered*, not if we were being hunted, not if *I* was wanted by men like Galan who would relish the opportunity to shove a rifle against my head and pull the trigger—

"Jaik…" His name emerged a desperate plea, a half-sob.

"Stay with me, Audra." His tone dipped, begging in its own fashion. "Stay in this. Tell me four things you feel."

I didn't know what else to do, so I told him: the tightness of his hands on my shoulders, the way I couldn't uncurl my toes in my boots, the stitch beneath my ribs, the cold licking at my skin.

"Right, sorry." Releasing me—leaving me adrift without that anchoring grip—he flicked out the cloak over his arm, then cast it across my shoulders. "Better?"

"Much." I tucked the new cloak under my chin, working to fasten its small clasp with my shaking, numb fingers.

"Here." Jaik batted my hands away and took to the clasp himself. "Tell me three things you hear."

"Besides your obnoxious voice?" My teeth still chattered, but it was more a consequence of the cold than the panic. That, at least, I could finally focus past. "Conversation, obviously. Most of it about the Shadre and Shadran visiting."

"Anyone talking about *us*?"

I listened for a moment, leaning my head against the cool wood side of the public house. "Not that I can hear."

"Excellent. Two more."

The way the wind moaned between the buildings in odd-shaped Kalvikan. The grind of hammer and chisel on buildings being repaired with fresh tools sent from the Shastah itself.

"All right. How about two things you smell?"

I breathed in through my nose, filling my lungs to the depths like bottles poured full of sweet cider, and the knot in my chest finally, *finally* released. "I can smell our food, I think. I left without it."

Jaik cocked a finger. "Hold that thought."

While he slipped from the alleyway, I breathed in deeply again. I smelled rain on the heavy clouds; I smelled oil and resin and fresh, powdered stone and wood shavings from the work taking place in the town square. I smelled *Jaik*, the spice that had ridden his breath when he'd grabbed me, the heat of his body even in his absence, the faint tinge of leather and smoke and pine that came from wilderness campfires and his vest.

By the time he rejoined me in the alley—nose reset, cloth tatters stuffed in both nostrils, food in hand—I was nearly calm. And when he handed me a loaf of fresh sourdough bread, I tore into it without pause, without even time spared for a *thank you*.

He grinned, and said in a congested, muffled voice, "Tell me something you taste."

"The best flipping bread I've ever had," I mumbled with my mouth full.

"Perfect." He tore into his own half-loaf, leaning across the alley from me. "We'll handle this, Audra. This is a big country, with a lot of wilderness to get lost in. The chances of them spotting us when we're not on the Spine, just out there tromping through bogs and getting tangled up in the trees?"

"It's not likely." I could see that, now that I was calm; now that he'd helped me return to myself. "Thank you, for what you did. Where did you learn that technique?"

He shrugged. "Couldn't tell you. Just something I've known about for as long as I can remember."

"Well, I'm grateful."

He cocked a smirk my way, softer than most of his barbed little grins. "Glad I could help. What do you say we go back to trying our luck against the wilds?"

I had never been happier to go.

CHAPTER 20
SECOND BEST

The land beyond Kalvikan opened itself up to us like a storybook pleading to be read. More than read, even...*experienced.*

The gentle, grading hills I'd first come to know near Rothmere steepened into sheer wooded slopes, veined with roads that had served as the ancient bloodpaths of the country, pushing foot traffic along with every heartbeat. Or so Naomi had explained when we were children, her eyes shining with the knowledge granted by her poison studies and the healing work that helped the rest of Mithra-Sha make sense to her.

Those veins had withered up now, bereft of blood ever since the Spine had been laid by spoken word; the few travelers we shared the trails with hardly paid us more than a passing glance, and never with recognition. We might as well have been alone—and much of the time, we were.

We walked through archaic, stone-bricked tunnels driven deep into the hills, their depths swallowed in shadows, their entryways framed with imperious pillars of the same rough angles as the towers in Krylan. We mounted high hills of rock and tree and slid down into valleys studded with the sort of hardy wildflowers that only thrived in the thick shade of the trees around us—trees consumed in a riot of wildfire color, dappling our path with tongues of flame.

We forded streams by way of fallen trees, an unspoken dare in how we pitched our balance, fighting to beat one another across. We watched the sun sneak away behind the distant crags of the coastal mountains to the west, fanning fingers of darkness along our way far earlier than if we'd walked the Spine beneath the open, uncluttered sky...but there was something we both appreciated about it. In silent accord, we were embracing this adventure out in the open, with our wits and the wilds paired against each other.

Jaik's love for the nature he'd tended for years with his hands sunk into the soil, coaxing life and sustenance from it—and my love for the story woven into the heart of the world itself, so much louder and more profound now that I was away from the Spine—was enough to quiet my nightmares a bit. It made surviving on less sleep and less rest overall far more endurable. Even *enjoyable*.

It was overall an experience I would have appreciated significantly more had Jaik not come down with a headcold.

Deep, congested snuffles and scathing moans punctuated our travels for some time, always reining me in from the fringes of true joy; it was difficult to lean into the beauty around us when my awestruck thoughts found frequent companions in moody protests muttered under another phlegm-soaked breath.

"It was that flipping tailor that gave this to me," he muttered one afternoon while we walked, banding the throat of the offending cloak more tightly around his shoulders. "I *knew* those chunks under her fingernails weren't glue."

"That's disgusting," I groaned.

"*This* is disgusting, tiger," he coughed, spitting a wad of mucus into the undergrowth as we trekked up the next hill in our path. "And her hand—flipping *Luck*, that hand. Corpse-clammy. I should've known right *then* what I was in for."

"Don't be rude, she was just trying to make a living. You know that with how things are, most can't afford a day of rest, no matter how ill they are."

"I noticed. You're the one who's been driving me like a plow horse."

I mimed cracking a whip at his back, but he only shot me a raw-eyed glower before he pulled ahead to conquer the next hill.

It had taken a week for Jaik's sickness to set in; now, after nearly another of the hacking and sniffling, I didn't know whether to be thankful I hadn't succumbed as well or furious it hadn't taken me instead. At least my solitary journey down the Spine had taught me to suffer in silence.

Jaik groaned and coughed his way through another hilltop ascent, and the irritation in my chest fizzled, giving way to worry. He really did look miserable; and while I'd learned by now that a good deal of Jaik's personality was pinned-together scraps of bravado and an exaggeration of every emotion, it tugged my heart to see his watering, red-rimmed eyes and nose bright pink from constant scrubbing and blowing.

Naomi drifted into my thoughts again as we crossed another narrow valley to the next hill—an inevitability, to be sure, with Dalfi on the not-too-distant horizon. Another several weeks of walking, anyway; but the nudge of our last encounter prodded other thoughts of her to the surface as we walked.

Naomi at Harrow Hall, and me at Fablehaven, stealing time between lectures to meet at a public house between our schools and teach one another what we knew: her, taking lessons on how to heal, drawing out poisons and illnesses from the body. Me, using tales to craft beakers and corked bottles and other vessels she could keep her cures in.

I wished I'd held on to more of what she'd taught me.

Jaik slowed on the next uphill trek, so much so that I reached the top ahead of him...and had time to fret while I fidgeted, watching him grip trees and undergrowth shoots to steady himself on the climb.

Perhaps I'd been a bit inconsiderate of his suffering. The truth was, I didn't *want* to think of him as ill. I didn't want to give worry a foothold in my heart.

Jaik was fine. He had to be. Anything else was a notion so strangely unconscionable, I didn't dare prod the edges of it.

Still. I didn't have to heap *more* pain on him with smart-mouthed remarks and aired-out irritation.

"I'm sorry," I blurted when he crested the hill at last. "You're right...Mistress Clammy-Hands should have warned you she had a plague before she wiped her snot all over you."

He cocked a brow, highlighting the red rim of it against the paler furrows of his tanned forehead. "Oh, so she has a name now? Planning to put her in your next tale?"

Ignoring his remark, I stepped forward to lay a hand on his forehead; dull, thudding heat met my palm, punching beneath my skin like a quill nib through parchment, straight to my heart. "You have a fever."

"*Agh*," Jaik moaned. "Your hand is like *ice*."

I snatched myself back. "Sorry—"

Calloused fingers wrapped my wrist in an iron grip; he trapped my fingers to his forehead, and beneath my palm, those furrows smoothed out when he leaned into my touch. "No. Don't. That feels *nice*."

We stood there for some moments—him gripping my wrist, my hand splayed to his brow. Nervousness pounded into the core of me; for lack of anything better to do, I swept my thumb over his forehead, finding the paths of old creases between his brows.

Finally, he peeked one eye open, hunting for my gaze. "Think the power is wearing off. Now your hand just feels like a hand."

"They do that, don't they?" I let my arm fall slack at my side, but that felt cumbersome, too; so I took him by the elbow and pirouetted aside, snugging his arm across my shoulders. "Can you make it one more hill?"

His pause was lengthy. "Sure, tiger. Maybe I can even make it two."

I wasn't certain from his tone if he was patronizing me, and I chose not to test the bait; instead, we walked through the gathering shadows that splintered around the faraway mountain peaks. The silence was, as usual, at least companionable; but something hummed under the surface like an unspoken question now.

"About Clammy-Hands," Jaik said at length, "I get it. I don't blame her. One of my sisters was the same way...she'd work herself to the bone, sickness or not, trying to make ends meet. Must be a tailor trait."

"You have siblings?"

"Oh, yeah, I've got four," he admitted. "Two brothers, two sisters. You've probably met a pair of them."

It took a moment for that to sink in. "They're Storycrafters?"

"Mmhm." His hand circled my upper arm, steadying us both against the drag of his weight as we ascended the next hill. "Adel and Lyam."

Confusion scratched at the back of my thoughts. "But, the night we met, didn't you say Storycrafters were—?"

"Bad luck?" His free hand tangled back through his hair. "Yeah, I shouldn't have said that."

"And you didn't even know what things were made by Storycraft, how Storycraft functions, how it can't be used to change *our* stories—?"

"Look, staying ignorant on purpose isn't something I'm prone to, but..." he grimaced, averting his face. "It skipped me, all right? However the Storycrafting talent works, whether it runs in families, it just...it passed over me and went to the twins. And maybe...I don't know, when they came along over a decade after my parents had me, and I went from first-born favorite to second-best..."

"You were jealous." I couldn't bear to tease him for that; in fact, the harsh dip to his tone echoed something that had chafed beneath my skin for years now.

"That about sums it up," he sighed. "So, for a long time, every spare coin my parents made went to getting them tutored, getting them shipped off to Vallanmyre...to Fablehaven, I'm guessing now, I didn't get that involved. I just made my own way, tried to stay clear of all things Storycraft, and then..." he trailed off, frowning, sketching a thumb over the latent furrow laid between his brows. "Then I ended up in the farmlands."

Compassion throbbed in the base of my throat. "What about your other siblings?"

"Nora and Caid. A tailor and a peddler." He shrugged, his hand bunching up and down my arm with the gesture. "About as plain as I am. Doesn't seem to bother them, but all they ever knew was everything going to the twins."

He was the only one who'd known another life. And the only one, it seemed, who missed it.

The notion strummed in my chest with the throbbing tremor of doors slammed in my face. Of frightened eyes and warnings to keep me at bay.

"I have siblings, too," I offered—a bridge between our pain. "A brother and sister, both older than me."

"No kidding?" Jaik stabbed his feet a bit harder into the downward slope before us, slowing our descent. "Storycrafters?"

"No, Raff's a lumberer and Marli is a wetnurse. We don't...we haven't spoken in years." Longer than I'd been estranged from my parents, even.

"Bad blood?"

I swallowed, gathering strength in the silence as the last of the sunlight trickled away between the trees. "I haven't seen them since I graduated Fablehaven. I think they resented me...for being a Storycrafter. For all the attention and accolades that came with my power."

I'd been too ashamed to reach out to them before I'd departed Vallanmyre. Too afraid I would see triumph rather than compassion in the eyes of my older siblings when I revealed that the Storycrafting power that had set me so far apart from them was gone; that I could do less for our country now than they could.

That, without my power, it turned out I had little to offer anyone at all.

Jaik was quiet for a time, and I peered up the next black hill in the continuum of them, a trace of oddness writing notes of unease in my chest; the waning light ahead of us had shifted, glowing a deep blush-pink rather than sunset-yellow over the next hill.

I tugged Jaik toward it.

"Well, I feel like an ass who ran into a fencepost," he said at length. "I guess the secret's out, huh? I'm not really all that different from your siblings."

"I don't blame you. I didn't blame them, either," I sighed. "Storycrafting is fickle...we don't get to decide who lays claim to it."

"You got any idea where it comes from?"

"From the Storymaker," I explained as we struggled up the hill—one of my favorite tales weaving deliciously off my tongue. "The One who creates all stories. The legend goes that His was the first Wellspoken story, that it shaped the whole world into being. And every tale a Storycrafter tells is a thread left dangling in the greater story we're all part of. Storycrafters can pull those threads, we can shape them into something tangible. An act of creation, like the first story ever told." My face heated as the words spiraled out of me, guilt plucking my ribs. It sounded far too much like bragging in the face of Jaik's resentment. "It's just that some people can weave those threads, and some people can't."

"And some people can't without *me*," he snorted, checking me with his hip as we ascended the hill. "Think I'd rather be me than you, tiger."

"Even with the plague?"

"Even..." He trailed off as we slowed to a halt at the crest of the hill.

Not that I would have registered anything more he'd said, my attention arrested by the sight that lay before us.

"Jaik," I breathed.

He let out a low whistle, hoarse with congestion. "Would you look at that."

I needed no lick of the skill that filigreed my veins to know we'd stumbled upon someplace touched by a Storycrafter's power. Here, rather than the firestorm of autumnal hues that had consumed our wayward path, the trees dripped a rich, lustrous magenta; their foliage was fashioned from overspilled clusters of flowerlike leaves intertwined with purple ivy, the cords of the climbing strands wrapped around the deep mauve tree trunks. At the center of it all stood a lamppost, guttering with a rich violet flame as if it had just been lit...or never stopped burning. And beyond that unusual beacon, a rippling silver-blue pond glinted coin-bright between the trees, its wind-stroked surface tossing iridescent ripples against the underbellies of the foliage.

Tears stung my eyes as I drank in the sight, and my storyteller's heart scrabbled at my ribs. I couldn't help but wonder what sort of tale had brought this place to life; it throbbed with an essence of peace and joy. Of sanctuary, built into the heart of the wilderness where few would find it.

I glanced up at Jaik; he looked down at me, and we said in unison, "Camp."

CHAPTER 21
A FLEETING LINE

The pond, we learned by delighted exploration, was not a pond at all; it was a warm spring tucked among the trees, its surface faintly steaming up close. I dipped in first, while Jaik occupied himself exploring the lamppost; the bathwater-heat made my skin cringe close to my bones at first, shy of the shift from the chilly sunset air. But once I'd settled, it was a relief to swim a bit, to dunk my whole head under the water and float cross-limbed in the silence.

But as a Storycrafter, even silence wasn't silent; my head hummed with tales waiting to be told, and this oasis beckoned them out of me. A kinship of creation—things breathed to life by the spoken word begging further utterance.

My thoughts clamored full of stories when I finally hauled myself from the spring, dabbed myself dry with my cloak, and slid back into my clothes. Then I padded toward that guttering lamplight flame, where I found Jaik sitting against the black iron post, head thrown back carelessly against it, gazing up at the treetops.

I nudged his thigh with my boot. "All finished. Your—"

"Shh." He laid a finger to his lips, gaze still hunting the bunches of tumbling purple-pink florals, and my heart stuttered its rhythm.

"Soldiers?" I couldn't envision them *here*, invading this sanctuary, but if it came to a fight—

"Nightbirds." Jaik sucked in his lip and whistled; somewhere in the vast canopy, a birdsong echoed like none I'd ever heard before—something so sweet and melodic, it wrenched tears to my eyes. Smirking, Jaik hauled himself up with an arm looped around the post. "I'll tell you, tiger…I've never seen anything like this place before."

He skinned out of his shirt right then and there, and I bit in a breath; not at he sight of his bare abdomen, precisely, but at the lateral scar that crossed his chest, lying just above the heart.

"That's…quite the mark," I croaked.

"Huh?" He glanced down, skimming his thumb along the raised ridge of skin. "Oh, right. Yeah, farming has its risks."

Something about the sight of that long-healed wound, with him in his sickly state, prodded my curiosity beyond the boundaries of propriety. "What happened?"

Balling his shirt around his fists, Jaik shrugged. "Slipped in the mud, took a plowblade to the chest, I guess."

"You *guess?*"

"I don't remember much of it. Blood loss and a few weeks of bedrest will do that to you," he snorted. "My parents, my brothers and sisters, they never even came to visit me. Woke up in the infirmary in Krylan and never even saw them. No one came to find me…then or after. I've learned to put things back together myself ever since."

He left me with that, winding away toward the spring, and I leaned back against the lamppost and watched for the shadowy flirt of wings between the boughs.

I tried to imitate Jaik's whistle; it didn't work.

For the sake of giving him privacy—and so I wouldn't think of his scar, or the bare chest it lay across—I set about building a fire, careful only to gather fallen boughs and old, crumbled foliage. It didn't feel right to remove anything from this sacred space.

While I worked, my mind drifted between the tales living in my head, and the one Jaik had told me of his scar…and his family.

Perhaps his misery these last few days, exaggerated as it had seemed, was more than a tactic to annoy me. Perhaps Jaik was seeking connection…someone who cared in ways his family hadn't. Whether for the bad blood stirred up with his siblings, or for being the first son overshadowed by what came after him, he hadn't felt he'd mattered enough to remember. To be visited—for his sickness or his wounds to merit a second glance from those who were meant to care about him the most.

Doors slammed in his face. The eyes of friends like family, turned to the wary gazes of strangers.

Commiseration pinched low in my gut, spurring my hands to work; if I could not absolve the pain along the path my own feet had trod, the shape of my life before I'd set out down the Spine, at least I could ensure that anguish did not repeat from the sharpness of my tongue.

By the time Jaik ambled back into view—still shirtless, wiping his neck dry beneath the damp ends of his hair—I'd built an impressive fire and turned up a few forest tubers and mushrooms to roast on spits. The pinch in my middle lessened somewhat at Jaik's return...and at the warm tone of his skin, less feverish and far healthier.

"Better?" I grinned.

"*Much.*" He pitched himself down at the fireside, rubbing his damp hands and holding them out to the flames. "How safe are those mushrooms, do you think?"

"I know how to forage, believe me...I've done it for years while I've traveled."

"Right." That single, soft word was contemplative in ways I didn't have the energy to explore.

We were silent while we ate, taking in the wild undergrowth, the bruise-blue dark above crusted with stars in streamers, the moonlight kissing the leaves. It was the loveliest place I'd ever made camp—such a far cry from the bushes I'd tucked myself beneath just off the Spine.

Some selfish part of me wondered what it would be like to let the wilds become my home. To forget Galan and his vendetta against Storycrafters. To forget any duty that came along with the power to weave stories from nothing, and the strange amplification that Jaik's presence offered.

To become an oasis myself—my own sanctuary.

It seemed impossible. Enticing.

So incredibly *lonely*.

Jaik finished his skewer first and tossed it into the fire, dusting off his hands. Then he rocked back on his elbows, tossing his hair from his eyes. "You know I don't resent *you*, right?"

Stirring from my reverie, I blinked, uncertain if I'd misheard him. "You—"

"Don't resent you," he repeated. "The things I said about my brother and sister, it's...you get that, right? It's sibling stuff, it's got nothing to do with you and me." Blowing out a long breath, he sank onto his back, staring up through the boughs entwined above us. "I've never met a Storycrafter like you, Audra."

He was right; I was like no one else. And that was the responsibility that weighed on my shoulders, that meant places like this could only be a fleeting line, a page at most, in my own story.

I had to move on. I owed it to Mithra-Sha, to all the other Storycrafters, and to the people harmed and crippled by the lack of our power.

Folding my knees to my chest, I balanced my chin on them and prodded the kindling with my own skewer. "I appreciate that. And I *do* understand...but I wouldn't blame you if you did resent me a bit. I clobbered you with a slag bucket."

He scoffed. "Not that hard."

"And dragged you into the wilderness with me."

"That was my choice. If I'd wanted to, I could have—"

"Dumped me like a sack of potatoes? I know."

"But maybe not right now." He sniffed—still a guttural, congested sound—then tucked both arms behind his head.

I curled over my knees, keeping my eyes on him; worry beat in the base of my throat, steady as my pulse. "How are you feeling?"

"Better," he echoed my wry question from before. "That spring is something else. This whole place is. Give me a day or two here and I'll be fine."

"We'll take as long as you need," I said fervently. "You tell me when you're ready to go."

He picked up his head a bit to peer at me—searching for sarcasm, perhaps. I met him, unblinking, with all the sincerity that hung in my heart; after a long moment, he murmured, "Thank you."

Quiet enveloped us again, warm and peaceful as the waters that had washed away our last few weeks of travel.

At length, Jaik broke it again. "Do you want to tell me a story?"

His tone was gruff, careful around the words. My heart skipped, and I picked up my head from my knees. "Do *you* want me to?"

He shrugged—a stilted motion with his shoulders flat to the ground and his arms still tucked away. "This place feels like it needs it, you know? Like it's meant for stories."

"You can feel that, too?"

He turned his cheek to the soil, eyes brighter than I'd seen them in days. "Sure can."

A flush of pleasure filled up my middle, and it was no effort at all to smile. "I'd love to, Jaik."

"Then go for it." His eyes tumbled shut, and a quiet sigh floated up from him. "I'm listening."

So I told him a tale of a seamstress shut away in a cellar, found by chance when a hunter stumbled in from the cold. I embellished it a bit—gave the hunter a headcold, described in detail his suffering until Jaik was sniffling in time with the tale, chuckling low in his throat.

But he was silent when I told of the father's return; of the battle between blood and heart, between the love that should have been and the one that might never have come if not for the deft flip of Luck's two-faced coin.

When the story's ending poured out of me, it was with the father disgraced, but spared; the seamstress choosing freedom and adventure over fingers washed in his blood. And with the hunter as her companion and guide, the pair of them struck off into the wilderness, seeking a place he'd only heard of—a forest oasis with magenta blooms and a warm silver spring tucked among the sacred trees.

From the last words tumbling off my lips, the warmth rising up in me, the making crystallized into shape. Into my hands poured a down-soft blanket— spun of words rather than a loom. Its threads depicted a starry sky traced through moonlit boughs, a lamppost jutting up to light the way for weary travelers and hunters and seamstresses looking for peace within their journeys.

Jaik's soft, hoarse snores painted the air as he slumbered; I didn't know when he'd fallen asleep, and I didn't mind. Rest would heal him. Rest would mean we could continue on.

Standing, I shook out the blanket and crept around the fire. Fluffing it with a snap, I settled it over Jaik, tucking it under his arms, tight against his ribs. He stirred at my touch, only faintly—just enough to rock his head my way, a faint divot creasing his forehead again.

Carefully, I laid my palm to his brow, relieved to find the tacky heat faded; his fever had broken.

Still, I lingered, my thumb absently tracing that burrowed-in frown until it eased.

"I'm here, Jaik," I murmured. "And I'll be here when you wake."

My throat tightened, strangling any other words I might have offered—any words beyond those few I'd yearned to hear myself before I'd left Vallanmyre.

I'm here.

No one had been there—no one had stayed for me.

But *I* would stay…and not only for the life he breathed into my stories.

Because Jaik Grissom deserved to be found.

CHAPTER 22
SUPERSTITION AND HOPE

When Jaik's health improved—as he'd predicted, after two days resting at the forest spring—we made far better time through the hills. Within another month of foot travel, our days full of easy talk and our nights full of fires built high to keep the cold at bay, we encroached on broader paths that turned to heavily trafficked roads.

I had no need to consult my map to know where we were approaching: Assida, a city I'd learned of in my studies at Fablehaven.

The very notion of it—the birthplace of so much legend within the realm of Storycrafting—raised the hair along my body as we approached. And entering it was necessary, despite our reservations after Kalvikan; our clothing was less and less fit for the cooling nights, and if our course necessitated a diversion up into the coastal mountains, we risked death against the elements.

So into the city it was, with silver coins and a straightforward mission. Thankfully, we were anonymous here among the clusters of other travelers, just two more hooded and cloaked on foot weaving in among the rest. Many of them were Storycrafters, evidenced by the color-leached gray of their cloaks and the hunger in their eyes. They had come for the same reason I had nearly diverted from the Spine to visit Assida on my journey south—and would have, if not for an acrobat troupe I'd saddled up with, passing the sideway to the city straight by.

Superstition and hope. Two things that danced around each other so closely, at times it was impossible to differentiate between them.

"Must be a good trade city," Jaik observed as we drew nearer to Assida's outer walls. "Seems popular."

"It's where the first Master Storycrafter was born." I matched my tone to his unease braiding into the excitement of seeing Assida in all its glory up close;

my eyes darted from person to person, hunting for any glimmer of recognition in the faces crowding past. "It's believed that Storycraft here is—or *was*—richer. More powerful, somehow."

"Ah." Jaik slowed, squinting ahead. "I take it that's your Master Storycrafter?"

I had to crane a bit to see what he indicated through the crush of bodies; a carriage in our path skirted sharply right, trundling around the base of a statue in the near distance, some fifteen or twenty feet high, rendered with an androgynous mask covering half of the face, and an unmistakable cloak cast in deep crimson dye.

A Master Storycrafter, neither man nor woman, but indicative of a position that could be held by either.

We halted at the base of it, as many did, peering up its impressive height. It wasn't rendered of any stone or precious metal I could identify; instead, it simmered with the same latent power that cavorted along the Spine.

A story had created this statue; likely the first Master Storycrafter's own tale. It explained why, all these centuries later, the cloak had not lost its perfect hue, nor the gray cast of the statue seen any weathering at all.

"Impressive," Jaik remarked. "So, who *is* the Master Storycrafter?"

Indignation flared in my chest, and I cut him a sideways glower. "You farmhands *truly* don't get out much, do you?"

"Hey! Cut me a break," he protested. "Where I'm from, folks rely more on the strong arm of soldiering over storytelling."

That was fair, and I did appreciate how he left off Krylan's particular name. We could never be too wary of who might be listening, who might be on the alert for a disgraced Storycrafter fleeing from the Tailbone City. After all, it wasn't as if Galan had left enough Storycrafters around there to mask my movements among theirs.

Resentment shivered down my spine. To calm it, I laid my hand on the statue's base.

A deep ache punched through me, as if a lifetime of sorrow lived within the foundation. The moment my fingers contacted it, tears seared across my vision and a sob built in my chest.

I wrenched my hand away, and my sight cleared. Jaik watched me, arms folded and brows lifted—expectant.

I scrabbled for a moment to recall what he'd asked me. "The Master Storycrafter was the most powerful—"

"No, that part I know," he cut across me with his usual caustic haste. "I mean, who is it *now*? Why don't I ever hear about them traveling around with the Shadre or trying to fix things up in Vallanmyre?"

"Because you don't hear much, apparently." My jab was halfhearted, my throat still tight. "There isn't a Master Storycrafter anymore. The trials were halted when stories lost their endings, and before that...with the last Master..."

I trailed off, nausea pinching in my middle. I'd hated these whispers from the moment I'd first heard them drifting down the Spine; worst of all was that I'd never found any *proof* of them, nor anything to discredit them entirely, which made it seem all the more likely they were real.

And that Sha Lothar was keeping the truth a secret to avoid mass panic.

"Well?" Jaik prompted. "Come on, tiger, you're not usually clammy about a good story! What happened...Sha Lothar terminated the Master Storycrafter's position when the stories dried up?"

"Actually, if you believe the rumors," I murmured, "the Master Storycrafter was murdered."

Jaik blinked, falling back slightly on his heels. "You're serious?"

"So they say." I rubbed the gooseflesh that pebbled my arms, peering up at the statue in whose shadow we stood. "It hasn't been discussed widely, just rumored by travelers. But I've wondered sometimes if the death of the Master Storycrafter was what severed all of us from the endings of our tales."

He let out a low whistle. "Any idea who—?"

"No," I interrupted swiftly. "Certainly someone who didn't know what havoc it would wreak, if it's true. The Master Storycrafter has always been the Sha's premier advisor and a crucial part of Mithra-Sha's balance. I can't imagine how much hate or greed or selfishness would have to lead someone to murder them."

But now that I'd met people like Galan, the notion seemed more likely than when I'd first heard those rumors.

"Did you know them?" Jaik asked after a beat. "The last Master Storycrafter?"

A sour taste saturated my throat; the dazed, slippery sensation of hot blood slithered so prominently down my palms that I skimmed them on my skirts. Jaik's eyes shot to me, and I focused on the curiosity lighting their tawny depths.

I hadn't had a nightmare in days. Why was the sensation of one prodding me now?

"I don't think so," I managed after several labored swallows, chasing down the bile that rose in my throat. "A Master Storycrafter wouldn't have time for someone like me."

Jaik frowned, but said nothing.

For a time, neither did I; we simply stood there, watching the statue, while others flowed toward and away from its base.

Finally, I jerked my chin at a pair of women in cloaks of mourning gray, laying coins face-up on the railing that surrounded the statue. "Storycrafters take pilgrimages to Assida from all over Mithra-Sha now. I can't count the number of them I passed on the Spine. There's some hope that because the craft had such powerful origins here, it might...rejuvenate the stories."

Jaik tipped his head toward me, almost conspiratorial. "You believe that?"

"Not enough to have changed course on my journey to Krylan."

And what luck I hadn't; the power I'd sought all along had awaited me at the end of the Spine, not in this city after all.

Finally, Jaik pivoted away from the statue, and that broke me from a daze like the rapture cast by a Wellspoken story. Cleaning my hands one last time on my skirts, I fell into step with him around the statue, toward the city gate.

He slowed—to wait for me, I thought at first. But then he leveled me with a look that sparked itself against the edge of my temper. "Where do you think you're going, tiger?"

"Into the city to find *clothes*?" I reminded him pertly.

"Thought we had an understanding about where you should show your face."

Heat colored my cheekbones. After Kalvikan, I *should* be hiding in the treeline we'd left behind at the crest of the last hill, miles from Assida's outer wall. But the notion of entering this city, rich and thriving with the history of my people, even if I didn't believe the superstition of its inherent amplification or the hope it failed time and again to bring...

It was irresistible. *Insatiable.*

"It's just one city, Jaik," I wheedled.

Skepticism was the hand that scripted the doubt between his tugged-together brows this time. "Right. But it's *the* city for Storycraft. If you were going to show yourself anywhere—"

"It would be here, I know. And they would expect me to know that. They would expect me *not* to come."

"They'd expect you not to be stupid? Yeah, pity them. They clearly don't know you at all."

"*Jaik.*"

He tossed up his hands. "Do what you want, Audra."

I could have let it go at that—victorious, despite his irritation. But the way he stomped off ahead of me made the chasm of loneliness in my middle crumble on the edges, stretching wider from end to end. And I thought I understood his frustration a bit, too.

We had agreed on the parameters of our own safety—both his and mine. And Assida was a risk.

It was a greater risk if we both ventured inside.

Lengthening my stride, I caught him under the arm. "Jaik, listen to me. I'll be careful. But I think we could both use a night indoors, a hot meal we don't have to cook for ourselves. A bit of comfort. And I trust you...I trust *you* to pick the places we go. I'll follow your lead to keep us safe."

Jaik slowed, then halted, so I halted with him. We gazed at one another while the crowd broke around us, ignoring the irate murmurs that floated our way.

"You're serious?" he asked.

I let go of his arm so I could fold mine. "You got us in and out of Kalvikan and free of Krylan with...well, as little trouble as possible, given the circumstances. I take it you have a knack for thinking your way out of tight spaces. So, yes...you can decide the where and how of things. Just know you can't stop me from going."

He stared at me a moment longer, an odd awe and even something like suspicion tingeing his gaze. Then, finally, his lips quirked up. "Compromise?"

I blew out a breath, relief loosening the tension in my spine. "Compromise."

Snorting, he draped his arm around my shoulders like he had on the uphills and slopes to the forest oasis, steering me toward the city gate. "Then let's have ourselves a look around, tiger."

It was strange, the shift in his tone and bearing as we approached Assida— as if our agreement had handed him a weapon he knew how to balance, the reins to a mount he was keen on steering. He flashed swift but self-sure nods to the pair of Mithran soldiers holding the gate, his grip tightening on my upper arm in a way that might have been reassuring or even a bit possessive...but I didn't mind. The soldiers looked away from that touch, and then we were past them, entering a city I'd yearned to see ever since I'd set out from Vallanmyre.

It was the colors of Assida that struck me first: everywhere I looked were deep stains of bloodred, the same evocative scarlet as the Master Storycrafter's cloak. This city reveled in it, from streamers banded between the whitestone buildings to cathedral spires and domes, to doorways and shutters all painted the same crimson hue.

It was a living, breathing tribute to the most powerful of all Storycrafters in Mithra-Sha.

"Do you think they know other shades of red exist?" Jaik mused, slipping his arm down from my shoulders as we wandered from one city plaza to the next. "Should we tell them?"

"Don't be rude." I backhanded his chest. "Let them have their fun."

And not just theirs...*mine*. Something almost giddy expanded in my chest at the sight of so much of that sacred color. And so much tribute to Storycrafting everywhere, from half-moon storytelling amphitheaters carved into every street, to shops selling wares rendered especially from tales told in times before, to bookstores splitting at the seams with handwritten tales still sprinkled with the memory of the power they'd once wielded.

It could not have been more different from Krylan, from Rothmere...from most of the towns and cities and even the villages I'd set foot in over the years. Here, the resentment for Storycrafters and our many shortcomings had not fully set in. An air of hope *still* seethed in the veins of beautiful Assida; something that beckoned Storycrafters to try one more time. To tell one more story.

And for some of these pilgrims, it just might work.

The thought slowed my stride and set my heart thundering.

If it was true that Jaik could amplify more stories than just mine, and knowing that there was indeed a range to his odd ability...

Somewhere in this city, he was bound to brush up against someone telling a story in the right place, at the right time. Someone else who would have a finished tale before Jaik walked away.

Emotions collided inside me like errant swoops of letters scripted by a drunkard's hand—a love-letter to my own fears and failures, my hopes and dreams, *my* shortcomings.

Worry. Excitement. Pity. Sorrow.

Jealousy.

"See something?" Jaik dropped back to my side, scouting the shops and homes stacked around us. "Audra?"

We shouldn't be here, my mind screamed.

Our presence was a danger not only to us, but to other Storycrafters; if word traveled that they'd found their miracle in Assida, it would draw Galan and his ilk straight to this city. They would fall like an axe on the necks of those unsuspecting Storycrafters and turn their luck with a flip of the coin.

People would be hurt. *My* people, my fellow Storycrafters.

But they were already going to be hurt. Because I didn't *want* to give them their miracle...I didn't want to share Jaik Grissom with the world. I didn't want to be just another Storycrafter touched by the impossible gift of his amplification; I wanted to be the *only* one.

Special. Set-apart. Someone worth remembering, for once in my life.

I was choosing to hurt them, to let them keep on hurting along with the rest of Mithra-Sha, by keeping this blessing all to myself. And the fact that they didn't know any better somehow made that choice more conscionable.

I was ruthless. Selfish. It made no sense at all that Storycraft had passed over someone like Jaik, who was honest to a fault, and settled itself in my hands.

Pastel-pink and practically worthless or not, I was making the wrong choices.

"*Audra.*" Jaik tapped the top of my head, abrupting my downward spiral of dread. "Anyone home in there?"

"I think..." My tongue stalled and stammered over the words. The confessions. The traitorous truths. "I think...maybe we should separate. I could find food and lodging, and you could find clothing?"

We would let Luck decide it, then...any Storycrafter meant to find him, would. Otherwise...

I desperately hoped for *otherwise.*

"Thought I was the one keeping us safe?" he teased without any real venom; but I winced anyway at the blow that landed twice as deep.

He was right. I was wrestling the choice away from him for my own gain.

I flinched again when he stepped into my space, his height crowding out the midday sun. "Audra, you're sure you wouldn't rather just wait outside the gate? I could have food and clothing sorted out in a few hours at most."

A few hours alone in this city, where any soldier or Storycrafter could grow suspicious and lay hands on him. And then I'd never see him again.

The thought troubled me so deeply, it stole my breath.

When I didn't speak, Jaik groaned, tugging a hand back through his hair. "Flipping Luck! All right, we'll separate. But try to find someplace in between squalid and luxurious to sleep in, all right? Extremes catch eyes. People with nothing to hide tend to walk the middle road."

Relief soaked my mouth in moisture; I fumbled out my purse and fished several coins free, tossing them to him. "Which part of farming taught you *that?*"

He caught the coins in his fist, gazing down at them for a moment; the light reflected on their edges, dancing in sheening stripes across his strong-boned features.

"I have no idea," he muttered, eyes flicking up to me.

Then he towed up his hood, pivoted on heel, and retreated down the road.

An air of annoyance lingered in Jaik's wake, tying knots of guilt and irritation, shame and indignation through my guts as I wandered Assida's streets alone. Without Jaik's eagerness to bolster mine, the marvel of the place began to fade, the dazzling red-tinged light suffocated by the shadows of my own selfish desires.

I found only the barest edge of consolation in the thought that once we reached Fablehaven—once we had our answers about what Jaik *was*, and why we affected each other this way—then I would be ready to let him go. To let other Storycrafters benefit from what he brought to the world.

I wasn't certain I believed myself. And with every step I took down the cobblestone roads, patterned with white and black and deep crimson bricks, I remembered how I'd argued passionately to Lio that no one deserved to use Jaik.

But wasn't I doing just that, by what I said and did…by what I *didn't* say?

The city streets my wandering feet found seemed a perfect echo to the darker paths my thoughts took—a prompting from Luck itself to watch how the coin flipped above me, how the light and shadow caught its edges.

Assida was not all whitestone and luscious scarlet beauty. There were dim alleyways and sidestreets; places where neglect had tainted the stone the same dull gray as the cloaks of the Storycrafters who leaned against them. Those without prospects, who hadn't met the same good folk who'd taken pity on people like me all up and down the Spine.

Gaunt. Derelict. Hopeless even in a city that breathed of hope. They pitched themselves against the sides of ramshackle shops and shabby homes, outside the cheapest inns that Jaik had warned me against. Only the faintest flickers of desire pulsed in the depths of their eyes when I passed them…then sundered when I didn't ask for a story.

And on boarded-shut storefronts and abandoned shops and crumbling, mold-soaked streetposts…page after pamphlet after bulletin, some fresh and sleek, newly-tarred to their places; others ancient and crumbled, years old.

All of them advertisements for amplifiers.

All of them promising the sort of power Jaik had given me unwittingly in the *Tankard*…a vow that couldn't be kept. But they were only posted here because they'd worked; because they had reeled in enough of these desperate, destitute Storycrafters to turn a profit for the thieves who manufactured those talismans.

We had to find a way to end this. Not only for those in close proximity to Jaik…we had to find a way to give the stories back their endings all across Mithra-Sha.

And right now, the person most standing in the way of that was *me*.

Tears branded my eyes. I plunged my hand into my coinpurse and fished out all but my last two silvers—enough to afford food and board for one night, and perhaps even a few meals to take on the road. The rest, I dropped into every beggar's coffer I spotted on my way back to the finer streets of Assida.

My stomach ached with contention to rival the pain building behind my eyes from too much thinking and justifying and self-accusation when I finally found an inn to suit our needs: *In the Pot and Pillowcase.*

The entry parlor bubbled with the scent of fresh goose stew, unmistakable with the usual herbal blend of rosemary, cumin, and special mountain salts meant for cooking fatty birds, all of which came in a unique and highly-coveted Hadrassi sachet. The tantalizing smells hinted that perhaps Shadre Calten had been to Assida recently as well, though I had yet to lay eyes on anything else that suggested her presence. Before the cauldron of a cookpot set in the hearth, a middle-aged, heavyset woman—presumably the innkeeper—sat stuffing the pillow shams with fresh goose feathers.

In the pot and the pillowcases, indeed.

"What can I do for you?" she asked tersely.

The last two coins rubbed together in my fist as I joined her by the hearth. "I'd like a room and two bowls of stew, please. And if you've got anything that will keep, goose jerky, hard biscuits, things like that…"

"I've got plenty." She rose, balancing most of her weight on one leg and grinding the heel of her hand into her opposite hip. "Name?"

I only deliberated a moment before I gave it. "Lio."

The woman arched a brow at the Ameresh name, but didn't question it. "Well, Mistress Lio, I've got one room free, and just for this evening. I assume it'll do you fine."

Relieved, I nodded. "And the food?"

"We keep some for pilgrims like yourself. But it'll cost you."

I bared the two coins in my palm. "Will this do?"

Silver flashed in the depths of her eyes with a gleeful shine like she'd seen Luck's own fickle coin flip in her favor. "More than. I'll bring the soup to the door when it's done and the rations once I've closed down for the night."

She snatched the coins from me like she thought I'd change my mind; and just like that, the last of my surety from Errick, the last glimmers of my own sundered dreams from Krylan, disappeared forever from my grasp.

My heart was heavier than my weary feet when I trudged up the steps to the last available room, and my muscles ached as if I'd caught Jaik's illness. When I shoved open the door and observed the room by the last hazy light of the fading day, I only had the energy to feel a trace of despair at the sight of the modest table, washbasin...and the single bed.

Someone would be taking the floor tonight. And it ought to be me.

Kicking the door shut, I wandered to the side table and lit the time-telling candle on it, coaxing a bit more warmth to the shadowy edges of the room. Then I dumped myself onto the bed, hugging my satchel to my middle as I stared sightlessly at the door.

Somehow, being in Assida—in the roots of Storycrafting—had unearthed something dark and tainted at the base of my own desires. My own *craft*. That ugly possessiveness felt like a stain worse than the blood on my hands in those unshakeable nightmares.

I hated that I'd even thought that way...about Jaik, about myself, about my fellow storytellers. And I hated that some part of me still did. And maybe it always would. That selfish, demanding portion of my spirit begged and kicked and *screamed* to be set apart. It pleaded not to be expendable, to keep this newfound propensity for finished tales all to itself.

But it didn't matter. It couldn't matter...that I'd be forgotten, lost in the tapestry woven of other Storycrafters reclaiming their endings. Just one miracle among many. I'd been forgettable, anonymous, nothing special for years now. What was a lifetime of that, if it meant there was life to be lived in Mithra-Sha?

It was time to stop this nonsense. Stop hiding in the temptation of being renowned, and give the stories back to the people. Give the choice back to Jaik.

I tied my fingers together, rested my forehead on them, and let a few rogue tears slip down my cheeks.

With a dull clatter, Luck's coin landed face-down against me. Against my chance to be something unforgettable.

But it had been lovely to imagine, while it lasted. Even if it had been a bitter and self-serving thing, too.

I sat there, cross-legged, hunched over, face pressed to my entwined hands, until the candle waxed low and night seethed against the windows. And then the familiar clap of boots sounded in the outer hall, and my head whipped up to meet the sound even as my stomach plummeted in retreat.

It was time.

The door punched open, and I bolted to my feet; if I didn't say it now, I'd never have the courage or the selflessness to say it at all. "Jaik, I think we should try to help—"

"We need to leave, tiger."

CHAPTER 23
CAGES OF BEAUTY AND BLOODSHED

aik and I halted, staring at one another—him on the threshold with two soup bowls in his hands and a new satchel strung across his front, and me at the bedside, fingers trembling, knees weak; the conflict of words clattered hollowly in the space between us.

Then, as one, we yelped: "*What?*"

"I just think we can do *good* for this city," I burst ahead before he could get in another word, taking two steps nearer to him. "I mean…that *you* can. With what you're capable of, Jaik, with the endings of the stories…"

"I know," he said tensely, setting the bowls aside and slinging off the satchel. "And I'm not the only one who does."

"Oh." I halted, the tangle of emotions tugging in several directions at once, sharpening the ache in my chest. "Did you—were you able to help someone already?"

"Not what I meant."

I blew out a swift breath, forcing my feet to unstick from the wooden floorboards, to stride toward him again. "But you *could*, and I think we should at least try to—"

He flashed up his fist, halting me in my tracks.

A pair of bulletins dangled from his hand, the fresh, dark ink reflecting the candlelight that flickered from the bedside table.

My own face this time, the plain and assuming angles of it rendered in perfect detail beneath the stamp of my name; and beneath *that*

One hundred *gold.*

My knees gave out, and I staggered back, collapsing onto the edge of the bed. Jaik followed me, arm still outstretched, baring the second *Wanted* notice.

Jaik's smirking countenance had joined mine. A bulletin wearing his face, his name, his bounty—the same price as mine.

A lack of sleep. The weariness of the road. That was the only thing that made sense, that explained what I thought I'd seen in Kalvikan—my name joined to a different woman's face. I'd been wrong back then, and the evidence lay before me now, trembling slightly in Jaik's grasp.

This was me...not just a wanted woman, a hunted one. And they were hunting Jaik, too...the Mithran army, and perhaps even the people of Krylan, pooling their resources to find us.

"Oh," was all I could manage.

"Yeah," he rasped. "*Oh.*"

Fleeing in that precise moment was the only choice that made any sense; yet neither of us moved, pinned beneath the suffocating weight of those innocent-looking parchment scraps still dangling in Jaik's fist.

When my words finally returned, they were abrupt, bursting out with all the potency of a last confession. "I gave the rest of my silver to some of the people in need here in the city."

An apology. Something that I absurdly hoped would lessen the blow of just how far into the wilderness we would be driven now. I didn't bother telling him the rest of it—the conclusions I'd reached about my power and his, and about myself.

It seemed we'd have no chance in helping the Storycrafters of Assida.

Jaik's eyes tightened slightly. "Yeah. Me, too. Only kept one coin. Dumped the rest with a few beggars and bolted when I saw these signs."

He sank onto the bed beside me, fisting the *Wanted* bulletin with his name and face between both hands.

"They made my forehead too big," he added. "Almost looks like I'm hiding a brain in there."

A strangled snort escaped my aching throat, and I buried my face in my hands so I wouldn't have to look at his countenance, wanted for a reward. "Have I mentioned I'm sorry for bringing you into this?"

"No." He paused. "Oh, do you mean *today*, or do you mean every single one since Krylan?"

"Jaik, this is serious."

"Well, thanks for clarifying that, Audra. Wasn't sure why this had you turning sea-green."

It wouldn't have surprised me if I was. My stomach roiled like stormclouds towing across the horizon. Still, I forced myself to stand, to retrieve the soup I'd paid good coin for. I sat at the back of the bed, cross-legged, leaning against the wall while I sipped what I could manage. Jaik didn't touch his for some time; then, finally, he cleared his throat, wadded the bulletins between his hands, and tossed them into my satchel.

"Look…the room is paid for the night, right? And so's the food." When I nodded mutely, he picked up his soup and stirred, keeping his eyes on it. "Might be tempting Luck, but I'd hate to waste the coin just running out the door."

His tone was forged of nonchalant swagger, but the way he leaned his weight back on the flimsy pillows told me just how much he wanted to sink into the mattress and never get back up. The same as I did.

Jaik deserved a roof over his head. He deserved one night of comfort.

I wiped my arm beneath my nose. "Did anyone see you? Recognize you?"

"I'm here, aren't I?" His mouth corkscrewed up into a lopsided smirk. "You'd think with that much gold in the lurch, they wouldn't wait until I bedded down somewhere to grab me."

"Or me." I finished my soup in a few hasty bites, then set the bowl aside. "And the rations I paid for won't be here anytime soon, either. What if we stayed the night and left between city watches near dawn?"

"Already marked them." His tone breezy, Jaik finished his own bowl with a hearty slurp, then tossed it onto the bedside table and reclined again, folding his arms behind his head. "Besides, we'll be quicker on our feet if we get some good rest."

I didn't even bother feigning a protest. Shrugging out of my cloak, I wadded it up and hunted for the most comfortable corner of the floor. Any one seemed as good as another, and I doubted I would do much sleeping, anyway; Jaik deserved to rest, but I'd gotten us into this mess. And someone ought to keep watch.

I stood, and he pushed himself up on his hands, frowning. "Where are you going?"

"To lie down?" I peered at him over my shoulder. "Where do you think?"

"Right." He smoothed his hand over the pilled bedspread, plucking a bit of lint from it and avoiding my gaze. "You know, it's…this is the only bed we're going to see for a long time. I don't really feel right being the one who takes it."

My heart stuttered. I unwound my satchel strap from my fist, letting it drop to the floor. "I don't need a bed, Jaik."

"You deserve one."

Three simple words should not have made my eyes brim with tears. I wiped away the absurd dampness, forcing a laugh. "Well, unless you can charm or intimidate someone in a two-bed room here to give up or share…"

"*We* could share," he offered.

My heart stopped altogether at that.

"I mean," he amended hastily, gaze shooting up to me as his hand formed a fist on the blanket, "build a wall of pillows if you want. We could stuff the cloaks and new clothes in between us, right? I just…I don't see why we can't both make the most of the last bed we're going to see for a while."

Protest grated against the backs of my teeth; for some absurd reason, I thought of how my mother, of all people, would feel to know I was contemplating sharing a bed with a man who'd been a stranger nearly two months ago.

But Jaik Grissom was not a stranger anymore. He was a friend…a friend offering a provision I didn't have the heart to want for myself.

I should say no. Propriety demanded I decline.

I opened my mouth to tell him as much, but what emerged instead was a quiet, laughably vulnerable, "Are…are you sure?"

He pushed himself up a bit more, gaze impossibly soft when he linked his arms loosely around his knees. "Audra, listen. You don't owe me some kind of penance by sleeping on the floor. Trust me…I know those kinks are hard to knead out."

I blew out a long breath; after all my inner turmoil today, I'd never felt less deserving of a hand of charity. But that was the sort of penitent self-sacrifice my body craved far less than my heart did.

With flying fingers, I undid the knot in my cloak and pitched it to him. "You build the wall."

While he did, I sorted my new clothes out of the satchel he'd bought for himself. Most were a deep crimson hue—little surprise in Assida, where scarlet dye was clearly in excess—but a few pieces were black, crafted of thick wool that would soak up the heat of the winter sun. A farmhand's knowledge of different hides and weaves, put into practice.

I couldn't find my way around the lump of gratitude in my throat when I turned back to the bed; Jaik had fashioned an impressive mountain range of stuffed cloth, dividing the bed in half. He took the outer edge, sprawled out already, eyes shut. I almost believed him asleep when I tugged on my new wool socks, blew out the candle, then clambered in at the foot of the bed.

The embrace of the mattress around my tired, aching body was good luck itself. I flipped onto my stomach, a giddy laugh bubbling out of me as I buried my face in the pillow, hugging it to my chest.

A snort of laughter rumbled above me. "All right over there, tiger?"

I peeked one eye open to find Jaik looming over the mound between us, propped on an elbow, his smirk forged of pure, wicked humor.

"Leave me *alone*," I moaned, burying my face back in the pillow.

"Fine by me. I was just about to drift off, myself." The bed creaked as he flipped over onto his stomach. Seams pulled audibly when he hugged his own pillow—then mimed a mocking, high-pitched giggle and an exaggerated moan, thrashing deeper under the blanket.

"Oh, would you—!" I tore my pillow out from under my head and slapped it blindly over the mound, striking skin and earning a real laugh from him this time, deep and rich like the soil that permanently stained his hands.

Hands that ripped the pillow deftly from mine. "Thank you, I'm keeping this."

"*Jaik!*" I rolled over and lunged for the pillow, and he contorted his body to keep it out of reach.

"No, no, no…penance for my suffering!" He roared with laughter, stretching halfway off the bed as I scrambled next to him, hunting for my prize.

"I hate you!"

He swept the pillow out of my reach again, pinning it over his chest this time. "Prove it."

I landed on top of him, trapping him flush to the bed with the pillow between us, glaring into his laughter-bright eyes.

And all at once, everything stopped.

My breath. My heart. His teasing.

We stared at one another, only our contours traced in moonlight. A silver glow that held secrets in this city where we weren't wanted. In this room where we weren't meant to be.

Something splintered and warped within me, deep, visceral as I took him in…like a story taking on angles I'd never planned. A path through the unknown—an unscripted, wild dash into everything a tale should and should not be.

Jaik gazed right back up at me, blinking when loose threads of my hair danced against his cheek and brow, tangling in his long lashes.

"You ever get this feeling," he murmured, "like you're in the middle of telling a story and all of a sudden it just…starts making sense?"

"Like you were looking for an ending and found it in the middle of the tale." I nodded faintly. "Yes. When you came into that tavern."

Another beat, where we only breathed, and didn't speak.

Then Jaik thrust the pillow up against my middle. "You win."

I didn't know what to do with that, with any of it—with *myself* and this yearning that blazed in my core. So I took the coward's way out he offered me, snatching my pillow and rolling back to safety on the other side of the mountain ridge built between us.

Suddenly, the pillow mattered less, and the comfort of the mattress was lacking somehow. The warmth of the blanket I slid under wasn't the warmth I craved.

I rolled over to face the wall, keeping my back to him. "Goodnight, Jaik."

"'Night, Audra."

And though the day and night tangled together into one snarled knot of confusion weighing heavy on my chest, somehow, that didn't matter. And the *Wanted* signs didn't matter.

The moment I closed my eyes, peace stole over me. And I was asleep.

Blood.

Blood soaked my hands. Blood spooled between every finger. Blood stained the bodice and belly of the finest dress I'd ever worn.

Gold built the world, the floors, the walls, the vault of the sky itself. Wealth and luxury, bright as the heart of the sun.

A gilded cage, smelling of foreign spice. Smelling of blood.

Reeking of death.

Let me tell you a story…

A prison of scarlet and gold. A dagger flash. Rifles cocking.

Let me tell you a story…

The world blurred in a mirrored image beneath me…my knees pressed to the gleaming tiles, my face swimming into focus as I pitched my weight to my hands, fighting not to buckle entirely, to break, to shatter into shards—

No. Not my face.

A sketch from a *Wanted* bulletin. A distorted outline of dark hair and full lips, glimpsed through waters chummed with blood.

Let me tell you a story…

You're a murderer, you're a murderer, *I despise you, I hope you rot, I will never, ever serve you again—*

A thousand severed threads. A hundred voices screaming my name.

Audra.

Blood soaking my hands, tears soaking my cheeks, screams filling my mouth—

It's all right, Audra.

Sobbing. Bleeding. *Dying* in a cage of beauty and bloodshed.

I'm not letting you go without a fight.

"Audra, *look at me!*"

Fight. Fight.

I thrashed awake, sobbing, cursing, *panicking*. The world was a disorienting black blur around me, gold plunged into shadow, blood leaching away in the dark—

"Hey! Hey, hey, look at me, Audra. It's me! It's Jaik."

His outline parted from the clotted ink that stained my vision; he hovered above me, one hand plunged into the mattress beside my head, the other cradling my cheek, fingers half-tangled in the hair at my temple.

"You're safe." His tone was low, husky with intensity. "I'm right here. Look at me…say my name. Tell me you're with me."

"*Jaik.*" It was just a sob. It was all I could manage.

In one deft motion, his hand left my face and his arm slid under my shoulders instead. He hauled me up against him, and I clung to his bare shoulders, his sleep-warmed back. I buried my face in the side of his neck, my forehead pressed to the wild, thudding pulse just beneath his jaw, and I willed myself to cry. To let go of the tension strangling my throat.

I couldn't weep. I couldn't breathe.

"Listen to me…listen," Jaik rumbled. "I need you to tell me five things you see in this room right now."

"All I can see is *you*," I panted.

"I know, and I count for five." He shifted, leaning back against the wall, pulling me into a sprawl across his lap. I was too shaken, too stunned with blood and gold and a face not mine to care for propriety anymore. "But try again."

And I did.

A candle. A window washed in moonlight. A pair of satchels tangled on the floor. A mound of fabric smashed down where he'd scrambled over it to get to me.

Four things I felt: the sweat on my skin. The blanket snarled around my tightly curled toes. The draft under the door. The scratch of his bearded jaw against my hairline.

Three things I heard: A dog baying in the streets. A distant cathedral bell ringing midnight. His heart thudding beneath my ear.

Two things I smelled: The fragrant smoke of the burned-out candle. The herbs from our soup bowls.

I tasted the tears that had begun to slide over my lips and stain my tongue while I spoke. Exhaustion hung thicker over me than the blanket that swaddled my feet. I couldn't even weigh the balance of embarrassment for Jaik finding me like this...again.

"I'm sorry." I squeezed my eyes shut.

"You don't have to be." I felt his words as much as heard them, grinding up from the depths of his chest where my head had slipped down while I talked. "I don't want you to be perfect around me, Audra. I just need you to be all right."

I wasn't. Not with these dreams circling me like carrion crows.

But I didn't tell him that. I didn't say anything at all.

When I blinked my eyes open again, it was the violet light of the coming dawn that greeted me; and I was still tucked in Jaik's lap, our heads propped together, his back to the wall.

Heat swarmed my cheeks like the prickling tips of a thousand quill nibs; and yet, even when I began to draw back, to shimmy from his grip, reluctance slowed my sleep-heavy limbs.

This was absurd. Falling asleep in his arms should not feel so comforting, so natural, so—

So *familiar.*

Legs still sprawled across his lap, my haunches pressed into the mattress and weight braced on my hands, I froze.

It *shouldn't* feel that way...but it did.

When I gingerly slid one leg free, Jaik woke with a start; his head rolled back against the wall, his throat bobbing as his eyes found me in whatever state of disarray the previous night had rendered me. I didn't dare seek my reflection in the sheen of his eyes.

Yawning and grimacing, he scraped the back of his neck with his fingertips. "Sorry. I meant to move before I nodded off, but every time I tried to shift you, you just…"

"Don't tell me." I wasn't certain my raw nerves could stand to know what I'd done to him; I forced myself not to search for weals my nails might have carved into his bare skin.

His face softened slightly. "It wasn't anything like that, tiger. You just held on to me."

I should have cursed my traitorous body for that; but I couldn't shake the sensation that the way I'd clung to him in sleep was the truest thing in this room.

"We ought to go," I whispered.

"Yeah." He slowly cocked his legs to his chest, stretching his back and freeing a groan. "Really, I'm sorry if things got a little too familiar last night."

I should have been sorry, as well.

But I wasn't.

Embarrassed, yes; exhausted beyond belief. But when Jaik thrust himself off the bed in a single lunge and went for his belongings, I found myself staring at the void he'd left behind.

And wishing, absurdly, that I hadn't woken us both just yet.

CHAPTER 24
A WHITE FLAG WAVED

We slipped from Assida at the watch change, the vestiges of my nightmare clinging to the air between us.

Once the woodland engulfed us, we ran.

Frustration and humiliation pulsed beneath my ribcage, building and building as we alternated between sprinting and walking where the hills allowed. The sky between the boughs paled, then brightened to a vivid sea-blue—and we didn't stop.

Always running. Always hounded by *something*. ..a feeling, a sense, a threat, a vow of retribution.

I hadn't stopped in years. I wasn't certain I ever could. And even if I did, would I be free of these dreams?

Despair weighed my ankles like shackles of pure iron, unleashing stabs of screaming pain through my tight calf muscles. The sky was dimming, nodding toward pink-tinged gray again, when I finally begged a halt.

A whole day of fleeing. And I wasn't confident we were far enough from Assida for it to matter.

Jaik and I paced slow half-circles to settle ourselves on opposite sides of a clearing, no doubt cut by local lumberers some time ago—a clean carving-away of trees, a few misshapen logs left behind. A remote, forgotten place.

Half of me wished we could be forgotten so easily, our faces erased from bulletins across Mithra-Sha; the other half despised the notion that I could matter so little.

My own indecision set my skin crawling. I ripped both hands back through my hair and pressed my palms over my ears to silence the nattering notions of what it would be like to vanish, to be untraceable...and the sly reminders that I already had, and no one had looked twice.

Jaik loosened his cloak, then shrugged free of it, letting it drop to the brushy forest floor. Deep thought scripted his face in the broadest quillstrokes, telling a tale of some emotion I struggled to name. Anger? Irritation? Or was he as conflicted as me?

Finally, he blurted out, "Are we going to talk about it?"

My skin cringed tight against my bones, recalling how I'd yearned to clamber back into his arms the moment I'd left them that morning. "About *what?*"

We each pivoted on our crescent track, circling each other in counter-crosses like wolves.

"Your nightmares." Those two simple words ripped my stomach free of its bindings, sending it plummeting to the soil—worse than the other subject I'd expected him to broach. "What was that?"

"Just bad dreams."

"*Bad dreams* don't usually wake people up screaming like a fishercat."

I halted, pinning him with the most withering glare I could manage. "Thank you for that, Jaik. On the worst days of my life, what I absolutely need, on top of *everything*, is just a *seasoning* of mockery."

"I'm not *mocking* you, I..." He cut himself off with a groan, yanking a hand back through his hair. His gaze dropped to the empty space between us for a long, breath-held moment; when it flicked back up to me, the sincerity there left me speechless. "I'm worried about you, Audra. I haven't said much, I figured it was your own business, but you can't tell me these bad dreams aren't getting worse."

I dropped backward onto the nearest log, rubbing my face with both hands. "You know, when we were in Kalvikan, I was sleeping so poorly I thought...I thought I actually saw a different face on my bulletin."

Jaik blinked, tipping his head. "It's *that* bad?"

"It's been a bit better since," I admitted. "But, still...every few nights, it's the same thing. Some dream where I'm soaked in blood, just *drenched* in it, and I always hear someone saying, *Let me tell you a story.*" I offered a miserable bob of my shoulders—the nearest I could muster to a shrug. "It's been happening ever since Krylan, and I don't know...I'm not certain if it was Galan, with his rifle against my head, but..."

The prominent kiss of the weapon tingled cold against my scalp again, and a lump lodged in my throat, choking off the rest of the words.

"Hey." He settled on the log next to me, palms braced on either side of his legs, shoving against the wood. "Who was there when he had that rifle cocked?"

"You," I sighed.

"Yeah?" His nearest hand crept over to mine, covering it in a warm cage of sweat-tinged skin. "And who disarmed him in a completely arresting, unforgettably sensuous way?"

"Listen to you and your fancy words." I dashed my free knuckles against my eyes before I rolled them, so no stray tears could escape. "It was *you.*"

"Exactly." He squeezed my hand. "It'll always *be* me, all right? I'm not going to let anything happen to you."

Perhaps that shouldn't have reassured me; by his own admission, Jaik Grissom was not a fighter, and even if he'd been kissed on the lips by Luck's smiling countenance, it didn't make him any sort of match for a seasoned soldier like Galan. Or for Mithra-Sha's most ruthless bounty hunters, some of whom were rumored to train in tracking and snaring in the Vensair Mountains in the far east.

There was more danger after us than we'd comprehended even two days ago. And yet, somehow, the mere promise that I did not face it alone—as I'd faced every trouble since Vallanmyre—soaked the slag of fear out of my core and left nothing but pure steel behind, ready to be forged into power.

"All right." I straightened, tossing my hair back over my shoulders. "It's time to get a horse."

Jaik straightened, teeth flashing in an awestruck smile. "You're serious?"

"Assuming your vow includes not letting me fall and get kicked in the head?"

He pressed a hand to his chest. "On my honor as a farmhand."

Scoffing, I tugged out my journal, surveying the map tucked within its folds. "We're not far from the farmlands in Leathris...they're known for breeding good stock there, people talked about them up and down the Spine. Maybe, with the coin you kept, you could find us a good mount."

"You're *serious*," he repeated...no longer a question so much as a testing of truth.

"Are you saying you can't barter for a decent horse?" Challenging him was simpler than challenging myself; I didn't want to test this bolt of courage lancing through me, to find it was weaker than it seemed.

"No, I'm just…"

"Jaik, we have to stay ahead of this." Desperation ripped free in my words. "Ahead of Galan and ahead of those bulletins. We can't do that on foot. I'm admitting you were right…can you just take the win?"

He watched me for a long moment, his gaze shadowy with thought. "You can't just tell a story, make a horse that way?"

"Storycraft can't create thinking beings with a spirit…a free will," I explained. "Humans, animals…if you try to forge them out of a story, that's how you make Misspoken manifestations, most of the time."

He paled slightly. "Right."

For a time, he was motionless—not as eager to go and find us a mount as I'd expected.

Then, at last, he said, "That bulletin, seeing my face on it…that doesn't make me feel exactly *excited* about going to haggle with someone. Even for a horse."

Incredulous laughter bubbled in my chest. "*Now* you're afraid of being recognized?"

He was silent again for a time. Then, his voice barely louder than a murmur, he added, "I have nightmares, too. Same as you, ever since we left Krylan. Usually where someone has a knife to my neck."

I swiveled to pay him my full attention; he gripped the log again, fingernails digging into the damp, peeling wood—the only sign of just how much the notion plagued him.

"Galan?" I whispered.

Jaik shrugged. "Don't think so. It doesn't sound like him. All I know is, I can't get away…and then the knife goes into me, and I wake up."

Pity banded my throat. "Why didn't you tell me?"

"Like I said a while ago, I'm used to putting the pieces together my own way." He peered ahead, into the undergrowth. "But maybe that's what's missing in all this. Maybe we're both looking past the fact that we don't *have* to do it alone. We can both win. We can help each other. I can do the things you can't…get in and out of places. Get us a horse without getting caught. And you can tell stories that pull us out of the tight spots these bulletins are bound to get us into."

The words stretched out like a peace offering, a white flag waved; but they were so much more than that.

"What if," I ventured carefully, fear hedging the words—the fear that he would mock me, reject me, disdain both the notion and the hopeless Storycrafter who spoke it, "we slept on the same side of the fire from now on? And if you wake up from a nightmare, you can take my hand and squeeze it...and I'll squeeze back." I tied my fingers between his, tugging his hand up from the log, and tightened my grip with a gentle pressure. "And I'll do the same. Then we'll both know we aren't alone."

Jaik peered down at our linked hands for a long moment, hanging in the space between us. When he swallowed, it was audible, and the fading daylight painted the pronounced arch of his throat as it bobbed. "Yeah. I think that'll help."

I gave another squeeze, then forced myself to let go. My palm chilled in the absence of his. "Good. So, if you're ready..."

"Yeah, yeah, tiger." Surging up from our perch, he dusted his hands off. "Flip a coin for luck, all right? I'll either be back with a horse, or you can come rescue my sorry damsel hide."

And with that, he disappeared into the shadows.

It was among the longest nights of my life, Jaik's fears swirling with mine in a thick blot that stained my heart. If his worries proved true, and someone in Leathris recognized him—if his *Wanted* bulletin had spread this far from Assida already—then whatever price he could pay would not match a hundred gold pieces offered for him.

He might return. Or I might never see him again, and both our worst fears would comes to pass.

The notion had me pacing for hours in the dark, consumed by agitation that grated like a stomachache. My mind conjured a thousand terrible scenarios that made me wish, despite my lack of love for horses and need to hide my face, that I'd gone along with Jaik; I couldn't rest, not even for a moment, while I strained to hear the faintest sounds of a struggle on the horizon. While I wondered if every gust of wind rattling the tree limbs above hid the sound of Jaik shouting my name, crying out for help.

I was a full-bodied knot of tension, trembling with every stride, when the distinct snap of undergrowth alerted me that I wasn't alone.

I knew by the gait and plod that there were two sets of steps coming toward me—one four-legged, one two-legged. But still, my heart danced a wild rhythm as I spun to face the ice-white, gray-dappled mare emerging from the shadows folded between the trees…and Jaik leading her by the reins, a smug grin capturing his mouth.

"I'm back," he announced…rather unnecessarily, but I'd craved the words so much for so many hours, I didn't mind.

All the breath rushed from me at once. "That was easy."

"Yeah, you would say that. You weren't out there." Jaik shook his head. "That wasn't farmland, it was more like a military compound. Good thing I know how to jump fences." He smoothed his hand down the horse's powerful neck. "And this is Hectra. Hectra, meet Audra…sorry I had to grab you a saddle, girl, because she'll be a pain in it."

Tears of relief blurred my vision as I beheld them both, but it was short-lived. The horse trotted nearer, the resonance of her hoofbeats thudding in my chest, and I flashed out my palms as a swell of irrational fear overtook me. "Stop!"

The mare skidded to a halt, then capered sideways, and my heart lunged into my throat as she knocked into Jaik. He stumbled, hand untangling from her reins, but she didn't bolt—and he didn't fall.

"Wait, wait. Easy." Jaik stepped to my side, wrapping an arm around my back, pivoting me to face Hectra. His hands pressed against both of mine from behind, palms to knuckles, and a shocked flinch clenched my whole frame when he bound our fingers gently together. "Easy, easy, easy…shh-shh-shh…"

His husky murmur wrapped around me and slid away, coaxing Hectra nearer. She plodded forward on hesitant hooves, halting just shy of us, and my breaths ripped out of me in frantic beats. "*Jaik…*"

"Take it easy, tiger, you're all right." His tone held its pace, just as low, just as soothing as before; fingers still twined in mine, he shifted us so my arm led, and his extended to its full length.

Our hands brushed Hectra's brow together, the short, bristly hairs dashing my palm and his fingertips like threads from the softest cloak.

My breath snagged again—in wonder this time. The strength of Jaik's arms enfolded me, a silent vow that if the mare so much as bobbed her head in a way he didn't like, he could tug me back and twist me out of harm's reach in half a heartbeat.

But there was no need; Hectra leaned into our joined touch, docile and somehow still elegant.

"She's beautiful," I murmured, tracing my fingertips along the splashes of gray on her round cheeks, like pond ripples cast on the underbellies of leaves.

"Yeah, she is," Jaik said hoarsely.

I twisted to glance at him, prodded by the subtle shift in his tone, but he released me and strode past before I could glimpse his face. He smoothed his hand down the mare's shoulders, side, and flank, keeping his gaze on her.

"Think she's a broodmare…no one was watching her, so grabbing her and he tack was easy enough," he added gruffly. "But they're bound to notice she's gone and start combing the hills for her, so let's make ourselves scarce before that happens, all right? Trust me, we don't want to be anywhere near that place when they realize someone stole a horse."

"You *stole* her?" I hissed.

"Told you I didn't feel like haggling. Besides, she's a riding horse, not a workhorse…and, believe me, with the size of that compound, they could afford to part with *one* broodmare." Jaik glanced back at me, brows arched. "You know I know horses, tiger. I wouldn't have taken her if I didn't think it was worth it. Besides, this way, we get to keep the coins."

He palmed Hectra's shoulder; then, in one swift hop and a lunge, he was saddled, gathering the reins and offering his hand down to me.

"Mount up," he urged.

Hesitation made one last desperate plea, rooting my feet to the clearing floor as I stared up—and up, and *up*—at his eager face. "I'm just…"

Terrified.

Jaik's gleaming gaze softened, and he curled his fingers twice, beckoning me. "Come on. You know I'm not letting you fall."

I gazed into Hectra's eyes, glimmering pure black with flecks of silver where the moonlight winnowed through the trees.

Riding a horse still scared me witless…but I trusted him more than I feared her.

I caught Jaik's hand, and with a bit of heaving and fumbling, he helped me mount; swiftly, he tugged his cloak around himself and laid the hem of mine back, creating the smallest distance between our hips—a thoughtful act that set my cheeks aflame.

Neither of us remarked on it; Jaik simply wove his fingers into the reins and nudged Hectra's ribs with his heels. "My feet are already thanking me for this."

Astride the back of a stolen mount, we returned to our northward course.

CHAPTER 25
OF BLOODY HANDS AND BROKEN HEARTS

Jaik had been right all along—we made *much* better time by horseback than on foot, particularly when the rolling hillsides morphed to shale slopes, the valleys steeper and the paths between them far more winding. The foothills of the Drennan Peaks on the western coast were encroaching, dark fingerlengths of stone winding out further and further east, until—after another month of travel—they caught us.

And, at last, it began to snow.

"See, this would be a lot more miserable if we were trudging through it in our boots," Jaik remarked smugly as we made our way northeast one day—fighting and failing to escape the shawl of tattered white clouds unleashing a gentle but steady tumble of snowfall across our shoulders.

Stubbornness clenched my jaw shut; I had already conceded that I'd been overly concerned about what Hectra could do to me. I'd let Jaik teach me how to ride properly, how to keep my balance and even guide the mare by the reins, though I still preferred to leave that to him. I'd even admitted, if only to myself, that my fears had slowed us significantly ever since that first day out from Krylan.

I wasn't in the mood, chilled and hungry, to also admit his urging to find a horse had been the best choice before the snows set in.

"I mean it," Jaik wheedled when I didn't take the taunt. "Probably we'd be soaked through to our socks by now. Not sure this footwear was meant for winter walks."

"My boots could pinch if needed," I muttered.

"I'm guessing they already do. That's why you're so grumpy half the time."

I speared an elbow back into his ribs—something I exceedingly enjoyed at this specific angle and height. I grinned when the breath gusted out of him, gratification chafing down the edges of my wounded pride. "Oh, look, now we can *both* be grumpy."

"I've got enough reasons to be grumpy with you," he groaned, breath puffing in icy streams next to my ear while he rubbed his ribs. "You didn't have to do that."

Mirth shriveled on the back of my tongue, a glib retort dashing itself to pieces on the cut of my teeth.

Sometimes, with Jaik, it was impossible to tell if he was joking or not. And though it shouldn't matter if he was grumpy, if he was enraged with me, even—

It did matter. It *always* mattered.

Despair branched through me like the tendrils of a spilled inkpot, and my lungs tightened. The absurd urge to apologize strangled me, though I wasn't even certain what his *reasons* were. The tangle of emotions lodged in my throat and refused to release until we made camp that night—in the shelter of a deep cave in the lofty foothills of the Drennans, tucked into a slice of the forestland my map named the Casmiss Wood. At last, we were safe from the snowfall that fell in quiet, soft fistfuls without relent.

It reminded me almost painfully of Lio…how she would expertly dust flour over a surface before she kneaded dough on it. I'd watched her at the task as often as I could spare time, fascinated with how intrinsically she seemed to know just the right amount of flour to sprinkle on the wood block and the dough itself, keeping a keen balance in the make of her breads and pastries. I'd asked her to teach me, and she had, just enough that I'd been able to dust right alongside her.

If only I'd had such a talent for maintaining the balance in my friendships. In any relationships at all.

Quietly, we tethered Hectra at the back of the cave and set about building a fire. It was a tandem effort, Jaik retrieving the kindling from small shrubs sprouting out of the seams of the cliff outside the cave, and me starting the blaze; we'd done this often enough by now that it required no words between us.

Still, the silence felt heavy, thick, full of more than just snowfall and crackling flames. As if it yearned for me to fill it with those apologies I didn't know how to say.

Once we'd consumed our evening meal—foraged chestnuts we'd roasted over the previous night's fire, and wild apples plucked from a few hardy trees further down the foothills, days ago—Jaik finally cleared his throat. "All right, tiger. Why are you plotting my death over there?"

The words poured over me like cold water, drenching under my collar and saturating my skin swifter than the snow could've found the gaps in my clothing. I straightened, swallowing to wet the sudden dryness in my mouth. "Why would you say that?"

Across the fire, he pitched himself back on his elbows and tossed his hair from his eyes, cocking one leg up while he measured me. "You're not usually this quiet for this long, *Storycrafter*." His mouth quirked up at the corner. "Besides, you look like you just practiced your wedding-day kiss with a lemon."

Indignation puckered my lips off to one side. "Do you actually put thought into your ridiculous insults, or do you just follow whatever words come out of your mouth?"

"Hmmm…the second one." Now he rolled fully to one side, prodding the fire so the flames climbed a bit higher, shedding light almost to the recesses of the cave where Hectra dozed. "Probably why I didn't get picked as a Storycrafter. I'm not much for having an idea how stories go…I like to just kick it off and see where that takes me."

If I hadn't had the fear of what he thought of me stuck like thorns under my skin, I might've retorted that he was Luck's favorite son—just chasing the stories he thought up and the things he said, without a care for how anything ended.

"So," he prodded when I didn't say anything, "what's eating you?"

A sigh heaved out of me; it seemed neither wry retorts nor stony silence would deter him tonight.

"Just thinking about what you said before we made camp." I didn't understand how storytelling could come so naturally even with shattered endings, but truth-telling—particularly truths that made me the vulnerable, needy, desperate one with something to lose—cost me a piece of my pride and soul every time.

"You're still riding with that?" Jaik snorted. "You know I was joking, right?"

"Right." My gaze and fingernails found a loose thread in the sleeve of my shirt, and I picked at the infinitesimal loop. "I know that."

Jaik added nothing, which seemed a mercy at first—a hole for my wounded pride to drag itself out through. But as warm, woodsy, smoky moments passed, the air lulled with a fine film of heat around us, the pressure built in me.

Finally, I couldn't take it anymore.

"It's just that you were *right*," I blurted out, and Jaik's eyes shot from the flames, straight back to me. "You do have plenty of reasons to be angry at me. And now I've been wondering if you are, and you're not saying it."

"If I am—?"

"Angry with me." Pain and humiliation flared in my chest to even hear the words spoken aloud.

Angry people did terrible things—righteous, sometimes, but often terrible for the one with whom they were furious. They moved on. They left. They shut doors in faces and threatened to call Mithran soldiers to arrest you.

Anger ended with bloody hands and broken hearts. I'd heard enough, seen enough, told enough tales of its consequences to know that full well.

"Not that you don't have any right to be," I rambled when Jaik held quiet, gazing at the flames. "I did cost you your whole life, and you've been on the run ever since you met me."

"Yeah, you did. And yeah, I have." But there was no scorn in his tone. "Do you want the truth, tiger?"

My heart fluttered between fragile hope and heavy resignation. "Let's have it."

"I meant it, what I told you that night we met. Before you—you know—whacked me in the head with the slag bucket." He pulled a face, this time of such exaggerated agony it yanked a breathy laugh from me; then he was serious again, his expression bracketed in earnest lines. "I had everything I ever wanted back outside Krylan. For as long as I can remember, that was the life I dreamed of. But, if I'm being honest…it didn't feel right."

Hectra shifted her hooves, punctuating his confession with a two-beat clop against the stone.

For a moment, I didn't even know what to say to that; and when I did speak, all I managed was, "How do you mean?"

He shrugged. "Couldn't tell you. All the trappings were there…quiet life, honest labor, somewhere comfortable to lay my head every night, as far as you can get from the chaotic parts of Mithra-Sha. But it was always missing something."

"Something like…?"

"I don't know. Maybe not something. Maybe *someone*. Like I was supposed to share it with a person who wasn't there."

I wrapped my arms beneath my bent knees, gripping my wrist in my opposite hand. "I'm sorry, Jaik."

"Don't be. I'm not," he admitted. "And that's what I've been thinking about while we've been trekking through these foothills, freezing our noses off. I should be a lot angrier about losing something I've loved all these years, about having my face plastered on *Wanted* bulletins, but it just feels...I don't know. I don't *know* how to explain it—"

"Like you were dreaming," I whispered. "And it was a beautiful dream full of all the things you craved...but now you're awake, and it matters less."

He stared at me for a long moment through the flames, his gaze pure, gleaming amber. Seeing pieces of me I'd never shared with another soul. Because, ever since the stories had sundered in Mithra-Sha, I'd never had anyone to share them *with*.

"You ever get the feeling like there's a part of your life that's just a story someone else told you?" he rasped.

My breath wedged in my chest; slowly, I eased out a nod. "Everything since Fablehaven, until I left Vallanmyre. I could tell you precisely every detail about it, the quiet life I lived just telling stories where I was needed, but in my head it feels...strange."

"Same with me, before I went to the farm," Jaik admitted. "I could describe everything, just about, until I left the house to get away from my parents and the twins. And then, after that...yeah, I know what I was doing, the odd jobs I worked, the plow accident, getting settled in Krylan. But it doesn't feel like me. It doesn't feel *real*."

I'd never heard anyone else describe their life that way—a story with a scribbled-in middle. Or like it was a *story* at all.

"What was the first thing that felt real?" I ventured. "That felt like you *lived* it?"

Jaik hesitated a moment, skimming his hand down his leg—dusting off a bit of snow that whirled its way into our shelter. "Ah...you know. Waking up in the infirmary." His gaze darted up to me. "You?"

"Waking up in my home and finding my cloak had turned gray," I admitted. "And then I went...I went to tell my parents, and they..."

The words stuck in my throat, even after all this time; one of the hardest tales I'd ever told.

Perhaps because it *wasn't* a tale; it was a beacon shining so brightly in a life otherwise dull since adolescence, memories that felt as ashen as the lifeless cloak I'd poured between my fingers that day—searching for a speck of color, tearing over every inch of things, to no avail.

"They let me ramble about my cloak, for a moment…about how my stories felt different. And then they told me they had no daughter named Audra Fashowin," I choked. "And they shut the door in my face."

The resonation of the falling latch, the clicking lock, burst through my memory so sharply I almost flinched; I hardly caught Jaik's low whistle beneath the ringing it set off in my head. "That's…flipping *Luck*, Audra."

My shoulders shook and bowed inward, and I slumped over my knees, shoving the heels of my palms against my brow, holding my hair clear of my face.

It sounded far worse when I spoke it aloud—and he was the first person I'd ever told.

It made everything so much clearer. So inescapable.

The indifference in the faces of the mother and father I'd adored. The cold regard as if I'd come to them completely deranged. And the way they'd wanted nothing to do with me, had abandoned me the moment I'd told them something was the matter with my Storycraft…

As if that was all they'd ever loved me for: the stories I could no longer tell.

The weight of it all crashed over me; as usual, the telling brought the tale fully to life, and pain wracked my chest.

I'd gone to my parents on the worst day I had ever endured—the day the color had fled my cloak and the endings had sundered from my stories. And rather than warm arms around me, rather than the words of comfort I'd craved, I'd had a door slammed in my face.

They'd cast me aside the moment I became broken. The moment I was no longer useful. And I'd been chasing my own meaning ever since.

"I lost everything." The words gasped out of me, pitiful and wretched, utterly humiliating; but now that I spoke them, it all broke free in their wake, surging out like a story that had waited too long to be told. "I lost *everything* that day, all of it at once…my status, my stories, my *family*. And no one even looked for me when I walked away. It was like I never existed. Like I *don't* exist anymore, not without my stories. And I hate how much I *hate* being a Storycrafter, sometimes. I wish I could throw off the cloak and title and be someone who matters if she doesn't have them. I never asked for this power, it tore my family apart, and now I'm nothing without it—"

"Audra…Audra, hey." Jaik shoved himself up on his hands, worry writing the dip between his brows again. He scooted himself around the fire to sit beside me, laying his hand on the curve of my back; but he offered no reassurances besides.

And that was good. Because I didn't *want* to be reassured. I wanted to be *heard*.

"I don't know what I did to *deserve* this!" I scooped up a handful of kindling from beside the fire and flung it into the flames, sending them bursting higher in a rush of heat and light. "Is there really *nothing* in me that was worth remembering, worth staying for and *caring* about, if I didn't have my stories? Was I just a tool for *everyone* I ever loved?"

Jaik said nothing, only skimmed his palm up and down my spine.

"Maybe that's what's *wrong* with this country," I ranted, dragging my palms along my tense, trembling legs from ankles to cocked knees. "Look at us…look at how we treat stories and the people who tell them! Like a good-luck talisman…like a piece of *commodity*." Flashing my palms beside my face, I adopted my deepest, most theatrical tone. "*Oh, look at me, I'm Farmer Flannery, I can't keep a wheat field alive if someone doesn't tell a story to make my crops grow!*"

"This Farmer Flannery," Jaik ventured, "he wouldn't happen to have long hair, brown eyes—"

"Would you shut your ramble-hole?" I rubbed my flaming cheeks with both hands, then slid my trembling fingers back through my hair. "I'm so tired, Jaik. I'm so tired of just being something *useful*. Most days, I'm sick to death of even being a Storycrafter. I'd give it all up if I could."

But even as the words left me, there was some lie that seamed them in cracks and grooves.

It was true I didn't want to be a commodity, or a tool, or even a Storycrafter somedays—but those things were needed. *Wanted.*

They were indispensable.

Frustration drew all the vitriol and vigor out of me at once, and I slackened, burying my face in my hands.

Were those my only two choices—to be worthless and expendable, or to have all of my value built into what I could do for people? What they could *use* me for?

Neither life seemed like the right one. Like the tale the Storymaker had woven for me and my kind.

But if there was a happier ending and deeper meaning for us all, I hadn't found it yet. Certainly not on my journey down the Spine, faced with the suffering of our people, their pity and scorn and helpless hope pinned on the likes of me.

"I hear you," Jaik said after some time—likely when he was certain I had nothing more to say. "I don't have an answer for you, because I've never stood in your pinched little boots, but...I hear you. It's not fair, things are unbalanced, and you didn't deserve to carry that on your shoulders. For what it's worth, I hear that."

A sniffle squirmed from my nose, and I dropped my hands to offer him a lopsided smile—the best I could muster. "It's worth plenty. Thank you for listening. I've never really said any of that before. I don't think I've ever told *anyone* I sometimes wish I wasn't a Storycrafter."

But it was freeing to speak it. Even if it changed absolutely nothing about our circumstances or what I was.

"See what I mean?" Jaik clapped me gently on the back. "Sometimes you've just got to open your mouth and say what comes out."

Grinding my heels into the stone, I circled my gaze back to the fire; I wasn't certain I could say the rest of what clogged my throat if I had to speak it staring into his eyes. "About...about my family. They're not terrible people, I just want you to know that. They loved me and supported me when I was at Fablehaven, and after I graduated..."

A pause stole my words, uncomfortably similar to the broken tales I'd become so acquainted with telling in recent years.

Because, now that Jaik had breathed it into being, that was precisely what that portion of my past felt like—a story someone else had spoken over me.

After I graduated, we were still close...suppers at their home every week, an endless stream of conversation between us. I always knew I was free to visit them, and they always welcomed me.

That was what I wanted to tell Jaik. It was what *felt* true. And yet...

"You don't have to justify anything with me." Jaik's words cut across my splintered, uneasy musings, offering merciful relief from the unsettled churning in my gut. "And just to put your mind at ease...I'm not sitting here holding a grudge against you, Audra."

My lungs emptied swiftly, and relief surged into the hollow of my throat. "You're sure?"

"I think I'd know if I was." Winking, he dropped his hand from my back at last. "If you're asking me if this how I saw things going when I agreed to run with you in Krylan…no. Not even close. But if you're asking me if I *regret* kicking things off anyway, or where it's taken me since?" His head tilted just slightly, eyes pinning me in the conflict between firelight and shadows. "Not a chance."

My tongue floundered in search of something to say to *that*—whether to thank him, or tease him, or confirm just once more that he meant it—

And then Hectra jolted, head shooting up, ears pricked and swiveling.

And Jaik stiffened, hand shoved again the stone behind me as he twisted to peer at the cave mouth.

And I *felt* it—dark, wicked aberration rearing from the void beyond our shelter, suffocating the night in shadow. Something that shrieked of *wrongness*, disfigurement, a misshaping of the very blood in my body, the Storycraft built into the core of who I was.

And before I could draw a breath for warning, to curse or call on the Storymaker for aid, a shrill, inhuman scream ripped through the air, putting to death the peace we'd built between us.

CHAPTER 26
MYTH AND MAGIC

Hectra reared, her equine scream colliding with the petrifying wail that echoed through the cave. Jaik and I moved in tandem: me, lunging to stand, Jaik spinning on his knees to kick out the fire and palming his way to his feet at my side.

"What in Luck's *flipping* coin—?" he began, but I silenced him with a cut of my hand, straining to hear over my racing pulse.

Somehow, the silence after that terrifying sound was far eerier than the scream itself.

Jaik backed to Hectra's side, soothing her with a hand braced to her twitching shoulder. But his eyes, like mine, were fastened on the cave mouth—both of us hunting for movement in the darkness that encroached beyond.

Quiet stilled the air for a time. Then Jaik murmured, "Maybe just some mountain animal?"

I opened my mouth to retort—then sucked in my breath as a thunderous *boom* shook the Drennans to their roots. The rock itself bucked beneath my heels, pitching me against the cave wall, and Jaik lunged to catch me around the waist before my knees contacted the floor.

That hurtling movement, after everything else, proved too much for Hectra. Our quicksilver mare bolted, hooves skittering and sliding on stone, straight out into the shadowy, snowswept night.

Jaik and I shoved apart and leaped after her, both reaching, grasping at nothing; she was a blur streaking down the foothill slope, already half-gone by the time we stumbled to a halt outside the cave mouth.

My stomach knotted, plagued with the wild negation of beholding something *wrong*, something that should not be. But there it was, framed with flickers of lightning in the volatile snow clouds, a pair of phenomena breaking against one another—one beautiful, the other utterly *horrifying*.

The *creature* loomed above the foothills themselves, the peaks of the pines on these lower wooded slopes hardly grazing its ribs; its head was higher than most cathedral spires I'd seen. It was all bone—or mostly that. A skeleton dripping with bits of slough and sinew, gaunt and disproportionate, its limbs too long for its body and its neck built of snakelike vertebrae, long and high and weaving. Finial tines protruded from its spine and neck and framed its wavering skull in a macabre crown; its empty eyesockets blazed with a violent reddish-gold firelight as it forded through the foliage like a sailor through rough tides, steady and relentless.

Coming toward *us*.

Jaik choked, stumbling back two strides. "I'm dreaming. I'm *dreaming*! There's no chance that thing is *real*."

"I wish it weren't." Somehow, his panic breathed calm into my core. I could vomit and weep and wrestle new nightmares later, that abomination dominating the narrative of every one. Right now, I had to concentrate.

To save us.

The skeletal creature opened its maw, shedding a spray of that firelight glow across the hills, and it screamed again; this time, without the cave walls to catch the sound and thrust it out, it nearly put us both on our knees.

Clutching his head, Jaik maneuvered across the snow-slick rock back to my side. "What *is* that thing?"

"That," I shrugged on my satchel, "is a manifestation of a Misspoken story." I planted my feet on the stone and breathed as deep as I could, filling my lungs with cold, clean air. "I think we may have some amplified Storycrafters after that bounty on our heads. Someone tried to craft a tale about giants, most likely."

I didn't want to think what havoc the story had wreaked on the crafter when that monolith of bones and fire had clawed its way into the world by knob-boned knuckles and gangly, misshapen limbs.

Jaik swore, snatching up his own pack. "Tell me you're not thinking about *fighting* it!"

"*I'm* not." I let my eyes tumble shut. "Someone else is."

And above the gusts of falling snow, the wind moaning in the passes, the boughs snapping beyond us as that terrifying, abhorrent *thing* towed them up and cast them aside on its way toward us, I reached for a tale of my own.

Let me tell you a story.

Jaik hollered, slamming into me, shoving me aside so we both tumbled to the stone cleft; a pine tree sailed into the space where I'd stood a moment before, impaling itself flush into the cave hole.

If Jaik had waited a second longer to move, it would have impaled *me*.

Terror threatened to choke me; but in the same instant, *purpose* burst alive in my veins. Jaik was on top of me, his weight forcing me down, shielding me…and that power roared awake between us, inspiration bursting into the creases where my back met his chest with every wild breath.

Snapping my teeth together, I spat the words as swiftly as they lunged to my mind.

There once was a land of myth and magic where wielders of mystic arts dueled to possess the greatest power ever known. Some fought for greed, others for glory…many for the sheer ecstasy of their own might. Rare it was, to find one who fought for anything but what the arts could win them.

Rare, but not unknown.

Syvee, she was named…a woman with an artistry whose depths were unplumbed. For she refused to search them…refused to be known only for her power. Refused to be defined merely by what she could do. Syvee desired a quiet life to raise her children, to remember the husband she'd lost.

But myth and magic spared none they touched for a quiet life. Fickle, merciless divinities, they were. And just as they had taken Syvee's husband—a good man fighting a losing battle to tame his own artistry—they came for the peace she'd built in his memory.

I fought not to envision Jaik as the man in the story this time; this one was mine to tell, mine to live.

Mystics thought Syvee the greatest threat in the land, for an artistry unmarked might be greater than theirs. So they hunted her, by powers both natural and those unnamed, the sort that misshaped and twisted them into beasts hardly human any longer. But to eliminate a mighty threat, they deemed it worthwhile to sacrifice even their very souls.

And so they sought her. And they found her, in the refuge she had built for herself and her family. Three innocent children, captured to draw their mother from hiding…to force her hand, so that Syvee might prove the depth of a power not yet measured by mortal eyes.

Another tree sailed above us, cast by the foraging hands of that snake-necked skeleton, smashing to splinters against the rock face above us and showering the ledge with sap and needles.

Jaik cursed, hauling me up with a hand under my arm. "All right, that's it…time to find cover."

We tore along the rocky hillside, footsteps striking stone in tandem with the words puffing from my mouth on bitter-cold plumes; to our left, the skeleton gained ground. The lower foothills only came even with the jutting of its hipbones, and its rangy arms cracked and tossed more trees and even clots of stone as it forded on. Another minute, two, perhaps, and its head would be at level with us.

Though a panicked, prey-like instinct urged me to keep the creature in sight, that meant it could see *us*. To ration out more time, to let the story build and grow…

"Jaik, we need to get below its eyeline." I snatched his hand and tugged to slow us both.

"I know." Grim. Resolute. By the way his eyes cast ahead, seeking a sure path down the snow-slick rock, he'd likely been thinking it already.

All at once, he released my hand and hurled me aside; then he whirled to face the valley, cupped both hands around his mouth, and *bellowed*.

My fingers clapped over my ears to silence the piercing shriek that echoed as the skeleton faced us full-on—beast calling to beast. "What are you *doing*?"

"What are *you* doing? Don't stop the story!"

A stitch pinched under my ribs, equal parts breathlessness and annoyance and terror; but I locked my trembling legs in place and forced myself to go on speaking.

Syvee returned from tending their crops one day to find their cottage ransacked, her children gone—a note nailed to their door, signed in blood, demanding her presence at the Mystic's Breach. A place of legend across the land…a mountain gap where countless battles had been fought, mystic against mystic, magic to magic.

There would be no better place to see Syvee's strength unleashed. No better reckoning ground to redeem all that had been taken from her.

Power thrummed in my fingertips as it might have thrummed in Syvee's heart; *this* was the tale my heart begged to save us. The story of a woman fighting to protect what was precious…a woman pitted against a force beyond reckoning.

But it was difficult to manifest the strength of the mystic from my tale when that skeleton shambled toward us, bones grinding, mouth agape. The next sweep of its arm sent another pine tree sailing toward us, and this time Jaik whooped with glee; then he ducked and rolled aside as the projectile slammed against the face of the mountain behind him.

"*Jaik!*" I shrieked, half in fear for his life and half in disbelief that he was *goading* that monstrosity.

"Ha! Perfect." Rocking back to his feet, Jaik slammed his foot into the tree's gnarled trunk, breaking off a sizeable chunk of splintered wood. Then he dove for my hand and yanked me after him, pushing me to sit on the wooden shield of sorts he'd knocked free. "How's your balance, tiger?"

Panic ripped through my middle. "*Why?*"

He planted himself behind me, cocked knees braced against my shoulders, and his brawny arm banded around my collarbones and towed me back to lean between his legs. "Just keep telling the story."

With his free arm, he shoved—and we *flew*.

Soaring down the foothills, skimming on the newly fallen snow and slick rock, we sailed wildly off-kilter on our wooden sled. Jaik steered us with one arm flung out behind us, palming the rock at random to pivot our course.

"Audra!" he bellowed over the harsh grind of wood on rock. "What are you waiting for?"

I slammed my eyes shut, dug my fingernails into Jaik's legs, and screamed the words:

Syvee made her way to Mystic's Breach and stopped for nothing—not to eat or drink, not even to rest! Even so, she arrived to find the Breach already full, brimming with countless mystics armed in weapons of mortal man as well as their own powers at the ready. All had come to bear witness to what she could do. And to put an end to whatever threat she might pose.

One woman, against hundreds of mystics. But she was not alone...for they held her children captive, there in the Breach. Two girls and a boy, with their mother's face and their father's eyes. The best of all the world Syvee had ever known...the world she had fought to hold together while the rest of it fell to the wars between the mystics.

Now they had made their war into her war.

And they would lose it.

The last words punched out of me with a groan as we struck level ground in the foothills, skidding to a halt; we leaped free of the cracked wooden sled, whirling to face the dense valley undergrowth—and the dull rasp of skeletal footfalls shaking the thick pines around us to their roots.

We were in the skeleton's path; there would never be a better chance to fight for our lives.

I jerked my head at Jaik. "Run."

And we did—straight toward our enemy.

CHAPTER 27
SWORD AND STORY

Syvee entered the Breach with neither armor nor weapon that any could see. She was a woman wrapped in robes and simple farm clothes…a mother's daytime attire. The mystics beheld her with scorn, and perhaps a bit of trepidation. But in none of them was a hint of respect for the power that stepped into their midst.

"We were told to expect a master of the mystic arts," taunted the man who held her only son. "Instead we find a farmer and a breeding sow!"

"Where are your weapons?" pried a woman armed to the last inch with blade and wood in all fashions. "Or do you think yourself so great a warrior that you need none?"

"I am not a warrior," said Syvee, halting before them. "I am an instructor…the teacher and guide of my children. And now I will teach you what you should have known before you ever crossed me."

She spread her hands wide before her, reaching for the depths of her power.

"The first lesson," Syvee said, "that bone is not stronger than stone."

y own power rose up in me in tandem with the story that spilled from my lips while we flew through the undergrowth. It was an unstoppable force, cresting, keening, crying for release. And just like Syvee, I widened my fingers, skidded to a halt, and dropped to one knee, slamming my palm against the ground.

The stone in the forest floor around us sundered with a thunderous *crack*, but it did not break apart and crumble; instead, it exploded *upward*, rearing into tangible shapes. Giants of my own.

Stone figures, as broad across the shoulders as Hectra was long from muzzle to tail, their great hands gripping granite battle-axes, their heads horn-helmed. And between their thick thighs were stone war-wolves, each one large enough to seat their nine-foot riders, their sandstone fur cast in sharp relief.

Jaik whooped at my side. "*Audra!*"

I'd never heard my name spoken that way—with so much wonder and exultation and *pride*. It sent tears slashing across my eyes, and I almost hated to blink them away. Hated to concentrate on the danger before us rather than the glee within me.

At Syvee's mere thought, a reckoning force of stone giants sprang from the rock that made up the Breach. They fell on the furthermost ranks, the cowardly among the mystics who held the rear flank. All the rest were driven flush toward her, and she raised a hand again.

"The second lesson," she rasped, "that blood does not flow more swiftly than water."

With a resonant *crack*, the foothills behind us broke apart; a floodway of inner springs trapped within the rock surged to meet the call of my tale, a deluge that roared into the valley, snapping trees like bones and tearing up the landscape behind us as it came. I shouted Jaik's name, and then we were up, scrambling together onto the back of the nearest stone giant and his war-wolf.

Rock hardly shifted when the avalanche of water slammed against it, forging whorls and wild eddies around the legs of our stone army, staked to the earth. But something *did* give way—tree and soil and skeleton legs, the rush of water sending that disproportionate, unbalanced thing reeling away from us.

Now we had time. And more distance.

"*Go!*" I shouted, and the stone wolves all lunged together in tandem, galloping through the floodwaters toward the skeleton. My mind raced in tandem through Syvee's tale, plotting, planning, seeking both a next step and one of those coveted, glorious endings.

Floodwaters poured into the Breach, wiping away a third of the mystics, wreaking terror over those who remained. For in no battle of mystics nor use of artistry in recorded history had such tremendous power been seen…power that nature itself heeded without pause.

Syvee was a mystic who required no weapon to channel her power. She was raw power itself. The world bent to her will.

The might of Syvee's tale thrilled in my veins as we reached the place where he floodwaters faded to a muddy slur. There we leaped down, splashing in the murky shallows, straining to hear in the darkness—listening for the skeleton's whereabouts.

"Think you could craft us some light?" Jaik murmured.

In that moment, I could do *anything.*

"The third lesson!" Syvee cried. "That—"

My words stuttered and broke off all at once, shock and fear dousing my voice like a candle wick trimmed to the waxline.

Sizzling white orbs flared alight all around us, pair after pair, empty, glistening—

No. Not orbs. *Eyes.*

Wild, white, wicked eyes, unseeing…but they did not need to see. Bloodred nostrils flared in the gloom; dozens of panting, slavering breaths rasped across the air, turning it wet with bloodlust, and icy slashes of pointed fangs parted the shadows between the trees.

Hunting hounds…Misspoken ones.

With a burst of burning light, lanterns struck alive in the undergrowth, shedding a horrific glow over the hounds' emaciated frames, their jutting ribs and dripping, sabertoothed mouths. And those holding the lanterns…

I almost emptied my bowels at the sight of them.

They were the waking dead, every one a man's shape with long, oily black hair, and two faces…likely some Misspoken attempt to forge Luck itself into the lines of a tale. But rather than one sinister side and one smiling, these two-faced huntsmen held twin countenances of agony stamped on either side of their heads: jaws growing down into sinewy necks where tendons strained in a soundless wail. Mouths melting off of their grotesque, half-rotted faces, their eyes bulging the same empty white as their hounds', ringed in blackened stamps as if they'd never slept a day. And when they strained as if to speak, a piercing, ear-shattering *scream* ricocheted off the trees, tunneling into our ears, sending us both stumbling back.

But the hounds knew that call. They lifted their hackles, rose to the tips of their hooked talons, and loosed a single, continuous snarl.

Courage fled me. I whirled on Jaik and met their scream with mine: "*Run!*"

We turned and tore back into the undergrowth, my stone army surging around us—our only defense as the hunting hounds gave chase. Distorted howls rived after us, warping through the trees, filling the night with a relentless, abrasive cacophony.

I could hardly think; panic pounded the insides of my skull, writing wild and distorted scripts of unfocused notions in my head.

We still had our army, but now we had enemies on two sides. And we could not afford to be trapped between them, particularly if any other Misspoken tales awaited…the sort that could shear stone apart.

Another thought occurred to me then: perhaps we were not being hunted…we were being *herded*. After all, the bounties were for both of us *alive*.

We couldn't keep running like this—not toward wicked Storycrafters lurking in the shadows, driven mad and misshapen by amplifiers.

"The third lesson!" Syvee cried. "The shield can be mightier than the sword!"

This she said, for she had seen the shift in the mystic who held her son; his shock, and his terror, and now his wrath. And as she spoke, casting out her hand, a shimmering web of power enfolded her children.

Not a moment too soon had she spoken; for just at that moment, the mystic drew the blade that channeled his own power, and stroked as if to drag it over her son's throat.

But the shield held true.

Our shield was not some mystic's power; it came from the stone giants themselves. As one, they wheeled back to us, and dove—locking bodies and battle-axes, forging a dome of rock that smothered us on every side. Only the faintest shard of lingering moonlight fell through the very top of the stone enclosure where the tips of their upraised weapons met.

For a moment, we stood panting, staring at one another in the slivers of snowy lightning that lit up the dark. Outside, the world shuddered with the skeleton's long strides renewed; the hounds bayed, the hunters closing in.

"We can't stay in here forever," Jaik panted after several heartbeats.

"I know that!" I snapped. "I just need time to *think*."

Tearing my fingers back through my hair, I paced in the shallow dome, guiding my mind through swells of panic—naming silently to myself things I could see, and touch, and hear.

"What else is out there, do you think?" Jaik propped one hand against the nearest stone wolf.

"The Storycrafters. They're running us straight toward them."

Cursing, Jaik straightened up. "How did they *find* us? If it was Leathris or Assida, you'd think they would've attacked before now."

I calculated our course rapidly, my heart sinking. "We're not far from Dalfi...half a day by horseback at most. They may have picked up the bounty there and started combing the hills."

Not only were the cities unsafe for us...so were the wilds *around* them now.

"All right...all right." Jaik dragged his hands over his stubbled cheeks and coursed them down the sides of his neck, then wound his fingers together behind his nape. "So those things, those are Misspoken manifestations, right? They're trying to pin us between them and run us straight to the Storycrafters who made them."

"That would be my guess."

He nodded once more, his profile framed in weak light as he pivoted and glanced up, measuring the height above with a sweep of the eyes.

Then he knelt, slung off his satchel, and started to root through it.

"All right, here's what we're going to do." Gone was the panicked Jaik who'd begged this all to be a bad dream; this Jaik was the same one who'd calmed me in Kalvikan and Assida, who'd turned on Galan without hesitation on that rooftop in Krylan. This grim, efficient Jaik spoke like a soldier and kept his eyes up even while he tore through his satchel—looking straight into me. "Two lines of enemies...safe to assume there's a third, because if you're hunting two people, you want to block three directions at least. We need to split our focus. I'm going to take the skeleton. You take the hounds."

A ragged laugh ripped from me. "*Jaik*, how in the Storymaker's *name* do you expect to——?"

He yanked a length of rope from his satchel—and a blade as well, which glinted sharp as the grin he flashed me. "The bigger the tree, the harder it falls...as long as you hit the trunk low enough."

I stared at him. "Where did you even get those?"

"Assida. Figured a few basic survival items might come in handy, and look what we're doing tonight...*surviving*." He measured the rope with a swoop of his hands, then nodded. "Should be enough to get across the anklebones, anyway."

Comprehension and disbelief collided in my aching chest. "You're going to *trip* it?"

"Get it down long enough for you to dream up some more of those lessons from Syvee." He looped the rope across his chest, then straightened, blade in fist. "Better make it good, tiger. Something tells me we're only getting one shot at this."

"*Jaik*." I lunged up beside him, seizing him by the bicep when he started to turn. "We don't even know if I can tell the story once you're gone."

His broad fingers covered mine, squeezing my hand hard against his arm. "I won't be that far away. They've almost got us caught, anyway. Hey," he added when I opened my mouth to protest, "we can do this. Sword and story, right?"

The words shattered past my defenses like a blade, gouging at something deeper than my skin, past my bones. It stabbed between my ribs and straight into my heart. "What——?"

With a smirk, Jaik shoved at the nearest war-wolf. It lifted its paw, and he was out—bolting into the trees, toward the echo of those cracking, skeletal footfalls.

"*Jaik*!" I shouted, but the hunting howls of the hounds muted my farewell. He was moving toward *them*, too.

No more time to rest, to think. I leaned into the instinct of my Storycraft—back into Syvee's tale.

The moment the mystic's blade fell away, Syvee bellowed, "The fourth lesson: all that was taken shall be restored."

Pain erupted through my head, flashes like the snowy lightning searing across my eyes, my head, my *heart*—

Hands on my hips. Forbidden truths whispered in the shadows. A kiss that tasted of brandy and spice and secrets. Fingers winding through my hair, a sweat-soaked brow burrowing against mine.

Safety. Warmth. Comfort. *Home.*

Audra. Audra Jashowin. Addie. Ayjay…

Blood on my fingers, a scream of hate and heartbreak ripping from my mouth, the world fracturing, *shattering* around me—

Howls and screeches and bellows.

Jaik, out there in the dark, hunted and running.

I had to get back. Had to drag myself away from whatever precipice this story was trying to hurl me off of.

Syvee's children…they all at once…broke their chains—

Every word was heavy. My tongue was swollen, clinging to the backs of my teeth. I couldn't open my eyes more than a sliver. But still I reached for the story and unspooled it from the depths of me.

For his sake. For mine.

And they ran to their mother's waiting arms.

Syvee gathered them close, then sent them behind her as she faced the last third of the army of mystics…the strongest of them all.

"We will never stop hunting you," said the man who'd nearly taken her son's life. "After what we witnessed today, we will not rest until the threat of you is stricken from this land."

Syvee looked at her children, bruised and gaunt from days of mistreatment, and she saw the truth: they would never have a quiet life again, so long as these mystics drew breath.

"It's to be a battle, then."

The moment the painful words streaked off my panting tongue, my stone army unfolded from around me; snow sifted down in pale freckles against my face and back, soothing my hot cheeks, my aching head. Slowly, I straightened, hands to my knees, thrusting myself upright. I turned and faced the hounds and their masters gathered among the trees, balanced on taloned toes and with heads twitching and slanting in odd, inconsistent jerks.

This was Krylan all over again; and I was not running. I would not be herded prey. And I would not go quietly for a purse of gold and whatever use this country had for me…and for Jaik.

The words escaped me a second time, lost in clouds of steam billowing on the air:

"It's to be a battle, then."

CHAPTER 28
SCARLET AND GILD

ive things I could see:

The trees, thrown into sharp relief in flickers of lightning dancing among the clouds; the sightless eyes of the hounds; the horrific aces of the hunters; the distant, distorted shadow flung by the skeleton's umbering approach; and the stone army gathered at my sides.

With the faces of her children in her mind, Syvee went to war.

With earth-shaking power, the stone giants surged past me on either flank, nurling themselves at the hounds in the same instant the beasts coiled and unged. The night tore apart with the slam of stone on ribs, talons shrieking on ock, slavering, lusting howls and the hunters' screams peppering the air. I lodged backward, hands up, mind racing over the rest of the story.

For every blow the mystics landed, Syvee landed two. Stone and water and shield were her allies…a battle she did not fight alone.

Stone, like her middle daughter's stubborn will; water, like her youngest son's gentle love; shield, like her eldest daughter defended her siblings and protected their home, as her father had taught her long ago.

Four things I could feel:

Faint pinpricks of cold dewing my skin as the water coagulated between the trees, spidering back toward us from where it had petered out in the downhill avalanche; the snap of a hound's razor-edged teeth clipping shut at the hem of my cloak when I swiveled out of reach, ducking behind the swinging axe that came to my rescue; the ferocious breath from a rotting maw dragging against my ear when a hunter leaped for me; the dig of its spider-legged fingers into my shoulder as it caught me and wrenched me aside.

Syvee fought with all her might, and one by one, the mystics fell before her. Their lust for her power and their fear of her strength were no match for the love that goaded her to battle!

Passion exploded behind the words, filling up every empty cavity in my chest that seethed with fear and longing and abandonment. All that was left was me—Audra Jashowin, battling for her own life. Battling for her friend.

And tonight—if *only* for tonight—that was enough.

I twisted in the hunter's grip and seized its open jaw, forcing the lower mandible down until the head had no choice but to duck. Then I yanked my knee up to meet its chin, snapping my hand free when the head cracked back.

The creature reeled on ungainly feet, and I shoved away from it, falling to my seat in the saturated earth that sucked at the paws and feet of the dueling hounds and wolves, the hunters and giants.

Three things I heard:

Canine cries of anguish, silenced forever; the crunch of bone beneath battle-axes and stone teeth; the crack of shattering granite when it was struck just right, spraying the heads of my stone army across the soil.

That day in the Mystic's Breach, it was not all the might in the world that won the battle—not the power of hundreds of mystics gathered with their arts at the ready. It was a mother's love, a woman's heart that felled the greed of her foes. And though her enemies crumbled, still she rose.

And so did I.

Shoving to my feet, I backed away from the fringes of the fight, drawing in the scents of pulverized rock and oily ichor that soaked the frigid air—two things I smelled.

And then, from the distance—far, but not so far that I didn't feel it within me as much as I heard it, piercing straight into my head—bone snapped. The skeleton shrieked so loudly even the hounds recoiled, shaking their heads with anguished yelps; and then the ground itself leaped and bucked beneath us as the bony giant fell.

Now. Now might be our only chance.

I let the rest of the world drop away and focused on nothing but the tale rearing inside me, begging to be told.

It was not enough for Syvee that the Mystic's Breach be a memorial of the battle fought there. She called instead on flame this time, such hot, consuming fire that it turned the bones of her enemies to dust…a dust swept away like fine, powdery snow.

Light seared through the trees, branding a sizzling teal glare across my vision; when I blinked, brilliant flares interrupted whole streaks of the world. I shook my head and smashed the heels of my palms against my eyes to clear them, grinding out the brilliance of the fire wrought by my own tale.

But the fire didn't abate…not entirely.

It was in *me*. It coated my hands, tarnishing my skin in a living, dazzling river of flame that did not burn as it rode just beneath the surface of my flesh.

Transfixed, I stared at the painless fire sheathing my hands for several moments…and one moment too long.

A hound gained its feet, then hurled itself toward me.

My arm rose in a seamless stroke, half on instinct…and cleaved downward.

The hound caught aflame, a Misspoken story consumed by a Wellspoken one, its edges crumbling like the parchment of an ancient book. It was gone before it even had time to cry out, and left nothing behind.

The hunters and hounds all swiveled my way at once, sensing a new threat…beholding the Storycrafted power in my hands.

It was time to finish this.

This time, *I* attacked, slashing out gouts of fire to consume these aberrations created by bounty-hunting Storycrafters. Anger fueled every strike of my cutting hands, and they fell, fell, fell...pieces of stories that should never have been, sent off not to the Isle of Misspoken Stories, but somewhere else. Somewhere broken tales went to die.

Perhaps into the same void where all of our endings had trailed off, before there was Jaik.

My eyes welled at the thought of him, and as if the scent of tears beckoned them, my stone soldiers rose to my sides. Axes and fangs joined flame, and together we cut down what remained of the Misspoken pack, leaving little more than the scent of charred paper and the impression of their perverted appearances stamped across my mind.

Exhaustion blew through me as the last of the flame simmered out of my fingertips. I bent, hands to knees, desperate exhaustion clawing through me. I wanted to lie down on the forest floor and not move until Jaik found me.

But I couldn't stop...not yet. We still had to find shelter, to leave this place before the rogue Storycrafters realized both their skeletal giant and their hunting party had been consumed.

And I had a tale to end.

Straightening, I wiped my mouth on my wrist and sucked in a deep lungful of the cold, clean air, charged with the hum of the fight and the lightning that still flickered in the bellies of the snow clouds.

And as Syvee beheld the empty aftermath of all she had done...all her hands had been forced to do...shame rose within her. She had taken the path she'd vowed she never would. She had made her power something to be feared, her hands themselves into weapons. She had followed the same path that had consumed her life's only love.

Yet even as she thought it, her battle-winning hands were taken by others...her children's hands. Her living, breathing, safe children, spared because of the impossible things she had rendered to life. Because of how fiercely she had fought for them.

It was then that Syvee knew why she had been gifted the sort of power all mystics craved. Why hers were the proper hands to carry that weight. For it was not the power itself she coveted...but how the power allowed her to protect what mattered most. The power of the mystics ought not to exist for its own sake. Instead, it was meant to——

Thunder cracked with the next flicker of lightning in the clouds, louder than the skeleton's fall moments before.

All at once, my voice was gone. Punched clean out of me.

The story was gone.

Something thick and hot salted my open mouth, shivering against my tongue as the breath dragged in and out of me.

Blood.

The only thing I tasted was blood.

My fingers rose to touch my parted lips, my mind sluggish, struggling to understand that rich, metallic, meaty flavor coating my teeth.

When I blinked, the world shivered brighter, pleated in gold.

Gleaming gold tiles beneath me. A prison of scarlet and gild.

Undergrowth rustled, and my eyes shot up to find the parting in the thick boughs—to glimpse Jaik's face when he shoved into the open and drew to a breathless, grinning halt.

I wanted to remember him that way.

I wanted to *remember*—

"How about that?" He spun the knife into his belt and jerked his head back the way he'd come. "I'd say we make an impressive team, but we already knew that, right? Tiger?"

Something urgent and desperate hurled itself up into a lump lodged in my throat, and his frame blurred before me.

"Jaik," I sobbed, stepping toward him—*stumbling* toward him. My legs wavered like quills snapped halfway down the shaft, holding on by a strand.

Jaik stiffened. "What's the matter, what—?"

He broke off. His eyes dropped along the length of me.

And widened.

"Audra. Your cloak."

I finally looked down. Finally had the courage to look, now that he was here with me, and I wasn't alone.

Blood soaked the front of my clothes. Blood that had sprayed in constellations across my face, dampening my lips, my cheeks.

My blood.

My eyes leaped back to his. "Jaik, *help me*—"

A second burst of thunder.

Not thunder.

This time, I *felt* the rifleshot when it tore into me, slamming through my shoulder, taking me clean off my feet and hurling my spine into the tree behind me so hard all the air tore from my lungs in a single, wailing scream.

"*Ayjay!*"

Agony ripped me wide open at Jaik's howl, and I arched up from the tree, gasping for air, grabbing for my shoulder, for my middle, panic and pain tying knots in my head.

"Hey, hey, hey! Ayjay—*Ayjay!*" Knees splashed in thick mud. Jaik tore the halves of my cloak apart, and heat thumped through me when his broad palm shoved into my belly, finding the place the first shot had made its mark. "Look at me—hey, *look at me!*"

His other hand curled around the back of my neck, a gentle pressure my whole spine caved into, slumping my chin to my chest. I couldn't muster the strength to lift my head again, so he did it for me, cupping my chin and forcing my eyes to meet his.

"Oh, hey, there you are, tiger. Look at me, it's not that bad…it's not that bad, I swear, I've seen worse, all right? I've seen a *lot* worse!" He flashed a smile void of anything but terror. "I've got this. I've got *you*, I can fix this, just keep your eyes open, all right? Keep looking at me—"

"Jaik…" All I could manage on a breath. Panicked. Pleading.

A harsh sheen coated his eyes. He pushed his forehead against mine. "Don't…don't you say my name like that."

But I needed to. I needed him to hear me; I knew when a story was losing its end. And mine was fleeing my grip, unwinding from around every finger.

"Dalfi," I choked, and his eyes widened a fraction. "Find…find Naomi Weathers."

"Audra." Jaik's hand circled the back of my neck again. "Audra, don't go to sleep—stay awake! *Ayjay!*"

But my grip on him wasn't as strong as his hold on me.

I tumbled into the chasm. Slid into a hazy gray dream of hands on my hips, a brandy-spiced kiss, and Jaik's voice, over and over, saying my name that way.

Ayjay.

Ayjay.

CHAPTER 29
THE SHROUDED PAST

*W*hat came next, I gathered from Jaik's own account. Some of the details, perhaps, were missing.

But let me tell you a story.

It begins with Jaik Grissom and the blood on his hands.

"*Ayjay!*" He bundled my cloak into my shoulder-wound, and though I twitched, I didn't wake; not when he tended to me, not when he shouted my name. "Ayjay, come on, please, I'm begging you…stay with me—"

Deafening bursts of rifleshot filled the night, three of them all in a row, and Jaik froze, looking down at himself, seeking a wound—but there was none. Not a single leadhole marred his body.

So he went back to tearing off his cloak and wadding it against my gut wound, and through all of it I thought perhaps he was still saying my name. Making a tether of his voice…something I clung to even in unconsciousness. Him, begging me to keep breathing, watching the rise and fall of my ribs until he'd stuffed the stiff fabric against the injury and bound it around me, then sat me up against the tree.

That was when he heard the rifle cocking and the footsteps toeing aside the undergrowth. When he heard the voice dripping with venomous glee. "Good. Got her. I wasn't sure that first time, when she didn't scream. But I figured the second one hit."

I could only imagine the rage in Jaik—how it would've darkened the bronze of his skin, redrawn the crease between his brows, set his hackles bristling when he settled me back against the tree and turned to face the redheaded, bearded Mithran soldier who'd bested us.

Galan, slinking from the trees, rifle trained at Jaik's chest.

"Little far from home, aren't you?" Jaik spread his arms, making a larger target of himself...and a smaller one of me, slumped in the shadow of his body.

"I could mention the same about you," Galan taunted.

"What can I say...I don't much like sitting around, twiddling my thumbs in a city where a soldier with a dancy trigger-finger is on the lookout for me."

Galan scoffed. "You lucking *know* what I mean, Grissom."

Jaik hesitated at that. The casual, cruel intimacy of the retort...that was new. Different from their rooftop scuffle in Krylan, even.

But confusion was a weakness Jaik couldn't afford.

"All I know is you shot my Storycrafter," he growled, "and you're aiming a rifle at me. Planning to clean this up right here, finish what you were threatening to start in Krylan?"

Galan edged nearer to us. "Not with a bounty of a hundred gold apiece on you now. That's good enough to leave even *that* one alive." He jerked the muzzle of the rifle my way, and Jaik shifted between us again. "I'm not about to risk this chance for anything...I had to put those amplified Storycrafters down before they started thinking of splitting the glory four ways."

"Two hundred gold's worth a soldier murdering three people in cold blood?" Jaik demanded.

"As if it's all about the coin," Galan shot back. "This bounty buys me far more than new boots and a way out of a pitiful soldier's salary...it lands me back in good graces. And that's worth more than the pleasure of seeing you both choke on your own blood for your last few breaths."

That prodded something in Jaik, too—it struck him far deeper even than the need to seem in control of the situation while he tried to scheme a way around the vicious end of Galan's weapon. "You two really hit it off badly in Krylan, didn't you?"

"Don't play coy, Grissom," Galan growled. "You know my business with *both* of you goes a lot further back than Krylan."

But Jaik didn't know that. And neither did I.

"Look, Officer," Jaik sidestepped again to keep himself between Galan and me as he edged closer, "whatever your problem is with us, you're not going to get any of that coin if Audra bleeds out. And seeing as your aim's about as good as your personality, that's the way things are moving. You need to uncock that rifle and let me help her, or you're going to lose out on a lot of gold."

Galan just stared at him, for so long Jaik considered rushing him, disarming him while he was frozen in wide-eyed, gape-jawed wonder.

Then Galan burst out, "*Whatever my problem is?*"

And then, more terrifying than the rifle aimed at Jaik's chest, Galan *laughed.* The rifle bobbed down as he cast back his head and *howled* at the snow-heavy sky.

"Oh, flipping Luck!" he crowed. "You don't remember, do you?"

And for perhaps the first time in his quick-witted existence, Jaik Grissom had no reply.

Before he could muster one up that made him seem the master of the moment again, a silver-white blur streaked between the trees; an equine scream knifed the cold air with the echo of a cloudburst breath, and both men whipped toward the sound at once.

Hectra had come back.

The mare slammed her hot, muscled shoulder into Galan, throwing him sideways into the mud. The rifle flew from his grip, and Jaik surged forward and kicked it with all his might, sending it skidding out of reach into the underbrush. Then he twisted, dropping to one knee, scooping me up; he met Hectra halfway through the clearing, cast me up onto her back, then steadied me with one hand while he swung up behind me.

By the time he turned Hectra, Galan was struggling up to his feet, fumbling after his rifle, his face warped with hate and rage and the sort of lust, Jaik said, that only vengeance could bring.

"The longer you run, the worse this will be!" the soldier snarled. "The more people will be hurt!"

"You already hurt the person I'm most concerned about," Jaik snarled. "You think I'm going to just hand her over to you now?"

Roaring, Galan forgot the rifle and lunged at us, at Hectra; Jaik turned her with a clip of the heel to the flank, yanked the knife from his belt, and slashed in one deft, backhanded cut.

Fresh blood slapped the soil, mingling with mine. Galan dropped to one knee, clutching his face, his screams peppering the air with new bursts of icy breath; Jaik's shout cracked like a whip, urging Hectra into a dead gallop through the trees and away from the clearing and the mud and the place where so much battle had happened—with only a bit of shed blood to show for it.

Clutching me tight to his chest with one arm and winding the fingers of his free hand into Hectra's reins, Jaik turned her northeast, toward Dalfi—city of industry and airships.

Toward the only hope I had.

We rode through the night, through the patches where snowfall turned to drizzle in the lower foothills. Of this, I had vague memories…stirring once or twice when the strike of hoof on stone or soil sent fresh pain bolting through my middle, my shoulder. I might've whimpered or cried out…all I knew was the rumble of Jaik's voice in his chest, a soothing murmur that vibrated against the back of my head where it lolled against his sternum.

All I knew was that I felt safe enough to retreat from the pain, to slide back into darkness, sheltered in his arms.

A steadier, colder rain fell, obscuring the outskirts of Dalfi when Jaik arrived, so he didn't even notice he'd entered the unwalled city until light pooled across the path ahead of him. A few lantern-keepers prowled the avenues, paving the way for the odd travelers and street-rakers, and they paused to stare in wide-eyed confusion at the man astride a mount, uncloaked, shivering, propping up an unconscious woman as he passed spirit-like through their midst. Like a figment of a story himself.

We'd be the talk of the lower streets come daybreak; but Jaik was only concerned with me surviving to see it.

He halted Hectra outside the first public house he came to and slid me down. Later, he would tell me he'd believed I was dead at that moment, limp in the cradle of his arms. I didn't stir when he jostled me; I didn't rouse when he said my name.

"Audra?" he repeated, pressing his forehead to mine, his breath blanketing the cold air between us. "Hey. Ayjay, come *on*."

I didn't wake; but I pulled in a shuddering breath, and that poured enough relief into him to unstick his frigid muscles and send him staggering into the public house.

It was not the only one he would visit. He would lose count of them, in fact…how many pockets of warmth he would enter and leave again when no one inside knew Naomi Weathers. How often he would pause to tighten his cloak around me, to ensure I was still breathing.

He would say it was, altogether, the worst night of his life. And I would believe him.

The sun had risen, but not quite broken the shawl of fog blanketing the city from the aftermath of the frigid rain, when he finally entered a public house where an elderly man could point him in the direction of Mistress Weathers. As relieved as he was desperate, Jaik staggered to the two-story edifice where the man directed him and rammed his elbow into the door—then adjusted his grip on me while he waited, muttering under his breath.

"Almost there, Ayjay, just hold on. Just keep breathing. *Hey!*" he shouted when no one answered his summoning knock. "We need some help out here! *Please!*"

That was when the door finally opened, framing her in the frame: Naomi, her mushroom-brown hair mussed, green eyes red-rimmed with sleep, banding her silk robe around herself. "Luck's flipping coin, *what?* Why are you *pounding* on my door?"

"Look, I'm sorry, I don't have anywhere else to go," Jaik rasped. "We can't pay you, but we need—"

And then Naomi said it—the word that changed everything.

"*Addie.*"

The way she breathed my name—the way she stared at me, senseless in his arms—it truly changed *everything*.

Because, to hear Jaik tell it…she said it like she'd seen a dead person come back from the grave. Like someone who'd been looking for me her whole life—and finally found me.

Then her eyes flashed to him, and she said, "Get inside and put her on my bed. I'll do everything I can for her."

CHAPTER 30
PURPOSE AND PLACE IN THE WORLD

I came back to my own story with pain throbbing low in my gut and shoulder, and the tangled curlicues of strange dreams fading from the script of my wayward thoughts.

The first thing I knew was someone speaking to me. A low voice, soothing—the sort that calmed wild horses and herded together rogue flocks. Power without a hint of threat; control untouched by cruelty.

Jaik Grissom brought me back to awareness, word by word, with only the rumble of his voice.

"…never seen an airship up close before." Those were the first words to distill into focus beyond the pain throbbing down the length of my body, twin hurts meeting somewhere in the middle just below my ribs. "Yeah, I know what you'd say…*No surprise there, Jaik, you bumbling, backwater farmhand.*" The pitchy tone he affected to imitate me might've been insulting, if he hadn't capped it with a chuckle. "But, flipping *Luck*, tiger, I've got half a head to just climb up one of the mooring ropes and see what it feels like for myself. Get the wind under my feet, see how it all feels from up there."

I wanted to chide him he was no backwater farmhand—he was the man I was certain, even in my delirious, half-awake state, had saved my life—but I couldn't reach my voice. It was as lost in the depths of me as the endings to all my stories before our paths had first crossed.

"Maybe I'd find a way to make a life out of that," he mused. "Jaik Grissom, sky soldier. It'd mean joining up with the army, which…*bluh,*" he mimed a far-too-realistic gag, "or becoming a peddler, and the only thing I can really sell is ny good looks." Another pause; then that high-pitched, combative tone was ack. "*Oh, I don't know, Jaik, you could probably sell a few sarcastic remarks until it bought you a punch to the face.*"

My insides twisted and tightened, curling around themselves at the brush of his hand covering mine, bringing to life the feeling of a rough, raspy bedcloth beneath my fingers. And then even that was gone, my hand cradled in the cage of his, every callous warming the stings and cuts I'd accumulated during the fight in the Casmiss Wood.

That memory unlocked some of the sleepy rigor from my muscles, pouring ease like hot wax along my bones. That nightmarish skeleton, those slavering hunting hounds and their misshapen masters, darted across my thoughts, and I choked on my next breath.

Jaik's fingers tightened around mine. For a long moment, he was quiet, but the weight of his attention hung on my face. If I could've just pried my eyes open, just *seen* him…

"Here's the thing, though, Ayjay," he murmured at last, that name sending a jolt through me—a sensation of brandied kisses, a sense of safety, a tether in the shadows— "I know what you'd say about all of this, but I really…" The breath shoved harshly from his nostrils, and he gathered my hand in both of his now. "I *really* need you to wake up and say it."

I scrabbled for my voice, reached for the words…but like sundered stories, they withdrew from me. The crushing weight of exhaustion numbed my tongue.

Brass hinges creaked in their fastenings. A door base brushed against a worn rug. The musical tingle of shimmering bells filled the quiet, and then someone spoke quietly to Jaik. "Let me see to her dressings. You, go and clean up…and for Luck's sake, have a shave."

My heart stuttered at that familiar voice, shifting from musical-sweet to demanding between one breath and the next. A voice that had goaded me to greater and greater heights in Fablehaven; a voice of girlish giggles, daydreaming fantasies, fathomless conversations about life and its meaning, the purpose of the world, our place in it.

Naomi.

A tear burned in my eye, then escaped, flickering in a hot path down my cheek. It didn't seem either of them noticed. I could envision them in a standoff, glaring one another down—Jaik's caustic stubbornness against Naomi's unshakeable will.

But she was the younger sister to four brothers. He'd lost that argument before she'd even stepped into the room.

"Fine," he grumbled at last. "Just...holler for me if she wakes."

"I'll perform my best damsel scream," Naomi said pertly, and then chair feet skidded and his grip on my hands tautened abruptly, as if she'd tried to drag him bodily back from the bedside. "Go, will you?"

Jaik's warm breath huffed over my skin, his dry lips brushing against our entwined fingers. Then he settled my hand gently back on the bed, and his footsteps thudded a reluctant retreat.

The silence in his wake did not last long. Naomi filled it with quiet humming, a song that plucked at every string of my heart. *I'd* taught her that song, a tavern tune turned love story, one of the most popular melodies I'd learned in Fablehaven.

She set about changing my bandages, her touch gentle yet firm with practiced ease. All of the disquiet was mine, flooding under my skin, heating every muscle she moved in order to minister to my rifleshot wounds.

I'd sent Jaik here because I knew Naomi Weathers like I knew my own name. She was the sister from a different family who'd loved me more than Marli ever had; the sister who'd risen through the ranks with me like climbing a stone cliff face together. We'd ascended hand over hand, always reaching down to pull each other up; she was as proficient in the healing arts as I had once been in Storycraft...if not moreso. I still remembered that final, flickering thought out in the Casmiss Wood, before the fear and agony had ended my consciousness like a tale cut short.

If anyone could save my life, it was Naomi.

And yet, when I'd seen her last, when I'd sought her out on my southern pilgrimage toward Krylan, she'd accused me of being a drunkard and threatened to call the city watch on me for harassment. She'd acted as if we'd never met, and she hadn't even bothered to hear my plight or what little explanation I could offer about my broken tales.

And now we were here, and she was treating me...and I was a coward. Because I couldn't bear to try and open my eyes, or to speak to her. Not when rejection awaited the moment I did.

I just wanted to lie beneath her gentle touch and pretend for a moment longer that we were still friends.

So I kept my breathing slow and even, and swallowed the whimpers of discomfort when she moved my shoulder and examined my gut. She muttered to herself about crackshot soldiers and—to my mounting unease—about Officer Galan Fiordona.

It seemed an eternity before she took her leave, the air in her absence sprinkled with the balsamic scent of the herb pack she'd set against my wounds. Still, I waited, counting my own heartbeats until I was certain she wouldn't return.

Then, finally, I pried open my eyes.

It took everything a moment to sharpen into focus around me…the steep, angled slants of the roof and walls, and the recesses along those walls where windows shed strong daylight through thick green drapes onto on the rug-swaddled floor. The beams of the walls themselves were exposed wood, a few of the seams packed with rich lichen boughs reminiscent of the power that had leaped from the end of my tale in *The Tiller's Tankard* the night I'd met Jaik.

A glistening crystal chandelier dangled above the bed, its prisms dancing on the walls. All of the mismatched furniture, the handcarved wooden chair at the bedside with the plush ivory footrest, the bed I was curled in, and the side table were assembled of different pieces that matched Naomi as I remembered her. She'd hardly changed, and yet somehow this life she'd built in Dalfi—after a swift and sudden departure years ago from Vallanmyre, before I had lost my stories—made no room for me. It held no place for me at all.

I was still huddled on my side, wrestling with that cruel notion, when the door opened again; and I took the coward's way again, squeezing my eyes shut, feigning sleep so I wouldn't have to face cold dismissal from her.

But the pad of footfalls wasn't Naomi's.

Jaik hovered behind me, silent for too long. Then he growled, "All right, this is ridiculous. She should be awake by now."

He pivoted, bare feet dragging on one of the rugs, and my heart leaped into my throat. Between the two of them, I'd take his concern over her cruelty.

"Jaik, wait." The croak of my own voice made me wince; I sounded like a sword-swallower who'd learned too late they lacked the talent for their craft.

But it did the trick; by the time I pushed myself over to face him, Jaik had whirled back to the bed. The relief in his newly-shaven face almost knocked me breathless—particularly in how stark a contrast it was to the dark circles scrawled beneath his eyes, the divot between his brows that seemed to have made a permanent home there.

He said nothing for a moment. He just *looked* at me, in a way that tied me up in the worst knots I'd ever felt; then he drew in a sharp, damp breath, and pulled on a smile that might've convinced me he'd never been worried at all.

"Hey, there, tiger." He ground his knuckles into his eyes. "I guess we don't have to wonder which side of Luck's coin *your* name's written on. You've got the good stuff for days."

"If this is what *good* luck feels like, I'm afraid to see the other side," I groaned, gripping my shoulder while I dug my feet into the mattress to push myself up. A yelp punched up my throat when my gut gave a deliberate, almost lazy throb, alerting me that *it* was the worst of my wounds.

"Hey, easy." Jaik conquered the space to the bed in a single long stride and plunked himself down at my side, one hand on my back and the other covering my bandaged middle. With his grip bracing me, I maneuvered upright against the headboard, finding a comfortable position with one leg drawn up and the other curled behind my ankle.

Only then did Jaik take back his hands, and not all at once; his palm slid down my hip and trailed up the bend of my thigh to grip my knee, which he held a moment, then squeezed before he finally let go.

All that time, his gaze never left mine.

"You've been asleep almost a week," he said at last. "I've been going crazy trapped inside this house. Must've walked up and down the stairs a thousand times."

Though I ached to apologize, to ask him how he was, that wasn't what he needed; so instead I arched a brow and trailed my gaze up the length of him: his dark pants wrinkled like he'd slept in them, his white linen shirt rolled to the elbows and undone to the third button. "So, that's why your legs look so muscular now."

"Noticed that, eh?"

"It's obvious, Jaik. You're disproportionate."

He snorted a chuckle, head dipping, chin knocking to his chest. I waited for him to lob back a witty retort—but he didn't. His head stayed bowed, and he huffed out a few more breathless chuckles; then his hand rose to cover his eyes, and he slowly shook his head. His shoulders jerked once, twice, three times.

It wasn't until his palm slid down to cover his mouth, pinching his nose shut, and he still wouldn't *look* at me that I realized he was overcome.

Shock rippled through me—then an odd, strangling gratitude that brought tears to my eyes.

"Hey." I dropped my voice to imitate that warm, soothing tone that had roused me from my weeklong slumber. Tugging gently on his wrist, I freed his mouth, winding my fingers through his. "Jaik, I'm all right."

He grunted, a noncommittal huff that seethed with unspoken emotion…something that made me feel oddly brave. Framing his face with my hands, I tugged his chin up from his chest until our eyes met. Tears lined his in blistering silver, a match for mine.

"I'm all right," I repeated softly, carding a bit of the tangled mess of chestnut hair from his brow and baring that frown to the light. Gently, I grazed my thumb over the divot. "And that's thanks to you."

"I didn't think I'd get you here in time," he croaked. "Ayjay…"

My hands burned with a sudden, clammy sweat. I let them tumble into my lap. "Why do you keep calling me that?"

He blinked. "It's your initials. *Audra Jashowin's* a mouthful."

"What about *tiger*? Or Addie?"

"Maybe sometimes I don't want to call you that. And Addie…Addie's what your friends call you."

Something dark and anguished bloomed in my gut. "Aren't we friends?"

"Sure we are, I just…" He trailed off, drawing in a deep breath and settling back a bit from me. "All right, I hear you. No more *Ayjay*."

I hated those three words more than any I'd heard since we'd met.

But there was no time to tell him so; Jaik shifted further away, boosting himself backward on his palms until he leaned against the baseboard of the bed. Arms folded over his abdomen, he crossed his feet at the ankles and looked me up and down. "So, you want to know how we got here?"

I tugged the blankets up to my chest, filling my head with a puff of Naomi's scent—line-dried cotton and freesia soaked in rose oil. The fabric's warm embrace felt like a perfect burial shroud for my festering disappointment. "I wouldn't be opposed."

That was when Jaik told me everything—his encounter with Galan, who'd wielded the rifle that blew through my shoulder and gut. How Galan had murdered the amplified Storycrafters in cold blood to claim our bounty himself. How that crazed soldier from Krylan claimed a history with me that went far deeper than our first encounter at the city gate.

"Know anything about that?" Jaik asked, one brow arching.

"No," I insisted. "I've avoided Mithran soldiers like a stomach plague ever since I left Vallanmyre. And I would have remembered if I'd crossed someone who despised Storycrafters as much as Galan...I always paid attention to the people who hated me on my way down the Spine."

An odd mingling of emotions rippled across Jaik's face. "That happen a lot?"

"What do you think?"

He snorted. "I know better than to step into *that* trap, tiger."

I couldn't muster more than a flicker of a smile, though it was good to see him in better spirits; I struggled not to miss that brief glimpse of vulnerability in him. "It happened occasionally. But I swear to you, I would have remembered a soldier who hated me this much."

Jaik tilted his head. "So, either he's really crazy...which, have you *met* the man?"

"Or," I volleyed back—then broke off as the door swung open.

No hiding this time. No cowardly games.

There she was, hair undone to the waist and eyes ringed in their usual dark-powder etching, her full-figured frame dressed in a sleeveless top of knitted lace draped over a tunic that cuffed at the wrists. Her layered skirts in shades of olive and tan brushed the floor, a sighing echo to the silver music that rang with each step from the bands around her ankles.

Coin charms, for luck. I'd bought them for her the day she'd undertaken her graduate's exam at Harrow Hall. After she'd passed, she'd sworn she would never take them off again.

And here she was. Wearing them still.

We stared at one another for endless seconds, me with the blankets bunched in my fists, held to my chest—ready to lunge from the bed and test my weight on my feet the moment she threatened to send for the city watch, now that I was awake.

Then, tentatively, she whispered, "*Addie.*"

My breath stilled. My eyes burned.

Jaik was right...only my friends called me Addie.

"Noni," I choked.

Naomi swept across the room and dropped onto the bedside, gripping my unhurt shoulder and turning me to face her; then both her arms were around my neck, and that cotton-freesia smell engulfed me.

"I can't believe this," she rambled, peppering the top of my head with kisses. "Addie, when I remembered...flipping Luck, I've never felt like a worse person. The way I treated you when you came here, asking for help...I swear, I

uld've thrown myself into the Alusia River right then. And then this *ruffian*
ows up with you bleeding to death in his arms…"

"Ruffian?" Jaik scoffed.

"Noni." I squirmed in her embrace, discomfort rising not from her
rangling grip, but from in my muddled head. "Noni, wait." I grabbed her hip
d pushed back until she released me, and we could meet one another's eyes.
What do you mean, when you *remembered?*"

Naomi glanced over her shoulder at Jaik, then back at me. Our faces
ust've reflected the same uncertainty, because hers shifted to match.

Slowly, she peeled herself up off the bed, settling back on the chair—a
miliar posture that made my skin crawl.

This was precisely how she looked whenever she delivered troubling news
o one of her patients.

"Addie." Her tone was deliberate, as if perhaps she'd spent the last week
lanning this conversation in her mind. "I don't think you understand…and
elieve me, that's the only reason I *haven't* thrown myself into the Alusia—"

Desperation shoved me up from the headboard, my good hand planted in
ie mound of the mattress on my left; Jaik lurched forward at the same moment
o steady my middle. I swatted him off, gripping my wound for myself. "Noni,
hat don't I understand?"

Naomi skimmed both hands down her cheeks, then pressed her palms
ogether, fingers balanced against her lips. Her eyes never left mine.

"Addie," she said, "when you came here last…I know how cruel I must
ave seemed. But I wasn't trying to shut you out, I swear by Luck's flipping coin.
was…" She broke off, tipping her head, shoving the heel of her hand beneath
er jaw. "Addie, I didn't *remember* you."

CHAPTER 31
A STORYTELLER FORGOTTEN

Naomi's words clattered into the hollow center of me…that place raked out by her rejection. By all the doors shut in my face and all the cold words and threats leveled at me over the past handful of years.

All I could manage was a flat, breathless, "What?"

Jaik's hand fell onto my knee, squeezing slightly; he watched Naomi like someone who'd wounded me and might try to again—something he would not permit in his presence.

"I didn't know you from a beggar on the street." Naomi's words rushed out now, hands dancing to animate her words. "You were an absolute stranger. I thought you were a drunkard or a madwoman, ranting and raving, and it terrified me that you even knew my name."

"How can you *say* that?" I hadn't thought I had enough places in me broad enough to encompass the heated swell of emotion that surged up at her confession. "*Naomi*! We were together every *day* while you were at Harrow Hall and I was in Fablehaven! We did *everything* together. How can you claim you didn't—?"

"That!" Naomi pointed sharply at me. "That's the thing, Addie…I remembered *none of that*. My time in Harrow Hall, yes. All the things I did in Vallanmyre before I came here, *yes*. But you weren't part of even a single one of those memories."

I crashed back in the pillows, skull thumping against the board behind me so hard Naomi winced. But I didn't feel the ache of the impact; there was too

"You said she *was* a stranger." Jaik's intense tone pierced the hum of shock that filled my head. "But that's not how you said her name when I showed up on your doorstep."

Naomi blinked, wet eyes trailing off of me to land on him. "Because she's not anymore. I remember her now."

I lifted my head with some effort off the headboard again. "You do?"

Naomi nodded. "And not just me. It was a few months ago, and all at once, I woke up one morning and I remembered Audra Jashowin. Not...not the *details* of you, so to speak, but I knew you existed out there in the world. I knew we'd been friends...like sisters. And not a week later, I received a letter from Vallanmyre. From Mama and Papa Jashowin."

Jaik's fingers tightened on my knee; it was the only thing I felt before numbness crashed over my body, the incredulous words spiking from my lips: "You're not serious."

"They were *frantic*, Addie. Asking if I knew where you were...claiming they hadn't seen you since you came to their doorstep years ago. They didn't know you then, either; they said they hadn't remembered until they wrote me that they even had a daughter named Audra. They only knew Raff and Marli until all of a sudden—"

We have no daughter named Audra Jashowin.

The last words my parents had spoken to me...the dismissal that had set my feet to the Spine, chasing Luck out toward the southerly horizon.

A callous refusal, I'd thought; abandonment for my lack of Storycrafting power, just as the craft itself had abandoned me.

I was wrong. I had been so flipping *wrong.*

They hadn't rejected me. They hadn't *known* me.

They hadn't remembered they had a daughter named Audra Jashowin.

"We've been writing letters back and forth ever since," Naomi went on, oblivious to the shock dragging me down hand over hand into a fathomless abyss. "We were searching for you everywhere. And then the *Wanted* bulletins started to appear, only...it was so odd, Addie. You're not how I remember you."

I startled up, biting back a groan at the pinch in my wounded middle. "What do you mean?"

Naomi tossed up her hands. "I don't *know*, and that's what's the most frustrating! I remember you, I do...but it's all blurry at best. I remember Fablehaven and Harrow Hall, I remember our schooling years. I remember you younger, and how *sassy* you were, so full of ambition. And then it all goes murky. It's as if, once we graduated—"

"The rest turned into a story someone else told you," Jaik said quietly.

My gaze darted to him; he was already watching me, cheeks hollowing with every pull of his breath. Something tightened in me as well, squeezing my lungs to withered shells. "What is *happening* to us?"

"I don't know." Naomi dragged her fingers back through her hair. "All I know is that, three months ago, the world remembered Audra Jashowin and Jaik Grissom existed. But not the finer details of you."

Jaik straightened up sharply. "I'm sorry...wait. You remember *me*?"

This time, I had a name for what seared through me: *shock*.

That shouldn't be possible. Jaik had no part in this story before our paths had crossed in the Tailbone City.

Had he?

"No, I don't really remember you...not *fully*," Naomi said, "but if someone else had come to my doorstep and asked if I knew a Jaik Grissom, I would have said yes. You're familiar, but not the same way Audra is. It's...it's indescribable. I'm not the one who's talented with words."

But in that moment, neither was I. There was only one thought that pierced through the hazy wreckage that disbelief had rendered of my mind; one shard that lodged like a splinter under my skin.

"You said it was just around three months ago," I croaked, "that you remembered. That Mama and Papa remembered, too."

Naomi nodded. "I'll never forget waking up that day. Addie, I'm so—"

"You don't have to apologize." I could coax no volume to my voice. "And I think I know precisely what day you remembered."

My eyes met Jaik's again, and in his stare I saw my own thoughts reflected.

"It was the morning after we met in the *Tankard*." His voice was husky, his hand falling from my knee.

In the absence of his grip, frigid incredulity swamped over me. I curled into myself to trap whatever warmth remained in my middle, a groan sinking through my gritted teeth when my stitched abdomen protested the movement.

Naomi and Jaik lurched forward, and I flung up a hand—then regretted it when my shoulder pulled as well, lancing fresh agony down into my side. I hoped Luck turned its wicked face toward Galan for the rest of his *life* for shooting me through my dominant arm.

"I'm all right," I managed—though my hoarse tone suggested otherwise. "I just...I don't understand how all of this is happening. To my parents, to *you*, Noni..."

Jaik crumbled back against the baseboard, fingers tangling through his hair. "It happened to Galan, too."

Naomi and I both swiveled his way, the air heating with our shared confusion. "What?"

"When we faced off, back in the Casmiss Wood...he was flipping kittens over how I didn't *remember* him. Didn't remember what his problem was with you." He folded his arms, thumbs snapping a wild rhythm against his elbows. "Might be he wasn't as crazy as we thought, tiger. Maybe he knows something we don't."

Spots dappled my vision, and I pressed my hand to my brow, squeezing my eyes shut.

This was so much more than I could contend with...almost more overwhelming than the notion of being abandoned. Cast out.

I'd been *forgotten*. And now I was remembered. By friends I recalled and enemies I didn't.

I buried my face in my knees. "I need some time to think."

"Of course." At once, Naomi's tone pivoted from friendly to professional. "I'll fix some tea for you. And food? You haven't taken more than thin broth by mouth all this week."

"What sounds good, tiger?" Jaik prodded.

My mother's homemade potato-and-cabbage soup. The halls of Fablehaven to lose myself in. Someone's arms around me.

"Whatever you can spare," I mumbled.

The chair scooted back, and Naomi's fingers brushed my head. "I'm so glad we found one another again, Addie."

Whispering coin-charms tinkled away. The door eased open and softly snapped shut again.

Jaik shifted. "Need me to go, too?"

I picked my head up from my knees, though my neck felt as wavering as that skeletal abomination's back in the forest, and heat pulsed behind my brow. "Jaik, they *forgot* me."

His confident countenance crumbled. He dipped his chin again, thumb raking his brow. "Yeah. I know. Wondering if my family forgot me, too...if that's why they never came to see me after the plow accident."

My gaze dropped to the hint of that scar peeping through the buttons of his shirt. "Why don't we remember Galan?"

"I don't know."

"And why in all of Luck's two-faced *fancies* did us meeting each other help them *remember?*"

"I don't *know*, Audra." Jaik's tone tightened, and I flinched; the last thing I wanted was him frustrated with me. He was the only person who could help me make sense of this impossible *thing* happening to both of us.

"I'm sorry," I mumbled.

His head jerked up straight again. "Why do you do that? Apologize whenever someone's angry?"

Despair cranked my throat shut like a twisted, damp rag. "So, you *are* angry."

"Yeah, but not with you. None of this is your fault."

"I just..." How could I explain to him that I didn't want to infuriate anyone so badly I would find myself facing another door shut in my face?

But that wasn't even why I'd faced the first one. Or the second. Something I'd been dodging, avoiding, fighting against for years, and it hadn't even happened the way I'd thought. For the *reasons* I'd thought.

Nausea churned in my gut, and I squirmed down to lie on my unhurt side. "I'm going to sleep. Wake me when Naomi comes back?"

"Sure." Jaik stretched out, his crossed legs fashioning a barrier between my back and the edge of the bed—then he shot upright again. "Oh, hey, before I forget...I found something in your bag I thought you'd want to see."

I rolled over to peer at what he was offering in his outstretched hand: a simple gold band studded with one bloodred ruby. A small, but likely expensive, ring.

I'd never seen it before in my life.

"This was in *my* satchel?" My eyes darted to Jaik's face—and my cheeks heated with a sudden, dizzying flush.

There was something about the vision of Jaik Grissom offering me a ring, however innocent the gesture, that stole my breath away.

"It sure as Luck wasn't in *mine*." He smirked, bobbing his hand a few times—urging me to take it. "Maybe it was tucked in the pocket of one of those pieces I bought for us back in Assida. But if it's not yours, maybe we could sell it."

Something cracked in my chest at those words, and I snatched the ring
way. "*No.* No, I…I like it. Maybe it *is* mine, maybe I just…"

Didn't remember it. Like I didn't remember Galan.

Jaik shrugged, settling back, arms folded and head craned to rest on the
delicate swoop of the baseboard again. "Up to you, tiger. It's your ring."

Somehow, that felt like the truth, even if I had never laid eyes on it before.

I rolled back onto my side, curling the ring in my fist and wedging that fist
under my cheek. Staring at the nearest cluster of lichen snuggled into the
wooden wall-beams, I let my mind wander over everything we'd discussed.

My parents and Naomi. Galan. The memories, lost and found. And how
those memories felt for my friend who'd only remembered we were close just
three months ago.

Memories that were only clear until we were of graduating age…eighteen or
so.

And it was there—wrapped in the familiar scents of Naomi's lovely home,
with Jaik a silent, steady presence at my back—that I finally let go. And I finally
did something I had avoided for years, evading the pain that came with thinking
of my life before I'd left Vallanmyre.

I didn't tell myself the tale of my past. I searched it out.

Those times where I'd felt truly loved and accepted. Where I'd had a
home…a family who cared for me. Who cherished me. Before I'd felt
disposable, expendable. *Forgettable.* When I'd known I had a permanent place in
the world, a stamp on the hearts of my loved ones that could not be smudged
away.

And as I lay there, awaiting Naomi's return, I saw the truth my clever friend
had already found out. That Jaik and I had touched upon in that cave in the
Tasmiss Wood.

I remembered our graduation, too; remembered Naomi's chiming luck-
pins and her strangling, enthusiastic embrace. Remembered my father's
woodsy-scented kiss on my head, my mother's hug full of citrus and sugar and
her tangible pride wrapping around me. I even remembered the half-grudging
sideways squeezes from Raff and Marli, how my brother had mussed my hair
and my sister had pinched my ribs and warned me I'd always be obnoxious,
accolades or none.

And after that day…

Haze.

A past that felt different. A quiet life that was not entirely tangible…as if everything had become so boring and mundane, it all blurred together.

That was what I'd assumed. What I'd *told* myself for all these years.

But it was as if the pages of my life had been torn out and rewritten with a shaky hand that did not quite match the rest of the script. A middle of a tome that nearly passed for authentic…but now I saw story after story laid out before me, and each one had the same pages missing. The same parts revised.

The sundering of story endings was not the only strange thing that had happened in Mithra-Sha. Something had happened to the memories of my fami and friends, as well. To Jaik's memories, and perhaps his family's, too.

And it seemed it all had something to do with me.

CHAPTER 32
THE INESCAPABLE MESS

B lood kissed the palm of my hand.

My knees kissed the polished golden tiles.

Blood and gilt. Ruby and gold.

Let me tell you a story.

It wasn't supposed to be like this.

Rifles cocked. My fists curled on my knees, my fingertips on the right pressing into something small and round swimming in the blood that splashed my palm.

I brought my trembling, stained hand up to eye level.

Let me tell you a story...

A ring lay tipped like a half-sunken vessel in the center of my hand; blood freckled its surface, stamped in fingerprints on the golden band, dripping from the red ruby like it had turned to liquid itself—melted beneath the heat of the fury rising and rising in me, bringing every sharp, gilded angle of my beautiful cage into sharp relief.

That was why. It has to be this way—do you understand that?

You're a murderer, you're a murderer, I despise you, I hope you rot, I will never, ever serve you again—

I captured the ring in the cage of my own fist and brought my knuckles to my lips.

Let me tell you a story...

The crack of a rifle jolted me awake, and I shot upright in the bed, pain blistering so hot through various points of my body that for a moment I thought

It took a moment with my free hand pressed to my gut to become aware of the bandages rubbing at my fingertips, to realize the woodsy smell in my nostrils leached not from living trees, but from the odd-angled walls of Naomi's bedroom. That the pain in my gut and shoulder were because of how I'd jerked up straight from my nest of blankets and pillows, the dull throb a residual ache rather than the searing agony of a fresh wound.

The new pain came from my palm...where I'd strangled the ring in my grip until it bit against my skin.

Sweating and shivering, I took in my surroundings; relieved that this time, at least, it seemed I'd awakened swiftly enough to avoid the screaming and sobbing that usually came with the nightmares.

And that was good, because I was alone. The room was as empty as the stew bowl I'd scraped clean and left on the bedside table the night before. As empty as I *felt*.

Flexing my sore fingers out fully, I gazed at the ring in the waxing daylight tumbling through the recessed window at the foot of the bed. It had certainly found its way swiftly into my dreams.

I held it up to the light, balanced between my thumb and forefinger; no fleck of blood was evident on the clean, polished gold. The ruby glinted bright and cheerful in the strengthening light of day.

An absurd compulsion overtook me, and I spread out my fingers again...then slipped the ring where a wedding band would nestle.

It was too large for me. Meant for a different woman entirely.

Of course it was. *I* certainly hadn't put it in my satchel...I would have sold the thing off during my desperate days along the Spine. Or in Krylan. There was no sense holding on to something that had no intrinsic value to me.

Yet I still slipped it into the pocket of my sleep trousers before I scooted for the edge of the bed.

It was my first time on my feet in days, and I wavered and strayed across the room like a new tale first being plotted. I splashed water on my face at the basin by the door, its contents spiced with sweat and something herbal. Jaik must've been washing here nightly...perhaps too concerned to leave my side.

The notion tugged a rueful smile from me as I scrubbed the tackiness of passing days from my own skin—the very vision of a damsel worth pining over.

If he hadn't known before, he was certainly aware by now that I snored. And drooled in my sleep.

I patted my face dry with a clean cloth that held Naomi's cotton-freesia scent—something she had spent so many years cultivating to perfection in Harrow Hall, I couldn't help but admire her dedication to it all these years later. It hung in every inch of her home.

Then I made my way to my own freedom…no gilded prison for me. The only cage I knew was my tired body; for a moment, I had to cling to the door and breathe through heaves of pain tossing themselves at my stitches. Like something living clawed beneath my skin, seeking a way out through the holes Galan had torn into me.

But oddly enough, it was the thought of him—a ceaseless foe with knowledge of me that I myself lacked, and despicable enough from what I *did* know of him—that poured enough strength into my weakened bones to push me out the door. Shoulder pressed to the wall, I trudged down the long hall peppered with a few other doors, then descended a flight of broad, dark steps to the home's lower level, where Jaik and Naomi's voices beckoned me.

I found them seated on either side of a long, narrow wooden table that ran the middle of the room. A low-mouthed hearth burned on the wall at Naomi's back, and over their heads, sachets and bundles of herbs shed an earthy aroma over the room. Cots were shoved to the walls—likely where she treated the invalid and wounded of Dalfi who were Luck-loved enough to know of her—and one door, framed in windows, led outside. Another led somewhere I didn't know.

I halted halfway down the steps, still masked in shadow, my heart lurching as if it had decided to continue on down the flight ahead of me.

It was such a quiet scene, domestic—the pair of them with platters of brown bread and meat, cups of cider and raspberry tarts between them. Peaceful, even. And it occurred to me as I hovered in the verge of light and darkness, pulse clipping painfully in the side of my neck, that Jaik Grissom insinuated himself so easily into this particular frame.

The quiet life he'd always wanted.

Perhaps he hadn't found it suiting, back in Krylan…but what of Dalfi, with its airship docks and blustering streets? What of Naomi, with whom he shared the easy rapport of a week in confines together? Even now, she murmured something, and Jaik chuckled, a smooth, warm sound that pinched off the breath in my throat.

For all they knew, I was upstairs, unconscious…and yet this moment played on. Would anything be different if I were erased from the narrative entirely?

Would they carry on as my parents and siblings had, as even Naomi had for *years* while I'd been forgotten?

Life could continue on flawlessly without Audra Jashowin. These last handful of years had proven that.

An indignant, aching portion of my spirit yearned to retreat back upstairs and feign sleep until one of them decided to come looking for me; and the masochism coupled to that ache wanted to measure just how long that wait would be. But hunger bubbled low in my gut, and now that I'd smelled some of Naomi's famous raspberry tarts...

I choked on my own hurt heart and wounded pride, then picked my way down the steps.

When I plodded into view, Jaik and Naomi both looked up; then Jaik was on his feet, chair shoved back, brow creased with that all-too-familiar frown. "Take it easy, tiger! What are you doing out of bed?"

"I was hungry." There was something gratifying, however briefly, in keeping the pain of my latest nightmare to myself; sullen satisfaction lifted its hideous head with a smirk. At least I could manage that much, if they all moved along without me again.

"Here." Jaik pulled out the chair beside him, and Naomi rose to fetch a platter of the same meat and bread and pastries.

Guilt swept my ankles, dumping me heavily into the seat. Here I was, lurking in the shadows, begrudging them a moment of peace and making that quiet exchange all about my absence...and yet as soon as I showed my face, they were tending my needs with an almost intuitive care.

Maker's tales. At least other people *could* escape the mess of me. I was trapped within the whirling spiral of my painful thoughts while Jaik spun his chair and sat, straddling it, watching me.

"How's the shoulder?" he demanded. "Stomach?"

"Sore, but I'll live." I didn't deserve his sympathy after my vicious thoughts in the stairwell, and I wouldn't hunt for it now—not even if it would buy me a moment's satisfaction of feeling irreplaceable.

"You eat." Naomi set the platter and cup before me. "I'll assess whether you're going to live or die."

I couldn't help the small smile that edged onto my lips at her usual pert tone, bubbling with thinly veiled humor. I'd missed the easygoing warmth of her friendship even more than I'd let myself feel when I'd thought she despised me;

it it rubbed at a small, raw patch on my heart that had yet to quite heal…a part at still missed Lio, and wondered often how she was faring in Krylan.

At least Galan was here, not making her life one long twirl of the dark side Luck's coin.

My mouth dried at the notion of him, and I grabbed for the cider cup, king several long gulps before I managed to school my tone into something asonable. "Any sign of our soldiering friend here in the city?"

Folding his arms on the seatback, Jaik shook his head. "Naomi's had her es peeled and her contacts keeping a lookout, but so far…nothing."

"I think we'd know if he was here," Naomi added gravely, peeling back the oad collar of my linen shirt to examine my shoulder. "It seems Jaik dealt him uite the blow…the sort a healer would need to see. But no one fitting his escription or his wound has come to any of us in Dalfi for aid."

"Maybe he bled to death out there," Jaik grunted. "Good riddance."

While I rarely wished death on anyone, even the lewdest vagrants I'd had e displeasure of crossing paths with on the Spine, Galan had proven himself a engeful and wicked pursuer from the first moment he'd cornered me in Krylan. wouldn't mourn a world bereft of the threat of him, whatever that said about e.

I couldn't see Naomi's face where she hovered behind me, but I could vision her puckered lips and creased brow by the way she answered: "Maybe. ut that's hardly a risk worth betting on."

"You haven't seen me gamble, sweetheart," Jaik scoffed.

"Actually, I have. You're betting on Audra Jashowin, which means you now a winning hand when you see one. So I suggest you don't break your reak by underestimating the likes of Galan."

Heat flushed through my heart, straight to my cheeks; Jaik shot me a delong glance and a crooked smirk, then leaned away, stretching his back and opping his neck. "I'm more worried about the bounty hunters here in Dalfi. We on't last long before they notice us."

"What's your plan, then?" Naomi asked.

I glanced at Jaik, conferring with a look that nothing had changed before I id, "We'll continue on toward Vallanmyre. We can't let Galan or the bounties op us."

Naomi's fingers seized around my shoulder so swiftly pain erupted down y arm. I flinched, a hiss escaping my teeth, and Jaik bolted up straight. "What as that?"

"I'm sorry!" Naomi's hand snatched away, and she circled around to face me, eyes wide. "Addie, I'm so sorry. But did you say you're going to *Vallanmyre?*

Warning clanged down every step of my ribs. "To Fablehaven, yes. For the answers we need."

Rapidly, I explained what had transpired that first night in *The Tiller's Tankard*—leaving aside how I'd assaulted and captured Jaik. To my relief, for once he kept his ramble-hole shut, though a smirk played at the corners of his mouth when he tore his bread in half and shoved it in.

Naomi's expression didn't lighten; instead, it fell from shocked to grave, twisting dread through my gut.

"I can see why you're desperate for answers," she allowed when I'd finished. "And to be fair, I haven't heard of a single other Storycrafter finishing their tales, so it does seem to be isolated to the pair of you...or to Jaik, at least."

"What can I say, this body comes in high demand," he gloated, and I tore my own roll in half, flinging a wad of warm brown bread at him.

"But that isn't what I'm concerned about," Naomi plowed on, capturing both our gazes and our full attention with her next words. "You can't go to Vallanmyre."

The bread wobbled halfway to my lips; it was an effort to force myself to bite and swallow, and one only managed by the thunderous roar of my appetite. Jaik set down the cider cup he'd just reached for. "Why not? Roads out?"

Naomi glanced between us, her brow furrowing so fiercely it wrinkled her nose. "You don't know? The bounty on your heads came from Sha Lothar himself."

CHAPTER 33
DANGER AND REWARD

The bite of bread bubbled right back up my throat, washing my mouth with the stringent taste of yeast and bile. I gagged it out into my napkin, and Jaik tipped sideways, resting a hand on my back even while his gaze stayed fixed on Naomi.

"You sure about that?" he demanded.

Naomi nodded. "I heard Shadran Arias and his mother were traveling from city to city, and everywhere they landed to bring aid and supplies, they left something behind."

"The *Wanted* bulletins," I choked. "Because of Krylan?" My mind filled with images of cratered, sundered streets—the destruction we'd left in our mad dash to escape Galan and his fellow soldiers.

"Perhaps it's nothing you did yet, it's because of what you *can* do." Naomi settled forward, elbows on the table, hands clasped and propped to her cheek. "Sha Lothar has been drowning with the effort of sustaining Mithra-Sha in the absence of powerful Storycraft. Of course he wants you."

And traveling to Vallanmyre would place us directly in his own city, teeming not only with potential bounty hunters, but with soldiers and even Storycrafters loyal to the Sha.

Nevermind Fablehaven, with its strict code and loyalty to the country…we wouldn't even make it past the city gates.

I fell back in my seat, appetite evaporating, despair pouring itself into every crevice that had ever thought of hunger.

The Sha *himself* was paying the bounty. He was hunting us from the opulent Shastah, his wife and son dispatched to personally nail our faces to the bulletin boards. It would have surprised me nothing if his daughter, Shadress Mahalia had sketched the *Wanted* notes herself; rumor on the Spine had it she was quite the talented artist.

The most powerful family in our country, by whose order the tales of life shaped themselves...they were personally seeking *us*.

"So," Jaik threw down his half-eaten roll and reclined, hands braced on his thighs, "what now?"

Naomi and I swapped a look that somehow—unbelievable though it seemed—held all the unspoken understanding that had carried us through our friendship before she'd forgotten me.

"There's another place we can go." My voice refused to be coaxed any louder than a murmur. "Somewhere even more likely to hold the answers we seek, but..."

"It's so dangerous, Addie," Naomi pleaded and cautioned at once, and both wrenched at my heart. I could hardly remember the last time anyone had sounded so worried for my sake.

Oh, hey, there you are, tiger. Look at me, it's not that bad...I've got this. I've got you, I can fix this, just keep your eyes open...

I swallowed and fixed my focus to the moment, meeting Jaik's wary, expectant gaze. "Fablehaven is considered a root of power for Storycrafting because—as the old tales go—it marks the place where the Storymaker built all stories. Where His essence hovered when the world was formed by His Wellspoken words."

"It's why the first Sha built Vallanmyre and his Shastah near Fablehaven," Naomi added—parroting tales I'd whispered with flourishes of grandeur over cups of cocoa in the light of the heated bonfire between Harrow Hall and Fablehaven so many years ago. "It's a seat of power for all the known world."

"Right, I'm following you." Jaik shifted his feet on the floor. "But you just said Fablehaven's out of the question, so—"

"It has a twin," I said, and his eyes blew wide. "The first *Misspoken* story was the antithesis of all the Storymaker intended the craft to be. Its speaking forged an island far off the coast of Mithra-Sha. Somewhere that became a...prison, of sorts, where all the other manifestations of Misspoken tales that can't be destroyed are sent to be caged."

"It's called the Illusionarium, or the Isle of Misspoken Stories," Naomi explained. "There are entire factions of the army devoted to corralling the Misspoken manifestations and dragging them there. It's the best pay, I hear. The most dangerous of all their tasks."

I nodded. "And the second tower lies at the heart of the island. It's called Erasure…and, according to the legends we learned in Fablehaven, Erasure holds the chronicles of life itself. The Storymaker's own outlook of the world, the interpretation of every tale Spoken or lived…all of it is there."

Jaik was silent for a long moment, his gaze drifting between us.

"So you're thinking," he ventured at last, "whatever made us like this to each other, whatever happened to everyone's memories of us, and to all the endings of the stories…"

"The written account lies in Erasure." I nodded grimly.

Jaik blew out a low whistle, sliding a hand back through his hair. "That night we left Krylan, when you mentioned that place you'd rather have faced a rifle than gone to…that's the Illusionarium?"

I folded my hands in my lap to hide their trembling. "Unfortunately, yes."

"Worse than the worst," he muttered. "Do we have any other choice?"

Naomi canted her head. "You *could* take your risk on asking questions…searching for someone who knows something. But given how all of us forgot Addie for *years*, I don't suppose the chance is strong you'll truly find the full tale anywhere else."

The last of my hope sputtered and perished at that; Naomi had always been the more practical one between us, her studies rooted in the clear definitions and angles of the world, while I'd played in the fantastical and creative. As usual, her perspective brought balance…the truth laid out with clarity, weaving into the dread I'd fostered quietly ever since Krylan.

Fablehaven's archives, perhaps, would explain the means by which Jaik's presence amplified my power. They might even hint at what could have happened to the minds and memories of our friends and families. But Erasure held the record as it truly was—*our* truth. Not guesswork or theory, but the actuality of what had become of us.

The danger was unmitigated. And so was the reward.

At long, long last, Jaik said, "I've got a friend…a ship's captain who sails in and out of the harbor at Fallshyre Bay, all the way down to Port Craythin near Krylan. Fallshyre's on the coast, so if we catch him at the right time, he might sail us out to the Illusionarium."

My pulse skipped and stuttered. "You want to do this?"

Jaik's gaze finally peeled off of Naomi, settling back on me; his eyes were rimmed pink. "Tiger, I'm a wanted man…and maybe not just by the Sha. My whole family forgot me, and now they might be out there, trying to find me again. You're not the only one that matters to. But if I'm going back, I'm not going emptyhanded. I want to know *why*."

His determination breathed life into the ember of my own resolve—that burning spark that had dimmed with the attack from the Storycrafters and Galan in the Casmiss Wood.

I squared my shoulders against the seatback, grimacing at the tug in my stitches. "So do I. This is our story…we need to know who altered it."

"One more week," Naomi urged. "Give yourself time to heal, gather supplies, and plan your route. Crossing the Drennans in full winter won't be easy…it's best if you have a plan."

"We'll need to pick up coin along the way," Jaik added. "Julas is a good man, but he's a businessman, too. He's not going to sail his crew to some Luck-forgotten spit of land out of the goodness of his heart and a few years of friendship."

"Especially if that friend is *you*," I snarked.

Jaik's brows rose, his grin spreading full-fledged across his face. "Welcome back, tiger."

Satisfaction shivered in my gut, teasing warmly at my wound.

I *was* back; doubts and insecurities notwithstanding, I was here. I was alive. I was *known*. And bad dreams or none, fears or none, I still had a purpose. A mission to fulfill.

Danger aside, I was going to the place we Storycrafters only ever envisioned and whispered about in the Academy.

I was going to the Illusionarium.

CHAPTER 34
SPECTACLES OF SPLENDOR

xcitement and dread still thrummed beneath my skin hours later when Naomi took her leave—dressed for the city, wrapped in a heavy cloak of green and silver, her hair knotted and the powder 1es refreshed around her eyes.

"I have your list." She snapped a piece of paper Jaik's way. "I'll see what of ese items I can find. We're still agreed on payment?"

Jaik snorted. "You'll get it, you crook."

I almost questioned them; but curiosity was not stronger than the envious ing that still curdled the meal in my guts when I thought of them bent over the ble when I'd come downstairs. And I preferred not to dwell on what payment aomi might have demanded under those circumstances.

I had other things to focus on: the sharp shift in our plans, the altered route at lay ahead. And what awaited at the end of that road.

Unfortunately, my burst of nervous energy was not enough to see me back bed unaccompanied.

"I can walk by myself," I grumbled as Jaik supported me up the stairs; as arefully as I'd conquered them in the descent, climbing back up sent a fresh jolt f pain lancing through my middle with every step.

"Yeah, and I can juggle raw eggs and balance on one foot at the same me." Jaik took a bit more of my weight on the next ascent. "Doesn't mean I do just to prove a point."

"I'm not trying to prove anything."

He was quiet, maneuvering up several stairs. "Luck's coin flipped your way ut there, Audra. You know that, right? I don't know what kind of shot Galan sually is, but that lead could've tor through organs if it had gone just a little to the left or right. No one's expecting you to be ready to plow off to the Illusionarium tonight."

Heat invaded my cheeks, miserable and prickly. I ducked my head and watched our feet mounting the upper landing in perfect lockstep.

"So," I murmured when we had been there a moment, catching our breath and waiting for my pain to subside, "you can really juggle on one foot?"

Rolling his eyes, Jaik tugged me down the hall back to my room.

I expected he would release me there and bid me goodnight, even though i was only nearing sunset. The other doors proved there were more than just a fe rooms in Naomi's home. Instead, Jaik followed me inside and shut the door. Then he went to his pack, tossed into a corner near the washbasin, and proceeded to empty it—letting me make my way to the bed myself.

Smiling, I hobbled over and settled onto the edge of the mattress, watchin, him inventory his things: clothes and rope and blade. The last of his rations fror our travels this far. No coin.

Sourness flooded my mouth. "Your...*arrangement* with Naomi. How precisely do you intend to pay her?"

"How do you think?" Jaik tossed me a smirk.

I fisted the ring in my pocket and forced a shrug. "Enlighten me."

"Look, I've got my ways." Rising, he pressed both hands to the small of hi back—and unleashed a groan so deep and powerful, it flared heat straight in my core.

"What was *that* for?"

"Back is killing me." He jerked his chin my way. "That chair's not exactly built for sleeping."

Disbelief punched my tone high. "You've been sleeping in the *chair?* For a *week?*"

He shrugged sharply. "What? It's not like I was going to leave you, with th(way things were. I wanted to be close by, in case you..."

He trailed off. Another shrug that insinuated all the possibilities the notion implied.

In case you died. In case you had another nightmare. In case you woke up alone, and scared, and needed someone to comfort you.

In case you needed me.

The warm wash of gratitude built in my throat and rinsed away whatever tartness remained from his deal with Naomi. I settled back, smoothing both hands on the bedspread. "Well, I'm awake now, as you know. And there s…well, not *plenty* of space on this bed. But enough that you don't have to murder your spine every night for a martyr's cause."

"You'd better be *really* offering, tiger, because I'm not ever speaking to you again if you snatch that little thread of hope out of my fingers."

Laughter burst from me, so sharp it hurt in both my wounds—the most pleasant ache they'd given me all day. "I'm really offering."

With a whoop of delight, he strode to the bed; giggling, I gathered up my limbs and tucked myself back against the wall, making room for him to sprawl out on the mattress. He collapsed, burrowing his head backward into the pillow and folding his hands behind his neck.

"Better?" I teased.

"Like you wouldn't believe."

Legs tucked under me, I watched his face easing into a relaxed grin. Comfortable. As if nothing beyond this moment mattered—not what we had endured before or what now lay on our horizon.

"Jaik," I murmured, "how do you really feel about traveling to the Illusionarium?"

He cracked an eye, sweeping a look up and down the knotted-up contours of my body. Then the line of his shoulders gave a single smooth bob. "Is what it is, tiger. I'm not going to lie and say I'm looking forward to an island full of things like we saw out there in the Casmiss Wood, but…is it worth it? I'm willing to bet it is."

"I think so, too." Particularly now that we knew there was more to the happenings in Mithra-Sha than sundered stories. Texts could tell us only so much of how something might have come about; chronicles would give us the precise reasons and ways.

"What about you?" Jaik asked. "This *Erasure* sounds like an important place to Storycrafters. Must be a big deal for you."

"It's daunting," I admitted, "but I'm not really afraid. It's hard to be afraid of anything when I'm going there with you."

His mouth crept up into a smile at one side. "I know what you mean." He offered me his fist. "Sword and story, tiger."

The words launched through me like a blow, the same as they had in the Casmiss Wood—and I didn't even really know why. There was just something *right* about them.

There was always something right about him. Something that made my mind prickle with wonder—with unease in not knowing—if perhaps Jaik and I had been acquainted, too. Before…everything.

But that still made no sense; if we'd shared any history, I would have remembered him, like I had remembered my family and Naomi despite everything *they* had forgotten. And he would have remembered *me* by now, like they had…even if it was only a patchwork recollection.

Yet to my memory, he remained a stranger I had first met in the *Tankard*…even if my heart was drawn to him in ways that made him feel like a perfect piece of my life's own story. As if he'd always belonged there.

As if I'd been waiting for him to be written into my pages, scripted on my heart.

"Sword and story," I echoed quietly, dismissing those tangled notions with a knock of my fist against his.

We both fell onto our backs, staring up at the ceiling. My heart clamored so loudly I almost missed when Jaik spoke again.

"So. This Isle of Misspoken Stories," he ventured. "You've always wanted to go?"

"Not particularly. It was something we dared one another about in the Academy. A bit like…you know how some of the cities and towns celebrate *Sinister Sundown*?"

"Right. One night every harvest when folks wear black cloaks and Luck's wicked mask, and they go on capers. Try to scare each other and play games." Jaik nodded. "I've done it a few times."

Of course he had. "Well, the Fablehaven students liked to pretend we'd go to the Illusionarium during *Sundown,* saying it would be the greatest caper of all. But no one ever did, to my knowledge…it was just too much of a risk."

"Figures that's where you and I are headed," Jaik snorted. "Someplace no one ever actually wants to go."

Curiosity nipped me, and I rolled onto my side, propping up gingerly on my wounded arm to face him. "Well, what about you? Is there anything you've *always* wanted to do?"

To my surprise, he wasn't quick with a retort; he freed a hand from behind his neck to rub his jaw instead, warm color darting across the bridge of his nose. "It's…ah, nothing."

"*Jaik*," I wheedled, pressing myself taller in the mattress. "Tell me!"

"No, you're going to laugh your head off."

"I will not! I swear on the hem of the Storymaker's own cloak, I won't laugh."

"It's not something you'd expect a farmhand to dream about."

"Of course, because that's all I see you as…a common farmhand."

He rolled his head sideways against the arm that still supported it, studying me with greater intensity than I'd intended from that glib remark.

"All right," he said after a long moment, his tone careful. "Truth is, I've always wanted to see this one traveling troupe…there are eight people in it, acrobats, they do all sorts of aerial stunts. Usually without a rope. I don't know…I always thought it would be worth seeing."

Familiarity wiggled beneath my ribs. "Wait. You don't mean *Four Brothers, Four Brides?*"

Jaik blinked. "You've heard of them?"

"I *love* them!" Eagerness lifted my voice, a memory of silks and gleaming lights lunging to the forefront of my mind. "The Arial Arena show? Absolutely *breathtaking.*"

"That's what I've heard!" Jaik grinned. "You've seen it?"

"Mhm. Twice."

He shot upright. "Get lost!"

"No, I mean it!" A laugh burst out of me, mischievous triumph rolling up my throat. "My parents took me to it as a girl, and again a bit later, before they stopped performing in Vallanmyre."

A bit of melancholy snagged in my chest. Seeing that show had been the first time I'd ever wanted to be anything but a Storycrafter; I'd told my parents forlornly on the long walk back through Vallanmyre's streets how, if I could be anything in the world, I wished I were an actor or an acrobat.

"The show was…beautiful," I admitted. "Breathtaking. It made me feel like I left for another world…how I suppose people must feel when they hear a Wellspoken tale."

"Wish you'd gotten to see them more often," Jaik said.

"So do I." The brilliant spectacle cooled in my mind, from hectic, heart-stopping splendor to something softer…something that crackled with firelight and kind voices, low as embers. "Actually, I traveled with the troupe for a bit on the Spine, as well."

Jaik slammed his palm into the bedspread. "*No,* you flipping did not."

"I swear on the hem of the Storymaker's cloak, I *flipping* did!"

"All right, so? What are they like?"

"Wonderful people. Truly. The brothers are close in ways I always wished Raff and Marli and I could be...like they'd do anything for one another." Sadness pinched my throat at the memory of nights of banter and teasing at the fireside that I'd always felt more a spectator to than a part of. "And they absolutely dote on their wives. I don't know if you're aware, but two of the brides are Hadrassi, and the other two are Ameresh. The brothers met them on traveling shows beyond the borders, and they refused to leave without them." I swallowed and shrugged. "Anyway, they looked after me for a bit, before our paths parted."

Jaik shook his head. "Can't believe you actually *traveled* with them."

"Neither could I. But they were truly just people." I ground my lip between my teeth. "I suppose everyone we admire, they really are all just...people. Flawed and wonderful in their own ways."

"Yeah," Jaik murmured. "That's true."

Silence strung itself around the room for a moment, telling tales of its own. I tried to keep my eyes to myself, but sitting this near each other, mostly all I could see was Jaik...and it troubled me a bit how little I *wanted* to look anywhere else.

After several unbearable moments, he shook his head as if stirring from a deep well of thought himself; his eyes focused back on me, a smirk toying with his lips. "So, what is it you like about the shows?"

"I don't know. It's a different sort of storytelling, I suppose. I bring tales to life one way, but what they do...it's Storycrafting in motion." I plucked at a loose thread in the bedspread clumped between us, then dragged my gaze back to his face. "And you?"

He didn't answer for a moment; an odd, pained emotion flickered through his eyes, and he blew out his breath. "Flipping Luck, tiger. I wish I could see the world the way you do. Just...stories, everywhere. The way it all weaves together and makes *sense*. Must be nice."

It hadn't always been—and in so many ways, it still wasn't. But it felt like the wrong moment, far too intimate and vulnerable, to admit the truth: the stories only made sense anymore when he was part of them.

"Well, you could try," I offered instead.

Jaik frowned. "What?"

"You don't have to have Storycraft to tell a story!" I beckoned to him. "Try it. Tell me a story, Jaik Grissom."

His mouth opened, then snapped shut. He scoffed, looking away from me. "his doesn't feel right...you're going to laugh."

"I didn't laugh about *Four Brothers, Four Brides*, did I?" I nudged his knee th mine. "*Please*, Jaik?"

His eyes snapped back to me, and something in that glance made my breath tch.

"All right," he said at length. "You get under the covers, I'll tell you a story. ıt I guarantee it'll have you asleep in two minutes."

It was the first vow he'd broken since we'd met; because one stumbling ɔry turned into two, then three. True ones, at first, of farmhand antics and *nister Sundown* capers; and then he wove them into fantastic, humorous ʌventures that had my middle aching with laughter.

Some things in life would never be fair, or truly make sense...the broken ʌds of all the tales in Mithra-Sha. The way our families and friends had ·rgotten us. Or that Jaik Grissom had not been made a Storycrafter. But night, he could claim a bit of that...not with tales that manifested power, only ith stories that soothed my frantic, weary heart. And I would never stop being ·ateful for that...or for him.

I was so grateful I'd met Jaik Grissom, it stung my eyes with tears.

Night had claimed the world when he tired of storytelling, and we lay on ur backs again, gazing at the ceiling.

"That was wonderful," I murmured.

"Yeah. Thanks for listening to me ramble."

"Whenever you'd like, I'll always listen."

He hummed low in his throat, eyes drifting shut. Curled on my side, I ɔudied his profile—made up of sharp and soft angles, inside and out.

"What do *you* love about that troupe?" I asked again, softly.

He shrugged, turning his face toward me. "I just like stories. Any way I can nd them."

The shadows that paved his features and hugged against my curves loaned ʌe a bit of boldness, to say what lurked in my mind: "I'm glad our stories ɔrossed over."

"Me, too, tiger." Jaik's voice was a husky murmur. "Me, too."

CHAPTER 35
LOST FOR WORDS

I slept better that night than I had in far too long; in fact, it seemed like a blink later that I was awake on my side of the mound of clothing stuffed between our halves of the bed, the strong daylight revealing the emptiness across from me.

Surging upright and bracing a hand to my middle, I scouted the room with a swift glance...and all the blood rose to my face in a single deft, dizzying eruption.

Shirtless and barefoot—wearing nothing, in fact, but gray linen pants tied low on his prominent hipbones—Jaik swiveled to face me. A bristle brush hung from the corner of his mouth, forsaken while he tugged his unruly hair back with both hands, securing it in a knot behind his head.

"Hey there, tiger." His raspy morning voice was congested with the brush jammed against his cheek. "Sleep well?"

Maker's tales. I was never going to sleep *again* without this image haunting me.

"I...I'm..." I coughed to clear my clotted throat. "What are you—?"

"Wait..." He grinned around the brush. "I thought I was supposed to *help* you get your words together. Where'd they run off to?"

"Shut your ramble-hole," I snapped, gripping the covers to fling them off; then, thinking better at the warning twinge in my shoulder and belly, I folded the fabric back with deliberate precision. "Why are you up so early?"

"Actually, it's almost sunhigh." Shrugging, he turned and spat into the washbasin, then tapped his brush on the rim a few times. "Guess we both needed a good night's sleep more than we thought. Anyway, time to rustle up some coin for Naomi and Julas at the gambling tables."

Relief spilled through me, hot and untampered, coaxing a silly grin to my face. "So *that's* how you're repaying her."

Jaik crouched by his satchel, eyeing me sidelong. "Yeah. How did you *think* was going to pay her?"

An image dashed across my mind—the pair of them bent together over her table, sharing laughter and conversation in my absence—and I shook it away. "I wondered if maybe you'd agreed to actually be quiet, for once in your life."

"Ah, tiger," he scoffed, rocking to his feet with arms laden in clothes, "no purchase in this country is worth silencing these golden tones."

He slipped out, and I took advantage of the solitude to do what I could: unlocking the window and shoving it open, ushering in the rich scents of Dalfi. For a moment, I simply breathed in that wind, spiced with a different note than any other city I'd visited.

Dalfi was an airship port, bleeding the sort of opulence that coaxed the flying vessels in—wealthy salesmen sniffing about for wealthy buyers. The structures here soared higher even than those in Krylan, ribbed with windows half the height of every floor; and to not a few of them, airships were tethered, their great iron-chain anchors a striking skein of darkness against the bright blue sky. Others were grounded on port-ledges, great half-moons of stern stone that jutted from edifices all across Dalfi.

In this city, one could almost believe there was no need for Storycrafters, and no lack in our absence. Dalfi maintained a rigid code of embellishment and strength; those who could not afford the city's excessive taxes did not stay long in it.

Likely the Storycrafters who'd taken the bounty on us were only passing through, just like we were now. We wouldn't draw any eyes if we were careful.

Rejuvenated by the clean breeze, I limped across the room, snatching up the washbasin and emptying it out the window, then refilling it from the pitcher on the stand. I'd just finished scrubbing the sleep from my face and begun finger-combing my hair when Jaik slipped back inside, fully dressed, lobbing his sleep pants onto the bed. "All right, time for me to earn my keep. Do you need anything before I'm out?"

I hesitated, glancing at my satchel.

Jaik pitched his weight back against the door, arms folded. "Ask."

Humiliation fought to name itself irritation instead as I yanked my hair off to the side. "I need to tie all of this up, but I can't..."

A few pained, gloating pulses in my side and shoulder thoroughly agreed: I could not.

Whatever mockery I'd expected for my silly plight, I found none of it in Jaik. With a curt nod, he strode to my satchel and dug up the leather ties for my hair at once—something else he must have found when he'd rifled through my satchel.

Perhaps the notion should have bothered me, but I knew him by now; he hadn't been snooping just to snoop. And besides, I had nothing worth hiding in there. He'd seen all my belongings that first night in Krylan.

For a moment, I considered asking him what my cloak looked like now; but I hadn't dared to look for myself, and I wasn't certain I wanted to know at all. I'd hardly teased my craft since I'd bundled the cloak away outside Kalvikan, except to save our lives in the Casmiss Wood; it wasn't worth taunting myself with curiosities, when the more practical problems lay at hand.

Jaik returned after a moment with the tie wound between his fingers. "Turn around."

I obliged, bracing my hands on either side of the washbasin and leaning my weight to my left, taking pressure off my injured side; Jaik halted behind me, his fingers maneuvering gently through the damp tangles of my hair, combing out what I'd failed to reach with pain abrupting my movements.

An unbidden sigh of relief floated to the backs of my teeth. His broad fingers felt so *wonderful* on my scalp; every tense knot in my neck and shoulders released beneath his ministrations. I bowed my head, my spine curving…then flinched when my back brushed his chest.

He was standing closer than I'd realized.

"Take it easy, tiger." A deep chuckle lived beneath his words.

Difficult. But the tension didn't settle in my muscles this time; it thrummed in my chest and stomach, sending my pulse staggering. Every breath drew in the woodland scent that still clung to Jaik's clothes, and I was maddeningly aware of each brush of his fingertips on my skin as he freed the tangles in my hair, then gathered it gently off of my neck. Callouses brushed bare flesh, guided along the curve of my shoulder, trailing up my nape, teasing against my hairline.

Shivers slammed through me, relentless.

"You seem to know your way around tying up hair." I begged the Storymaker that my voice didn't sound as breathless to Jaik as it did to me.

"Sure do." Concentration muted his tone as he twisted more hair gently into his fist. "Used to do this for Nora and Adel."

The heat in my cheeks abated a bit, cooling with sympathy at the mention of his sisters.

I wondered if they remembered that now, the way Naomi remembered me; if they had woken one day and suddenly known they had a brother named Jaik, whose skilled hands had once banded up their hair as deftly as they did mine.

I wondered if they missed him.

"All right." Jaik wrapped the leather twine around my hair several times, then knotted it off and dropped his hands onto my shoulders. "You're all set."

I didn't move. Neither did he—except his thumbs, tracing gentle, absent circles against the back of my neck, just above my shoulderblades.

My fingers dug into the underside of the basin stand. Another, longer shiver unraveled through me.

Jaik's hands glided down to grip my hips for a heartbeat, and his nose brushed the shell of my ear. "I'll see you, tiger."

Then he was gone, striding out the door, shutting it carefully behind him.

All the breath rushed out of me at once, and I sagged against the basin stand, burying my face in my hands.

What was I doing?

What in the Maker's many tales was I *doing*?

CHAPTER 36
HIDDEN OBSESSION

aik was mercifully absent when I descended the stairs nearly an hour later; Naomi greeted me with a smile from where she sat on her table, feet propped on a chair, a mortar and pestle trapped between her knees. "Good morning, Addie. There's biscuits and gravy inside the hearth. You eat, I'll look after your stitches."

The silence was not entirely devoid of discomfort while she changed the dressings and I navigated the platter of food with my weaker hand. Naomi snorted out a few giggles when my fork bested me, and I shot her dirty looks she met with an innocent smirk.

Maker's tales, I'd missed this. And likely we were still missing other things—gaps within that void of displaced time after graduation.

It felt safer to tiptoe around the matter, for now.

"You seem to be doing well for yourself," I offered, giving a chin nod to the cozy warmth of the room around us. "Healing in Dalfi pays well?"

"Better than you would believe." A seam of relief opened up in Naomi's tone, as if she'd hoped for a breach in the thick silence between us. "Airships are wonderful things, but flipping *Luck* if these sky-sailors aren't still learning as they go. I have burns and broken fingers to treat every week, and that's besides all the usual injuries that come with daily life in a city of this size…"

She chattered on as she worked, her eager tales thawing out whatever unease remained. She reminded me about her father—a wealthy peddler himself, from Vallanmyre, who'd doted fiercely on his only daughter after four sons and paved a path for her to pursue her passions without restraint.

He'd purchased this home for her outright, but she'd maintained everything since, paid the taxes herself, and still had a bit left over for comfort and charity

"I was always surprised he supported you leaving Vallanmyre," I admitted. "eing so far away from him, from your brothers…and especially when you left abruptly."

She hesitated a moment, then slowly maneuvered the hem of my shoulder idage into place. "It's like I told you back then, Addie…they needed more lers in Dalfi, and I needed a bit of breath away from…everything in the iital."

The words danced around things unsaid—or unremembered.

"It seems you found it," I offered lamely.

Naomi brightened—then grimaced. "I do hate the feeling that I'm profiting the suffering of others," she admitted, shifting to sit across the table from me ile I polished off my second helping of biscuits and beef-gravy, "but these last v years in particular, healing has been…lucrative." She rolled her sleeves back m her wrists in careful measures. "Poison studies as well. There's no end to k who will eat anything they find just to take the edge off their hungry lies."

"Well, and you live just off the Spine," I added, "and believe me, I know m my own travels how tempting a bright red berry-bush can be when you ven't had a decent meal in days. But you're not profiteering, Noni…you didn't for all of this lack any more than they did."

Glumly, Naomi dropped her chin onto her fists, staring past me into the iber-filled hearth, kept just warm enough to heat the biscuits. "So many sick d starving people, Addie. They come from all around Dalfi, hoping I can cure :m…but I can't mend what's wrong in this country." Her eyes flicked to me, urpening. "We need the stories back."

"I know." And I truly did. "Jaik and I are trying."

And we were. But hearing those desperate few words from Naomi :indled the same resentment that had seethed in me while Jaik and I had ;ued before the skeleton made its appearance in the Casmiss Wood.

It always returned to Storycrafters…our duty to ease life in Mithra-Sha. en Naomi saw it that way.

Stories were tools. How much moreso those who crafted them?

Neither of us spoke for so long, the awkwardness insinuated itself between again. Then Naomi cleared her throat and straightened, tapping her well-mmed nails on the tabletop to draw my attention. "I didn't mean to imply that u're not doing the best you can. It's just such a desperate need."

"I know." The words wrenched from me, half-growl and half-sigh. "But there's nothing I can do while we're here…it would draw too much attention with bounty hunters in the city if I told a story to its end."

"I agree." She glanced toward the closed door across the room. "But, if you'd like to do *something*…"

"I won't turn down the opportunity to be useful."

As if the eagerness in my tone could ever suggest otherwise; I nearly cringed at my own enthusiasm.

But Naomi laughed, pushing back the bench and rising, both hands splayed on the tabletop. "I have some bandages that need washed and folded. Will you help me?"

Heat crowded the corners of my eyes; we might as well have been back at Harrow Hall, one of the countless nights I'd crept inside and helped her tidy up while we traded tales of our days, our exploits, our latest topics in class and even individuals of romantic interest. "If you'll tell me everything you've been up to these last few years."

And she did—with a level of enthusiasm only Naomi Weathers could muster. Alternating between boiling the cloth strips in the herbal water over the fire and folding the mounds of them already dried—depending on which task my shoulder felt better fit for in the moment—I listened raptly to tales of her life in Dalfi.

Between her today, and Jaik last night, I was beginning to enjoy being the one hearing stories rather than speaking them. And how strange, that moments like this were precisely what had stuck my feet to the Spine when I'd wanted to give up walking, all the way on my journey south; notions of sharing cups of bone-broth cocoa and mint cookies with Naomi while we reminisced and laughed and folded laundry and simply lived life together.

"I wondered if I would ever have the chance to do things like this with you again." Naomi echoed my thoughts while we rested after our task. The mound of washed, folded bandages teetered at her side, and we were each on our second cup of cocoa. The milky warmth seeped through me, rendering me just another sleepy complement to the cozy room as I stretched out on one of the lounging sofas beside the door. Naomi sat with her legs curled beneath her in the chair across from me, sipping her drink while she peered out the window.

"I'm glad we had it." I circled my thumbs over the mug's lacquered sides and fought not to remember Jaik's thumbs brushing my skin the same way that morning. "Particularly before we strike off for the Illusionarium."

Anxiety cut across the soft contours of Naomi's face. She sat taller, shifting her weight over her legs, peering at me from beneath heavy brows. "I wish you weren't going, Addie."

"Because it's dangerous?" I teased lightly; I'd always had more of a taste for recklessness than Naomi, which was significant considering I wasn't inherently reckless at all.

"Because it's *strange*." Naomi's quiet retort put to death my humor. "Straightforward danger is one matter. But what you and Jaik can *do* together, and how you're being sought for it…" Shaking her head, she set her mug on the wicker side table. "Sha Lothar is not an unjust ruler. He cares for the people, for the wellbeing of Mithra-Sha. I don't know why he's put out a *bounty* for the pair of you, of all things, but that he has…and that *Galan* is taking it so personally…"

"How do you know him?" A bit more suspicion leaped off my tongue than I'd anticipated; that was twice she'd spoken of the maddened Mithran soldier—and with far more recognition than a mere tale told by Jaik at my bedside.

Naomi sank back slightly against the plush seatback, tracing her thumb over the coin-strung leather band around her ankle. "Galan had…some interest in me when I schooled at Harrow Hall. He was a soldier-in-training, I was a healer-in-training…our paths crossed now and again."

A frown pinched my forehead. "Why didn't I know this?"

"It was a harmless flirtation, at first…and entirely one-sided. He was the precise sort of man I've avoided all my life, the sort I vowed to my mother on her deathbed I'd never marry." She pressed her lips thin. "As we neared graduation, it became far more obsessive. He followed me to and from Harrow Hall. He left threatening notes and frightened a few of my friends. But he was also very accomplished at covering his tracks, so few ever suspected…even my brothers couldn't pin the notes to him, and believe me, they tried."

Just as he'd hidden his trail in Krylan, erasing Storycrafters from the Tailbone City like he'd threatened to do to me.

Nausea bubbled in my throat at the thought of Naomi holding that man's attention; and beneath that, something bitter and heartsick simmered and heaved.

She's been pursued by him. Harassed by him. And yet she'd never told me; my memories before graduation were still free of the shadow of Galan. I could only think of a single reason why that would be.

"Noni," I murmured, "did you hide him from me to protect me? Was he *using* you to try and find his way closer to me?"

Naomi held my gaze for a long moment; then her chin dipped. "I suspect so. Particularly because I don't entirely *remember*...that bit is blurred, too. All I know is that one day, Galan disappeared from Vallanmyre. I have no more memories of him shortly after we graduated."

One shared look told me we both knew why.

Galan had become tangled up with me, somehow. And now it had given him shadowed pathways to slip through, back into good favor—just like he'd told Jaik.

Likely the *Sha's* good favor, given who'd posted the bounty he pursued.

"Do you know what he wanted with me?" The whisper stuck to my lips, hardly louder than a breath.

"I don't. And I'm sorry I can't give you more clarity than that."

"No, it's not your duty to clean up my messes...however many they may be." I offered a small half-smile, tipped my cup—then jerked upright on the sofa when the door opened and Jaik swaggered in.

At first glance, I didn't recognize him; his hair was no longer chestnut, but ink-dark...even his eyebrows and the day-and-a-half of stubble that shadowed his jaw. He wore different clothes than the ones he'd left in that morning—finer, fancier threads better suited to a peddler. And his eyes were a different shade, muddy green rather than rich brown.

"What a day!" he groaned, kicking the door shut and leaning back against it. "Dalfians sure know how to gamble."

"Jaik," I started.

"What did you *do* to yourself?" Naomi spoke over me, shooting to her feet.

"What—this?" He tugged at his gaudy, filigreed sleeve. "Yeah, tell me about it. Sign me up for the next circus troupe."

"What happened?" I set aside my cup and stood, steadying myself with a hand to the swoopbacked sofa when my side pulled uncomfortably. "Did you lose a bet?"

"*Several* bets?" Naomi added.

Scoffing, Jaik ducked his head, popping off the glass lenses over his eyes; when he peered up at us again, it was with his usual—albeit bloodshot—tilled-soil stare. "You ladies have never heard of a *disguise*, have you?"

Comprehension crashed over me, and I studied him more closely—this time, trying to see him with a stranger's perception. He certainly no longer looked the description on the *Wanted* bulletin; and while his face held the same angles and contours as the sketch, that rendering had been recreated from a ecollection. Even if someone looked twice, the change in his coloring would no doubt give them pause.

And a pause was all Jaik would need to slip away.

"You gambled like this all day?" I asked. "And no one recognized you from the notice boards?"

"Not even when I was playing right beneath one in *The Lucky Coin.*" Jaik grinned—then added hastily when I sucked in a breath, "They didn't recognize me, tiger. Trust me, we were playing for coin pots a lot smaller than that bounty, and no one batted an eye."

Naomi folded her arms, cocking one brow. "Impressive."

"I know my way around a gambling table." Jaik fished a small coinpurse from his pocket and lobbed it her way. "That ought to cover it. You get everything I asked for?"

"Rations, clothes, those ridiculous threads," she eyed him up and down a moment, then added more grimly, "a rifle, ammunition, and a set of blades."

My ears crackled and hummed with the echo of the rifleshot that had torn through me. *Twice.* "I didn't know you could shoot."

Jaik ducked his head and shucked off his peddler's vest, but not before I caught his grimace disappearing beneath the high collar.

By the time he reemerged from the tangle of attire, he was smirking again. "What can I say? I'm a farmhand of many talents."

"Apparently." Naomi put out her hand, wiggling her fingers, and Jaik pitched the vest to her as well. "I'll wash these up. If you intend to make more coin, you'll need it again. And, Addie, get out of those clothes, will you? It's been days."

By some sheer force of will, I resisted sniffing at the wrinkled, wide-mouthed fabric bunched over my hurt shoulder. "Fine. I'll need some help."

Jaik breezed past me on his way to the side room, curling in as he passed to breathe against my ear, "Need some help with that hair, too?"

A shudder of heat punched down my spine, and I glared after him as he ducked into the side room—presumably to change.

Naomi glanced between us, lips curling mischievously. But she only said, "Come upstairs. I'll help you."

CHAPTER 37
KNIVES IN THE DARK

*U*ndressing was an awkward affair, even with Naomi's skilled assistance; the contortions it required had my side and shoulder throbbing by the time we'd maneuvered my injured arm into the fresh shirt Naomi fetched for me. It was another of hers that gathered across the clavicles and hugged the upper arms—perfect for access to the wound, but the cold raked my bare shoulders when we returned to the room below.

Jaik had beaten us there, already dressed in sleep clothes: a long shirt over his sleep pants this time, thick and shabby, the sleeves so well-worn they stretched over his scuffed knuckles and dirt-stained hands. I tried not to notice his pants were the same ones from that morning.

I didn't want to think about that morning at all.

"I have a few patients to see to," Naomi said as she snagged her medicine bag from its hook behind the front door. "I shouldn't be home before dark, but there's stew chilling in the side room. Help yourselves."

"Thank you, Noni." The words rushed out of me as I tumbled gingerly into the seat she'd vacated earlier, navigating my limbs until I found a position that neither pulled my side nor set my shoulder twinging.

Jaik glanced up from sorting through the items Naomi had purchased at market that morning, and his gaze lingered on me for a long moment before flicking to her. "Let me know if you hear anything out there."

My blood chilled a bit, and I shivered.

Jaik rose to stoke the hearth, squeezing Naomi's arm in passing—a silent show of gratitude, perhaps. But my heart sank lower at the casual ease between them.

Storymaker have mercy, I wished it all came so easily to *me*.

We were silent when Jaik returned, and he folded aside the clothing, stacked
rations, and then picked up the rifle. Something pinched in my gut at the
ht of him handling it—an odd blend of intrigue and disquiet.

"Jaik," I murmured, "why did you have Naomi purchase that?"

He was silent, still, for a long moment—a sign as clear as script scrawled
ore my face that he would not give me a flippant response.

Absurdly, I wished he would.

"After what just happened in the Casmiss Wood," he said at length, voice
low and husky as when he'd spoken over my sickbed, "I'm not too keen on
ng unarmed. Or barely-armed. Rifles might not do much against Misspoken
nifestations, but Galan bleeds the same as the rest of us."

I swallowed a surge of nausea at the notion of Jaik and Galan with rifles
ined on one another. "But he's a soldier, and you're…"

"A farmhand?" he concluded where I trailed off. "Yeah, I know."

Yet there was something decidedly unlike a farmhand in the meticulous way
oiled that rifle and checked its parts, then loaded ammunition into it.

We were silent while he worked. Then Jaik cleared his throat. "You know
w I told you I've been having nightmares, too."

A casual response floundered on my tongue. I could only nod.

Smoothly, Jaik racked the rifle bolt and set it into place—like he'd done it a
ousand times.

His gaze darted up to meet mine. His chest swelled with a deep breath.
hey're changing." Pushing one hand against his knee, he rose from the sofa.
ately, I've been facing someone down in a hallway I've never seen before in
life, but I could swear I know where it leads. Could swear I know who's
asing me down it, too. And when they attack me…when they shove that blade
o me, now I can look down, and I'm…" It was his turn to swallow, harsh and
ift. "I'm wearing a soldier's uniform."

Chills raked up my shoulders like filthy hands, raising the hair on my body
d my hackles at the same time. I gaped at him, lost for words.

"Yeah," he muttered, tugging a hand through his hair. "Could be
thing…could just be my head trying to make sense of Galan. But, Audra…I
ear to you, I know how to use this thing." He gave the rifle a jolt in his hand.
nd I don't remember ever picking one up before."

The knife and rope in his pack. The way he'd tussled Galan for his weapon
Krylan. Even the way he'd defended us from the deranged soldier when their

paths had crossed while I wrestled my own death in the Casmiss Wood, slashin his face so precisely...

Jaik Grissom was more than a farmhand. I'd always felt that in him, alway speculated it, from the first night he'd helped us escape from the Tailbone City

But why was that *speculation*? What else didn't we know about ourselves— about each other?

I buried my face in my hands. "I hate this. I hate that everything is so tangled up and *nonsense*."

"You and me both, tiger." Breathlessness touched his laughter, and the rifl stock audibly tapped the floor. When I lifted my head, I found Jaik standing before me, hand offered. "Maybe it'll make more sense in the morning."

An empty hope—but I needed something to hold onto. So I took his han

We made our way slowly up the steps, my arms laden with his lighter purchases, his fingers grazing my elbow to support me when my muscles tightened in silent protest at the ascent. Once in the room, he leaned the rifle against the washbasin and went to the chair, where he motioned me to bring th clothing and rations.

I did, setting them aside and then sliding under the covers. The mattress settled audibly when Jaik kicked his heels up on its edge; in the pronounced silence afterward, his stomach growled so loudly he jumped and cursed.

A smile crept over my mouth. "You can go find food. I'm not going to be exciting...I'm going to be asleep."

"Yeah, I know." Wood creaked as he repositioned himself. "But I want to make sure you get to sleep all right. Until then, I'm not going anywhere."

Four simple words. Words I had craved from so many people, that I'd wanted to hear for so long I couldn't even put it to true time. It should have thrilled me to hear them. Should have made me feel safe.

Instead, dread spilled through me, sickly and blighted and fever-hot.

I did not sleep after that. I huddled with my back to Jaik and stared at the wall, heart thundering, bowels weak with fear.

He kept his word; he didn't leave.

And somehow, that made me more unsettled than if he'd abandoned me i the dark.

CHAPTER 38
A TERRIBLE AND BEAUTIFUL THING

Jaik's words haunted me all through the night. They plagued me during my frequent wakes and chased me from the room while he still slumbered well before dawn. Padding downstairs, I stoked the hearth and curled myself on the sofa, rubbing my temples, struggling to *think*.

I couldn't make sense of my thoughts; how long had I yearned for people like my parents and siblings and Naomi to tell me they wouldn't leave me? Yet hearing those words spoken aloud set my nerves rioting and introduced a vicious panic that crackled in my veins like the flames in the flue.

Not only was I forgettable...to be bonded to me was to *be* forgotten. Galan and Jaik both were proof of that. And now Jaik was casting aside his life's own pursuits to travel with me to the Illusionarium...a place scripted into being with the darkest Storycraft. A place where all stories, good and ill, went to lose themselves. He would throw himself headlong into that danger because of *me*. And a plow to the chest might be the least of all the scars he ever wore afterward...if he survived at all.

The notion of Jaik cut down on the Isle of Misspoken Stories freed sharp-clawed terror that raked my throat. He wanted to come along because he cared for me; but because I cared for him, too, I had to find a way to stop this.

He'd changed his appearance already, to go gambling at *The Lucky Coin* the day before...and he'd succeeded. No bounty hunters or soldiers lurked at the door while I pulled apart my thoughts like parchment stripped at the seams.

Jaik didn't draw the same gazes I did. He never had. So he could stay here, in Dalfi. Rebuild his life...perhaps even with Naomi, if he stayed long enough to get to know the brilliant friend I'd loved for so much of my life. He could be anonymous and discreet and *happy*.

And I could carry on to the Illusionarium alone. I wouldn't have to put his life in danger anymore.

Simple. Sensible.

My heart would shatter.

It had to be done.

And I had to do it now, before things worsened. I had to part with him on good terms, while he still thought well of me, before my neediness in this wounded state convinced him to come along out of charity. Before he talked himself into coming to my rescue…and got himself killed for it.

Another thought, equally as disturbing, joined the churn in my racing mind: perhaps my needs would have the opposite effect entirely. Perhaps he was already tiring of aiding me up and down the stairs and helping me accomplish mundane tasks like tying back my hair. Perhaps those things would do the work for me, and he'd walk away himself.

The notion absolutely strangled me.

No. I had to do this—separate us out of strength, not weakness.

And then, perhaps, if Luck flipped the coin just once more in my favor, Jail would let me return and tell him whatever I discovered in Erasure.

It was a struggle to behave normally while the three of us shared a silent breakfast of maple-cinnamon porridge; while Naomi told us of her work the previous day, and the state of her patients as we laundered Jaik's new threads and prepared meals for ourselves and the widows, widowers, and orphans Naomi saw to—those whose loved ones she had not been able to save.

My silence weighed heavy on my tongue; I didn't know what to say. And even had the proper words occurred to me, I almost preferred my own quiet. I waited for one of them to notice what was simmering beneath my surface. To ask if I was all right.

Neither of them did. And absurd as it was, that ignorance transformed my heartache to fury by the day's end.

I retreated upstairs the moment supper was finished and the dishes put away—my conscience wouldn't allow me to leave them burdened with the mess, even if I couldn't spare them my scowl. Still, it was a breathtaking blend of relief and misery to be by myself in the room, to breathe of the silence and fight to calm my churning insides.

Somehow, the whole painful day made the thought of carrying on alone to the Illusionarium more palatable; a nasty voice told tales in my head as I washed my face, banged the window shut, and threw down the mound of pillows that separated the two halves of the bed.

If so little about me was worth noticing, would they even notice I was gone? Could I spare the entire conversation and slip away unseen?

It would be simple enough. I'd done it in Vallanmyre.

A boldness born of hurt scathed the back of my throat, guiding me to plan precisely how I'd do it—how I'd leave unnoticed. And I was still fabricating the notion in my head, telling the story to myself of my deft potential to disappear, when the door creaked open and footsteps brushed the bare wood floor.

"All right." Jaik shut the door and sacked his weight against it, arms folded. "So. You ready to tell me what I did wrong?"

Heat rushed to my head so potently my temples throbbed. "You didn't do anything *wrong*, Jaik."

"Really? Because the way you've been acting today feels like the silent punishment I'd get from my sisters after I told them their clothes looked ridiculous."

In the span of a single heartbeat, all but a slim sliver of my fury and determination peeled away. What remained was a depthless blend of embarrassment and shame.

So, he *had* noticed. And what a fool I must look like…immature and childish in the extreme. Here I was, saddled with all the power of crafting words into life-changing tales, and yet I couldn't make use of them to convey my own struggles like a reasonable, grown woman.

When I found my voice again, it was little more than a croak. "I'm tired, that's all."

"Mmhmm." His arms tightened in their cross. "Except I've *seen* you tired…so tired you could barely keep putting one foot in front of the other, climbing up and down the foothills in the Drennans. This isn't tired, Audra. What's wrong?"

Vulnerability tore me wide open, swifter and sharper than Galan's rifleshot. "Nothing is wrong." I put my back to him, if only to spare what little dignity hadn't been consumed by the fire raging across my face. "I just want to sleep."

"You really expect me to accept that?" Callouses scraped scalp—Jaik towing his hand back through his hair. I could envision his agitated grimace without even risking a glance. "You've got to explain this one to me. First you spend half the morning clammed up, looking at me like you're waiting for me to start a conversation. Then, when I do, you're *glacial.* Now you storm off to bed the second dinner's cleaned up, and you want me to believe that was just you acting *normal?*"

Bile climbed my throat. I wished I could curl into a wad of flesh so small no one would ever see it again.

"Well, I'm here," he said when I didn't speak. "So, say what you want to say."

I steeled my jaw and shut my eyes.

It was now, or never.

"I'm going to the Illusionarium alone."

The words emerged stronger than I'd expected. Nearly devoid of any of the doubt that writhed beneath my skin.

Jaik was quiet for several long moments. Then his feet shifted audibly on the floorboards. "That's insane, and you know it."

"It's not. The Isle is dangerous, and you've put yourself through enough."

"Yeah? And how is it *you're* going to reach that tower without any stories to tell?"

"I'll sneak."

"Audra…"

"I don't *want* you to come with me, Jaik."

There was the faintest stagger in the next breath he drew. But somehow, he kept his calm when he said, "First you *capture* me to make me come with you. Now you're trying to shrug me off into a city where my *Wanted* bulletins are strung up everywhere?" His hair brushed his collar—I could envision the slow shake of his head. "Help me make sense out of this, tiger. Are you trying to spare me, here, or are you throwing me to the dogs?"

I could muster no retort for that.

"We both need answers. We both decided we were willing to take the risk." Jaik's tone sharpened with every word. "We decided that *days* ago, and now you think the best way to get those answers is for you to just take off on your own?

at changed—that I can wield a rifle? What, am I too much like *Galan* for
?"

Disbelief ripped me back around to face him swifter than a hand wrenching
shoulder. "How can you even ask me that? You two are *nothing* alike!"

"What am I supposed to think?" Jaik tossed his hands up, anger and some
otion I couldn't quite name warring through his eyes. "Yesterday, things were
e. Today, you're treating me like dead weight. And the only thing I can think
that changed was our conversation last night! So help me understand,
dra…what do you *want* from me?"

Guilt punched a shout from me. "I want you to leave, Jaik!"

He stiffened, but he didn't fling back a retort; for a long moment, he simply
red at me, the tension rolling out of him, his chin lifting slightly—a look so
p and intent, I wanted to cower from it.

Then he said, simply, "No, you don't."

Indignation stole the air from my lungs. "Excuse me?"

"You *don't* want me to leave." Jaik crossed the room to stand before me,
s narrowing, voice pitched low. "But you think I'm going to anyway, right? So
're trying to beat me to the punch…get the upper hand. Be the one who
lks away instead of the one who gets left behind."

Fresh heat flared in my cheeks. "I'm not…that is *not* what this is about! I'm
ncerned for your *life*, Jaik—"

"I know you are. But that's not what we're discussing *here*." He stabbed a
ger at the narrow gap between our feet. "This, right here, this fight…this is
cause you know I'm *with you*, and after all these years alone on the Spine, you
n't know what to do with that. You don't think you can trust it, so you're
ing to shove it off before it hurts you."

The room swam and sparkled along the corners. My eyes heated, and I
rdly felt the twinge in my shoulder when I thrust my hands onto my hips,
ing him with a glare. "You're being ridiculous."

"Yeah?" He slanted his head. "So, tell me your life wouldn't make more
nse if I said I was done, and I turned around and walked out that door."

My fingers spasmed, tightening on my waist.

Nothing in my life made sense anymore. Not the person I was or the things
ould do. Not the people who had forgotten me or why they remembered now.
t the way my stories and my heart knew Jaik, though sense told me we hadn't
t before that tavern in Krylan. And certainly not how I felt, knowing I had

Naomi back, and that my parents had searched for me…and knowing they might forget again, because I didn't know why they had forgotten at all.

It was terrifying, that Jaik had drawn his line in the sand. Because my family had done the same…and then they'd slammed the door in my face. And I had survived that, and survived Naomi's threats and her slamming the door, too.

I wasn't certain I could endure the same from him.

And I couldn't want him so desperately to stay, and beg for him to leave in the same breath. How could any one person be such a mess of contradictions? And how could such a mess ever be deserving of the friendship he and Naomi had shown me?

"I'm sorry," I choked, and Jaik's eyes widened a fraction. "I'm sorry I'm so fickle and needy and *desperate*. And I'm sorry that I don't know how to *want* you to stay, so the easier way is just to do this alone."

I was saying *far* too much, baring far too much of my raw heart to him. Tying myself to him in ways that would rip me apart when he was gone, however he left and whenever it happened. But I couldn't seem to stop, now that the words were escaping.

"No one wants this." I gestured down the length of my body, and this time Jaik's brows crashed down. "No one *wants* a life like this—hunted by men like Galan, running from the *Sha,* going somewhere they're almost certain to die. And I'm afraid if you stay with me like you promised, you're going to realize it, too, and you'll walk away when I least expect it, when I…"

When I need you most.

Jaik stepped forward, snagging my wrists and tugging my hands off my hips. He brought them together before me in the grip of one fist; then his free fingers slid under my chin until I found the strength to lift my head and meet his gaze.

"Audra, I need you to hear this, all right?" His voice was rough, but not unkind; passion girded every word. "I'm not going anywhere. You can't scare me off…not with being on the run, not with those Misspoken nightmares or your Storycrafting power…not with whatever is going on in this country. You hear me? I don't scare easy." He snorted a laugh, tucking a wayward strand of hair behind my ear. "*You* don't scare me, tiger."

The sob that burst from me blew apart every wall I'd erected to keep me safe since Vallanmyre. Jaik's words poured through the breach, washing over me like the tide that broke the dam—a wave of roaring force that knocked me off

ay feet. I buckled forward, and his hand wound into the hair at the back of my
ead, pulling my face into his collar.

And I leaned against him, hands fisted in his shirt, and I wept.

For my parents, who had forgotten me, and remembered—and feared for
ne.

For Naomi, who I'd lost, and found again—and still had to walk away
rom.

For Jaik, tangled up in this by no fault of his own—and adrift in this
vilderness with me.

For myself. I cried for *myself*, for the awful wretchedness that I could no
onger ignore, that horrible tugging between the safety of loneliness and the
nguish of being seen, and wanted, and *held* like this.

What a terribly beautiful thing it was, to be cared for…knowing so many
hings could change that forever.

And then I cried for the road ahead—for the unknown, for the danger that
vas certain, for the pain of knowing we had to go, anyway. That it was my duty
o go. And I cried for the relief that despite my faults, I would not travel by
nyself to the place of haunted tales and nightmares shared among the students
it Fablehaven.

I cried out the fear of men like Galan, of bounty hunters and skeletons and
hunting hounds. I cried over every little thing I'd stuffed away for so long so that
I could move forward. So that I could keep myself from shattering on the long
road I'd walked alone.

Here in the quiet, in Jaik's embrace, I *did* shatter. But I didn't fall apart…he
held the pieces gently, cradled them as carefully as he cradled me. His fingers
tangled into my hair, his other arm looped over my waist, his chin brushing my
temple as he murmured quietly into my ear.

"Hey, hey. You're all right, Audra. I'm right here. Let go, it's fine, I've got
this—I'm here."

I'm here. I'm here. I'm here.

Somehow, that was true. Despite my fickle, flighty heart.

It would take some time to trust that. But tonight, Jaik held me when he
could have walked away. And that was more than enough.

It was something to believe in.

CHAPTER 39
THE SOLDIER RETURNS

The days were short and cold in Dalfi, the sky carved the sort of chilly, rich blue that only the coldest months of late winter could bring. So it was no surprise that Jaik spent much of our recuperative week gambling, gathering coins for thicker cloaks, sturdier boots, and the sort of smothering, wooly socks that begged to be worn in front of the hearth.

That was where I spent a great deal of *my* time—helping Naomi with her work, bottling tinctures and sorting out medicines, and building a route by my map through the Drennans to the bay at Fallshyre. And while we worked, we unraveled years of our lives, prodding at the edges of that odd, dreamlike time between graduation and the day when stories had sundered.

Or at least, when I'd become aware they had.

Life was a tangible contradiction; though mind and memory insisted we had seen little of each other since we'd left our separate academies, that we might have drifted apart, even, my heart refused to believe it. And so did hers.

Another contradiction unmasked itself like Luck's turning face as the days wore on: I did not want to leave the warm, quiet domesticity of Naomi's home. I didn't want to walk away from my friend again. Yet there was a disquiet that breathed beneath the surface of every meal, that punctuated the silences of our days spent at work together.

Naomi Weathers had lived years of her life that I was not part of…not even as a thought, not as a fleeting figment spared a nod while she went about her days. Suitors had come and gone, men whose names I had never heard; new friendships had been forged which she spoke of with gleaming eyes and reminiscent smiles. She had confidants and close relations who she turned away during our stay, feigning busyness or contact with a plagued patient to avoid anyone learning of the fugitives calling her bedroom their refuge.

Naomi and I did not fit into one another's lives as seamlessly as we used to. And there was a part of me that yearned to be away from the constant, aching reminder of that.

I beat a cowardly retreat from another strained silence after our conversations lulled one afternoon; and for the first time in our whole stay, I made my way outdoors instead of back to the room.

Naomi's roof was hatched, like many in Dalfi; the small door, fitted into the ceiling above a short flight of steps at the end of the upper hall, gave way to a flat span jutting up among the angles of the roof itself. The railing was low, the rooftop sparsely decorated except for the many planters where Naomi grew her own herbs in the warmer months. Most were empty now, only a few pots of brave, cold-hardy plants framing the corners of the rooftop, shedding their crisp scent over the bare wood when I shouldered free and pulled myself up onto the beams.

I was not alone.

Jaik lounged in the center of the roof, arms banding his knees loosely, head craned back to gaze up at the nearest tethered airship, only two buildings away. We were cast in its shadow, steepening the chill when I shut the hatch and came to join him.

"I thought you'd left for *The Lucky Coin*," I remarked, balancing my hand on his shoulder while I settled cross-legged at his side. The motions twinged far less than they had in days, and while my arm remained stiff, Naomi assured me that would heal in time.

Jaik shrugged, and I let my hand slide away. "Believe it or not, gambling gets old after a while. It's a lot of playing a part...telling a story." He flashed me a crooked smirk. "Don't know how you Storycrafters manage it, day in and day out."

"As if we do. You've seen how often I've told stories since we left Krylan."

"That's fair." He leaned his head back, dye-darkened hair swept away from his eyes by the angle as he gazed up at the belly of the airship.

A memory flashed to mind—his tired ramblings about these airships. His hands cradling mine.

Warmth churned in my middle, and I tilted toward him, dropping my voice to a conspiratorial whisper. "How long do you think it would take us to reach the coast aboard one of *those*?"

Jaik scoffed. "The *coast?* We could ride one straight to the Illusionarium…two weeks, tops."

I had to admit, the thought was as tantalizing as it was utterly impossible. To be there and done, without another month of travel at least ahead of us…it would have dulled the edge of mounting panic that was certain to sharpen while we rode.

But it was also wonderful to have all that time to prepare before we confronted the Isle of Misspoken Stories.

I nudged my shoulder against Jaik's. "Couldn't you have had the decency to befriend a sky-sailor instead of a common shipman?"

"Ha." He nudged me right back. "Trouble is, sky-sailors are a rowdy, self-absorbed bunch of skinflints. Don't think I could have gambled enough coin to pay off even one of them…and that's if they *weren't* in the Sha's back pocket. We'd be buying their silence as much as our passage, and at that point, we'd have to turn in our own bounties just to afford the voyage."

"I know," I sighed. "Airships are such a commodity, Sha Lothar almost has to be selfish with them."

"I'd have a lot more sympathy for him if I didn't know he put out a bounty on my head." Jaik ruffled a hand over his hair, then twisted to peer at me. "How are you feeling?"

"Better." And that was the truth—not only for my wounds. Though we hadn't broached the matter again since my emotions had erupted all over him, something had lightened considerably in me with Jaik's vow to remain at my side. Though it required near-constant prompting on my part, my heart was slowly beginning to accept that we *were* in this together, come what may.

"That's good." Jaik's head bobbed slowly, his gaze drifting skyward again. "We should be on the move soon."

I sighed. "I'm as ready as I could ever be."

"So am I. I figure maybe one more gambling session, and then—"

The slam of a fist on a door below—*Naomi's* door—sent us both jolting up from our seats. With one swift glance at Jaik, I bolted for the edge of the rooftop, sliding down in a crouch to peer down into the street.

There was no band of Mithran soldiers or armored bounty hunters gathered outside her home; only a lone man, slumped against the entry frame, raising his fist to pound again.

But I knew him. Knew his build even when he wasn't looming above me, eatening violence. Knew the shock of red hair peeking from the edge of his turned hood.

My heart plummeted, and I rolled onto my back just as Jaik reached me; he mbled, sliding down on his knees, straddling my hips and planting his hands either side of my head to keep from pitching over the rooftop's edge.

"*Galan*," I hissed.

Jaik's palms struck the wood paneling silently beside my ears; then he reared ck, snagging my good hand when I offered it, hauling me to my feet.

Flighty and silent as shadows, we descended back into Naomi's home; she et us in the stairwell, eyes rounded with despair.

"It's Galan." Jaik's grim announcement was half-buried under the next lley of ferocious knocking. Galan must still be wounded, or else he would've oken down the door already.

"I know." Naomi's tone was equally grim; when her eyes landed on me, she ifted her weight, peeled back her shoulders, and set her jaw. "Both of you, go to the supply room...it's the only one I can lock from outside. I'll do what I n to deter him."

"Noni, wait!" I snagged her wrist as she turned back down the steps. Three of us can manage him. You don't have to face him alone."

Her harasser. Her obsessor. The man who'd haunted her life for years, ying to reach *me*.

Naomi's gaze softened, but her grip was pure steel when it covered mine, rying my fingers off. "Even back in Vallanmyre, you always made my enemies ur enemies. But this one put holes in you I was just barely talented enough to ose." Pain shuttered the brightness in her eyes. "Let me fight for you, for once, ddie."

Then she was gone, scurrying down the stairs; my feet did not unlock to llow her until Jaik gave me a shove, and I had no choice but to descend the eps and bolt for the room where she kept her bandages and tinctures and dried erbs—the door off to the side of the main room.

We slipped inside, and Jaik shut the door behind us. The seam was just ide enough to catch a glimpse of Naomi securing the latch with a twist of her rist and then pivoting to bark at the pounding on the front door, "I'm oming!" She paused to dunk her hair in the water barrel beside the hearth; then he scurried to the front door, undoing the locks and chains across it, calling as he worked, "Patience...*patience!* You caught me washing my hair!"

My teeth snapped together; I didn't want Galan thinking of Naomi bathing Maker have mercy, I didn't want him breathing the same *air* as her.

But it was too late for all the things I didn't want; the front door raked open, and Galan barged in—not dressed like a soldier, but like a woodland hunter. A *bounty* hunter. And that dark attire was rusted with long-dried blood; sash of makeshift bandages, equally stained, hung across the slant of his face.

"*Galan Fiordona?*" Naomi's surprise was almost believable; but I knew her well enough not to mistake the lilt in her voice for startlement. She'd poured her rage, not her shock, into the vaulting syllables of his name. "What in Luck's flipping *coin* are *you* doing here?"

"Not here for your company, obviously." He shouldered past her into the warm room. "I would think even a healer who won her title through her father' connections would recognize a *wound* when she sees one."

Naomi pivoted after him, her hands curling into fists at her sides; mine mimicked, imagining themselves around Galan's throat.

"I don't understand," Naomi snapped. "What are you doing *here?*"

"You're still considered a healer, aren't you?" He shucked off his shirt and dropped straight-backed onto the bench seat of her table. "*Heal this.*"

Every muscle in my body coiled tight; it was his *face* that was wounded, not his torso. He had no reason to be disrobing before her.

But Naomi was ever the professional; she gathered a bowl of herbal water, cloth, and tinctures. Her frame flickered in and out of the narrow gap…but not his. I was as riveted on Galan as he was on Naomi—and abruptly, viciously conscious that she had likely ushered us into this room, not only for our safety, but to keep us from lashing out on her behalf.

She was determined to manage him alone.

Jaik's hand pressed the door beside my head, all his weight bearing into his arm as he loomed behind me, and I swiveled halfway toward him; I didn't dare speak, but I flicked my gaze from the seam back to him in silent question.

Could he break through, if Galan proved too much of a threat?

Jaik measured the door with his eyes, studied the hinges for a heartbeat; then he offered a clipped nod.

The pressure in my chest eased a bit; I turned back to peer through the gap

Naomi deposited her tools on the table, then took up position before Galan, unwinding the bandage lashed around his head. Her positioning was flawless, affording us a glimpse of his face.

A glimpse of the damage Jaik had dealt him.

All Mithran soldiers received instruction in triage—it was necessary for times of peace as well as times of war. But it was likely Galan had spent more of those lessons fixated on the healer before him than the skills being taught; his wound was an ugly, brutal mess of jagged flesh held together by rough black stitching. Somehow, Jaik had missed blinding him entirely; but he'd raked through the left brow, across the bend of the nose and into the fleshiness beneath the eyesocket, down the right cheekbone and all the way to the jaw.

He puffed a soft breath of bitter satisfaction that stirred my hair, even as nausea churned my gut; the swollen, oozing mess of marred skin was a sight I would never be rid of.

"How did this happen?" Naomi demanded, fingertips hovering at the edge of the wound with an appropriate amount of feigned intrigue.

"Luck flipped its coin on a losing bet."

Jaik's next breath was a scoff. I barely restrained myself from throwing an elbow into his ribs.

"Hmm." Naomi retrieved a thin blade meant for snipping sutures; she'd threatened me in jest with them so often, I could have wielded them myself. "I would say this has the look of a knife wound."

"It was Jaik Grissom."

My breath caught. Naomi hesitated for a heartbeat.

It was a tactical blow—one intended to unbalance. To trawl Naomi's depths and uncover just how much she knew.

Galan suspected we were here.

CHAPTER 40
FESTERING HATE

I jerked back from the door by sheer instinct, and Jaik's arm snagged around my waist, halting me. A strange sense of safety barreled through my body at that one-armed embrace. It cleared my head enough to watch as Naomi carefully set about removing Galan's self-inflicted stitches.

"Jaik Grissom," she said slowly. "I feel as if I should know that name. *You* clearly think I should."

"You don't remember him?"

"Vaguely."

"Well, it was him." Galan fitted his palms backhand to the table's edge, heels grinding in, fingers braced to the underside. "Him, and Audra Jashowin."

This time, Naomi's ministrations snagged to a stop.

"You want to know what I'm doing here, when we haven't seen one another in years?" Galan growled. "I was out there in the Casmiss Wood, tracking the two of them. I caught them up…and I shot her. Straight through the belly, like an animal."

Jaik's breath stopped; that silence was all I heard for a moment over the roaring in my ears.

"Is that so." Naomi's tone remained level as she resumed her work—a healer's practiced calm.

"It sure is. And she was a bleeder."

"I wouldn't know." Naomi turned for her materials, and Galan snagged her chin in the cradle of his hand—a hand I knew best manning a rifle, aimed at my head. My belly. My shoulder.

I sagged a bit; Jaik's arm tightened around my waist.

"I know you remember *her*." Galan's voice was a pain-harshened rasp. "Because *I* remember the pair of you...an arrogant Storycrafter and her sniveling, sycophantic friend." His fingers visibly tightened, shadows sprawling from the indents they made on Naomi's skin. "And somehow, that never made you any less enticing."

Hatred set my blood simmering.

Naomi didn't even flinch; she held Galan's stare steadily. "Why are you wasting what little excuse for a life you have on finding her?"

Galan's eyes narrowed. "You don't even remember what she did, do you?"

"Do *you*?"

"I remember *enough*." Galan shoved her aside by the jaw, and Naomi's head snapped right back to meet his bared-toothed glare. "I remember the contention back in those academy days, when you two were at Harrow Hall and Fablehaven. When Storycrafters called soldiers *footmen* and *footstools*. I remember that swollen, self-obsessed little girl who ground my face into the dirt for a few cheers. And I remember spending every day, year after year, planning how to make an example of her."

Jaik's arm tightened sharply around my waist, towing me back a bit from the door—as if he could defend me from the ruthless intentions of a far younger Galan.

My mind struggled to make sense of his memories. It was true that Storycrafters and soldiers had been at odds during my years at the Academy; some of the commanders had feared the Sha was placing far too much faith in Storycraft to fight his battles for him, particularly with tension brewing between our country and Amere-Del.

During that time, I'd had my share of scrapes with soldiers-in-training, boys and girls who'd come to the Fablehaven grounds to taunt us, to pick fights because they *knew* we were forbidden to use our Storycraft for sparring...and they held all the advantage with their weapons in varied encounters.

I'd been disciplined by the headmistress at Fablehaven a handful of times for proving with my power what Storycrafters were capable of...but not a single one of those encounters had made an impression in my mind. They all blurred into a single streak of vicious insults, the jeers of my schoolmates, the slap of blood on the courtyard cobblestones, the sizzle of power in my veins.

Was Galan truly so weak a man, so insecure, that being bested by a Storycrafter as a boy had twisted itself into this lifelong grudge against all of us—against *me* in particular?

"Well," Naomi's taut, furious voice dragged me from my shocked reverie, back to the quiet room and the door looming dark before me—separating me from my dearest friend and the man who loathed me with undying passion. "Then I suppose you feel particularly proud you exacted your vengeance in the Casmiss Wood, don't you?"

Wood creaked as Galan shifted. "Not how I'd always intended it, but I won't lie…it was ecstasy."

This time, Jaik's weight barreled forward, not back; I hardly had time to swivel in his hold and press my hand to his chest, thrusting him away before he reached the seam in the door.

"*Enough*," I mouthed.

His furious gaze pinned to mine; my breaths hitched, but I held his stare, shaking my head until the rigor in his muscled chest eased. After a long moment, he nodded, and I swiveled so I could peer through the seam again.

Naomi was tending Galan still, but I read the tale told in every sharp maneuver of her fingers, dabbing and swabbing and rinsing his wounded face. Nevermind the rage that darkened her features. Neither of them said anything more until she retrieved a needle and sutures—the very ones I'd boiled that morning.

I almost wished I hadn't…I wouldn't have minded being the cause of Galan's weeping, bleeding, infected face.

Naomi threaded the needle, her back to Galan, guiding the suture by the firelight; and even at such a narrow angle, the hungry manner of his stare was blatant, observing the curves of her body.

"I know that *you* know where they are," he said at last, so softly I nearly missed the words. "She would have run off to you. She always did."

Jaik and I both stiffened; Naomi didn't so much as twitch.

"What you think you know of us doesn't change what *I* know," she said, "which is that I haven't seen Audra Jashowin in years."

"He was riding this way."

Naomi swiveled back to him with a shrug. "Perhaps they found aid elsewhere, or they were waylaid…they never reached my door, that's all I can say for certain." She advanced on him, laying one hand to his cheek, bracing the needle tip against his freshly-rinsed skin—and then she paused. "But ask yourself this, Officer Fiordona…do you truly want a woman near your eyes with a needle if you murdered her dearest friend?"

He snagged her wrist, staying the first stitch. "I'll ruin you."

"Please," she scoffed. "You're a pathetic, incompetent man who's built his
ire life's pursuit off a single humiliation from a schoolgirl. A girl who needed
weapons to best a *soldier-in-training*." With a deft swivel, she freed her wrist
m his grasp. "The only thing you have ever succeeded in ruining is yourself. I
r a common cold more than I fear you."

His teeth gritted in a wordless snarl, and he surged upright, forcing her back
h the sheer breadth of his soldiering brawn. "Then you won't mind if I search
s home your father *gifted* to you?"

"If you have the proper papers, signed by the local city watch, then, no."
omi regarded him steadily, but the way she clutched that needle in her fist
de it seem more a weapon than a healing tool. "Despite your grudge, despite
ur *lust*, you are still a soldier of Mithra-Sha. And I am a citizen and a healer
h rights of my own. So, you're welcome to search every inch of my
me…once you return with the city's approval."

Galan bent toward her, and Jaik nudged me aside, hands braced on the
orframe—ready to kick it down, break the lock, and lunge to Naomi's aid.

Though Galan didn't strike Naomi—he whipped a hand past her instead,
zed a handful of bandages, and snapped them loose from the pile—the swift
t of those movements achieved precisely what he'd intended.

Naomi flinched.

"This city is crawling with healers," Galan hissed, so near her face she
inkled her nose at his breath. "Plenty of them who *earned* their merit, rather
in inheriting it from their well-connected fathers. I'll have my face seen to
ere…and *you*, I will be seeing with papers in hand."

He strode to the front door, wrenched it open, then glanced back, tapping
e finger on its polished edge.

"You're right that I'm a soldier. And soldiers aid their own. So I'll have eyes
 this place until I return."

He slammed the door so hard the whole frame of the house rattled—a
iver that echoed the one crawling along my bones.

I gripped the door handle around Jaik's hip and shook it. "Noni. Let us
t."

No answer; only an audible, tremulous inhale.

"Naomi!" Her name cracked in my mouth. "Let us *out*, right now!"

"Don't make me break down this door!" Jaik's tone sharpened with
irtling ferocity. "*Naomi!*"

"Just *give me a moment!*" she snapped back; but every word shook, and my need to reach her poured through me like a tipped inkwell, spidering into the cracks of my composure.

"Noni, *please*—"

The lock rattled and unjammed, and the moment the door swung open, I surged forward, wrapping my arms around Naomi; hers enveloped me in turn, and for a long moment, neither of us spoke, or broke the embrace. Naomi leaned into me, and I stroked her hair; Jaik dodged around us, locking the front door, drawing the curtains.

"He's so much worse than I remembered," Naomi choked out at last. "He been festering like an infection all this time, Addie."

"He's sick in the head," Jaik growled.

I darted a glance at him over Naomi's shoulder. "Do you remember him yet?"

"No." Jaik leaned his back to the door, dragging a hand down his face. "And I don't like that."

Neither did I; because it suggested that I had been wrong, in what I had dismissed so eagerly before. What I couldn't bear to look at any closer, because was the greatest, most confusing mystery of all.

It likely meant that Jaik's memories of Galan were somehow bound up in memories of *me*.

CHAPTER 41
EITHER ONE A WIN

It was nearly an hour before Naomi stopped shaking. Jaik sat with her on the sofa while I steeped the herbal packs, his low voice guiding her through the same tactics he'd taught me: helping her name things around herself, to attune to her senses. She was far calmer when I finally sat at her side, pressed tightly together on the sofa. Jaik took the chair facing us, turning his teacup slowly in his hands.

"So," he muttered, "no leaving the house."

Naomi shivered, and I shot him a glower. He rolled his shoulders in a haphazard shrug.

"Jaik is right," Naomi mumbled. "Galan likely caught the ear of every soldier he passed on his way to Dalfi's watchtower. The pair of you won't be able to set foot outside without being spotted."

I'd been thinking about that while I brewed the tea; the notion no longer made me shake as it had while I'd stoked the fire and added the herb sachets to our cups.

Every single problem in all of Mithra-Sha had a solution; I'd been solving my own for years, with no one else to rely on. Now there were three of us, and I'd meant what I'd told Naomi: together, we were more than a match for Galan.

We didn't have to outshoot him. We had to *outthink* him.

Staring at the door where Galan had made his abrupt departure, I gave over to a notion that had prickled at the back of my mind while I'd stood at the hearth, listening to Jaik guide Naomi back to calm. "I have an idea how we can evade him."

Jaik paused with the cup of tea halfway to his mouth. "Love to hear it.

"He already suspects we're here in Dalfi. He's looking for *one* Storycrafter with the power to finish a tale…and an amplifier who makes it possible."

Jaik's brows tugged together, reading the precise enunciation of my words. "You want to give him more than one Storycrafter with that power."

I couldn't help a smile, hearing my own thoughts from his mouth. "Galan i a miserable, life-leaching roach. Fear is his greatest weapon…so we outwit him with something more powerful than fear."

"Hope," Naomi whispered. "And joy."

I pointed at her around both edges of my cup. "Precisely. Do you know anywhere in Dalfi where Storycrafters might congregate?"

As one, they chorused, "Cathedrals."

"I played against a few of them at *The Lucky Coin*," Jaik explained. "Most were on their way there or just coming back."

"It's the tradition," Naomi added. "More Storycrafters than anyone else lay coins at the feet of Luck's two-faced statue. They're desperate for something to change their fate."

"Something is about to." Determination mounting, I set aside my mug. "Here's what we'll do: Jaik and I will creep out and make a show of running for the hills. When Galan's friends catch us, that will leave you free, Naomi…you can run to the cathedral and bring the Storycrafters to the watchtower. "

"And then?" she prodded, lowering her cup as well.

I winked at Jaik. "That's a story that will tell itself."

Jaik didn't match my grin; the slant of his brow and set of his mouth were troubled. "I like it, but it's missing something."

"It's that you're both going to be in Galan's hands." Naomi rubbed her upper arms. "And he clearly does not let go easily. I'm not certain even the distraction of a dozen or more Storycrafters will be enough to keep his eyes off of you two."

Some of my excitement guttered, the edges roughening with irritation. "What else can we do? Any way out of this is a risk."

"Right," Jaik said. "Which is why I'm not opposed to the plan. But how about this: Naomi's got to have some solution in here that can strip the color out of hair, the same as the dye soaks it in. So let's have her stand in for you."

Horror unhinged my jaw, but Naomi was already nodding. "Galan likely told his lackeys to be on the lookout for a man and woman leaving the house together…I doubt if he'll have taken time to describe you both in detail. With the proper attire and hair color, and if I carry myself as if I'm wounded…"

"That won't work!" My tone vaulted frantically at the notion of Naomi slipping back into Galan's grip. "Galan knows your face even better than mine."

"But it isn't him we need to fool. It's the soldiers working with him." Jaik sipped from his cup, then bent forward, elbows on his knees, twisting the porcelain idly between his hands. "And we only need to do *that* long enough to buy you time to get out of the house and to the cathedrals."

"And what if it fails?" I demanded.

Jaik's eyes anchored to mine, resolute and steady. "Then I go wherever they take me, and you get out and get to the Illusionarium. Either way, I win—because you're safe from him."

Dizzying heat swarmed my face, and I hid it behind a deep slug of tea.

"You're ridiculous," I mumbled into the dregs, waiting to emerge until the threat of fainting from the warmth had passed.

Maker's tales, was this why women in my tales swooned? Far less an embarrassing trait than I'd envisioned, it was a health malady over which I had no control.

"Ridiculous, maybe. But I stand by it," Jaik said.

"Addie, you're right. Galan knows my face," Naomi added gently. "But that means I can protect Jaik. If something goes awry, and you run, Galan will have no grounds to detain me once he recognizes me. And I can get Jaik out."

That was likely true…Naomi was as resourceful as she was well-connected. By her own deft wit, her father's influence, and even her brothers' notoriety in their various trades, it was likely she could free Jaik before Galan brought him in for the bounty on his head. And I'd trust no one else to do it the way I trusted her.

But I'd be sending them both into the hands of the man responsible for my half-crippled shoulder and wounded middle…and their greatest hope would be how fast I could move and how convincing a speech I could give.

"You might be willing to gamble on me," I said to Jaik, "but I don't share that courage."

He set aside his cup and offered his hand, palm up. Carefully, I laid mine in it, and he stroked his thumb over my knuckles.

"I can be brave enough for the both of us," he said. "Just trust me on this, tiger."

It was fair of him to ask—after all, I was asking them to trust *my* plan with the Storycrafters. And in the end, the risk was not my choice to make…that belonged to them.

"All right." I forced the words out in a tumble over my numb lips. "Let's clear a way out from the city."

Smirking, Jaik took back his hand. "A whole herd of Storycrafters getting their talents back all at once should really throw things into chaos. I'm looking forward to it."

"I'll make my way from Dalfi, as well," Naomi said—and added when I swung my stare onto her, "my father remains well-connected in Vallanmyre...in fact, he gives reports directly to Sha Lothar of the state of peddling and merchandising throughout the country. I might be able to catch the Sha's ear, or at least the Shadress or Shadran's...I could possibly persuade them to leave off the bounty."

"Whatever buys us time to get to the Isle of Misspoken Stories." Jaik clapped his hands on his knees and pushed himself upright. "Want to point me in the direction of that stripping solution?"

Naomi gestured to the room where we'd huddled, waiting for Galan to leave; the moment he slipped away, fresh heat consumed my eyes.

It felt as if I was looking at Naomi for the last time.

"When you arrive in Vallanmyre," I croaked, "will you find my parents? Tell them I'm sorry that I can't come home yet...not until I know why we all forgot one another."

The last of the fear gentled from Naomi's gaze. She reached for my hand. "Of course I will. I'll assure them you're all right...because you will be. All of us will be. I still have faith in that."

The heat built and built, consuming my face; tears slid down my cheeks before I could blink them back.

"Oh, Addie. Don't cry." Naomi snared both my hands and tugged me around fully to face her. "If these last few years have proven anything, it's that you and I always find a way to see each other again."

"I just hate this." I strangled her fingers in my grasp, and she didn't even flinch. "I hate that you're leaving your life behind to help us."

"Don't despise the gift." Naomi kissed my brow. "Your friends love you, Audra. Trying to protect you, to save you, even...that's not a burden. It's a privilege."

My eyes swept shut of their own accord, every fragment of my aching heart clinging to those words. *Needing* them to be true.

They were the only thing that would sustain me if this mad scheme led to me leaving her and Jaik behind.

CHAPTER 42
A FABLE OF LACK AND LUXURY

*N*aomi's clothes fit strangely to my body, every lace and cord tightened to compensate for where the fabric cut for her curves met my sharper angles. I could hardly fathom bolting into the fields in these skirts, this top, this corseted boning…but that was what I would do, if this all went according to plan.

And as I hovered near the dead hearth, watching Jaik usher Naomi out the door, the only comfort I had was the scent of my dearest friend pressed into the folds of these clothes that would make me seem, from afar, just like her.

Jaik paused briefly on the threshold, glancing back; it was all the ruse would afford us, though the way his gaze raked over me imparted infinitely more than a cursory moment could say.

"Thank you," he murmured, and somehow that didn't seem to be merely the parting words for Naomi, meant to distract any listening ears.

My throat tightened, and I nodded him on his way.

The moment the door shut, I flew to the window, finding the crease in the pleated drapes where I could glimpse a sliver of the world outside. It was nearing sunset, the city spun in blush tones and scarlet hues, the street soaked in long shadows cast by the clusters of homes and shops on either side; the perfect time to attempt an escape, if they were making one in earnest.

It was little surprise that Naomi so perfectly affected my limp; how many hurts like mine had she treated? How many wounded had she stitched back together and watched them walk away?

I hated to be another one who walked away. But it was all set into motion now.

That was clear the moment the shadows peeled off the walls of the alley near the mouth of the street, slinking up behind Naomi and Jaik.

My hand fitted to the doorknob, and my heart rent in two; my instinct screamed to lunge to their aid, even as I crossed the threshold and angled my feet up the street. Even as their shouts echoed to me—Naomi's cry as a hand clamped on her right shoulder, Jaik's bellow of, "Hey! *Get your hands off of her! Watch her shoulder!*"

Something thrilled in my gut at that furious roar, even if it was only feigned on my behalf; then I dragged the door shut and bolted the opposite way, our provisions smacking against my body like a pack mule's burden.

No one pursued me; likely because, by the sound of things, Jaik was putting up quite the fight. The crunch of fists on bone shattered through the streets, and my heels snagged, slowing my stride; but I didn't dare falter to a full stop. I only paused after I'd gone a mile unpursued, and in a waste street, I stashed our satchels and Jaik's rifle.

Finally unencumbered, I ran with all my might.

Whatever Jaik and Naomi were enduring now, and would still endure between her home and the watchtower, it would be for naught if I didn't reach the cathedrals.

In my mind, I held the map Naomi and I had reviewed while I'd worked the stripping dye through her hair, turning its memorable mushroom shade the same unremarkable brown as mine: a maze of streets that intersected in the shape of a mask, the eyehole pools ringed in four cathedrals each and the magnesite-and-ebony-quartz statue of two-faced Luck posted on the bridge of the nosepiece.

The Masquerade Quarter, they called it. If Assida had been a tribute to all things Storycraft, then Dalfi hung its wealthy pride on the fickle strings of Luck; and I hoped beyond reason the coin would flip in my favor today.

Patterned strands of cloaks and clothing sifted past me on either side as I pushed through the bustling Dalfian streets. Hawkers shouted and vendors chattered; the clamor of sound was thicker than any I'd heard since Krylan, and every speckling of shadow respired with the hint of Galan's sinister presence. My skin prickled with the fear that he might appear around each corner that loomed ahead along the ribbon of street leading to the Masquerade Quarter—that he knew, somehow, this deception we'd plotted.

There were few things more terrifying than a man who knew so much more ut me than I did about him. Who seemed to know more about me, in some ys, than I knew about *myself.*

We couldn't leave him behind swiftly enough.

Relief bloomed in my chest when the crowds around me thinned at last, urrying away from the strand of an avenue that opened at last into the asquerade Quarter.

The jagged spires of the two-toned cathedrals rived against the last blush ip of daylight on the horizon, tufted with deep purple clouds; each was as lendid as its was intimidating. On their steps, candles burned, shedding urulent wax that puddled along the cobblestone way. I dodged those thick cks and the long, tracing fingers of caramel-thickness that spread off from em on my way to the edge of the nearest pool, where I could see everything at lay around me.

Where I could scheme with the railing at my back, avoiding any sneaking oldiers.

The water winked in the dying daylight with the damp sheen of countless oins flipped inside, bound to prayers and pleas to the Storymaker for a turn of uck. For a story with a happy ending, or any sort of ending at all.

I knew those wishes like I'd made them myself. I *had* made them myself.

And I knew the Storycrafters who'd made them, flocking to this twisting istrict of Dalfi by their drab, colorless cloaks, their slumped shoulders blending ith the rising dark while they lit more candles and tossed more coins. Some ffered tales to desperate souls come to plead for a better tomorrow at the feet f Luck's half-smiling, half-scowling statue.

There were so many of them; so many yearning for something better.

And for once, I could give it to them.

Threads of gold and glister burned my tongue like a fresh sip of hot cider when I gripped the ankle of Luck's looming statue with my good hand and swung myself up onto the base where its feet were anchored. In its shadow, I set my own feet; and in the suffocating dark, I raised my voice.

Let me tell you a story.

Countless heads turned toward that clarion call, innumerable gazes striking me like blows from every side. Surprise, irritation, intrigue, desperation, sorrow, even anger flashed on the faces of my fellow Storycrafters and those from whom they'd begged coin for tales of their own.

My heart cringed at the barrage of so much attention, but I held my body fast; I had only this one chance. For them—and for Jaik and Naomi.

And for myself.

So I raised my voice to a shout—I *shouted* my story.

I cried out a tale of a poor and downtrodden merchant in a land of lack. A man whose sharp edges of arrogant surety had shorn down over the years as the world took and took and gave so little back. He was a romantic at heart, suffering as he watched his future bride forfeit her faltering business to care for her ailing mother; he was a desperate man beguiled by a rumor sold to him for his wares...the promise of a spring in the desert that could turn his lack to luxury.

So for the sake of the woman he loved, and her family who were all like his own, he struck off on the journey to the spring.

It was not a remarkable story—truly, it was more a fable than anything. But I built into its spine the very things I saw around me: the hunger, the need, the desperation. I bolstered its brevity with truths plucked from the audience I told it to.

I gave the merchant the rags off the back of an elderly Storycrafter seated on a cathedral step, head in hands. I handed him the cart pushed by a girl some years younger than me, her thin frame shrouded in a colorless cloak. I fed into his person the ruthless determination of a woman who dogged the heels of passersby, crying her stories after them even when they turned away. I steadied him with the hope in the eyes of a young man who passed by the base of the statue, flipping me a tired, encouraging half-grin.

It was a fictious tale, but once again its hero wore Jaik's face in my mind. And across his shoulders he carried the same burdens as the Storycrafters who dabbled about this district...slowly, meticulously making their way toward the statue. Just as I'd suspected they would.

Because these were my people. And they, like me, could not resist a good story.

So I sent the merchant off on his quest, my tongue stumbling a bit over the haste of ushering him from one place to the next. The sun was sinking low

neath the forestlike fringe of rooftops, not even my story enough to hang it a
oment past its measure in the sky.

Time was against us. So I turned it against him, too.

Threads of dune-gold wove in my hands and head at the man's arrival to
e spring; I did not think it was coincidence, either, that the fountains feeding
to the pools seemed to burble higher when my tongue touched on the ethereal
aters the merchant beheld. For the first time, I was keenly conscious of the
fference in my tales when I'd first met Jaik in the *Tankard,* and as his power
uched me from afar now, across Dalfi.

That night in the tavern, no manifestation had eked out of me until the end
f the tale; but the nearer I was to Jaik, and the longer we traveled together, the
vifter these surges of power emanated. As if my talent was becoming
ccustomed to his, awakening sooner in its presence each time, grinning,
asping fearlessly for the amplification he offered.

For now, it was as subtle as sand sprinkling like gold dust from my
ngertips and water surging to meet my words. And that was good—I needed
mething unforeseen, something truly grand, to capture the attention of all my
llow Storycrafters.

So I sent the merchant into the spring, where a voice warned him of the
st of power—that want and lack were a river that could not be entirely
ammed, only channeled away. But the man was fearless in his pursuit; and
king that weight onto himself, he drank from the spring and returned home to
is village. It was a solitary pilgrimage, one I hastened through once again,
emarking pointedly on the absence of another soul to cross him all the way
rough the desert.

When he returned to his village, it was with great aplomb; and here I slowed
yself, measured my words carefully. I wove the tension into the words, my eyes
kipping around all of the Storycrafters who drew nearer to listen.

They knew, just as I did, that this story would not have a happy ending. But
e difference was, they thought the unhappiness came from a lack of any ending
t all.

Flexing my hands loose at my sides, I gave them their tragedy.

*The merchant's beloved ran to greet him, and as she neared him, he cried out, "Look at
e, my love! I've been granted the power to turn lack into luxury! Ask me for anything, for the
oin to raise your family out of poverty and find your mother the finest physician...it's yours!"*

Laughing with pure joy, she leaped into his arms...and the moment their skin touched she burst into a shower of coins.

So it was for everyone and everything the merchant touched ever after...every object, ever item was reduced to coin. And it was true that no one around him lacked for the things they needed to survive. But the lack became his, for he could never touch another soul again. He himself became a curse to bring about their blessing.

For all power comes at a price.

The insatiable might of Storycraft rose within me, and I clapped my hands together, then flung them apart.

From my fingertips spilled coins.

A veritable shower of two-faced Luck charms cascaded over the base of the statue and smashed off the cobblestones like steel raindrops.

All across the Masquerade Quarter, shouts and whoops and disbelieving, cursing cries vaulted toward the darkening sky, snaring every bit of attention not yet captured by my fable. Passersby dove for the coins—though they were not good for trade, they could certainly be sold to metalsmiths for a decent price.

But the Storycrafters had their gazes fixed on a greater prize.

The tale still hanging on my lips. The moral lesson—*completed.*

Now they swarmed me, gripping the base of Luck's statue, their faces upturned in rapture. In disbelief. In the same shocked, greedy hunger and urgency for truth that had possessed my hands to wield the bucket that had struck Jaik unconscious that first night in Krylan.

"How did you do that?" A man's strident voice rose above the clamor. "Tell us!"

"I can do better than that!" I cut across all their upraised demands with my own shout, and several of them stilled. "I can show you how to do the same."

They all quieted at once, a breathtaken hush so absolute and sudden it raised every hair on my body.

"You...you can?" A woman whispered from off to my right, shattering the brief silence; I followed the waft of her voice and found a Storycrafter little younger than me, face gaunt and lined with the weariness of sundered tales that didn't rake in a living anymore.

The precise sort of person I'd been when I'd traveled the Spine.

My heart wrenched in my chest; I descended the statue's base with a slither 1 a plunge, catching my weight carefully on my left leg to spare my wounded e.

Soon I would be demanding much more of it than it might be ready to give.

I nudged through the throng until I reached the woman's side—and I ered her my hand. "Let me show you."

Her smile broke free, dazzling with hope, and she laid her hand in mine.

CHAPTER 43
COLORS RESTORED

I could only begin to fathom the sort of sight we made—a dark-cloaked stream of bodies moving with a singular purpose toward the watchtower that loomed only a handful of streets from the Masquerade Quarter. Any soldiers on patrol might have looked twice, might've felt the hairs on their napes rising. They might have trailed after the cluster of Storycrafters jogging down the main thoroughfare of Dalfi with an air of intent as if for battle.

They might have…but I saw no soldiers as we ran.

Not a single one.

When we drew near the watchtower, I understood why.

The cacophony of upraised voices reached out like a beckoning hand, grasping around my throat, tugging my feet relentlessly down the cobblestone way. A stitch built below my ribs; gasping, I skidded to a halt in the mouth of the street, the Storycrafters all fanning out at my sides. Their air of confusion collided with my horrified panic.

The soldiers of Dalfi were fighting one another over Jaik and Naomi.

Hands bound behind their backs, my friends were crashed down on their knees in the plaza's broad center, cast in the watchtower's shadow. The soaring monolith of ebony quartz was almost a cruel nod to ill luck…a promise of the fate that awaited anyone who crossed the army of Mithra-Sha.

The promise of the fate that awaited Jaik and Naomi if this scheme of mine failed.

Soldiers clustered all around them, faces dark with resentment toward their brothers and sisters in arms, all flinging bitter words at one another, their hands to rifles and blades. I could hardly discern one voice from the next, but the

tent that soaked the square screeched louder than sharpened talons on
rroded steel.

This was about the bounty.

I could only glimpse a sliver of Jaik's face from this angle, but it was enough
catch the crooked, cutting edge of his smirk.

He'd mentioned the bounty himself. Clever. Now the unrest would
uble—a thicker veil for us to slip behind.

I turned to the Storycrafter on my left, the girl who'd been the first to show
flicker of faith in me. "Spread the word: all of you, start telling stories."

Her wide eyes tracked from the commotion ahead to me; doubt burned in
eir depths. "To whom?"

"To anyone. To each other." I squeezed her arm gently. "Keep them
uick...and raise your voices high. You'll see soon enough."

"You don't have to tell us twice." She grinned, curving her fingers over
ine for a moment; then she whirled and slithered in among the rest of the
orycrafters, passing along my missive like a tendril of smoke spreading from
:w fire.

Soon, it would set this plaza aflame.

No sooner had the excitement bounded up into the base of my throat than
e watchtower doors burst open, and Galan thundered down the broad steps,
fle slung across his back. Half of his swollen gash was held together by fresh,
rk thread; the other was padded beneath bandages speckled in blood.

I melted back among the Storycrafters when his boots slammed the plaza
agstones, and he strode toward Jaik and Naomi; but there was no distance I
uld put between us that would mask the grisly sight of his countenance. Not
erely his wound, but the gruesome, triumphant twist of his features when he
ught sight of my friends, the sneer that bunched bandages and banded-
gether flesh alike.

When I beheld Galan in this place, believing victory and riches and status
ere floating just at the edges of his grasp, embodied in a pair of prisoners put
wn on their knees...I saw the truth in the tales both he and Naomi had told.

This was a petty, cruel, cutthroat man who hungered for vengeance decades
the making. And tonight, he believed he had it.

"Creeping out in the coming dark seems dramatic even for you, Grissom."
is taunt whipped across the squabbling in the plaza, silencing it for a moment;
hich made the soft murmurs around me abruptly clear. Dozens of voices

chanting stories under their breaths—but the soldiers took no more notice of them than a crowd of simple onlookers.

Jaik leaned his head back and somehow rocked out a shrug, even with his arms bound at his back. "I'd do something dramatic every hour of every day, if spared me having to see your hideous—"

Bone and bone cracked, this time quieting some of the Storycrafters as well—and choking the air off in my throat. My hand clapped to my mouth to smother a shriek as Galan followed the blow to Jaik's face with a fist to the gut, doubling him up in a retching heap over his own knees.

"Let that serve as a reminder while we're making our way to Vallanmyre," Galan's hoarse hiss carried in the moment's pause. "No *antics*."

"Straight to Vallanmyre, is it?" The soldier behind Jaik bristled, tugging his shoulders back as he squared off against Galan. "To collect the bounty for this pair?"

Galan's eyes snapped back to Jaik, then landed again on the soldier as murmuring budded all around the plaza again. "I found them here, I sniffed them out. It's my bounty to claim."

The soldier hooked his thumbs in his belt, settling back on his heels. "Seems to me we did the work for you, catching them both, bringing them in." He tipped his head at Naomi. "That one put up quite the fight before we got our fingers into her shoulder like you said."

Jaik unleashed a timely, half-snarled curse, and my heart collided against my ribcage.

"So, the way I see it," the soldier went on with a sort of blithe confidence I could never have managed if Galan were glaring at *me* that way, "we're owed a cut."

"A *cut*," Galan snarled.

"That's right. What's the bounty—a hundred gold apiece?" The soldier glanced down at Jaik. "I'd say, one hundred and sixty to go around the watch. You keep the other forty."

Warning tolled like Dalfi's belltower in my head as Galan stepped nearer, smothering Jaik in his shadow. "Is that what you say?"

In one blow to the throat, he had the man on his back on the flagstones, clutching his windpipe and choking for air. Half the soldiers in the square shouted their protests, but with a swift cut of his arm, Galan silenced them all.

"Who was out hunting these runaways while all of you were drinking and dining without a care here in Dalfi?" he shouted, and around me a handful of

ɔdies rippled with winces. "You turned me down when I came through looking
ɔr aid in the search…I had to rely on lucking *Storycrafters* instead!"

A shiver rattled down my spine. For the very first time, it occurred to me
iat the amplified Storycrafters whose Misspoken tales we'd faced in the Casmiss
'ood had likely been a part of this fold I'd brought with me from the
ithedrals. All that had separated us from an alliance with them had been Luck's
ʌer-turning coin, a handful of days, and the brittle edge of desperation that
ung in every face around me.

They'd been pushed so far. Now they were pushing back.

"This is *personal*," Galan went on, shifting his bearing toward Naomi. "This
 about more than the bounty. These two belong to me, their *fates* belong to me.
nd I'll be stamped on the dark side of Luck's flipping coin before I let even
ne of you greedy, lazy luckers take a *scrap* of *my* glory!"

His vicious words were still not half as horrifying as the snarl that tore
cross his features when he gripped a handful of Naomi's hair, wrenched her
ead back—and caught sight of her face.

His curse embodied pure violence, a tone only half-human that fractured
rhen he slammed her head downward so hard her face nearly met the stones.
earing backward, Galan whirled to take in the whole plaza.

"You incompetent, lucking—" He choked on his own rage, hurling his
ngers back through his hair, whipping into a sharp pivot back to face the rest of
ie soldiers. "You brought the *wrong woman!*"

The men nearest to Naomi were already staring at her, recognition dawning
leakly across their faces. Perhaps they knew her in passing; perhaps they'd even
een treated by her skilled, selfless hands. And now, in the firelight-harshness of
ialan's burning fury, they were placing the familiarity. Realizing they knew her,
ot from *Wanted* bulletins, but from here in Dalfi.

"Tell me where she is," Galan snarled, planting a boot on Jaik's knee and
iclining toward him. "Or I swear on Luck's coin, this one dies."

Jaik spat blood from Galan's last blows off to the side. "Gone. You think
'd let her stay in this city, knowing you were on the prowl? She got out…she got
way from *you*."

Galan opened his mouth to retort—then stiffened when one of the soldiers
osted along the plaza's edge moved to pick at Naomi's bonds. "What do you
iink you're doing?"

"We're holding her unlawfully," the soldier said. "I recognize her…this is
lealer Weathers. She isn't under arrest."

"Don't you *touch* that one!" Galan jabbed a sword-sharp finger at the man. "No one moves until I have my hands on Audra Jashowin!"

Jaik's whistle was low and wobbling, congested with blood. "Hope everyone brought a change of clothes, then, because we're going to be here a *lon* time."

"You're so full of slag. She wouldn't abandon you."

Jaik snorted. "I'm not the one who has a hard time seeing how all of this is bigger than me. I convinced her to—"

Another blow, this time to Jaik's temple, flung him against Naomi and nearly tore a furious shriek from my throat; she shrugged him back up on his knees, her glare pinned on Galan.

That look was a chilling reminder that Naomi knew poison studies as well as healing.

Rocking back to his feet, Galan spun to take in the whole plaza. "Where is she? Where's the lucking *Storycrafter*?"

No one answered—I wasn't certain they could hear him above the weaving of voices that took advantage of the silence. It was a chant, a song, a story rising around us. No...it was *dozens* of stories all braiding together, barreling forward at a feverish clip. The sound prickled the hair on my nape, and exultation bubbled in my core.

Their power was rising, reaching out, growing all around us. Some shimmered in flickers of mirage-silver, the tales already fighting to come to life. Soaking in the imminent might in this place...soaking in *Jaik*, the living amplifier, who gazed up at Galan with triumph blazing in his bright brown eyes.

And in *Galan's* eyes, for an instant, uncertainty pushed through.

And on the heels of it...*fear*.

"Get them out of here!" he roared; a few soldiers shifted toward us, but most kept their gazes pinned on him. As if they suspected he might lay hands on Jaik and Naomi and haul them off the moment they all turned their backs.

Good. They were learning to see Galan Fiordona as I already did.

"*Shut them up!*" When no one moved to obey, Galan shrugged the rifle from across his back and spun, darting the muzzle across the crowd. "Scatter, all of you—this ground belongs to the Mithran army! You will vacate the premises *now*, or else you'll—"

All throughout the plaza, color erupted.

CHAPTER 44
THE POWER THEY DESERVE

A painter's palette of pastels burst to life around the watchtower plaza, like wildflower meadows blooming and stars tumbling from the sky, striking body after body on every side of us. Mellow shades of warmth, peaceful pockets of blue and green, secretive purples and moody rust sprayed across the cloaks of my fellow Storycrafters.

At the riot of colors, they screamed. Joy, shock, wonder all rose in a torrent of whoops and wails, and the face of the whole world changed in an instant.

Greenery spewed through the cracks in the flagstones—fruit trees rearing to life, living waters pouring out of gaps between the buildings at the plaza's edge. Threads of roughspun wool and silk and cotton burst from the open hands of the Storycrafters. Baskets of food. Crops of all kinds. Blankets and coins and carts and carriages.

All at once, the space forged into an oasis, a forest grove resplendent in life and beauty. The watchtower itself turned to an ivy-wrapped trellis, creeping vines sprouting melons and squashes from its face.

They'd been clever, my fellow Storycrafters; what they'd spun to life with their tales was all practical. Useful. Each and every bit of it cut against the teeth of the poverty and lack and *need* that had festered in every inch of Mithra-Sha for far, far too long.

Tears blurred my sight, and a desperate ache to give *back* reared up in my chest.

These were good people. *My* people. They deserved this power. They deserved this moment, however fleeting, more than *anything*.

At that instant, glorying in the majesty of what their tales had wrought, the Storycrafters were undefeatable—and the soldiers lost control of the crowd.

And Jaik took advantage of the chaos, like he always did.

He barreled his weight forward, slamming his shoulder straight into Galan chest; the man staggered, choking up his air, and Jaik's boot crunched into his knee. Galan collapsed, cursing and howling, and the crack of his body on the stones freed me from my wonderstruck reverie.

Surging forward, I hauled Naomi back by her shoulders and loosed her bound hands where the soldier had frayed the twine; then I yanked her into an embrace, pressing a kiss to her brow. "Go. Run."

She framed my face briefly with her hands, flashed me a bleak smile brimming with determination and heartache, then bolted away into the pandemonium that had overtaken the plaza.

I whirled, seeking Jaik in the crush of bodies—and found him with a soldier on each arm, thrashing and writhing to reach Galan. The man had hauled himself up on one arm, teeth bared in a snarl, fingers wrapped around his grotesquely bent knee.

He shouted something I could not hear; but the hate in his face was enough to launch my body into motion.

Hurtling forward, I tugged Jaik's knife free from my waistband and swung in a single, deft cut—severing his bonds from behind while I flung my weight into the soldier on his right arm. "*Jaik!*"

He tore his wrists from the twine, swinging one arm in a vicious punch straight into the face of the guard on his left; the man staggered back, losing his grip, and Jaik hooked me around the waist and swung me away from Galan. "*Run, tiger!*"

And I did; with Jaik's arm curved around my back, we bolted for the mouth of the nearest street, losing ourselves in the storm of color that swarmed the plaza. Stumbling into the safety of the avenue, I paused just a moment to glance back, to commit to memory the sight behind us—the first time I could ever recall seeing so many colors together since my graduation from Fablehaven.

A pang of guilt lanced through me; I didn't want to imagine the faces of these Storycrafters when they realized their talent's revival was only temporary. When they ran or rode out of Jaik's reach, and their stories dried up again.

But that was why we had to go…had to carry on to the Illusionarium. To Erasure. We had to uncover what was happening in Mithra-Sha, so we could give the stories back their endings for good.

Heart in my throat, I whirled and darted after Jaik, losing myself with him in the twisting streets of a city that would never be the same again.

The chaos clung to our heels all the way to retrieve our provisions, and yond there to the stable where Jaik had boarded Hectra. We tacked her up and ounted in a flurry, and by the time we emerged on horseback, the sizzling .ergy of Wellspoken tales spiced the air even to the edge of Dalfi.

My tongue practically burned with the brand of Storycraft, a tantalizing ste I'd all but forgotten in my years of travel. Now the keen memories of tales ld at whim in Fablehaven, relishing a power we never thought we would lose, ⸱gged me on the descent from the stableyard to the city's outermost fringe.

Once there, we slowed, glancing back.

The script of Storycraft had extended itself far beyond the watchtower ⸱uare. Garlands of cloth clashed against acres of full-bodied crops. The city ⸱arkled with greenery and flourished with abundance, all thanks to my fellow ⸱orycrafters.

I wondered what shade their cloaks had turned by now. And what color ey would be come dawn.

Guilt nipped at my heart; I was glad they had all of this, at least. All these ⸱ngible witnesses that their power, however briefly, had returned.

Jaik whistled lowly. "Would you just *look* at that? They really made ⸱mething good here. One little taste of power, and they used it to make enough ⸱ovision for this city and everyone around it for the rest of the winter. ⸱at's…that's flipping *impressive*."

But there was more than admiration in the lopsided grin he cast back ⸱ward Dalfi; there was pride, too.

And he had every right to it. Dalfi's sudden prosperity, the weight lifted off ⸱ese people's shoulders tonight, was only possible because Jaik Grissom had ⸱en in that square. He was as much to thank for this as any Storycrafter.

Feeling the heat of my gaze, perhaps, he glanced down at me seated before ⸱m, snugging Hectra's reins around his fist—and I winced. In the light of the ⸱oon shedding unencumbered now that the city spires and heights lay at our ⸱cks, the bruising on his face from Galan's battering fists was all the more evident. A cut on the corner of his lip stood out stark scarlet against his sun-bronzed skin, still weeping a small thread of red.

"Here…" I tugged my sleeve down over my knuckles, sent a silent though of penance to Naomi for sullying her beautiful shirt, then dabbed the blood from Jaik's jaw.

"Agh," he hissed. "You know, the last woman who wore that shirt had a better bedside manner."

"Shut your ramble-hole." My ears warmed at the brush of his breath over my knuckles. "We can't have you leaving a trail of blood when we run."

Though it was a halfhearted jest at best, Jaik's eyes gentled, and his smile widened—which tugged at the edges of the gash, setting more blood running free.

"I'm fine, tiger." His chuckle was soft, his touch even softer when he captured my hand, guiding it down from his face to settle over his chest. Over his thudding heart. "It's just because this hasn't stopped trying to sprint out of my ribcage since we got out of there."

His pulse leaped against my fingertips like a greeting from a familiar friend. "Thank you for giving the Storycrafters back something they've missed so much."

His thumb stroked the back of my knuckles, my palm hovering over his heart. "Not that I had much of a choice, but…it's my pleasure. Wish I could do it more often."

And as we turned Hectra west, my heart echoed that wish—wailed it to the power-peppered sky.

So I started to scheme.

CHAPTER 45
A WORLD IN SUFFERING

aik and I traveled for five days before we saw the smoke.

In those days, we put Dalfi far at our backs. We rode through the fringes of the Casmiss Wood that had nearly been the death of us and entered a deeper pine swath; there, we angled our track toward the well-established woodland paths and the inhabited passes above them.

It was a risk, straying so close to civilization, but neither of us were mountaineers, and we agreed we would fare better following in the footprints of the hardy folk who called the Drennans home, rather than trying to forge a new way through the perilous crags of the mountains that peered over the horizon.

And then we spotted the low, smoldering haze.

A sick pit yawned in my gut when I first discerned it from the clouds, blotting grayish-black against a pink sunset. I ignored it as best I could while we made camp that night, darting glances at Jaik now and again to see if he'd taken note of that distant plume.

He didn't seem to. But when we woke on the cusp of sunrise with a faint dusting of ash on our clothes, sitting up sharply next to one another on the same side of the fire, there was no use even speaking. A single glance between us hung heavy with unease that tiptoed toward dread.

We gathered our things in silence and mounted just as mutely. And Jaik didn't ask, nor did I protest, as he turned our course toward the column of smoke joining frigid earth to scarlet sky.

My imagination played havoc with my heart, drumming up notions of entrapment between walls of fire, of Misspoken blazes immune to water that might wall us in on an unchangeable course back the way we'd come, straight into bounty-hunting hands.

But that was not what awaited us at the source of the smoke.

I almost wished it was.

Instead, by the deep, bloodred hue of a smoke-choked morning, we behelc the remnants of a village devasted.

Smoke billowed in sluggish plumes from what had once been homes and stables, the acrid touch of flame scouring even the low brick walls between wrecked wooden structures. It had not been a large village—a dozen shells of dwellings remained, at most—but that only made the ruination stand out more starkly.

I pressed my sleeve to my mouth, sheltering from the stench of charred ha and flesh; the motion muffled the sharp intake of breath that forced itself down my throat anyway as horror vaulted the steps of my ribs and wrapped itself around my heart.

Bodies littered the single path among the ransacked homes, blanketed und€ the same fine layer of ash that clung to our clothes.

Cursing, Jaik swung down and jogged to the nearest corpse— a man face-down in the dirt, the ashen veil still not enough to mask the stark stain of blood spread between his shoulderblades.

A mortal blow.

I slid from Hectra's back as well, clinging to her saddlehorn by a fist as pain lobbed itself along my injured side. The ruined village pressed itself against my senses, telling a tale I couldn't ignore; after all I'd seen along the Spine, all the stories I'd told and heard, there were bits and pieces that wedged themselves gracelessly into my understanding.

Things I wished I couldn't fathom.

There was no marks of soldier swords or bandit knives; no rifleshot peppered what structures remained. The injuries on the bodies nearest were not clean, neat slices like an army-issued blade would deal.

When Jaik rose from his crouch beside the body at the mouth of the village's winding path, his hoarse pronouncement confirmed what I already feared: "This was a sickle wound."

A farming implement.

The evidence was everywhere as we picked our way among the char and corpses; fires had been set to erase evidence of wrongdoing, but the bodies fellec in the open, or those who had crawled or stumbled out to the path and died there, bore wounds from plowblades and saws, hooks and hoes and tools. The wounds, Jaik confirmed lowly, were not delivered by some skilled hand; they

re almost brutal in their inefficiency, weapons laid to skin again and again,
g after death was assured.

I hadn't asked him since Dalfi about his dreams of finding himself in a
dier's uniform, nor had we discussed his uncanny way with weapons; but now
as grateful for whatever wisdom those nightmares imparted to him.

It helped make sense of the wreckage around us.

Village had turned against village; the drag-marks in the snow beyond the
age proper indicated where baskets of goods and useful items, as well as
all, kicking feet, had been hauled away—food and supplies taken, children
red and carried off for their own salvation. The hoofprints stampeding the
ow flat belonged not to some raiding party or vagabond band of hungry
diers, but to desperate people who'd chosen slaughter over starvation. Those
o'd sooner cut down their neighbors than watch their own families waste
ay.

They'd taken the children of their victims as some small shard of mercy,
haps...a penance, a plea to the Storymaker that they were not made utterly
nstrous by their desperation.

But this *was* a monstrosity. It was an injustice.

It was a mark of the wild need that seethed in these treacherous climes,
onger than in the heart of Mithra-Sha.

Some strange penance of my own, a Storycrafter's offering of remorse for
eds we had all failed to meet, finally freed my grief-tied tongue enough to say
Jaik, "It's good you have those farmer's arms. We need to dig graves."

Jaik leveled his gaze at the ashen sky, the round of his throat bobbing.
eah. It's worth the time."

All that day, we dug and dragged and dumped the bodies into a low pit,
oring the pain in our own still-healing wounds, shutting out the ache of
obbing shoulders and battered middles. Then we covered the corpses with
t mercifully thawed by the fires. Those fires we doused with armfuls of snow,
they wouldn't spread; then we set our course opposite the retreating
ofprints and skidmarks of the raiding villagers.

Neither of us wanted to know what they would do to a pair of travelers,
ving seen what havoc they'd wrought on their neighbors.

Winter closed around us like a fist, its biting wind gnawing beneath our clothes and frequent snowfall powdering us like fresh ash as we trekked west again, further and further from Dalfi…further from that first unmistakable sign of the desperation that prowled the passes.

And as the hills steepened and hardened into the footpaths of the lowest peaks, the suffering we encountered grew teeth and talons of its own.

Villages strung with pearled strands of icicles from a late and unexpected freeze; a quilt of frost-burned crops fanned out limp and bleak for miles in every direction. Small towns and cities where canals that cut through the rock of the Drennans had frozen over completely, the ice chipped by pickers hoping to reach sustenance below. Graves littering the edges of the paths we traversed, some large and some far, far too small…places where families had broken and agony had cut its mark into the earth in the form of beloved bodies left behind.

Suffering. Pain. Things that could be remedied with a Wellspoken story— things that *had* been kept at bay by Storycrafters for so long.

The weight of responsibility sprawled across my shoulders thicker than my winter cloak, heavier than the snow we shook off most mornings before setting out from our ramshackle campsites. So few knew what Jaik and I could do together—and fewer still I trusted with that truth—so these villages and towns and cities were never the wiser how near a helping hand brushed by them.

But *I* knew. And it ached whenever we stopped to rest Hectra, those brief lulls in our progress where Jaik practiced with his rifle. Not shooting; he didn't like wasting the ammunition, nor could we risk the thunderous crash of rifleshot attracting hunters of any sort.

But he shrugged off, then shouldered the empty rifle, and pulled the trigger again and again while we were stopped, aiming at imaginary foes. Likely seeing Galan's face among the shadow-flocked trees.

And I watched him, seated at the bases of the pines, warming my hands between my bent knees even while ice glazed over my heart.

At least he was *doing* something—practicing. Preparing. Meanwhile, I was as good as useless without my craft. All I had to keep my insides from freezing with

spair was the scheme that had occurred to me when we'd ridden out from
alfi.

Finally, I couldn't bear it anymore.

After three weeks of riding through the passes—nearly a month of
itnessing the suffering around us, and doing nothing about it—I couldn't keep
y desperation to myself another day.

CHAPTER 46
VISIONS AND DREAMS OF IMPOSSIBLE THINGS

*W*e have to do something for these people," I announced one night when we paused to make camp; I spoke these long-rehearsed words matter-of-factly, though my heart raced to hear them aloud, and my fingers trembled slightly when I bound Hectra's reins around a hardy shrub.

Jaik snapped low-hanging branches from the nearby trees, then peeled off a handful of bark for tinder. "We *are* doing something. That's what this journey to Erasure's about, right?"

"Do you think that us finding the answers to the missing endings of all these tales means *anything* to the people in these mountains we're riding through?" Conviction sharpened my tone like a stone knife, pricking Jaik's back that he kept to me while he worked. "They're suffering *now*, Jaik. They're dying *right now*, and if we don't do something for them, they won't live long enough to learn about what's made the world like this."

"Fair point." He returned to the cleared patch of our campsite and handed me an armful of sticks; I stood, and together we broke them over our knees for kindling, the dull snap of twigs peppering the air like shattering bones. "What'd you have in mind?"

I teased the words around my tongue for a bit, weighing the thoughts that had haunted me ever since we'd left Dalfi. "Storycraft could help them."

Jaik was already shaking his head before I'd spoken the second word. "That's not going to work, Audra. Galan and the other bounty hunters are sniffing for a man and woman traveling together, wielding that exact kind of

ower. Wherever they may have scattered after Dalfi, they'll be on us like stink
n a manure heap the second they catch wind of this."

"What if we're careful? We'll warn people not to breathe a word of it before
even start—"

"Too dangerous."

"You don't know that!" My frustrated shout rattled the snow-heavy boughs
round us. "Some people are actually so *grateful* for help that they can be *trusted!*"

"I don't care if they stitch their lips together!" As usual, Jaik's passion flared
o meet mine. "Audra, I've seen enough of this to know how these stories of
ours speak for *themselves*. You think Galan or those Storycrafters with their
mplifiers aren't going to *notice* where the crops are coming back and canals are
nawing? You're going to lead them right to us!"

"So you think *our* safety matters more than these people's lives?" I cast
own my handful of kindling, rage searing in my fingertips stronger than the
pinning of a tale coming to life. "They're suffering, Jaik! I'm trying to save
nem!"

"And I'm trying to keep *you* safe!"

"I didn't ask you to be my bodyguard! You're my *amplifier!*"

The kindling tumbled from his arms, and he stepped into my breathing
pace in a heartbeat, backing me against the nearest pine and laying one hand to
ne jagged trunk beside my head. There was no threat in his nearness, but fervor
lared from him hot enough to thaw the snow around us. "*Don't* you use me.
Don't you *dare* use me just to make yourself the hero."

My mouth dried out. Shame punched through me so fiercely, vomit
limbed my throat.

"You're right," I croaked. "You're right, Jaik, and I'm sorry. I didn't mean
o say that, I just…" The first few tears escaped over my lashes, and I swiped
hem hastily away with the backs of my knuckles. "I just want to fix this. I want
o save them, and I can't help wanting to be loved for it, too. You know how it
eels to be completely forgotten, and I'm glad that rolls off your back, but it
loesn't for me. Not when the whole world goes on without me and I'm—I'm
ust…" The words stuck like thorns in my throat. "If I don't have this, I'm
nothing. I'm *expendable*, Jaik."

He should have yelled. Should have lectured me. Should have walked away,
ven.

Instead, he slid his hand down to cradle the side of my neck. His gaze fastened on mine so fiercely, I could see nothing but him. "No. Not to me. Not anymore."

For a moment, only his breath clouded the air.

"I don't care if you never tell another story again," Jaik added. "You're worth more than what you can *do* for people. Even the ones who need it most. You know that's the truth about me, and I'm saying it's the truth about you, too."

For the first time I could ever recall, *I* was the one hanging on someone else's words—enraptured by them. Desperate for them to be true.

Jaik Grissom needed no Storycraft to beguile me. To make me see visions and dreams of impossible things, and to want to see them spun to life when he was finished.

I'd been daydreaming and wishing and wanting since the first night I'd met him. And I didn't know precisely when I'd begun to hope—beyond all reason, forsaking the knowledge of our world without endings—that somehow, this would end with him staying with me.

But I could do nothing about that. I *would* do nothing about it, until I could trust my selfish heart not to use him.

"All right." The concession made my chest cave in. "We won't use Storycraft."

Jaik regarded me shrewdly for a long moment. "Are you saying that because you think it's the best choice, or because you're afraid I'll be angry if you don't?"

My teeth caught around a sheepish grin. "Can it be both?"

"Flipping *Luck*, Audra!" Jaik rocked back on his heels, spinning away from me, dragging both hands through his hair as he took several paces through the snow; before I could truly taste the bite of fear that I'd pushed him too far, he whirled back. "Listen to me, all right? I'm not out to make you agree with me because you think that's the only way I'll be your friend. I want you to pick something to stand for without worrying about how someone else is going to think of you. Fight for something, all right? *Fight me!*"

His voice rose, his hands slamming into the pine's broad trunk on either side of my head; he leaned his brow so near mine, the tendrils of his hair brushed my forehead.

"Look. You were the one who told me the Storymaker gave *you* this power. Do you think helping people out here is what He wanted you to use it for?

cause, if you really believe you're doing what He sent you to do, why do you
e a flip of Luck's coin what anyone else thinks? Even me."

I had no answer for that.

"If you use your Storycraft to please people," he rasped, "you're more likely
do it the wrong way, in the wrong place, at the wrong time. You're more likely
get *caught*." His hands slid down a bit, wrists brushing the tops of my
oulders. "Now, put all that aside. Forget being remembered for helping these
ople. Now tell me what *that* looks like."

My chest constricted. Desperation clawed out of my heart, digging its talons
o that tantalizing notion of being *coveted*. Even revered as the only Storycrafter
o could save the desperate folk who called the Drennans home.

If I laid that aside…laid *myself* aside…there was still a whole world of hurt
t there. A vast expanse of need we could meet. And if I didn't have to be
unked for it, didn't have to be Audra Jashowin, Storycrafter and savior…

Dying to my own desires would spare countless lives. The only thing
nding in the way of that was the ache to ride into cities and towns and show
face there…to be their salvation.

But that was my own need before theirs. The people in the Drennans and
across Mithra-Sha needed no hero. They needed to be cared for, and
lped…rescued in ways only Jaik and I could manage until we unraveled the
stery behind the sundered stories.

Wasn't that what Storycrafting was about? Talent wielded for the sake of
ers—not for the pride of the wielder.

It was what *I* was meant for. It was only a matter now of whether being
at the Storymaker had fashioned me for was enough to forsake being loved
everyone else. Enough to push back against Jaik's disbelief and concern.

If it was worth fighting for, even if it cost me everything.

I held Jaik's gaze, breathing in the sacred swelling of emotion that came
th letting go…and releasing all my pride, and my wishes, and my ache for
roism and notoriety that I'd fostered in silence for three long weeks. And for
ars before that.

In its place, I let the faith in his gaze fill me up…and the words he'd spoken
at mattered more than all the rest.

The Storymaker *had* entrusted me with this gift. In these peaks, at least, I
ew how to use it best.

"It looks like never being seen." I could muster no more than a whisper behind the words, but I knew he heard me. "It looks like leaving without any glory. But, Jaik, we're supposed to do this. I can feel it in my bones."

Nodding slowly, he slid his hands down from the tree and stepped back from me. "All right. How do you want to dance this?"

I pushed up from the trunk, my body tingling with the brand of his near heat. "What if I tell stories—just small ones—once we've passed through? Not enough to be truly remarkable, but enough to help whoever we can. And we could stagger our course…keep to the established trails, but instead of traveling this one straight to Fallshyre Bay—"

"We detour. Keep the bounty hunters and Galan, if he's out there, cutting back and forth across the mountains, too." Jaik grimaced, rubbing a hand over his bearded jaw; he hadn't touched a razor since Dalfi, and I didn't think he minded the beard he'd sprouted. Not with the cold wind that nipped our faces relentlessly, staining our cheeks a permanent rose-red. "It'll add time to our journey, sure…but if you're convinced about this, then I'm with you, tiger."

An ache built in my chest—the need to know that this would not somehow be torn away from me. This believing. This support, even though I hadn't conceded.

Still, I framed it in humor—the only thing that would soften the blow for us both. "Are you sure about that?"

"Oh, I'm sure." For a heartbeat, his knuckles brushed my jaw. "I'm with all you all the way."

Then he slipped past me to build the fire.

For the first time in weeks, I was glad of the cheek-biting cold slipping beneath my cloak. It made my blush far easier to hide.

CHAPTER 47
A BANNER OF HOPE

*M*y plan was not without flaw; in fact, it slowed us far more than we'd anticipated. We squabbled and bickered over the map, pitting Jaik's calculations of our safest travel against the pockets of hurt that spread like bruises through the mountains.

We couldn't help them all. But I was determined to do my best, even if it left me toppling from Hectra's back in exhaustion most nights, stories still half-tangled on my tongue. And to Jaik I entrusted all the rest; our safety mattered, too—enough that whenever he told me it was time to switch tack, I learned to argue less and less.

If I was to become the Storycrafter I'd been made to be, then Jaik Grissom would have to be my bodyguard.

Once I accepted that, everything became easier. I surrendered the concerns of bounty hunters and rogue soldiers to Jaik's keen mind and sharp eyes, and simply focused on seeking out the places of need along our path; I selected strategic cities to divert our course toward, knowing aid for them meant aid for the smaller towns and villages within their purview.

We conquered perilous clefts and sheer vaults, every day ushering in a new, breathtaking view of mountain peaks and stone-and-wood valleys cupped between the passes. We descended forest slopes along treacherous descents, Hectra's hooves skating on bare rock, Jaik's hands anchoring my hips to keep me from pitching off her back. We found cities forged entirely of stone, carved from mountain faces—tiered hives of civilization so remote and ancient, I wondered if storycraft had shaped them.

For weeks, our roof was the capricious sky, our bathing pools the crystalline ponds beneath waterfalls that still surged from the rock, fed by heated geysers within the Drennans against which most towns and cities and villages were sculpted. We ate what game Jaik trapped, and in our wake we left a varied array of gifts, subtle as I could craft them.

A burst of warmth that thawed the manmade canals channeling between valley abodes high in the mountains, which might have otherwise remained frozen for weeks yet.

A small rockslide in the still-unnavigable upper passes that forced game down through the hind trails, closer to the towns fringing the path below.

A fresh gust of vigor breathed into the winter crops scorched by brutal frost, offering the life-giving harvest a second chance to thrive.

A swift melt working its way in behind a hard late-season freeze, so livestock did not succumb and fragile bodies weren't wracked with sickness while they waited for warm weather to find these mountain clefts and ease their lungs again.

I hid my work behind the errant flip of Luck's coin; enough coincidences would still draw the eyes of our antagonists, but I attempted nothing that would reshape the landscape entirely or twist the seasons out of shape. Just enough to lend a bit of strength to the bent backs and bowed heads we encountered now and again on the way, to lessen the burden of survival in these mountains where spring always looked last.

Yet something more than my power thawed the way around us. Tales trickled through cities and towns, pooling in the taverns where Jaik ducked every now and then, wielding his brick of dye expertly to alter his appearance and purchase supplies…and to listen for a hint of soldiers or bounty hunters crawling the mountains.

He heard far better than that.

He brought back tales of Dalfi; of the Storycraft that had consumed it. Even in the absence of more Wellspoken tales since our departure, all was not lost; travelers carried words of encouragement in their mouths, passed along to Jaik and anyone else who would listen.

If it had happened once, it meant the ends of stories were not lost forever. They could come back. They might be making their way back all the time.

It was a flame in the dark, a candle's flicker in the vast trench of despair that had swallowed Mithra-Sha for so long.

And Jaik brought tales, too, of the villages and towns that lay behind us. Even the mountain stronghold cities we'd skirted the edges of rippled with the grazing hand of passing Storycraft. Though they didn't call it such, it was a inder end to winter and an earlier touch of spring by far throughout the Irennans.

Fewer deaths. Fewer natural disasters. Fewer funerals and pilgrimages from ained villages and snow-buried towns.

There was *hope*.

Hope went before us. Hope trailed behind us. Hope left me smiling each night, no matter how heavy exhaustion hung on my face, when I curled with my back to Jaik's beside the fire. Hope had me leaping up to greet him at his return from every tavern, his tired smirk and my unstoppable grin heating the air between us.

Even my nightmares slaked. My dreams were better, kinder...more precious than I could ever say.

Sometimes I dreamed of a world full of stories again. Sometimes I dreamed of every city in Mithra-Sha coated in the manifestations of Storycraft. Sometimes I dreamed of the hope in that girl's smile back in Dalfi.

But often—more often than I could bear—I dreamed of Jaik.

He featured in my mind's sleeping fantasies as much as in my tales now. Adventures we had together, impossible scenarios we conquered, jokes we told that sometimes had me waking myself with laughter I couldn't explain to him.

Embraces we shared, and sometimes more than that...things I could never bear to ask for when we were awake. But I wanted them just the same.

Something had shifted in me; I knew better than to deceive myself. Our passionate discourse in Dalfi, the tender gestures by which he'd cared for me in my time of hurt; the way he'd shouted at the soldier who'd manhandled Naomi, pretending she was me. The brand of his heartbeat that still lived in the center of my palm; the way his arms snugged around my waist while we rode, and how neither of us could fall asleep anymore until we both lay on the same side of the fire, curled back-to-back.

The way he'd encouraged me to fight. To fight *him*, even, if it meant doing what the Storymaker had fashioned me for. To become what I was born to be.

Jaik Grissom saw me. He saw the truth of me, not only as I was, but as I was becoming. And he fought for that as fiercely as he fought to keep us both alive. He fought to bring me to him, and to get back to me, whatever came against us.

And he stayed.

He *stayed*, even on the nights when danger lurked so near we didn't sleep at all; when footsteps prowled outside the shelter we'd taken in clefts and beneath

prickling foliage, sometimes human, sometimes animal. He never left my side; h
assessed the danger, then turned us away from it. And in the safety of his
presence, my power was free to flourish.

The security Jaik provided was a sanctuary for my imagination and strength
to bloom.

And it was enough—though it took some weeks for me to make peace wit
that notion. It was enough to do good, to leave hope in our wake, even without
the accolades. Without the heroism. Without a single person ever knowing
Audra Jashowin was responsible for it all.

Doing good in secret while traveling on the next gust of wind through the
mountain range...it was far more than enough.

It was what I was meant for.

And that truth sustained me all the way across the switchback, staggered
path we made, through the passes, winding between the highest peaks, braving
the most treacherous twists in the road through the Drennans...until the jagged
fangs of rock began to abate. Until the horizon smoothed out, its craw yawning
wide.

Until the weather warmed, turned almost balmy compared to the stinging,
persistent chill of the upper mountains. Until the trees budded with new growth
and the soil warmed, and a new sort of life breathed across the world.

Until, after many weeks of travel and storytelling, Jaik and I rode into
Fallshyre Bay.

CHAPTER 48
THE BAKER'S FATE

The Bay itself was like nowhere I had ever seen before, captivating from the first moment I laid eyes on it.

The foothills framed it on every side, their jutting stone fingers piercing into the water where lower slopes met steady tides. The necklace of pine and rock worn around the Bay's jagged neck only ended where the town of Allshyre itself began—a distant gleam from where we emerged onto a spit of rock hanging out over the water, but the echoes of revelry within were cupped perfectly by the mountains at our backs.

Notes of fiddle reels and melancholy violins and some other, throatier strings saturated the air. Lanternlight gleamed in windows at staggered heights, from street-level wharfs to the illumined face of a clocktower proclaiming the evening hour. Faraway laughter and drunken toasts met the veil of night spreading out from the mountain peaks, the sun taking its final breath before the plunge over the western horizon.

The air skirling off the waves was warmer than any we'd encountered crossing the Drennans—proof that, beneath those high passes we'd traveled for so many weeks, spring was finally settling in—and I loosened my cloak with a sigh of relief.

It swiftly soured into melancholy when Jaik loosened the grip he'd kept on me and shifted backward, giving me more breathing room than I truly wanted.

"We made it." He nudged the back of my head with his chin. "Not bad for a runaway farmer and a mid-level Storycrafter, eh?"

"Don't make me shove you off this horse," I warned.

"What you call a *shove*, I call *the gentle breath of a butterfly's wings*—ow," Jaik grunted when I drilled my elbow back into his ribs. "Really starting to regret giving you those lessons, tiger."

We'd engaged in a few grappling sessions during the crossing—something Jaik had insisted on for my safety, in case Galan or another bounty hunter caught up to us while we were apart. It was a reasonable concern, one I'd happily agreed to for his sake as much as mine.

There'd been something else living in Jaik throughout the Drennans, awakening in a slow, leisurely curl…this boundless energy that seemed to seep out of the rifle and into his arms. He was hardly ever still anymore, tapping his thigh, bounding his foot against Hectra's side, humming under his breath.

He'd needed the sessions to calm himself, to direct that energy before it burst out of him. And I hadn't minded them, either—for too many selfish reasons to tally. It had certainly kept us warm on the coldest nights in the Drennans…and I hadn't regretted a single moment of Jaik's arms banded around me in a threatless cage, the excuse to breathe in the wild, campsmoke scent of his clothing and the hard soap on his skin while he'd talked me through breaking his hold.

But more than all of that, like a persistent itch that demanded to be plucked at, was the vague notion that I'd once known these things. Now and again my minded wandered back to Kalvikan, when Jaik had crept up on me outside the tavern and I'd turned absolutely feral, scrabbling to escape him.

Some of the maneuvers he'd taught me in the mountains were eerily similar to that. And even he was impressed with how swiftly I took to them—less like was learning.

Far more like I was remembering.

I shivered off that uneasy notion, and Jaik's hand settled on my hip, steadying me. "Hey. I was joking. Whatever awful scenario you're thinking about right now, I'm glad you've got the strength to scrap for yourself."

I rolled my eyes, though he couldn't see it—and though it was a dull gesture against the prickling heat of his hand on my waist. "I can't think of any scenario worse than having my face wedged in your sweaty armpit while you explain all the ways I failed a leglock."

"Below the waist *is* your trouble area."

Groaning, I rapped my heels on Hectra's sides, urging her toward the town—toward my mind's own escape.

It was strange to return to civilization after so many weeks with only one other for company—and I had seen even less of another face in that time than ik had. A portion of my heart thrilled at the notion of conversation with meone whose edges were softer and whose tongue was more tactful than his; ıt there was a bite of melancholy beneath my excitement, as well.

In ways that had absolutely nothing to do with amplification or heroism or orycraft…I would miss having Jaik all to myself.

But there was no turning back from the only road that led into the town of ıllshyre; by full dark, we were clopping on cobblestone between a winding reamer of lampposts the same iron make as the one we'd encountered in the oodland oasis. A fresh shard of nostalgia pierced my chest at that thought hen we rode between the lamp rows, our way cast in the dazzling impression of e etchings in their frosted-glass cages: sailboats and sea creatures, waves and icked things from the deep.

All of it awaiting us on the next leg of our journey.

My heart pounded by the time we emerged into Fallshyre proper; it was a wn of wattle-and-daub houses in contrasting shades, grading gently into a sea-one marketplace and business district, every rock rounded by the kiss of the aves.

Between the jutting corners of the modest rooftops and thick lumber wnings, garlands of silver tinsel clung in proud bunches, and gilded glass omegranate lanterns sparkled amidst the glittering clusters. Cut pines dotted ınd-hewn pots on the market edges, freckled with decorations: candied rope, ts of fishing twine, coins stamped with Luck's two faces. Offerings of ıppiness and hope, tokens of a year's delights and the silent petitions for even etter things to come.

My mind struggled for a moment through days and weeks, shock drenching ıy bones. "Jaik, did we miss *Spirited Sunrise?*"

I couldn't fathom that the time had already come and gone—the elebratory daybreak after the last day of true winter. It was the most festive day ı Mithra-Sha, one I'd even ducked off the Spine to enjoy on my long journey own toward Krylan: a time of feasting on potted meat pies and rich citrus uddings imported from the border near Amere-Del, roasted vegetable platters orinkled with sharp cheeses and fresh cracked pepper, and cider so warm it had ıade me forget even the notion of ever being cold, sleeping alongside the Spine.

Not to mention the dancing. The singing. The storytelling, back in my days : Fablehaven…back home in Vallanmyre, before that. It was during a *Sunrise* that I'd first discovered my own talent for Storycraft, entertaining Raff and Mar long past our bedtime with tales of a winter wonderscape that had blanketed ou room without warning in a gale of fresh snow.

I'd counted down the days to it in my journal every year. I couldn't fathom that I'd let it slip by unnoticed this time; but the festive decorations drooped a bit, and the white gourds and pine-bough wreaths fashioned in the shape of Luck's smiling side were sagging in the forgotten way of the melancholy that set in after celebration.

"Flipping Luck." Jaik's tone hung as heavy with surprise—and disappointment—as my laden chest. "I think we *did*."

And it seemed we'd missed that brief window of joy the celebratory day carried on its flocked cloak-hem, regardless of the dire straits across Mithra-Sha. The cheeriest faces we beheld as we trotted along the lamplit streets were still engraved with exhaustion, and hands worked to the bone toiled onward at their labor despite the late hour, lifting only a scant inch in greeting.

We might have left the most hazardous mountain paths behind, but the lac had followed us—or fanned out ahead. And here there was even less we could do, with the risk of being found out by any bounty hunters in the town the moment I flexed a finger of Storycraft.

My hands curled into fists against the warm arch of Hectra's neck, tensing at the helplessness and the urge to be *useful* that strained between every finger.

I was glad of Jaik's levelheaded leading that kept us moving through the winding streets of Fallshyre, down toward the bay itself. The moping decoration and wilting cut-tree displays gave way to practical, unadorned structures where sailors and fishermen made their trade: taverns, seafood stalls, boarding houses for those who came and went from the sea.

A bristle of unease rubbed my spine as we passed those public places, little different from the ones I'd frequented in towns like Rothmere. Places where notice boards were abundant and *Wanted* bulletins littered their surfaces.

Jaik guided Hectra away from them, winding through the darkened avenues until at long last—and seemingly at random—he drew her to a halt. "This is the place."

I squinted at the stone-and-wood edifice off to our left; it perched halfway over the waters of Fallshyre Bay, propped up on sturdy stilts, and the sign above the door carved in the shape of a fish boasted the name of the establishment.

"*The Song Beneath the Sea.*" I swiveled to glance up at Jaik; the strong line of is jaw flickered in the soft light spilling through the building's frosted-glass indows. "*What* place is this, precisely?"

"The tavern Julas always rambled about whenever he was in Krylan. *Best wordfish soup you'll ever enjoy, Jaiky...or, no, you won't, since you'll never leave this boring bit of a city.*" Jaik dismounted with a smooth hop, offering a hand up to me as he often did when we finished a day's ride. "If they're in port, this is where we'll find him."

"*Jaiky?*" My lips tugged up at the absurd nickname—a simpler thing to ocus on by far than how my stomach lurched when I took his hand.

Rather than holding on loosely, palm-to-palm, Jaik swiveled his hand to lace his fingers between mine. In one smooth motion, he tugged me down from Hectra's back to land on the sea-stone road beside him. "Fair warning...if you spend enough time around Julas, you'll earn yourself a name, too. I take it that's an Ameresh habit."

He didn't release my hand. I didn't pull away. "I think I'm all right with tiger."

Jaik studied me for a moment; then the side of his mouth cocked upward. "Yeah. It suits you."

We looped Hectra's reins over a fencepost that separated stone path from seaside; then Jaik led the way into the tavern, still holding my hand.

A gust of cool harbor breeze followed us indoors, speckling the air with the smell of brine at war with the warm notes of salted meat, cheese biscuits, and what must have been the swordfish soup—a savory marine scent my rumbling stomach found oddly appealing.

"Don't do that," Jaik warned at the audible burble from my middle. "Don't give him the satisfaction."

Scoffing under my breath, I took in the rustic details of the welcoming establishment. There was plenty to admire: the gleaming teakwood walls and tabletops, the deep teal accents that striped the walls and wrapped the serving counter, the matching fabric that topped seats and stools, the handcrafted wooden instruments hung between old netting and various figureheads poached from vessels—ancient, retired ones, judging by the state of the dozen or so barnacle-crusted, weathered busts that kept vigilant watch over the room.

A pang of melancholy dug into my heart.

More than anywhere we'd set foot since fleeing Krylan, this place reminded me of *The Tiller's Tankard.* Its angles and corners and the very shape of it reminisced of the few weeks I'd worn a barmistress's attire and worked beneath Errick's stern but fair gaze; when my days had filled with labor and my nights with Lio's company, learning to play Ameresh games and *Poor Man's Dice.*

The ache of missing her seized my throat in a tight fist, and my next breath wobbled its way down to my lungs.

Maker's tales. What would she think of all the adventures I'd had since we'd parted ways in Krylan—and of all the ways things had shifted with Jaik, the stranger she'd only ever met bound to my bed?

The sheer absurdity of that memory loosened the tension in my chest, and my gaze leaped to Jaik just as he settled his stance, lifting our entwined hands to point across the tavern. "What did I tell you, tiger?"

I followed the gesture, passing over the staggered variety of clientele until my gaze landed on a table full of men and women gathered around tankards and cards. There was nothing about their shabby, sea-stamped appearance that stood apart from the rest of the taverngoers, but Jaik strode toward them with that air of swaggering charm, towing me after him, his hand still wrapped around mine.

It was no mystery why he did it; the stares that tracked us varied from curiosity to keen interest. There was no way of telling which of these might be honest traders and which traded in flesh at the fabled and never fully disclosed slave markets rumored to lurk off the coast. Or which might even be bounty hunters.

In the bay, wisdom won over luck.

So Jaik and I kept close together until we breezed into the space warmed by the boisterous crew. Then Jaik released me, stalked up behind the burliest of the bunch, and snared the man's card-holding hand, jerking it near his own face to study the weathered cards.

"Yeah, he folds." With a low whistle, Jaik gripped the man by both shoulders and shook him roughly. "Tough break, my friend."

The sailor cursed—an Ameresh turn of phrase I'd heard Lio utter over particularly stubborn loaves of bread, though I didn't understand precisely what it meant—and then he swiveled to his feet, shoving his chair aside.

I decided right than that Jaik Grissom was the greatest charlatan I'd ever met; he certainly didn't have a wise bone in his body, provoking this giant of a sailor. Each of his biceps was broad around as Jaik's head, sloping into forearms just as brawny. His ink-dark hair was tugged back into a severe topknot and braided down the dip of his back, and his beard was tasseled the same way, draped down his chest. Dark kohl encircled his eyes in hoops as broad as my allest fingernail, deepsetting the ferocity of a stare so pale blue, it was nearly ⌐er.

I lost my breath and couldn't even croak Jaik's name as the sailor towered ⌐er him, lips curling back, teeth baring in a nearly lupine snarl—

And then it transformed all at once into a grin so broad, those black-ringed ⌐es nearly crinkled shut. I lost count of the laugh lines and dimples that hewed ⌐o his cheeks as he lunged forward, thrusting the chair aside and catching Jaik ⌐ an embrace.

"*Jaik Grissom!*" the sailor roared, pounding him on the back.

"Yeah—all right—good to see you, too, Julas," Jaik gasped, clapping him ⌐ the elbow...the only thing he could reach.

I choked on a whoop of relief, grabbing onto the nearest seatback to steady ⌐yself—then snatching my fingers away when I realized the chair was occupied. ⌐*his* is Julas?"

"Jularius Cathan," Jaik coughed out a laugh as Julas released him, gripping ⌐m by the shoulders and shaking him just as fiercely as Jaik had shaken him ⌐om behind. "Best captain to sail in and out of Port Craythin in our lifetime."

"I'm blushing, Jaiky!" The childish nickname fit so strangely in the depth of ⌐las's voice, which resonated like a shout into a thick oaken barrel. "Look at ⌐u—here, in Fallshyre! I can't believe it...how in the wicked, blasted depths *are* ⌐u?"

"Wicked. Blasted. The usual." Jaik raked out a pair of seats from the nearest ⌐mpty table and dropped into one, straddling it; to the other, he motioned me. I ⌐t, touched with lightheadedness, feeling as if I was living through one of my ⌐wn stories. "Who's the crew today?"

Julas gestured around to the gathering of sailors, most of whom wore ⌐olite, if confused, smirks. "Henriet, Reinera, the twins—Nix and Nash, here— ⌐anah, and Syd." A flurry of chin-nods and hand-flips showed which of the ⌐notley bunch was which. "Other half the crew's with the ship. You lot, this is ⌐aik Grissom."

"*The* Jaik?" Nix—the narrower, more sunburnt of the pair of blond twins— ⌐ngled forward, arms folded on the tabletop. "The one who bailed you out of ⌐he Krylan Riots last year?"

"I was in the right place at the right time," Jaik said modestly, slinging his ⌐rms over the seatback and fixing Julas with a pointed look. "I'm assuming you ⌐old them who *started* the Riots?"

Julas pulled at the back of his neck; contrition was an ill-fitting mask on th grinning face. "Sometimes, you kiss the wrong woman."

"Sometimes the wrong woman kisses you," Jaik fired back, smooth as a rifleshot; it gave the impression they'd shared this exchange before. "And sometimes you flirt with the wrong woman, who just so happens to be the wife of the highest-ranking army official in the Tailbone City, and then she tries to take her husband's pension and run away with you—"

"But enough about me!" Julas cut in hastily, dropping back into his own seat after hailing the barkeeper for a fresh round of tankards. "Jaik, what in the depths are you doing here in Fallshyre? You're a long way from home."

My gut twisted a bit at that word.

"It's a long story," Jaik said—then paused to nod and accept his tankard o mulled cider from the barmistress who scurried to our table.

I took mine as well, flashing her a wide smile; I knew all too well what it was like to tend a rowdy bunch like our table alone on a busy night, nevermind the rest of the bustling establishment.

"Mostly," Jaik added when we had some semblance of privacy again, "it's *her* story." He tipped his head my way, then tossed back a mouthful of cider while the rest of the crew swiveled their curious stares onto me. "And believe me, she loves telling them."

Heat crowded the nape of my neck, and I slapped the back of Jaik's head, shoving his face into his tankard so hard he sprayed cider and dissolved into a coughing fit.

"I'm…Addie," I said hastily, smothering my embarrassment at the state I'd put Jaik in.

Julas blinked. A small frown tightened his thick, black brows. "*Addie.* Not…Addie-cat?"

My heart jolted at the way his Ameresh accent, far fainter than I was used to hearing, wrapped around those two precious words. My haunches half-left the chair as I shoved nearer to him, my knee bumping his beneath the table. "How in the Maker's name do you know about that?"

Julas's eyes jumped to Jaik, who'd recovered swiftly at the sharp pivot of atmosphere around the table, his narrowed gaze cutting between Julas and me. Then the Captain said, slowly, "Our last voyage was…let's just say, not the *usual* sort. We were paid a handsome sum to ferry a pair of women from Krylan to one of the bays in Amere-Del."

My heart lunged into my throat. "*Lio?*"

"That was her," Reinera nodded, a tinge of melancholy alight in the depths
f her charcoal-dark eyes. She balanced her chin on her fist, shaggy black hair
lling against her brow as her posture slumped with a weight I knew all too
ell…the pain of missing a long-lost friend.

"Who was with her?" I demanded.

Syd grimaced. Reinera scoffed. "That, I wish we truly knew."

"But Lio mentioned her story-loving friend, Addie-cat," Julas added. "More
han once."

The whole tavern washed away in a teal-and-teak blur, and I clapped a hand
 my mouth to muffle my trembling breaths.

She'd made it out. Escaped Krylan. After all this time, I knew for certain
vhat I'd fought to believe for the sake of my own sanity: that Lio was free. She'd
scaped Galan and the eyes of the Mithran soldiers.

And by the sound of things, she'd made friends along the way.

I thudded back in my seat, wrapping my shaking hands around my tankard.
"Thank the *Maker*."

"So, you're the same Addie?" Julas prodded.

"That's her." Jaik's edged tone reeled me back from the throes of relief,
oricking my spine with a blade of wariness. "How much did Lio say?"

"She said her Addie-cat was a Storycrafter who fell on hard times…that she
und her friend were on the run out of Krylan." Julas's gaze sprang between us.
"Wait. *You're* the friend?"

"Can you believe it?" Jaik mumbled into his next mouthful of cider,
shooting me a wry look.

"Small country," Reinera remarked.

"Getting smaller all the time." Julas wrapped one arm around his ribs and
raked his opposite thumb along his lower lip, looking levelly between Jaik and
me. "Still on the run, then?"

"More like running toward something," Jaik said…then clammed up,
nodding me on.

I forced a sip of the cider down into the pits of my churning belly, buying
myself a moment to frame the words properly. "Things haven't been right in
Mithra-Sha for years now. I'm not certain how much has changed out on the
seas, but inland…"

"Oh, it's the same on the water," Lanah cut in wearily, scrubbing at the
freckles spangling the sunburned bridge of her nose. "Used to be every ship had

a Storycrafter sailing with them, to change the weather patterns and save them from pirates if need be. Now we have to rely on wind and our own wits."

"Barbaric, if you ask me." Syd tugged the twine from his ink-splash of a short ponytail, then cast his arm around Lanah's chair and tugged gently on her golden curls. She blushed, but affirmed him with a vigorous nod.

"Not to mention, less product to move," added Nash—the broader and paler of the twins who otherwise looked so alike they might have been the two sides of Luck's coin.

"We were wintering here," Julas admitted. "Or at least, riding out the last few months of it. Pay was good enough from that run to Amere-Del that we could afford the board and meals, and things have been so slow we didn't feel like sparring with the other ships for coin, anyway."

"But the coffers are drying up." The anxiety that touched Henriet's tone and the restless way she wound her fingers into her graying chestnut hair suggested those coffers were her personal—and greatest—concern. "Only a few more weeks' worth, at best."

"So if you're here looking for me," Julas winked at Jaik, "and if that coin purse rattling under your cloak might have my name on it, then I'm already interested, Jaiky."

Jaik glanced at me, his shrug offloading the burden of convincing them from his shoulders to mine.

Oddly enough, I relished it. This was my quest of sorts, my journey. My story to tell.

So I set aside my tankard, turned to Julas, and held his curious stare. "We're looking for a captain with enough salt to sail us to the Illusionarium."

CHAPTER 49
MAKING A WAY HOME

enriet's breathing snagged. The twins stared at me, wide-eyed. Lanah and Reinera swapped glances. Only Syd maintained an air of boyish confusion, glancing from me to Julas, whose countenance was abruptly clean, cold, without a flicker of any emotion at all. "The...what?"

"Illusionarium," Julas and I spoke in tandem, and I added hastily, "the Isle of Misspoken Stories."

"Somewhere most sailors wouldn't sail if their own skin depended on it." Julas folded both arms now, which accentuated the contours of his muscles. "Now, what are you looking for out there?"

I hastily explained our hunt for answers to the sundered stories, to our own strange recollection of the latter halves of our lives, and why we believed Erasure, of all places, held the truth that had so long evaded all of Mithra-Sha. The crew listened with rapt focus, their tankards all as one forgotten; when I finished speaking, the Captain settled forward, resting those brawny forearms on the table. "Can I have a word with the pair of you, privately?"

I glanced at Jaik; he shrugged, tossed back the rest of his cider, and stood. Together we led Julas to a quiet corner of the tavern, beneath the shadow of a leaping-horse figurehead, half its body lost in a swirl of artfully-hewn waves.

Jaik and I ducked beneath the bust; Julas wrapped a hand around the hook of an intricate cut of seafoam, leaning his impressive weight into the hang of his arm.

"All right, listen to me." The intensity of his barreling voice snagged my whole attention. "I know about the *Wanted* bulletins for you, Jaiky...I saw them when we first made port. And I tore them down."

Jaik blinked. "You did *what?*"

"I wasn't about to have a whole gaggle of sailors off trying to bounty-hunt Jaik Grissom before I got to him and heard the truth…but I didn't think I'd have the chance to make it back to Krylan before the spring thaws came. So I was biding my time." Julas raked his gaze between us. "Now, here you are. And want to know what you're not comfortable saying in front of my crew."

This time, Jaik looked to me with questing eyes—a search for permission.

Though my bowels weakened at the sensation that we were cornered in every possible way, my faith in him was still stronger than my fear; if he was willing to tell Julas, I was willing to trust he had a good reason for it.

I nodded.

Drinking in a deep breath, Jaik faced his friend again. "Truth is…Audra can tell stories."

"That's nothing too—"

"She can finish them." At that, Julas's eyes blew wide. "Because of me. Somehow. Every Storycrafter we've crossed paths with can."

"That's what we're traveling to the Illusionarium to uncover," I added quickly. "Not just what broke Storycraft in the first place, but why Jaik can mend it just by being near us."

"Bounty hunters, soldiers with a grudge, the flipping Sha…they're all after us for coin or just what we can do." Jaik skimmed a glance my way, then focused on Julas again. "But we're not throwing up our hands until we solve this for ourselves."

"We don't just need to know that stories can be finished…we need to know *why*," I added. "And what it has to do with Jaik."

"We need a ship to get to the answers," Jaik said. "We need *your* ship."

Julas sucked in the longest, deepest inhale I'd ever heard, dropping his hand from the figurehead to rub the back of his neck. He blew out all his air just as gradually, glancing over his shoulder at the crew who milled and muttered at the table, staring our way with blatant intrigue.

"I could turn the pair of you over to the town watch," Julas mused aloud, and tension cut through my body at his casual tone; I recoiled from him, but Jaik laid a hand on my shoulder, shaking his head the barest inch. "But that gold wouldn't last long, divvied up between the crew. Getting stories back…that would create more product. More paying jobs. More runs means more food in our bellies and coin in our pockets for longer than one measly bounty."

"Two measly bounties," Jaik reminded him.

"Yours is measly, because *you're* measly. This one…she's a Storycrafter."
as winked at me when he swiveled back to face us fully. "I won't do this one
free, Jaiky. Show me the coin."

Jaik unhooked the coinpurse he'd carried ever since the taverns in Dalfi,
ching it underhand to Julas. The Captain caught and weighed the small
chel, his full lips pursed in thought.

"This should just about cover it," he said, "but let's top it off with a bit
re. The crew's going to want surety for a voyage this dangerous. Even the
s around that Isle are a threat."

Jaik's mouth opened, carved for protest, so I cut across him. "I can tend
here, or at one of the public houses for a few nights. It's good coin."

Jaik hesitated a moment; then his shoulders crumbled into a mutinous
uch. "I could sell Hectra off and do some day labor. How much do you
ed?"

"Give it until week's end," Julas said. "That'll give us time to turn this coin
o sailing rations and plot a course to the Illusionarium. Whatever you make by
:n, we'll call it enough."

Jaik stuck out his hand, scowling. "Flipping *pirate*."

"Still as keen a flirt as always, Jaiky." Breaking into another of those eye-
nkling grins, Julas shook his hand, then mine. Over mine, he lingered, his
lused fingers tightening slightly. "I think…Lio would've wanted you to know
: was in good hands."

Hope fluttered in my chest, and I nodded. "I think we both are."

Nodding curtly, Julas strode back to his crew, barking them up from their
its with a flurry of orders I didn't quite understand. Jaik turned to me in the
adow of the bust, eyes gleaming in the slight gloom that gathered beneath it.
ou sure you're all right with this?"

I set my shoulders and nodded, bulking up my courage. "I have to be. They
serve ample pay for what we're going to face out there."

The last of the tension in his face softened, and his hand wandered over
sently to tuck a thread of hair behind my ear. "You're a good woman, Addie-
t."

Then he brushed past me, striding for the door…leaving me touched with
eathlessness, my face tingling on the path his fingers had taken across my skin.

CHAPTER 50
THE THREAD OF KNOWING AND SEEING

*T*he week passed in a whirlwind of relentless labor; it was to our advantage that we were seeking work in a sailing port, where there were never enough hands to complete all the labor the town required, or to scavenge sanity out of the mess the sailors made.

I hardly saw Jaik during that week; though we used the few coins Naomi had tucked away with our provisions to secure the smallest, shabbiest room at the boarding house nearest the docks, he was always arriving just as I was leaving. And each morning, when I tumbled into the only bed with aching feet from a night of serving travelers and sailors coming to and from the public house for food and drink, Jaik was climbing out of it to make his way to the docks for more manual labor.

I curled up every dawn in the warm nest his body left behind, his scent chiseling away the loneliness and lulling me to slumber.

Fortunately, I had little time to dwell on Jaik—or on the crew we would b sailing with, or the journey that loomed on the horizon. The public house kept me busy, body and mind…tending the pots of stew and cider kept over the hearths behind the serving counter, chatting with the endless rotation of patror who came to warm themselves, pointing them in the direction of the things the needed.

Clothing, board, food, weapons, textiles…Fallshyre was a modest town, b there seemed to be at least one trader of every sort clustered among the close-fitting streets. It was no wonder Julas and his crew had chosen this as their hav to finish out the winter and welcome the spring.

The public house also proved the perfect place to gather news as it tunneled down from the mountains. While I swabbed tables and scrubbed out old dishes, I listened intently to the hive of chatter swarming the common room, keen for even the mention of Galan or of bounty hunters in the passes…or worse, in the town itself.

But there was no talk of either; the bulk of the week passed with little affair, even though every moment was crammed to the teeth with working or sleeping. And even then, some portion of me didn't mind the long days and opposite nights.

It made it all the sweeter when, the day before our intended departure, a gust of tepid wind signaled the opening door of the public house in the late afternoon, and I glanced up from scrubbing the counter to find Jaik framed in the doorway, tugging off his leather workman's gloves with his teeth.

My pulse stuttered, and I sucked in my breath, drinking in the sight of him etched against the backdrop of broad windows, the notice board, the various seating areas where visitors warmed themselves and planned their next steps through Fallshyre.

I could almost imagine a life like this.

A quiet life, like Jaik always said…simple work and honest labor. No storycraft, no lack, no bounty hunters or vengeful soldiers on the prowl for us. A farmhand and a woman from Vallanmyre with nothing impressive to offer the world, but content to simply be a part of its comings and goings, its gentle breathings.

To have stable footing, a place to come home to. And someone to greet at the end of the day, someone the heart nearly burst with joy at seeing…the way mine nearly burst when Jaik sauntered to the counter, nodding to a handful of sailors on his way over.

"Hey, there, tiger." He planted himself on the nearest stool, eyeing the empty mug at my elbow. "Got anything to drink?"

"That depends…what are you *doing* here?" Delight strangled whatever playful outrage I fed into my tone, and I hid my grin instead by turning away to fill the cup to brimming with fresh orange-rind cider.

"Ended my contract for the week early, figured I'd stop by and see you before I go and pass out on that torture-rack the inn calls a bed." Jaik shrugged as if it were the most casual thing in the country—that after a hard day's toil, his first desire was to seek me out. His posture was easygoing, his grin almost flippant when he caught the mug I slid to him. "I hear this spot has the best stew and cider in Fallshyre."

"Oh, is that how it is?"

"It'd better be. I've been sending every day-laborer here." He winked, crossing his arms around the mug and situating himself more comfortably on the stool. "Been busy?"

"I hate you." I slapped the buffing rag against his arm, and he laughed.

"You don't, but I appreciate the intent." Head tilted, he considered me in my bartending attire—a laced corset over a long-sleeved tunic and skirt in the warm cream-and-scarlet tones of the public house. The wood paneling, linens, and drapes were all the same hues. "You know, this suits you. In a way. Maybe because it reminds me of when we first met."

"I know," I groaned, "when I hit you with the slag bucket. Hasn't that healed yet?"

"Oh, the bruise is long gone. I wasn't talking about that." Jaik shifted forward on his seat. "I think about that night all the time."

I braced my fingertips against the counter's edge to quiet the tremor that wrung my bones out. "You do?"

"Mmhm. You want the truth?" His swiveled the cider mug I'd shoved to him, but didn't drink; he stared into it instead. "Truth is, when you said your stories knew me that night...I felt it, too. The second I walked into the *Tankard* and saw you up on that mounting block. You glowed, Audra. It was like you were the only thing I could see in that room. And it scared the breath right out of me." He chuckled lowly, took a slow sip, and finally raised his eyes to mine. "All my life, I'd never felt anything like that. I don't have a single story to tell, but whatever's in me, whatever I'm made of...it knows you, too. And I'm some kind of luckless coward, because all I wanted to do was run from it. I had to get away as fast as I could, because, right then, I knew my life wasn't going to be the same. Even if I'd dodged you, you would've stayed with me. I would've gone back to the *Tankard* and looked for you every night, even if you never knew I was there."

I could hardly believe the *truth* in those words, as tangible as that tie between my storytelling heart and the look of him the moment we'd first laid eyes on one another.

Heat coiled itself around my throat like a noose. Like something so wonderful could only be fatal in the end.

Before I could muster any sort of noteworthy retort, the door burst open behind Jaik, interrupting our conversation—and that unfathomable look he still pinned me with—and ushering in the unmistakable, pert voices of pouting children.

I'd never been gladder of grousing adolescents; swinging around to face them afforded the perfect excuse to hide my flaming cheeks and addled mind—something that happened with alarming frequency around Jaik these days.

It was unbefitting a Storycrafter to be so flustered that words failed her...but here we were.

Three children slid onto vacant stools down the counter from Jaik, their matching scowls as alike as the dark hair on two and the luminosity of their bright brown eyes. The eldest, tallest boy stripped off his fingerless gloves and slapped them down on the counter with the sort of force that begged for a challenge; his sister kicked her feet moodily against the wooden facing on the lower bar, every strike like a death knell. The younger boy simply swiveled his chair in half-crescents, staring vacantly at the hearth behind me.

"Difficult day?" I laughed, ladling warm cider from the pot over the hearth behind me and sliding the mugs into three pairs of fidgeting hands.

"Difficult *year*," the oldest boy grumbled, burying his nose in the drink. "Haven't had any snow. It's all just been ice, keeping the ships in harbor. That's it."

"We never have a season without *any* snow!" the girl added, indignation peaking every other syllable. "Now Mother says it's too late...it's springtime, we won't have any snow until next winter."

"We were supposed to go skating, and make snow-people, and build snow-houses. We had all these *plans*, and what are we supposed to do *now*...build them out of mud?" her brother complained.

The girl shuddered at the notion, resting her chin on the rim of her cup. "It's not *fair*. *Sunrise* is supposed to be the best, snowiest day of the year, and this time it was just *gray*."

"Yeah, we never got snow much after *Sunrise* where I used to live, either," Jaik offered, half-turning in his seat to face them. "That never stopped us hoping, though. Like your Ma said, there's always next year."

The girl stiffened and her older brother blinked, both of them casting a glance at the youngest boy. He sat with his chin cradled on the crook of his arm, his cider untouched, his listless, half-lidded gaze still fixed on the hearth; for the first time, under the burden of his siblings' stares, I noticed how thin he was.

How the yellowish tint of his flesh clashed with the warmth of the firelight that filled the public house. How his eyes protruded slightly though the sockets were sunken deeply, and the snug way he fit his cap to his head, as if he concealed something beneath.

My heart crumbled to the vicious blow of understanding that nearly took my feet from beneath me.

Naomi had told me during our schooling years of a disease she despised more than any other. One that did not discriminate between the young and old, the fit or the frail; though it disguised itself often behind the most innocuous symptoms, just as frequently it protruded in mounds beneath the flesh, making itself known by greedy knobs that overtook bone and organ alike.

I'd held my friend through so many tearful nights when men and women, mothers and fathers, even children had slipped through her desperate, clinging fingers and succumbed to this disease. I'd attended their funerals to support Naomi...I'd seen their bodies.

I'd seen far too many bodies just like this boy's, disappearing under heaps of grave dirt; and all at once, the hopeless yearning in his brother and sister mad sense.

This was not merely the farewell to a snowless winter; it was the last winter their littlest brother might ever see.

Grief seized my heart in a vicious fist, twisting and squeezing, and I traded glance with Jaik; his drawn brow and the dismal downturn of his mouth spoke of an understanding just as grim as mine. Even without Naomi's tales to fashion an explanation, there was no denying the unique sort of desperation that corded through the older brother and sister while they gazed at their sickly sibling.

And desperation, I had done plenty for. I had just spent weeks soothing it in faraway tales told across the mountains.

But it was different. Here, in a town, even one we were so near to leaving..

Busying hands that ached to curl into fists, I snatched up my bar rag and scrubbed vigorously at a stain in the wood that was likely older than me—then hesitated when Jaik caught my wrist, his eyes fastening to mine.

There was so much sorrow in that single, slow blink, his eyes rimmed in silver...and in that sorrow, so much agreement to the desire that wailed in my heart.

I offered him a tentative half-smile...a last chance to argue sense over sentiment. My own sanity was already lost.

Jaik dipped his head and freed my wrist.

Loosing my breath, I turned to the children. "You never know! Some years, snow just takes a while to come. Where *I'm* from, sometimes we had snow as ⁞ as near the *end* of spring."

"Really?" The girl asked, but her older brother scoffed, rolling his eyes.

"That never happens here. Not even this close to the mountains."

"You might be surprised, that's all I'm saying." I beckoned them, hands still ⁞zzing with the need to do *something* more helpful than scrubbing at stains. "In ⁞ meantime, would you three like to hear a story?"

The little boy perked up a bit, head rising from his bent arm. "What *kind* of ⁞ry?"

"Mother says stories are good for nothing anymore," the girl complained. ⁞e stopped telling them at bedtime when Laith was still…"

"Before he was walking," her older brother corrected sharply.

"Well, this is a different sort of story." I tilted my head, motioning them to ⁞low me to the cluster of thick seating nearest to the hearth. Laith slid off his ⁞ol first, then glanced up at the height of the tall counter where he'd left his ⁞nk, frowning.

"Um," he mumbled. "Help?"

Jaik was on his feet in a heartbeat, catching the boy's cider mug and ⁞nding it to him before his siblings had even dismounted their seats. "Come on. ⁞mething tells me you three won't want to miss this."

"So, you're Laith," I addressed the youngest when I settled into a plush ⁞nchair at the hearthside, the roaring heat painting my right side. "And you two ⁞—?"

"Lainey and Ziek," the girl said. "Who are *you?*"

Jaik dropped onto the sofa opposite me, caught Laith under the arms, and ⁞ed the boy smoothly into his lap, careful not to spill even a drop of cider. ⁞he's a Storycrafter."

Ziek's chin jutted up, his gaze dark and suspicious. "Mother says ⁞rycrafters are worth even less than bedtime stories."

The words were delivered with all the bluntness of a child's faith in their ⁞rent's opinion; still, they twisted like a blade in my heart. With so much ⁞ejudice being taught even to the youngest of Mithrans, would finding the ⁞swers to the sundering stories even be enough to put things right?

My gaze drifted to Laith, and the wound made by Ziek's words pulsed…it ⁞ught to stitch itself back together.

Hope. It was there in the boy's eyes, the same as it had traveled before us and behind us in the Drennans. Ever since Dalfi.

"Why don't I tell you a story," I offered, "and you can decide what you think of it?"

Lainey and Ziek swapped a look far too heavy for their ages…a look shar by siblings who'd learned to lean into one another while the world crumbled around them.

Then, with a shrug, Lainey sidled onto the sofa next to Jaik. Huffing, Ziel lowered himself at his sister's side.

I held Laith's wondering gaze, offering him a smile that ached from the corner of my heart I pulled it out of, all the way to my cheeks.

Let me tell you a story.

CHAPTER 51
STORIES SCRIPTED IN SNOW

Once, in a time forgotten, there existed a magical kingdom full of mystical might. Each of s provinces was ruled by a powerful family, and each family was in command of one piece of an ancient relic.

Some claimed the unified relic was the heart of the world itself, from which every land was born…and that it was split into shards by a powerful elder who feared what would transpire were anyone to wield the whole heart of the world for themselves.

That was the story all the kingdom believed…for they all knew the relics were more than a mere heirloom, passed down within the families. Each of the shards contained a season, and by their might, the land thrived, generation after generation.

Until the Vizier came.

iek's eyes widened. Lainey sat forward, chin balanced in her hands. Laith gulped an impressive, loud wash from his mug, then balanced it again on his knees while I wove the threads of he tale before them.

The Vizier was a man of great knowledge from faraway lands…and also one of great ambition. It wasn't long before he became an advisor to the King…and then the chief advisor. And then the King began to doubt his other counselors…the heads of the provincial families, he relic-holders. Until, at long last, steeped in suspicion, the King did precisely what the Vizier

*had intended all along: he dispatched the man to revoke the status of the families and gather t[.]
relics to be housed in the royal treasury.*

*So off the Vizier went, to Summer and Spring and Fall, and lastly he traveled to the
Winter House…to visit the Lord and Lady Winterhart, and their only son.*

*Now, the son was a brave lad, and clever, his wit matched only by the strength of his
heart. He did not trust the Vizier from the moment he laid eyes on the man; but he was youn[g]
and the courtiers often doubted him for his youth. They paid him no heed when he told them t[o]
Vizier seemed fixated on the treasure house where the relic was stored.*

*But the boy was too courageous to be daunted by their doubt. This is his tale, after
all…the story of how a boy named Laith Winterhart saved a kingdom.*

"That's the same name as mine!" Laith crowed, drumming his heels into
Jaik's legs.

I tipped my head, feigning awe. "It *is*, isn't it? Are you certain you're not
named for him? Descended from Laith Winterhart, perhaps?"

His eyes widened, brightening against their darkened sockets as he swung a
glance at his siblings. "*Am* I?"

Ziek peered around Lainey at him. "'Course you are. Where else would
Mother have gotten your name?"

Jaik snorted into the side of his fist, and I shot him a grin; then I focused
on Laith again, spinning the next silver threads of story to match the gleam in hi[s]
eyes.

*Laith didn't trust the Vizier, not even when he claimed he'd come on orders from the
King. The purest hearts are often keen to the darkness in others, and Laith's eyes were wide
open. He warned and warned, but no one listened…they were too fearful of angering the King[.]*

*So Laith crept to the treasure-house on his own the day before the Vizier was intended [to]
depart, his only companion his noble feline friend, Sheeba. He watched, and waited all throug[h]
the night, Sheeba at his side. And just as dawn began to encroach from the east, the Vizier
appeared.*

He came without guard or escort. He came without the Lord and Lady Winterhart. All *carried were the special keys to the treasure-house, which were seldom ever apart from Laith's* *parents. And while the boy and Sheeba watched in dread, the Vizier stole the last relic for* *himself…and he fled, forsaking the royal escort who had brought him to all the Houses.*

And just like that, the world plunged into chaos.

The words hitched on my tongue a bit, for no other reason than that I *felt* nem; I felt the weight of the chaos in the world as if it was my cloak to wear.

But I couldn't afford to stop; not when even Ziek watched me with awkish intensity now, awaiting the next turn of the tale.

Shaking myself back to clarity, I carried on:

There was no sign of the Vizier anywhere in the kingdom, but the mark of his cruel theft *was written across the world. The very seasons themselves were uprooted. The world became a* *dark, dismal place, perpetually between times, both too warm and too cold all at once. Trees* *withered and crops shriveled. Animals sickened and poverty spread. Farmers could not farm,* *traders could not trade.*

The very heart of the world had been broken. Taken by greed.

Laith could not stand by. He alone had seen which way the Vizier went. And when no *one would listen to him, he took matters upon himself again.*

Laith lashed on his sword and training armor. He harnessed Sheeba and packed his *satchel. And then he cast out into the wilds to hunt the Vizier.*

From there, I wove a tale of an heir on a quest and the companions who oined him along the way: the surly swordsman who became his guardian and uide. The thieving girl with a compassionate heart who became his friend. The rickster traveler who he saw as a hero…and who betrayed him to the Vizier for oin.

The siblings hung on the words; even Ziek, whose doubtful scowl faded when the tale didn't trip to a halt. And Jaik watched me, elbow propped on the sofa's back and temple leaned on his fist. The power that strung between us moved in effortless synergy; so long as he was here, the fictitious Laith was immortalized. His tale was without flaw.

I had lost track of time completely when the story began to near its end; I only knew the light was dimming beyond the windows and another tender had come to relieve me. I paid no heed to the filthy glances he shot my way…what I was doing here mattered far more than the counters I'd neglected scrubbing for the latter half of my final workday.

Laith was content, his mug and half of Ziek's polished off, his knobby knees curled to his chest as he leaned back against Jaik. That was all I cared for as I spun the end of the tale.

Creeping into the Vizier's stronghold was no small feat. But with Jorg's swordmastery and Dera's lockpicking skills…and of course, Sheeba's tail-flicking distractions and Laith's courageous heart!—soon they were running through the halls of the black glass fortress Neirir had told them of when they captured him with the Cords of Truth.

Laith was determined to return the relics and to free the trickster-traveler from the Vizier's cruel employment. He was so determined, he could not fail.

But the Vizier was waiting for their arrival. And when they reached the center of the stronghold, they found a room plain as anything…and four crystal shards smashed to pieces across the floor.

"As if I would let you win!" cackled the Vizier as he drew his own blade to meet them. "If I cannot possess the heart of the world, no one can!"

Jorg and the Vizier began to duel, and Dera ran to aid their swordmaster guide. But Laith looked around at all of the shards scattered across the floor, and in his brave heart, he felt the truth.

So he and Sheeba hunted all around the room, dodging Jorg and Dera and the Vizier, looking around at the most plain, unremarkable things that littered the shelves and hearths.

This was not the end. The kingdom could not fall like this. For Laith was a Winterhart, and he was certain of just one thing: the relic was still there, still alive in that

...m. He would know it when he saw it, though he'd never laid eyes on it before...and then he need only touch it, and it would return winter to the lands.

And when one season was restored, the world could begin to balance, and the Vizier ...uld be defeated. Then Laith would bring back all the relics, and the other heirs could touch theirs, and the kingdom would be saved.

"That's like Mithra-Sha!" Laith slithered out of Jaik's lap, turning to his ...lings. "Don't you see? We have to go find *our* winter relic so we can make ...ngs right again! Then maybe that healer will come back, the one who ...omised Mama he could make me better!"

Lainey's eyes tightened at the corners. Ziek shot me a foul look, but it ...dn't stir up the shame that such frigid judgement had wreaked on me in the ...st.

There was still hope in the hearts of these children. In Laith's heart, despite ...w sickness had ravaged him.

And a good story could still feed hope, just as it had in the mountains.

"Laith, I haven't finished the story yet," I reminded him gently. "Don't you ...ant to know what the winter relic looks like?"

He hobbled around to face me, wide eyes full of rapture. "Yes, please, ...istress Storycrafter, please."

Sliding from my chair, I settled on my knees before him, gripping both his ...ands in mine. "It was something plain. All of the most precious things in the ...orld tend to be. Tell me what it was, Laith...I think you know."

His eyes darted around the public house, landed on the hearth behind ...e...then widened. "Was it a glass bird?"

I shot Jaik a look; wordless, he pushed up from the sofa, retrieved one of ...ne ornamental winter doves on the mantle above the hearth, and passed it over ...aith's head. Cupping it in both hands, I offered it to him. "Just like the story ...aid...Laith knew the relic the moment he saw it."

Ziek snorted—then broke off with a grunt when Lainey's elbow audibly ...ontacted his ribs. I didn't look their way; I kept my eyes on Laith as his bony ...ingers closed the space between us, taking up the glass dove and turning it over ...n his hands.

"And the moment Laith held the winter relic for the first time," I ...vhispered, "what do you think happened next?"

His gaze met mine, and the smallest, secret smile pulled up his lips—a tir grin so full of faith, it freed tears from the corners of my eyes.

Jaik whistled lowly. "Would you look at that?"

Lainey twisted on the couch to follow his stare toward the wide windows the front of the public house—then bounced onto her knees, shrieking. "It's *snowing!*"

"What?" Ziek snapped, shooting up beside her. "No, it's not!"

But it was; thick, heavy flurries cast themselves against the windowpanes, the sills already cupping a full mound of white powder.

Laith gasped so deeply it swelled his belly; then he hugged the dove to hi chest and tore for the door, his brother and sister on his heels. Grinning, Jaik offered me his hand, towing me up so we could dart after them.

The opening door ushered in a frigid gust of wind and the sight of dozen of other doors opening as well. The people of Fallshyre stepped out, faces upturned in disbelief toward a spring sky overcome with white-bellied clouds…and toward the deluge of snow they unleashed. Already the rims of fountains and stoops of homes were disappearing under a veil of fresh powde the water within the basins icing over, the pine trees fringing the edges of tow crowned in pale flocking.

It was one of the most powerful stories I'd ever told, with how swiftly it brought the stroke of winter over springtime in Fallshyre. The sight stole my breath away.

"Winter is back!" Laith raised the dove overhead in both hands, screamin his triumph to the sifting clouds. "*Winter is back!*"

He took off at a half-limping run, smashing between the townspeople clustering in the midst of the plaza, murmuring in wonder. Lainey tore after hi laughing and whooping; but Ziek lingered beside us, raking his arm beneath hi reddening nose.

"That was some story," he mumbled.

"Still don't think they're worth much?" Jaik teased lightly, cuffing the bac of the boy's neck and shaking him gently.

"You gave my little brother a snowstorm." Ziek laughed breathlessly, craning his head back to meet my gaze. "That's worth the whole country. *Than you.*"

He wound one lanky arm around my waist; then he bolted after his siblin calling from them to wait up.

A sharp, wet inhale dragged itself through my nostrils; Jaik wrapped an arm
ound my shoulders, tugging me to his side in a fierce embrace. "He's right.
his one's worth it, tiger."

And it truly was—not only for Laith, but for all of the townspeople who
ame piling out in their scarves and mittens and winter furs to enjoy the fun
ey'd been deprived of all season.

By the time we changed clothes and retrieved our own cloaks from the inn,
e squares were piling up with snow-people and snow-fortresses, the drifts
eckled with a vast array of multihued characters talking and laughing, their
onder hanging thick as our icy breath on the air.

Sailors toted driftwood up from the shoreline to stack for a bonfire.
averners and the owner of the public house brought out casks of cider and
eated milk with melting chocolate. Laughing children leaned on their parents'
ms while they strapped on skates and wobbled out onto the frozen fountains.

Not one face held a glint of suspicion. No eye brimmed with anything but
y. It seemed the people of Fallshyre were as welcoming of a miracle coming
own from the mountains as I was glad to give one the only way I could—a gift
anded from the Storymaker, straight to them.

Fragile as glass. Beautiful as a dove.

Jaik nudged me, and I glanced up just as he plopped a red knit hat on my
ead, snatched from a passing hatmaker handing them out. Tugging the same
ggy sort of cap over his own hair, he grinned. "What are we waiting for?"

And we dashed into the fray.

CHAPTER 52
A TALE BEYOND ALL REASON

or several glorious hours while lampposts ignited and fire burned high against the coming night, we forgot all of the trouble that encroached on the world outside of Fallshyre Bay. Fiddle music and deep strings rose to meet the snowshowers, and in the radiant glow, we ate and drank and danced our way to warmth.

We skated and made snowbirds flat on our backs, our laughter pluming the air. We helped roll great mounds of snow for the largest snow-people, and crawled on our hands and knees, chasing children through ice castles while their shrieking laughter wove with the music on the muffled air.

Once, pausing at the edge of the square near the public house to sip drinking chocolate and warm my numb knees after scuttling around in the snow for nearly an hour, I caught a glimpse of Laith and his family. Their parents had joined the festivities, all of them bundled in hefty cloaks. I could hardly see Laith's face through the cowl and cap he wore, but the squint of his eyes suggested a smile never-ending while his father spun him to the fiddle notes, and his mother looked on, one arm banded around her middle and her other hand to her heart. Tears coursed ceaselessly over the two deep dimples carved by her grin—a perfect match to her youngest son's.

For a moment, I considered approaching her; considered hinting to her that this was no mere act of nature—it was for her son. For *her*.

And perhaps, selfishly, I wanted her to know it had been me. To see her gratitude when she heard the truth.

But I dug my heels into the cobblestones and shook my head to dislodge the notion, wrapping my fingers more tightly around my mug. This needed no thanks, and I would not pursue accolades on a night like tonight. Everything round me was the *purpose* of Storycraft…not only the necessity of it, but the joy could bring.

They didn't need to know I had done it. It was enough to know I uld…and that I had a friend, an accomplice in this who made it all possible.

I glimpsed Jaik across the square, dancing with Lainey, and over her bright merald hat, our gazes met.

Jaik stiffened. Then he shot me a wicked grin.

It was the only warning I received before a deluge of snow dumped all over ay head, sending me staggering off the curb.

My inarticulate, yelping curse crying bad luck on whoever had crept up ehind me drew eyes all over the square and brought the music to a screeching alt. Now I was indeed the focus of attention—and the worst, most mbarrassing sort—as I danced and flapped snow out of my collar and whirled ack to the edge of the street.

Captain Julas faced my wrath with his hands spread before him—fingers till pulsing bright red from the cold of the snow heap he'd dropped all over me. It's not my fault you have a very prankable presence!"

"Right?" Jaik crowed, doubled over with his elbow propped on Lainey's houlder, laughter exploding behind every syllable. "That's what I've been hinking!"

Startled rage morphed seamlessly into mischief; I scooped another handful f snow from my hood, whirled on heel as I wadded it between my fingers, then ent it hurtling straight into Jaik's head.

It was a good throw—one of the best I'd ever made, and likely something I wed to all our practice grappling in the Drennans. But I didn't feel like handing im that victory; I wanted it entirely for myself when the snowball blew the knit ap straight off his head and sent him reeling into the drift behind him.

Collective gasps and *oohs* of sympathy and admiration curled from the rowd. Jaik shoved himself to his feet, both fists sunk into the snowbank— merging full. Packed. Ready.

I backed away, baring my palms, but I couldn't fight the grin that dragged tself across my lips. "Jaik, wait—*mercy*—"

"Too late, tiger! Julas, hold her!"

Brawny arms wrapped around me from behind, lifting me off my feet and queezing a scream of laughter out of my chest as Jaik pelted me with his andfuls of snow—and caught another one to the side of the head himself.

Ziek was already forming a second snowball when Jaik rounded on him. "That's my *friend* you're holding hostage!"

Snow slapped the side of his face, strung with the threads of his sister's mittens as she shouted at him, "And that's my *dance partner!*"

That was all it took; only a few moments, and chaos erupted to new height

Suddenly, snow was flying *everywhere*. Snowballs struck elders and youths alike, squeals of laughter and barking battle-cries lighting up the night. The fiddling began again at a fevered tempo, the wild setpiece of a troupe show as w all devolved into slinging snow like our lives depended on it. I kicked free of Julas and tripped him into the snowbank, and the crew scattered around him, pummeling every other sailor they saw with handfuls of snow as if it were some personal vendetta.

Julas hopped up only to take a full, entire barreling *Jaik* to the waist, hurling him back into the drift where they wrestled and fought to bury each other's faces.

Snow fortresses and snow-people were sacrificed as ammunition. The beautiful, glistering world we'd built turned to a slushy havoc, pairs slipping and helping each other up again only to be pulled back down, children sliding and knocking into each other, forgoing a badly-thrown snowball to shove handfuls of ice down each other's backs instead. For the first time in longer than I could recall, nothing but delight saturated the air. It was joy on top of joy.

It was perfect.

Cackling, I whipped away from the trio of children who'd just peppered my front with fresh powder, my eyes seeking Jaik in the throng; he'd escaped his struggle with Julas and was hunting through the snowball battle, too.

His gaze locked on mine, and that wicked grin lit his face again. He stalked toward me, and I bolted for him, raking snow off a window-ledge when a brief thickening of the crowd hid me from his view. I packed the snow into my fist and concealed it against my side as the bedlam broke, and there he was—

Jaik caught me around the waist before I could even bear down a breath to lunge forward and smash the snow over his head. He spun me off the square and into a pocket of alleyway still strung with *Sunrise* streamers, backing me up against the bricked side of a bakery. "I don't think so!"

Sticking out my tongue, I wriggled my arm free from behind my back and aimed for his face; his hand snapped up, catching my wrist quicker than I could lob the snowball, pinning my arm against the bricks beside my head.

"Nice try, tiger."

His wild laughter set every part of me aflame as it gusted across my
e...the rich smell of spiced cider on his breath. The mirth dancing in his eyes.

The snowball crumbled in my fist when it contracted...then dribbled to the
und when Jaik grazed his thumb over the thudding pulse on the inside of my
st, coaxing my fingers wide.

My knuckles were pressed against the cold wall beside my head. For a
ment, I could feel nothing else but that and the clash of heat from his body as
settled his weight, leaning toward me.

His thumb still stroked the inside of my wrist, and something shifted in his
e.

A question. Curiosity.

Permission.

Fear choked my breath for a moment.

I'd wanted a moment like this one so badly, for months now...and yet the
lision of curiosity and desire in his gaze was far beyond intimidating.

What if we tested and tried and he found he didn't want this, or anything
n to it—didn't want *me*?

I'd endured so much rejection in its countless forms ever since my parents
1 first shut their door in my face. But never that sort; I wasn't certain I was
ong enough to survive it with my heart intact.

Jaik's brows drew together, that familiar, beloved little frown scripting
:ween them.

"Hey." He settled his other hand on the side of my neck. "Look at me. Tell
· what you see."

"I see..." My chest constricted. "I see a miracle we made together. I see
ldren playing, I see parents smiling, I see a whole town forgetting to be afraid.
.d I see how you're looking at me right now."

His mouth curled up at one side. "What do you feel?"

The kiss of cold brick on the back of my body. The heat of him everywhere
e. The calluses on his thumb where it met the softness of my wrist. The glide
his fingertips trailing down from my neck, across my ribs, to my hip,
choring me lightly back against the wall.

"Everything," I whispered.

Jaik slanted his head, his gaze dipping from my eyes to my mouth. "What
you hear, Ayjay?"

Maker have *mercy*. "Everyone laughing out there. My own heart. The way
u just said my name."

"Hmm." The growl of breath in his chest weakened my knees. "What do you smell?"

"Woodsmoke, and...and pine." And the cider on his breath again as it grazed my cheek, my lips, the tip of my nose.

His gaze flicked back up to meet mine. "And one thing you taste?"

I surged forward off the bricks, seizing the nape of his neck with my free Firelight and scarlet heat erupted through my mind, a wilder, more exultant joy than I'd ever known; it spun my head into a story without words. A tale beyon all reason.

Jaik's hand skimmed off my hip, his arm wrapping around my waist as he shifted me gently back against the alley wall, and he kissed the breath out of me—but with such a gentleness it *ached* in my fevered heart.

Jaik Grissom kissed me like he'd been waiting his whole life to do it. Like he was memorizing the moment, cherishing every shift when we pulled back to gasp in breath and then pressed in again. His hold on me was tender, protectiv somehow—as if he feared I'd melt like the snow from our dripping clothes, gone forever, a memory of a miracle rather than the truth of one.

His other hand crept up from pinning my wrist at last, our fingers lacing together, still resting against the bricks beside my head. The tip of his index finger grazed absently over the inside of mine, an almost drowsy tic that thrille fresh heat through my whole body.

We settled for lazy, nipping kisses when the need for air demanded it; and then, at long last, Jaik slid his hand up the small of my back to the back of my neck, and pulled away to rest his brow against mine. Labored breath plumed th narrow gap between us, and he shuddered from head to foot, leaning his weigh into our entwined hands against the alley wall.

"Flipping *Luck*." The rapture in his tone nearly dizzied me. "I've been wanting to do that since Assida."

Shock clawed out of me in a few staggered giggles. "That long?"

"Ever since I realized we both gave up our coin for the people back there. It felt like the first time I really knew who Audra Jashowin was, and after that.. He shrugged, fingers dancing gently along my nape. "I've been falling in love with you ever since."

Heat scorched my eyes. I didn't know when, precisely, I'd begun to see Jai the way I did now...when he'd sidestepped my loneliness and aggravation and made himself a home in my heart. Somewhere between the oasis and Assida an Dalfi, and every small, inconsequential, unforgettable moment between.

A hundred things. It had been a hundred things for the hundred ways I
red for Jaik Grissom.

"Why didn't you *ask*?" I wound my fingers into his snow-soaked collar and
ttled my forehead more tightly against his.

"You're not the only one who's been left out in the cold before, Ayjay." His
ngers played with a tendril of loose hair trailing against my neck. "I figured it
as safer not knowing than risking...you know..."

"A door in your face." I settled back on my heels, leaning into the curl of
s hand around the column of my neck and searching out the flickers of anguish
his eyes. My stomach twisted, a keening pain that echoed the sight of his; I
d my hand on his cheek, relishing the freedom to do something I'd yearned to
r so long...simply to feel his stubble rasp against my thumb as I traced it back
d forth from his jawline to the corner of his mouth. "I'm not going anywhere,
ik. Not without you."

His slow blink introduced a sheen of tears across his eyes; then he tugged
e against him, wrapping both arms around my waist.

For a long time, we simply held one another, swaying beneath the tapering
nowfall to the tune of strings echoing beyond the alley haven. And though no
ne came to look for us, for once, it didn't matter.

We had found each other.

CHAPTER 53
THE MEMORY OF MURDER

R ed and gold. Scarlet and gild.

Let me tell you a story.

A golden cage. A swimming sea of shocked faces.

A blade in my hand, soaked in blood. A knife, wielded deftly. Fatally.

Let me tell you a story…

I was down on my knees, hunched over a figure…a frame.

A corpse.

A bloodied corpse, face-up on the stained tiles. A face blurred by the tears and the blood warping my vision to red and gold, scarlet and gild—

Let me tell you a story.

The knife tumbled from my fingers. I glimpsed the face as I buckled sideways.

A flash of wide eyes, fixed in death.

A countenance rushing up to meet mine.

Dark hair. Lovely features. Full lips, spread apart, no waft of breath passing between them.

A cloak of scarlet—a Storycrafter's cloak—stained in blood.

The same blood on my hands.

The knife in *my hands.*

The knife, bloodied and stained, that clattered beside me as I struck the floor.

What have you done?

I gasped awake, tearing myself from the cage of Jaik's embrace in a world of shadows, floundering across the bed and tumbling to the floor. My cheek struck

ne swollen wood of the inn's uneven paneling, but I hardly felt it; there was
ickness, burning, *vomit*.

I purged all over the floor, all over myself, then fell back on my haunches to
scape the spray of sick. Pain stabbed through my fingers, and I realized dimly I
vas raking at them while I crawled backward, clawing off the blood, panicked to
uproot the half-asleep thought that was already winding its cruel threads around
my heart.

This wasn't real, it couldn't be happening, it *couldn't* be—

Feet slammed the floorboards, then knees crashed down in my line of
vision. "Audra, stop, you're going to tear your skin off!"

I couldn't muster anything but a sob as I ripped at my own hands,
powerless to rid the soaked sensation of that thick blood spidering into every
crack—

"Audra!" Jaik snatched my hands, pulling them apart. "Ayjay, you're scaring
me! What's wrong? What's going on?"

"I think...Jaik, I think I..." The words stumbled out of me, and I broke
down in a half-huddled curl, woozy from my reckless, gasping nausea.

Jaik propped me back up. "Breathe. Deep breath, tiger. Tell me five—"

"That isn't going to help!" My shout knifed through the room, and Jaik fell
back slightly on his heels, hurt flashing across his face.

I couldn't do that to him. Not even in this.

I fumbled for his hands and brought them down from my shoulders,
gripping them in the narrow gap between us—clinging to him for all my life.

"Jaik," I choked, "I think...I think I killed the Master Storycrafter."

CHAPTER 54
ENDURING TRUST

The grating, dull rasp of wood on wood stirred me from rubbing my fingers absently on my sleep-trousers. I glanced up at the mug of tea Jaik slid to me across the small seating arrangement for two at *The Song Beneath The Sea;* we had both accepted we would be sleeping no more tonight, so we'd abandoned our board at the inn, packed satchels slung over our chairs while we waited for the sky to lighten enough for the journey down to the docks.

The world was quiet, the snow from last night's celebration muffling all of Fallshyre. I wasn't certain what felt most like a dream now…that revelrous celebration, Jaik's head-spinning kisses in the alley, or this dark, uneasy hour after my nightmare.

A nightmare that, in truth, felt more like a memory.

"I just don't *get* it." Jaik sank into the seat across from mine and balanced his own mug of tea between his broad hands. "You really expect me to believe *you* murdered someone…and the *Master Storycrafter,* of all people?"

"I know how absurd it sounds," I mumbled. "But it also makes sense. Why else would the Sha be hunting me for a hundred gold?"

He arched a brow, glancing over his shoulder at the snowy plaza beyond the windows. "Can't imagine."

"But it's a *bounty*," I argued. "We've both agreed this all feels larger than what we can do with Storycraft. And I told you there hasn't been a Master Storycrafter for years, since—"

"Around the time you left Vallanmyre." Jaik sat back, his bleak gaze settling on the tabletop between us for a long moment; then his focus snapped back to me. "Look, Audra, I've gotten to know you over the last few months. Believe

, the way you've handled people like Galan, not to mention that skeleton and hounds in the Casmiss Wood…it's impressive, I'm not denying that. But I don't see you committing murder."

I brought the tea to my lips, sipped, then cringed; I'd rarely been one for tea he best of times—Lio's Ameresh dessert blends being the rare exception—tonight, everything tasted like rot. My own breath made me nauseous.

I cleaned the taste from the backs of my teeth with my tongue while I ved the mug aside.

I had an answer for Jaik…the notion that had first set me shuddering in a erish panic when I'd roused from that dream. The thing that had settled into us with harrowing clarity in the hour since.

"If these nightmares we're both having are somehow pertinent…somehow e," I said, "then I killed *someone*. And I've seen her face before."

Jaik blinked; then his eyes narrowed. "Where?"

"On *Wanted* bulletins, while I made my way down the Spine."

Avoiding his incredulous stare, I tugged down the too-long sleeves of my rt…*Jaik's* shirt, one he'd flung to me to replace my sick-soaked top while we'd tily packed and cleaned up the mess of our room.

I hadn't truly needed it—I had plenty of clothes of my own—but the ratty eads enfolded my body like an embrace, and the scent of him tangled in the ave of fabric calmed my nerves some. Enough so that I could go on, quietly, thought she was being hunted. A criminal. But then I saw her again, Jaik…in lvikan. On the same *Wanted* bulletin as my name."

Jaik's jaw flickered with tension, but for once, he had no swift retort.

"I didn't stop to read it." I pulled the sleeves taut over my knuckles on both nds, hiding the faintest pale freckles where the skin had rubbed raw against :yway brick the night before. A daydream swallowed by this latest nightmare. thought they mistook my face for someone else's…or that I'd imagined it. But nv that face in my dream. What if that woman was the Master Storycrafter, d all those *Wanted* notes along the Spine were searching for her murderer, not : the woman herself?" The next words stuck in my throat, but they demanded be spoken no matter how brutally they tore: "What if my name was tied to rs because I killed her?"

"Would you stop *saying* that?" Jaik dragged a hand through his hair, cutting wift glance to the only other patron of the tavern—the barkeeper, lining up sses and preparing some sort of stew for the day's menu. "All right, let's say you *did* somehow manage to kill the most powerful Storycrafter in Mithra-Sha. We both know you didn't do it without a good reason."

A nasty laugh tore from my mouth. "I don't think anything we've seen in this country is a good enough reason for *that*."

"You're assuming her death was the reason the stories broke in the first place, like you told me back in Assida. There's no proof of that."

"Not here, there isn't. There would be in Erasure."

Quiet settled in the wake of my words, and hopelessness panged in my chest. Because, truly, even if this was the cause of the broken stories, we still h to go. We had to know for certain. All that this nightmare had shifted was the burden of responsibility, placing it squarely onto my shoulders.

Now, it was no longer a matter of what a mere Storycrafter needed to do for the sake of Mithra-Sha; it was what someone owed to the country she migh have thrown into turmoil in the first place.

Jaik and I were silent for some time, neither of us touching our tea.

"Would..." Jaik cleared the gruffness from his tone. "Would the death of Master Storycrafter affect memories?"

"I don't know," I admitted. "Naomi would say that if it were just me, if I was the only one who didn't remember things, then perhaps the trauma of killi someone made my mind wall itself off. To protect against the shame."

"But that doesn't explain *me*. Or why everyone forgot *us*, not just the othe way around."

I nodded miserably, then buried my face in my arms.

"Hey." Jaik's fingers tangled in the hair at the back of my head, applying a gentle, steady pressure until I picked my head up again to meet his eyes. "We'r going to figure this out, Audra. No matter what you did, or why you did it, I've still got faith in you."

I let those words be scaffolding—let them prop up the pieces of me that wanted to fall apart.

Then I reached for my satchel, tugged it over my head, and pushed back n chair. "Let's go. It's almost dawn."

We cleared our table, shoved the seats back into place, and left the tavern side-by-side. Jaik took my hand when we halted on the stoop; and then, slowly, giving me plenty of time to withdraw if I wished, he bent to kiss me.

I didn't pull away; I leaned into him instead, pressing my free hand over h beating heart. I let him kiss me back to solid ground, standing there in his tooge shirt, my hair undone, the fraying threads of my sanity undone even rther.

I could hardly trust the world beneath my feet or the memories in my head aymore. But I still trusted Jaik Grissom.

That trust kept me walking, one foot in front of the other, all the way down the edge of Fallshyre Bay.

CHAPTER 55
THE ATHALION

I had never seen ships up close like the ones that wintered in Fallshyre Bay, with banding around the sails and what appeared to be a cold-weather varnish that had kept the snow from sticking to the railings and decks. The sheer height and breadth of them was enough to make me forget my nightmare…and the taste of Jaik's tea-leaf kiss on my mouth.

When we descended toward the bay, other vessels stood out among the dormancy…the few that were sea-ready. Even the way they bobbed on the calm waters seemed different; not lazy and slumbering, but eager. Broad bodies bouncing on their heels, readying to run.

We wandered some ways through the mariner's plot, our ears filled with gull cries and sailor shouts. Fishing vessels were already casting off to greet the dawn, and I was grateful for the ceaseless activity that hemmed the docks. It eased the sensation that we were sneaking off in a manner that might draw eyes.

We were not fugitives being hunted; we were a simple couple taking a stroll to admire the ships in port. And when we turned aside toward one, what other reason could it be than that we were beckoned by an unfamiliar deckhand?

Except he wasn't unfamiliar.

Winding a mooring rope around the bend of his elbow and up into his hand, then back down in a proficient coil, Syd leaned against the bollard at his back and smirked at us. "Restful night, you two? Or a memorable one, at least?"

My ears heated so swiftly they burned at the cold nip of the damp bayside wind. "How is that *any* of your business?"

"Just need to let the Captain know how many hammocks to reserve." Syd straightened up, winking. "Or maybe you lot prefer something more private…the Captain's quarters themselves?"

"Hey," Jaik growled. "Enough."

Relief loosened the harsh knots budding between my shoulderblades. I had no interest in being so intimate with Jaik when we'd only indulged in a handful of kisses—and I certainly wouldn't explore beyond that on a ship full of nosy sailors. It wasn't something we'd discussed before toppling, deliriously happy and kiss-drunk, onto our separate sides of the bed last night. But it was warming to hear Jaik defend the boundaries of our private affairs, no matter how intimate they were...or weren't.

Syd was still grinning when he leaned aside, gesturing up the plank behind him. "Might as well climb aboard, if you're not going to be any fun."

Jaik tugged me toward the ship; I dug in my heels a bit to shoot Syd a glower. "Before you go sniffing around in other people's affairs of the heart, you might as well make yours right with Lanah."

I left him there, gaping, and dragged Jaik up the plank after me.

"You know, I'm starting to like seeing you bite someone else's head off for a change," Jaik chuckled as we boarded the vessel.

I sacrificed a retort in favor of drinking in the sights around me: the three broad masts, the supple rigging, the crew—some I recognized and some I didn't—climbing and scaling and dismounting like trained troupe monkeys from the ropes.

Up at the helm, Julas was a man transformed; gone were the simple trousers and the plain white tunic that had strained mercilessly against his musculature when we'd met him in the tavern. Now he wore a crisp, loose shirt and a Captain's cloak tossed over it—deep blue, trimmed in gold, and pants the same color.

Jaik dropped an arm around my shoulders and nodded up at his friend. "Naval hues. Blue and gold demarcates him as a Trade Captain, first rank."

Now, this was a pattern I was unfamiliar with—and one I didn't mind learning about, particularly if I could find use for it in a tale. "What are the other ranks?"

"Blues are all Trade Captains...they get bronze, silver, and gold trimmings. Army Captains wear red, same trim. Ferry Captains are green, I think. And then there's..."

"Pirates." Julas's voice rang out against the cold, crisp air as he descended from the helm to join us, clapping a hand on Jaik's shoulder and shooting me one of those eye-crinkling grins. "They wear all black."

"Lovely." I mustered a smile for him despite the exhaustion that hung from every bone in my body. "And what do you call this vessel, Captain?"

"*The Athalion*." Julas knocked his temple against Jaik's. "And it's good to have your feet on her boards again, Jaiky!"

"You've been aboard this ship before?" I demanded.

Jaik shrugged. "Not out to sea. Julas took me up to the crow's nest once, after we had too much to drink."

"Poor boy rallied all over the deck down below," Julas guffawed, clapping Jaik on the back so mightily he winced.

"Heights?" I offered with all the sympathy Julas lacked.

Jaik shook his head. "Motion. Feels like the ship's going one way and you're going the other from up there."

"Ah, you get used to it!" Julas shook him by both shoulders this time, then thrust him toward me and spun on the crew. "All right, you sorry slag pot full of sailors, all cargo's aboard! Let's make way!"

"I take it we're the cargo?" I teased as we slipped past the flurrying crew, finding a pocket of empty railing to tuck ourselves against, out of the way.

Jaik leaned his elbows back on the polished wood, grimacing. "Strictly speaking, Julas isn't cleared to ferry us anywhere, much less to the Illusionarium. He could lose rank if he was caught, so…yeah, for their sake, we're cargo."

Shock punched my throat. "Why is he risking his *rank* for us?"

"Because, if you forget all the bluster back in the tavern and the coin we're saddling him with…he believes in what we're doing." Jaik stared across the deck at his friend. "He's always believed in me."

I could think of no words to console him for the risk his friend was taking on our behalf; so I slipped my hand into the crook of his elbow, holding on as lines ran up and anchors were weighed. At Julas's shout, Reinera flew a deep cobalt standard edged in gold rope and tassels—another mark of their rank.

Another blow to my heart, a punch of knuckles biting with gratitude and regret.

If my dream told the truth, all of this risk was my doing. My fault, for my mistakes.

I would have to ensure the reward was equal.

When we cast off, the first lurch sent me staggering against Jaik; he smirked, wrapping my waist and spinning us both to face the water and the mouth of Fallshyre Bay. Lines chafed and sails huffed as the crew worked them, and we picked up speed, moving toward the split in the land that fed out to open sea.

"It's a good wind today, lads and lasses!" Julas announced from the helm. ᴐming in sharp and cold off the mountains—think we can thank our lucky ꞥ for that!"

"He means you," Jaik murmured against my ear. "What you did yesterday ꞥnt a lot to this crew, tiger…they know there's real power in your words."

Hope raised its weary head within me as we barreled free of Fallshyre Bay ꞥ put out to sea; I let myself absorb the expanse before us, an endless gray veil ꞁhoppy surf, a wide-open world of water ahead.

And somewhere out there, lurking in it…the Isle of Misspoken Stories. The ꞧwers to all the questions we carried, even the ones that had just awakened the ꞥt before.

At long last, we were on our way to the truth.

CHAPTER 56
STAGING THE BOOKS

*T*he breathtaking beauty of the sea only lasted as long as my constitution did.

I spent much of the first three days of our voyage belowdecks, my stomach heaving too much to risk any motion more demanding than rolling from side to side in my hammock. I all but lived in the woven netting, strung in square with three other hammocks belonging to Lanah, Reinera, and another sailor named Valori. Of the trio of women, Valori most fit the sailors I'd envisioned; in fact, I found her charmingly similar to Captain Lyndra from my tales, fit with fiery red hair, broad curves, and nearly six feet of height. Her laughter filled the whole room when she unleashed it, which was quite often when she realized how poor a card player I was.

Those games were how we passed the time, when I could bear it between their shifts abovedecks and when Jaik popped his head in to check on me every few hours. I insisted the first day—with what little vigor I could muster while upending my guts into a bucket—that he not sequester himself in the crew's quarters with me.

This was our first opportunity to be wholly ourselves—without looking over our shoulders in fear of Galan or some other ruthless pursuers—since Krylan; at least one of us ought to make the most of it.

The only small mercy, perhaps, was that my seasickness withheld me from deeper sleep. So there was no risk of sinking back into that cage of crimson and gold, to the bloodied knife in my hands and the knowledge of what I'd done. Or the assumption of what I had.

Often, I lay awake, visited by that woman's countenance in my mind—the

If Erasure proved my suspicions true, then returning to Mithra-Sha's shores ould be more than complicated…it would be nearly impossible without the hole country aiming a rifle at my heart. I couldn't begin to imagine what the future held for someone who'd murdered a Master Storycrafter, but I would certainly never be free from looking over my shoulder again.

The thought left me so gutted and fretting, I couldn't discern what was seasickness and what was nerves. But at the fourth daybreak, restlessness won over the wooziness that had held my body in a smothering fist; so when Lanah and Reinera woke at shift change with Valori to man the daylight lines, I struggled up on my hammock as well.

"Are you *certain* you should be moving?" Lanah demanded, watching me with shrewd eyes while she braided back her pale hair in swift strokes.

"We're already moving," I joked weakly, stuffing my feet into my boots and slinging my satchel over my head; I didn't need it, but it was a comforting counterweight whenever I was upright. And it was wise, I'd already learned, to keep a change of clothing with me on this ship. "I might as well do it under my own terms."

"Fair enough. Lying down does make the nausea worse, for some."

"I know, I know," I groaned. "So you told me." But I'd lacked the strength after that first day to be upright for more than a handful of minutes at once. "I think I've adjusted enough to make the attempt, anyway."

Reinera lashed on her cutlass for no reason I could fathom; we were utterly alone on the waves. "Just don't expect any of us to thrust a bucket under your face if you go green in the middle of a conversation again."

"That was only *once!*" Mortification pitched my tone higher, and even Valori, rolling over to face the wall and giving her hammock a kick to set it swaying, burst into laughter.

"All I can say is, thank Luck I have quick hands." Reinera flashed them at me, palms and then knuckles. "Otherwise, you would owe me a new deck of cards."

She jogged from the room, but Lanah lingered at my side, making the journey abovedecks at my slower pace. I clung to walls through the narrow halls and bent nearly double up the broad steps, shouldering through the hatch onto the deck.

It was nearly as disorienting above as below; though the rocking motion was mitigated somewhat on the topdeck, the vastness of the world knocked me reeling. There had been shoreline still visible in a narrow strip at our backs when

I'd stumbled belowdecks that first morning for a prolonged session emptying my stomach; now there was none, not even a speckle of land in the distance. Vast, brilliant teal-blue water spanned in every direction, captivating and consuming.

No stories I'd told of the sea—not even the hasty tale of Captains Kidd and Lyndra—had ever done it justice. I wanted to absorb every drop of it to add credence to whatever tales I spun in the future.

I wandered toward the railing for an even better view, ears humming with the shouts of the crew and the blended harmony of shanties sung from deck to crow's nest. I'd made it almost to *The Athalion's* edge when a gleeful voice shouted, "Ayjay!"

Bare feet clapped wood as Jaik dropped from the rigging and straightened before me, arresting my entire focus. He'd traded his winter garb for trousers slashed at the knee, and he was shirtless, his long chestnut locks banded back by a handkerchief; despite the tepid spring air, he sweated, beads gathering along the thin scar that puckered his chest.

"About time you popped your head out of your den, tiger!" He mussed my hair gently, then hooked his hand behind my neck and brought my face to his shoulder, pressing a kiss to my temple. "How are you feeling?"

"Like I swallowed a barrel of live fish, and they haven't had the decency to suffocate and die yet," I admitted. "But it's good to be in the sun."

"I hear that." His hand slid down to the small of my back, and he guided me to the railing. I leaned into it, grateful to steady myself against the wood rather than rely on my own balance, and craned my head back to peer up at the weaving ropes and billowing sails that cast their early-morning shadows across the deck.

"What were you doing up there?" I asked.

Jaik shrugged, propping his elbows back on the wood and lounging beside me. "Earning my keep."

I eyed him sidelong. "Julas dared you to learn how to sail, didn't he?"

He cocked two fingers. "*Twice.*"

"Well then, how were you to resist?"

"Oh, I think I've already proven I'm a luckless fool for someone who challenges me." He winked. "Besides, it kept me from harassing you all day."

"I didn't mind." Stringing my hair behind my ear, I heaved a sigh to steady my tossing middle. "But I'm glad you've felt useful."

"Hey. You're useful, too. And I'm sure if we'd needed it, you would've awed your way up top and crafted whatever story we needed to carry us out of anger. I'm just glad we didn't have to."

Though I hadn't been seeking his reassurance, it still warmed a piece of me that had wrestled with a sense of inertia and unworthiness, huddled in my hammock all these days. "I likely would've vomited in the middle of telling the tale."

Jaik snorted. "Would've been interesting to see what *that* brought out of the narrative."

Heavy strides crossed the deck, and we both swiveled at Julas's arrival; he'd tied his own shirt but still wore his Captain's coat. Astride the back of the waves, I doubted if he ever went without it. "Well, look who decided to brave the topdeck at last! All right there, Addie-cat?"

Melancholy stubbed itself against my heart at the name; I was absurdly glad to hear it again after all these months. "Better. Put me to work, Captain."

His grin was as dangerous as the sea itself. "Thought I'd never have the chance."

To my relief, Julas didn't assign me a position in the crow's nest; of all the tales Jaik had ever told me, that brief anecdote had dug itself in the fiercest, settling into my tossing stomach. Instead, the Captain put me to task under Henriet, the ship's bookkeeper—and the only one, I learned, who had her own quarters besides Julas himself.

"Thank Luck you're here," she groaned when I ducked inside the small, lanternlit room. "I wondered if you were going to sleep away the whole voyage!"

"Only most of it." I swept the small cabin with a glance. Though it was indeed her own space, it seemed Henriet used it for little; most of the tiny room was taken up with logbooks and charts, a bed, and a small, two-stool desk bolted in the corner where she sat, poring over a book at my arrival. The bed, too, was heaped with tomes. "Captain Julas said you requested me specifically?"

"That I did." Henriet waved me inside with a stroke of her hand, a quill balanced between two of her thickly veined fingers, her hair escaping its sharp tie behind her head. "I need your storytelling acumen."

Picking my way through the mess, I settled onto the seat across from her. "In what way?"

"Staging the books." Henriet slapped down the one she'd been feverishly working through and spun it to face me. "Captain needs a story about why we'r sailing out the way we are…and a good one that will hold up to scrutiny, should there ever be questions after we return to port. Or if we're caught out here, Luc forbid. And," she scratched beneath her hair with the shaft of the quill, then jabbed it toward the book, "it has to account for all that coin you paid us."

"Ah." Already my mind was plucking up possibilities for a winning tale— something to keep the scrutiny from falling onto this crew long after Jaik and I had gone our own way.

"I have a mind for numbers," Henriet added after a long span of quiet. "I always have, ever since I was a little girl. Numbers are simple and sensible, they do what you tell them to do. Everything concludes properly with arithmetic, so I've never struggled with the books before. But tales are harder to tell, and I'm afraid I don't know precisely how to craft a good one."

I offered what I hoped was a reassuring smile, not a queasy one. "I imagin you struggled with how to explain your foray to Amere-Del as well."

Her breath gusted out, and she settled forward, burying her face in her hands. "I sweated every day we were wintering in Fallshyre Bay, begging Luck that the portmaster wouldn't audit us."

A laugh burst out of me as I tugged the book closer. "Luck heard you begging, Henriet. I happen to know just enough about Ameresh trade to make this look real."

It was a different sort of Storycraft for me, but it was peaceful, and it challenged me—both things I was grateful for. While we worked, Henriet told me of their many voyages along the western coast of Mithra-Sha…the ports they'd put into, the things they'd witnessed that even my story-bent mind couldn't dream of. The places both dangerous and beautiful they'd seen; the excess they'd stumbled upon and the lack that had gnawed at its edges.

The greed…and also the generosity.

"Sometimes, I wonder if the world isn't a bit more in balance than people suspect in their own suffering," Henriet mused as we made our way to the galle for an evening meal I hoped would be as well-cooked as the books we'd just finished forging. "Certainly, there's lack, and people who take advantage of it. But if you look about, you'll find people in pockets of need striving to make it ter. Balance…I don't think it's an absence of struggle. It's brought about by ople who dive headfirst into the problem and set it right."

Something about that notion eased the tightness in my middle. It made me ldenly, sharply aware that perhaps my sickness all this time hadn't been owed ly to bad dreams, or even to the movement of the sea.

Perhaps it was owed just as much to dreading where the sea carried us…the oblem Jaik and I were braced to dive headfirst into.

I was grateful for the distraction the galley offered, providing me a few oments more not to think of the Illusionarium or what awaited us there. The om hummed with chatter, lively and brisk when we entered its long, narrow nfines. I caught the echo of Jaik's voice at once, but to my disappointment he s already sequestered at a table with several deckhands, playing cards for a ize pot of what looked like fresh apples.

I swallowed a surge of melancholy as I followed Henriet past him, to a table crewmates I better recognized.

"She survives!" Reinera crowed, shoving out the seat across from her with e boot. "How was the cave?"

"Must you call it that?" Henriet mumbled, sliding into her own chair and aving the one across from Reinera for me.

"It was wonderful," I grinned, settling at her side. "I suspect the stories we un will hold up to any portmaster or soldier's scrutiny."

Particularly the latter; I'd held Galan's detestable face in my mind while I'd oven the lie to keep the crew of *The Athalion* safe. If he came stalking on our eels even months from now, going chest-to-chest with Julas or any of these eople, I wanted their alibi ironclad.

I would not see him harm them on our account.

"Well, that's worth drinking to!" Syd toasted a mug of grog with one hand; e other was looped casually around the back of Lanah's seat, and her cheeks eld a stain of permanent blush. "To the Storycrafter!"

"To the Storycrafter!" Reinera, Lanah, Henriet, and Nix and Nash all oasted after him—Henriet with an empty fist but the broadest smile of them all, rimming with relief. I ducked my head, warmed half by their gratitude and half y the embarrassment of holding their attention; my gaze skirted sideways, and I aught Jaik glancing our way at the cheer.

He raised his brows, tongue poking between his grinning teeth and chin ilting up; then he threw down his next handful of cards, winning himself an pple and a round of groans from his shipmates.

The ship's cook brought bowls of stew, a plate of fresh sourdough bread, and a broad smile that never slipped from his face while he chatted and made his way around the galley. The others tucked into their meals at once, but I danced around the edges of mine; my stomach and I were just becoming friendly again, and that was one balance I was not eager to test.

"If you aren't going to eat, would you tell us a story?" Nix demanded while I carefully sipped my stew. "Been a long while since we heard one."

"Let her eat, you rogue," Reinera snapped.

"It's all right...I wouldn't tell one if I didn't want to." I slid another peek Jaik's way, a bit of mischief striking along my spirit when he hoarded the next apple in the set. "It just so happens I *do* have a tale I could tell."

I kept it brief, another fable like I'd told in Dalfi—but I began it with a focus in mind that made it come alive from the first word. The cautionary tale—of an orchard owner whose greed overwhelmed his acreage and destroyed both his trees and their crops—rolled out of me between careful bites of stew.

"And the moral of that story," I grinned at the captivated faces around the table, my skin humming with the power curling at my fingertips, "is that, if you covet too much, you may just find you have so much of a blessing, it turns to a curse."

At my last word, a door across the galley burst open, mops and brooms tumbling out—no, they were *shoved* out by a deluge of crisp red apples that came flooding from inside the storage room. Shocked shouts and laughter burst above the crooked tumble of fruits thudding across the floor, and sailors dove from their seats to retrieve the sweet treats, throwing grins my way.

Jaik launched to his feet, then froze, hand on the table, shooting me a look of such disbelief that I doubled over in side-splitting laughter.

He may have won a few hands, but I'd bested him at his own gamble.

Hands pounded tables all around, a chant rising from the sailors—first at my table, then at the array of them scattered throughout the galley.

"*Audra! Audra! Audra!*"

A cheer. A shout of delight and gratitude. Hope, finding me yet again in this gloomy, lanternlit room.

The edges of my humor melted into something teary and pure for which I had no name; it heated me from the inside out. And I found my grin matched on Jaik's face when he slipped around the table and strode toward me.

Dipping my head to the others, I stood, tugged my satchel from the atback, and pushed through the throng of fruit-gathering sailors to meet him. ɔe-to-toe, we halted, and Jaik offered the pair of apples he'd won at cards.

"Let's get out of here," he said. "I want to show you something."

CHAPTER 57
TO THE NEXT ADVENTURE

*U*p abovedecks, *The Athalion* drowsed for once; not quite slumbering, but it was certainly less lively than the galley. Julas's first mate—a woman I'd met only in passing named Frixia—manned the helm with a precise hand, steering our course between the lonely pockets of far-flung isles toward our destination.

She offered us a curt nod, the stern black bob of her hair hardly shifting with the motion, and we returned it before we wound our way between the barrels and crates strapped to the railings and mounted the ship's forecastle.

There, strung between the rails at the narrow point of the prow, was a lonely hammock creaking in the breeze.

I slowed, blinking. "What's this?"

Jaik shrugged as he strode to the hammock, fidgeting with one of the ropes, tightening and tying off the left side more securely. "Julas mentioned being belowdecks makes the seasickness worse. Lasts longer down there. I figured maybe if you slept under the stars, it would get your rhythm back by morning."

Touched by his tender care, I banded my cloak more tightly around myself. "It's lovely out here."

"Even better when you're leaning back." Dumping himself sideways into the hammock, feet brushing the deck on one side and head cast back over the opposite hem, Jaik opened his arm to me. I let my satchel slide to the wooden boards and eased myself in beside him, the hammock half-swallowing me in its woven cords.

With a shove of Jaik's foot, we were off, rocking lightly above the deck—and I felt better at once. Something of the hammock's countersway to the ship's rollicking motion over the water was grounding. Comforting.

I nestled my head back against the hollow of Jaik's shoulder, and he tilted his neck over the hammock's edge, watching the stars.

I had never seen them so numerous—not even while we'd trekked the wilderness in the Drennans. The darkness of the sea was absolute, the light immaculate above us, sculpting the sky in silver. I picked up trails carved of stars I'd never distinguished before, as vivid as the footpaths stomped into the snow we'd followed through the mountains.

I'd never felt so infinitesimal. So small and lost in the great scape of things.

Jaik's thumb brushed a circle on my upper arm, anchoring me when my thoughts wanted to drift through that wide-open void. "Julas says we're probably close already. To the outskirts of the Illusionarium's waters, anyway. He thinks we're probably a day, day-and-a-half out, with how the wind's been at our backs."

I nodded absently. "Tell him to keep an eye out for a pair of watchtowers. They used to be manned by Storycrafters…to keep anyone from coming in or anything from slipping out. That's the mark of the Isle's boundaries."

Jaik stiffened, craning his head in such a way that I knew, even without looking, he was staring down at me. "You were going to mention this—when?"

"It doesn't matter anymore. When the stories sundered, the Storycrafters were called back. It was deemed too dangerous for them to be on the watchtowers without the power to craft defenses."

"Wonderful for us," Jaik muttered under his breath—then grunted when I found a piece of his side to land my elbow on. "I'm just saying, tiger…you're going to be our *only* defense once we get near that island."

Nervousness swooped through me, sharper than the nausea. "I know."

We were silent for a time, moved by the occasional idle push of Jaik's foot, sung to peace—despite what lay ahead—by the quiet; the rhythm of the world.

Then Jaik added, quietly, "Whatever happens out there, you know I wouldn't change a thing."

My heart vaulted into my throat, and I pushed myself up a bit, buckling on the awkward gaps of the hammock's weave when I half-turned to face him. "What?"

"Any of this." There was a strange fervor to his voice; to the way he watched me, the way he reached out to shift my hair behind my ear. "Meeting you. Having this Luck-flipped adventure. I wouldn't trade it for anything, Ayjay. Not even the worst parts of it."

Choked with a hundred emotions, I whispered, "Neither would I."

I slipped my leg over his waist, hooked my hair behind my ears, then lowered myself to kiss him—mindful of the crew in the rigging who could undoubtedly see us, but far too grateful for Jaik Grissom in that moment to entirely care.

We kissed slow and leisurely as the night wore on, pausing now and again while I rested my head on his chest and his fingers stroked my back in drowsy patterns, up and down again. Here and there, he told me stories he'd thought up while he worked the rigging and ran lines with the crew, his voice so low and husky it married with the rasp of the waves cutting back from the prow. It was such a quiet practice, something that felt like it was truly just ours…almost a private joke.

The Storycrafter, being told stories she could have listened to every night for the rest of her life.

Now and again, on the hems of his tales in the absence where his voice fell away, I thought I might sleep; and then I tugged myself back up to find his lips, to lean into the pleasure of his embrace rather than risk the threat of nightmares.

He seemed no more inclined for slumber than I was; we were one with the stars, making our way across the face of the night without intention of missing a moment. And somewhere between one spell of kissing and the next, I realized how much I'd missed him, just in the few days I'd been belowdecks and it had not been only us against the world.

I'd missed his humor. Missed his stories. Missed his warmth and his sturdiness and everything that was Jaik Grissom.

"What do you think happens after this?" I murmured, nuzzling my head beneath his chin as we paused to rest our kiss-swollen lips.

"What—after life?"

"After the *Illusionarium*, Jaik."

"Ah. Right. I was hoping that's all you meant." His fingertips resumed their lazy exploration of my back. "I don't know, tiger. It could go a lot of ways, depending on what we learn. Whether or not your stories can be fixed at all."

"Are you going to help me, if there's anything that can be done for them?" I propped myself back up on my elbow to peer down at him. "Come with me on the next adventure? Even if…even if I'm wanted for…"

I couldn't form the word. It was one that would always fail when it hung on my tongue—when it hung between Jaik and me.

His hand brushed over my cheek, smoothing back my hair again, fingers sliding gently behind my jaw. "Just *try* and keep me away."

Before I could truly fathom my own relief that he would still be with me, ∙n if I was proven a murderer, those bold fingers twined into my hair, ∙turing the back of my head, towing my mouth down toward his.

This time, a gust of wind arrested our kiss, halting us with our noses ∙shing. Jaik shivered, shifting beneath me, and I couldn't bite back a laugh. ∙ld?"

"All right, so I didn't exactly account for the weather with this plan," he ∙ttered. "Got anything we can cozy up under?"

"Just my Storycrafter's cloak."

But then, there was no reason to hide it here; the crew knew what I was. ∙d none of them were hunting me.

I swung up off of Jaik, heat punching my core at his groan in my absence. ∙h, be patient, will you? I'll be right *here*."

"Too far," he mock-grumbled as I knelt by my satchel, hauling out clothing ∙ rations to scour the depths. "Come back, I miss you already. Let's just freeze ∙death. It's all right."

Rolling my eyes, I felt around at the bottom of the satchel until I caught the ∙niliar woolen corner of my cloak. With a puff of triumph, I tugged it out—and ∙ght sight of it for the first time since I'd bundled it away after Kalvikan.

I froze.

It felt as if the whole world stilled around me. I could no longer hear the ∙p creaking. The hammock swaying. The wind sighing in the sails and lines. I ∙ld not even hear if my own heart still beat beneath my breast.

I couldn't look away, at first. Could not tear my gaze from the fabric or ∙arate my shock from my distrust of what I beheld, from the *denial* that roared ∙hin me, not comprehending, not *believing*—

"Ayjay?" Jaik pushed himself up in the hammock. "Hey. You just went ∙ite. What's wrong, are you about to get sick?"

"Jaik?" His name clawed out of me—a question that stumbled and punched ∙ward as I hauled free enough of the cloak so that he could see.

It spilled over my hands like blood. Like a stain that never washed clean.

A Storycrafter's cloak…spun of pure, perfect *scarlet*.

CHAPTER 58
FEAR THE DEEP

No breath penetrated my lungs.

Jaik and I stared at the cloak cradled across my arms, eve[ry] inch I'd bundled out the same deep, bloodied shade of red gathering shadows [in] its creases.

It wasn't possible. It wasn't *possible* that my paltry Storycraft, flexed so sparingly over the last handful of months in clandestine aid of my country, had darkened my cloak from blush tones to burning scarlet.

Yet I'd never known a Storycrafter's cloak to lie.

"How in flipping *Luck* is that possible?" Jaik doubled forward, gripping th[e] fringe of the hammock on either side of his legs.

I sucked in a breath, choked, fought for words—

And a warning bell clanged, slicing through our shock, bringing my head snapping around toward the helm where it rang.

"Movement off the starboard bow!" Frixia's throaty bellow—deep as if she'd lived with a pipe between her teeth most of her life and rolling with a rich Ameresh accent—thundered in the dark.

We bolted to our feet; then I hesitated, stringing the impossible cloak between my fists, uncertain what to do with it.

Jaik squeezed my elbow, a silent vow we'd come to this again later. Then [he] was past me, lunging to the right-hand railing, the chilly spring wind ruffling his hair as its zephyrs poured off the sea.

Something about that gust felt strange…unnatural. Like moist breath, cut with a warm, fetid undercurrent.

Swallowing a curse against Luck's ever-turning coin, I lashed the cloak ove[r] my shoulders and darted after Jaik. Pitched sharply against the railing that essed into our ribs, we leaned over *The Athalion's* side to glimpse what Frixia's awkish gaze had caught in the dark.

And there, by the shimmer of lanterns dangling from posts strung along the ipdeck, I glimpsed it, too.

Sickness of a different sort pitched through my body at the motion beneath e waves: a slither of ghastly, green-tinged, larch-hued flesh rippling along the ip's side. Something flickered back along its current like hanks of seaweed ailing in *The Athalion's* wake. A knobby, protuberant spine broke the waves in a eft slide, bony ridges arching into a frilled dorsal crest—then flattening as the reature dove.

A last flicker, a snap of some limb that set the waves churning, and all was lent again.

Jaik drew back slowly, spanning his hands on the railing. "Either that stew's arning on me, or—"

"It looked human," I choked.

A creature. A sea-beast.

I met Jaik's gaze, the memory riding the air like lightning between us: a keleton too large for the world. Slavering hounds and their ghoulish masters.

A Misspoken manifestation.

Without Storycrafters at the watchtowers to keep them penned, these reatures were spilling out into the seas.

I jolted when feet clapped the main deck below us; Julas surged out into the pen, summoned by the bell, buttoning his Captain's coat over his muscled chest vhile he led the stream of sailors to the railing. So many of us clustered against he starboard side, I wondered for a moment if we would capsize *The Athalion*.

Movement streaked along the ship's shoulder again, setting a handful of the crew back on their heels with cries of shock and disgust. A split, whale-like tail broke the waves, then slapped down again, propelling the creature deep beneath the surface.

It moved swiftly. With intent.

"What is that thing, Ayjay?" Jaik growled.

My mind stumbled through various notions—what a Storycrafter might've been trying to create with such a sleek, humanlike body, those tendrils of hair, and the *tail*...

The crew bolted along the deck, following the streamlined arch as the beast's body reappeared; its dorsal spines flared, its shoulders pumping above the

waves, head cresting for a moment to bare a dripping curtain of black hair befo:
it dove again, rocking the ship in its wake.

"What in the blasted depths are we looking at?" Julas howled to no one in
particular.

Daring Luck, I fitted boot to wood and lurched up onto the railing. Jaik
grabbed for my ankle, but I kicked his hand away, winding my arm into the
rigging as I leaned out over the waves for a clearer glimpse of what we were
facing.

Staring straight down into the chasm of the sea, I saw *light*.

The creature floated below the surface, face turned upward, its skin
emanating a sickly olive glow like a lantern smothered beneath a sheet. Black
locks fanned in oil-slick tresses around its skull—a behemoth skull, broad as hal:
the ship itself, made up of jagged angles. Sword-sharp jawlines carving back fron
a hollow neck; bladed cheekbones like razored shelves cutting against the
currents; a nasal cavity piercing like bone hollows dug into stone.

I coughed up all my breath as terror jabbed into my deepest parts.

With a low, vibrating *thrum* like a prison door clanging shut, the creature's
eyes pulsed into view.

White, lidless, vacant orbs gazed up at me from sunken sockets. And
fuming from that stare, blank though it was—

Malice. Wickedness incarnate.

I knew precisely what this was meant to be. And what it had done to us.

Air rushed back into my aching lungs, then cracked out in a scream. "All of
you, scatter! *Get off the starboard side!*"

Those eyes snuffed out.

With a mighty surge, water belted in a tidal blast up beneath the ship's right
side, rearing it skyward. My feet left the railing, and I lunged with all my might,
tangling my limbs into the rigging. A shriek cut free from my chest as I found
myself dangling face-first toward the water, strung up in the ropes—only their
chafing twine between my body and the abyss.

Jaik roared my name. Screams hammered against my ears as sailors pitched
over the railing, clung to what they could—then slipped and plummeted.

Straight into the open maw of the beast rising up from the depths, her
emaciated frame lit from within—a glow that guided sailors to the depths. To
their *deaths*.

The Misspoken siren devoured the members of Julas's crew who'd lost their
grip, her fanged jowls split wide, utterly consuming; the shadows of their corpses

inked against her inner light, tumbling down her throat, winking out like blackened stars where they fell.

For a moment, *The Athalion* was suspended on nothing, the water cascading away from the belly of the ship; only from my vantage point, dangling in the rigging, did I see what kept us aloft.

We were balanced on the slick, rotting arch of the siren's tail, framed by the jagged crests that jabbed out from the lean, muscular twist of her lower half.

Those white eyes blinked open again. A gruesome grin split her mouth wide open to the jutting angles of her jaw, her craw craving, a clawed hand rising from the sea to pluck us up for a meal—

Rifleshot slammed into her left eye.

The siren's shriek made it clear where the Misspoken tale had first warped her; there was no allure to that sound. Discordant and head-splitting, it tore a hole in the world and half-deafened me as the creature reeled backward, black ichor showering the sails and rigging.

I had half a heartbeat to twist in my web of rope and glimpse Jaik, feet planted, rifle at his shoulder, still raised from that perfect shot.

In that moment, he had never looked more like a Mithran soldier.

With a snap, the siren's tail unbent, and *The Athalion* was falling.

I lost sight of Jaik. I lost my sense of *everything*. The world was a plummeting havoc of rope, seaspray, and screams. The crew's screams. My screams. The siren's screams as she tumbled backward, smashing beneath the waves.

The ship struck the water aft-first. Then the bow slammed down, tossing me up, half the ropes releasing me, the other half snapping taut. A brand of fire wrapped my throat; pain flung itself down my right shoulder, biting into the healed riflewound there.

I couldn't breathe. I couldn't grip anything or plant my feet. Pain noosed my throat, the world falling out beneath me—

Noosed.

The rope was around my *neck.*

Thrashing, gasping, I floundered for the twine, desperate to haul myself up and lessen the tension that lashed under my jaw, that spun my head into silken, shadowed tatters—

And then, all at once, the pressure released. And I was *falling.*

A brawny arm snagged me around the waist; dimly, I was aware of the world bouncing, flipping end-over-end, my hands fumbling weakly for anything to latch onto.

Wood slammed against my knees, jolting my lungs back to life. I gasped in air, choked, retched, and hot breath bellowed against my ear. "I've got her, Jaik, I've got her!"

Julas. The hilt of his knife—the knife that had severed the noose—pressed hard against my belly as he pounded me between the shoulders with his other hand, forcing me to heave air in and out. I sagged over his arm, my forehead nearly smashing the deck.

Familiar fingers gripped my cheeks, raising my head up. "Ayjay! Don't you dare."

Wheezing, I fumbled to feel the ropeburn beneath my jaw, looping over the bend of my throat. Jaik's touch followed mine, then brushed my ear. Pain pulsed in my head at his touch, and I raised my eyes to find his fingers dampened with blood.

Blood that matched the trickle of it sliding from his ear, too.

The siren's scream had plunged the world into a thudding, muffled cacophony. Through it, I hardly heard the waves breaking again; but behind Jaik, I saw her rising.

One-eyed and wild with rage, the siren had returned.

"Burning, blasted, drowning depths," Julas huffed against my ear.

"Go," I choked, shoving his knife-wielding arm away from me. "Sail us..."

My aching throat allowed no more words, but the Captain already knew.

Stabbing the knife into its sheath, he shot to his feet and hurtled down from the forecastle, leaving Jaik and me bent over, clinging to one another—staring as the siren broke water, shooting for the ship.

"Get her," I croaked.

Jaik tensed, glancing down at me. I settled for a nod—it hurt far less than speaking.

For a moment, his eyes darkened with concern; then his fingertips brushed the collar of my cloak. "Suits you, tiger."

Shoving to his feet, he hurtled after Julas, winging down the steps and landing on the deck just as the siren's clawed hands swiped the portside, tearing from prow to hull.

Wood splintered and snapped, ripping my mind back to focus; my fingers tangled in my cloak, feeling the space where Jaik's touch had lingered.

It *didn't* suit me...not that I could feel.

But the Storymaker's power imbued these cloaks with color. That color could not be falsified, imitated, or Misspoken.

My feelings, my belief, my own fickle measure of my talent did not define
value of the tales I told.

He did.

And this cloak was not a lie.

Fumbling for the railing, I dragged myself to my feet, fixing my gaze on the
sspoken siren; and though my voice churned like grave dirt, dark and gravelly
l grim, I choked the words out beneath my breath.

Let me tell you a story.

Down below on the main deck, cannons loosed and rifles fired; the siren
1t and swayed away from their shots, wise to the threat they posed now. Julas
ok the helm, buffeting Frixia aside, barking commands she hastened to pass
ng to the crew of bloodied-eared, panicked sailors.

And on the forecastle, I told the tale I prayed to the Storymaker would save
all.

CHAPTER 59
A THOUSAND SCARLET THREADS

In a world wrought to fashion by a long-ago flood, where islands were few and resour[c]
fewer, power was shaped on the high seas. Rank and status were writ by cannonfire and cut[t]
lash, and every sailor was built of swashbuckle and steel, with saltwater veins and shiplap sk[in]

Every captain and crew was pitted against the other, for they all sought the same treas[ur]
a hoard of power some claimed could restore land. It could grant the finder powers beyon[d]
reckoning.

And Captains Kidd and Lyndra held the sole map to it.

A heady thrill tore through me at revisiting these same characters from the first night I'd met Jaik—though in a different world entirely. Still, their familiarity leant strength to my voice as I picke[d] my way down the steps toward the main deck, focus torn between the tale in m[y] head and the battle unfolding in cannonfire and rifleshot around me.

They set sail for the treacherous waters demarcated by a map inked on leathered siren
skin...a warning unto itself of the beasts who lurked along the way. But the Captains had n[o]
fear, only courage that bordered on recklessness.

Above all else, they sought the hoard for themselves and their crew. They sought the

And so they resolved to endure anything on their quest: the unplumbed ocean depths. The duplicity of the pirate lords who ruled the waves. The greed of their fellow Captains. And the undying storm that lay between the known waters and those marked on the map.

Far off the portside bow, lightning flickered, churning in the depths of the clouds and painting the siren's soaring frame in brutal lines. Jaik twisted toward the storm, beheld it for a moment, then spun back my way just as my feet struck the main deck.

He dipped his chin in a sharp nod; then he caught a fresh rifle Reinera tossed him, shouldered it, and took aim. For a heartbeat, he hesitated—masking his own shot behind another sailor's. When the siren dodged that man's strike, he fired a heartbeat behind, tunneling into her ribs and showering fresh blood into the sea.

Biting back a savage grin, I plowed on.

The threats on the open sea were vast, but Captains Kidd and Lyndra were utterly fearless. They cut down those who boarded them in the night. They sailed through storm and raging sea, turning the punishing rains and roaring thunders to their advantage; by lightning stroke and endless deluge, they cut around their enemies, the map-hungry ship-boarders and pirates aplenty.

And when the undying storm was upon them, they did not hesitate. Hands to helm as one, they drove into it.

With a sonorous *clap*, thunder tore above the sea. A rush of black clouds spilled across the face of the stars Jaik and I had admired from our hammock only moments before. Rain whipped free of the tattered veil, turning the deck to an ice-slick...but it slowed the siren as well, blurring *The Athalion* in a drumming haze.

Julas and Frixia's orders echoed more clearly in the rain, dispatching sailors like seasoned soldiers. Jaik leaped up onto the railing, wound his foot into the rigging for balance, and fell into a mind-numbing pattern of firing, reloading, and firing again while I pushed my way across the deck toward him. Every stride his

way sent fresh power pulsing through me, heightening the tale until it darted of
my tongue with the same sizzling energy as the charged, stormy air around us.

*The maelstrom thrashed their ship at first. It dared them. It punished them to the
uttermost. But the Captains and their crew would not be cowed. They turned their faces into t.
wind and rain and dared them in turn to do their worst. For every gust that ripped the rigging
for every stroke of lightning that beat the sails, they mended and stitched and repaired.*

*For days, they sailed under cover of cloud and darkness unending. And they never once
gave way, never once gave quarter, until their boldness left a mark on the world. The path the
carved through the storm was a wound on the pride of nature itself.*

*So the tempest became their ally. It guided them without map or star or chart to the way
they should go. And at last, they emerged into the unsailed seas.*

The wind blew in a foul, furious rush, snapping the knotted rigging loose,
sending the sails beating like drums against the might of the storm—but I didn't
share the fear of the sailors rising up in cries all around me. My hair stood on
end, the wind tearing my scarlet cloak behind me in a bloodied trail off my
shoulders. Fear perished as exhilaration fought to sweep my feet from beneath
me.

Undaunted, I stared up at the siren as she reared back her arm to swipe at
The Athalion again—and I freed the next words with a grin.

*And there they confronted a great creature of the deep…a serpent built of the backwashed
waves, life breathed into the refuse cast aside by sailors. It was said the treasure hoard itself was
its lifeblood…and it defended its own existence by tooth and claw.*

Twines of scarlet power unspooled from my words, a call sent out into the
world itself—and a mighty roar answered, louder than the break of shattering
waves.

Jaik dropped his rifle, strung his arm through the rigging, and gaped open-mouthed along with half the frozen crew as a mighty, snakish figure surged from the water.

It was indeed built of the ruined things beneath the waves: a leviathan crusted of shipwrecked wood and battered stone, its skin dripping seaweed, its head fashioned of a battered ship's figurehead—a bellowing, scaled sea-serpent carved of amber wood, with fixed, jeweled eyes.

A beast without life. A puppet of my own making.

And it lunged without fear for life or limb, clamping its two-rowed stone jaws around the siren's arm and abrupting her blow.

The sea-serpent was Luck-sent! For the map denoted the beast itself as Waymaker to the island where the hoard lay…the serpent's own trove. Fearless Captain Lyndra lassoed the beast and lashed its lines to the prow, so that it drew them straight to their destination.

At long last, the treasure was theirs!

A crazed whoop lifted from the deck, and laughter burst out of me, equally wild. Jaik lunged off the railing and darted up the steps to the helm; I raced after him, gripping the masts as I passed them to steady my feet on the slippery wood.

"Julas!" Jaik's shout rang louder than the siren's ear-cracking shrieks as it swiped and wrestled with the serpent. "Sail us out of here!"

"Doing my best, Jaiky!" Julas snapped.

Captains Kidd and Lyndra cast ashore, their crew keeping watch over the sea-serpent while they conquered its cove. Through numerous traps, they quested, kept alive only by their unshakeable faith in one another. No other captains, no other crewmates would have breached the trove…but there were no other captains like Kidd and Lyndra.

At long last, they beheld it…a room stacked to the heights with treasure. And at its very center, simple enough as it seemed, sat the most precious possession of all: a ring on a pedestal.

Innocuous it was, a gold band studded with a single ruby. And yet, when Lyndra touched it—

I broke off at a snap of wood and shattering stone, spinning back halfway up the steps.

Shock yanked the words straight from my mind and mouth, silencing me with a hoarse gasp.

The siren's talons had pierced my puppet's throat. Wrapping her fist around the false serpent's amalgam frame, she tore its wooden head clean from its body and cast the halves of it aside in a shower of useless shards.

And worse, pieces that turned to projectiles as they whizzed down from above.

Wood and sea-rock, seaweed and silt slathered the deck, smashed the masts and punched holes in sails and siding. Bile scorched my throat, and I doubled up cursing as I whipped back to the steps, clambering up them to the helm.

A shadow passed over me—the siren reaching aboard. Reaching for the wheel.

I crashed atop the deck, and my heart stopped altogether.

Jaik slammed into Julas, thrusting him out of the siren's reach—and her clawed fist closed around him instead.

Skin shredded. Blood slapped wood. Jaik's agonized cry ripped apart the world, tore straight into the belly of my tale, halted it on my lips.

The siren bore him backward, leaving streaks of blood on the wood. Then she lifted him up and brought him to her gaping maw, fixed wide in a sinister grin—

My arms flung open, holding the jaws of the world itself apart. The next words exploded out of me, a surge of scarlet-dusted power, the exact shade of Jaik's blood.

ALL OF TIME STOPPED!

With a sucking rush, sound deserted the world.

Rifleshot hung suspended between unmoving droplets of seaspray.

Cannonballs churned in place, every individual spark of the lit powder that sent them flying still littering the air.

Sailors froze in midshout, midswipe of their swords.

Julas, propped on his elbow, halted half-turned toward Jaik, mouth split in anguished cry of denial.

Jaik.

Caught in a thrash in the siren's fist, beadlets of his blood hung among the zling foam of the sea peppering the air. I could have counted them ..gathered them all. I *wanted* to.

His face was a rictus of pain. But in this pause, this moment of held breath broken time, his eyes were fixed on me.

I held his gaze. And then I blinked, and I brought another layer of this zen reality to focus.

A thousand scarlet threads spun the world together. They hung it pended—they held the siren stationary, the sailors, the ship. The wind and ves themselves.

They held *me* captive.

I reached for the threads that snaked around my wrists and ankles. That and my body to this single moment stretching on and on, forever. And I ced the words from my lips.

But not for her.

And I cleaved into them.

The scarlet threads snapped away from my body, and I slammed to my es—then bounced back upright, ignoring the pain clapping through my body he impact. I scrambled across the deck, tore the knife from Julas's belt, then ved off from the helm, caught the railing, and vaulted onto it.

And I leaped.

For a moment, I was weightless, wild, *aware*. Cognizant of every drop of ter and blood that broke against my form—my body the only thing that ved through the unbreathing world.

Then I slammed into the siren's fist. Clinging to her bulging knuckles, I nged the knife into the meat where bony thumb hinged to palm. Julas's well-ned blade tore through the flesh and sinew like butter, and I peeled back the mb beyond its limits, loosening her grip on Jaik.

The world pulsed, tilted as I ducked my head beneath Jaik's arm and haul him free with the deft shove of my right shoulder; it twinged, pulsing a warnin deep in my muscles that I ignored.

I'd sever the whole limb if it saved his life.

We tumbled back onto the curve of the siren's fist, and I raised my weak, wobbling head to squint through the shadows and the shivering spray.

I was losing time...losing the story.

Was that because of me? Or was Jaik—?

I shoved the thought away. I wouldn't even permit my mind to stray dow that path. He was here, my arms wrapped around his chest from behind, holdi him up against me. And that was where he stayed as I hauled him to the edge the siren's fist and cast my gaze to the snapped rigging that hung in twists abo our heads.

Stretching up to such a height that my shoulder popped and panged—a sharper, fiercer warning still ignored—I snared the rope and wrapped it aroun Jaik's waist. Around mine.

Then I shut my eyes against the dizzying height, and breathed out the words.

Lyndra peeled off the ring, and...with a clap like thunder...time restored.

The world boomed back into focus, and with a gut-rending *snap*, the rope resumed its skyward thrash—carrying Jaik and me with it, up from the siren's grip, careening wildly above the deck.

Jaik's grip scrabbled around my middle. He cursed, cried out, shouted my name.

Then we were falling, and I shoved out an arm, catching at the rigging, slowing our fall until we struck the deck and tumbled down in a rolling heap against the railing.

Boots pounded wood. Julas shouted Jaik's name; Syd barked mine.

Cannonfire ruptured the daze in my head, and I peeled my eyes open to find the siren reeling backward among the waves, her bloodied hand splayed open, thumb hanging only by the hinge.

Vomit climbed my throat. I rolled to my side, fumbling for the words to end my tale...

My eyes fell on Jaik instead.

He lay motionless, fetched up against the railing, hair falling across his eyes d obscuring his face.

Blood pooled beneath him.

"Jaik," I panted, digging my elbows into the wood, crawling toward him iile fire and thunder erupted above our heads. "Jaik?"

My hands were damp.

Damp.

Soaked in his blood.

Scarlet and gold.

Blood on my hands.

Let me tell you a story…

My arms buckled, my chest striking the deck.

Darkness overtook me.

CHAPTER 60
WATCHERS OVER THE WORLD

I woke to a world that shifted and swayed like a lullaby.

Exhaustion was slow to release its grip over me—and even when I blinked my heavy eyelids apart, the pall of deep slumber still cocooned my limbs. I lay prone for a time, awareness sprinkling back over my senses: the bend of dim lanternlight above, the scent of some herbal pack that reminded me achingly of Naomi. The near-inert slap of water on wood, the creak of the ship's shifting bones around me. The scrape of canvas against my back and the uneven skeleton of a poorly-welded cot grinding into my bones.

A gruff throat cleared somewhere beside my head. "You just lost me a bet, Addie-cat. Thought for sure you'd wake up second."

I cranked my head painfully to one side, my wet gaze finding the shape of Julas in the shadows, perched between my cot and the next one over in the ship's small sickbay.

And on that other cot…

"Jaik?" Fighting my heavy fingertips to find purchase on the steel frame that cradled me, I leveled myself upright—then buckled as a hazy gray deluge of weakness surged through my limbs.

"Easy, there." Julas moved swiftly to my cotside, his broad fingers closing over my shoulder. "He's all right, just asleep. Gave him a hearty dose of seaman's swill…it put him right under."

"But…all that blood," I croaked, fixing my eyes on the unconscious slump of Jaik's body. I couldn't breathe easily until I measured the rise and fall of his ribs.

I'd been dreaming of his blood. Had nightmares about it while I was unconscious, though the details grew sparse the longer I was awake.

"Oh, that beasty got him good, there's no arguing that." Julas's strong jaw as boulder-stiff as he settled on the foot of my cot, facing toward Jaik just as I d. "But Hasser sewed him up and packed him over with herbs and tinctures d some truly depths-smelling stuff. He shouldn't have any infection, and after e stopped the bleeding, that was the worst concern." His kohl-stamped eyes ifted my way. "Well, that, and how you dropped like a rock let loose from the ow's nest. Can't stand blood?"

"It wasn't that." I'd thoroughly exhausted myself with the Storycraft I'd leashed against that creature.

We were quiet for a time; then Julas said gruffly, "With that hand crippled, e siren cut her losses. Haven't seen hair or tail of her since. Think you scared e life out of her."

Relief settled me back against the thin, stiff pillows; I let my mind wander a oment, wondering when the siren had been made, and by whom; and why she d been dragged off to the Illusionarium rather than killed, when it was clear e bled.

Perhaps the soldiers who'd driven her off to the Isle of Misspoken Stories d feared for their own safety more than they feared for those who would cross at siren again someday. Perhaps, unlike me, they had not had someone whose e had mattered above their own when they'd faced her.

"How long have Jaik and I been here?" I mumbled.

"Few days. We've been drifting, mostly…sails and rigging were almost a ss, so the crew's been making repairs. Keeping a watch out for anything worse rking under the waves."

I swallowed at the notion, and pain throbbed in the swollen angles beneath y jaw where the rigging had noosed me. My fingers crawled up to graze the rasion…to relearn the feeling of the twine burn for themselves.

A latent trill of panic whispered through my body, and I let my hand fall, eeting Julas's gaze. "Thank you for coming out there into the rigging," I sped. "For saving my life."

The mounds of his broad shoulders arched—as if the choice to leap out ver the perilous waves and cut me free had cost him no thought for his own ellbeing at all. "You matter to Jaik, more than anyone I've ever seen. Don't ink even you could spin a story where I wouldn't take that risk for him." He anced at Jaik on the opposite bed, the stern ridge of his brow softening. "That ight at the helm wasn't the first time he's saved my hide…that's just the sort of friend he is, the kind he's always been. I'd do anything for that man. That's why we're here."

This time, the heat in my throat burned like gratitude for both our sakes. "He's Luck-blessed to have you."

"I could say the same." Julas folded his arms over his muscled abdomen, straightening up until his back cracked unreasonably loud in the close, quiet bay. "We saw what you did out there, even if none of us can claim to know how you did it. And this?" He reached over the backside of the cot and tugged up a fistful of scarlet—my Storycrafter's cloak. "This tells me we're *all* Luck-blessed to have you on our side and on our ship, Addie-cat."

Before I could muster another word of thanks—for his belief in me, misplaced and mostly unfounded thought it might have been—the drum of footsteps echoed through the room. Julas snapped to his feet when the sickbay door sailed open, framing Frixia against a hall full of swinging, lit lanterns.

"Captain." Her middle-aged face cupped shadows in every sun-squinted fold. "Land, ho."

Julas and I swapped a glance; then he thrust a callused hand beneath my face. "Coming?"

Ignoring the weakness that still thrummed in my body, I let him haul me from the cot. Snatching up my cloak and bundling it around my shoulders to ward off the chill, I cast one last glance at Jaik—still inert, his face angled our way, the frame of his jaw and brow smoothed with lanternlight.

Then I plodded after Julas and Frixia.

The Captain took the lead, his First Mate falling back to keep watch over me. As we walked, she murmured, "It was magnificent, what you did with the storm and the serpent. It gave the crew more hope than you can fathom, to see tales manifest their might again. And it has helped to ease the grief, some."

Swallowing ached more than just my wounded throat this time. "Who—?"

Frixia named a handful of sailors I hadn't known—and I regretted it. "Nix and Nash," she added, and the anguish that weighed her voice pierced my chest even deeper when she went on, "Valori. And we found Henriet in her quarters when the chaos settled. Hasser suspects she struck her head when the ship fell from the siren's tail."

A swell of sorrow nearly knocked my legs from beneath me, my gaze dragging irresistibly to Valori's empty, swaying hammock in the square we'd made with Reinera and Lanah as we passed through the crew's bay; the echoes of the laughter we'd shared while I'd clung to the edges of my wavering stitution haunted the walls, winding after us the last hall and up the steps to topdeck.

In the murky gray gloom before dawn, I staggered down the deepest breath uld manage around the fist-sized holes punched in my gut from the tragedy crew had suffered—personal losses. Deaths endured for our sake, for the e of putting the world right again.

And then, for the first time, I beheld in earnest the damage the siren had aked in all its terrible rampaging.

Railings on both sides of *The Athalion* were snapped like kindling, the sails run down for mending with talon-length tears rived down their middles. Syd l Lanah were settled in rope harnesses with buckets of pitch and wood ckets in arm; another pair of sailors I'd had yet to be acquainted with braced noist them up the tallest mast to do repair work on its battered length.

But they were not hoisting. And no one was moving. Every eye was nsfixed off the starboard side.

For a moment, panic plunged through me; a vision of sharp, skull-like tures and a stream of ink-trail hair darted through my mind so swiftly I sucked breath in through my teeth, and Frixia glanced my way.

She was the only one able to tear her gaze from what we'd drifted upon, at mercy of the currents…as if the world craved our coming here.

The watchtowers were not mere stone and mortar. They were works of —perhaps even Wellspoken ones, stories brought to life in such a shape to m a cage around the most dangerous pocket of the known world. Fitted to e stone walls rearing out of the sea, the towers were half-shrouded in the ness and fog, but their features were distinct.

It was a man on the left, a woman on the right; monolithic figures rendered precise detail, down to the carven thatch of the man's forward-cropped hair l the woman's granite tresses trailing so distinctly over her shoulders, they ght have even been wind-stirred. Each stood with their Storycrafter's cloak t up in hand, their noses leveled in the crooks of their elbows, chiseled eyes ering with lethal vigilance over the bars of their arms. Their fists met in the ce between their towers, knuckles to knuckles, the articulate detailing of their aks gathered up in their fingers and then cascading back across their bodies, eeping down to rest in perfect rendering where their legs plunged steadfast o the stone.

Guardians. Defenders. Watchers over the world, protecting what lay yond from what awaited inside.

The hair rose on my neck as I squinted through the shawl of early-morni
fog that shrouded the lower portion of the stone walls from which they reared
the sea beyond lay in shadow, but there was something sinister about that mist
Something just as watchful as the towers themselves.

Something that lurked. Something that bided its time.

"The Illusionarium." Julas's tone was equal parts reverence and trepidatic
echoing the churn of emotion that engulfed my chest.

We moved to the broken railing together, our gazes pinned to the towers
we drifted before them; the gap between was broad enough for a half-dozen
ships to sail through abreast of one another, and somehow that made the notic
of sailing a single one alone seem all the more intimidating. Particularly a ship
crippled as *The Athalion*.

"The Isle lies beyond that wall." The words croaked out of me, a gift of
logic lit like a candle against the miasma of unease gripping the ship whole. "If
weren't so dark, or so misty, we might be able to see Erasure from here."

"Ah," a dry, pain-riddled voice floated across the deck from behind me,
"something tells me it's always got that ominous fog out here."

Shock beat through my blood, and I wrenched around on heel. "Jaik!"

I took swift stock of him as he limped across the deck to join us—dresse
in a shabby sailor's coat thrown over his bandaged chest, hair mussed, eyes
stamped with exhaustion.

But he was upright. Awake. No longer marred with blood, as he had been
at the helm…and in my nightmares.

Swallowing the swell of emotion that blotted out my composure, I manag
to choke, "We thought you would be asleep for a while yet."

"Yeah, well…here I am." He grimaced, tucking one hand over his ribs
beneath the shelter of the open coat as he leaned an elbow on the railing
between Julas and me, squinting at the watchtowers. "So, that's why we're not
moving."

"We aren't moving because my blasted ship is broken, you bad-luck coin,
Julas muttered under his breath.

"That's not what Audra calls me." A hint of humor touched Jaik's voice,
then faded as he bent further against the railing, craning his head back to take i
the sheer vault of the stone figures soaring above us. "All right, Ayjay. How dc
you want to do this?"

"Clearly we're not sailing *The Athalion* in there." I eyed his bandaged middle, bating our choices—which were few. "If there's a smaller craft, I could row us "

"There is," Julas said. "Though you don't quite have the rower's build."

"I'll make do." I would swim the nightmare-infested waters bare-skinned, if ad to; we were far too close to turn back now, and I wouldn't risk the lives of e *Athalion's* crew beyond what sanity demanded.

It certainly did not demand dragging a limping, pieced-together ship into most dangerous waters any of us had ever sailed.

"We'll go slowly," I offered. "That will attract less attention, anyway."

"And a smaller boat will draw a lot less attention than this hulking beast." k clapped Julas on the shoulder with his free hand. "No offense."

The gesture seemed only genial at first; but there was no mistaking how avily Jaik leaned into that hand, or into Julas's shoulder, as he pushed himself refully up straight.

Julas shot me a look, then pivoted to face Jaik so smoothly he didn't disturb grip at all. "Sure you don't want a third crewmate along, Jaiky?"

"You're the one who taught me most rowboats are only good for two."

"Right, well," Julas rubbed the back of his neck, "that was because I wanted have Lissa Havercraft all to myself on that romantic rowing venture, and your nely heart wouldn't take *no* for a good answer."

Jaik snorted. "I figured." His fingers tightened over Julas's shoulder. "I preciate it, but Audra and me is all we need. Any more than that could just ɔw us down."

Julas's jaw shifted, his gaze darting between us. Then he tugged his fingers rough his dark beard and cursed. "Flipping *Luck*. All right, I don't know what n thinking, sending two of our injured off on their own…but we could use the st of the hands getting *The Athalion* back in shape."

He whipped his chin toward the mast, and with a tug of ropes, Syd and nah were aloft; the grind of twine in its fastenings broke the fetters of awe and lease locked around the rest of the crew, and they flew to their tasks with newed vigor.

"We'll drop anchor just around the side of the wall and wait for you to sail t," Julas added gruffly, not sparing us a glance. "How long should this take?"

I studied the mist ahead, squinting for even a hint of land in the distance— ɩd finding none. "It shouldn't take more than today."

"Tomorrow, maybe, if we run into too much trouble," Jaik added.

"We'll make it the day after," Julas offered. "Three days will be enough to get this ship in sailing order, anyway, and we can put in at one of the outlying islands to finish repairs after. If the pair of you don't need to go running off to your next suicidal quest right away."

"I can take a few days off from suicidal," Jaik said. "Audra?"

"At least a few. Possibly several."

"It's settled, then." Julas beckoned us. "Meet me off the port stern, and bring your effects. They're in the sickbay."

CHAPTER 61
INTO THE ILLUSIONARIUM

We made our way silently belowdecks, where Jaik dropped an arm around my shoulders, snugging me against the side of his chest. He leaned against me a bit more heavily than usual while we navigated the narrow corridors back toward the sickbay. "Are you ready for all those answers you've been looking for?"

"Mostly," I mumbled, flecking sweat from my palms on my trousers; a wince twisted my muscles taut when I grazed against a spot of blood on my knees.

Jaik's blood? Or mine?

"Hey." His arm tightened, tugging me to a halt in the press between two walls. Lanternlight contoured his face as he rested one hand against the rough wood beside my head, taking some of the strain off his injured side. "What you did with that siren, Audra—"

"It was nothing—"

"No. That's not *nothing*. You stopped time."

My breath hitched around the offhanded dismissal that wanted to fly from my tongue.

Hearing him say it—knowing I'd *done* it, though I was fighting not to relive those terrifying moments when the world had hung at a standstill and I'd been the only one moving, the only thing standing between Jaik and death—

"You stopped time with a story." Wonder rolled through Jaik's tone as he chafed the scarlet collar of my cloak between his fingers. "And you saved my life."

Pride blistered in my throat, and I cracked a wavering smile. "And I'd do it again if I had to. A hundred times over."

His fingers fell away to my shoulder, his thumb smoothing gently against my clavicle. "Come here."

He guided me into his embrace, and for a moment we stood in the breach of light and shadows, dark and dawn, his arms around me and his chin on my head, my face buried over the scar on his chest. We swayed to the motion of a ship at the mercy of the currents, taking power from a pause spared between th far more powerful currents that guided our lives...that had brought us here.

Together. To the answers we craved and feared.

"I'm not scared of what's out there." Jaik's words vibrated through me wit so much heat and conviction, I couldn't doubt them for even a heartbeat. "I'm not scared of anything as long as I'm with you."

My eyes warmed at the echo of the words I'd offered him that night in Dalfi, when we'd first discussed this mad venture. All I could offer now was a kiss to his chest, to his throat, to his lips in silent agreement; then I pressed my forehead to his, tying my arms lightly around his neck. "Let's end this, Jaik."

His hand slid along the back of my arm, tracing the muscle there, creeping up to weave into my hair. "Right behind you, tiger."

The sun had risen, turning the world tawny-brown but little brighter, when we stood on the port stern saying our farewells.

I kept mine brief; not for lack of gratitude, but because the crew was pressed for time, and I had cried enough in recent weeks to last me my whole life. It was strength we all needed now, and resolve. So I embraced Reinera and Lanah with all my might, kissed Syd's cheek, and hugged Julas until every bone in my body creaked like the belabored ship's hull from the strength of his arms.

"We'll see you soon, Addie-cat." He mussed my hair, then helped me aboard the craft, which swayed from its moorings suspended above the sea.

Eager as I was to conquer that breach between boat bottom and waves, I didn't urge Jaik. Instead, I tightened my satchel strap across my cloaked front and watched him and Julas face on another, their gazes averted.

Jaik, predictably, grew uncomfortable with the silence first. Rasping a hand along the side of his neck, he muttered, "Don't drift off while I'm gone."

"Don't go tangling with any more sirens while you're away," Julas shot back chely.

Then their arms were around each other, fists pounding each other's backs, d I barely caught Jaik's hoarse whisper. "Take care of yourself. See you in a w days."

Julas gripped the back of his neck, shaking him gently. "See you then, ky."

They drew apart, and Jaik stepped up on the railing, then dropped heavily o the rowboat beside me. I gripped his arm to steady him when he buckled at e impact, and at that brief graze of contact, for a moment I was standing in aomi's home in Dalfi again.

It was Jaik who was injured this time. It was my turn to carry him.

I flashed him the most reassuring smile I could muster as Syd and Lanah let wn the ropes, lowering us to the choppy waves; and when we were there, cked by the sinister arms of the sea, I fitted oars to fastenings and rowed us ward our fate.

Into the Illusionarium.

CHAPTER 62
RUN AGROUND

*J*aik and I didn't speak as the boat cut through the waves. All of r
attention was fixed on rowing—something that took several
unwieldy minutes to find the rhythm of, and once I had it, I was
frightened of losing the monotonous beat.

So I timed it to my breaths and fastened my gaze on the wall surrounding
the Illusionarium, then on the mist swirling beyond; it was the only thing that
kept me from holding in my air altogether when we passed beneath the arched
arms of the statues and into the island bay.

Beyond the wall, I still could see nothing but that foul miasma curling off
the water. When we passed into it, suffused in its fumes, I wondered for the fir
time if perhaps it was some Misspoken creation, too. It certainly seemed
irreverent of the rising sun.

We rowed deeper into the bay, unhindered. Jaik's heel tapped in the
footwell. My shoulders began to ache at the repetition of rowing, my right in
particular panging deep in the muscle, snug to the bone.

Gritting my teeth, I rolled the oars harder.

"What do you think's out there?" Jaik wondered aloud at last, his foot
jittering swifter still.

"I don't think we *can* think of what we'll see," I admitted. "So I'm trying n
to."

"Fair enough. No sense fighting the same enemy twice."

I eyed him between the shifting oars, pricked by the tension of his body as
well as the odd calm in his voice. "Where do you think up these things?"

His heel stilled in the footwell, and he stiffened, straightening to grip both
sides of the rowboat so sharply it rocked beneath us. "You hear that?"

The moment his words tapered off, I did.

It was an echo like rainfall—brief, small splatters of the bay's surface turbed. I couldn't fathom what made it, nor could I see anything that did. st still enclosed the craft...and fear enshrouded my heart.

"That can't be good," Jaik muttered, plunging a hand into the belly of the wboat where he'd cast his effects. Snapping the rifle free, he twisted on his at, surveying the waters before us.

Still nothing but that luckless, choking *mist*.

The splashing turned abruptly to skittering. Clicking.

Jaik cocked his head. "Does that mean what I think it does?"

And then, like a torch struck in the night, all at once I saw what lay ahead.

When I first beheld Erasure, I thought of Fablehaven; they *were* twins after , true to the tales told, in height and breadth and in their sable shade. But when asure peeled back the fog like a cruel talon, allowing for the jagged eyes of its permost crest to peer down at us, the similarities ended.

Fablehaven had always exuded warmth, from its jutting side-turrets with eir cottage-like roofs to its many roaring hearths and red-draped windows en to welcome in the warmest summer days, and shut to the gathering snow the coldest winter nights.

Erasure was all frigid, all severe angles with black iron lances jutting from its les. Its only windows lurked more than halfway up its height, their yawning, eel-toothed maws looming darker than the blackness of the stone that encased em. It was a thornbush to Fablehaven's hedgerow, a warning to the Academy's ckoning.

It was meant to keep people *out*. And yet it held greater knowledge than any blehaven offered.

I hauled at the oars and thrust them out, driving us nearer to that island at e heart of the bay on the momentum of my own desperation; my visceral *need* possess the truths that lurked in Erasure, waiting to be claimed.

It was the cut of the oars that silenced all other sound until it was too late.

I heard nothing. Saw nothing amiss, my eyes fixed on that tower.

But all at once, between one heave of the oars and the next, pain erupted rough my back, wrenching a scream out of me so piercing it ripped my throat w. Pressure doubled on my spine; and before I could make sense of the blur of stant Erasure, and Jaik's horrified face whipping back my way, it was all gone. ost in a streak of mist and a glimpse of shrouded sky before I plunged toward e water, yanked over the rowboat's side.

Clarity slammed into me the same moment the frigid water did, piercing pure panic through my whole seized-up frame; I flung out an arm, grasping wildly, and my fingers clawed at the lip of the rowboat's side, anchoring me just as needle-sharp fangs latched onto my ankle beneath the water and yanked with all their might.

Deep in my shoulder, something gave with a sickening, stomach-flipping *tear.* I choked on another scream when my head plunged beneath the waves.

For a wild moment, I had no sense of up from down, of my own body that refused to heed my commands. There was only pain, clawing up my leg and thundering down my shoulder—the shoulder Galan had shot, the one that had been giving me grief ever since the siren's attack, and now—

Now my whole arm failed me.

My tingling fingers separated from the rim of the rowboat.

A hand closed around my wrist, and pressure ripped me two ways, pulled apart at the seams. The scar across my middle gave a single warning throb, threatening to sunder just as my shoulder had—perhaps irreparably this time—and with that punch of agony, I lost my air in a halo of bubbles closing over my head.

Something brushed against my side, thrusting downward; the grind of fangs in my leg vanished, and with a violent *heave* I was rising up through the water, the world a dizzy spiral of bubbles and murky waters and *blood* chumming the waves.

Jaik's other hand closed over the back of my cloak, and he hauled me out of the water, spilling us both into the rowboat's footwell. All of the seawater I'd swallowed and breathed in surged out of me at once, and I vomited all over our things. But Jaik didn't let go of me; his shaking arms were an anchor bringing me back into myself, back into my shuddering, spasming body crashed across the belly of the rowboat with him.

Back to my aching shoulder and throbbing leg, and to that raindrop echo drumming on the water.

"*Jaik...*" I croaked.

"Think I know what's been following us." His grim breath grazed my ear; then his arms vanished from around me. A moment later, rifleshot popped, deafened by the mist.

Wiping my dripping face with an equally-soaked sleeve, I rolled over and squinted to see what had attacked us through the shroud of fog—and my stomach flipped, curling into a horrific twist.

These Misspoken manifestations had the bodies of the angler fish I'd seen
r sale at novelty fishmongers down by the wharfs in Fallshyre Bay: crooked
d arched, their eyes wide, lifeless black holes sprinkled with silver flecks like
ars. Those misshapen jaws with their daggered teeth would've fit perfectly to
e slices screaming in my mangled calf.

But they didn't *swim* toward us; they *skittered* on spiderlike legs atop the
aves, so swift and light and buoyant they hardly disturbed the water as they
rted across it.

"*Maker's tales!*" I scrambled back in the craft as one of the creatures boarded
e side in a crablike crawl and scuttled down the rim toward me; my hand
pacted one of the oars—ripped from its fastenings, the weapon wielded by
ik that had freed me from the beast trying to drag me into the depths—and I
ung it with a clumsy strike of my left arm, flinging the abomination into the
epths.

Standing over me, shoulders squared, his wounds forgotten, Jaik fired,
loaded, and fired in a blur of muscle memory and sheer fury; but that would
ot sustain us for long. The rainfall drumming of these Misspoken
anifestations on the approach spiked fear straight through the center of my
est.

I needed a story of my own; but with the pain in my shoulder and leg
inning my head into cobwebs, I couldn't begin to think of one.

Then I heard it again—more skittering and clicking, coming from behind
s, in the direction we had been rowing.

This time, the pain in my back didn't surprise me; I was already ducking
rward when the knifelike heat erupted across my skin, the creature's talons
king over my cloak as it tumbled into the footwell. I smashed my good foot
to its face, then walloped it over the side with the oar; before its body even
ruck the waves, I was spinning toward the direction from which it had leaped.

And there, through the mist, I saw the stone shoreline at last, spearing its
cky fingers out into the water. The clicking was the echo of more of those
reatures storming the verge of sea and land, awaiting our arrival, their teeth and
earlike legs both dancing for the kill.

There were far too many to shoot or beat back, particularly when we were
oth injured. And they knew it…it was why they were herding us from the
ater.

A plan swirled rapidly to focus as the momentum of our small, insatiable
ttackers bore us toward their kin waiting on the shore. I snatched up both our

satchels with my unhurt shoulder, strung them on, then shoved myself upright and snared Jaik's arm as he paused to reload. "We have to jump!"

He didn't argue, didn't even ask; his arm curled around my back, the rifle bumping my hip. Then he tugged me up onto the rowboat seat and stepped off, plunging into the bone-breaking cold of the water just as the rowboat plowed aground.

CHAPTER 63
A WORLD OF WICKED WHIMSY

O ur vessel shattered into the heap of Misspoken creatures, sending half flying and rolling, the others scurrying from its path. Seizing the advantage of their distraction, Jaik and I crawled onto the shore and fled into the Isle of Misspoken Stories.

The ground itself was formed of no common sod and stone; its surface was spongy, an odd, soaking *give* to it that squelched and sucked at the soles of our feet while we staggered for the nearest semblance of shelter: crumbled ruins that might have once been a home, its Misspoken angles piercing blade-sharp against the murky sky.

My bones trembled at the resonant *crack* of the beasts falling on our rowboat, tearing it to splinters. When I chanced a glance over my shoulder, neck stinging and arm throbbing at the angle, it was only to see our way back to *The Medhalion* vanish beneath a needle-mouthed flood of chomping jaws and soulless, venous eyes.

Heart in my throat, I skidded after Jaik, tumbling into the shadow of the ruins. He didn't hesitate for even a moment, plunging into his satchel to retrieve the healing gifts Naomi had sent with us; while he did, I craned my head carefully around the barbed angle of our shelter to catch my first true glimpse of the Illusionarium.

A long, lonely road curled through lingering pockets of fog that traveled off the water to saturate the inland reaches, stretching toward the faraway lance of Erasure shredding the clouds with its vicious fingertip. Blighted snatches of land and Misspoken crops, hollowed out from the face of Mithra-Sha and discarded here before they could spread to all the rest of the growing food, had wound their treacherous fingers across the island.

The face of the Illusionarium was draped in vicious, throttling vines thick around as a tree and sporting thorns as long as a blade; rotting vegetation that drenched the air with a pungent, sickly odor; blackened fruits, reeking of a poison not even the most skilled Hadrassi assassins could have replicated. All these horrific, twisted attempts to spare our people from starvation now dangle from the fetid ropes of buckling trees that edged the road to the tower.

There were more ruins, too…plenty of cratered stone heaps, the remnant of homes Misspoken in recent years, bought for likely some ludicrous sum by those driven to desperation when they lost everything. But these structures were all as lethal as the one we crouched in, its inward-jabbing barbs telling of the horrific end its inhabitants had likely met—impaled on the shelter that was meant to be their sanctuary. Pulverized by the army and carted off here by ship to spare the country any lingering effect of their presence, these homes scattered the horizon like corpses, stained in the blood of the residents they'd betrayed.

And on either side of the path were the figments of Misspoken stories that no soldier or Storycrafter had yet learned how—or never managed—to destroy.

The largest ones caught my eyes and stopped my breath first: hulking, bare skinned figures, huddled in egglike curls over their knees, wicked weapons plunged into the dead soil before them, ready to be taken up at a moment. Like some guardians raised for the Shastah long ago…and disfigured in the making.

The distant, wicked howls of hounds shook the silence loose, the warped manifestations of canine companions, I could only assume, miscreated by false amplifiers. Their throaty hunting cries and eerie yelps, turned tinny by the thick veil of fog, blended in a stomach-churning contortion with the creak of carousel hinges.

The army had cast an entire Misspoken circus off near the shore, a smashed, battered array of half-broken troupe carts and structures warped between whimsy and wickedness. Someone had no doubt commissioned it to make swift coin, paying a Storycrafter to speak to life an entire entertainment array without a bit of building effort…but something had gone horribly awry.

Skeletons were tangled among the pieces of it, cyr wheels strung into rib cages, the tentposts tipped in blood and rammed through skulls. A calliope played an off-kilter tune, the same handful of notes repeating to nausea from somewhere amidst the seaside wreckage. The carousel alone still stood, making grinding revolution beneath the wind's duress, and seated upon it…

I knew what they were. I had heard plenty of tales of them, though I'd
considered myself fortunate until this moment to have never laid eyes on them.
Misspoken children.

The creations begged to life by barren men and women, or those whose
empty arms had once or nearly held their children…parents like Laith's, facing a
loss that could never be healed, their sanity torn wide by a pain beyond fathom.

In Fablehaven, our instructors had told us how loss and lack could make
desperate believers of even the most sensible people; those who knew a story
could not create or resurrect living people were still eager to try, their faith
turned to reckless determination when what they desired most was denied them.
The proof of that rode the carousel in tattered rags, slope-backed and bent-
headed, a waft of sound floating from them every now and again that swirled
sickness in my gut: high-pitched, discordant cackles and low, guttural moans.

Nearby shambled other Misspoken beings, their jointless bones all out of
symmetry, their necks far too long and sloped with elongated jaws to chests;
their bodies void of all color, leached to blankness, hair dark as the ink spilled
hopelessly across the pale parchment of their flesh.

Loved ones recreated in some soulless imitation. These were not people,
but marionettes puppeted on the cords of Misspoken stories. They were only
here, amidst the wreckage and rubble, because the soldiers had been too pained
at the notion of beheading them—or too frightened of what they could do if
provoked—to deal with them properly.

We had been warned in Fablehaven how the Misspoken manifestations
always hungered. Always hunted. The lust that had first envisioned them was
built into their flesh, desperation incarnate. They had felled seasoned soldiers
with their pain-blind thirst to consume; they would never stop hurting, hunting,
taking. Some could be destroyed by mortal weapons; some, like the skeleton we
had faced in the Casmiss Wood, could only be felled by powerful Storycraft.

In the absence of it, this island had become far worse than a place for the
rare refuse of indestructible, mighty manifestations to be sequestered. It was a
haven for *all* Misspoken manifestations…and it appeared the Sha and his people
had been far busier than I'd realized, with how many they numbered.

There were dozens of them between us and the road. And those were only
the Misspoken stories I could *see*.

Pain wrenched my focus off the creatures, a yelp bitten behind my lips
when chilliness splashed over the inflamed flesh of my leg. I tore my gaze down

to the wash of blood soaking my trousers, a nearer problem we at least *could* dea with.

My stomach flipped at the mess of my calf—ribboned and pulsed by the jaws of the beast that had done its best to drag me to the depths.

"Those teeth," Jaik cursed, rinsing my wounds with the water Julas's crew had packed for us. "Some of these go almost to the bone, tiger."

"It feels like it," I gasped with false humor, armor padded around my shaking voice. Pain burned and crackled like a lightning strike from my ankle to my knee, and rogue threads found a way to pierce as high as my hip.

"Deep breaths," Jaik warned. Then he dumped a powder from his satchel onto the rinsed wounds.

I bit the side of my fist to hold back a sob; the powder lent a whole new dimension of agony to the wound, and necessary though it was, I wished I'd never even seen the stuff.

"Sorry." Jaik produced a spool of bandages and hastily wrapped my lower leg. "Want me to check that shoulder?"

I reclined against the ruins, sipping air through rounded lips for several moments before I had control of my nausea enough to answer him clearly. "No, I know what happened. The muscle, where Galan shot me...it tore. I can feel it."

Jaik cursed, thumping his head back against the rock as he collapsed across from me. "Sling?"

"I think I'll have to." And it would leave me all but useless, apart from my stories. Wounded on both sides of my body before we'd even made landfall. "I'm sorry, Jaik."

"For what? I didn't see you dousing yourself in herbs and serving your skin up on a platter." Despite the flippant words, intensity sparked in his gaze. "This place isn't made for people, Audra...I'm not a Storycrafter and even I can tell that. Don't feel guilty because we didn't get in unscathed."

Clinging to the reassurance of those words, I bent forward, wrapping one hand around my bandaged calf; the pressure helped ease the pain some. "But we did get in."

"Right." Jaik slid a hand around his side, guarding his ribs—they were likely throbbing as fiercely as my leg and shoulder. "So. What now?"

I strained to the limits of my overtaxed muscles, leaning around the ruins to catch sight of Erasure's height in the distance. "If the tales are true, Erasure's door won't admit anyone from outside."

"So, why even have a door?"

"There used to be a Storykeeper, or so we were told. Someone who kept watch over the Isle and made certain no one came to do…well, precisely what we're doing."

Jaik snorted. "Luck sure loves us, doesn't it?"

I offered him the faintest tilt of a smile—the only one I could manage. "I don't know if they're still alive, or if there was more than one…I've never heard of anyone else being sent since Erasure first began to collect tomes. So there isn't likely anyone to let us in."

"If they even would." Jaik leaned with me, bracing one hand on the slab of stone beside my head as he peered at the faraway taunt of that tower. "But there's the windows."

I measured him with my eyes. "Are you planning to grow a few hundred feet in the next several minutes?"

"No, I wouldn't have enough boots for all of them." He shot me a smirk at the hysterical giggle that tumbled free. "I'm thinking climbing."

I pondered the notion—and the dilemma it presented, with the pain thudding through both sides of my body. "Jaik, I'm not going to be able to climb. You know that."

Pain pulled through his gaze. "I'll help you."

"With this?" I nudged his side, and he grimaced. "If *you* can climb to the windows yourself, it will take all of your strength."

"What about Storycraft?" he demanded. "Can you get us both up there with something? A staircase, maybe?"

"If I can focus that much," I said. "But the trouble is these Misspoken manifestations. If they see us on the tower, they're all likely to rush us at once…and we won't have a free hand to defend ourselves."

Slowly, Jaik pulled back to face me. "Why do I get the feeling you already have an idea I'm not going to like?"

"Maybe because I can't look you in the eye," I mumbled, chafing the corner of my cloak between my thumb and forefinger until a shred of scarlet courage soaked into my skin. "If I focus, I can get you at least halfway up to the windows before you're too far for your power to amplify my stories. Then I can raise a distraction from below while you get inside and unlock the door."

Jaik's hand fastened over mine, stilling my fidgeting. His tone was low, brittle with seething emotion when he rasped, "You're talking about distracting an *island's* worth of those abominations. Without your Storycraft."

"I can be scrappy," I offered weakly.

"Ayjay. You've got a torn shoulder and a shredded leg."

"That makes me the weaker prey. The easier target."

"*That's* what concerns me!" His voice punched upward, impassioned with fear. "I can't just leave you on your own to—"

"Jaik. You're not my bodyguard, remember?" I freed my grip from his and laid my hand on his jaw, willing steadiness to fingers that wanted to tremble at the magnitude of what we faced…and the pain we had already endured. "We're in this together…we have to be true to ourselves about what we can and can't do, if we want to succeed at all." His mouth sprang open for an argument, and I cut across him sternly. "*You* can climb that tower. *I* can get you most of the way there…and once you're inside and moving down to level ground, you should come back into reach for your power to feed mine."

Anguish haunted his eyes. "What if I'm not fast enough?"

"You will be, Jaik. I trust you."

It was blind faith, perhaps; but for all the times he'd offered it to *me*, ever since he'd taken my hand that first night in Krylan when he'd still worn my shackles, I wouldn't allow myself to doubt him in this moment. To doubt what we could achieve together.

A shudder wracked visibly through his body; then his hand pressed over mine against his cheek, and he turned a kiss to the inside of my wrist. "Come with me."

"*Jaik.*" I framed his face with both hands this time, forcing him to look at me. "Let me do this. Let me carry *you* this time."

A crooked breath dropped through him; and behind it, the tension severed from his body. Resignation spilled into its place, the sort that wracked me full of guilt…even though I'd won the argument.

"You take the rifle," he growled. "You take everything except my knife. And you *stay alive*."

"I had no plans to the contrary." I offered him a wider smile this time; he didn't meet it, only snatched the back of my head and pulled me in for the fiercest kiss he'd given me yet. A kiss soaked in regret and fear. A kiss that begged me to remain with him every second I could.

It was over too soon; a quake shook the whole Illusionarium, and Jaik peeled back from me, craning his head to peer around the ruins.

He paled in a way that drained every drop of confidence from my body.

"*What?*" I snapped.

"You don't want to know." All at once, he was pure focus. Snapping a scarf
of my satchel, he tied a complicated knot and slipped my arm into the cradle
it, then tucked it over my head and freed my hair from the strap. "Let's get
ide that tower."

I didn't realize I'd begun to saw my lower lip between my teeth in sheer
ves until his thumb grazed my chin.

"Hey." He tugged my lip free, then followed the throbbing indent my teeth
l made in the tender flesh. "No, listen…you're right. We can *do* this, Ayjay.
ord and story."

Except that, inevitably, once he was on the tower face, we would have
ther.

It was my plan. I was resolved to it.

It still terrified the life out of me.

But I let Jaik guide me by his gentle grip on my chin, our lips meeting again
a slow, lingering kiss I wished could last for the rest of our lives. A moment I
urned to hide myself in until all the necessity of this passed away.

Jaik drew back first, and in the absence of his warmth, duty crashed over
—a weight far colder and heavier than the cloak knotted around my throat or
sling strapped around my arm. Gritting my teeth, I gripped a tine of the ruins
hind me, rusted with blood, and bobbed to my feet with Jaik beside me.

I finally saw what he had seen: it was the largest Misspoken abomination
, so large I could hardly see both ends of it. Its emaciated frame sloped over
path, a bridge of rotting flesh frozen as if in mid-crawl…facing our way.

It sensed us. Scented us. It pointed our way, braced to strike.

For a moment longer, we were still—silently steeling ourselves. Watching
creatures that lurked in the mist-shrouded shadows of the Illusionarium.

"You've got a story that's going to be enough for them?" Jaik muttered.

I brushed a tingling hand down my thigh; though that cleared the
mminess, power built against my skin, a tale begging to be unleashed the
ger I looked and the more I considered what lay ahead. What had made this
, and the things on it…and what they should have been. "It's going to be
ough for *all* of it."

Laying my hand against the rubble, I breathed out all the fear I'd carried
re with me…and the beginnings of the tale to see us through.

Let me tell you a story.

A STORY SPUN IN SCARLET

In the beginning, shadow was separated from light. The vastness of darkness and the brilliance of day were kept at bay by the hands of the Storymaker, who stood as the breach Himself between the realms; and in the breach, He waited, crafting the tale of the world He would make.

Time as we know it—time as it is today—began the moment the Storymaker decided how the tale would be told.

In that flicker of an instant, the gates were open, and light splintered through the dark.

As one—sensing their antithesis, the opposite of the sundered craft that had rendered them from the fabric of the world—the creatures of the Illusionarium took heed of us.

The calliope and carousel halted. The creatures froze in their fastenings to the island. And then, in a single shivering, ghoulish sweep, every head of every beast, Misspoken child, and warped Storycraft puppet cranked around toward us in a twitching tide.

"Here we go," Jaik hissed.

Then he grabbed my hand, and we tore down the path.

CHAPTER 64
A TOWER OF IRON THORNS

risly cackles, ear-splitting shrieks, and predator howls rose up from the ruins across the Isle as we plunged into the heart of the Illusionarium—and like their tethers had snapped all at once, the banished inhabitants gave chase.

Flesh puppets of misshapen adults and children dropped to their chests and crawled after us with spiderlike speed; half-formed infants clawed up from the soil and barreled on their heels, jaws snapping, crowded with fangs. The behemoths unfurled from their resting places, their boulder fists smashing the soil behind us, peppering our backsides with a spray of sod. The whole face of the island arched at the impact of their blows, nearly tossing us to our knees; but we clung to one another, shoved our shoulders together, staggered up, and kept running when they struck.

We never let go.

And while we ran, I set the story free.

With death rising up on either side of the path to pursue us, I spoke life. With the end clawing at our heels, ripping clots in the ground, erasing the road that had led us here, I cried out to the beginning of us all.

I spun a tale of a birth—a dawn, the making of the world. I brought the power of the Storymaker near to me, leaning into His acts of creation as I had been taught them, as I had always believed them, learning and shaping my own strength in the image of His.

And from the story I told of a land first being born, strength like I'd never known pulsed in my core, shoving out from my fingertips not in threads, but in *flows.*

The stones along the path punched upward in jagged prongs ahead of us, lances of rock to match the iron thorns protruding from Erasure's imperious height; they blasted into Misspoken manifestations that charged us head-on, throwing them off our course, launching them halfway to the horizon—clearing the way toward the base of the tower.

To our left and right, columns of soil and stone warped upward from the ground, encasing beasts by foot and neck, caging them away from us. At our backs, the tale of creation ripped chasms into the Illusionarium itself, plunging pursuing creatures into the belly of the island in shrieking, bellowing twists of fallen flesh.

Over the echo of a sundering land, Jaik's breathless whoop reached my ears. *"Don't stop, Ayjay!"*

I barely paused to drink in air, the story spiraling out of me in blazing scarlet glory, my cloak staining the wind behind me as I clawed my way up and over the cracked landscape of my own making. The pain in my leg was nothing, the persistent ache in my shoulder falling silent beneath the exultation that swelled from my core. It pushed everything else aside even as it drove the words from my lips, the power from my fingertips.

We dashed across the island in snatches, pausing here and there to breathe between the ruins, ducking behind sheltering stones cropped up from the tale itself while the shadow of Erasure lengthened and deepened—the sun shifting behind the zenith of the tower. The gloom it cast was eerie, ominous, world-consuming...like a perpetual eclipse.

The nearer we drew, the deadlier its barbs seemed, serrated and sinister as the tilt of Luck's darkest side. And the more breathless I was, the harder I struggled to form the words for the tale that kept us safe; bent with my hands on my knees behind yet another shroud of crumbling soil, I closed my eyes and hid from a suffocating wave of dizziness that spiraled through my head.

"Ayjay?" Jaik's fingers fastened to my hunched shoulder, and only then did I realize I'd swayed forward, too near to acquainting my face with the ground. "We need to keep moving."

"I know," I panted. But the island crawled with horrors my mind could hardly comprehend, scarcely held at bay, and my shoulder and leg were a fiery mess of anguish now that we'd paused. "I'm so tired, Jaik."

"Hey." He swung in front of me, gripping both my shoulders now, propping me back against the sod where we sheltered. "We're almost

ere…another half-mile at most. This story's not finished. *Our* story isn't
ished."

I held his gaze while I drew those words deep down into myself—deeper
an air, a fresh pulse of life, a breath igniting the coals of my resolve. My
ssion. Awakening a new corner of vigor I hadn't even known I possessed until
found the reflection of it in his eyes.

Seizing his wrists, I tugged his hands down from my shoulders to my hips,
d surged forward to press my mouth against his; then I ducked beneath his
m, whipped from hiding, and measured the distance to the tower.

"Give me the rifle," I said, "and the rest of your weapons. Then start
nning, Jaik, and don't stop. Not for anything."

He hesitated for only a heartbeat; then that ironclad faith straightened his
ine, and he swung the rifle from his shoulder and tossed it to me.

"See you in there, tiger." His smile was pure confidence—precisely what I
eded to shore up the breaches in mine.

Then he took off at a sprint, one hand bracing his ribs. I gathered my
eath and bolted after him.

I spoke no more of the tale as we ran; saving my air, storing up my power, I
llowed Jaik in a swerving dash for Erasure. We outpaced the scrabbling
ominations hindered by the tale of the Storymaker; we dodged around
hemoths far slower than us, ducking the swing of their weapons, evading their
asping hands that would crack us in two with a simple squeeze.

No more beasts capturing us in their mortal grasp. No more stopped time.

We only had now. Only us, and the distance to Erasure that we gobbled up
ith stumbling strides, scrambling on our hands and knees over the notched
kes of stone protruding ahead, pointing the way to the handleless doors of the
wer.

They grew definition as we approached, pure obsidian slabs, hardly a fringe
f silver to demarcate their seams. No knockers, knobs, or hinges; there was
uly only one way to open them.

Erasure eclipsed the horizon. Skeletal fowl lifted off from its joints and
rotrusions, spanning their membrane wings, every thread of pulsing veins
ithin lit up by the sun crawling around the tower's side as they took flight.

By that light, I saw why the Misspoken puppets had not caught up to us
om behind.

They'd changed their tactics. Disjointed limbs akimbo, they spidered up the
ce of the tower ahead, their elongated necks weaving in serpentine slaloms.

They twisted to peer back at us, colorless skin reflecting the sun, needle-sharp, overcrowded teeth flashing in the light—daring us to approach.

My heart lunged into my throat as the distance shrank from us to them. T the face of the tower. A quarter mile. Then half that.

"Get ready, Jaik!" I threw all my breath into my scream—then bore down another, deep as I could, and let the story loose with a thrust of my words and my hands, showing the power precisely where to go.

A story of mountains rearing to life from smooth soil erupted out of me— and with it, the ground itself grew fangs.

The first layer bucked upward beneath Jaik's boots, and he rode it like a sled, skimming forward, balancing himself with his arms outstretched; then he lunged to the next talon of rock as it burst upward. Then the next. And the nex

Slamming to a halt at the base of Erasure, I unleashed the tale of the worl coming to being, its utterance forging a path for Jaik up along the tiered spines protruding from the tower's face, until—

The power guttered in me. The words sputtered in my mind and stumbled on my tongue.

I grasped for them desperately, sowing every last shred of my failing voice into casting out the story of the world's beginning, bringing the notion of the Storymaker close to my heart even as I scrabbled for the last flicker of Jaik's power reaching back to me.

And then it sundered, his next hurtle up the stone juts I'd created putting him out of my reach.

Jaik jammed his knife sideways between his teeth and lunged for the tower face, as if he'd sensed that tether snapping loose between us and was already braced for it.

For a heartstopping moment, he hung suspended in his leap, the Misspoke creatures pulling in their wings to dive after him.

Then he slammed against the black rock between the jagged lances and began his ascent toward the windows, hand over hand, knife gritted in his teeth.

With a shout, I braced the rifle's stock against the soil, plunged to one kne and pulled the trigger.

The blast half-deafened me, the weapon lunging upward with the recoil. Bu the shot was enough to bring the creatures whipping my way—turning toward the Storycrafter, a maker like theirs, an enemy in their empty eyes.

All of them wheeled my way. From every side.

My courage ran like ink on a damp page. Shoving upright with the rifle as a ancing staff, I swiveled and hobbled down the curve of the obsidian tower— ıy from Jaik.

And away from the Misspoken beasts whose gruesome hunting cries rived fog-wreathed air.

CHAPTER 65
A CATHEDRAL OF CHAOS

I had never run so recklessly before…not even from Galan. Nor had I done it injured.

With the power fully unspooled from my center, there wa plenty of space for pain to make itself known again. It came in pops and bursts shredding through my damaged calf, hailing blows into the muscle of my shoulder, spiking through my ribs and into my chest. My leg buckled with ever other stride; the air gouged like pure steel into my lungs.

But they were pursuing me—beasts incensed by blood. Behemoths drawn by movement. Misspoken nightmares of every shape and size skipping, clawing scuttling after me.

They left Jaik to climb.

The pure exhilaration of success lent strength to the leg that bore most of my weight; I half-hopped, half-dragged myself around Erasure's side and plunged into a blighted field of perpetually decomposing crops. Gagging on the putrefaction that sucked at my ankles, filled my boots with sludge, and saturate my lungs with every gasping breath, I led the creatures on a wild chase toward the only shelter I could see.

The knobby bones of the ruined cathedral jutted just beyond the shadow the tower; the way they buckled inward suggested someone had tried to craft ar homage to two-faced Luck with the words of their mouth rather than the work of their hands…and it had fallen in on them.

Its pure ebony ruins were a tribute only to the dark side of Luck's flipping coin, a brutal irony offering salvation as I slowed my mad, wound-warped dash with a hand to the cratered doorway, sliding through the rotten muck and ducking inside.

Sable stone crumbled in my hand, skinning my palm. Cursing Luck, I
opped to my knees and crawled into shelter behind one of the walls. Hands
tling like a sick woman in a snowstorm, I trapped the rifle between my knees
d reloaded it the way Jaik had taught me in the Drennans—but with a single
nd, newly cut, and not my dominant one.

Outside, the echoes of pursuit were relentless. The footsteps of fleshy
ints shook the island to its belly, racking loose depraved laughter from the
alformed marionettes of children humming macabre tunes, begging me to play
th them. A baby's sinister cry warped in and out of tune; the hissing, damp
eaths of the flesh puppets curdled on the air, played in nauseating harmony to
e vicious panting and throat-deep snuffles of beasts scenting for me on the
nd. Wingbeats sent the mist whirling as the scavenger birds circled above my
elter.

"Come on, come *on*," I pleaded with my shaking fingers, jamming in the
d and racking the rifle bolt into place. A hiss slid between my teeth when the
etal scraped my wounded palm.

Something squelched to my right—rotted vegetation giving way beneath a
ep. A many-layered moan echoed off the crumbled, Luck-abandoned walls, and
engorged head on a snaking neck curved into the belly of the cathedral,
ipping thick locks of rancid, night-dark hair.

Bracing the rifle stock against my hip this time, I swung the muzzle level
th that head just as it snapped my way.

For an instant, I was staring down an unhinged maw, the chin stretching
d stretching to meet the petrified soil, a bloodcurdling shriek erupting from
thin as the creature shot toward me.

I fired straight through the back of its head.

The abomination recoiled in a tangle of long limbs and wobbling neck...but
did not die. There was no life *in* it to take, and that shot had not been enough
put it off the hunt. It surged back a heartbeat later, rearing for me, that
orrific mouth wheeling wider.

I swung the rifle like a club this time, like I had the oar, clipping the beast in
e head. It smashed against the cathedral wall, and I surged up on my good leg,
oving deeper into the ruin as the beasts gave chase behind me.

Behemoth hands plucked away the crumbled residue of rafters and marble
olumns that sheltered me from above. Debris smashed down on every side,
lting the sodden earth beneath my feet. I gripped smashed pews and dented
tars around the rifle's barrel to thrust myself ahead, bearing as little weight on

my leg as possible; and when the wind brushed my back, I ducked, slamming to my knees on the sheer granite floor, sliding forward beneath the grasping talons of a predator bird's outstretched, bony legs.

The snap of its body against the dented pool at the rear of the cathedral—full of coins all flipped sinister-side up, grinning at me with a promise of death—resounded off the walls. Several beasts pulled up short; seizing the pause, I rammed more lead into the rifle, set the bolt, spun on my knees, and fired at the broad behemoth hand plunging down through the shattered roof nearest to me

The shot punched its grip off course, and I went careening back, ducking under the shadow of its palm, aiming for a side door hanging half-off its hinges The opening was narrow, broken and caved, shrunken by abuse enough that the creatures who lunged after me all at once tangled themselves in the gap. They blockaded the rest behind the writhing knot of their grasping, elongated limbs and malicious faces punching through the doorframe.

Gasping with pain and terror, I staggered out into the open—and met the spine-rending snarl of pure obsidian tolling against packed earth from afar. Then the cry of my name pierced over the raspy wails and guttural moans of my pursuers, cleaving across the face of my heart.

Jaik.

He'd made it.

Stabbing the rifle stock into the soil, I gathered my wits and leaned into the toss of Luck's coin one last time.

Then I dodged between the legs of the slow-turning behemoths and pelted back for the tower doors.

CHAPTER 66
A FIGHT FOR FREEDOM

The rifle was my crutch, helping to pluck my feet free from the mire and lending strength to my crumbling leg. I refused to spare another glance behind me even when the cathedral's granite doorway collapsed with an audible *crack*, the triumphant caterwauls of freed creatures cing against my ears.

Even when the ground tossed with the pound of pursuing footsteps that uld have trodden me flat, I didn't tear my eyes from the tower.

The door loomed wide, a slab of shadow against the gloomy horizon. And ere, gripping its edge, wedging it open with his shoulder and hands, was Jaik.

A sob of relief wrenched in my chest—then bubbled over into a scream hen something icy and sharp closed around my ankle.

Muscle and tendon ripped deep in my wounded leg even before the pain nk its hooked talons into my hip and tore me down. A dimmer, distant agony udded in my hands and knees when they plunged into the frigid, decayed il—all the way to the elbow.

It was boggier here, the cold mud sucking at my limbs. And when I jerked nto my side, tugging against whatever had snared my ankle, it wasn't those horn-riddled vines I found.

Ash-white arms rose from the mire like reeds from a lakeshore, dozens of hem tearing out of the bog—tearing at *me*. One gripped my ankle in the frozen age of its long fingers, unpared nails tugging down my bandage, seeking the uncture wounds beneath.

When those taloned fingernails plunged into my injured flesh, I couldn't raw in enough air to scream. A feeble sob huffed out of my lips, my world ashed in sparkling silver-black stains. My hands dug into the mud as I clawed backward, kicking with my free leg, fighting against the grip that towed me deeper beneath the bog.

Fighting for life—fighting to reach Jaik.

But that hand was iron-strong, relentless, joined by a half-dozen others winding into my clothes; and as the pain tossed over my head in brutal swells, I lost my sense of height and depth.

The bog sloshed at my chest. At my chin.

And then something sailed down on my right side—a book, a tome half the height of my body. It cracked down on the hand that held my leg, crunching bone at the elbow; then Jaik aimed a vicious kick into the abomination's wrist, snapping its hold on me.

Another blow. Another grip released. Then another. And another.

"Jaik," I gasped as he hooked his hands under my arms, hauling me up from the devouring bog and into a slithering hobble back toward the tower. My eyes were fixed on the creatures hurtling after us from the cathedral. "Jaik, the door!"

"I've got it!" he bellowed against my ear. "Just use your *flipping Storycraft!*"

His words—half a plea and half a snarl—righted the world around me.

Thrusting my unslung arm up before me, I squeezed my eyes shut so the fear of what pursued us would not be my voice's undoing. And this time, I spoke not only creation, but *separation*—the only thing I was certain could save us now.

My tale of an island's birth cracked through Erasure like the sundering of a spine. The ensuing earthquake threw Jaik and me to our seats in the mud, and this time we didn't bother rising. We scrambled on our hands and knees out of the quagmire, an awkward two-armed maneuver with Jaik clutching my elbow still in the sling.

Behind us, from imperishable tower to distant shore, a chasm rendered open on the face of the Illusionarium. Clots of stone and soil and foul water poured audibly into the abyss of my making, and though I dared not look again, I felt the breath of the ever-widening expanse howling at my back.

With one last thrust of limbs, Jaik hooked his hand around the door's sharp edge. With a roar of agony, he slung me up around the side of it.

And the crater fell out from beneath him.

His name tore from my throat, a cry of defiance against this world that seemed so Luck-bent on taking him away from me; wedging my shoulder to the door, I caught him with my good arm hooked around his waist, my fingers tangled in the loops of his belt. And I did not let go, even when strain hurtled ough my ravaged back, and the awkward bend of my body around his sent all blood cascading into my head.

Jaik's hands clawed at my knees, found the door and the soil beside my leg, d then he dragged himself up over the lip of the ground, his weight barreling backward. At the last instant, his palm caught my head, cushioning it from pact with the path where it met the half-open door.

"Get inside," Jaik panted against my face, agony seething beneath the rds.

On both knees and with a single hand, I dragged myself over the threshold o Erasure. Jaik tumbled in after me, wheezing, cursing, both of us sprawled on floor.

The door scraped shut at our backs...though neither of us had touched it.

And in the absolute silence that ensued—not a creature cry from outside so ch as whispering at the walls—the sound of clapping hands was deafening.

"Very well done." The warm, sincere, and richly accented voice came from ind us. "And welcome to Erasure."

CHAPTER 67
IN THE HEART OF THE STORY

Shock bolted fresh vigor into my limbs—enough, at least, that I could flip onto my back and behold the figure who leaned again the door. He no longer clapped, but rubbed his weathered palms together, regarding us with the kindest smile I'd ever seen.

His age was difficult to determine, but he must've been older than us by a least a handful of years; smiling lines weathered his tanned face, his black hair falling in gently tangled curls to his shoulders. His attire was utterly unremarkable, even a bit shabby: a tunic and trousers in harmonious shades of parchment-brown, a thick black sash bound around his hips to complete the raiment like a score of ink marked across a page.

I had never seen him before in my life. And yet something in his gentle gr rang familiar, like a tale I'd known since infancy.

"You…" I cleared my throat; it did little to soften the words when I tried again. "Are you the Storykeeper?"

"That is quite a fascinating question, Audra." He laid his index fingers together, tapped them to his smiling mouth, then angled both at me. "I am not But let me see to you and Jaik, and I will explain."

Shrugging up from the door, he stepped gingerly over us and made his wa into Erasure; I rolled to follow his movements and took in the height of the tower for the first time.

The look of it clashed so absolutely with the jagged exterior that for a moment, it truly felt as if we'd been conveyed to some other, remote corner of Mithra-Sha.

Unlike Fablehaven, with its many floors and grand central staircase wrapping through the spire, Erasure was cavernous; the walls were lined from adowed vaults to the broad, circular span of the floor with bookcases flocked balconies. Thread-thin, spiraled staircases joined the overlooks together, and re and there the shelves were arrested by thick floes of obsidian stretching up m the floor in spidering black veins.

And everywhere, there was life.

Clusters of herbs and lichen and ivy spilled from the balcony edges in cadent, floral clumps. Birds flitted and floated from edge to edge across them. y humming ears picked up the distant tumble of a fountain—or a waterfall, en—buried somewhere among the twists of books and this impossible inner rden. My wide eyes distinguished several trees lurching in hardy wooden knots and among the record cases, their twining limbs serving as the shelves on ich the books were settled.

It reminded me achingly of Naomi's home in Dalfi. And of the story I had ld in the *Tankard*.

I saw no bed, no side room, no place for making meals. Only a broad desk ing up half the base of the tower, backed by a hearth with no visible flue; and s enigmatic stranger making his way toward it, utterly unawed, it seemed, by w *impossible* this place truly was.

"Who *is* he?" Frustration overturned disbelief as I hooked Jaik beneath the m, helping him up from his chest to his knees.

"Couldn't tell you. He was waiting when I came in through the ndow…just snapped his book shut and told me to come help him get the door en." He hesitated a moment, then added gruffly, "He offered to hold it while I agged you out of the bog."

Gratitude blunted the serrated edge of my suspicion, but not my curiosity; I ould have gone straight after the man, lobbing whatever questions occurred to e first, had Jaik's pained, quiet grunt not arrested my focus.

He'd slipped a hand beneath the sailor's coat hanging open over his chest, essing into the bandages that tied his injured middle; when he peeled his gers back, they came away stained with blood.

"Flipping Luck," he muttered.

"*Jaik!*" I snagged his collar when he wavered—then flinched as strong, llused hands closed over mine.

"Here." Our mysterious benefactor knelt beside us, settling Jaik back ainst the wall. He uncapped a tincture tin, set it on his knee, and dabbed his gers within; then he flashed them at Jaik. "May I?"

Panting through gritted teeth, Jaik grunted, "If you think it'll help, you can bathe me in the stuff."

"I've always appreciated that sense of humor about you," the man chuckled; then, ignorant of the disbelieving glances we both pinned on him, he slid his fingers beneath Jaik's bandage.

"Flipping—*cold!*" Jaik cursed, writhing aside.

"Not so good for bathing in, then, hm?"

Jaik settled—not out of stubborn pride, but with a sudden, full-bodied looseness I hadn't expected. As if his wounds no longer pained him. His hooded eyes were fixed on the stranger's face, searching him with the same distant familiarity that thrummed in my chest. "Who are you?"

"Someone who cares very much for the quest you both are on." The man scooped out more tincture, turning to me this time. "I see your pain, Audra."

Something about the words—the way he said them, how precise they were—cut me to my core. It was truth laid bare.

He *saw* me...not only the pain pulsing in my leg and shoulder, sharpening with every throb now that Jaik had stopped bleeding through his reopened stitches. But the pain that had brought us here. The guilt. The confusion.

He bore his palm out to my shoulder first, but did not touch me. His gaze was trained on mine, brimming with compassion so fierce it was nearly tearful. "Will you allow me?"

"Yes," I whispered.

The tincture *was* cold, burning like fresh ice when it touched my shoulder...but because of Jaik, I'd expected that. I sucked breath in through my teeth and held it until warmth followed the chill—warmth that traveled to the bone itself. Then I let the air out in increments while he moved to my leg and applied another generous slather to the skin.

Before my eyes, the swollen, puckered holes from those needle teeth began to knit themselves shut. In moments, only pocked scars remained where wounds had festered with the stain of the bog, gashed by those vicious talons rising up from the silt.

I yanked my leg back and scrambled to my feet, shock pounding in my temples like a raging headache. "What was *that?*"

"Something I like to keep on hand." Dusting off his palms, the man rose as well, offering a hand to Jaik; he ignored it, gripping the wall behind him and sliding upright.

"Storycraft can't *heal,*" I countered.

His thick brows rose. "Who said that I was a Storycrafter?"

My next volley of argument caught in my throat. It was true, he hadn't said at...I'd assumed. Latched on to that kindred familiarity between us, the ~~~eness in this place and the stories I'd told myself.

"But...you aren't the Storykeeper." I stumbled back over the same question ~~om before.

"No. It was the Storykeeper whose Misspoken tale forged this island." The ~~an settled back on the corner of his broad table, one foot on the floor and the ~~her leg cocked, swaying gently as he lifted his gaze to the height of the tower; ~~s eyes burned with pondering. "He was interred here long ago to chronicle the ~~les of others, in hopes he might learn humility and put away his pride in his ~~wn craft. But he aspired too greatly for far too much power in Storycraft, and ~, the end, for the sake of all the world, he was sealed away."

A chill scrawled down my spine at the quiet pain in his voice. It was a ~~rsonal anguish built into a tale I'd never heard before.

"So if there's no Storykeeper," belligerence framed Jaik's words, false armor ~~ver the ignorance we shared, "who's watching over the tower? Who made it ~~ok like this?"

"I am. And I did." The man's gaze darted back to us, mirth simmering in ~~e depths of his eyes. "Writing the tales as they are told. Chronicling all that I ~~e."

Shock ripped my legs out from me, this time—not pain. My knees clapped ~~e obsidian floor the same moment the words left our benefactor's mouth.

"I am the *Storymaker*."

CHAPTER 68
WHAT TALES ARE MADE OF

I t was not every day one came face-to-face with the power that had set the world in motion.

A power like their own.

On my knees was the only way I could face Him—gazing up at that benevolent face that held a collision of pureness and agelessness. Impossibility screamed in my head, the insensibility of doubt that came from a world I'd thought I understood.

And yet…

I knew Him. My craft knew him even better than it knew Jaik, almost painful in its poignance. The very folds of my cloak strained toward the one who'd imbued them with their power.

"I quite enjoyed the tale you chose to reach the tower." The Storymaker winked at me. "It is very much the Audra Jashowin thing to do, to use creation for her defenses. You have always been a rare and memorable scholar of Storycraft…one of those sorts who reminds me why I shared this power with mankind to begin with."

"Wait," Jaik croaked, flashing both hands—blood still on the pads of his fingers. "Wait. You can't—you don't honestly expect us to believe you're—"

"Disbelief becomes you, Jaik Grissom." Pushing up from the desk's edge, the Storymaker strode back to Jaik, taking gentle hold of the sides of his neck. "But faith does so even more. *That* is the steel penned into the core of your story."

Jaik's breath choked off audibly. He did not pull away.

"How…how is this possible?" Tears lined my eyes and soaked my stammering question. "You've just…been here? For how *long*?"

"Time is not the same for me as it is for you." His gaze traced the
dowed crown of the tower again; then His hands fell from Jaik's neck as He
oted my way. Behind Him, Jaik buckled, pressing the side of his fist to his
uth; tears pooled over and vanished into the beard that lined his cheeks. He
nothing to wipe them away. "Ever since the Storykeeper failed in his task, I
e chronicled the stories spun by Storycrafters with my own hands. Centuries
hem. And then, all at once, they were no more."

Shame like nothing I'd ever known bowed my forehead to the cold obsidian
or; that did nothing to calm the heat raging in my skin. "I am so, *so* sorry—"

A hand slid under my chin—calloused from writing stories the same way
tongue bore marks from telling them. "Do you even know what you
ologize for, Audra?"

Embarrassment braided into my guiltstricken heartache; I hardly had the
ength to shake my head.

Sadness framed His smile now; taking my hand, the Storymaker guided me
my feet. "I know why you have come...what you are seeking. The story you
g to hear."

One hand on Jaik's shoulder, the other holding mine, He guided us to His
le.

At first, I had believed it to be disorganized chaos—which had fit,
nehow, with the image I'd built of the recluse in the tower, without even a
I to lay in. But now that I knew who He was—who He *truly* was—I saw
thod to the disarray. Order within the chaos of different covers, how they
re stacked together, books paired off one with another. Stories joined, side-
-side.

And there, at the heart of it all, was a leather-bound volume as thick as my
d from wrist to middle fingertip. Situated near the Storymaker's chair at the
k, it was as if He'd been reading it—or writing in it—when we'd arrived. And
hitch in Jaik's stride suggested this was the book the Storymaker had shut
en he'd slipped in through the window.

And now He released us, drew ahead of us, and halted before the book.
wly, with a tenderness that set off a deep pang in my heart, He smoothed his
d over the cover.

"Of all the stories I have written here," He murmured, "yours has been
ong my favorite."

He opened the chronicle and turned it toward us, and my breath snared in
chest.

Scripted in gentle, articulate lines at the head of the first page was my nam
Beside it, Jaik's.

But the contents were scorched. Blackened. As if the Storymaker had
tossed this book into the fire and then retrieved it out of a guilty conscience.

"What did you do to it?" Jaik's tone was brittle—reluctant to accuse the
maker of the world, but desperate to fling blame somewhere. To make sense c
all the impossible things we were beholding today.

"It is far better if you read the tale first," the Storymaker said. "After that
perhaps the state of the book itself will be made clear."

I grasped for Jaik's hand like a drowning woman, and my fingers met his
already reaching for mine. Together we sidled nearer to the desk, while the
Storymaker settled into His seat, braced his elbows on the armrests, and laid F
steepled fingertips to his mouth.

Regret. Sorrow. And also a deep, aching affection—all of it lived in His
gaze when it settled on us.

"Read it," He invited us. "It is your story."

I beheld the page with mounting trepidation and insatiable hunger.

The beginning of a story. *Our* story.

And there, in scorched filigree beneath our names, I found a date scrawle
into the margins.

The day after I'd graduated from Fablehaven.

Confusion crashed through my head, and my gaze flicked to the
Storymaker. "How could *our* tale begin back when I left the Academy?"

"Read," the Storymaker urged with that quiet, convicting intensity.
"Please."

Chastened, I dropped my gaze back to the page. And I did as He said.

I read the tale time had forgotten…the story of us.

CHAPTER 69
THE FRACTURED PAST

*J*aik's hand slid onto the table's edge as he crowded in behind me; for a moment, the heat of his body, the ebb and flow of his chest ~~pr~~essing against my back with every shallow breath. were the only truths I knew ~~be~~yond the book.

And then, as my gaze skimmed the page—

I saw the threads. Scarlet and silver. Gold and black. They danced along the ~~pa~~rchment, curling up from the blackened loops of the letters themselves like ~~cu~~rls of smoke. Like whispers from the past, beckoning us nearer.

We leaned as one over the book, over that first page. Knitting my fingers ~~be~~tween Jaik's, I raised both our hands together to press against the parchment.

And the moment I did, everything within me *broke*.

Memory cascaded to the surface of a fractured history, a geyser cracking ~~th~~rough every layer of false storytelling built over it. A cry strangled in my throat, ~~an~~d my stomach struck the table's edge, the wood biting against my hips when I ~~st~~umbled. Jaik fell with me, his other hand still braced on the table's edge, his ~~gr~~eater weight and height swaying against me as we plummeted.

And over our heads, color erupted.

Everything I saw in my mind's eye, every flash of memory hurtling to the ~~su~~rface, vying against the others to reach freedom…through squinting eyes, I ~~sa~~w them repeat in twists of Storycraft cascading through Erasure.

Built of that same scarlet dust that had freckled from my palms aboard *The* ~~Aca~~*thalion*, figures clashed and collided; they swaggered and strutted. They ~~co~~nquered heights and plunged to depths. They walked halls that burst to life ~~an~~d dissolved in the same heartbeat; but no matter how swiftly they were gone, I ~~co~~uld not forget them.

They were branded on my mind. On my *memory*.

"*Ayjay…*" Jaik's voice was a gasp against the back of my head as he buried his face in my hair, and my heart seized in my chest.

He had never said my name like that before. With exultation and wonder and so much heartbroken *relief*, like a man finding something he'd believed was lost forever…

No. No, he *had* said it that way before.

But I'd forgotten until now.

I wept in the face of all that had been forgotten as it poured back into me, drenching every dark corner of my mind where cobweb beliefs of the past and present had taken up the musty emptiness. Glister and glamor and power incarnate; fear and shame and desperation.

Love. So much love I became a vessel overflowing with it, one body far too lacking to hold it all…

And then, scarlet halls dipped in shadow.

The darkest of nights. A missed appointment.

This memory…

This memory…

Jaik stiffened against me; and then a ruthless heat—brutal, *lethal*, knife-sharp—plunged through my chest, and Jaik hurtled backward from me, slamming onto his seat on the floor of Erasure and scrambling to escape the table.

No. Not the table. But the memory that built between us when I floundered around on my knees to face him. The memory of a man's armor-clad figure forged of scarlet sand, looming over Jaik, a bloodied blade in hand.

A blade I *knew*.

Both of us cried out as the dagger descended, a shower of crimson powder shattering against Jaik's chest.

Directly over the scar bared through the parted halves of his cloak.

I fell back on my seat as well, my spine striking the table, jolting another memory loose like a picture rattled off a wall.

Red and gold. Scarlet and gild.

A golden cage. A blade in my hand, soaked in blood.

That same dagger.

But I hadn't thrust it into its target. I'd torn it *out* from its mark.

From Jaik's heart.

With my next sob, warm hands cupped my face—not Jaik's. The
countenance that swam into view was full of sympathy and compassion that set
loose all the bottled emotions I didn't know how to face. And I cared nothing
for propriety or impossibility as I leaned into the arms of my Maker and
wept…and He held me, as no one had when I'd first lived through the worst day
of my life.

A day I'd forgotten until now.

I dimly knew when Jaik dragged himself to join us. When his hand laced
into mine, his forehead pressed to my temple. We huddled there against the
table, weeping, for so long that time forgot us. It could have been minutes or
hours, even, while memory wrung Jaik and me to the edge of snapping apart.

And then, slowly, the dizzying grief and shock ebbed; the memories settled,
and the things around me became more tangible. Realer than the images
skittering the walls of my overchurned mind.

Sniffling, panting, I slowly lifted my head; the Storymaker released me, but
Jaik did not. And there, on our seats beside His table, the Storymaker linked His
arms loosely around his knees and pinned me with a look of such knowing, it felt
as if every lost fragment of me had been found.

"Tell me a story." His tone was calm, beckoning…inviting us into
remembering. Into knowing the truth of who we were.

I glanced at Jaik; his fingers strangled mine, shaking, clammy as if with
fever. His throat bobbed when he swallowed, and he shook his head.

So *I* told the Storymaker first—the very first thing I remembered.

CHAPTER 70
SWORD AND STORY

I didn't meet Jaik Grissom for the first time in Krylan," I croaked. "I met him in Vallanmyre...after Fablehaven. I graduated at the top of my class, and the Sha took interest in me. He wanted me to complete the tests alongside a few of my classmates, to try for the title of Master Storycrafter. And Jaik..."

I swiped my tongue along my lips, readying them for words that would have seemed utterly *impossible* if I did not remember the event so clearly—as if it had just transpired today, not over a decade ago.

"Jaik was a newly-graduated soldier who was assigned to protect me during the tests in case of sabotage. We all had one...a bodyguard. Jaik was mine."

"I signed up for the role because Galan sent me." Jaik's voice blistered with a rage as forgotten as all the rest of it. "We were soldiers in training together...he riled me up about the Storycrafters, the way they were stealing the Sha's focus off the army. He wanted me to get under Audra's skin, skew the tests so the Sha wouldn't trust the next Master Storycrafter."

The notion was almost nauseating. To imagine Galan's treacherous chokehold on my life, on my craft, even *then*...

"And what happened in the tests?" the Storymaker goaded us quietly.

"I passed." The whisper tumbled from my lips, an awestruck breath swallowed up in the vastness of Erasure. "I *excelled*."

"And I helped her," Jaik added, a faint edge of his familiar arrogance creeping into the words. "I was supposed to be hurting her chances, but I couldn't stop *helping* her instead. Galan tried to step in, rig it himself and get us both killed, so I talked to Arias. We were starting to be friendly, at that point. He'd told me he had his reasons for wanting Fiordona out of commission, and

at I brought him…that was the last piece of evidence he needed. We went in
ether and turned him over to the Sha."

I blinked, snapping my head his way to find a grim smirk tilting his lips.
..you never told me that."

He didn't glance my way, but there was an apology in the faint bob of his
ulders. "Raz didn't want his name on it, and I didn't want you to think I was
ing the credit just to get back in your good graces."

It *had* taken some time for him to win my full trust again after he'd revealed
role in the tests at the very start…but I'd forgiven him enough to vouch for
1 before the Sha. And I'd begged to keep him on as my bodyguard when I'd
en the title.

Master Storycrafter.

Choking out a wondering breath, I chafed my cloak between my fingers. "I
n't…I didn't murder the last Master. I *was* the Master."

"I have always loved that part of the story." The Storymaker shot me a
owing wink, a lopsided smile. "And then what happened?"

What *hadn't* happened? For eight years, Jaik and I had taken Mithra-Sha by
rm. We'd infiltrated and broken up fabricated Storycrafting rings; we'd built
strongest alliance of soldiers and Storycrafters in generations, a trusted circle
friends reporting directly to the Sha. We'd faced and thwarted conflict with
ere-Del and prevented wars with marauders and traders trying to capture and
ry off Storycrafters to sell. We had even devised strategies to fully unite the
ny and Storycrafters…to train them all as one, to make them a blended force
to fully eradicate Misspoken manifestations wherever they encountered them.
eliminate the need altogether for those abominations to be left intact on an
e where they might one day escape…just as the siren had done.

Swords and stories, irrevocably joined. The greatest defense of Mithra-Sha.

And somewhere along the way—between long journeys across the country,
m military outposts where we'd been forced into a single tent to cabins in the
note peaks of the mountains where we'd met informants and plotted to raise
e standards of our stations higher and higher in Mithra-Sha…

Somewhere, all of the teasing and bantering and berating that had filled the
ys of a cocky soldier and Master Storycrafter had given way to something
rmer. Something so intimate, it had turned us both inside-out, our deepest
rts exposed to one another.

Jaik Grissom had become my closest confidant. My best friend.

And then he'd become the man I'd fallen in love with.

"We started a clandestine romance," I murmured, tightening my grip around his hand, "because tensions with Amere-Del were on the rise again, an the Sha was growing anxious. He wanted me at his side at all times...no more journeys across the country. No more outpost visits. He kept me in the Shasta day and night, calling me his choice weapon, the only thing that could turn the tide in our favor if the Del didn't keep to his own borders."

"You felt like he was suffocating you." Jaik's thumb traced over my knuckles, his voice laced with the anguish of watching me crumble during thos painful days. "Like he didn't see you as a living thing anymore, just the power under your skin."

"I wanted to disappear." The absurdity of that notion punched a laugh from me. *Me*, Audra Jashowin, who craved heroism, who dreamed of being se as the savior...I'd once had *everything* I coveted now, and I'd yearned for nothi more than to escape it.

And perhaps that was *why* I fought so hard to feel useful, and wanted. Perhaps there was a portion of me that remembered what it was like to have been the one holding the balance between war and peace in Mithra-Sha...the Master to whom all Storycrafters had looked for guidance. The tilt of their compass. The truth north of the craft.

"We came up with a plan to get you out of there." Jaik's words dragged tl time, hoarse and unsteady, hauling me back to a painful present. "To leave the Shastah and disappear up to one of those cabins we found in the Vensair Mountains. Then we'd get across them to Hadrass-Drui and lay low until the S gave us up for dead."

"We had everything settled." The words dropped hollowly from my mou "But..."

The phantom feeling of blood lapped at my hands.

"The Sha found out we were courting behind his back," Jaik rasped. "An he found out how serious it was."

My hand clapped over my breastbone, meeting the small, innocent angles the ring I'd strung on a chain around my neck, so I wouldn't drop it from my pocket on our way across the Drennans.

"I was going to ask you to marry me." Jaik's gaze was fixed on my hand, where marriage bands were worn. "But the night we were supposed to leave..."

His eyes slammed shut, and he grimaced, grinding the heel of his free han over his scar.

Not from a plowblade. Not an accident.

"The Sha had you murdered," I choked. "Left in a corridor to bleed to ath. And Raz…Shadran Arias found you, and he brought your body to the astah's Convening Chamber, because he recognized the blade was Hadrassi."

I could still see Arias's face when he'd shoved through the door of the ded chamber where we were in council; the anguish, the tears spilling down cheeks, Jaik's arm slung across his shoulders—the knife still protruding from at heart I'd cherished so much.

I remembered the numbness slamming through me when I'd finally derstood why Jaik hadn't met me that evening so we could escape the Shastah together.

The echo of Arias's knees cracking the floor as he'd finally buckled under k's deadweight—and the clap of mine next to his when I'd fallen beside them, pping Jaik's face in my hands, screaming and screaming and *screaming* his me—pierced through my head, pinning my eyes shut.

"I pulled out the knife." Tears built again behind my words, and I did thing to stop them. "I knew—Naomi had taught me enough—"

"You recognized death when you saw it." Empathy rounded every word the rymaker spoke; it still did nothing to sand down the edges of my jagged grief, sh as if I'd just laid eyes on Jaik's corpse for the first time.

"The Sha told me how sorry he was, what a good man Jaik had been…a at soldier, the best bodyguard in all of Mithra-Sha. But he said it had to be ne, to keep the country from falling apart. He said he'd had no choice." The rds tore from me, each one swifter than the last, hysteria building and bbling in my chest. "He used your death to *leash* me to him…as if I'd ever stay d serve the man who *murdered* you, Jaik—"

That was why. The Sha's heartbroken voice tore through my memory, no ger muddled as it had been in my nightmares. *It has to be this way—do you derstand that?*

You're a murderer, I'd screamed in the face of the man I'd trusted, vered…who I'd given everything to. *You're a murderer, I despise you, I hope you , I will never, ever serve you again—*

"And then," the Storymaker murmured, "what did you do, Audra? With the t I gave you."

I staggered a damp breath in through my parted lips, nausea tying my mach in a horrible, throbbing knot. "I…I tried to tell a story that would bring k back. I told a story *about* him, about *us.* I broke all of the rules, everything I'd ever been warned about the limits of Storycraft...I tried to create life, real *life* from a story."

And after that moment, the defiance that had ripped from me, with Jaik's blood on my hands and my faith in the Sha forever shattered, and all the rifles in the Convening Chamber aimed my way...

I'd woken in a simple home in Vallanmyre, believing I lived a simple life. And I'd found my cloak colorless and drab that day.

Jaik's fingers flexed around mine—then sprang away. "Flipping *Luck*. That's why I'm not dead. You actually *did* it, tiger."

"Indeed, she did. I always knew she would do wondrous things with the double-portion I assigned to her." The Storymaker's voice hung with a smile, though all I saw was the light-speckled darkness behind my squeezed-shut eyes...still hiding from the tragedy that had become of our story. "Though the rules of Storycraft should never have been altered. Still, the truth of the craft remains...you reshaped nature by your own design. And that story has been imprinted on your heart ever since."

Of course it had been. I could see it all now...the scarlet threads of a single tale spidering through the amalgamation of them all.

I was Syvee and Lyndra and the Frost Queen. The entombed spinner and the Enchantress.

I hadn't merely been telling sundered stories all this time. I had been telling *my* story, in pieces and fragments, bits of it branded into my very essence despite the way the world had rent in half.

And I had been telling *Jaik's* story. The hunter, the pirate, the savior, the Prince of Mirrors...the man betrayed. They were all *him*, a shattered reimagining of the man I'd lost. The man I'd *loved*.

That I'd found a way to love twice in one lifetime.

I blinked my eyes open to see Jaik's ashen face, to read the horror and disbelief written into his stare...and my heart dropped.

Slowly, the Storymaker rose from His seat. "I have spent many years piecing your story back together. Ever since you set your feet to the Spine, Audra, you have walked toward Jaik...not because I forced you to do it, but because your heart and your craft alike are drawn to him."

Tears ran recklessly down my cheeks, ravaging me in their escape.

I could not deny the truth in His words—not any more than I could deny the tale I had remembered for myself while we'd read it from the page.

That horrific day in the Shastah, I had done far more than reckon back life ▸r the man I loved; with my Storycraft, I'd written Jaik Grissom into the very ⸱bric of the world. Immortalized him. He'd become a figure in countless stories, constant, an amplifier incarnate.

In trying to keep him with me, I'd given him to everyone.

And I'd also taken *everything* from them.

CHAPTER 71
MAKING IT RIGHT

ou knew this power was not meant to be," the Storymaker said when I did not speak for a time—as if He saw the course my churning thoughts had taken. "You know conscious life cannot be created by Storycraft. But your freedom of will and the strength of the gift I gave you bent the rules…it caused a tearing so mighty that it rewrote the very story of the world."

As one, our attention swung the same way—to Jaik, still frozen, pale, unspeaking.

"And," the Storymaker went on softly, "it wrote Jaik's life back into the tale of time, but it required far more than your own strength to do it. It drew on all the might of Storycraft given to the world. To rewrite his ending undid all of the endings around him. It rendered every memory of you both from the minds of those who knew you, and rewrote you utterly…Audra, in your appearance and mannerisms. And Jaik, in the very essence of your design."

Another undeniable truth; for with every memory of myself that reared to life in my mind, I saw a far different girl growing into a far different woman…not plain, not forgettable. Someone of striking appearance, with dark hair and taunting smirks and lively eyes.

A woman whose face had been smudged and distorted, but plastered on *Wanted* bulletins sprinkled all down the Spine. The first face joined to my name in Kalvikan…when the Sha, it seemed, had begun to remember me as I had once been, as the woman in service to him.

Before someone—likely Galan—had informed him of my new face.

I'd written her into anonymity. Written her a fresh start with everything I'd wanted at the end of my tenure with the Sha…the freedom to strike out on the

ne, unhindered, unsought after. And so achingly lonely for someone I hadn't
n known I'd lost; for a life I'd scripted away in the rewriting of life as we
w it.

I'd been entrusted with so much power by the Storymaker standing before
. And in the end, I'd used it to tear a wound into the heart of the country I'd
n delegated to protect.

Jaik moved at last, jerkily, burying his hands in his hair, his gaze wrenching
to the Storymaker. "What *am* I?"

"You are Jaik Grissom," the Storymaker said. "But you are a Jaik who
bodies all the power of the gift I gave to Storycrafters. The endings to stories
bound up in *your* ending…and your rebirth. The moment life flowed into
, it left the stories of the world. Now they only possess their power to create
en you are near them."

Suffocating weight bore down on my chest with every calm, truthful word
t fell from His lips.

I *had* done this—not through murder, but *because* of murder. I had stripped
ry Storycrafter of their power and given it all to Jaik…to make him live again.
broken the world to mend him.

Worse than being told this tale…I *remembered* now. I remembered the
ttomless abyss of grief that had opened up beneath me when I'd knelt on the
stah's golden floor and held his limp, lolling head in my hands. When I'd
n that beloved face slack in death. When I'd kissed those cold lips and found
pressure, no eagerness rising to meet mine.

And I sensed the edges of that hole still stripped into my heart…a hole I'd
ributed only to the loss of my craft. The sundered stories within me.

I'd never once considered that the ache *I* bore in their absence might differ
m what my fellow Storycrafters felt…that I might be mourning for something
re than my shattered power.

I'd only known the ache had disappeared that day in *The Tiller's Tankard*,
en I'd seen Jaik on that stool.

"How do I make this right?" Pleading strangled my tone. I would do
ything—*anything*—to fix the world I'd broken.

The Storymaker was quiet for a long moment. Then He said, "There are
ny paths from this tower. Many possible tales yet to be told. Some have good
dings…others have tragic ones. But I will tell you this much: what you read in
s book, what you have seen and remembered, is not the entirety of the story.
is only what the tearing took away from you. There are other answers you still

seek…but you may not need them in order to choose what is the best way to write the next page of your story."

My gaze hunted for Jaik's; in his shimmering stare, I saw my conviction already reflected.

"We have to go back," I rasped. "back to Mithra-Sha. To help people and warn them about what the Sha did to us."

The Storymaker drew in an audible breath. "That is one way to write it, yes."

Jaik's focus snapped past me, straight to Him. "Are you saying it's the wrong one?"

"I am saying that it is your choice. And that every choice you make from this moment forward will write a different ending."

The hair rose on my nape as cold brushed down from my hairline to my tailbone. "Then how do we know if we're choosing *right*?"

The Storymaker closed the gap between us—a motion so oddly merciful, after what I'd done, that it freed fresh tears from my eyes. He took my hands in both of His, swaying our arms between our bodies. "I gave you such a great portion of this craft for a purpose, Audra. Because I believe that whatever mistakes you may make, however you stumble along the way, you are still capable of choosing to wield it wisely. My belief in you has not wavered, despite what you have done."

Every word snagged through my heart like the piercing of a suture needle, jabbing where it struck, but mending as it passed. Knitting the tattered halves of me whole again.

"You know what lies ahead," He added quietly, "and though you believe you have counted the cost, you have not. Not yet. Someday it will be clear enough for you to face it…and that is the strength I wrote into *your* story. You will uncover it in time."

Another wave of unease feathered down my back. "Can't you just *tell* me what—?"

He pressed a finger to my lips, shaking his head, his smile small and sad and so achingly *sure*. "You will discover it as you turn the proper pages. But know this: I gave you this craft to fulfill a purpose. When you walk in that purpose, you will know your times and seasons. You will learn how to let go."

He freed my hands and turned from me, to Jaik; offering a hand down, He drew him to his feet and steadied him with strong fingers clasped around the back of his neck.

"I have seen the heart of you, Jaik Grissom. Your story might have ended ɔ soon in death, but now it is being rewritten. And I have not finished putting ƴ quill to the parchment of your tale. Keep the faith and continue ʇking…you will find what you desire as you prove yourself worthy."

Turning, He laid a hand on my head as well; for a moment, all three of us ɾe bound. Joined. The power of the One who made the stories themselves, ɐ one built of stories, and the one who had changed Storycraft forever.

"I can see in your faces that you have made your choice," the Storymaker ɪrmured. "Now it is time to write it."

His grip on us both tightened for a moment, and a throbbing shock of wer, of strength, of *love* surged into me, so potent I wept afresh; and then the ɔrymaker released us and brought His hands together with a resounding *clap*.

The walls of Erasure bowed; thunder boomed through the cavern of it, and ɐ wind whipped a flurry of loose-leaf pages off the desk, blinding us both, ◦ping the dampness from my eyes. I scrubbed my face hastily on my sleeve, ɴked, squinted as the breeze settled—

And we were alone.

The hearth still burned. The books were precisely as they had been. The ᵥves rustled in the trees winding above our heads. But the Storymaker was ɴe—as was the tome of our history. The tale of Jaik and me.

My eyes lunged to him, frenzied to know I hadn't hallucinated all of it…and ᵥvas a relief and dreadful all at once to see my shock reflected in his ashen face.

As we stood there, rooted in our disbelief, from outside the door a ᴄophony of sound clawed in to find us.

The hunting cries of the Isle's prisoners, lurking outside the tower doors.

CHAPTER 72
WHAT'S NEVER CHANGED

The Storymaker did not return.

It was difficult to discern if that was why we waited, huddled by the hearth, taking stock of our belongings and grazing our wondering hands over wounds newly-healed.

We kept our silence. Even when night slithered its long shadows through the windows and the Misspoken manifestations raged outside, beating against the tower doors that held true, we did not discuss our escape.

We said nothing at all.

The silence was so absolute, it held all the grim chill of being buried alive. Over and over, my mind burst like a struck flintrock, spitting sparking memories of Jaik's dead body beneath my hands. My own scream, a chant of *No, no, no, no* shredding my ears. The precise weight of his lifeless corpse cradled in my arms. The taste of the blood on his mouth when I tried—failed—to kiss him back to life.

I hooked my finger through the ring that hung around my neck...Jaik's ring. One of the few things I'd carried with me, though I hadn't known I'd kept it...a piece of the life I'd lived before, tucked in the hidden pocket of my cloak. A scrap of him I'd kept even when I'd lost everything else. Even when I hadn't recognized the ring for what it was.

"Would you have said yes?"

His question rumbled in the dark, breaking hours of quiet and jolting me from my harrowing memories. I snapped my attention from the fire burning in the hearth—the only light in the night-swallowed tower—and found him staring into the flames still. His jaw was so tight, the muscles feathered down the side of

"Jaik…" His name throbbed in the way I whispered it.

His eyes darted to me, watching me chafe the ring on its cord; then they bounded to the fire.

"Not that it matters anymore." He rasped his palms together as if to ward f a chill, though the fire was almost unbearably hot. "I just…"

"Yes." More strength banded that word than any I'd managed to choke out 1ce memory had returned to us from the pages of that book. "I wouldn't have en hesitated. No matter what it cost me, even if I'd had to live the rest of my e hiding it from the Sha…it was always *yes*, Jaik." I shifted nearer to him for e first time since we'd sunk into the shock of our shared past, nudging my 1oulder into his. "It still is."

His head jolted my way, wide eyes paved with firelight. "What—?"

I captured his mouth when it came near enough to mine, planting my hand 1 the stone behind him and grazing my fingers along the line of his jaw; then I ew back just enough for him to feel me whisper the words against his mouth. Marry me, Jaik Grissom."

His breathless laughter fanned against my cheeks. "After everything that 1ppened today, *that's* what you're going with?"

I pressed my forehead to his shoulder so he could feel me nod. "I member what it was like to lose all the time I ever thought I'd have with you. I 2n't want to waste a second more."

His fingers played with a lock of hair brushing against my neck. "You 1ow, Captains can officiate marriage vows when they're out to sea. Since the aters belong to no one. It doesn't need a Sha or a Del or—"

"Is that a *yes*?" I teased, drawing back to meet his eyes.

His stare was fathomless and freckled with tears. "That hasn't changed, ger."

I had never found it more difficult to hold his gaze; not for that endless, iercing love in his eyes, but because for the first time in years, I remembered hat it was to have lost him. To have lost that love…and the desperation it had riven me to. The things I had broken to fix what the Sha had done.

Swinging one leg over both of his, I straddled Jaik's waist and buried my ace in his collar. My fingertips crawled up of their own accord, tracing the utline of the mark on his chest…the mortal wound that had changed verything.

"I *lost* you." The words dripped miserably from my lips—the first time I'd ver been able to say them. I hadn't conceded that truth before the Sha, even when I'd heard the emptiness in Jaik's chest where his strong heartbeat had lulled me to sleep on so many of our journeys across Mithra-Sha.

His arms tightened around me. "I remember the last thought in my head before I was gone: how flipping *scared* I was of leaving you behind."

And then, for some time, we leaned into one another and wept.

They were healing tears, cleansing years of strange feelings and false memories; they washed away the lies that remained, making way for the truth of us to bloom in the cracks.

But they were wretched tears, too...tears of grief and anguish, of fear and regret.

They were the last tears Jaik had cried, alone in a hall in the Shastah while he'd bled to death, his thoughts on me. They were the last tears I'd shed before I'd made the choice that had shattered our world, my thoughts on him.

But the mourning made way for clarity; and in the ever-thickening shadow of Erasure, when I'd spent the last of my sobs and only had dry, quaking breath and the reassuring *thump* of Jaik's living pulse under my ear again, certainty settled in.

I'd given myself back what I'd lost. But others had not been so fortunate.

"We have to go back." I pushed up from his chest to meet his shimmering gaze. "We...*I* have to help wherever I can."

"I know." His fingertips traced up my spine. "So do I. I mean, flipping *Luck*. Everything that's broken is because of us."

"Then we'll make the mending because of us, too." The words emerged with more strength than I felt; but strength would come in time. "We'll do like we did in the Drennans...fix as much as we can. Even if it draws bounty hunter and unwanted attention, I owe it to the people not to leave them stranded because of my choices."

Jaik brushed his lips against my brow. "I'm with you, Ayjay."

But it would not begin tonight; not with both of us so griefsick, reeling from the day's struggles and revelations.

Instead, we curled up before the hearth, my back tucked to Jaik's chest, his arm looped around my waist; we watched the fire crackle and smolder and yet never dim. And in that silence, my mind traced the new paths of memory laid open before me...all the people and places and things I'd traded for the belief in a false life.

"Tell me what you remember that means the most to you," I murmured.

He was quiet for a time, his contemplation filling the silence in its depth; n he said, "I remember Arias. Raz. I remember how much I struggled to trust self with befriending anyone after Galan…I was pushing everyone aside, even 1. But Raz wouldn't let it go. And the more he held on, the more it taught me at friendship should've looked like with Galan. It showed me what I missed, I could be better."

"I remember my friends, too," I admitted. "Not just Naomi, back when we ed in the Shastah together while she served his family. But Shadress Mahalia, d Reiko."

Jaik snorted. "*Reiko.* That pain in my saddle…"

A sharp laugh burst from my nose. "The perfect words for her."

"You were trying to put me through it for working with Galan. That's why u chose your biggest rival from the tests to be part of your inner circle of orycrafters."

"Maybe so," I teased, half-rolling onto my back to flash him a smile. "No, eiko gave me a run for the Master Storycrafter title…even when she tried to botage me. She didn't have to do that, she was powerful enough as it was. I anted that power kept in service to the Sha."

"She did help us out of a few rough patches," Jaik conceded grudgingly.

We talked for some time about those dangerous years, and of the Shadran d Shadress, my fellow Storycrafters, the soldiers Jaik had brought into his fold. hen the reminiscing strayed to solemn paths: journeys we'd taken, just the two f us; places we had seen and long forgotten. And then, the things we'd hoped o do and see once the Sha no longer held my leash.

"Do you remember what you were going to do," Jaik murmured, playing ith my hand in his, tracing my knuckles with his thumb, "once we got out of allanmyre and made it into the mountains?"

I did; the notion was a physical pain throbbing under my breastbone now. Do *you*?"

Jaik's head thudded onto the rug, and he groaned, low and deep. "I was oing to start *farming.*"

Laughter bubbled out of me again, and I nudged an elbow backward into is ribs. "At least I gave you that."

The words stopped my breath a moment. I couldn't find a way around the veight lodged in my throat.

Jaik's hand shifted up from mine; he balanced himself on his elbow behind ne, taking my chin, half-turning me to lean against him until our eyes met.

"You wanted to tend bar." The words floated across my face, warm as embers. "You learned how for one of our missions, and it sat right with you. Talking to people all day long...hearing their stories."

"It was a way to be surrounded by tales...true ones and fables," I breathe my mind darting back to the *Tankard*, and to the public house in Fallshyre Bay where I'd had just that—a hundred people telling me stories, just like Jaik love to do, "and to earn coin at the same time."

"And at the end of the day, instead of hours of meeting with the Sha, you could just head back to the farm." A note of depreciation slid into Jaik's tone— scrap of armor slapped on over the notion of a perfect future we would never have the opportunity to build.

I slid my hand behind his head, relishing the silkiness of his hair threading between my fingers. "I was always coming home to you."

His expression shuttered a bit; he rolled onto his back, staring up at the tower recesses. "And I forgot you."

"And I forgot *you*." I slid over to mimic his posture: flat on our backs, fac offered up toward the shadows. "Why do you think *Galan* remembered us mor clearly than everyone else?"

Jaik's shoulder tugged upward against mine. "Who knows? Maybe he held on tighter to us because of how much he hated us. Blamed us for everything. W already knew how he felt about you back in Dalfi, but me...I betrayed him. An thanks to Raz, he got shipped off as far from Vallanmyre as you can go. I gues he hung on to that when everything fell apart."

Hatred had clung on harder than love...that was almost impossible to accept, at first. But the longer I dwelled on it, the more sense it made.

My parents and siblings, even Naomi and the others, had loved me intrinsically; it was never something they had to foster, it had flowed naturally between us. Galan, on the other hand...banished to Krylan, he'd fed and fuele his hate. He'd nursed it and grown it. Who knew how much uglier and how cru it had been *before* the tearing had ripped it away from him, if he'd held on to so much of it afterward?

The things we held onto the hardest were the things we'd brought with us into this strange, broken world. Like I'd held onto Jaik, in those last moments. His ring. His vow. Even his body.

I hadn't remembered him...but I'd been walking toward him ever since th tearing had flung him to Krylan. I'd been traveling home for years, and never known.

Those quiet musings of hate and love were the last words either of us spoke
at night, though the tightness in how we held one another spoke infinitely
ore.

When we woke, daylight splintered through the high windows of Erasure;
e hearth was dark, and an odd mustiness hung about the tower...as if it hadn't
en touched in years. Centuries, even. The trees had shed their leaves and the
hen and ivy had begun to crumble. The sound of falling water had dried up.

It was time to go.

Jaik and I rose without packing and strode for the tower doors. Between us
ng an unspoken understanding of precisely what we had to do...and just how
pable we were of doing it.

Hand in hand, we faced the doors.

"Ready, tiger?" Jaik muttered.

Somehow, the sound of that flippant name cradled in his usual caustic tone
eathed fresh strength into me; with a grim nod, I slung my satchel more tightly
ross my front, shut my eyes, and reached out for that spark of power that
ned Jaik and me to one another.

And with my Storycraft, I built us a bridge.

CHAPTER 73
ABOARD THE ATHALION

The story that rolled out of me this time was of a world divided in suffering, and of crafters determined to save it through unity; a realm of scattered islands and the thinnest thread of hope that bound them together. And from the telling, though I couldn't see it taking shape, I *felt* it: a broad obsidian arch that pulsed out from above the entrance to Erasure, traversing the span of the Illusionarium in a long, dark artery that soared above most of the Misspoken manifestations caged here.

There was no fear in me that the story would fail, no hesitation when I spoke. Memories of my power wove into the truth of the scarlet cloak draped over my shoulders, making no room for doubt. I held in me the same might that had laid the Spine and crafted airships from pure imagination long ago; the only obstacle in my path to seeing us safely from the Illusionarium was my own uncertainty.

And for Jaik's sake and my own, I gave no ground to it.

Somewhere in the telling, a bright, carving silver glow etched itself into the wall of Erasure above our heads; and from those sweeps and angles, a second set of doors manifested above the first, the deep scarlet wood splashed like blood against the black stone.

With a swift glance and a nod, Jaik and I scrambled up one of the staircases to reach it; then we thrust our way out into the daylight, the tale still tumbling from my lips as we ran.

It was a harrowing dash down the obsidian bridge, placing us at eye level with the behemoths that still roamed beyond Erasure; but whether by the sheer spectacle of us careening past their faces, or the fear of the Storycrafting power that had fumed ahead of us, they did not attack. The burning depths of their

zes tracked us while we bolted past, their fiery maws gaping—but nothing
ore.

Spine prickling, I did not look back.

We crossed the island from above, and as the seaside loomed into view, I
as already sending the words of the story out ahead of us—launching the
afters within it on a quest by boat to reach the outlying islands their bridges
d yet to join together. My heart leaped at the vessel that surged up from the
pths at the sloped end of the bridge—a rowboat not unlike our last, but larger,
eker, and framed all along the rim with jagged wooden tines to keep depths-
velling Misspoken creatures at bay.

With a mighty leap, Jaik and I launched from the bridge, crashed into the
lly of the rowboat, and grabbed an oar each, thrusting out to sea.

Howls and distant cackles and grating, discordant calliope music rose again
om the island when we had rowed some distance away; my thundering heart
d not slow until we drew even with the sentinel watchtowers unpursued.

Then I slumped, pressing my forehead to my hand wrapped around the oar
andle, letting out a long, shaky breath.

Jaik clapped me gently on the back. "See, that wasn't so bad, was it?"

"If it wasn't, I don't want to see what *bad* is, Jaik."

"Fair," he chuckled, peeling my fingers from the oar and nudging me into
e bow of the boat. "You spot for the ship. I'll row."

I was glad to let him do it; though the Storymaker had mended the majority
f my hurts, an ache still thumped in my leg and shoulder, the tangible reminder
at no wounds—not those dealt to us or those we'd dealt to others—could be
ompletely erased. And that was a truth I leaned into as we crossed back out into
e open sea, scouting for *The Athalion*. It was not a lesson I could afford to
rget ever again.

For more than an hour, we rowed against the sea's currents, quiet, vigilant;
d when I first caught a freckle of darkness against the span of the dim early-
orning horizon, for a moment I thought it was a mere scuff on my vision from
raining too long to see what lay ahead.

Even when that blot took shape—even when I was certain I wasn't
magining it—it still made little sense. And less as we drew nearer.

"Jaik," I murmured. "Look at that."

It was indeed *The Athalion* we'd rowed into sight of, still drifting at the
ercy of the currents—still crippled from the battle against the Misspoken siren.
ut that was not what set my stomach pitching with disbelief.

An airship hovered in the clouds above *The Athalion*, the vessels tethered b a rope loosed from the airship's belly.

Jaik frowned. "Could be sky-traders saw *The Athalion* was crippled. They might be bringing the help the crew needs."

Relief sent the breath surging out of me in a gust, and I slid back onto the rowing bench, seizing one of the oars from him. "Let's move, then."

"You're just eager to get married."

"To you?" I wrinkled my nose. "What gave it away?"

Our laughter rolled with the wake of the rowboat until we passed into *The Athalion's* shadow, where Jaik braced two fingers in his mouth and whistled. After a moment, a rope ladder descended the ship's hull, and I gripped its wove frame—then hesitated. With one foot dangling above the sea, I looked back.

The vigilant watchtowers seemed to train their stony eyes on me; there wa an eerie sort of life to them. A weighty intensity to their stares.

Do better. The bidding, the warning, was scripted onto my bones. *Do right b what He gave you.*

Setting my teeth around the determination that bubbled like an overflowin inkpot in my center, I scrambled up the ladder, reaching the top with Jaik a rung below. Snagging the railing, I hauled myself over, dropped onto the deck—

And met the gaze of Officer Galan Fiordona.

Pure malice. Pure hate held in stormy gray eyes.

That was all that pierced the shock, at first. Then I realized he was not alone. That Mithran soldiers held the railings, rifles trained on me.

And Galan had Julas.

He was down on his knees, the soldier's fingers tangled in his matted black hair, wrenching his head back—and his face was such a mess I hadn't even recognized him at first. Eyes swollen, mouth ripped, throat bruised and breath heaving around a gag biting his cheekbones bloody, he couldn't shout. He couldn't speak. He could say nothing, but his eyes said it all.

A plea. An apology. A warning screamed silently in the space between us. *Run.*

And then Galan's blade ripped across his throat, spilling the Captain's lifeblood onto the deck of *The Athalion*.

CHAPTER 74
SILENT SHACKLES

—hock and horror held me captive a moment too long, my feet stuck to the decking, tears slashing across my vision—blood painting my rld.

Scarlet on gold. Crimson on umber.

One moment was all it took.

"*Julas!*" Jaik's bellow—half heartbreak, half world-reckoning *rage*—jolted me m my stricken stupor; yet by the time I blinked, jolted, snapped toward him, was already moving. Already lunging down from the railing and tearing ard Galan even as the soldier thrust Julas's lifeless body aside.

A rifle reported. A single, lonely shot.

Jaik slammed to the deck with a bark of agony, blood spraying from his leg.

This time, the red I saw was all fury. The same sort that had shattered rycraft.

I lunged for Jaik—then drew up short when the soldiers along the railing ned their rifles again.

Not toward me. But toward the figures they'd sidestepped for me to see— prisoners I had not yet noticed, my whole focus consumed by Julas.

Reinera and Lanah, Syd and Frixia, and the whole of the remaining w…all bound and gagged like their fallen Captain, with rifles aimed at their art. Lanah wept silently, tears soaking the cloth that chafed the sides of her uth bloody. Syd had angled himself halfway between her and the muzzle ant for her, holding the attention of two fatal shots on his own chest. Frixia l Reinera faced these marauding soldiers with unflappable strength, chins ;ed, shoulders squared…but fear and grief shone in their eyes.

And Galan watched me, braced between the railing and Jaik, his smug gri saying all his measly mouth would not.

They were expendable.

We were not.

And I had never hated that truth so much in all my life—not even when i was the Sha who'd wanted me.

I held my ground, hands flexing in and out of fists, gaze leaping back to Jaik; he clutched his leg and dragged himself to sitting, blood spooling between his fingers, hate knifing on the jagged edge of every breath that escaped him.

"You're a *dead man*," he spat.

"Who, him?" Galan toed Julas's body aside. "I think he knows, *Jaiky*."

Snarling profanely, Jaik palmed the deck and lurched up on one leg—ther broke back down with a cry that ripped through me, a shout of agony that cut off breathlessly when Galan stepped forward and drilled a fist straight into his gut.

I nearly coughed up my air, too. My mind raced, scrambling for a story, a tale to crush these bounty-hunting soldiers, to rescue all of us—

"This is the fate of those who help fugitives against the Sha," Galan adde stepping over Jaik and strolling toward me. Behind him, a pair of soldiers converged, hauling Jaik up by the arms, twisting them behind his back. "Once I'm given a command in the Mithran army, I'll be sure the same punishment finds its way to Fallshyre. And to everyone who looked kindly on the pair of yc there."

Rage spiked in my head, so hot and vicious it rammed a blade of pain behind my eyes. "If you lay a hand on *any* of those people—"

"You know, I like you far better when you aren't talking, Jashowin." Galan's eyes raked over me, full of so much contempt my skin couldn't contair it all; my flesh crawled with it. "Whatever you were doing in the Illusionarium…well, it worked. I remember everything about you two, now. I remember what a failure of a soldier Grissom was…and I remember what it wa like with you. Arrogant, cruel little prodigy of Storycraft." He halted before me—near enough that I could smell tobacco on his clothes and stale rations or his breath. "You always did hide behind your talent in a fight."

"Oh, you've convicted me," I hissed. "I'll be certain not to use my strateg advantage, so that you feel we have a fight on *equal footing*."

Galan arched a brow. "Who said anything about *having* a fight?"

I barely registered the flash of his fist, and then—

Pain.

Agony exploded through the lower half of my face, bone grinding bone, ~n separating with a tangible *crunch*. My teeth reared against each other at all : wrong angles, and by the time my knees hit the deck, by the time I retched I vomited for the pain, but couldn't open my mouth wide enough to let it e, I realized what he'd done.

Galan had unhinged my jaw.

I couldn't *speak*.

Down on my hands and knees before him, sick seeping from my crooked >uth, with Jaik howling my name between threats aimed at Galan, I was lpless to craft a single story.

Galan hooked his boot tip beneath my chin, thrusting my head back; I ;ged and arched at the pain splintering through my jaw, a fresh spew of bile nbing my throat and dribbling from the sides of my lips.

"Now, this is how I like you best," Galan murmured. "Silent and in your ice. Showing everyone how little you have to offer without your Storycraft."

He crouched on my level, gripping my chin and tilting my head back even :ther; black dapples erupted across my vision, and for a moment, I floated. ily the distant thread of Jaik's voice chanting my name in anguish and fury pt me tethered to myself.

"No witty retort?" Galan taunted. "No story to outmatch my soldiering?"

A smattering of nervous laughter beat against my ears in a distant, thudding e; perhaps whatever he'd offered these soldiers—likely in Dalfi—to fly him :oss Mithra-Sha in pursuit of us, they had not anticipated his cruelty. How rsonal of a grudge he held.

But no one intervened. No one dared, with the deck paved in Julas and k's blood.

Finally, Galan snorted, "Pitiful."

He released me, and I slumped to the deck. Dimly, his orders penetrated ? fog occluding my senses.

"Get the pair of them onto the ship," he barked. "Leave the sailors adrift, .t take their rations and pitch their sails. They'll have plenty of time to consider ? consequences of treason against the Sha before they starve to death."

I twisted my head toward the crew, hunting desperately for their faces—for d's enraged scowl and Reinera's furious weeping. For Frixia's grim stare and .nah's tearstained eyes.

I'm sorry, I wanted to sob. *I'm so sorry for all of this—*

But I could not form the words. I could not even weep when the soldiers surged over me and hauled me after Jaik toward the rope ladder. One of them flung me over his shoulder, and then we climbed—and I could only squeeze m eyes shut and cling to the man's flimsy shirt with both hands, shutting out the ship bobbing away below my overturned head.

Shutting out the friends we had no choice but to leave behind.

CHAPTER 75
STORIES IN THE SHADOWS

There was no time and even less desire to admire the soldiering airship they hauled us onto. Galan's accomplices dragged us across the topdeck and down into the belly of the skyborne vessel before my pain-addled head could register more than the darkwood veneer or the sheer number of soldiers who gaped at us as we passed.

The heart of the airship was far colder than any corner of *The Athalion* I'd visited. An amalgamation of wood, metal, and churning parts, its inner walls emitted a bone-chilling fume that magnified the pounding in my head so brutally I gagged. The soldier who'd hauled me over his shoulder up the ladder tossed me ahead with a disgusted grunt through an unmarked door and into a metal-walled brig, the far wall full-fitted with narrow, iron-barred cages.

My knees threatened to meet the floor, but the soldier was ready for me; another thrust of a boot to the back, and I staggered through one of the open doors, my ears ringing with Jaik's curse, hollering at the soldier to leave me alone.

Our cells clanged shut in synchrony.

"Next port…Vallanmyre." The soldier locked my cage with a pivot of the wrist and an equally sharp swivel of his lips. His eyes cut between us, brimming with hunger…hunger for the pot of coins he saw reflected in our wounded bodies.

We were less than human to him; we were pure profit. And he, like his fellow soldiers on this airship, was ready to collect.

The moment the soldiers retreated from the brig, Jaik rolled onto his haunches in his own cell; he ripped off his coat sleeve with a few deft yanks and knotted it around his leg, then thrust himself to the wall our cages shared.

Winding his fingers between the slats, he pressed his brow to the iron mesh. "Ajay. Ayjay, hey…"

Whatever words of comfort he might have thought to offer, he choked before they escaped; digging his forehead against the iron, he breathed deep, the sound rolling damply with the tears that slid down his cheeks.

The cold walls shuddered like a vicious respiration around us; then the airship *roared*, so deafening it stabbed through my eardrum on the wounded side of my head, knocking me reeling against the ship wall.

For a moment, I clung to the cold metal, the icy bite just barely soothing the pain that flared from the mark of Galan's wild blow to my face; and that was the only thing that kept my stomach from deserting me when the airship lurched forward, tearing free of its bond to *The Athalion*.

Leaving our friends stranded. Carrying us off toward the last place I ever wanted to go—back into the hands of Sha Lothar. Jaik's murderer.

Desperation surged through me all at once, snapping me back to focus…back to the brig, back to the pain hurling through my face, back to where we were now. Back to the people we were leaving behind to starve or sink, adrift in the sea, while we were carried off captive to the Sha's clutches.

I couldn't do this. I couldn't abandon the crew. Nor could I watch Jaik be dragged before the Sha and executed *again*.

Shoving myself up from the wall, I crawled to the door ; ignoring Jaik's uneven croak of my name, the warning that bracketed his pain-roughened tone, fitted my fingers to the slats and heaved myself up onto my knees. I fixed the faces of the crew in my mind.

And I struggled to form words.

Let me tell you a story…

All that emerged were pathetic puffs of air, half clogging in my bloodied, sick-stained mouth, half jamming in my nostrils. I coughed, choked on them, but I struggled to find more. Struggled to form a story that would rip the bottom out of this sky-pirating vessel and return us to *The Athalion*, its crew robbed of their Captain—robbed of so many friends during this voyage on *our* account…

"L-L-L…" My tongue fumbled over the single letter and would go no further; heat flared along the hinge of my knocked-crooked jaw, a warning shot fired down the line of my face.

I ignored it. I could not afford to be powerless now.

"Audra—Ayjay, *stop!*" Jaik snarled. "Listen to me…"

Ignoring the slam of his palms on the iron between us, the way he bellowed
name, I still struggled to speak. I fought to force the words out past the pain
lating from before my ear, out across my face, wrapping the side of my
d—tried to muster the strength to choke out some story that would save us.

I failed.

I came to hours later, judging by the darkness dripping through the
thole window.

My body was slumped upright against the door of the cell where agony had
t me crumbling senseless, still fighting to speak. My head was angled toward
's cell, and in the gloom, I caught a glimpse of his fingertips—stained with
own blood and with Julas's from the topdeck—shoved between the slats, as
r to me as he could reach. His shoulder was wedged into the corner where
cages met. He could have been no closer unless he was in my cage with me.

It was a blessing to register these things before the pain resurged.

When it came, it came with startling force, the anguish of my damaged jaw
l swollen, contused face barreling over me so swiftly I sucked in a staggered
ath. Even that hurt; my cheek throbbed and my line of vision was narrowing
the side where Galan had struck me.

Jaik's fingers tightened, curling around the iron slats, fingernails dragging on
metal floor. "Don't do that again."

I wouldn't. I didn't even have the power to tell him so.

Galan had finally done what he'd yearned for ever since I'd beaten him in
t schoolyard duel in our youth: he'd found a way to silence me.

But he could not silence Jaik—and that was the only comfort I found as the
vs changed by rising sun and waxing night through the porthole window. As
e *Athalion's* crew faded on a horizon we could not reach, and the world shrank
the endless moments in the cold brig without food or water to speak of, Jaik
d me stories.

True stories of his past—stories I remembered now, and some he hadn't
divulged of his time in Krylan. Stories of the mischief he'd gotten into with
as, and how Julas had become Captain of *The Athalion*...stories that brought
out tears that were not yet able to heal. It was all raw, wretched grief, with

Julas's murder still unavenged and his killer carrying us off to the man responsible for *Jaik's* death.

Jaik fell silent for a bit on the day he ran out of stories about Julas. And then he rasped, his voice choked with tears, "Flipping *Luck*, I should have let him come ashore with us."

After that, Jaik pivoted; he told stories to take us away from the frigid prison aboard the airship and our looming fate. Often I drifted to sleep to the murmur of some fantastic tale that would rival any one of mine, and woke to hear him still speaking, almost to himself. Almost to the Storymaker, as if a Wellspoken story told even by one who was not a Storycrafter would draw Him near.

It seemed impossible we had met Him in the flesh in Erasure only days ago. And now we were prisoners being carried off for coin.

I wept, the hot tears aching on my equally hot face. When I lay near enough to the iron bars, Jaik reached through to brush the tears away. And he still told me stories.

It had been a small handful of days—though I could not count how many—when I woke with a jolt one morning to silence. And stillness.

Panic flared through me, and I floundered fully awake, hunting the other cell, heaving for breath—searching for Jaik.

He was standing, for once, arm looped into the iron bars to hold himself upright; his head was lifted, body rigid, a man on alert.

A soldier scenting for trouble.

I croaked out a whimper—the only sound I could make through my parched throat and slanted jaw.

Jaik's eyes cut to me, carved bright with grief and touched with fear; and then he breathed the words I had been dreading since we'd touched down on *The Athalion's* deck.

"I think we just docked in Vallanmyre."

CHAPTER 76
A WORLD OF GLASS

he capital city was a memory imprinted on my mind and body—an impression not even rewritten history could have blinked away.

I knew it before I saw it; knew by the scents that permeated the g while Jaik and I huddled against the curve of the wall, awaiting the vitable.

The decadent aroma of the many markets, from fishmongers to the exotic it-peddlers who clustered on the edges of the city, attracting travelers from Spine and the smaller, outlying villages that hung in Vallanmyre's shadow.

The abundance of Hadrassi spices mingling with the clean, clear smell of e-flowing water that poured from the shallow, flat-topped hills backing the y—atop which the Shastah had been built—into the canals that sliced through llanmyre proper.

The herbaceous undercurrent of the sprawling gardens that bordered arrow Hall and kept their students in supply of all the tinctures and remedies ey could possibly require.

And if I could have pulled in a deep enough breath past my swollen jaw, I ght've caught a trace of the perpetual must of old parchment and the sharp or of new ink from Fablehaven.

A portion of my spirit longed to lay eyes on that tower; but the stronger bits me never wanted to leave this brig or set foot into the city where I'd grown . Where I'd lived for so long. The place I'd fled from when I'd sundered all e stories in Mithra-Sha.

I was meant to be doing something about that…putting right what I could. lping where I was able. Instead, I was huddling against the brig wall like a poached creature, guarding my jaw behind the tilt of my bowed shoulder when the door creaked open—and Galan strolled inside.

Hate lanced through me, vicious and white-hot, at the sight of his gloating face; Jaik hopped away from beneath the window, squaring his stance as well as he could with a rifleshot through the leg. "The second you open that door, you better—"

"Should've broken *your* lucking jaw," Galan cut across him with the breezy arrogance of a man who'd achieved all the desires festering in his gruesome imitation of a heart. "You never were much of a soldier…just a vat of hot steam." He slid the key into the lock on my cage, gave it a half-twist, then eyed me through the slats. "Here's how this will go: you're walking with me, and if either of you gives me grief, the other one bleeds."

He wrenched the door open and stepped back, slinging the rifle from over his shoulder, aiming the muzzle at level with my hip. My shoulder and midsection twinged deeply, a vicious reminder of this soldier's aim—how he could incapacitate me without harming his own gains.

"Out," he growled.

I shoved myself up from the brig wall and wove toward him, despising how the mess he'd made of my face affected my whole body—my vision occluded, my ear still ringing, pain thudding dully through the side of my head and throwing off my center of balance. Galan's lips curled with cruel pleasure at my unsteady gait, a smirk that only grew when he pitched me the keys…and I fumbled, hardly catching them before they hit the floor.

"Unlock his cage and lend him a leg."

I obeyed, for no other reason than that my hands ached to be on Jaik already; he met me at the gate, his fingers shaking slightly where they wrapped the bars, and the second the latch gave he wrenched the door open and took my face gently in his broad grip. The first brush of his frigid palms was an icy shock, startling at first, then so soothing against my inflamed skin that a tear escaped from the corner of my eye.

Jaik thumbed it away and drew me in close, his lips pressing hard and swift to my brow; then he wrapped his arm around my shoulders and leaned into me as we hobbled in a half-circle to face Galan.

His rifle trained on us, he jerked his head toward the brig door. "Shall we?"

I glanced at Jaik, gauging what sort of plan he might have; but his face revealed only his loathing for Galan.

So we went, arms around each other, back through the halls the soldiers
d dragged us down days ago. Every tandem stride of our three sets of feet
sed the hair on my neck for how they echoed in the silence. Absolute, gutting
ence.

I glanced at Jaik and found my same unease reflected in his eyes.

His hand tightened around my upper arm. Then he called back to Galan,
s tone taut and surly, "What, you line up and shoot the rest of the soldiers
ce they got you here?"

"A true soldier doesn't murder his own," Galan sneered. "They're all
eping...peacefully. Once I've gathered the returns for the bounty, I'll leave a
rtion for them."

"You think they'll just accept that?" Jaik scoffed.

"They won't have a choice. By then, I'll be their superior."

Disbelief blistered in my throat. He truly believed he would redeem every
istake he'd made through a single bounty?

Then again...the Sha had killed to possess me. He might instate Galan into
e country's hierarchy out of sheer gratitude.

Stomach sinking, I held tighter to the only man not desperate to tame or
vn me as we ascended the topdeck and looked out from the airship dock, high
 one of the capital's fringe towers, toward the looming Shastah in the near
stance.

It would not be a far walk, which was good for Jaik's wounded leg—and
sential if we were to have any hope of escape once an opportunity presented
elf. The skydock lay just in the shadow of the flat-topped hills, affording an
broken view of the span of waterfall-laced rock where the Shastah perched,
eaming in the early-morning sun.

And behind us...Fablehaven.

My heart lurched at the sight of it; it was precisely how I remembered, just
 sleek and inviting amidst the sprawl of the outer complex where we students
d lived and learned. And it was indeed the more beautiful twin to Erasure's
posing shadows, though I would never forget now what beauty lurked within
e tower of iron thorns.

I yearned for the Storymaker's touch on my jaw and on Jaik's leg as we
parted the ship and crossed the dock at the tip of Galan's rifle, bound for the
ty's skybridges.

The high, glass arches with their translucent gemstone walls were another
ake of Storycraft; they allowed an unmitigated view of Vallanmyre's buildings

and avenues below, but permitted foot traffic between skydocks and the Shasta without tangling in the bustle of the capital's inner streets. Passing through ther before dawn on the way to another mission with Jaik had been among my favorite quiet moments as Master Storycrafter…a held breath between one cris and the next, the world shattering with sunlit beauty where the first rays of daw turned gemstone and glass to the heart of a star.

Today, I despised it all; because these high bridges ensured we saw no one on our way to the Shastah. No one who would look twice at the injured captive being led along at riflepoint by a sneering, triumphant soldier.

Outside the bridge walls, the stone cliff loomed nearer and nearer—and then we were there, crossing the final arch of shimmering glass and catching sight of the pair of doors through which Jaik and I had intended to flee the nigh everything had fallen apart.

The night he'd died.

My feet slid on the smooth glass a moment, and both of us stumbled. Jaik' thumb grazed my arm, a swift, reassuring pressure before we fixed our focus ahead on the broad, golden doors and the soldiers who guarded them.

It was impossible to know why they stiffened: if they recognized us, or if it was the sight of Galan's rifle that sent all dozen soldiers in their twin rows of si shooting upright, hands to their own weapons.

"At ease, gentlemen," our captor purred. "Officer Galan Fiordona…I'm one of you. And I'm here to collect the bounty for Audra Jashowin and Jaik Grissom."

CHAPTER 77
WRATH AND RETRIBUTION

*W*e were not delayed at the Shastah's lower doors nearly long enough; I couldn't even begin to devise a plan, my head torn into a thousand tatters that had not stitched themselves back together by the time the guard escorted us through the doors and into the tunnels that ribbed the k below the Shastah.

Incandescent ore spidered through the stone, marrying in winking gleams h the lanternlight that paved the way; it would have been beautiful if it hadn't n so tomblike. If this had not felt like walking to my own execution.

Jaik's nearness was my only comfort…and the posture he took, watchful not strangled with tension. I wished I shared whatever faith kept his feet eath him, even his injured one, as we wound through the heart of the hills I emerged at last up a flight of steps into the belly of the Shastah.

I nearly went to my knees at the assault of sight and sound and scent that eted us in the halls of our old home. It felt as if no time at all had passed. le had changed…not the scent of Hadrassi potpourri and cooking spices, d-pressed oil perfumes and the polish of the weapons stashed all throughout Shastah. The imported artworks and carvings that lined the gold-and-scarlet ented walls…many of them painted by Mahalia herself. The ivory-and-guild r tiles. The tapestries and chandeliers and fountains.

Except, the nearer I looked…there were bare patches where valuables were ssing. Perhaps even sold back to our neighboring countries for funds to aid hra-Sha.

Tears danced along the surface of Jaik's eyes, too, when they swept the ls—walls that had once been so familiar and beloved to us both.

The walls that had been his grave.

"Go, Wyat," one of the soldiers spoke curtly to another, and the young m
broke away at a jog; Galan scowled after him.

"Where is *he* going?" he grumbled.

"To inform the Sha."

Galan scoffed under his breath; no doubt he'd hoped to make a scene, to
catch the Sha off-guard and impress him with the shock of our capture. It was
small satisfaction to know he'd be deprived of that, at least.

But now the Sha would be expecting us. And if he intended to repeat wha
he'd done to Jaik when we'd last been here...

My heart seized and stumbled. I wanted nothing more than to bury my fa
in Jaik's neck and hide from this gilded cage and the captors who held its locks
on all sides.

Servants throughout the halls slowed to stare at the procession we made:
cluster of soldiers, one of whom strutted and leered more broadly than the rest
Another, a soldier-turned-farmer; and a Storycrafter made mute, a scarlet cloak
hanging limp from her shoulders.

It was a spectacle I would never have dreamed of telling. But if I could ha
told any tale now, it would have been another that slowed time...that would
have stretched out the far-too-familiar journey to the Shastah's Convening
Chamber, holding this moment in abeyance forever.

Until I was ready. Until I had a better plan to save Jaik...and myself.

But I still had nothing, only half-formed pleas and a jaw that would not se
them free, by the time we reached the Chamber doors.

Galan barged ahead and threw the deep-relief crescents wide, swaggering
inside like a man of station and title. "Sha Lothar, Your Excellence!"

And there he was.

Tobyrus Lothar had changed far more than the Shastah he called home. F
dark hair, which had hung to well below his shoulderblades when I'd seen him
last—a defiance, I'd always thought, in the face of his over fifty years of age—
was cropped in a short, tangled weave hardly reaching past his ears; and it was
salted with more silver than black now. His always-articulate facial hair had
grown to a ragged beard, and the icy blue of his eyes had gentled, the creases
lined with perpetual exhaustion.

That same grooving weariness stooped his shoulders beneath his fur-lined
cloak and bent his back—a burdened slouch that only eased somewhat when o
gazes locked.

And all at once, the rage and disgust that had fomented in those moments ?'d last seen one another gave way, like the floor dropping out beneath my feet. nd all I wanted to do was weep.

This man had been my friend, my mentor. He'd seen potential in me and stered it beyond anything I'd ever hoped for myself. He'd loved me like a :her alongside his own children, indulged my interests, entrusted his country in y hands…and then he'd betrayed me. Broken my heart.

So I'd broken his world.

A gulf of bitterness and paranoia, heart-wounds and hate, filled the air tween us. And yet in his eyes, I found none of the hunger and possessiveness I anticipated. Nor did he raise a hand to motion any one of the soldiers ustered in the chamber to take aim at Jaik…or me.

He stepped away from his governing seat, walked as if in a dream down the igth of the Chamber where we and the Shadre had discussed the best interests Mithra-Sha so many times…and halted still some distance away. His hands ew his cloak across himself as if a bitter chill lived in his bones.

And then he spoke, his voice achingly soft: "Addie."

I raised my chin as high as I could, bordering on a flinch—always keeping y gaze fixed on him.

The Sha's eyes darted to Jaik, and pain cracked through his features so tently it knocked the breath out of me; he did not behold him with the shock a man seeing his cruelest work undone. He stared into his face for a long oment; then he glanced down at Jaik's leg nearest to mine, bearing none of his eight.

A frown cut into his brow. His focus shot back to me. Slowly, his fists leased his cloak, the creases falling straight to brush the floor.

"What happened to you two?" The steely note of the Sha's far-reaching wer slithered through his tone.

"They attempted to escape custody." Galan brushed forward, taking a low w. "Sha Lothar, it is truly an honor. You remember me, I was—"

"The soldier who informed my wife of Audra's altered appearance, yes." he Sha stepped nearer to us, his frown deepening. "Addie, will you speak to e? Please?"

The way his voice cracked over the last word made me desperate to obey. ut I could only hold his gaze.

"Her jaw's broken." It was impossible to be certain whether the rage in Jaik's tone was meant for the man who'd murdered him or the one who'd struck me. "Ask your *friend* Galan how *that* happened."

The Sha pinned his furious stare on Galan—and for the first time, the ruthless soldier flinched. "Like I said," he grumbled, "they tried to escape."

"After you *murdered* my friend," Jaik snarled, "you luckless, flipping—"

"Enough," the Sha cut across Jaik firmly, but the dislike in his face was aimed at Galan. He beckoned one of the soldiers behind us. "Give this man his bounty—reduced to one-third."

"Your Excellence—" Galan began sharply.

"The bounty was for them both unharmed and well-treated," Sha Lothar growled. "Since the requirements were not entirely fulfilled, the bounty will not be entirely rewarded. And you," he nodded to another of the soldiers, the same young man who'd come ahead of us springing up sharply now from near the wall, "fetch Healer Weathers from her rooms. Inform her she has work to do."

For the first time, something like hope flared in my chest.

Naomi had made it here. And she was being brought to *us*.

"I'm sorry," Galan snapped, without a touch of apology in his tone at all, "what is *happening* here? A *healer* is being brought for—?"

"For the damage you've done," the Sha replied coolly. "Not that I am under any obligation to explain myself to you, *Officer*, but the Master Storycrafter and her bodyguard will be given the utmost care available in this Shastah. And you will be leaving forthwith."

"You're *rewarding* them?" The irreverence in Galan's tone fired through me like a warning rifleshot. Jaik tugged me aside so that we both faced him, our backs no longer exposed to his palpable fury. "After everything they've *done*?"

"What was done was no one person's fault." The Sha's eyes were trained on me. "And what will be done now is no concern of yours, Officer. You will have your reward. And you are dismissed."

"Dismissed?" Galan barked. "*Dismissed*, after I hunted them down for you, after I told you how to *find* her, what she looked like…after I warned everyone for *years* what these Storycrafters are capable of? She *remains* in the Shastah while I'm tossed out into the street?"

"What did you expect? Accolades and esteem?" the Sha countered coldly. "Did you think I'd forget how you sabotaged our tests and undermined me? How much personal loathing my son holds for you? I may have forgotten these two for a time, but I never forgot *you*, Officer Fiordona."

For one moment, the room held its breath while all of Galan's schemes shattered in his hands.

And then he leaped.

My body registered his direction before my mind truly did, and I wrenched Jaik away a stumbling half-step…but it wasn't Jaik he was reaching for.

Galan's clobbering weight plowed into us both, but his slap rang against my broken jaw; a wordless scream hurled itself out of my throat as silver-white apples burst across my vision. My ringing head lost its control over my limbs, and Galan ripped me from Jaik's grip, hauling me against his chest as he backed toward the door.

The next sensation I was aware of in full was the kiss of his knife under my crooked jaw.

"I am not going to allow this!" Galan's breath burned slick against my ear, still stinging from his slap. "Even after you saw what their kind are capable of, you're intending to let her into your halls…and she's the *worst* of them! I didn't bring her here to see her reinstated, I want to see her *hang* for what she did to our country!"

I choked at the jam of rifle bolts into place—at all of the muzzles leveled our way by the other soldiers lining the walls. Soldiers whose aim I couldn't trust.

Scarlet and gild. Rifles cocked.

And Jaik…Jaik stumbled toward us a step, then stiffened when the blade tightened under my jaw.

It couldn't end like this. Not with Galan's knife under my broken jaw. Not with Jaik staring into my eyes and the Sha pinning Galan with the most glacial glower of mortal wrath I'd ever seen from him.

"How do you suppose this will go?" He stepped back to his presiding seat, hands upraised toward Galan as they'd been toward me.

"I know how it's *not* going," Galan spat. "It's not going in her favor. She deserves to—"

"*Jaik!*" the Sha barked—and slung a rifle from over the edge of his seat, throwing it to him one-handed.

Jaik didn't even hesitate; flawless as a dance, he spun on his good leg, caught the rifle, racked the bolt into place, aimed as he planted his injured foot—and fired.

Blood exploded against the side of my head; deft instinct brought my hand up, gripping the knife and shoving it away before it could slice my skin. I kept pushing with all my might, thrusting Galan's corpse away as it folded down, bloodsoaked and grisly, at my back.

Scarlet on gold. Blood on my hands.

I plunged to my knees beside his body, holding tightly to my throat where the wild, desperate scratch of my nattering pulse against my palm told me I was alive, I was alive, I was *alive*...

Galan was not.

He was dead. Gone. Crumbled in a heap on the same floor that had once drunk Jaik's blood.

Now it sated itself on the blood of the man who'd stalked our steps all the way from Krylan, whose ever-burning fury and disgust had seared at the corners of my life in the Tailbone City, curling the edges in dark cinders day after day. This floor was saturated already in the last vestiges of the shadow of a forgotten past who'd made himself so much larger than he'd ever deserved to be. The man who'd harassed Naomi, *murdered* Julas and left the crew to die…

He looked so insignificant, sunken down on the vast span of the Convening Chamber's floor, his head an oozing gape. Without his petty hatred filling him up like parchment scraps soaked in ink, ready to catch alight at the merest lick of fire, Galan Fiordona was indeed a small man. Small and simple in his desires. Things that would be forgotten, his story untold now that he was gone.

I didn't know if he had a family. A lover. Anyone who mattered.

Certainly, nothing that had mattered more to him than vengeance for a childhood slight.

There was no grief knocking against the beat of my thundering pulse. Only a cold, clear satisfaction that belonged to the woman I'd once been.

The relief of a threat removed from my door. From Naomi's door. From Jaik's door.

Jaik.

His name bolted through me like the slash of a quill tearing through feeble parchment, and all at once I came aware of a steady pressure exerting against my wrist, towing my hand down from my neck. The familiar, burning brush of Jaik's thumb coaxed a tumble of gooseflesh from my jugular in a spill down over my collarbone as he wiped away the blood on my throat.

Galan's blood. Not mine.

Jaik's breath rushed out all at once, and he cursed, arms linking around my shoulders and waist, crushing me against him. "You're all right. Hey, tiger, I've got you…"

"Deal with that," the Sha ordered the soldiers, jerking his chin at Galan's
dy. "We've had enough blood on this Chamber floor to last lifetimes. As for
e bounty, disperse it among the neediest on the rosters in the city. And
meone find me Weathers, for Luck's sake!"

My eyes found his over Jaik's shoulder, and I tensed as he strode toward us.
ood squeezed between my fingers when they curled into fists, pressing against
k's hips.

But the Sha only bent, catching Jaik under the arm, hefting him gently to his
et—and me with him, as if we weighed nothing. Yet he gazed at us as if all the
avity of the world hung over our shoulders. As if all his hopes and failures
ere embodied in us.

And when Jaik shrugged him off with a violent twist, the Sha let him
...uncontested. Unhindered.

"Help is coming," he vowed, stepping back from us.

And somehow, though he was a murderer, though he'd destroyed my life...
Somehow, I believed help was precisely what we were about to receive.

CHAPTER 78
UNBROKEN BONDS

aomi met us halfway between the Convening Chamber and the Shastah's guest wing, the singing of the good-luck coins on her ankles announcing her arrival before she skidded around the end of yet another gilded corridor and all but crashed into us.

For a long moment, she held onto us both, an arm around each of our backs; and with the soldiers clustered awkwardly behind us, I clung to my friend and trembled so fiercely I feared my legs would give way.

It was nearing midday when we made our way at least to the guest wing, a lengthy complex sprawling more than a mile down the craggy cliff that overlooked the city. I'd never spent an inordinate amount of time in this span of the palace—I'd usually kept to the opposite wing where permanent residents dwelled, myself among them—but it was gilded in the sort of opulence I'd forgotten to miss during my years of travel.

Strangely, I no longer had a taste for it.

I was almost unsure where to place my feet on the costly scarlet carpeting down the middle of the glass-bright hall; Jaik followed after Naomi and me, supported by Wyat, who took his weight from his injured leg with a sort of a reverent eagerness I would've teased them both for if my jaw had been functional.

Now and again I gave into the compulsive urge to rub the bloodstained side of my head, the crack of the rifleshot that had killed Galan echoing through my skull.

I'd never been so glad to see a man dead. Nor would I likely sleep well

When we reached Naomi's rooms—assigned by Shadran Arias for the ration of her visit, she explained—the soldier left us. Naomi reached for my ~e, but I tugged back from her and gestured to Jaik instead; I was far more ncerned with the rifle-wound in his leg.

While Naomi set about cleaning and patching his injury, all three of us ated on the edge of the fine bed taking up the back wall of the modest arters, she told us of her journey from Dalfi to the capital; the concern of rsuit from Galan and his accomplices paling into relief while she'd ridden by rseback and walked where necessary.

Then the fear had come—the worry that he'd caught up to us rather than rsuing her.

"I worried myself sick," she admitted, knotting off Jaik's bandage and cking the edges gently beneath the cloth. "I'm not certain I slept more than a w hours at a time until I arrived and heard the Sha hadn't seen either of you."

"Not many folks were seeing us at all." Jaik's tone, though heavy with haustion, curled into a humble brag as he stretched his leg and tested the ndage. "We were weaving through the Drennans, helping whoever we could."

"I'm sure." Naomi swiveled to face me where I huddled against the pillows, ns wrapping my ankles, hugging the warmth into my core after the day's illing events—and the cold that had come long before it. "You always did love e people in the mountains. I remember that now."

I wished I could muster a smile for her.

Jaik's eyes narrowed slightly; gripping the corner post of the bed, he swung mself to his feet. "You got her, Naomi?"

"I've got her," she confirmed, eyes sliding his way. "But where are *you* ing? You know you're supposed to hover and fret while I see to her."

Jaik smiled widely enough for both of us, but it perished rapidly when his ze darkened. "I've got to see the Sha about a ship left out near the usionarium. The crew needs our help."

Hope jolted my heart like a kick to the sternum, then tangled and fell away th a surge of slick unease. The thought of Jaik wandering these corridors ne, after everything...and to see the *Sha*, of all people...

"Be careful," Naomi warned.

"Trust me...never been more on my guard." Jaik brushed his knuckles ntly over my cheek, then hobbled rapidly from the room.

In the silence, Naomi crawled to sit cross-legged before me. She flashed her fingertips in silent question, and when I edged out a nod, she began a gentle palpation of my jaw.

"I'm assuming none of this went how you expected," she murmured as she worked, her gaze trained at level with my mouth. "*I* didn't expect it, either. I thought I would have trouble gaining entrance, at first…but the moment the soldiers told Arias and Mahalia I was at the doors, it was like coming home." A deprecating smile curled her mouth. "I had my audience the same day. And though I'd feared the Sha would be nearly impossible to convince of your good intentions, it seems he was never hunting you to imprison you. He asked me to remain on as a guest until we found you. And then, a few days ago…"

The door jolted open without warning, and Naomi jerked her hands back and a sultry drawl spilled over the threshold. "Everyone, all at once, became obsessed with Audra Jashowin all over again. Ah, well, the reprieve was wonderful while it lasted."

My heart tumbled all over itself at the sight of Reiko Nayori, shoving off the doorway with both hands splayed, taking up as much space as she always did. Her dark hair, cut into a forward-feathered crop and shaved short on the sides, burned almost blue-black in the lanternlight; but it was longer than I'd seen it last, the tips nearly grazing her weary amber eyes.

Our time apart had aged my once-rival, my most trusted fellow Storycrafter before the world had fallen to ruin. Though she was only a year older than I, she wore the strain of these last few years in service to the Sha in the new frown lines and a tighter scowl that sharpened her severe features.

Behind her, quieter, but bearing no less presence in a different way, Mahalia Lothar eased the door shut; her dominant left hand painted a smudge of lead and charcoal on the doorpost, a sign that she had been drawing vigorously and often of late. She hugged her sketchbook against her chest like a shield and flashed me a teary-eyed grin, her russet curls springing wildly against her pert nose and plump cheeks.

She was the shortest and youngest of us, soft in many ways we were not, several years my junior; but her tell-all gaze flashed with a newfound wisdom only struggle could bring.

Struggle heaped on her—on all of us—by the choices I had made in this very Shastah, years ago.

"We all remembered you at the same moment," Naomi went on quietly, her gaze fixed on our friends. "We remembered each other, as well...how you brought us together in the interest of bettering the country."

"How you beat some of us—not necessarily fairly, might I add," Reiko scoffed, gripping the same post Jaik had used for leverage and winging herself round to tumble to her seat on the bed. "But it explained some things I couldn't make sense of...like how I'd come to serve in the Shastah in the first place. It always seemed like it happened in such a boring way."

"And we all know that with your appetite for the dramatic, it would never have occurred so casually." Her Hadrassi accent as rich as the mother she'd earned it from, despite a lifetime lived in Mithra-Sha, Mahalia lowered herself on my other side. "Addie, flipping *Luck*...what happened to you?"

"Not now," Naomi scolded the Shadress with the practiced ease of a long-time friend. "Now is for resetting her jaw. Will you two help me?"

And they did—curling up on either side of me, gripping my hands and pressing me down by the shoulders. I shut my eyes, steeled myself as best I could, to the very core...and still couldn't keep from bucking and thrashing at the scorching arc of agony that shot through the side of my face when Naomi maneuvered my jaw back into its hinges.

"There! Not broken," she announced, yanking her hands back the moment the deed was done; her words hardly penetrated the tinny ringing in my ears, but at least in the wake of that horrific surge, the relief was nearly instantaneous; not painless, but certainly better. "We'll need some cold for the swelling, and I'll mix a poultice to pack against the skin. But...can you speak?"

I worked my jaw gingerly, a few more tears leaking from my eyes at the distant, thumping vibration of anguish along the bone lines. But when I untangled my tongue from where it had been trapped for too long behind my grating, slanted teeth, two words slid out—two words for all of them at once. "*Thank you.*"

Barely a breath later, all of their arms were around me. And that was how we stayed for a long, long time.

CHAPTER 79
RUNNING HOME

*N*ight hugged the windows, draping itself in luxurious bruise-blue against the glass panes, when Naomi finally fetched her medicine satchel and began her new ministrations over my jaw. Mahalia rang up for soup from the Shastah kitchens, and Reiko remained at my side on the bed while Naomi worked, arms folded, scowling.

"I can't believe you made this much of a mess and left it for *me* to clean," she complained, fiddling with the corner of her drab gray cloak. "Actually, no, I can. Typical Audra Jashowin."

"None of that," Mahalia scolded. "She can barely speak, this isn't the time for an argument of wits."

"She's never fit for an argument of wits. That hasn't stopped me before."

"How bad?" My throat was still raw from days of disuse, and my teeth tingled from striking against one another at the wrong angles all that time.

"It's been…" Reiko glanced at Mahalia, then shook her head. "It's been a long few years, Addie."

"So many Misspoken manifestations to contend with," Mahalia fretted. "So many people suffering from lack. Desperation has made villains of even the well-intentioned."

"Beginning with the Sha himself," Naomi muttered, dabbing a chilly poultice on my jaw.

I swallowed. "How much do you…?"

Naomi pressed her smallest finger to my lips, silencing me while she

"Arias told us," Mahalia explained. "The moment he remembered, he told what became of Jaik at the Sha's orders. That was nearly a week ago, now. I ven't spoken to my father since."

Shock pinned my gaze to her; Mahalia had always adored her father, and 'd been doting and attentive almost to a fault. To hear that she had severed all ntact with him on my account, and Jaik's...

I wasn't certain if the ache in my heart was gratitude for her steadfast endship, or an echo of the pain in all of us, for so many different reasons.

"So Naomi says you can tell stories again." Reiko palmed herself upright d shifted to the side to face me. "Ones with power, and endings?"

"Not alone," I admitted. "Jaik—"

"They know. And no bedtime stories," Naomi warned, and Reiko rolled her es. "Audra needs to rest her jaw before she leaps back into Storycraft. Even broken, this will take some time to heal."

Time that demanded to be spent here, in the Shastah...looking over my oulder. Fearing for our lives.

And Sha Lothar would not be content to wait forever.

Before I could sink too deeply into the inevitability that loomed on the rizon, a knock sounded at the door; Mahalia leaped up and hurried to meet at I could only assume were servants bringing the food she'd asked for.

"We *do* need you well," Reiko conceded grudgingly, laying back into the lows beside me with arms cinched over her waist. "We have work to do, tting this country back on its feet. I know I said I wanted the title, back in the ts, but...flipping Luck, you can *have* it. After what I've seen these last few ars, I never want to be Master Storycrafter."

"Sorry to intrude," a smooth voice reached us from the doorway, "but we me bearing gifts."

I lurched upright as Mahalia opened the door wide—ushering in Shadran ias first, who had changed the least of any of them: still tall, muscular, and nning as if not a care in the world dared write itself into his story. His vivid een eyes gleamed beneath a thatch of thick, dark curls, the definition of his gh cheekbones cutting against his amber skin when he smiled at me, the same ay he always did...with confidence none of the rest of us would ever fully aster.

My gaze leaped almost irresistibly past him—to Jaik, limping on his heels. lief crashed through me at his return, at his stalwart face and the lack of blood anywhere on his skin. Both men carried satchels and platters of food, the scent of hot bread and salty cheese wafting from beneath the steel cloches.

My mouth watered at the notion of eating for the first time since Erasure—but even hunger mattered less when my gaze met Jaik's.

Setting the tray of broth bowls on the small chest-of-drawers near the door, he hobbled rapidly to the bedside and sank down on the edge, facing me. His fingers tenderly explored my reset jaw, a tilt of relief curving up one side of his mouth. "Say my name?"

An invitation I'd never been gladder to meet. "Jaik—"

His mouth covered mine for the briefest, most chaste of kisses—one that curled my toes in my boots and left me desperate for more, even when sense knew my jaw couldn't endure it.

"About time," Reiko crowed; a muffled squawk raked my ears when Mahalia jabbed her...presumably with the tip of her drawing pencil.

"Hey, there, tiger," Jaik murmured, ignorant of their banter as he drew back to rest his brow against mine. "Glad to have you back."

"That is an understatement." Arias came to kneel on the floor at the bedside as well, taking my hand and pressing his lips to my knuckles with the sort of suave, self-sure ease that had made me swoon like most women when we'd first met. "Ah, Audra, look at you...scarlet is much more your color than bruise-blue."

Naomi rolled her eyes. Mahalia mimed a gag.

"Would you lay off?" Jaik scoffed. "You're embarrassing yourself."

"How can I, when I have you to do that for me?" Smirking, Arias withdrew, pushing himself upright and returning to the chest. "We have plenty to eat, fresh from the kitchens."

"The crew?" I croaked to Jaik while Reiko slipped from the bed to help Arias arrange the meal.

"I met Raz on the way back to the Convening Chamber." Jaik rolled across my legs to take Reiko's place at my side, winding his fingers into mine. "We talked to the Sha...said he'll dispatch an airship and see what they can find."

I hoped, perhaps beyond reason, that the crew had endured this long. That they would hold on just a bit longer until help could reach them.

And I hoped it was truly coming.

"You believed him?" I mumbled, keeping my words curt and my breathing shallow as Naomi packed chilled leaves onto my jaw.

"Well, he didn't give me a new scar to match the one on my chest, so…" k shrugged, though Arias's frown cut deep at that, darkening his pale green es to the shade of a storm-shrouded forest. "I'm willing to dance this a little ager before I make any judgements. He said he'd get us rooms of our own and y out of our way until we're ready to speak with him."

"The rest of us, however, are far less noble and possess a good deal less straint." With a smirk to clear his shadowed gaze, Arias dropped onto the foot the bed next to Naomi, offering a bowl of spiced-cheese-and-potato soup to ch of us. I nearly fumbled mine, snatching it from his hands. "So I'm afraid ere is no escaping us until we hear every bit of your lives the last several years."

"*You* start," Naomi said to Jaik, taking her bowl and shifting away from ias. "Let Addie rest her jaw as much as possible."

"Or should we forget about Audra again, and *I* try Storycrafting?" Reiko ked innocently, nudging her shoulder against Jaik's.

"You should try shutting up, actually." He shoved her right back.

"Still haven't learned to be charming, even after all this time."

"Following your example, Nayori."

"Shall we place a bet on which one draws weapons first?" Arias intoned to aomi and me.

Naomi offered an innocent, edged blink. "Can your family afford your bad mbling habits anymore, Shadran?"

"It's never a poor gamble when one bets on Jaik Grissom."

"Proven false," Mahalia said around a delicate sip of soup. "Though the ntiment is sweet."

"You know what, I don't think I missed all this abuse." Jaik shoved a hand to the bed as if he would lurch up; I gripped his elbow, towing him back down.

"Sit." I plucked his soup bowl from his hand, settling it into mine. "Speak."

He imitated a baying hound, and Reiko and Naomi burst into laughter.

It was breathtaking, to be sitting with all of them here, bantering and telling es as if no time at all had passed. As if we were not years older, and in many ys, far more scarred. As if Jaik had never died, and I had not been running m all of this for so long.

And somehow I had still run home to *all* of them—to this unit we'd once ade, pooling all our distinct talents for the sake of Mithra-Sha.

So we ate together, and we told our stories one by one; of a Shadran and adress helping to hold the country together. Of a Storycrafter left with a mess attend, and a healer cast off to her own devices, a hole gaping in her heart.

We told each other everything. And they were the sort of stories I would never forget: the tales of my friends fighting to survive in a world I'd broken with my own power.

CHAPTER 80
THESE WORDS WE MUST SPEAK

or nearly a month, we lived in the Shastah.

All that time passed in odd lurches and lulls. There were brighter moments: when we took word that the crippled *Athalion* had been found, the ship returned to Amere-Del—the country of s origin—for repairs, and the surviving crew as well for recovery; and when I ould finally speak without excruciating pain flaring in my ear and jaw; and every oment we spent with our friends.

But I spent a good deal of that month in spine-tingling vigilance, waiting for blow from the shadows. Testing the Sha's patience, in some ways…waiting to ee when he would grow weary of the pause. When he would seek *me* out. When e would try to coerce me back into his service.

But he never did.

He kept his word to Jaik and Arias, and he did not impress himself on me; e seemed content to spend all the rest of his days waiting for me to reach across he gap between us.

And for almost a month, I had no desire to.

I rarely left the room Jaik and I shared, at first; I practiced the use of my oice in quiet conversation with him, curled on the bed together, hands joined nd brows together while we talked of Erasure and Julas and Galan. We spoke of he stories the others had told us…their lives since we'd parted ways.

And we pondered aloud what to do next in this strange world where we'd een hunted, not for sport or vengeance, but simply to return us to Vallanmyre.

After the first fortnight, restlessness possessed us; we crept from the hastah after dark, occasionally with Arias and Mahalia, sometimes with Reiko nd Naomi…but often alone. Just the two of us, fingers entwined, walking the streets with our love on display—the way we'd always feared to before Jaik's death. There was nothing to hide anymore, and no one to hide it from; the Sha had already done his worst, and we had survived it.

Yet I couldn't bring myself to seek out my family. And Jaik did not go to see his.

It felt as if we were waiting in the balance. Waiting for something to permit us those reunions.

Flighty and reckless, I tested the Sha even further; I showed my face to everyone in the Shastah but him. I even flirted with the possibility of leaving Vallanmyre altogether…but that reeked of pettiness even in my head.

I was foregoing the inevitable. And that made me all the more resistant to it.

That notion woke me in the dead of dark one night, chasing me out of the room Jaik and I shared, into the halls, and finally to one of the scattered crescent mezzanines arrayed out from the Shastah's bold face.

I remembered now how often Jaik and I had sought solace in these places, particularly during my trials for the title of Master Storycrafter—alone at first, each of us haunted by our own thoughts, our own fears and failures. And then, gradually, we'd begun to seek one another out on these secluded balconies, to rely on the predictability of encountering one another.

Private conversations. Secret uncertainties shared. Our past was a tale woven of mystery and desire and a foreboding sense of the tragic, as if we had always known our story could only end one way.

But tonight, those sensations were dimmer. Perhaps because it was only me seated on one of the many chaise sofas arranged at the edge of the balcony. Arms wrapped around myself, hands stuffed into the sleeves of Jaik's overlarge shirt I'd never returned to him after the day we left Fallshyre Bay, I reclined on the wingbacked wood and stared up at the shutting eye of the moon.

Absurd as it was, I felt trapped again; trapped in this sprawling Shastah, with anywhere in the world to go. Trapped in this city, though no one had halted me venturing into it. Trapped, not by the constraints of those around me, but by the hook in my middle that drew me inexorably back each time I considered fleeing. Each time I sought my own path.

It was as if my feet already knew the right road to take—though every other part of me resisted it.

"Do the stars give up their secrets tonight?"

I jumped at that smooth, teasing voice, twisting on my seat to spot the man aggering across the balcony toward me; he was dressed down for the dead of ght, his fine collar undone, sleeves rolled to his elbows. A blanket hung in the ook of his elbow—a piece his mother had made by hand.

I knew because she'd made it for *me*.

"Arias." Hooking my hair behind my ear, I fumbled between the familiarity nearly half a lifetime of friendship and the odd awkwardness that years of rgetting had introduced between us—between all of us.

"Well, if they do, perhaps you could inquire of them for me." He halted reast of the sofa, hands thrust in his pockets, breathing deeply of the warm, dly summer air. "Because I have certainly been bereft of guidance these last veral weeks."

Pity unfurled through my chest. "Your father?"

He eased himself onto the far end of the chaise, freeing his hands from his ockets only to trap them between his knees. "Have you been to see him?"

"No," I confessed. "I think I've done everything *but* that—well, just about erything."

"Hmm. Haven't you gone to see your parents?"

Sheepish, I shook my head. "It feels like I'm waiting for something."

"Aren't we all. May I?" He held up the blanket, and when I nodded, he ffed it loose and flung it over my shoulders. Though time had turned its reads somewhat musty, there was still the faintest tinge of a perfume I'd once orn, folded into the creases.

A perfume Jaik had stowed away for me as a gift—something the Sha had ver known about.

Banding the fabric tight to my throat, I glanced sidelong at Arias. "Why are u here?"

"Well, one of the servants mentioned he saw you come out this ay...apparently, everyone is waiting on tenterhooks for you to flee."

I couldn't even muster a snort. "I've considered it."

"I don't blame you for that. So have I."

I whipped my head his way, shock catching my breath in my chest. "*You?* rias Lothar, the perfect son and heir?"

"She remembers," he groused under his breath—but his smile, though slim, as genuine. "You know, back before...well, everything, I found you to be a end with a unique perspective on struggles similar to mine."

Memory prodded the words from my lips. "Both of us carrying titles that felt too heavy for our shoulders."

He nodded, angling his gaze back to the crystalline moon, the dim crust of stars above. "Astonishingly, that weight has not abated in recent years. And in fact, with my father's choices, the burden weighs all the worse."

"Are you afraid to become like him?"

"Oh, Luck, yes." His breath gusted out. "And what a change that is, when all along I worried I would never live up to his reputation." Flinging an arm along the seatback, he tipped his head conspiratorially my way. "As it turns out, it's even *more* difficult trying *not* to become someone than it is to step into their boots. How ironic."

Dropping my gaze, I prodded my fingers between the linen links of the crocheted blanket. "I feel the same, only…"

"It's the Storycrafter you *were* that you both fear becoming again…and fear to fail."

Scowling, I elbowed him through the blanket. "Where is all of this wisdom coming from?"

He shrugged, smirking, but the warmth of it did not touch his eyes. "I sometimes feel as if I've lived a lifetime in these short years."

It was my turn to lose my breath, swiveling back to gaze over the city. "In some ways, we have."

We were quiet for a time, both mustering our thoughts in private; then Arias said, quietly, "I suppose that's why we're all afraid to move ahead. The path out there, in a world with your sort of power in it, with what Jaik is made of now…that territory is entirely uncharted, isn't it? We don't know precisely where we stand there. Who to *be* there."

Heat pricked the tip of my nose; I rubbed it hastily on my blanket-swaddled wrist. "And some of us are more responsible for creating that world than others."

"True. Is that why you've been avoiding so much of your past? Why you haven't even been to visit your parents and siblings?"

Huffing a sigh, I spilled the blanket's articulate hem between my fingers. "I don't know how to face them. I don't know how to face *any* of this…it all still feels a bit like a dream. Or like a story I'm telling myself, but I haven't decided if I believe it's true yet. And in the meanwhile, all I can do is…exist. Breathe. Try to make sense of everything."

"How is that going for you, then?"

"Not well," I confessed. "The quill is on the page, but I can't bring myself write what comes next."

"As if you're waiting for something." He was silent for a moment, then ded, "Not that I'm one to judge or advise—Luck knows I've been avoiding e man myself—but I suspect what you're waiting for is what you're running om: a conversation with my father."

Groaning, I slumped back against the seat, dumping my neck against his m when I craned my head back to stare at the stars. "I was afraid you would y that."

"It's entirely within your rights to keep him waiting," Arias offered. "In ct, I applaud you for this whole month you've drawn it out. But if it's keeping u shackled—keeping you from moving ahead—"

"Then I'm not punishing him. I'm punishing myself."

Punishment. That was it...that was the word that had haunted me on all our ty jaunts, all of our time spent reminiscing with our friends.

A part of me did not feel it deserved this. This reunion, this uncontested cceptance from the friends I'd abandoned to clean up my own forgotten mess.

It did not feel *right,* that no one ever spoke of my mistakes, that no one lamed me. That the world had not yet held me accountable. That no further ost had been paid.

"It seems that way to me." His hand crawled to my shoulder, squeezing ghtly. "You were never really one to lose sleep, as I recall...quite the opposite, n fact. I suspect if you're out here, it's because you know the time is coming. If ou ever want to move ahead with the rest of it...if you want to choose your vay forward from here..."

"It all goes through him first." A bitter, dejected laugh surged in my throat. How ironic, that after so much time—after I had risked everything and broken he world, escaping his plans for my life and the length he would reach to enact hem—the next step forward still rested with the Sha.

"Keep your chin up," Arias urged. "At the very least, it happens on your terms."

If it were truly my terms, I wasn't certain we would ever have a conversation at all; but even as that thought grazed my mind, I weighed the lie in it.

I had been avoiding this confrontation ever since we'd disembarked in Vallanmyre...but not entirely because I was reluctant to have it. In many ways, the opposite was true. I wanted to scream and rage at Tobyrus Lothar. I wanted to deal back the pain he'd dealt me a hundredfold.

So long as we remained in the lurch, I could avoid all of it—the true pain and the imagined sort. The ache for vengeance. The guilt. The shame that had kept me from seeking anyone else in the entire city who knew me…even my parents.

I didn't know how to apologize. I didn't know how to explain it to anyone who hadn't walked the road of Storycraft with me, with Jaik, before it had all come undone.

There would be no leaving the Shastah, no seeking out my loved ones, no having a life beyond this moment until I was *beyond* this moment.

It was just like the Storymaker had told me…there were plenty of roads. But my feet were set to mine.

It was time to walk it now.

"Thank you, Arias." I dragged my knees to my chest. "For taking the time to speak with me."

"My pleasure, Addie."

We lapsed into silence again, watching the city that would someday be his. That had once been one of so many under my protection.

"Why are *you* awake?" I ventured at last. "You were always a fairly heavy sleeper, too."

His free hand—the one not trapped behind my head—ruffled through his thick curls, and he slanted his gaze away. "Shockingly, I haven't slept well in some time. I find my days consumed with work, and my nights…well, that's when my mind chooses to race over everything it hasn't the time to ponder during the day."

"You could speak to Naomi," I offered. "She might have a sleeping tonic that could help."

Rich chuckles bubbled out of him, and he cast his head back into the seat of his hand, flinging his laughter up toward the stars. "I could ask her, couldn't I?"

Bemused, I craned my head to study his face; but though his voice brimmed with mirth, tension pulled the lines of his countenance.

Something about it was familiar, but in a way that made me feel as if I'd never paused to truly look at it before. Another mystery kept by the family Lothar.

"We both deserve to sleep at night," I said when his laughter finally subsided.

Thumbing his eyes, Arias glanced down at me. "That we do. So, while I'm discussing my sleeping woes with Naomi, what will you be doing, Addie? What are you tired of running from?"

I held his gaze, keen and sharp and so painfully like his father's.

Right then, I knew the ruse was over.

The next morning, I sent word to the Sha. It was time for us to talk.

CHAPTER 81
THE ONLY WAY

Sure you don't want any company?"

Wiggling my toes into my boot, I let my foot clap down on the polished stone floor of the chamber Jaik and I shared, and pinned him with the driest glance I could muster. "What do you think has changed in the two minutes since you last asked that would make me say *yes* this time?"

Sprawled out on the bed, arms folded behind his head against the nest of beaded pillows, Jaik shrugged. "You're quiet. Who knows what's going on in that head of yours?"

"Nothing you'd happily be privy to," I sighed, pushing up from the bed and snapping my cloak from the corner post. I'd hardly slept after my conversation with Arias the night before, stomach a riot of nerves and knots, knowing my confrontation with the Sha was looming on the near horizon; yet I felt oddly alert, and strangely calm now.

Not peaceful. But as if I was holding my breath, waiting for something to erupt.

"Ayjay." Jaik propped himself up on his elbows, fixing me with a look so penetrating, it rooted me in place, my fingers still in the motion of knotting my cloak. "You don't have to deal with him on your own."

"I know that." And I did. My other reason for seeking no companionship—not his, not even Arias and Mahalia's, when I'd had no qualms in the past about bringing them as my advocates to help sway their father—was purely selfish.

I knew what this discussion would involve. And I wasn't eager to have any of my friends present when I laid my own mistakes bare before the Sha.

So I simply kissed Jaik—murmured against his mouth, "*Stay here,*"—then slipped out alone for the first time into the Shastah halls.

I no longer quite expected to be ambushed here, carted off to some remote
rner of Vallanmyre, or held prisoner to the Sha's whims. But my skin still
ckled with awareness at every soldier I passed, my heart not quite trusting
eir dipped heads, the anxious reverence in their eyes.

I had once walked these halls like a member of the Sha's own family. Now I
owled them like an intruder, keenly aware that every mark of suffering I saw—
ery hollowed pair of eyes in every visitor who'd come to appeal to the Sha—
s my blame to share.

It was a long, grueling journey from the guest wing to the Convening
amber, my darting gaze soaking in all the haggard faces, all of the shaking
nds rattling with too small a stipend from the Sha along the way. It appeared
one in need was turned out to the cold, but there was still not enough to go
ound.

Still so much lack, so much need, even in the planting and growing seasons.
mmer was proving no kinder than winter had been.

My heavy heart weighed every step down by the time I reached the
amber, where two pairs of soldiers drew wide the doors—then shut them
th a clatter behind me.

The moment my gaze fell on the Sha's seat, I wished I'd brought *someone*
th me. Just as he had.

Shadre Calten was seated next to her husband, full of the same long-limbed,
stere grace I'd always envied…and been a touch intimidated by, despite her
rmth and the gifts she'd given me over the years. But she, too, had been
vered and lined with the toils of keeping Mithra-Sha alive during these arduous
st years; and her skin was even browner than I remembered, kissed by sunlight
oard an airship deck.

A mark of all her travels to all of the places we'd just barely missed one
other while Jaik and I had journeyed north.

My heart pinched at the sight of her, and her chin lifted at the sight of me.
flash of tears lined her eyes, then vanished with a single blink.

The Sha rose. He strode across the room toward me, every step clapping in
poignant echo along the high walls, and it occurred to me for the first time that
ere were no soldiers present…and that perhaps I should be concerned about
at.

Tense, I halted, and came no further; I let him come to me.

And he did. He crossed the room without a pause in his stride, until he was
fore me.

And there he plunged to his knees and pressed his face to the floor.

Shock jolted me back a step, my gaze cutting to the Shadre again; this time she was not swift enough to blink the tears at bay. They rolled down her cheeks as she beheld her husband—the most powerful man I'd ever known, the one who'd gone toe-to-toe against the Del's ruthless threats, who'd held his ground against Calten's cunning, saccharine-sweet Hadrassi family without so much as a blink—crashed down onto his knees.

In front of *me*, a Storycrafter who'd remembered her place in the world for scarcely a month.

It was head-spinning. Utterly disorienting.

"Audra," Tobyrus mumbled toward the floor, "I beg...I *beg* your forgiveness."

"You..." I choked after that single word. In no world—not for any approval, not for anyone to accept me in any way—could I *ever* bring myself to say he did not need to do this. That he had not done something truly horrifying, truly in need of being forgiven.

Nor was I certain I could give him that.

"My actions, my choices, were...inexcusable." The Sha's voice heaved with emotion. "I was a man obsessed...obsessed with the fear of retribution from Amere-Del, obsessed with your potential. Where the two met, I became paranoid. Irrational. I treated you precisely how an enemy would, the way I was protecting our Storycrafters from being used if they went to our neighboring countries. And when I heard what you and Jaik were planning, I acted out of my hurt and panic, not the way a ruler should. Nor certainly someone who considered you a friend, a prodigy, and a wise counselor."

He raised his face at last, and tears streaked his bearded cheeks; he did nothing to brush them away.

"For what I did to Jaik, I deserve to lose my title, if not my own life," he croaked, "and I would have abdicated already were I not offering Arias a land in crisis. I have held onto this position by the tips of my fingers and have resolved not to make a single decision that is anything but generous to my people. All of the rest, I have entrusted to Calten and Arias. You may ask them...or ask Mahalia. She will tell you if I'm being truthful, she has no reason to lie on my account. She hasn't spoken to me in a month."

Pain wrenched through his words and twisted itself equally in my chest. The ripples of agony from our actions, our choices, still fanned across the surface of our lives. They still touched us as much as others, years later.

"I give you my solemn vow," the Sha added, "and I will do it in writing, if I ust, with as many witnesses as necessary…once all of this is resolved, I will ep aside and give Mithra-Sha the ruler it truly deserves. I will hand Arias a juntry no longer in chaos. But I believe I need your help to accomplish that, udra. One last time."

A chill rippled down my spine, and my gaze tugged irresistibly to Calten, ho had dashed away her tears. "What do you mean?"

"We'll come to that," the Sha assured me. "For now, I need to know that ju hear me. That you understand how sorry I truly am."

I forced my focus back to him—forced myself to truly take in the rawness f his eyes, the tearstained flush of his cheeks. This man I had loved and espected, who had taken what was most precious in my world because he had elieved it would keep me from taking *myself* away from him.

"I don't know how to forgive you for any of this," I rasped. "For what you id to Jaik…for how you treated me before. Or for sending out a *bounty* on my ead."

"I wanted *no* harm to come to you," the Sha said swiftly. "The purpose of he bounty and how it was to be carried out, those were both explicitly clear. There was never intended to be anyone hurt in returning you to Vallanmyre."

Disbelief narrowed my eyes, blurring the room until I could only see him. "There was plenty of destruction and havoc wreaked for someone who didn't vant his people harmed. Those amplified Storycrafters outside of Dalfi could 1ave killed hundreds of people."

"I know." The Sha rubbed his brow. "I doubt if I have to remind *you* of all beople that what they did was illegal. I never authorized amplification of Misspoken stories as a means of bringing you home."

Home. As if the Shastah could still be called that.

"I personally saw to the arrests of all amplified bounty hunters." Shadre Calten spoke for the first time, her tone crisp, the set of her eyes and mouth sincere—not hoping, but *demanding* to be believed and respected.

"But Galan was working on your orders," I countered.

"For our *bounty*," she corrected me. "Those are hardly the same thing."

"He spoke with you. He gave you the truth about me…how I'd changed."

"It was a necessary wickedness, taking his counsel, to know how best to find you. But I made it clear to him what our demands were for your return when I spoke with him. I gave no room for doubt of that."

"And even those demands, he broke," the Sha added. "I ordered you brought unharmed to me, and cared for. He allowed his own hatred to cloud hi judgement, and I am sorry you and Jaik suffered for that."

I didn't want to concede, or accept his apology; but with each passing moment, the sincerity rang clearer, and I could find fewer corners of my heart t plunge into and hide from the light shed on their shadows.

I knew Tobyrus and Calten. I had known them since I was an arrogant young woman of nineteen, leaping into the Master Storycrafter's tests, leaning into their faith in me. I had seen them lie and seen them lay bare their truths—t their children, to their country, to one another. And to me.

They had waited a month for this. Tobyrus had helped saved me from Galan's last blade. And they had poured themselves out into the salvation of Mithra-Sha so utterly, it had marked their bodies with age and distress in ways that nearly rendered them strangers.

These were not the actions of heartless people. Nor unrepentant ones.

I gave in at last to the shaking in my legs…let myself fold down on level with Sha Lothar, who I'd feared from afar, and then hated when I remembered him for all he was.

But there was no strength left in me to hate, to flee from him as I'd ached to after Erasure.

Not from this man whose sins matched mine.

"I just wanted to be happy." The words escaped me as hardly more than a cracked whisper. "I couldn't find a way to be that *here* anymore."

"I know." Tobyrus raised his hands before me, then hesitated; when I didn't draw away, he framed my face gently in his broad palms. "You were only girl still when you came to us, and you carried threats and duties on your shoulders that seasoned Storycrafters before you had never faced. I should have focused on helping you through your overwhelm…or set you in charge of finding a successor. A new Master Storycrafter. I'm so sorry for all of it, Audra."

"As am I." Calten descended from her seat to kneel at her husband's side. She gripped my hand in hers…more physical affection than she had ever showe me. "I know better than most women what it is to be shackled to duty. Luck flipped its coin in my favor, that being Shadre has proven itself a blessing, not the curse I thought it would be. Yet when the coin turned against *you*, I didn't intervene. Forgive me."

"I don't know how to," I croaked, my hand sweating in the strong cage of ers. "I don't know how to forgive either of you. But I have to believe it's ossible, because I need you to forgive *me*."

"We forgave you the moment we remembered why this all happened," obyrus said quickly. "There was never a moment either of us blamed you for shing out. We…*I* had just ordered Jaik's death. And then my soldiers turned eir rifles against you. We tore the world out from under you. Of course you ied to tear it back."

It would be so simple to accept the allowances. The excuses. But the torymaker's admonishments rang clearer in my heart than my own need to be ared.

"No." I shook my head. "I knew better. I knew the limits of my gift, but I ared more for my own heartbreak in that moment than for what my actions ould do to anyone else. We're exactly alike, you and I."

With a tearful smile, the Sha released my face, his hands settling gently on y shoulders instead. "We were never truly right for one another, I think."

That was true. We'd been a powerful pair, Sha and Storycrafter…but on the ther side of things, all the broken bones and open wounds showed through. All f the many places where my youthful arrogance and his ambition had chafed gainst one another. The permanent bruises and bleeding gaps where our ubbornness had damaged the country we'd sought to defend.

"Do you…" Tobyrus trailed off, then cleared his throat. "Do you know hat happened, precisely? How you did it?"

I explained it to him then, crouched on the floor, the three of us brought w by our mistakes. I told it to him as best I understood it…as the Storymaker ad helped me to understand. Tobyrus and Calten listened with rapt attention, nspeaking; and when I had finished my tale, the Sha rubbed his bearded face ith both hands and murmured, "I was such a fool."

"We were all fools," Calten agreed. "But it's our people who suffer for it. ood people, and Storycrafters like Reiko."

Guilt gnawed relentlessly on the pit of my stomach. "I want to make this ght, but there's only so much I can do."

Tobyrus and Calten exchanged a glance; her brows arched, meeting some nspoken question in his gaze like an adamant wall.

Slowly, my stomach slithered down, lower and lower. Dread puddled in its ake. "What—?"

"I think," Tobyrus said carefully, "given what you've told us, that there is a way, perhaps, to mend it. But you haven't...or, rather, you don't *want*—"

"There is a reason you fled rather than coming straight to us from Erasure, in your own words," Calten cut across him curtly. "You want to help, but not in the way Mithra-Sha truly needs."

My pulse thumped in the base of my throat. I had never hated anything as much as I did the knowing look on her face. The piercing fixation of her gaze.

"But I *am* helping," I croaked. "The villages in the foothills...up in the passes...and Reiko and I, together, if we travel with Jaik, we can—"

"Audra. We both know that is not enough," Tobyrus said gently. "One or two Storycrafters can't do the work of an entire country. That was the very burden that set us against each other, and you can't shoulder it now any more than you could back then. We need to put this right."

And I despised him more in that moment than I ever had.

I despised him because he was *right*.

All those villages and towns, suffering in the harsh winter of the Drennans, who'd been spared this season but might not survive the next. All of the Storycrafters in Dalfi, who'd overflowed with joy that their stories had endings again. All the ones flocking to Assida, hoping for a kiss of Luck to put their world right again.

They were not like me...not most of them, anyway. I'd struggled so much to make my Storycrafting larger than myself. To let go of an Audra I'd forgotten...one who'd been so important, so beloved, that the need to be wanted had impressed itself on her heart and carried on through the tearing. I'd taken that with me when I'd lost hold of everything else...even Jaik.

I'd made my Storycraft all about me. What I was to Mithra-Sha. What *I* could do and how I could be praised and wanted and loved for it.

The others were not like me. Those Storycrafters loved the craft for the craft's own sake. They craved the wholeness of their talents restored.

I had taken that joy from them. It was only me who could restore it.

Such a bitter irony, that the one thing for which I could be coveted and revered would steal everything back from my hands.

"You think...that I have to do it again?" I could barely force the words out, my jaw rattling with the emotion building up in my throat. "Tell the story *again*?"

"Or untell it," Calten said. "I do not understand the particulars of Storycraft, but if what you say you learned in Erasure holds true..."

"You wrote the power for ending stories into Jaik," Tobyrus rasped, "so it ⸺nds to reason that you must…write it back out of him. Give it back to the ⸺rld."

"But what will that do to *him*?" My voice cracked shrilly as I lurched to my ⸺t, stepping away from them—from the truth that pooled between us, ⸺evocable. Unescapable. "You're asking me to put things back the way *you* had ⸺em, not knowing if it might hurt him, if it might—"

Kill him. *Again.*

"I know." The Sha rose as well, but made no movement closer to me. ⸺egret scripted the lines of his face—too real. Too heartbreakingly true. "This is ⸺ impossible burden to bear, and the fault is mine that you have to carry it. I ⸺ould take this from you if I could, Audra…if *my* death would rewrite the way of ⸺ings, I'd offer it up without hesitation for this country. In penance for what ⸺ve done, and to spare you the grief I've already put you through."

Calten's fingers laced through his, her head shaking off the mere notion, ⸺er anguish at his proclamation booming in the breach between us; I knew it ⸺ecause I *felt* it. Because, if it were Jaik saying these things…

Agony arched through my chest.

We *were* discussing Jaik in that very way.

"No one else can do this, Audra," Calten whispered. "Because no one else ⸺as done it yet. You are a powerful, talented Master Storycrafter, more deserving ⸺f the title than anyone I have ever heard of. But *you* did the tearing…only you ⸺an do the mending."

Even as my heart rebelled, my mind found the truth in those words.

The Storymaker had told me He'd given me this power for a reason. And ⸺hat He trusted I would wield it wisely, when the time came.

He was right. Of course, He had been right all along.

I *had* known what lay ahead…the inevitability of this road. I'd known the ⸺moment I'd remembered the entirety of the past. That was why I'd chosen to ⸺lee back to *The Athalion*…why I'd urged Jaik to strike off into the wilderness and ⸺ry to help with our own hands.

I'd known that coming here—facing the Sha—would mean facing my own ⸺responsibility in this. And facing the resolution only my power could bring.

But I truly had not counted the cost. Not in that moment. I had been ⸺terrified to do it.

Because mending the stories—setting everything right again—was something I could do. I could *feel* how to do it, the same way I'd felt through the tearing…recklessly, but with purpose.

And if I did it…

If I did it, I would write Jaik out of the narrative.

I would lose him forever.

CHAPTER 82
FIGHTING FOR JAIK GRISSOM

I had no memory of leaving the Convening Chamber.

I did not recall walking the Shastah halls, or for how long I did it. From the moment I faced the cost—truly looked it in the ...e—the world became a blurred slate, tarnished and numb. I did not know if I ...d goodbye to the Sha and Shadre, or if I simply turned and walked away from ...em, crushed beneath the first blows of grief raining down on my heart.

Some force, whether my own feet or the hand of the Storymaker Himself, ...oved me through the world. All I knew was that it was dark when I came back ... myself, and that I was standing on the threshold of the room Jaik and I ...ared; and he was there, halting in his pacing stride near the window, spinning ...ward me with his hands laced back through his hair.

"Thank *Luck*," he swore. "You've been gone all day, I was about to…"

He trailed off. His hands slid out of his hair, arms swinging loose at his ...des when he took me in—truly took me in.

"Ayjay?" His voice cracked over my name.

There was fear there. Trepidation. The gentlest invitation to explain…and ... break, if I needed to.

I could not afford to break again.

I toed the door shut and leaned back against it, dimly aware that my feet ...hed. I must've been walking for quite some time. "I spoke to the Sha and ...adre."

Jaik's arms slid into a cross over his middle. "And?"

"They…*we* think that…" I fumbled for the words. Swallowed to see if they ...ould tumble back down my gullet.

They did not.

"It's possible that...the tearing—" the name lent so much weight to it. Made it so much more tangible, this thing that I had wrought, "—can be undone. I've thought that might be possible since Erasure. But to do it, Jaik..."

"You don't know what happens to me."

Quiet. No shock. Only resignation.

I stared at him until his form blurred before my eyes; I could hardly make out the motion when his arms tumbled back out of their cross, and he slicked a hand through his hair.

"Yeah, I figured," he murmured. "Ever since we talked to the Storymaker, haven't been able to get it out of my head, either. It makes the most sense, right. Whatever's in me, you'd have to pull it out to fix the stories. And this past month, I got to thinking the Sha must've suspected it, too. It's why he wanted u brought in together, safe."

"Why didn't you tell me what you were thinking?" I rasped.

His mouth and shoulders arched as one. "You would've just argued with me. You had to face it on your own terms."

He was right. I would've fought him with every last inch of me if he'd raised the suggestion. Even now, my heart kicked and scrabbled, trying to tear itself away from the cold, harsh truth sinking deeper and deeper into my core.

I could do it. With the double-portion given to me by the Storymaker, I could unbind this patchwork world I'd made. I could write a whole new narrative.

But Jaik...

I slashed through that line of thought before it even had time to fully form

"I'm not doing this." When Jaik's mouth leaped open, I stumbled over myself to add, "*No.* I'm not playing with Storycraft that way again. There must be something—"

"Yeah, you'd think the Storymaker would've showed us, back in Erasure."

"He told us there were different paths!" The words cracked as they cut free of me. "This can't be the only one. I'll...I'll go to Fablehaven. I'll look at everything, I'll read every book there..."

"Even you aren't *that* quick a reader, tiger."

"Jaik, don't you dare fight me on this." I spoke it desperately, pleading, when all I yearned for was ironclad armor around my words. Around my heart. Anything to bulwark against the inevitability that encroached at our sides, scribbling out an ending in cramped scrawl like there was not enough parchmen left, not enough pages, not enough *time*...

Jaik didn't speak. He slouched against the bedpost, tipping a hand back through his hair again.

"I've already lost you once." I stepped toward him, begging in every stride. "Give me this chance. Let me fight for you, Jaik. Let me do everything— everything I—"

"Ayjay. Hey." He snagged my hand, snagged my words to a halt with a graze of his palm to mine. He tugged me against him, my face buried in the hollow of his throat, his chin on my head. His deep sniff vibrated through me, and his arms folded around my back, hands gripping my biceps. "All right. This what you need?"

You're *what I need*. The truth clamored through me, a piercing, wailing echo I couldn't bear to speak. I simply nodded, keeping my face hidden in the shadow of his neck, where nothing Misspoken or frightening or world-ending could ever reach me.

"Then let's do it," he said. "Every book?"

"All of the relevant ones," I mumbled, and the chuckle that shook us both warmed me from the inside out. It was a small candle against the shadow cast by my conversation with the Sha and Shadre…but for now, it was enough.

Jaik nudged me out gently at arm's length—just enough to twine our fingers and brush away dampness I hadn't even felt escaping down my cheek.

"I'll find the others," he said. "Let's go read some books."

CHAPTER 83
LESSONS IN LETTING GO

Returning to Fablehaven was like a dream tilting on the edge of a nightmare.

So much about it remained the same. The broad, thick stones that paved its face, the thatched roofs of its branching turrets, the rich red drape that flapped in the breeze through the open, painted-glass windows…they beckoned us all as we crossed the inner courtyard together. Six friends of varying status, all bound by the same brutal determination.

And, buried deep within our bones, unspoken through clenched teeth and stiff jaws…the same fear.

The rustic, roaring hearths, the deep inlay of wooden beams, and the endless bookcases greeted our arrival within the tower doors. The headmaster hastened to greet us—not Ovalia, the fierce but fair woman I'd tutored beneath in my schooling years, but a harried, middle-aged man with a raspy voice like the scrape of crumpled parchment wadding tighter with every word. He didn't look twice my way from beneath his bushy, silver-streaked black brows when he greeted us; his eyes were only for Arias, Mahalia, and Reiko, and that was sensible. I looked nothing like the Audra Jashowin he might've heard tales of; and, mercifully, none of my friends spoke my name.

We were not here for me. Not really.

I fell to the rear, glad to blend behind the others as I took in the surroundings I had once called home; melancholy scrawled lazy loops across my heart when my gaze swept the thick rugs and lounging sofas where Storycrafters had often sat, reading and writing and telling tales to one another.

Things were pitifully quiet now, the sofas empty, the hearths kept bright for ow rather than necessity; there was little need for students of Storycraft to ger in an academy for a shattered talent.

So many lives ruined, so many futures altered, because of the Sha's choices. cause of *mine*.

Jaik fell back a bit, nudging his hip against mine. "Hey. We did it, tiger. nally made it to Fablehaven."

A strangled laugh bubbled in my throat, and I stuck my tongue out at him.

A flash of Arias's charming smile at the flustered headmaster—who troduced himself in a rush at last as Vyan Thiago—and a bit of Reiko's famous flaunting to smooth out our purposes, and the man granted us access the staggering breadth of Fablehaven's inner library.

My feet recalled the way there even as I walked in an utter blur, head on a vivel, taking in all of these familiar impressions of empty corridors and pandoned rooms. It was a relief to arrive at the library, through a locked door hiago opened with his own key.

Another laugh nearly escaped me at that, edging on hysterical. It was true at with the bounty still raised, Jaik and I would never have reached this place.

Another vicious twist of inevitability speared me straight through the heart.

The library encompassed the whole of the innermost tower, level after level fter level of shelving entwined with intricate, Storycrafted staircases. For those nprepared to brave the endless flights of steps, a hewn disc fixed on levers and vinches rose and descended an iron chain at the heart of the tower, reaching rom the floor to balconies at every level. Mercifully, that was the way we chose o go; gratitude framed Jaik's tight smile when he leaned against the railing that ircled the broad stone disc, taking his weight off his still-mending leg.

The headmaster saw us off at a balcony nearly half the height of the library, vhere tales and storybooks gave way to lore and history. A cold, musty tmosphere consumed us as he ran back down the chain, leaving us in lanternlit limness among the rows of shelves.

It should have intimidated me, witnessing the vast breadth of all the ground we had to cover; but I couldn't stifle the odd relief that simmered in my core, taking in what lay ahead. Knowing just how much time it would required to pore over these pages.

I just wished it didn't all feel borrowed. Against what Mithra-Sha needed. Against—

Arias clapped his hands together, startling me from the downward spiral r thoughts tended toward these days. "Right! Lots to do. Shall we?"

"Funny. I didn't think you could read," Jaik snarked.

"I've been able to read *you* since the day we met."

"You say that like it's worth putting on your accolades. Ask Ayjay, I'm an open book. Right, tiger?"

Gritting my teeth, I stepped forward and slid the nearest book from the shelf, tucking it tightly to my ribs until the edge bit against bone. "Raz is right. We have work to do."

The others dispersed—Mahalia wandering off among the rows, Reiko striding away with purpose, Naomi gripping Arias by the elbow and leading hir off to load him down with whatever volumes she deemed best. I ducked into th nearest aisle of historic texts on Storycraft; Jaik stepped after me, hands in his pockets.

"We'll gather more if we split up," I pointed out.

He slumped his shoulder to the sturdy wooden bookcase, chafing the knuckles of one hand along the woodgrain. "Ayjay...look. I know we're doing this, and I'm glad to do it, just..."

He grimaced, trailing off.

Unease sparked along my bones, and I faced him fully, slipping another halfway-promising title into my arms. "Just *what?*"

Pain flickered in the depths of his eyes, and he shrugged up from the shelf closing the distance to brush his thumb along the cleft of my chin. His gaze hel mine, unblinking; uncompromising. "I don't want to see you lose your head trying to save mine."

It was some effort to draw in a full breath. "Don't say it like you aren't worth the sacrifice."

A small smile, sad—far too sad, unraveling something in the core of me— pulled at his mouth. "I just think enough's been sacrificed on my account. So either we find a way to win this, or—"

"I told you when I found you in that tavern back in Krylan," I cut across him firmly, "I'm not letting you go without a fight."

"Right." His thumb changed track, gliding along the curve of my jaw. "But don't fight with *them* either, all right? Everyone's here to help us."

I eased out my breath, willing my anger to disappear in the puffs of dust that exhaled up from the shelves in tandem. "You're right. I know you're right, Jaik. I'm trying."

"That's all I'm asking for." His lips brushed my brow, and then he was ne, vanishing between the shelves…just another figment of a story, lost 1ong the aged pages of time.

Another tale that the world was already beginning to forget.

The days all ran together, a single, joined-together scrawl scripted by an hing, exhausted hand.

It was a small relief not to have to return to the Shastah in all that time. Not face the shame in the Sha's eyes, the expectation in the Shadre's. I was free to se myself among the books and the shelves I knew so well, to read of orycraft's past and present. To seek a way to rewrite the future.

My friends came and went, Arias and Reiko dancing with the ebb and flow their duties elsewhere. Mahalia and Naomi stayed for longer stretches, reading d retrieving and returning books to the balcony where we'd made ourselves a me. We slept on bedrolls and brought in food, which Thiago allowed with a ave of his inkmarked hand.

I suspected he was simply relieved to have someone in the academy halls ain, after years of sundered Storycraft.

That notion—the aloneness of it all, the void space once filled by rgeoning Storycrafters I'd called both peers and proteges as I'd grown in my vn craft—poured new strength and fresh determination into my search.

For the first time since my youth, I called Fablehaven my home. I never left e confines of its library, ripping through book after book, searching for mething—*anything*—reminiscent of the tearing. Anything that would give me arity on the next steps to take.

Jaik was the only constant, the only one who stayed even when the others ere called away. We floated in the same strange in-between we had called our me when we were forgotten, the world as we knew it shrinking to only the ace we filled.

And the days we filled with us; with lounging against the balcony railing, rning pages until our fingertips dried and split, stealing bites of one another's eals brought in from our old favorite haunts. Pastries and beef platters and egg dishes we'd once indulged in at our whim; lemon-berry water and warm bone broth cocoa, which Naomi brought with a knowing look and a wicked wink.

It was so much like the life we'd left behind. So much like all the years we'd forgotten. Outside the Shastah walls, it was easier to forget why we were here and what awaited us.

Easier, but never fully possible. Not with every day that passed, every page that turned, all manifesting devoid of answers.

Devoid of *hope*.

Determination waned and anxiety waxed stronger as the first week mounted into the second. With every sympathetic glance my friends shot me when another book proved pointless. When nothing revealed some secret way of restoring Storycraft. The burden on my shoulders bent my back, leaving me hunched over yet another book when Jaik's rousing cough drew me from my wandering thoughts one day—and snapped my watering gaze from the blurry text, back to him.

He sat up on the bedroll he'd fallen asleep on after sunrise, only a few hours before. Pinching the bridge of his nose, he squinted at me in the flickering lanternlight. "Anything?"

"I'd have woken you if there was," I mumbled, shutting the book much more softly than I really wanted to. But this ancient tome on long-forgotten Storycraft didn't deserve to bear the brunt of my frustration. "Nothing. Not in any text, about *anything* pertaining to lost Storycraft—"

"Or how to restore it." Jaik stretched, arching his back with a groan. "Listen, Ayjay—"

"Why don't you go back to the Shastah?" I offered swiftly, setting the book aside and choosing another from the tower of tomes at my side. "Go and bathe. Eat some food that isn't from a street vendor. I'll...I'll join you soon."

If he was aware of the defeat that dripped through every word, Jaik wisely chose not to comment on it. Instead, he simply said, "Yeah, all right. If you're sure."

"I am."

Because another conversation was looming like low-bellied stormclouds corroding the air between us. And I wasn't ready for what came after *Listen, Ayjay*.

Not with the heaviness sulking in my heart and leaking into the hollow cavity of my chest.

Jaik stood, flexing his leg; then he moved stiffly to my side, squeezing my shoulder and pressing a kiss to the top of my head.

I leaned into the tender motion, hating how fiercely my heart clung to every sensation of it...the strength of his fingers, the stroke of the callouses against my bare skin where my collar had slipped down, the heat of his breath stirring my hair and the soft warmth of his lips.

I hated how it felt like a stamp on my heart, something to carry on after—Jaik was gone.

I was alone for the first time in Fablehaven; and for the first time since I'd crossed its threshold again, I simply sat amongst the books. Unmoving. Unseeing. I did not tear frantically through their contents for a cure, a remedy, a solution. I did not turn to them for guidance and strength.

I simply sat, my back to the railing, gazing up at the heights of the tower looming far, far overhead.

"Please." The word trickled from my lips with the first tear that escaped down my cheek. "Please, there has to be some other way."

I hadn't meant to choose this path. I hadn't wanted to face my shame, my guilt, my role in all of this...

Not if it meant losing Jaik.

"You have to show me!" I begged the Storymaker, my voice knifing the silent gloom, my hands balling into fists pressed against my thighs. "You have to show me how to fix this, *please*—I'll do anything, I'll give *anything* if You show me how to save him."

Only silence. Only shadows.

"I don't know how to give up. I don't know what to tell Jaik," I choked, digging the heels of my hands into my eyes. "I don't know how to do this. Help me. Help me. *Help me.*"

Those same two words poured from me again and again...the end of a tale. The tapering off. The only words I had left.

After a time, they failed me as well. And then it was only me. And the silence. And the *knowing*.

And as I sat there, the minutes passing like turning pages, each one a whisper closer to the end—

Peace. Peace stole over me, deep and calming and absolute. Not acceptance, not resignation of my pain.

But surrender. Surrender to my own endless fight...and the truth that it would change nothing, in the end.

I was not ready. I would never be ready for the farewells looming on our horizon.

But I had taken so much for myself already. Stories and time and second chances. And for every one I stole, someone else went without.

Headmaster Thiago, whose hopeful smiles I hadn't deserved the whole fortnight I'd spent here. A man grateful for the halls to breathe again, after years of loneliness.

The Lothar family, waiting for power to pass to a more worthy hand. Their family torn and incapable of healing until something changed again, for better or far, far worse.

Naomi, still here in this city she'd left long ago, because she was loyal beyond reason. She wouldn't leave me for the life she'd built in Dalfi, no matter how deeply it pained her.

Reiko, carrying a burden I'd foisted on her, desperate for relief but too noble to shrug it off. The better of us, after all this time.

Jaik, who'd resigned himself already. Whose focus had been outward, not inward, ever since Erasure. Who had been here all these long days, forbearing and fighting the losing war, for *me*. Helping me limp and crawl toward the outcome he'd accepted before I'd ever spoken to the Sha of it.

All of Mithra-Sha, suffering. Suspended. Begging. Praying. And perhaps I heard no answer to *my* prayers because my impossible choice was the answer to theirs. And that was my penance for all I'd set in motion with my choices years ago.

There was a whole country beyond these walls, waiting for me to be ready. And I never would be.

But it was time.

Time for Mithra-Sha. Time for me.

It was time to let go.

CHAPTER 84
VOWS AT THE WORLD'S END

entered the Shastah with heavy steps, but a heart that had finally found its iron armor.

Surety. Certainty. I knew what needed to be done. And ough every fiber of me rebelled, every inch screamed against the notion…I d done my seeking. I had searched for another path. And now I stood halfway wn the only road left, the one I'd already chosen with the first steps we'd en from Erasure.

There was nothing left to do but walk it now.

After dark, I slipped into the same room where I'd made Jaik vow to let me for this…to try and save him. I found him asleep again, sprawled on the bed, e arm curling the pillow to his face. The other hung over the edge of the bed, gers brushing the floor…just within grabbing distance of the rifle he kept neath it.

Shutting the door, I barreled my weight back into it, soaking in the sight of s. Of *him*.

The vision I'd wanted to come back to every day. A quiet life. A simple one let myself dream of, just for a moment, in Fallshyre Bay.

I wished I'd let myself appreciate it a moment longer back then.

His name slid from my lips—little more than a breath. All I could manage. But he still heard me. He always did.

Snapping awake, Jaik rolled to one elbow, drowsy eyes finding me in the midark. That familiar, heartbreaking furrow wedged itself between his brows en lucidity found its way through the haze of slumber.

"Ayjay?" He shoved himself up from the bed. "What are you doing back re? I thought you—"

"I'm letting go."

The words brutalized my throat; they ached worse than anything I'd tried choke out after Galan had broken my jaw. And they halted Jaik in the motion taking that first step toward me.

"The Storymaker said I would know my seasons," I choked, "when it was time…and this is it. For me, for Mithra-Sha, I don't—I *can't* keep looking for something I *know* isn't there—"

"You're right." Jaik rasped a palm over his stubbled jaw. "I was just laying here, thinking that…yeah. It's time. We're not going to find anything, because there's never *been* anything like this. Like us."

Us. There was an odd surety in that word. It always *was* us…sword and story. And even in this, Jaik would not be alone.

The notion threaded strength into my limbs, opened my chest wide to bea in a steadying breath—to say what needed saying next.

Slowly, I lurched up from the door. "Jaik, whatever happens to us…"

"Wait." Jaik flashed up a hand, that frown cutting deeper between his brows. "What do you mean? I'm the one the endings are tied to. Whatever happens, it happens to me, right?" When I said nothing, his voice pitched highe "*Ayjay?*

"I don't know," I admitted, halting before him. "I don't even know what *will* happen to you, Jaik…if it will take your life or if I can unbind the stories from inside you without turning things back how they were at the tearing." The words came more swiftly as I spoke, nearly tumbling over themselves on the wa out. "But the story last time cost everyone their memories of us. I don't think it will be any different this time."

"So you're telling me even *if* I survive, somehow…I lose you again." The confidence in his tone turned brittle. His countenance was ashen.

"It's the price," I whispered. "The cost to put things right."

Jaik seized my shoulders, thumbs pressing into my sleeves, his gaze fixed mine. "*I* don't want a story where I keep forgetting you. I don't want *any* of this without you."

I nearly lost my tight rein on my heart just then. Because *that* was what gav him pause, the only thing he hesitated over.

Not his own death, not his undoing. But that he might forget *me*.

"I owe this to the world," I said—then barreled on when Jaik shook his head, "Jaik, I did this. I put my broken heart before my home, before its ople…before *everything*. I can't afford to make the same choice again. Mithra-a *needs* Storycraft."

"And I need *you*." His palms rose to frame my face. "Ayjay, you don't serve to be forgotten. The world's not asking that from you."

"It's asking for someone to save it, Jaik." I gripped his wrists, tipping my ad into his touch, wishing I could brand the precise feeling of it forever into y flesh. "Traveling with you taught me that I don't need recognition or colades to do the right thing. To be the hero of my own story. I've told so any tales like that, and now…now it's my turn to live it. I just need you to help e do that."

Because I would not take the choice away from one more person; I would ot force Jaik to choose this with me. Not when his very existence and erything he'd ever wanted hung in the balance, and neither of us knew what ould endure beyond this choice.

"So I die," he rasped, fingers tightening in the hair hanging loose against my ce, "or I lose the woman I love. Again."

I pressed my lips together. I had no reassurances to frame our predicament any fairer light.

No matter what happened, we lost. Even if Mithra-Sha won.

Jaik's hands slipped from my face, slid down my arms and wrapped around e to clutch my back as he plunged to his knees, his face buried against my omach. At the damp heat of his tears against my skin, my composure umbled: I buckled, bowed over, clinging to his shoulder with one hand and nothering my sobs with the other.

I squeezed my eyes shut, though it did nothing to keep my tears at bay. But I looked down at him now, broken before me…then I, too, would shatter. So stead, I held on to him as we both wept; it was his moment to break, to truly ount the cost. And all that kept my feet beneath me was that Jaik needed me. nd Mithra-Sha needed me.

I'd fled that duty once before. Never again.

I held him as the shadows deepened and the hearth dimmed; and mewhere in the ink-dark night, Jaik's weeping tapered. He still clung to me, it the span of his hands widened, and the way he gripped my back shifted.

Determination. Resolution. There was new strength to the splay of his agers when he dragged them up from my waist to my shoulders, pushing mself slowly upright again; he still leaned into me, but this time his height guided me to sway against the small supper table where we'd shared nearly every meal this past month.

"All right." His tone was rigid, a mainstay against the gravity of the choice he'd parsed out in his own head, in his own grieving. "You're right, Ayjay. We've got to do this."

I breathed in those words—the finality of them. The resignation.

The choice was made.

"I'm sorry," I choked. "I'm sorry it wasn't enough to save you."

I crumbled this time, and Jaik caught my chin in his hand, guiding me back upright, his weight leaning me back into the table's edge.

"Hey. Look at me," he urged. "I'm not going into this angry. I don't blame you for anything. You gave me this incredible gift…I got the chance to do everything I was too scared to do the first time." He brushed a strand of hair behind my ear with his free hand. "Got to try farming, got to have a cat, got to make my own way in the world. I got to meet Julas and his crew…I got to fall in love with you all over again." A smirk tugged his lips at the reluctant laughter that burst from me. "So if I have to give it back now…you're not going to catch me regretting it, tiger. Not one flipping *second* of it."

I surged up to wrap my arms around his neck, and he banded his around my waist again, hauling me so near every line of our bodies met and matched. And for a long moment, we simply swayed there in the darkness, clinging to one another while the choice loomed larger and more sinister beyond us with every beat of our hearts.

And then Jaik's husky voice brushed my ear, harsh with tears unshed. "I, Jaik Grissom, take you, Audra Jashowin, as my wife."

Squeezing my eyes shut, I whispered into the fluttering pulse on the side of his neck, "I, Audra Jashowin, take you, Jaik Grissom, as my husband."

"To love and support, to protect and defend…"

"To encourage and uplift, to guide and advise…"

There was only us, and the vows breathed in the dark; there was only one night, and no one else I wanted to share it with. And somehow it was more sacred than anything I'd ever known…to have a promise that would be so short lived. Knowing I wanted a thousand years of him made this tenuous time so much more precious.

I was Jaik Grissom's, body and soul, by oaths and promises.

And in the morning, I would be no one. And there might not be a Jaik Grissom to belong to anymore.

CHAPTER 85
WHERE I ENDED AND HE BEGAN

In the dark before dawn, we lay tangled together. The ring on my finger winked in the banking firelight.

It was like Erasure all over again—only our bodies and the flames in the hearth—yet everything hung heavier. The warmth. The weight. The press of Jaik's arm around my waist, his palm sprawled on my abdomen, his thumb circling against my hip. His other arm was tucked beneath the arch of my neck and curled over my chest, his hand cradling my opposite shoulder—holding and guarding the scar there, where Galan's lead had punched through.

"Do you have any idea how incredible you are?" Jaik's drowsy whisper stirred my hair, unleashing a shiver that coiled up my spine.

I burrowed my back into his chest, tucking my nose against his arm where it sloped over my still-racing heart. "Odd choice of words to describe the woman who did…all of this."

"Hey." He flicked my hip. "That's my *wife* you're talking about."

A small thrill swiveled in my chest, like the last flourish of an artfully penned love letter…one that would soon be cast into the fire. Burned up with nothing left to show for it.

Perhaps we would never have a written deed or a celebration to officiate this. But I had made my vows, more precious than any other words I had ever spoken…and I wore Jaik's ring on my finger. And I would be his for the rest of our lifetimes…even if those would end far, far too soon.

I choked on a fresh surge of emotion, shutting my eyes. "Are you afraid?"

He nuzzled his face into the back of my head. "Scared out of my mind, actually. But walking into it with you makes everything easier."

Pressing a palm into the bed we shared, I levered myself over onto my back; he released me just enough to prop himself up, temple on his fist, hand sti splayed over my belly…shielding the scar there, now. His depthless eyes burned into mine with springlike warmth…the heat waiting beneath the newly-churned soil, inviting fresh growth. Whispering tales of new life to come.

Agony wrenched through me.

I didn't *want* a new life without him, either.

I brushed the sweat-tangled hair from his brow, and at the pass of my hand everything altered; his steady expression crumbled. The lines at the corners of hi eyes tightened, that divot reforming between his brows. His mouth trembled as if he might cry; and then his forehead fell against mine, and his broad shoulders bowed inward. So near to breaking.

Swallowing the heat that blistered in a hard lump at the base of my throat, I worked my arm from between our bodies and took his unshaven cheeks between my clammy palms. "*Hey*," I whispered, and his back arched in a damp, strained inhale. "Jaik. Tell me five things you see."

The steps of this dance he'd learned long ago…to help *me*, I remembered now. Because I had suffered so many nightmares and moments of panic after the trials to become the Master Storycrafter, buckling beneath the burden of the responsibility on my shoulders and the tasks I'd undertaken to prove myself worthy of it.

So he had gone to Hadrassi scholars here in Vallanmyre, and he had learned how to do these things. How to ground a frantic mind, how to find a center of calm. For *me*.

Using those steps to help him in turn was the very least I could do for him. For my Jaik.

My husband.

"Tell me, Jaik," I urged, smoothing my thumbs over his stubble. "Please?"

Another shuddering breath. "Right now, just…you. How beautiful you are. How flipping *perfect* you look."

Heat scorched my cheeks. "You're ridiculous."

"Known. Established. Beside the point." An uneven chuckle burst from him. "I can see the fire's going out. Someone ought to do something about that."

"Later." I curled my leg over his waist, trapping him with me. "That's two. Three more?"

"Can we skip to what I feel?"

"*Jaik.*"

A rumbling laugh, and he drew back a bit, planting his free hand against the low beside my head. "I see the most powerful Storycrafter of our time. And I see the love in her eyes…and that's for me." A fresh tremble stroked the line his jaw. "I can see my ring on her finger, and, flipping *Luck*…that's everything wanted."

I wrapped my hand into his hair, bringing his brow back to mine. "Four ings you feel?"

"You. Every inch of you." His hand traced a path from my hip to my oulder and back again. "I can feel the places where I let people past my ard…places people like Galan hurt you. And I can't stop thinking, if you make out of this, what's going to happen when I'm not there to—"

"Jaik." I tugged his head up this time, forcing him to meet my eyes. "Stay in is. With me."

His words on my lips. His mouth curled at the irony, too.

"I can feel a draft coming in from the window," he said. "And how flipping ratchy these sheets are. You'd think the Sha could do better, but, hey, times are ard all around."

A laugh burst from *me* this time. "What do you hear?"

"That giggle I love." He brushed the tip of his nose against mine. "Your reathing. Your heartbeat." He paused, eyes gathering a silver sheen of emotion. That makes this all worth it."

I dragged the corner of my lip between my teeth, biting back tears of my wn. "What do you smell?"

He captured one of my hands, still balancing effortlessly on his elbow as he rought my knuckles to his lips. "The ink that's always in your nailbeds. Always as been, no matter how many times you tried to pick it all out for formal linners. And you'd keep picking at the stains in meetings with the Sha." A hroaty chuckle swelled through him, coaxing heat that moved in synchrony hrough me. "I teased you about it, but I was always glad you couldn't get it out. That smell was *you*. Just like that shampoo Naomi used to make for you…what was it?"

"Patchouli and clove." A fragrance that had always calmed me after long days full of fear and tension, reviewing Mithra-Sha's innumerable needs and debating how Storycraft might meet them.

"Right." Jaik dipped his head, his nose gliding along my neck and grazing behind my ear. "Still smell that, too. It used to collect right back here."

I fought not to squirm, resting my hands over his prominent hipbones and shoving him back lightly so I could meet his eyes. "One thing you taste?"

He bowed, pressing a kiss between my eyes. "How about that mouth?"

I shoved myself up on my palms and kissed him, a hungry, fervent meeting of lips and tongues, and we fell back among the sheets again. We kissed until desperation dulled back to the resignation that defined our next steps...the inevitability that loomed on our united horizon.

Then we simply held one another, so near I no longer knew where I ended and Jaik began.

"Promise me, whatever comes next," he murmured, his chin on my head and his hand stroking the frayed ends of my hair that draped against the dip of my back, "you're not going to forget yourself again, Ayjay. Don't you ever let anything make you forget what you're worth...who you are."

"I won't." And even if I had no choice, I intended to keep that promise. I would cling to it with all my might...to remember the lessons I had learned on our journey together.

The truth of who I was—in myself. In the Storymaker's eyes. And in Jaik's.

"And you promise *me*," I whispered against his bare chest, "you do everything you can to hold on, Jaik. You don't have to be mine, with whatever comes after...I just need you to *be*."

"I'm not letting go without a fight, tiger." He drew away just enough to grip my chin, tilting my head back against the pillow until our gazes met. "But I *am* yours. Nothing can change that."

His lips captured mine again—once. Twice. Then he snugged me tight against him, my leg hitched over his hips, my arms linked around his back. And with my face buried against his chest, I felt as much as heard the words he spoke next:

"Let me tell you a story, Ayjay."

And he did. He told me tales of adventures we would never have and places he wished he could take me, until sleep finally laid claim to me...until I couldn't hold on any longer.

To consciousness. To our last night together.

To *him*.

CHAPTER 86
A TEARING TOLD IN TRAGEDY

I left our bed after sunrise, my nerves already shredded, my heart following suit. It was painful to watch Jaik sleep, stretched out on his stomach on the bed, face buried in the pillow I'd abandoned…not knowing if this was the last dawn he would see. Nor if I would remember him, or care beyond common courtesy, if the day ended with his body lying on the Shastah floor again.

I stole away with those thoughts like a thief, keeping them to myself as I walked the halls yet again, wearing his shirt for the last time. I stopped servants here and there; I asked for things. Asked them to go places and do things for me.

And they all agreed. Out of respect. Out of reverence. With an adoration I did not deserve.

One that would be gone, with me, by sundown.

I found a quiet corner of the Sha's home that I'd once loved: a window in the western wing that allowed an unbroken view of faraway Fablehaven. Seated on the broad sill, I tugged out my journal with its loose-leaf pages and maps and stories…*my* story, broken into so many parts. The mark of all the places I'd been, the things I'd seen, the tales left unfinished before I'd met Jaik.

And I wrote all of the things I couldn't bear to say.

Declarations of love that might have no ear to land on after today. The things I'd always wanted to do, and never been brave enough to. The things I might find the courage to accomplish when I was alone again.

In silence and solitude, my cheeks stained with tears, I buried my face in my hands and begged the Storymaker for just one thing: that wherever my story took me next, I wouldn't waste so much time craving the affirmation of others.

That I could learn to embrace being expendable. That He would help me to live if living were possible.

But that, above all else, *Jaik* would live. Even if that meant our lives never entwined again.

When the page was marked with all the tears I could spare and still keep m courage, I finally pushed myself from the windowsill and made my way to the Convening Chamber to see if the servants had done as I'd asked.

It was not quite a relief that they had; I nearly wished I could have stretche out this moment forever.

But there they were—the Sha and Shadre, waiting for me. Arias and Mahalia with them, near but not quite next to them. Reiko and Naomi, lingering off to the side.

Everyone in the Shastah I'd once thought of as family…all but one.

Naomi hastened to meet me the moment I entered the Chamber, ignoring how the rest of the conversation quieted behind her. She snatched my hands an peered into my eyes, hers glossed with tears on the brink of falling. "Some of th servants brought us here, and the Sha…the Sha said you were going to…"

I nodded.

"Oh, *Addie*," she sobbed, tying her arms around my neck. "You don't have to do this. We can find another way—"

"No. I started this." I tugged her arms down to her sides and fastened my gaze on hers. "I have to set it right."

"You don't know what it will do," Reiko warned, striding across the Chamber to join us. "You played with Storycraft like this before, and look what happened. You really want to try again?"

"It's just retracing my steps. I can find my way back to where we started from."

"What about Jaik?" Naomi demanded, and across the room Arias flinched. "What happens to *him*?"

My mouth wobbled. I breathed deeply, anchoring my feet to the choice Jai and I had made together, weighing all the costs as one. "We don't know. But it's a risk he's willing to take, and that's his decision to make."

To think we had once made judgments like this every day, lives balanced in our hands, and hardly thought twice about it…

I yearned for the strength of the Master Storycrafter I'd once been…but by the same stroke of the quill, I resented her. She had not known the cost, either; she had never faced loss like I had.

She had played with lives and risked far more than I would ever bring myself to, knowing now how heavy the grief hung when things went awry.

"What about your parents?" Mahalia demanded, sweeping over to join us. "Your siblings? Don't you want to see them?"

"She's right." Reiko gestured to the Shadress. "I know you've been here a month, but you haven't really *been here*. You've been going out in secret, avoiding them, avoiding *everyone*. Take some time, think this over—"

"I don't need to think. The people of Mithra-Sha don't have any more *time* for me to think," I amended. "And I'm not going to put my parents through having me, just to let me go again."

We would only gather pain we couldn't measure. And memories we couldn't be able to carry with us, anyway.

And I could not afford for them to dissuade me. It was better they never knew they'd had me back before they lost me again.

"Addie, please," Naomi choked. "*We* need more time."

I bore down another deep breath to fortify the pieces of my heart that wanted to crack and crumble at the misery in her voice, in all of their faces. I looked around at them all, lost for words for one of the few times in my life.

Reiko's countenance was steely, but her jaw shivered with the tension of bitten-back emotion. Naomi wept openly, fingers interlaced and pressed over her mouth. Mahalia clung to practiced stoicism so like her mother's, arms tucked behind her back, chin raised—but a single tear sparkled in the corner of her eye.

With a blink, my own tears blurred their faces into others I had come to know. And come to care for.

Julas, smirking at me beneath lanternlight and ice, his hands dusted in snow. The crew, begging for a tale around a table of good food. Laith and his siblings, gazing in wonder at the fresh winter world built of stories. Arias, seated beside me on the chaise, sharing a weight we knew better than most of our friends. Lio, her faith in me so resolute, it had taught me to begin to believe in myself again.

These people who had grown to love me, or always had...and we had all fought our way to each other, only for our lives to amount to this moment. This choice.

I finally knew what to say to them...and the words weren't even my own.

"I love you, my friends," I whispered, and Naomi sucked in a harsh breath. Reiko cursed, and Mahalia shook her head wildly. "Trying to protect you, to save you, even...that's not a burden. It's a privilege."

Naomi's voice cracked over a sob of my name, and she lunged forward, wrapping her arms around me; the others surged to join in, and for a moment I was surrounded in a haven of warmth, an endless embrace. A love that time and tearing and sundered life-tales had not fully broken.

I wished it could last forever.

But then they peeled away, one after the other, catching glimpses of something inevitable. Something as wonderful as it was devastating.

Naomi was the last to let me go, half-turning me as she did.

And there he was.

Jaik pushed into the Convening Chamber where I'd held his bloodied body years ago. He did not look at the Sha and Shadre; he met Arias halfway through the room, and the pair slung their arms around one another, their embrace so tight the ache of it echoed in my chest. Jaik gripped the back of Arias's head and muttered something in his ear, too low for any of us to hear. But Arias held him tighter at that, his back shuddering in unmistakable sobs.

It was several moments before they drew apart, and Arias remained where he was, laced-together fingers smothering his eyes. Jaik squeezed his shoulder tightly, then brushed past him and made his way to me. His gaze and stride were fixed and sure, like I was a lodestone. The center of his story.

There was no fear in his face. No hesitation in his steps. Whatever power he'd found within himself as he'd fallen apart on his knees before me the night before, he retained it now.

He halted, hand outstretched, face steady. And for the last time, he asked me, "How do you want to dance this, tiger?"

Swallowing back my own tears, I took his hand. "The same way I want to do everything: with you by my side."

His cool mask cracked a bit, his mouth wobbling up at the corner. "Yeah. Me, too."

He drew me away from my friends, toward the center of the Chamber; we passed the Sha, who reached for my shoulder, his eyes brimming with tears. "Thank you."

"I'm not doing this for you," I said, tucking my arm out of his reach. "I expect you to keep your word."

His gaze skipped to Arias, then back to me; he nodded curtly—he knew his penance to be paid. And I hoped Arias and Mahalia would hold him to it.

In the very center of the Chamber, Jaik and I halted. With my free hand, I tugged my journal from the waistband of my sleep pants, offering it out to him.

k frowned as he took it, staring at the tooled leather cover, well-worn by the
ush of my hands. "What's this for?"

"Hope," I said. "And something to remember me by, if…"

If he survived and forgot me anyway.

He shoved the journal into his own waistband and claimed both of my
nds this time. We knelt where I'd once held his cooling corpse; only warmth
rrounded us now, our fingers tied, our brows resting together. A grim echo of
e way we'd left the world when it forgot us.

I heard the words in my head. The words of a nightmare and a life turned
pside-down, broken forever even before I'd completed its shattering.

Let me tell you a story.

Panic ripped through me as the precipice loomed…the point from which
e could never return.

A story to be told. A choice made, but not yet carried out.

I couldn't do this, I couldn't *end* this, I couldn't end *him*…

"Hey." Jaik nudged his forehead gently against mine. "You've got this, tiger.
ist one word at a time."

His faith was gut-wrenching. Breathtaking. And I would miss it, even when
forgot who I was. And who *he* was.

"I don't regret any of it, either." The words freed a few tears to scrape
own my cheeks.

"Yeah, I know," he laughed, bearing his weight more fully into me. "Come
n, Ayjay. Don't leave me in suspense. I'm dying to know how this one ends."

"Close your eyes, Jaik," I whispered. "Let me tell you a story."

And I told him the story of us.

Our own names, our own selves laid bare. I told the story precisely as we
ad lived it…from Krylan to Vallanmyre and everywhere between. I told the tale
f the man made of story endings and the woman who'd helped spin him from
he power gifted by the Storymaker Himself.

And I told of stories going home…endings returning, power flowing back
o its source.

Even when Jaik flinched, even when he stiffened and groaned, his fingers
wisting in my grip, his brow aching in its fierce press against mine, I did not
pen my eyes.

And I did not stop.

I met the power building and building within me, and I gave it all up. I shoved it away from me with all my might, toward him…I held onto none of it for myself.

It was time to let go. It was time to be free of this double-portion, this weight, this power the Storymaker had given me. And it was the only thing I could think of that might somehow, in some way, give Jaik the happy ending he deserved.

I cut and severed and clawed my way free of the scarlet cloak of power that hung over my bones. I floundered through its folds, tearing off the patchwork, knitting something new with the tale of us. Reshaping who Audra Jashowin was. Who Jaik Grissom was.

And even as the words unspooled out of me, ripping, separating from the core of me, my very essence—something reached back. Something branding, white-hot, electrifying.

Something that imprinted itself on my bones and blood. Like the story I told was *memorizing* me. And across the raging cord of it, the tendrils of the last tale I would ever tell…

I felt him.

Jaik.

The man made of stories. My talisman, my amplifier. My love.

Memorizing me. Holding on with every inch of him.

Taking me with him, wherever Luck would send us now.

And then, in a blaze of white fire and scarlet power, the world erupted. I erupted with it.

The tearing ripped into me.

I was unmade. Made new.

I was…

I was at the end.

I had become *the end*.

Let go, Audra. The Storymaker's whisper echoed from Erasure, all the way to me. *Let go.*

And with Jaik Grissom's name blazing in my mind and heart, I finally did.

EPILOGUE
FUTURES ENTWINED

n the space between dreaming and waking, the world was spun
in scarlet.

The harsh brand of flagrant color seared my eyelids when
struggled to open them, blinking until the roof of the small, humble room
arped into shape above. For several moments, I held perfectly still, every
uscle rigid and every other sense reaching out in their stead…grasping,
inging, scrabbling to remember a dream held closer than breathing. A vision of
ld and gore, tawny light and shadow…

But it was gone.

I never could recall more than a blink of my dreams. Every morning of
very day for the year-and-a-half since I'd made the pilgrimage by airship from
allanmyre to Krylan, my sleeping mind was the same musty, hollow void
ickering with dust-mote dreams. Whenever I tried to grasp them, they slipped
vay.

This morning was no different.

It could have been worse. I could have woken with one of those pounding
eadaches splintering into a keening whistle in my ears and fractals of agony
riven behind my eyes. I could have woken with tears on my cheeks.

At least today, all that lingered was the ache in my gut—a sorrow
nshakeable. One of my only two constant companions.

Plunging my hands into the feather-soft mattress—the first luxury I'd been
ole to afford after six months of scrimping and shuffling aside my wages—I
oisted myself up from the nest of pillows, then dug my knuckles into my eyes
clear the last dredges of sleep from the corners. When I squinted the room

into focus, its shadowy corners hung in sharp contrast with the daylight pouring through the only window.

The walls were bereft of ornamentation and trinkets. I'd left Vallanmyre with nothing to my name but a satchel slung across my front, filled with sparse clothing and an heirloom ring stashed in the bottom folds.

I'd sold that the moment I'd stepped off the airship into one of Krylan's ports, and the coin from that exchange had paid for half a year's board in this modest three-room home...long enough for me to secure employment and shed every reminder of the city of my birth. Long enough for Krylan to begin feeling like some semblance of home.

After all, I'd had nothing to pin the title to in Vallanmyre; my family wanted nothing to do with me, and hadn't for some time. My siblings were cold toward me, my parents shutting their door in my face. I'd been sleeping for Luck-knew how long beneath the bridge where I'd woken to the roar of the falls in my ears one morning, grass and dew woven into my hair, wearing a shirt too large for me—and determined to finally make something of myself.

I was finished being one of Mithra-Sha's many victims, another poor, impoverished destitute living out beneath the stars. I felt like I'd been running away from my future for so long.

So I'd come here to claim it.

The reminder invigorated me, a stark notion of the precious moments already wasted chasing fathomless dreams and painful memories around the murky corners of my mind.

Arching my back, I stretched until my shoulder twinged...an old scar from an attack in an alleyway I hardly even remembered. Easing out of my bend, I surveyed the chaos of last night's work arrayed around me—the task I'd fallen asleep in the midst of.

Books of lore and fable. Books full of epic quests and romantic forays. Things I had never—and likely would never—experience for myself. But it was enough to read them, to let them carry me away; at times, when I whispered the words aloud to cut the silence of another night of solitude, my exhausted mind conjured sensations of cool breezes on my skin, a brush like grass and leaves along my palms, a passing scent of chilled stone and campfire smoke that teased the inside of my nostrils.

These books and the sensations they invoked were a wonderful escape, most nights. But with the break of day, reality beckoned.

I wiggled my feet to wake them fully, bending my knees toward my chest—
then winced when pinprick claws unsheathed from the mound keeping my feet
warm.

"*Sheeba*," I groaned, hooking my arms beneath her fluff and hauling her off
my ankles, "we've had this discussion. *Both* of us can't stay bundled in the
blankets all day." I held her up at eye-level, her brindled body drooping toward
the bedspread, disparaging gaze holding mine. "So. Either you can return to your
roots and start mousing the corners, or you let me get up and earn our keep."

She seemed to consider it a moment before a brush of corrosive tongue
against my thumb's second knuckle sounded her surrender.

Grinning, I deposited the cat back into the patch of sunlight sprawled
across the bed, sliding free of her lazy reach. I dressed hurriedly in the same
clothing I'd shed before tumbling among the sheets the night before, fresh from
another night working at the same tavern I'd return to this morning.

By the time I turned back, she was a snoozing mound of purring
contentment, a scrap-fattened shadow of the farm cat she'd once been.

I'd found Sheeba not long after I'd arrived in Krylan, during a sleepless
night when I'd wandered out to the farmlands embracing the outer limits of the
Tailbone City, desperate to clear my head. She'd been a sleek, happy thing back
then, prancing after me through the grass and dry cornfields until we'd found a
path and lanternlight again.

When I'd wandered across a pair of farmhands finishing out the night,
they'd gazed at us like spirits emerging from the shadows.

"I've never seen Sheeba take to anyone like that," one of the men had
remarked. "She's always been standoffish, ever since…"

He'd lost the thought mid-word, something I'd found strange until his
companion had shrugged. "Ever since I've known her, anyway."

That night, she'd followed me all the way back to the house…and now she
barely left, even to accompany me back to the fields I still wandered on occasion.
Sheeba had found her purpose in a life of softness and days spent in the sun…a
quiet end to a lifelong tale of hunting in the fields.

A simple story, maybe. But as I scratched her ears and slipped out to greet
the endless bustle of the workday, my heart warmed with fresh gratitude that she
was part of mine.

Two things could always be counted on to come through the door of *Ale Alley Pourhouse*: customers and gossip.

Today was no exception. The late-summer breeze chased countless hungry faces through the open door of the low-roofed establishment on the verge of th Ameresh district, ushering in murmurings from across Mithra-Sha with them.

Most of the faces belonged to traveling vendors, peddlers…even Mithran soldiers just beginning their rotation in the city. And all of them had stories to tell from their travels.

Crops were flourishing for the first time in years. Cures were making their way into even the poorest hands, now that there were plenty enough herbs to go around. Innovation pressed us ahead into the future at breakneck speed, crafting new jobs left and right. There were far fewer homeless, luckless mouths to feed—mine among them, a notion that always kept my feet moving even when I ached to pause and soak in their tales.

Those were just a few of the many stories that had made their home in our country again.

Storycraft flourished. After so many years of bedtime tales without end and an absence of power throughout Mithra-Sha, now I heard stories about stories every day, a storm of chatter populating the dustiest corners of the *Pourhouse* while I filled tankards and mounded warm, dill-and-mustard smashed potatoes and braised roast slabs onto plates.

The work came as simply to me as breathing; though I'd never worked a true day in my life after I'd graduated from my studies—I'd wandered aimlessly, trying piecemeal crafts until I'd finally decided my life was worth turning around—still, I'd taken to the tasks of a barmistress like it was in my blood.

Pride glowed in my chest when I whirled a platter of plates to one of our most populated tables, cheerful smile as quick as my hands. Two of the men seated there flicked a silver coin each to me with nods of appreciation—and perhaps a bit more.

I knew how to be the character who earned herself extra coin. And the rest they paid with went straight into the hands of Leatrix, the owner of the

rhouse—a no-nonsense, talented businesswoman who'd softened to me over
months once I'd proven myself capable despite my lackluster past.

Now she offered a nod, a swift smile, and a wink as I slipped the extra
er into my pocket—a flash of approval that sent warmth cascading through
veins. It was a swift surge, mellowing almost at once into the fierce
ermination that had breathed in my core ever since I'd abandoned Vallanmyre
l all the things there that had made me feel less-than, unworthy, shut out.

I *was* worthy. My life itself was a gift to celebrate. I was through wasting
and I required no one's approval, no grand life achievements, to make the
st of it.

That truth felt as if it had been scripted on my bones the day I'd woken
neath the bridge and decided to reshape my life. It had carried me through so
ch of the uncertainty since then. It had given me the strength to barter,
ggle, then demand a place aboard the airship that had brought me here. It had
used into my marrow the courage to fight for myself against Leatrix's doubt.
its might, I had crafted the woman I was today. And on its quill-tipped wings,
rossed the *Pourhouse* floor yet again, back to the serving counter to ladle up a
ping of bone-broth stew, the stories about stories following every step I took

I caught Leatrix's next glance—an eyeroll, a pointed yawn—as she added
re coin to the coffers, finally free of another vendor who'd lingered to chat
ut the world outside Krylan. I couldn't help a sympathetic smile in return.

We didn't really need to hear for the fifteenth time about Sha Arias Lothar,
d how he and the Mithran army and the many, many Storycrafters in service
ngside them were working together to reach every corner of Mithra-Sha. All
gossip about the tales told, the things created, the new bridges and roads and
ships forged—and about how, when the endings of the tales had returned,
y'd brought with them a vast array of colors, an artist's palette splashing every
nceivable hue across the face of our country again.

All but one. The most notorious color. The most gossip-rich subject of all.

There was no singular scarlet cloak to speak of. There was no more Master
rycrafter...or at least, none that had come forward in the year-and-a-half
ce the endings of the stories had made manifest again.

There was a different color the gossips liked to whisper about instead.

To hear peddlers and sailors and even Storycrafters themselves tell it, the
y all the endings had returned to Mithra-Sha, a simple Storycrafter's cloak,

entirely ash-gray, had ben discovered inside the locked doors of the Shastah's Convening Chamber.

No one knew how it had gotten there. Or why, of all the Storycrafter cloaks, its color had never returned.

That had still been the favorite subject among tavern patrons for months after I'd landed my position at the *Pourhouse*. In fact, it had only recently been buried beneath chatter of other exploits and mysteries and the reckless feats of the Sha's right-hand Storycrafter and her soldiering companion, the head of the Sha's personal guard. Rumors had swirled for the last fortnight of how he'd taken a pilgrimage alone to the Isle of Misspoken Stories, where Storycrafters and soldiers had been meticulously and swiftly destroying all the Misspoken manifestations banished there, hand-in-hand under the Sha's direct orders.

I had yet to hear a whisper if he'd survived. Or why the Sha's own bodyguard had traveled to such a dangerous place.

I shuddered at the thought. I had never had the displeasure of encounterir a Misspoken manifestation, but by the tales customers told of the soldiers and Storycrafters rounding them up and shipping them off to that island, I was bett off that way. And I could hardly wait for the gossips to find something new to jabber about.

Battering those notions aside, I plunged back into the slapdash fray of tavern life.

It continued on like that for some time, the hours leaking by, the rotation customers near-constant, keeping us busy without end. Not for the first time or one of the *Pourhouse's* more bustling days, I wished Leatrix would hire another pair of hands. Talented a team though we were, my feet twinged and desperate thirst smoldered in my throat when I paused to gasp for breath and take stock of the ever-filling room at midday.

And that was when I saw them.

A new group had arrived and seated themselves at the table nearest to the door—not our usual clientele. Those who *were* usuals ogled, whispered, and gaped at their presence. All talk in the tavern seemed to break around them where they huddled with the intimacy of old friends and an air of pure purpose.

I could only tear my eyes from them when Leatrix cleared her throat besid me at the bartop—so loudly there was no mistaking she'd been trying to captur my attention for some time.

"That table is now your *only* table." She slid the newest of our serving platters into my hands. "Go."

Before I could even ask who in flipping Luck they *were*, her weathered fingers tugged me around the bartop and thrust me toward their table; my feet, though clumsied from the hours of serving I'd already done, handled the rest.

I marked their attire as I approached: silk and bright hues, badges and brands I'd never laid eyes on before. There were five of them—two men, three women, but they'd dragged over two more chairs. One of the women wore a vivid, layered blue skirt cut jaggedly from one hip down to her opposite ankle; another was ash-pale, a stark contrast to the dark hair cropped and feathered forward on her head. The third was perhaps the softest woman I'd ever seen in the *Pourhouse*, shaped as though she hadn't labored a day in her life. But a journal lay before her—a sketchbook, perhaps—and the side of her left hand bore a permanent rash of an inkstain while her gaze darted around the tavern; likely seeking a subject to draw.

Both men had their backs to me; one had shaggy hair the same charcoal shade as the smudged ink on the woman's hand. The deep russet curls on the other bounced a bit when he tossed his head and laughed at something one of the women said.

Nausea and dizziness surged in me all at once when the collision of fine, perfuming scents wafted from their bodies to greet me at the tableside: herbs and leather and ink, flowers and spice all mingling as one. I halted behind the two men, balancing the empty serving tray on one hip and my hand on the back of the nearest chair.

"Good afternoon!" The cheer in my voice cracked, and they all stiffened at once. "How are all of you today?"

Two of the women flashed me wide smiles, the other a smirk so riddled with abrasive enthusiasm I nearly stepped back from it. Dead wolves I'd seen hauled in by trappers for stuffing often wore less vicious grins.

And then the man in the seat before me swiveled to a flash a rakish smirk of his own, and all the breath rushed from me at once.

Of all the faces I had ever seen at the tables in the *Pourhouse*, his was the least expected…the most *impossible*. He had no use for taverns, for food and drink of any cost at all. The most I'd ever witnessed of his countenance was the announcement bulletins that had hung to rotting on all the notice boards across Krylan when he'd taken power from his father.

Sha Arias Lothar—here, in the *Pourhouse*, of all the luckless, *flipping*—

"You—You're—" I had never been particularly talented for words, but the sputtering gasps that tripped over my tongue were pitiful even for me.

To my undying humiliation, the Sha's smile only widened. "Take your time."

"What are you—*why* are *you*—?"

He laid a hand over mine on the seatback, the motion so utterly, arrestingly familiar I stopped fighting for absent words and simply gaped at his knowing smile.

"Did you really think I would miss this? For anything?"

Miss what? My tortured, overwhelmed mind cried out into the abyss of my hollow chest.

What was *I* missing?

They all gazed at me, faces upturned and expectant. *Exultant*, even.

And all at once, I remembered.

Who I was. *What* I was.

Shaking my head, I cleared my throat and settled back into my familiar skin. "What can I get for you and your companions, Your Excellence? We'll handle the cost, of course." Leatrix wouldn't be thrilled, but we couldn't very well demand payment from the *Sha*.

The whole table went on gazing at me, but not one of them asked for food or drink; and then the anticipating in their expressions morphed, one after the other, as if they'd been awaiting the brunt of a joke left to hang in the wind.

Slowly, frowns carved into brows. Eyes narrowed. Mouths pinched off to the side.

The woman in the serrated skirt, hair tamed beneath a frayed handkerchief, tipped dizzily against the edge of the table, elbows to the stained wood, hands covering her mouth. "Addie?"

"Something is wrong." Her wolf-wicked companion graced me with a gaze so sharp, it stripped me open from flesh to bone.

"Audra," the third woman began carefully, setting her sketchbook aside, "do you...do we seem familiar to you?"

"Of course," I fumbled, and the skirted woman brightened a bit, sitting tall from the tableside again. I gestured to the man before me. "This...this is Sha Arias Lothar, and judging by the likeness in you, I think you must be Shadress Mahalia?" She blinked, her expression flattened, and an inky slash of *wrongness* knifed through my veins.

I'd done something...misspoken, somehow.

Rolling my quill in sweating fingers, I gestured unsteadily to the dark-haired woman. "I think I know you…Reiko, the Sha's right-hand Storycrafter? I've heard about you in the stories they tell around—"

"*Audra.*" The skirted woman bent again, her eyes glistening in the light of the lantern at the center of the table. "What about *me?*"

I held her gaze, though it was a painful effort when her stare warned me my answer held the balance of whether the tears would fall from the corners of her anguish-tightened eyes.

Was she a regular? Someone I'd served early in my time at the *Pourhouse*, made some sort of impression on…and forgotten?

Leatrix wouldn't appreciate that. Not when this woman was clearly a friend of the Sha, of all the Luck-loved people in the country.

And all at once, I knew what I had to do.

"Fooled you!" I chortled, and the woman jerked back in her seat, an unbidden grin tearing across her mouth—a look of such relief that guilt consumed me at once. But I'd begun the act now…I couldn't let it go. "Flipping *luck*, you've always been easy to rile up. I'm sorry, all of you, I've just been so distracted today, I needed a little humor." I put quill to paper, meeting their peaked brows and widening grins with fresh shame welling in my gut. "Let me get your food, and I'll come by and chat when my shift ends."

"*Chat?*" Mahalia laughed. "That seems a bit casual for everything we need to discuss!"

Mouth dry, I forced another chuckle. "It does, doesn't it?"

Reiko tilted her head; then, curt as the cut of a blade, she lifted her chin at the man seated next to the Sha. "Do you know *him?*"

I had no choice but to continue playing this odd game of theirs…this ruse I'd fallen into to avoid losing their patronage. So I sidestepped neatly, taking in the man's face: younger than the rest of them by some years, wearing typical Mithran soldier garb. His stubble, the same inkblot shade as his hair, barely filled his jawline; but his shoulders were broad and his body was well-built.

I'd never seen him before in my life.

"Of course I know him!" I scoffed, and they all blinked at once, trading wide-eyed glances; I ignored them, resting a hand on the soldier's seatback. "How are you? It's been some time since—"

"Ayjay. *Stop.*"

I didn't know how that voice, coming from the tavern doorway—and speaking a name I'd never heard before—cut through all the chatter in the room like a brand.

I didn't know how I knew he was speaking to *me.*

But my gaze tore away from the table, alighting on the man who'd crossed the threshold of the *Pourhouse,* standing framed in vivid daylight burning through the open door. Its glare burnished the edges of his deep gray cloak as he tipped the hood back, laying it to his shoulders with a deliberate, careful movement—revealing his eyes already boring into mine.

My breath caught at the sight of his face, bearded, stamped with laugh-lines and flushed as if he'd been weeping. Recently.

I *knew* him. I had seen his face plastered on notice boards throughout Krylan, too, at the public house where I occasionally treated myself to a meal, and even on the announcement panel that hung behind the bartop in the *Pourhouse.* That long, chestnut-gold hair, his fine threads, the deep gray cloak lashed around his shoulders…

The Sha's most powerful, talented soldier, his own personal bodyguard, head of the defenses in the city of Vallanmyre. The most renowned of his kind.

Captain Jaik Grissom, in the *flesh.*

Standing in *our* doorway. And staring at me like I was the ending to some story he hadn't known how to finish all this time.

I blinked first, looked away first, reclaimed my breath first—all difficult to manage when he was looking at me that way. Should I pretend I hadn't recognized him…hadn't gawked at him?

"I don't understand," the woman in the skirt whispered. "What's happening? Why is she—?"

"She doesn't know us." Grissom stated the truth bluntly—the very thing I'd known the moment the Sha and his people had gazed at me with a foreign familiarity.

It shouldn't have ached the way it did, hearing him declare the obvious; it shouldn't have stung like I'd betrayed them somehow. Like I'd *been* betrayed by the dismissal in his tone.

"That must've been the cost," he added quietly. "The price for…everything. To fix how it tore the first time, and for me to be here. She gave her power for them, but for me…"

Confusion dragged my gaze back to him; a secret, private grief and frustration braided into his tone and danced in the deep brown of his gaze.

Slowly, he stepped forward, winding between the tables. Brightness from
doorway at his back splashed across the threads of his cloak, turning the
.dows in its creases so deep, it was as if they'd been dipped in ink.

And just for a flicker, a blink, the *Pourhouse* shimmered around him like a
:age.

The walls paved themselves in shades of teal and gold; ships' figureheads
.red in the corners, leaped from the walls in such lifelike relief, I flinched.

But Captain Grissom still moved toward me the same way, bending
ween tables that shivered from full to empty in my distorted sight. The
.sion only dispelled when he halted before me, hand to the empty seatback,
ween the Sha and the woman in the skirt.

"Sorry about that." His breath was salted with emotion, grazing my face.
·on't let us bother you."

He swung the seat out and dropped into it, his back to me.

I didn't know why, but I wanted to kick his seat so hard it skidded and
.mped him out. And I wanted to scream, *Look at me!*

But I couldn't speak. I couldn't *breathe*.

I could only take the coward's path.

I fled to the counter and turned their table over to Leatrix's far more
·able hands.

The rest of the day passed without incident; the Sha and his cohort floated
: figments of imagination on the corners of my vision while I hurried from
·le to table, mind only half on my work, no more silver offered up for my
·entiveness.

I couldn't bring myself to mind the lack of extra coin. Nor could I bring
·self to breathe deeply until their table sat vacant again…and then, the air that
·l through my gritted teeth and crashed to the bottom of my lungs was tinged
·h bitter disappointment.

It shouldn't have mattered…their presence then or their absence now.

But the memory of all their faces—of Jaik Grissom's countenance,
·stfallen, tearstained, hope dying in his eyes—was branded into my mind long
·er the light faded and the bustle of the *Pourhouse* ebbed to a trickle.

By the dimming glow of the last handful of lanterns lit for the customers
·gering at the bartop, Leatrix counted the day's earnings. I swabbed the sleek,
·otted wood absentmindedly with a cloth in one hand; with the other, I
·ttened open an adventure tale against the ledge beneath the lip of the counter.

It was an unusual struggle tonight to lose the day between these pages. There was little I didn't love about this sort of reading, yet my thoughts wandered if I gave them even a bit of rein.

I had just found my rhythm—consumed by the words sliding off the page and digging into my head, making a home for themselves in my memory—and annoyance reared in my chest at the telltale splash of the tipped cup affixed to the *Pourhouse* door. The spattering signal of a new customer arriving just as the last one made her exit.

Irritation burned in my throat; it was so near to closing, I practically had a foot out the door. But Leatrix had made it clear the day she'd hired me that we would turn no one aside with coin in their purses, unless they were belligerent o dangerous.

Stool feet slid on dull wood directly before me, swinging full around. A crimson-tinged shadow flexed in the corner of my vision, straddling the seat. "Got anything to drink?"

"This is a tavern," I replied pertly, stabbing a finger beneath the line I'd been reading and jerking my gaze up from the book. "What do you—?"

The words perished in my throat.

Jaik Grissom folded his arms over the stool's swooped back, one brow arched, waiting for the remainder of my ill-timed retort.

"I'm sorry," I cut myself off. "That was incredibly rude."

"If it makes you feel better, there's a more-than-decent chance I deserved it." He straightened a bit into the lanternlight, allowing me a clearer view of his face—enough to see his cheeks were dry this time, no trace of dampness sliding among the stubble. "I know it's late…about to close up shop?"

I couldn't hold my hackles up at his innocent tone; sighing, I shut the book. "In theory, yes. But we don't lock the doors until the till is balanced, and before *that's* finished…"

"Fair game." He smiled crookedly. "So, how about that drink?"

I retrieved the last pitcher of cider from beneath the counter, shifting my book to the bartop while I pulled him a stein. I had scarcely set it before him when his fist flashed from his cloak pocket, and he deposited a handful of silver coins before me—*far* more than a stein of day-old cider was worth.

The *plink* of spinning, scattering silver held all the whizzing chatter of Luck's own coin being flipped on its sharpest edge…ready to fall either way.

"That," I croaked, watching the coins twirl, flashing in the lanternlight clustered on the bartop edge, "that's *far* too much—"

"It's not just for the stein." He dragged it toward himself, but didn't drink t. "It's payment for the food and drink earlier, too. Your employer wouldn't let cough up the coin, but Arias doesn't take anything for free. Not when the untry is still climbing back to its feet."

The casual way he spoke the Sha's name—*Arias*, like a friend rather than e newest ruler of Mithra-Sha—spun my head more wildly than the last few obbling coins.

I suppose being both the Sha's bodyguard and the head of his soldiers in e capital of the country, he had every right to it.

"Besides," he added, a tilt of mischief to his tone, "I figure it'll take a while add those to the till...which means a little more time on this stool."

Slamming my hand down to halt the lazy whirl of the last few coins, I raped them moodily toward myself and emptied them into my hand. It only ok a moment to bring them to Leatrix, huddled at the shadowed table in the r corner of the drinking floor where she did all her numbers and kept an eye 1 me for any trouble with the last patrons.

She seemed to sense none from Captain Grissom; in fact, her eyes were as ide and bright as the silver I handed over before making my trudging retreat ack to Jaik Grissom and the book I'd left behind.

He'd gotten interested in my absence—cocking his chair forward on its et, craning to read the title upside-down. He withdrew when I slid back into y place and raised my brows his way. "Sorry. Light reading?"

"Not anything a soldier would find intriguing...much less one of your ation." The words tingled on my tongue—the absurdity that not only the Sha, ut his most trusted inner circle, had been here in the *Pourhouse,* of all places...

In a fluid movement, Captain Grissom balanced on one foot and swung his air around to face the counter properly. Then he laced his fingers together, opping his hands on the bartop and inclining toward me with a full-bodied rnestness that caught me off guard. "Try me."

For a moment, I kept my breath captive, considering. But what was the orst he could do with the truth—spread word through the army ranks here in e Tailbone City of some lonely barmistress and the silly stories that kept her ompany?

Shoving out the air from my lungs in a gust, I swiveled the book and ushed it toward him. "It's just a storybook. Not even meant for grown women, ut..."

He didn't scoff. Instead, he smoothed his fingertips over the colorful cover. "I know this one. An adventure story about a farmer's daughter." A fond smile tugged up the corner of his mouth. "That figures."

A strange chill sparked down my spine. "Does it?"

His gaze found me, peering up through his lashes. "It's a good story. My wife used to love stories like that."

Intrigue and pity twisted in my core at the faint crack in his voice. I had never heard of the head of the Sha's guard having a wife; perhaps because, judging by the tilt of his tone, that tale had not ended happily.

"Anyway," he cleared his throat, "you seem like you know a good story when you see it."

Heat flared in the tips of my ears, and I hooked my hair behind them, enduring the surge of pleasure with the praise from this powerful, infamous stranger—and settling into the quiet that waited in the wake of his commendation. "Thank you. Yes, I do."

"I like the confidence." His eyes crinkled at the corners with the broadness of his grin. "Out of everything, I was hoping that's what would stay with you. Glad it did, even if all of us didn't."

I couldn't discern for a moment if he was joking or not; mirth lived in his tone, but his eyes shone with sincerity that made little sense.

Unless he was *flirting* with me, of all things. But why in flipping *Luck* would a man in his position pursue a barmistress who dreamed of the impossible...and one he'd only met in passing today?

"Why are you here?" I muttered, scrubbing furiously at a spot on the bartop that would never wipe clean.

"Thirsty." He toasted to me with the stein of cider, took a swig, then cleared his throat and added more quietly, "I wanted to get the coin to you. And to, you know, apologize...if we set things off with you earlier. That wasn't the plan, they just...everyone had an idea of what it would be like when we came here."

"What were they expecting, precisely?"

Anguish rippled in the depths of his gaze, so profound it halted my hand altogether.

"Something different than I was," he rasped under his breath, dropping his gaze to the stein. "Which is why I'm sitting in this chair instead of nursing a hot meal and a headache back at the public house with everyone else."

The quiet offering of a shared agony among that smiling tableful of faces icked the breath from my chest.

Whatever this was—whoever they thought *I* was, for whatever reason hey'd set their eyes on me—they had come all the way from Vallanmyre to the *Pourhouse* for it. They'd sought me out, behaved as if they knew me, treated me ike they believed my worth as much as I did…from the moment they'd first laid *yes on me.*

And ever since they'd walked through the tavern doors, I'd had those lickers in the corner of my mind, like I *did* know them…but I'd forgotten them all. Like I'd seen them in that scarlet void between awake and asleep, where I could never remember anything at all.

Dodging the swell of emotions lobbing a harsh lump into my throat, I summoned a gruff question in a wild grasp for clarity: "What are *you* doing in Krylan? Aren't you supposed to be at sea, on an island somewhere?"

"Tried it. Came back." The pain in Captain Grissom's gaze cooled slightly; he raised his brows over the lip of the stein and took another sip. "Ship was pretty fast. Maybe you've heard of her…used to be named *The Athalion*. Now they call her *The Cathan*."

A fresh chill skittered beneath my skin, that name prickling at me like a piece of a bedtime story I'd heard long ago. "I…don't go to port much."

"Figured." He set aside the stein, then produced a book of his own—a weatherworn journal—from the pocket of his cloak, and cast it down on the counter. It landed with a dull *clap*.

Brushing my fingers across its face proved a mistake; a surge of melancholy spiked through me so fiercely, it stole the breath from my lungs. My throat turned to a barren waste—an empty path down to my hollow chest, full of nothing but miles of walking, alone, bereft, unwanted—

I jerked back, and Captain Grissom's hand replaced mine, caressing the leather with a reverence often reserved for headstones and grave dirt. "Working here, I'm guessing you've heard the stories about the cloak they found in the Convening Chamber. Strangest flipping thing—"

"I know." Such a fickle toss of Luck, that the subject I'd been bored of this morning proved the safest waters to swim with him. "About how it was found behind locked doors. No broken windows. No sign anyone had entered the Sha's Convening Chamber…or left it."

"Right. But there's a part no one ever talks about. Because no one ever knew it except me." Captain Grissom's brandied gaze flicked up to me. "This journal was in the cloak pocket."

I blinked. Straightened a bit. "Why would the leader of the Sha's armies tell no one of that? It seems like it could've led you to the whereabouts of the cloak's owner!"

"Yeah. It finally did." Tenderly, he undid the tie on the cover and laid the well-loved pages apart, baring a tale penned neatly on the lines partway through: *The Prince of Mirrors.*

His fingertip traced the letters, every loop and swirl, with the sort of careful intimacy that captured my attention. I couldn't glance away.

My chest burned as if he was scripting the words on the bruised face of my weary heart.

"You know, someone told me once that every story has two sides to it...like Luck's coin," Captain Grissom said softly. "There's the story on the page, and the tale behind why the teller told it."

His finger strayed to the middle of the writing, lingered—tapped.

"The story I was looking for was right here, all along."

My eyes had already picked up on the aberrance he indicated—the place where the handwriting changed. Where the words became tighter, neater. Sharper, somehow.

He turned to another story: *The Seamstress in the Cellar.*

It was the same—the elaborate script that shifted pattern halfway.

Half-mindful, I traced my fingers over the letters myself, brushing against his. Tingles sparked along my nerves like a splash of hot oil on my hands, but this time I lacked the propriety to pull away. "You wrote these?"

"I finished them." His voice was husky. "Every story without an ending. Every single prayer someone else prayed without knowing what to ask for. But I was praying them, too. I'm no Storycrafter, but I didn't have to be. I felt like I'd heard all these stories before." He swallowed, but it did nothing to soften the rasp of his next words: "I've spent the last year filling in the pieces someone else left behind...the holes in me, too."

My gaze wrenched up to his at last, and my stomach lost its bottom at the look in his eyes—something unfathomable, aching beneath the surface of his mirthful mask.

"You still haven't answered my question honestly," I croaked. "What is the leader of Mithra-Sha's armies doing here?"

"I was looking for you."

I stared at him; he stared right back, and abruptly, his expression shifted. e teasing smirk dropped from his lips. Pain and yearning flashed in his s…the same vulnerability I'd witnessed when he'd laid his hood back on the eshold today, and met my gaze.

There was desperation there. A plea.

See me. Know me. A need my heart echoed with such painful force, I could rdly speak a single, strangled word. *"Why?"*

"Because, Ayjay," Jaik murmured, "it's your turn to be found."

I stopped breathing altogether.

"You gave up everything for the world," he went on quietly. "You gave ay your power to every person who ever needed it. You gave up your *life* for . And I just spent the last year and a half of *mine* remembering things that felt e real memories underneath some story I'd been told…a hammock on a ship ck. An adventure out in the Drennans. Some snowy back alley in a portside vn."

Shock kicked through me at every word—notions that carried the same st-mote essence as the dreams I could never remember. Like impressions nded on my eyes from a glorious blink of time, lost to the carving threads of e and Luck.

"Finally, I got tired of it. So I took my chances…I went to the Isle of sspoken Stories, and what I learned out there…Who I *met* out there…" nistling lowly, Jaik shook his head. "Now, *that's* a story."

Storycrafters who came through Krylan always said there was power imaginable in a few small words. I'd never fully believed them until now.

"Why do I feel like I know you?" The whisper fell hoarsely from my lips as ounded the counter to step into his space…somewhere that burned with longing. Like coming home. "How do you know *me?*"

"It's a complicated story." Jaik offered his hand to me, palm up on the rtop. "Do you want to hear it?"

Yes, my whole heart cried. *I want to hear everything.*

I could only muster a nod as I laid my hand in his.

His fingers tightened and a smile overtook his face, his gaze tied to mine e futures entwined—never letting go.

"Audra Jashowin," he murmured with a voice of mystery and adventures d epics waiting to be crafted, "let me tell you a story."

CHARACTER GUIDE

Audra Jashowin (AW-druh JASH-oh-win): A disgraced Storycrafter on ᵉ hunt for purpose in her life.

Galan Fiordona (gay-len FEE-or-doan-uh): An exiled soldier serving in ylan. Audra and Jaik's nemesis.

Lionyra Vara (lee-oh-NYE-ruh var-uh): A talented baker from Krylan d one of Audra's closest friends. Imigrated from Amere-Del.

Jaik Grissom (Jake Gr-ISS-um): Farmhand from Krylan. Possesses the wer to reanimate stories.

Naomi Weathers (nay-OH-me): The most talented healer of her class d one of Audra's closest friends.

Jularius Cathan/Julas (joo-LAIR-ee-us/joo-LAHS cath-ann): Captain *The Athalion.*

Frixia (frix-ee-uh), Syd (sid), Reinera (ray-NAIR-uh), Lanah, Nix & ash, Henriet, Valori (vah-LORE-ee), Hasser: Key members of *The* ᵗhalion's crew.

Sha Tobyrus Lothar (toe-BYE-russ low-thar): Ruler of Mithra-Sha. ᵤsband of Calten, father of Arias and Mahalia.

Shadre Calten Lothar (sha-dray kal-tehn): Wife of Tobyrus, mother of ᵗias and Mahalia. Hadrassi by birth.

Shadran Arias Lothar (sha-drahn ah-RYE-us): Son of Tobyrus and ᵤlten, first in line to rule Mithra-Sha.

Shadress Mahalia Lothar (ma-HAY-lee-uh): Daughter of Tobyrus and ᵤlten, second in line to rule Mithra-Sha.

Reiko Nayori (ray-co nay-OR-ee): Close advisor to the Master ᵒrycrafter and one of Audra's closest friends

LOCATION GUIDE

Alusia River (ah-LOO-shuh): The river that winds from the foothills, beside Dalfi, to the Spine

Amere-Del (AH-meer dehl): Country to the south of Mithra-Sha. Ruled by the Del and Della

Assida (ah-SID-uh): Birthplace of Storycraft

Casmiss Wood (caz-miss): A forest running alongside the Drennan Peak

Dalfi (dal-fee): Airship port and trade city

Erasure (ee-race-sure): The dark tower of records, located in the Illusionarium

The Drennan Peaks (dren-ann): The mountain range spanning the western coast of Mithra-Sha

Fallshyre Bay (fal-shire): A port town where ships tend to winter

Hadrass-Drui (ha-drahs droo-ee): Country to the east of Mithra-Sha. Birthplace of Mithra-Sha's Shadre

The Illusionarium: The Island of Misspoken Stories, where manifestations are sent that cannot be properly destroyed

Kalvikan (cal-vih-can): A woodland city known for its trade in lumber

Krylan (cry-lan): The militant city at the base of the Spine

Leathris (lee-ath-riss): A farming location near the Drennan Peaks

Port Craythin: Bustling harbor near Krylan

Rothmere (rawth-meer): A small town along the Spine.

The Sha (shah): Ruler of Mithra-Sha

The Shadre (shah-dray): Wife of the Sha, co-ruler of Mithra-Sha

Shadran (shah-drah-n): Son of the Sha, heir of Mithra-Sha

Shadress (shah-dress): Daughter of the Sha, co-heir of Mithra-Sha

The Shastah (SHA-stuh): The Sha's palace

Vallanmyre (val-en-mire): The capital of Mithra-Sha; home of the Shastah and Fablehaven Academy

The Vensair Mountains (venn-sare): The mountain rage spanning the eastern border of Mithra-Sha; separates Mithra-Sha from Hadrass-Drui

ACKNOWLEDGMENTS

Some stories just live for us.

We never quite know if they're going to, before we put pen to paper (or in my case, fingers to keyboard). Like Audra, I set off into this tale without knowing if I would ever find the ending. But I am eternally grateful for those who supported me and came alongside me from beginning to ending…and beyond.

To God, for the neverending reminders that He is with me, that He is co-creating and working in this labor of love with me. That He gave me this craft for a reason. I will always do my best to be worthy of it…and to hold on and let go as I'm led. Thank You for this one…for another book of my heart. I consecrate it to You. May it be *established* in Your will.

To my family, for never forgetting me, forsaking me, or thinking I am a madwoman for this life I choose. For helping me make this dream come true through encouragement, guidance, listening ears, and many, many hours spent keeping a toddler happy while I explored Mithra-Sha. And to the toddler tornado himself, the one, the only JD—for being the best part of my life's story and patiently enduring me playing the same songs over and over on every car ride while I drafted, and letting me slow down at the zoo to write down Audra's name when it came to me, and for celebrating with me the million other quirks that come with having an author for a mom.

To Kristin, Lina, and Cassidy…best of CPs, best of editors, dearest of friends. For telling me how to improve this story from start to finish. For the art of all kinds and the encouragement that came out of it, for connecting with and loving Audra and Jaik and their story so much. So thankful you three are a part of MY story.

To my early readers who gave me their insight, their encouragement, their honest feedback. You are what makes this process possible! And to the illustrators and artists who helped bring the corners of Mithra-Sha to life, from cover to map to illustrations…I could not be happier or more grateful to work with you!

And to every single reader who picks up Audra's tale, and between its pages, find something that resonates. Something to believe in. I wrote this story when I was at one of my lowest points as a writer, wondering if I would ever find the courage to finish a story again. It has impacted me like no other book to hear how many readers and fellow writers see themselves in Audra…and how we see our struggles reflected in each other.

May we all keep telling stories in our own way. And may we all continue to find, each and every one of us, the truth and love pressed between the pages of the tales we read and those we share with others.

ABOUT THE AUTHOR

Renee Dugan is an Indiana-based author who grew up reading fantasy ɔks, chasing stray cats, and writing stories full of dashing heroes and evil sterminds. Now with over a decade of professional editing, administrative ɾk, and writing every spare second under her belt, she has authored several tasy standalones and series. Living with her husband, son, and not-so-stray s in the magical Midwest, she continues to explore new worlds and spends her e in this one encouraging and helping other writers on their journey to illing their dreams.

ALSO BY R. DUGAN

You can find other R. Dugan books, including…

The Chaos Circus (YA Portal Fantasy)

The Starchaser Saga (NA Epic Fantasy Series)

The Curse of the Blessed (Adult Fantasy Trilogy)

at online retailers Amazon, Barnes & Noble, and more,
and at **reneeduganwriting.com/shop**

Find Renee Dugan online at: **Reneeduganwriting.com**
And on social media: **@reneeduganwriting**

If you have enjoyed this or any of my books, please consider leaving
review on Goodreads, BookBub, Amazon, and other online retailers.
These will help new readers find and fall in love with my books!

You can find more information on my books, including sneak peeks,
special giveaways, shop discounts, and more by subscribing to my
newsletter at

Reneeduganwriting.com/newsletter